THE ALPINE MYSTERIES OMNIBUS

THE ALPINE ADVOCATE

THE ALPINE BETRAYAL

THE ALPINE CHRISTMAS

MARY DAHEIM

THE ALPINE MYSTERIES OMNIBUS

THE ALPINE ADVOCATE

THE ALPINE BETRAYAL

THE ALPINE CHRISTMAS

Wings Books

New York

This 2006 edition is published by Wings Books, an imprint of
Random House Value Publishing, by agreement with Ballantine,
divisions of Random House, Inc., New York.

Wings Books is a registered trademark and the colophon is
a trademark of Random House, Inc.

Random House
New York • Toronto • London • Sydney • Auckland
www.randomhouse.com

Printed and bound in the United States of America.

A catalog record for this title is available from the Library of Congress.

ISBN-13: 978-0-517-22853-1
ISBN-10: 0-517-22853-X

10 9 8 7 6 5 4 3 2 1

CONTENTS

THE
ALPINE
ADVOCATE

To all those who lived the real Alpine story, and in the process, created a legend. These courageous men and women embodied the spirit of the Pacific Northwest.

Author's Note

THE TOWN OF Alpine no longer exists. But from the early part of the century until the late 1920s, it was a small but thriving mill center off Stevens Pass in western Washington. The mill's owner, Carl Clemans, was a relative of Samuel Clemens (a.k.a. Mark Twain), though a discrepancy in spelling the family name had arisen between the two branches early in the nineteenth century.

Alpine, which saw the doughboys pass through during World War I, was consumed by such patriotic fervor that sales of victory bonds far exceeded the quota for any other community in the state. Old Alpiners still take pride in their contribution to Over There.

My mother grew up in Alpine and returned as a bride when my father took a job with the mill. When the logging operation was shut down, the town was intentionally burned to the ground so that transients off the freight trains wouldn't start forest fires. In over sixty years, the second stand of timber has obliterated all signs of the town.

But since Alpine anecdotes have played a large part in my life, I felt this rustic, picturesque place deserved to be revived. Thus, the background is genuine Pacific Northwest history, and now the town lives again in more than just the memories of those hardy souls who embodied the spirit of Alpine.

Chapter One

In my dream, Vida Runkel had her clothes on backward. In real life, Vida only wore her hat the wrong way to. Obviously, the poor woman had regressed in my subconscious. Maybe people who spend a lifetime working on small-town newspapers tend to deteriorate in every possible way. Maybe, I thought hazily, as the phone rang, that will happen to me. . . .

"Emma Lord here," I mumbled, trying to make sure I wasn't talking into the earpiece. "Who died?" A call at two A.M. had to be bad news. Unless it was my son.

It was. "Nobody's dead, Mom," replied Adam, his usually strong young voice sounding a bit reedy over the five-thousand-mile cable between the shining sands of Honolulu and the foothills of the Cascade Mountains. "What are you talking about? You working on a story for the paper?"

I sat up, fumbling for the light switch on the lamp next to my bed. "Why else would you be phoning in the middle of the night unless there was a disaster? Are you in jail?"

Adam laughed, and I relaxed a little. "Hey, everything's fresh. It's not the middle of the night. It's only eleven o'clock. How come you're asleep so early?"

Single mothers, married mothers, even stepmothers are basically a patient lot. They have to be or they would devour their offspring early on, like guppies. I repressed a sigh. "Gee, Adam, you've only been going to the University of Hawaii for two years. When are they planning to teach you about time differences? The earth is round, re-

1

member? You're three hours behind us, you nitwit. Are you broke again?"

"No." The incredulity in Adam's response struck me as incredible. This was the kid who could lose money as fast as he could spend it. He could lose just about anything, if it came to that, having once misplaced his baby-sitter when he was eight. She thought it was the other way around, but it wasn't. So if Adam wasn't broke, he must have robbed a bank. Ergo, he was probably in jail after all. I finally managed to locate the light switch. "It's Chris Ramirez," Adam was saying, as I blinked against the brightness of my cozy little bedroom. "He's coming home. Can you put him up at our house?"

"Chris?" I sank back against the pillows. A cool breeze blew in through the two-inch span of open window. I could smell the evergreens and the damp earth. As always, they gave me strength, like an elixir. "Why on earth is he coming back to Alpine after all these years?"

"He's quitting school." Adam made it sound simple. He also made me sound as if I were simple, too. "He wanted to quit even before his mom died. He registered, but he didn't go to any of the classes. He can get his money back, but it's a big hassle."

My son's attitude toward extra effort rankled, as usual, but I decided not to run up the phone bill by saying so. Undoubtedly, Adam had charged the call to my credit card. "Okay, when will he be in?"

"Let me see . . ." Obviously, Adam was consulting an airline schedule. I marveled that he'd bothered to pick one up. "It's a six-hour flight. He'll be there in about . . . uh . . . five hours. But you don't have to pick him up at the airport. He'll hitch a ride up to Alpine."

I bolted upright, clutching at the phone. "What? You mean he's on his way? Hell, Adam, it's over a two-hour drive to the airport! I've got a paper to put out! It's Wednesday!"

It was Adam's turn to exhibit patience, a virtue he seemed to reserve only for parts on his '82 Rabbit and his considerably older, if more reliable, mother. "Yeah, I know. That's why I called now, to give you some advance notice. But you don't have to go clear into Sea-Tac. I told him it'd be a cinch to find somebody driving over the Pass."

Visions of various serial murderers danced through my mind. In my opinion, hitchhiking should be outlawed not only on the freeway, but everywhere. "Never mind," I said grimly. "I'll go get him."

"That's up to you," my son said, and I could see him shrug. "Hey, I gotta run. I got some dudes with a half-rack waiting for me, okay? I'll write this weekend and tell you about Deloria."

"Deloria?" But Adam had hung up.

I put the phone back and ran a hand through my short brown hair that somehow had not yet turned gray, despite a conspiracy by the rest of the world. Instead, my teeth kept trying to fall out. Thank God for Dr. Starr and giggle gas, I thought as I reset the alarm for four-thirty. The Seattle-Tacoma Airport was over ninety miles from Alpine, but at least I shouldn't run into much traffic.

Unfortunately, I was now wide awake. Even if Chris's plane was on time, I wouldn't get back to Alpine until ten. As for Chris himself, I had seen him twice, on trips to Honolulu to get Adam settled in at the university. He was dark, spare, handsome, and more moody than most young men his age. A bit of the poet about him, or would have been, if he, like the rest of his generation, didn't seem to be semiliterate. But then I was prejudiced. You get that way when you spend a lifetime in journalism and watch the circulation figures drop. I keep waiting for *The New York Times* to make the endangered species list.

Or at least *The Alpine Advocate*. Granted, except for the fact that both are printed in English and appear on newsprint, there isn't much of a comparison. But then Alpine isn't New York. Originally, the town where I live and work was called Nippon because of the Orientals who helped build the railroad. Later, a sawmill was opened by a relative of Mark Twain's, one Carl Clemans, whose father had changed the spelling of the family name back to its Welsh origins. Carl, in turn, had rechristened the scattering of buildings along the railroad tracks as Alpine. The town thrived, if that's the word, from the pre–World War I era until the Depression when it should have folded and disappeared, like other railroad semaphore spots along the old Great Northern route, such as Tonga and Korea. But a farsighted entrepreneur named Rufus Runkel joined forces with a Norwegian immigrant called Olav the Obese, who decided that putting boards on people's feet and letting them fall down steep hills could be fun—and profitable. They built a lodge in the early 1930s and saved the town from extinction. The mill had closed in 1929. Logging had continued in the vicinity but was jeopardized in the last two years by the controversy over the spotted owl.

Sixty years ago, when both owls and trees had still seemed plentiful, the former mill workers who didn't want to log found other jobs, first in building the ski resort, and then in staffing it. Meanwhile, the silver mines that had originally lured Mark Twain's relative continued to draw visitors who were more curious than greedy. A good thing, since nobody I know has found any silver worth having assayed since 1942.

I turned the alarm off, got up, and got dressed. The *Advocate* office is less than a mile from my house, and I often walk. But, since I'd need the car for the trip to Sea-Tac, I drove. Many of the four-thousand souls who live in Alpine are now commuters to Everett and Seattle. The spectacular beauty of the Cascades, the sharp, fresh mountain air, and the comparatively cheap real estate prices have kept Alpine—well, thriving. During ski season, the town is full of visitors, but in late September, we can still call our souls—and our grocery store—our own. The first snows weren't due for another two weeks, at least.

The *Advocate* office is small but up-to-date. We have three word processors, though Vida Runkel insists on banging out her House & Home section on an old Royal upright. Every Wednesday at nine in the morning, we ship the finished layout off to a printer in Monroe, some forty miles away. It comes back around three, ready for our carriers to deliver and the post office to mail. Then we sit back and wait for the irate phone calls to the publisher and incensed letters to the editor, both of whom happen to be me. I love it. Usually.

My desk is always a mess. At three A.M. it looked even worse, like Adam's room. Fortunately, I had almost everything in hand before I'd gone home last night about seven. I checked over my editorial on the need for a public swimming pool adjacent to the public tennis courts and the public park, and then revised the layout. Twenty-four pages, which was the usual, except during holiday season. For the next hour and a half, I proofed the ads that Ed Bronsky, our one-man business staff, had solicited; tried to make sense out of Vida's column on recycling potato peelings; and corrected the numerous spelling errors on all the copy supplied by my young, eager, and dizzy reporter, Carla Steinmetz. Carla is straight out of the University of Washington, and so zealous that she makes me tired. Maybe I was like that once, too, before the world caught up with me. Maybe that was before I fell in love and got pregnant and had Adam and neglected to acquire a husband in the process. Maybe that was how it was in that brief springtime of my life when I still thought all things were possible, and then discovered that even *probable* usually didn't mean anything good.

Except for Adam and the half-million dollars. They were both better than good. After nine months, Adam didn't exactly come as a surprise, but the five hundred thousand did. I never dreamed that my ex-fiancé, Don Cummings, would forget to remove me as the beneficiary of his life insurance policy with The Boeing Company. But then I didn't expect him to die at forty-five, either. When he did both, I ended up with a windfall—and the cash to buy *The Advocate*.

I left a detailed memo for Carla, a brief note for Vida, and a question for Ed on the Harvey's Hardware and Sporting Goods Store ad. I headed for the car, finding Front Street as deserted and dark as should be expected so early in the day. Alpine is set a mile off Stevens Pass, twenty miles below the summit where the Tye River joins the Skykomish, and smack on the Burlington Northern railroad line. The town founders built compactly on both sides of the train tracks, there being a dearth of level ground and a tendency for residents to walk a bit like mountain goats. Hills surround us, and mountains tower over the hills. In winter, Alpine is cold and dark and often isolated, with the tang of sawdust and woodsmoke carried on the wind. In summer, the town is fragrant with wild flowers, and the sharp, clean air is intoxicating. I love the place, though it's not Eden. Small towns have vices, too. When you run the local newspaper, you know every one of them by name.

I crossed the bridge over the South Fork of the Skykomish River and found first light about ten miles down the highway. I loved this part of the drive, where the road was still narrow and the tall second-stand evergreens framed the asphalt like stalwart sentries. Seventy years ago the original inhabitants of Alpine had hacked down the Douglas fir and the red cedar and the Western hemlock and the white spruce, but their heirs had done more than inherit the earth—they'd reforested it. I blessed them every time I drove this stretch of road.

One of those farsighted Alpiners had been Constantine Doukas, known for reasons I've never heard as *Neeny*. His parents had come from Greece at the turn of the century, and his father had gone to work in the mill. The family was prone to saving and scrimping; by the time the mill was shut down, Grandpa Doukas was able to buy up most of the town. Neeny had been selling it off by bits and pieces ever since. His grandson was Chris Ramirez, and if Neeny was as rich as everybody said, it was no wonder Chris wasn't worried about getting his tuition money back from the state of Hawaii. Neeny could probably afford to buy Waikiki.

But I wasn't sure that Chris would ever see any of that money. His mother, Margaret, had married "beneath her," as Vida Runkel and half the town were fond of saying. A handsome Mexican laborer had passed through Alpine twenty years ago to help put in a new sewer system. He had swept Margaret off her feet—and Neeny Doukas had tried to sweep the romance under the carpet. Failing that, he had threatened to disinherit his daughter if she married Hector. She did—but, as far as I knew, Neeny didn't carry out his threat.

That, however, resulted from Hector's abandonment of Margaret when Chris was about six. Or so the story went. I rely on Vida for Alpine's history, since I arrived in town only a little over a year ago. A small town's past is very important, I've discovered, since its inhabitants seem less concerned about the future than their city counterparts. Maybe that's because they figure their towns don't have a future. Or else their lives have become so intertwined that a local history is more like a family album than a text-book. Whatever the case, Vida Runkel was the current Keeper of the Archives.

According to Vida, Margaret was overcome by grief. Furthermore, she had never liked the rain. Or her father. So she bundled up young Chris, left Alpine, and moved to Hawaii. About a year ago, she died of cancer.

Adam had made friends with Chris Ramirez at school, the two of them having the common bond of an association with Alpine and growing up virtually fatherless. Later they discovered a mutual fondness for basketball, surfing, girls, and half-racks, though not necessarily in that order. Now Chris was coming home after fourteen years. I wondered how much he'd remember. I also wondered what his grandfather would think of him after all this time.

The fragile silver sky of the past few mornings was dimmed, promising rain later in the day. Over the mountains and above the trees, the sun came up behind me, looking wan in the early mist.

It was beginning to drizzle when I reached the freeway. I turned on the windshield wipers and realized I was not the only driver on the road. It was after five A.M., and the commute had begun, a thin trickle of cars headed for Everett to the west and Seattle to the south. I'd avoid city traffic by taking the Eastside route through Bellevue.

Or so I thought, always forgetting that Bellevue was a city. In my youth, it had been a sleepy little suburb. But that was almost forty years ago, and time and invading Californians had changed all that. I kept driving in traffic that grew more dense and aggravating. A year in Alpine had spoiled me; twenty years in Portland had been dismissed as if they had never existed.

The flight from Hawaii was a mere fifteen minutes late. Chris emerged into the terminal wearing a Hard Rock Cafe T-shirt, a Dodgers baseball cap, and a sullen expression. He registered no surprise at seeing me in the role of his personal chauffeur but at least had the grace to mumble something that passed for thanks. His luggage, he told me glumly, consisted of one suitcase and a gym bag.

"How long will you be staying, Chris?" I asked when we finally collected his belongings and had reached the dark green Jaguar that is, next to Adam, the light of my life.

Chris's black eyes roamed somewhere in my direction. "I don't know," Chris said. "A couple of weeks, maybe."

"Oh." Call me crazy, but I can never figure out how the hotel-motel industry keeps going when nobody I know supports it. My house is small, with two bedrooms and a den. When Adam is home, the only place guests can stay is in sleeping bags on the front porch. Or that's the way it should be, but I have been known to put up a family of five in the living room, the dining nook, and even the laundry room. Of course that was my cousin, Trina, and her brood, which hardly counts because I figure they usually sleep in trees and eat out of troughs. "Sure," I conceded, "you can sleep in Adam's room. He might even have made the bed before he left."

"Cool." Chris's voice was remote. His gaze was fixed on the passing traffic, now bumper-to-bumper, mostly headed for Boeing—where Don worked until his fatal heart attack and fortuitous insurance policy. I would have felt guilty about the money had he not also taken out a second personal policy in the same amount which covered his wife and three children. As it was, I counted my blessings. I might not have wanted to be Don's bride, but I never wished him ill. Ironically, the reverse may not have been true. Don was not a happy man when I told him I was carrying Tom's child. Come to think of it, Tom wasn't too thrilled about it either. At least he never told his wife.

"Do you remember much about Alpine?" I asked as we swung onto the Eastside freeway and found ourselves going against traffic for a change.

Chris gave what I assumed was a shake of his head. "Just the trains going through. And the snow."

"It's grown some," I offered. "Your uncle Simon has two new partners in his law firm now."

"I don't remember him." Chris's voice was uninterested.

"Your cousins are both still in town." I was struggling to make conversation, raking up a past that I wasn't sure meant a rat's behind to Chris. Except that it must, somehow, or he wouldn't be coming back. "Jennifer is married to Kent MacDuff. He works at his dad's used car lot. Mark manages property for your grandfather. He had a girlfriend, but they broke up."

"Mark used to lock me in the cellar at Grandpa's." He spoke matter-of-factly, but the fact that he mentioned the incident at all spoke volumes.

The rain was coming down harder; I switched the windshield wipers on to high. "Will you see them while you're in town?" I asked, trying to sound casual.

I sensed rather than saw Chris shrug. "I don't know. They've never come to see me." He was silent the whole time I drove past Bellevue.

Resisting the urge to ask about Deloria, I kept closer to Chris's home turf. "Your grandfather isn't too well," I remarked at last. That was what Vida told me, anyway. She'd run into Neeny Doukas at young Doc Dewey's office about a week ago. He'd definitely looked *poorly* to her, but so did Sheriff Dodge's Siberian husky.

"Neeny's old," Chris replied in a tone that assumed anyone over seventy was expected to be ailing. "He never liked me."

I slowed down as the first of the logging trucks pulled onto the highway. "Chris," I began, a bit surprised at the annoyed note in my voice, "if you don't think much of your relatives, why are you coming back to Alpine?"

Chris glanced at me, then looked down at his battered but expensive gym shoes. "That's my business." He scuffed one foot against the other and relented a bit. "I've got a score to settle with Grandpa. I hate him so much I could kill him."

Chapter Two

Now BOYS WILL be boys, and all that, but I still found Chris Ramirez's response disturbing. I hardly knew the kid, but he struck me as too unmotivated to do much of anything, let alone stage a face-off with Neeny Doukas. I laughed, a bit lamely, and gave him a quick sidelong glance.

"Just wait awhile. Vida Runkel already has him halfway to death's door."

"I don't know her." Chris was staring straight ahead through the rain-streaked windshield. The freeway felt vaguely slick, for it hadn't rained since Labor Day. Indian summer had held sway until this last week of September.

"Chris . . ." I began, then stopped. I sensed his seriousness and recalled my description of him, however inaccurate, as a potential poet. But moodiness can beget other things than verse. "Did he and your mother ever write or talk?" I posed the question with less than my usual professional aplomb.

"Sometimes." He resettled the baseball cap on his head. "Afterward, my mother would be mad for a week."

"Is that why you're so angry with him?"

Chris shifted in the leather-covered seat, his feet now pigeon-toed. "He wrecked my mom's life. She died sad. She lived sad. He sent my dad away. He owes me. And them."

This was serious stuff indeed. I recalled the time I'd been sent by *The Oregonian* to cover a story about a woman who was going to jump off the roof of a down-

11

town Portland hotel. The policemen and firemen weren't
having any luck talking her out of it, so they dispatched
me, as the only woman on the scene, to give it a try. I
hadn't had the wildest notion what to say to her. I vividly
remembered walking out onto the rooftop and wracking
my brain for words of wisdom. The first thing that popped
out of my mouth was "Where'd you get those green
shoes?" She had gone right over the ledge. A decade later,
I didn't have a lot more confidence in my abilities at persuasion.

I hedged a bit. "You never saw your father again?"

"Nope. Neither did Mom. Never heard from him either.
He just . . . disappeared." Chris paused, fidgeting with the
baseball cap. "Whatever my grandfather did to him must
have been pretty freaking grim."

Whatever, according to Vida Runkel, had involved a
large amount of money. At least that was what she and her
fellow town gossips had figured. But nobody knew for
certain.

"Maybe he went back to his own people," I suggested,
veering further away from the topic of Neeny Doukas.

"Maybe." Chris fell silent. We turned off the main freeway, heading toward Monroe, where I hoped this week's
Advocate had arrived an hour ago. If only Carla Steinmetz
could screw her head on the right way long enough to get
the paper properly routed, I'd have my faith restored in her
and, to some extent, in the younger generation in general.

"Say, Chris," I said, reverting to more practical—and
comfortable—matters. "Have you got enough warm
clothes?"

He shrugged. "I can buy some."

"Okay." I suddenly felt weary. I'd been up for eight
hours, and it was only ten A.M. I cursed Adam for sending
Chris to me; I cursed myself for being sappy enough to
drive all the way to the airport. I wondered why Chris had
confided in me. Maybe it was because I, like his mother,
had raised an only son on my own. I experienced a familiar pang of regret, not for my sake, but for Adam's. Chris

had had a father for the first six years; Tom had never seen Adam. I wouldn't let him, and sometimes I was sorry.

"Hey, this is fresh!" The young man beside me had suddenly metamorphosed into an enthusiastic passenger. He was straining at his seat belt, staring out the window at the dark green hills and the occasional fertile field. "This is like forest! Are there any deer?"

"Sure. We just went by a deer crossing sign a couple of miles back. Your uncle Simon used to hunt before he got some environmentalists as clients."

Chris didn't react to his uncle's change of heart. He was still gazing out the window, the faintest hint of a smile touching his wide mouth. In profile under the bill of his Dodgers cap he looked very young. I hoped it was only bravado that was setting him up for a confrontation with his grandfather. Maybe, once we were settled in and I'd fried up some chicken and made milk gravy and mashed potatoes, I could talk some sense into him.

I shot another swift look at his face. It was set in stone. I'd be better off talking shoes to would-be suicides.

To look at Ed Bronsky, you wouldn't figure he could sell mittens to the three little kittens. Almost as wide as he was tall, Ed had the gloomiest face this side of a basset hound, and his ears were nearly as long. He was the most negative man I ever met, except for my seventh grade math teacher. I'd actually heard Ed try to talk advertisers out of buying space in *The Advocate*.

"The town's too small. There's no competition. You've been around forever. Everybody knows you already." I still shudder every time I hear Ed chatting with one of the local merchants. After ten years in the job, it's a wonder the paper isn't in worse financial trouble than it already is.

Which, I must confess, is bad enough. Marius Vandeventer, who started out as a raving Socialist in the 1930s, had evolved into a patriarchal capitalist by the time I met him in 1990. At eighty-five, he was still sharp, but he had lost his crusading zeal along with his hair. He was also ready to retire. I thought the asking price of $200,000 cash was a steal. As it turned out, I was the one who got robbed. A kindly newspaper broker told me later I could have acquired *The Advocate* for $150,000, with one-third down and ten years to pay. I guess it was the Jaguar that gave me away.

My debut was not auspicious. I was an outsider; worse yet, a City Person. At first, the locals assumed I was divorced or widowed. While I didn't flaunt my status as an unmarried mother, I didn't hide it either. There are, as my mother used to tell me when she was especially mad at my father, Worse Things Than Being Married. Some of the Alpiners didn't agree, and the usual spate of outraged letters ensued. I printed every letter in full. Without rebuttal. The letters stopped. But of course I was still an Outsider.

So, in fact, were two members of my staff. Carla had been on the job for only three months, but Ed had worked on *The Advocate* for almost a decade. He was gradually assimilated, but acceptance took time in a small town.

So we muddled along under my untested managerial skills. We weren't losing money—yet. But we were teetering, just making ends and the payroll meet, but I was determined to make a go of *The Advocate* and had actually upped the circulation by almost fifty subscribers, most of them in outlying areas. The same, alas, could not be said for the advertising income.

"The Grocery Basket wants to cut its ad to a half page," Ed reported in his rumbling, mournful voice. "No more coupons. They're losing money on the fifty-cent eggs."

"Promotion," chimed in Carla, whirling around the office like a wind-up doll. "The Grocery Basket needs to promote its specials more. Take squash. It's the season. Do you know there are twenty-eight varieties of squash available this time of year?" Her long black mane sailed around her slim shoulders.

Ed looked affronted. "I hate squash."

"Pumpkins are a squash," Carla went on blithely.

"They'll be in next week. The Grocery Basket could sponsor a jack-o'-lantern carving contest."

Ed was shaking his head, his heavy jowls undulating. "Halloween is getting dangerous, even in a town like Alpine."

"Ed, you're a ninny," asserted Vida Runkel, who had just stumbled across the threshold carrying a megaphone. "You think Arbor Day is dangerous."

Ed gave a mighty heave of his body and got up from his desk. "It can be, around here. All that controversy with the environmentalists and the loggers. A bunch of nuts want to picket Old Mill Park."

I sighed. The park was the site of the original sawmill, complete with a small museum and a half-dozen picnic tables next to the railroad tracks. "How can you picket a memory?"

"Symbolism." Carla nodded sagely. She turned to Ed. "Besides, that's only a rumor, probably started by the loggers. There are too many rumors in this town. It's impossible to verify everything if you have to make a deadline. Like finding that gold this morning."

I frowned at Carla. Ed swiveled slightly, his hand on the coffeepot. "Gold?" I echoed. "What gold?"

Carla was taking off her suede flats and examining the heels. "These are really worn down. Maybe I should put on my running shoes and go to the shoemaker's."

"Carla . . ." My voice held a weary warning note. Carla's attention span was as fragile as her five-foot frame.

"What?" The big black eyes were wide. "Oh! The gold mine!" She giggled. Carla was a world-class giggler. "I got a call when I came in first thing saying that Mark Doukas had found gold in . . . some place."

"Bunk," Ed said, sloshing coffee into a Styrofoam cup.

"Rubbish," Vida said, tapping the megaphone with her stubby fingers.

"Who called?" I inquired, feeling that familiar unease I often experience when Carla goes off chasing wild geese.

"Mmmmmm." She danced a bit in her stockinged feet.

"Kevin MacDuff, I think. He said Mark Doukas was tripping out. Isn't Kevin the kid with the pet snake?"

Kevin was. In addition, his eldest brother was Kent, who happened to be married to Mark Doukas's sister, Jennifer. Despite the snake, Kevin was as easygoing as Kent was touchy. Kevin was also one of our carriers.

"That snake eats mice," Vida declared, putting down the megaphone and taking off her ancient velvet cloche which, as usual, she'd been wearing backward. "I don't care for mice, but I think that's disgusting."

I was bearing down on Carla, which only took about four paces, since our front office is quite small and very crowded. "The gold, Carla. What exactly did Kevin say?"

Carla turned vague. "Oh—that Mark had been panning or digging or delving and he'd hit pay dirt, or whatever you call it, and he came racing out of the woods looking half nuts. Kevin said Mark must have found gold. You know how he likes to play prospector."

Mark did indeed, though *playing* was the word for it, as he expended no more energy on prospecting than he did on any other endeavor that might qualify as work. Neeny Doukas's oldest grandchild had never held a steady job in his twenty-six years, despite the family's efforts to make him a responsible citizen. As far as I could tell, his alleged duties as property manager for his grandfather consisted of harassing tenants he happened to run into in various bars around the county. It was no wonder that Heather Bardeen had dumped him the previous weekend.

"I doubt it was gold," I said. "Nobody's ever found any around here, and not much silver, either, in the last forty years." I glanced at Vida for confirmation, but she was wiping off the mouthpiece of the megaphone with a tissue soaked in rubbing alcohol. A sudden horrible thought assailed me as I turned my gaze back to Carla. "You didn't write this up, did you?"

Carla's long lashes flapped up and down like spider legs. "Well, of course I did! I made room for it by pulling that two-inch story on the zoning commission meeting.

They meet every two weeks and never do anything. Who cares?"

"Oh, Carla!" I didn't try to hide my exasperation. It wouldn't faze Carla anyway. Nothing ever did. "Where is it? Let me see your hard copy."

Undismayed, Carla obliged. The short article was fairly innocuous—for Carla:

Bonanza days may be in store again for Alpine. Mark Doukas hit the jackpot yesterday when he struck gold outside of town near Icicle Creek.

According to a colleague of Doukas, the local resident was prospecting close to the old silver mine shafts and found a large deposit of gold. An excited Doukas returned to Alpine to report his findings to Sheriff Milo Dodge, but the local law enforcement agency was out to coffee. As of this morning, Doukas was unavailable for comment.

I handed the story back to Carla. At least Carla hadn't misspelled Dodge's first name this time. In her first article involving the sheriff, she'd made a typo, calling him *Mildo*. Fortunately, I caught it in time, telling myself that it could have been worse. "Okay," I said to Carla, "this probably isn't libelous, unlike your piece on Grace Grundle's bottle cap collection—where you insinuated she stole it from Arthur Trews. You're very lucky that Arthur died the week after that story came out."

"Not so lucky for Arthur," remarked Vida.

I ignored my House & Home editor. "However, you shouldn't have pulled the zoning commission story. We'll catch hell from Simon Doukas for that, since he's the chairman. As for the gold: you have only the word of a fifteen-year-old boy. And you didn't contact Mark Doukas. Where was he when you called?"

"I didn't call." Carla's eyes were so wide and innocent that I thought her face might split. At least I hoped it would. "I didn't have time. I had to get the paper off to Monroe."

"Monroe's getting too big," said Ed, sitting back down. "You see that new development going up? Thirty houses, at least. They'll ask an arm and a leg. I couldn't afford one of those three-car garages."

I also ignored my advertising manager. I hadn't yet finished with Carla. "Look, I appreciate your initiative. But this isn't the kind of story we need to get in at the last minute, if at all. Next time, wait until Mark runs in here with a ten-pound nugget, shouting—"

"Eureka!" Vida blasted the word through the megaphone, and both Carla and I jumped.

"What on earth are you doing with that thing?" I demanded, sounding more cross than I really was.

Vida shrugged, her rumpled blouse quivering over her big bosom. "I interviewed the high school cheerleaders this morning. They gave it to me as a souvenir. Actually, I stole it. I've always wanted one." She started to give me her smug little smile, but stopped when a car door banged outside her window. Vida glanced through the rain-spattered pane. "Oh, swell, now I'm under arrest. It's Sheriff Moroni. The old fool."

Enrico Moroni was actually the former sheriff, having given up his office on account of his diminishing eyesight, and, according to Vida, his diminishing hold on the electorate. Moroni's impaired vision didn't keep him from driving a battered old Cadillac de Ville, but his status as an ex-sheriff kept him out of jail. Nothing else could, since he averaged about one accident per month. No doubt he was now parked on the sidewalk. Moroni and Neeny Doukas had been chums since boyhood, and Enrico was known as *Eeeny*. Some day I intended to ask Vida what had happened to Miny and Moe.

"Che bella!" Moroni burst into the office, making straight for Carla. His parents had been immigrants from Palermo, and while Eeeny had been born in Seattle, he retained a few fragments of their native tongue, especially

when he wanted to impress pretty women. "Hey, Carla, you want to make pesto with me?"

Carla giggled. "I can't. I have to interview Henry Bardeen about the improvements at the ski lodge."

Moroni, who was spare and sinewy, looked over the top of Carla's head to Vida. "Vida, *cara mia*, let's go in the broom closet and make beautiful music, eh?"

Vida gave him her gimlet eye. "I'll play the dust mop on your head, Eeeny. Why don't you marry one of those silly widows who are always having you to dinner?"

Moroni pulled a long face. "You're a widow, Vida, but you never feed me. How come?"

Vida's expression was sour. "Because you're an idiot, that's why. Isn't Moroni the Italian plural for moron?"

The former sheriff laughed and made a slashing gesture with his hand. "Ahhh! You never forgave me for arresting your husband as a Peeping Tom, right, Vida? Give up the grudges. Think of the good times we could have."

Vida shot back in her chair. "Ernest never peeped! That was his brother, Elmo! And that halfwit cousin of theirs, from Skykomish!"

Eeeny leaned on Vida's desk and wagged a finger at her. "Now, Vida, you know what I always say—'The Family That Peeps Together, Keeps Together,' eh?"

Vida was about to boil over with outrage, but Moroni had already swung around to face me. "Say, what's this I hear about young Chris? Harvey Adcock just told me he showed up at the hardware store not half an hour ago. Where'd he come from?"

"Hawaii," I replied as the phone rang and Ed answered it in his lugubrious voice. I'd dropped Chris off at the house about an hour earlier. He hadn't mentioned any plans to go out, but there was no reason why he shouldn't. Yet I somehow felt uneasy. "I brought him in from the airport this morning."

Moroni was studying me closely through his thick glasses, his usual leer displaced by a scrutiny that I felt he'd probably reserved for hardened criminals in bygone days. "Does Neeny know?"

"I don't think so." I glanced at Ed, who seemed to be trying to talk Driggers Funeral Home out of its standing four-inch ad. "Chris came over here all of a sudden. He quit school."

"Aaargh!" Moroni made another slashing motion with his hand, this time more emphatic. "These kids! No staying power!" His dark, lined face displayed a grimace. "So why come to Alpine? Does he expect a big welcome-back party?"

I shrugged, trying to ignore Ed's doleful arguments and Vida's aggressive typing. Carla had slipped out the door, presumably to interview Henry Bardeen up at the lodge. "Alpine is home, after all. Where else would he go?"

Eeeny Moroni seemed to take the question seriously. He rocked back on his heels, rubbing his hands together. "Damned if I know. But why is he trying to buy a gun?"

I blinked. Unfortunately, I thought I knew. But I was not going to say so to the ex-sheriff.

Chapter Three

WEDNESDAYS ARE USUALLY set aside for catching up. The paper is finished for the week; the reactions haven't yet started to come in; and the next edition is just beginning to take form in my mind. After Eeeny Moroni left, I went into my cubbyhole of an inner office and sat down to look at the books. It was the end of the third quarter, and I needed to assess *The Advocate*'s current financial position. A cursory scanning of the columns told me we weren't in any worse shape than I feared. But we weren't any better, either.

Ginny Burmeister had come to *The Advocate* directly from high school three years ago. She ran the tiny front office, which had its own entrance and led to the former back shop, which was now mainly used for storage in this age of high tech. Ginny answered the phone, took classified ads, sold stationery supplies, filled out small printing orders, and handled the books. A tall, thin girl with auburn hair, she was far more reliable than Carla but had no literary gifts whatsoever. Money was her metier, and I was glad of it.

I opened the drawer of my old oak desk and took out some gum. No wonder my teeth kept trying to fall out, but at least I wasn't smoking a pack and a half a day anymore.

It was almost noon, and I suddenly realized I was starving. I also knew I should go out looking for Chris. Handguns—if that's what he was trying to get—were sold in the sporting goods section of the hardware store, but I convinced myself that he wanted a rifle. For deer, or

21

maybe birds. The season was upon us, after all. I didn't care to dwell on its being open season on Neeny Doukas.

Not that I was an avid fan of Neeny's. Like a lot of big frogs in small puddles, Neeny was borderline obnoxious. He was accustomed to getting his own way, whether buying people or things. Since his wife's death in 1986, he had lived alone in a big old stone and stucco house on what was known as First Hill, beyond the high school. Frieda Wunderlich, maybe the homeliest woman I ever saw, came on a daily basis to cook and clean. It was said—by Vida—that employer and employee rarely spoke. Frieda, in fact, might have been the only person who ever got the better of Neeny Doukas.

Before heading for the Venison Eat Inn and Take Out next door, I called my house to see if Chris was there. I didn't get an answer, except for my own voice, babbling on the recorder. Buzzing Ginny on the intercom, I discovered that she'd already left for lunch. Still stalling, I checked the little mirror above the filing cabinet. I looked awful, with circles under my eyes and the faint mark of a cold sore lingering on my lower lip. Not that I could ever put in a claim to beauty—but there were days when I was quite presentable. This just didn't happen to be one of them.

The rain had stopped, but the clouds hung low over the town, gray and heavy. The trees that marched up the hills into the mountains looked black and somehow sad. Above the dense forest, Mount Baldy brooded, its long ridge not yet wearing its first cap of snow. In late summer and early fall, Baldy's crest boasted wild flowers and heather. The colors had faded now, leaving the mountain dark and seemingly bare. I tied the belt to my black trench coat and wondered if autumn had really arrived. Judging by the gold and red and russet of the maples and birch, it had. I didn't mind; fall is my favorite season.

Front Street was busy, at least by Alpine standards, with a half-dozen cars and twice as many pedestrians. A couple of scaffoldings and several ladders were lined up along the sidewalk, evidence of the third annual Clean-Up, Paint-Up, Fix-Up project. Obviously, the merchants who had postponed their refurbishing would have to hurry before the bad weather set in. Not for the first time, it occurred to me that we should have made some improvements to *The Advocate*—other than getting a new doorstop for the front entrance.

The noon train, a freight bound for Chicago, slowed, whistled, and kept going. So did I, but not to the inn. Instead, I tramped across the street in the direction of Harvey's Hardware and Sporting Goods, two blocks away. On the near corner, I glanced up at the marquee of the Whistling Marmot Movie Theatre. Oscar Nyquist, the bombastic owner, was contenting himself with having the glass on the outside poster displays washed. Originally, the Marmot had been housed in the social room above the old pool hall on Railroad Avenue; but during the 1920s, Oscar's father, Lars, had built a real theatre on Front Street at Fifth. A miniature, if less lavish version of its art deco city cousins, the Marmot had also undergone a name change early on. Carl Clemans had mused in his droll manner that Lars Nyquist ought to choose something more imaginative than the Alpine Bijou, perhaps a name that would evoke the majesty of the surrounding mountains and forests.

"Goddamn, Carl," replied Lars, whose origins on the edge of a spectacular Norwegian fjord had hardened him against any less dramatic beauty, "look out the vindow and vat do you see? Nothing but trees and more trees and those goddamn pesky warmints that pop out of the ground and act sassy. Yah, sure, you got it—Vistling Marmot it is, and vill serve you right, py golly!"

Clemans, finding himself hoist on his petard (or perhaps secretly amused), didn't argue. The grand opening had taken place in 1924, with Greta Garbo's first film, *Gösta Berling's Sagg*. The show was a big hit with Alpine's Scandanavian population, but residents of different nationalities demanded Hollywood movies. Lars Nygnist never booked another foreign film. Over seventy years later, Oscar Nyquist was offering *Dances with Wolves*. It, too, was popular, though some of the old-timers ventured that Kevin Costner couldn't hold a candle to William S. Hart.

The hardware and sporting goods store, which was divided into two separate sections, smelled of sawdust and paint thinner. Harvey Adcock was a pixie of a man, no taller than I am, with pointed ears and a balding head and quicksilver movements. He was behind the counter of flooring samples, waiting on, of all people, Mark Doukas. I considered beating a hasty retreat, but figured Mark couldn't stick around forever. Besides, I really should talk to him, too.

Harvey looked past Mark and smiled with lots of small, perfect teeth and twinkling green eyes. "Mrs. Lord! Don't tell me your hallway panels have come unglued!"

I smiled back. "I'm the only one who has come unglued, Harvey. No, I wanted to get . . ." I paused, and nodded at Mark, realizing that there was a considerable resemblance between him and his cousin, Chris. Mark was older, taller, and heavier, but the long mouths were the same and so were the jawlines. Both had dark eyes, but where Chris's were vaguely hooded, Mark's were faintly shifty. Still, Mark was the better-looking of the two, possibly owing to style, rather than substance. In fact, Mark Doukas was incredibly handsome. That, coupled with the inheritance he would no doubt one day receive, should have made him the catch of Alpine. Yet he remained single, reputedly antagonizing young women such as Heather Bardeen at regular six-month intervals.

"Hi," he said in a laconic voice, leaning against the counter. His brown bomber jacket looked new; his faded blue jeans looked old.

I was still pausing, now waiting for Mark to mention his cousin's arrival. But he said nothing about Chris. Harvey was looking at me expectantly.

"Oh—I wanted to get some attachments for my cordless screwdriver," I said, latching on to the only excuse I could think of, despite the fact that I already had two extra sets, one courtesy of Adam, the other, a birthday gift from my brother, Ben.

Mark kept lolling against the counter. "Go ahead. Harvey and I were just shooting the breeze."

"Okay. Thanks." I smiled at Mark. "By the way, we've got a small story in the paper today about your prospecting. Frankly, I'm not sure if we got all the facts." Never admit you're wrong when it comes to reporting—that's one of my basic rules of journalism. Allow a margin for error or a lack of detail, but don't suggest you might be mistaken. I tried to look ingenuous, but at forty, I don't do it very well.

To my surprise, Mark drew back. "What about it?" he asked.

Since the paper would hit the streets in less than three hours, I opted for candor. "Carla Steinmetz got a call this morning from Kevin MacDuff. He said you'd found gold near Icicle Creek."

Mark's face darkened, and he banged his fist down on the glass counter. "Hell! That kid's as big a jerk as his brother! Wait till I get hold of him. . . ." The rest of the threat faded as Mark rushed out of the hardware store.

Harvey Adcock's eyebrows, which were only a sketch of red-gold hairs, lifted quizzically. "Gold? Mark never said anything about gold. He wanted to buy a crowbar."

I considered buying one myself and using it on Carla. "Did he mention his cousin, Chris?"

Harvey leaned both elbows on the counter and looked unusually solemn. "Oh, Mrs. Lord, I just about fell over when that young man came in here and told me who he was. He didn't want to, you know, but I had to ask when he inquired about handguns."

I tried to keep my voice casual. "Did you sell him one?"

Harvey shook his head with vigor. "Of course not. I had to ask to see his driver's license. He isn't twenty-one. Even if he were, there would be a sixty-day waiting period since he's just come in from another state." He looked up at a newcomer I recognized only vaguely from the Grocery Basket and called out a greeting. "Hello, Virgil. I've got your lumber out back. Do you want to bring the truck around?"

Virgil did, and Harvey called to his nephew through the door behind the counter. "Jason will help Virgil load up. I didn't say anything to Mark about his cousin. Do you think I should?"

I shrugged. "I'm sure his arrival is all over town, or will be, before the day is out."

"Neeny will have a stroke." Harvey came out from behind the counter and headed in his sprightly manner for the tool section. "Unless he's already had one. Mrs. Runkel tells me he's in very poor shape." He hesitated, his hand on a large cellophane-sealed package of more screwdriver attachments than I could ever find uses for in fifty years. "Gibb Frazier told me Mrs. Pratt left town last week. Do you suppose she and Neeny had a spat?" Harvey spoke in a near whisper, though there was no one to hear us.

"I doubt it," I said, automatically lowering my voice, too. "I saw her Monday driving on the ski lodge road." There was no mistaking the upswept hairdo of Phoebe Pratt or the bright red Lincoln Town Car she'd recently acquired. The car, along with most of Phoebe's other expensive possessions, was rumored to have come from the indulgent hand of Neeny Doukas, her longtime lover.

"People are odd," remarked Harvey, fondly looking at the screwdriver attachments as if he found tools more reliable than humans. "This set has everything," he asserted.

I was dazzled. "Gee, it sure does. Can it decorate cakes, too?"

Harvey laughed, much harder than the comment warranted. He looked more like a pixie than ever. A loud crash out back wiped the mirth from his face. "Oh, that Jason! He's so clumsy! Let me ring this up, and I'll go see what I can to do to help."

"Never mind, Harvey," I said. "Just hold it for me. I'll get it later." Maybe I'd forget. With luck, so would Harvey. "Say—do you know where Chris went after he left here?"

Harvey was already at the back door. "No, I can't say that I do. He should be easy for you to find, though."

"Oh?" My curiosity was piqued. "How come?"

From the doorway, Harvey gave me his impish smile. "Because he's driving your car. That big green Jaguar is hard to miss."

Sure enough, I sighted Chris, pulling in down the street at the Burger Barn. I ran along the uneven sidewalk, calling his name against the wind that had blown off the mountains.

He stopped in the parking lot and waited for me. When I got closer, I noted that his expression was more sullen than ever, and that he didn't seem very glad to see me.

"Chris!" I started to shout, but thought better of it. Two members of the local Chamber of Commerce were just emerging from the Burger Barn. "Chris," I said, mustering calm and waving at the merchants, "why the hell didn't you ask if you could use my car? Where did you get the keys?"

Chris looked almost as vague as Carla. "I thought I did ask," he mumbled. "Do you mind? The keys were underneath, by the left rear door."

They were, of course, since I always kept an extra set with the car in case I locked myself out. Or more likely, if Adam lost the keys, which he had already done four times in two years, despite the fact that he had spent twenty of those months in Hawaii.

I sighed. "Okay. But be careful. I love that car, even though most of the people here think I'm a snot for owning it."

"Most of the people here *are* snots," Chris said. He scowled at the length and breadth of Front Street. "They're worse than that. They're pricks."

"Some are, that's true. One thing about a small town: at least you know who's a prick and who isn't." I tried to keep my voice light as I put a hand on Chris's arm. "Have you eaten lunch? I'm famished."

With only a minor display of reluctance, Chris let me lead him into the Burger Barn. It was busy as usual, with two women clerks from the drug store; the local insurance agent; Dr. Starr's dental hygienist and her new beau; the Episcopal rector and his wife; a quartet of loggers who were passing through—and Heather Bardeen with a girlfriend I knew only as Chaz.

Now and again I have been accused of having a perverse nature, but I prefer to call it puckish. Thus, I steered Chris over to Heather and Chaz, which wasn't difficult since they were seated in the booth next to the door. They were also about to leave.

I introduced them and watched Heather's cornflower blue eyes narrow. "So you're the long-lost cousin from Honolulu," she said, sounding pleasant, if not actually friendly. "You must have heard that Neeny is about to croak."

Chris regarded her coolly. "You said it first."

Heather's pouty mouth opened slightly. "Huh?" She gave me a questioning, sidelong glance.

"Chris just got in this morning," I explained a bit too hastily. "He hasn't seen any of his family yet. He's staying with me."

Heather picked up her purse and the bill. "Well, if you run into Mark the Shark, tell him to go screw himself. For a change," she added with bite. "Come on, Chaz, we're going to be late getting back to work. Dad will flip his toupee."

Heather and Chaz flounced off. I decided not to make an awkward moment any more so by standing around waiting for a booth, so I sat down in the seat Heather had just vacated. The waitress, whose name was Kimberly and who was some relation to Vida, came over to clear the table.

"Heather's the girlfriend?" Chris inquired after Kimber-

ly had departed in a clatter of dishes and rattle of silverware.

"Ex-girlfriend." I picked up the menu, though I knew
exactly what I was going to order. "She works for her dad
at the ski lodge. He runs it for the Norwegians. They all
live some place else now—Seattle or Palm Springs."

Chris seemed even less interested in the Norwegians
than in Heather. Still, I thought he'd shown a spark of life
when Heather had put on her pout. I congratulated myself
on my puckishness. What irony, I told myself, if Chris and
Heather should fall into each other's arms. What goofy
ideas I could get, I reminded myself as Kimberly resurfaced with an order pad.

Making small talk over burgers, fries, and shakes wasn't
easy with Chris Ramirez. He evaded any queries about
calling on his relatives. He never mentioned trying to buy
a handgun. He didn't say where he'd been in the past two
hours, except cruising around town. And, like ninety-nine
percent of the people I meet, he never asked me anything
at all.

"My treat," I said when the bill arrived. Chris didn't argue. I calculated the tip for Kimberly and said hello to the
rector and his wife as they went out. "What are your plans
for this afternoon?" I asked without much hope of getting
a direct answer.

Chris put his baseball cap and his denim jacket back on.
"I'm going to see Neeny."

My heart gave a little lurch. "Chris—why don't you
wait? He's sick, really he is." Vida might be right. Certainly the rest of the town seemed to agree with her. "Why
don't you talk to your uncle Simon first? His office is just
down the street, in the Clemans Building."

"I didn't come here to see my uncle." His jaw was set,
his eyes staring straight past my shoulder.

I leaned across the table. I wondered if I should ask him
why he wanted to buy a handgun, but since he hadn't been
able to get one, I decided to let that question slide. Instead,
I urged caution. "Damn it, Chris, you're staying with me.

You're my son's friend. Don't you dare do something foolish! At least take time to think things through."

"I've been thinking for fourteen years." He barely
moved his lips when he spoke.

"Then keep thinking for another fourteen hours. Please
talk to your uncle. If you don't go see him, you can bet
he'll come see you." I sat back, my own lower lip thrust
out.

Chris seemed to waver ever so slightly. "Maybe not."

"No maybes about it." I was gaining confidence. "You
don't know small towns. You don't know your family. I'm
surprised Simon Doukas isn't combing the streets for you
right now."

Except that was precisely what Simon Doukas was
doing. He stood in the door of the Burger Barn, and there
were tears in his eyes.

The tactful maneuver was to leave uncle and nephew
alone. For once, I gave in to my better nature as a human
being, rather than my professional voyeurism as a journalist. I made my exit as discreetly as possible.

The office was in its usual midweek hiatus. Ginny
hailed me on the way in, repeating her frequent argument
that we ought to insist on prepayment for household items
in the classifieds. "If they don't sell the stuff, they think
they don't have to pay for the ad," she asserted, pulling
back her curly auburn hair with an elastic band. "I've already talked to four deadbeats this morning." It was an old
argument in the newspaper business, but I was sticking to
Marius Vandeventer's policy of publish first, collect later.
Unfortunately, it didn't seem to be working. I tried consol-
ing Ginny, but she remained adamant. Not for the first
time, I considered her as Ed's replacement.

Carla was fretting over her story on the ski lodge renovations. Ed was complaining that the Hutchins Interiors
and Decor ad was too big. Vida was singing the Alpine
High School fight song as she pounded out her cheerlead-
ing article.

"Fight on, ye Buckers;
    Chop down their trees!
Turn them into suckers;
    Bring them to their knees!
Saw off their . . ."

Miraculously, she stopped. "My grandfather wrote that," Vida announced, using the keys of her typewriter to tap out the rest of the melody. "Back in 1916. There were six pupils in the school, four of them were Blatts."

Vida had been a Blatt before she became a Runkel. It was her father-in-law who was responsible for the original brainstorm about building the ski lodge, but he'd sold out to the Norwegians just before World War II. Ernest, Vida's husband, and the fourth of the Runkels' six children, had been in real estate, working first for his father, and later for Neeny Doukas. Ernie, as he was known, might never have been a Peeping Tom, but he'd had some other curious hobbies, including going over waterfalls in a barrel. It was on one such excursion ten years ago that Ernie had met his demise on Deception Creek. The falls weren't that treacherous, but the truck that had driven off the road and run over his barrel was.

Vida had been left a widow at forty-four, with three children to raise. A natural font of information about everybody and everything in town, she asked Marius Vandeventer for a job. Marius had complied, and Vida had been a fixture at *The Advocate* ever since. She wasn't much of a writer, but she worked hard and had a genuine nose for news. Her only vices, as far as I could tell, were chocolate truffles, her sharp tongue, and the propensity for wearing her endless variety of outdated hats backward.

In the beginning, Vida and I had only one problem: she despised Democrats more than anything else in the world—except Catholics. I was both. Having been forewarned by Marius Vandeventer, I predicted that when Vida learned I'd borne a child out of wedlock, she would be the first to pin a scarlet letter on my raincoat. But Vida had surprised me. On a snowy afternoon last January when the subject came up and I'd casually remarked that Adam's father and I had never been married, Vida had taken off her glasses, rubbed her eyes like mad, and said, "Good for you. You've got spunk." We had been forging a tentative friendship ever since.

"Hey," I asked, as Ed hung up on his latest advertising victim, "what's with Phoebe Pratt? Harvey Adcock said she left town—but I saw her Monday."

"Phoebe!" Vida gave one of her magnificently eloquent shudders, her bosom heaving. "She probably went to Seattle on a shopping spree. With Neeny's credit cards. I still can't believe she convinced him to take her to Las Vegas last month. Neeny hasn't left Alpine in four years. The old fool. He dotes on that brainless hussy. I always said I should have married Clinton Pratt. He asked me first, you know. Even then, Phoebe was fast. She got caught with boys in the boiler room at the high school at least four times before we graduated. Poor Clint, it's no wonder he died young. He'd have been better off with me."

Ed looked up from the classified section he was working on. "And you'd have been Vida Blatt Pratt. You wouldn't have liked that, Vida. *I* sure wouldn't."

Easily diverted as usual, Carla turned away from her ski lodge article. "I thought your own husband died young, Mrs. Runkel."

Vida lifted her sharp chin. "He didn't die," she said with dignity. "He was killed. It's not the same."

Ginny Burmeister had noiselessly entered the editorial office, bringing with her a couple of legal notices for the next edition. "My father worked for Mr. Pratt's plumbing company," Ginny said in her nasal voice. "Dad thought Clint Pratt was really nice, but a wimp."

Vida harrumphed. "He certainly couldn't stand up to Phoebe. She wouldn't give the poor man children, either. I hoped that when she went away after he died, she'd keep out of Alpine for good. But oh, no, back she came not even a year later, looking like the Queen of Sheba, and ready to sink her claws into Neeny Doukas. In fact," Vida added darkly, slamming the carriage of her typewriter for emphasis, "I wouldn't be surprised if she'd been carrying on with Neeny even before Clint died."

"I don't know why our generation is always being criticized," Ginny said, exchanging glances with her peer, Carla. "Think of people acting like that back then. That was twenty years or so ago, when I was a baby. Dad had to get another job after Mr. Pratt died and my folks were really broke. Mrs. Doukas was still alive. Wasn't she heartbroken?"

"About forty times," retorted Vida. "Poor Hazel didn't have the gumption to make a fuss about how Neeny couldn't behave himself. She just sat at home and baked apple pan dowdy."

Gibb Frazier stood in the doorway, thumbs hooked in his suspenders, plaid flannel shirt not quite meeting over his paunch. "Damned post office," he muttered, letting the wind rattle the door. "They're talking about raising the rates again. They'll put you out of business, Emma."

I gave Gibb a wry smile. "Me and *The Christian Science Monitor*."

Gibb banged the door shut and stumped over to Vida. He had lost a leg ten years ago in a logging accident. At not yet fifty, he'd been too young to retire, so after acquiring an artificial limb, he'd traded in his logging rig for a pickup truck and hired himself out as a Jack-of-All-Hauling-Trades. One of his jobs was to take *The Advocate* to and from Monroe every week.

"What's this I hear over at the post office about the Doukas kid coming back to Alpine?" He addressed his question to Vida, who was commonly known as the source of all vital information.

"Ramirez kid," I corrected, but neither Vida nor Gibb paid me any heed.

Vida took off her glasses with the tortoise-shell rims and rubbed her eyes with both fists in a typically vigorous manner. "How should I know?" she replied crossly. Above all else, Vida hated not knowing. "Ask Emma. He's staying with her."

I gave a little shrug. "He quit school. You know how kids are these days. I suppose he figured it was time to get reacquainted with his family, now that Margaret's dead." The fib slipped easily off my tongue; sometimes you have to be glib to protect your sources.

Gibb's wide faced creased into a frown. "If I were Chris Doukas or Ramirez or whatever his name is, I wouldn't bother myself. That arrogant sonovabitch Neeny will give him a bad time. And Simon's a stuffed shirt. As for your Mark—" Gibb stopped and spat into his hand. "That's for Mark, the dirty little creep. He may be rich, but he's still a bum."

It wasn't the first time I'd heard Gibb Frazier cast aspersions on the Doukas clan in general, and Mark in particular. Before Gibb could further revile Mark Doukas, the phone rang in my inner office. I left my staff and hurried to take the call. It was Chris. He wanted to know if he could leave my car at the Burger Barn. He was going to have dinner with Uncle Simon and Aunt Cece and his cousin, Mark, at their house on Stump Hill.

"Sure," I replied, a sense of relief flooding over me. "That's great, Chris. Do you remember Cece? She's very sweet." She was, too, so much so that she frequently made me gag.

"Kind of. Doesn't she have moles?"

"One mole, on her cheek. People find it charming." That was true, too. People found everything about Cecelia Caldwell Doukas charming, especially her enthusiasm for Good Works. "Will you be back later tonight?" I hoped not—I didn't mind having Chris stay with me, but I'd much prefer that he made peace with his family. Spending the night on Stump Hill might very well lay the foundation for a new relationship.

"I guess," said Chris. "Uncle Simon or Mark will probably bring me to your place."

"Okay." My euphoria over the happy Doukas family reunion slipped a notch. "Have a good time. I'll wait up to let you in."

"You don't have to," said Chris in his taciturn manner. "I've got a key."

"Oh." I didn't bother to ask how.

For the next hour, the phone never stopped ringing, which isn't unusual at *The Advocate*. I fended off the president of the Burl Creek Thimble Club, who was threatening to disband the organization; listened patiently to a long-winded diatribe from the Chamber of Commerce's executive secretary; took complaints from two members of the zoning commission abut the deletion of their story; explained why Vida's account of a recent wedding had not included the fact that the bride had set her wedding vows to rap music (Vida had been adamant about leaving it out); and jumped in my chair when I heard Neeny Doukas's deep, gravelly voice at the other end of the line.

"What kind of an outfit are you running there, Emma? What's this bullcrap about my grandson?"

I wasn't sure which of his grandsons he meant, so I hedged. "You know me, Neeny. I just try to do my best."

Neeny snorted into the receiver. "There's no gold around here. That's the trouble with you newcomers. You don't know siccum about Alpine. Mark wasn't prospecting. He was digging up maidenhair ferns for Cece's rock garden."

The resonant growl of Neeny's voice suggested he wasn't as feeble as Vida had reported. I could picture him at the phone, broad-shouldered, barrel-chested, a shock of white-streaked hair with a big mustache, full beard, and black eyes that could bore holes in tree trunks.

I don't like admitting I'm wrong, especially in print. But Carla's flighty reporting had put me in a tight corner. "Look, Neeny, we went off the deep end, I'm afraid. The story should have been verified. It wasn't, because we were right against deadline. I've already spoken to Mark about it. He blames Kevin MacDuff for calling it in, but we take responsibility for running it. We'll do a retraction next week, okay?" A faint smile twitched on my lips. On metropolitan dailies, editors and reporters worried about war and rumors of war, with statements checked out through the White House, the Kremlin, and Vatican City. In small towns, we sink into turmoil over maidenhair ferns and teenaged paper boys.

Neeny was grumbling over the line. "Oh . . . hell, I suppose. What else can you do, unless you rerun the whole damned thing. Could you do that?"

"No." I was emphatic. It wasn't just the expense of printing another three thousand copies of *The Advocate*. It was the principle. Neeny's request was tantamount to asking God to start the day all over again. It occurred to me that he'd probably done just that somewhere along the line.

"You gotta understand," he was saying, apparently for once taking no for an answer, "that it isn't just because of Mark that I'm upset. Do you wanna bunch of half-assed gold seekers tramping all over the woods and tearing the place up? It'd be worse than all them damned hikers and bikers."

I hadn't considered the wider implications, but Neeny was right. Every week, at least three hundred copies of *The Advocate* were mailed to former residents who liked to keep up with the doings in their old hometown. We had subscribers in twenty-seven states of the Union, as well as in Canada, Mexico, Japan, England, Belgium, and Sri Lanka. I had a sudden vision of all of them descending on Alpine with pickaxes and gold pans.

"You're right, Neeny," I said, resorting to a phrase that he'd no doubt heard ten thousand times in his seventy-two years. I felt obsequious and vaguely ashamed of myself. "I apologize." Hearing a rumble of assent, I broached an even more delicate subject. "Are you going to have dinner at Simon's tonight?"

"Paaah!" Neeny seemed to be fumbling for words. "How the hell did you get mixed up with that kid? As far as I'm concerned, he don't exist. Let Simon and that lamebrained wife of his feed the little punk. I'll bet he looks like Hector."

"He looks like Mark."

"Bullcrap. He looked just like his old man when he was a kid. God help him if he acts like him, too. I don't want any part of that Ramirez tribe."

Obviously, the antipathy was mutual. I marveled that Margaret Doukas Ramirez had maintained any contact at all with her father. No wonder she got a case of the glums whenever she heard from him. Still, my conscience was needling me. I decided to put Neeny on the alert. It was the least I could do.

"Chris has a chip on his shoulder, I'll say that. He was very fond of his mother." I spoke carefully, hoping Neeny wasn't in one of his purposely obtuse moods.

"Kids should like their mothers," he said with a grunt. "How old is he? Twenty? They all got chips on their shoulders at that age. Don't worry. He'll get it knocked off soon enough." He paused, and I heard a sound in the background. "Listen, Emma, I got company. Let me see what you're gonna do to fix up your dumb-assed story."

Ordinarily, I never clear copy with anyone, but I decided it wouldn't hurt to make an exception. "I'll do it right now and read it to you over the phone later, okay?"

"Huh?" Neeny was obviously distracted. "Yeah, sure, fine. Goodbye."

Before he hung up, I heard a female voice in the distance. I was almost sure it belonged to Phoebe Pratt.

Ed Bronsky was about to go home to his long-suffering wife and hyperactive children. "Another day, another half-dollar," he said, putting on his wrinkled raincoat. "I haven't had a raise on this job in three years."

I gave him my brightest smile. "If we took in more money, we could pay more. It's that simple, Ed. Why not bring in some new accounts?" Instead of losing our old ones, you dumbbell, I thought in secret annoyance.

Ed was searching in his pockets for his driving gloves. He didn't find them. He never did. Frankly I didn't think he owned a pair. "Now who would I get? A lot of the stores at the mall would rather advertise in the shopper that comes out of Monroe. Those other new places are too far out of town. Some of these merchants want to do inserts, and stuff *The Advocate* full of four-color tripe that just falls out on the sidewalk." He gave a forsaken shake of his head. "You wouldn't believe what advertisers can come up with."

I could, and wished I had the nerve to get rid of Ed and hire an ad manager who shared my imagination. Like Ginny Burmeister. But I was too good-hearted—and weak-willed—to fire Ed Bronsky. "What about Driggers Funeral Home?" I asked, hoping for the best but fearing the worst.

Ed was shuffling toward the door. "I talked them out of running that weekly ad. Once a month—that'll hold them." He tugged at the doorknob, which needed fixing. "Heck, it's the only funeral home in thirty miles. Besides, nobody has died here since July."

It was funny that Ed should mention that. No, it wasn't funny at all. Within twenty-four hours, it would be quite sad.

Chapter Four

WITHOUT CHRIS COMING to dinner, I wasn't inclined to fry up a batch of chicken. I hate cooking for myself, though I'm fairly competent around a stove. I left the office at six, heading for the Venison Eat Inn and Take Out. Except for a new French restaurant ten miles down the highway, the inn had the best kitchen in the vicinity. I often ate alone, which I usually preferred. I brought the printout of *The Advocate*'s financial statement. The conversation with Ed had goaded me into a serious analysis.

Unfortunately, I'm not very good at managing money. In the eighteen years I worked for *The Oregonian*, I succeeded in saving a grand total of $2,146.85. It was just enough to send Adam off to his first semester at the University of Hawaii.

I ordered the broiled halibut cheeks and rechecked the columns of figures. The good news was that the holiday season was upon us; the bad news was that Ed would probably try to cancel Christmas.

Over my green salad, I considered my personal finances. Out of Don's $500,000, less taxes, I'd spent $200,000 on *The Advocate* and $30,000 for the used Jaguar. I'd sold my two-bedroom house in Portland for $145,000 and paid just under $100,000 for the stone and log cabin in Alpine. I'd paid off all my debts and still had a small nest egg. I certainly didn't want to use it to keep *The Advocate* alive. Capitalism wasn't supposed to work that way. But if Marius Vandeventer had updated his technology, he'd let the building run down. In heavy rain, the roof leaked. When the snow piled up, ice covered the inside of the windows. The floorboards in my office creaked ominously. The exterior and interior were badly in need of paint. I figured I was looking at an outlay of at least $25,000. Given our current hand-to-mouth existence, renovation wasn't feasible.

The halibut arrived, snow-white and tender, with just a dusting of charcoal on top. Should I pony up that twenty-five grand? Once I got Adam through school, he'd be on his own. Maybe. I knew a lot of parents who'd congratulated themselves at commencement and four years later were still providing free room and board. Or worse yet, had found their children on the doorstep with *their* children.

I layered my baked potato with butter, sour cream, chives, and bacon bits. Luckily, gaining weight isn't a problem for me. I have too much nervous energy, and I tend to burn off calories. It's a good thing, because I consider physical exercise a deplorable waste of time. I could be eating instead.

The *Advocate*'s spread sheets depressed me. Chris Ramirez's hostility depressed me. Gibb Frazier's comment about the increase in postal rates depressed me. Ed Bronksy's negativism depressed me. Carla Steinmetz's careless journalism depressed me. I should have ordered a drink. Instead, I ate like a pig and watched my fellow diners, which depressed me even more.

There was Dr. Starr's dental hygienist again, holding hands with her boyfriend. There was Harvey and Darlene Adcock, looking devoted after thirty years of marriage. There were the newlyweds whose wedding Vida had just written up. Two other couples I didn't know sat at tables across the room.

Couples. The world was geared to pairs, not singles. I cup up my potato skin and ate that, too. I'd never really been part of a couple. I'd been engaged. I'd borne a child. In the past twenty years, I'd had two more lovers and another fiancé. I wasn't given to casual romance. I never loved anybody but Tom Cavanaugh.

I met Tom when I was an intern on *The Seattle Times* and he was working the copy desk. I was twenty, he was twenty-seven, and we fell for each other like a ton of bricks. My plans to marry Don Cummings after we graduated from college evaporated. Tom talked about leaving his wife of five years. We were wildly, briefly happy. Then I got pregnant. So did Tom's wife. He made a heart-wrenching choice and stayed with Sandra.

I went to Mississippi to have my baby. My brother, Ben, had received his first assignment as a priest in the home missions along the delta. A capable black midwife with a seamless contralto voice delivered Adam, and the two of us struck out on our own.

My parents had been killed in a car accident coming from Ben's ordination the previous summer. I finished my degree at the University of Oregon, instead of at Washington, and took a job on *The Oregonian*. I'd stayed there until a year and a half ago when I inherited Don's insurance money and realized I could fulfill my seemingly impossible dream of owning a weekly newspaper.

I'd stopped dreaming about being half of a couple a long time ago. My last romance was with a twice-divorced professor of philosophy from Reed College who was brilliant, charming, and so claustrophobic that he wouldn't even go to the movies. We went on so many picnics that I developed a phobia of my own—to potato salad. We split up in January of 1987 after I caught pneumonia from eating lunch in a hailstorm.

My depression lifted with the presentation of the dessert menu. Either I am very shallow or I have great resilience. Whichever it may be, cheesecake restores me. I was polishing off the last bite when Eeeny Moroni came into the restaurant.

"Emma, *mio cor!*" Not wanting to show favoritism, he gave the hostess a slap on the backside before gliding up to my table. Eeeny Moroni was light on his feet for an older man and reputed to be the best dancer in Alpine, though Vida insisted it was only because he'd taken professional lessons in his youth. "I thought you had a date with a younger man," said Eeeny, sitting down in the vacant chair opposite me. "Was that Chris Ramirez I saw outside of the Burger Barn with Simon?"

"Probably. Dark, not quite six feet, denim jacket, and baseball cap?" Given Eeeny's lousy eyesight, I marveled that he could tell Chris from Vida. Except, of course, that Vida would have worn the baseball cap backward.

"That was him." Eeeny nodded. "I kept my distance. They seemed deep in conversation. So where's the kid now?"

"He's safe in the bosom of his family," I said as Eeeny stared unabashedly at my bosom. "Simon and Cece asked him to dinner."

Eeeny scowled. "Simon's going to make Neeny mad." He paused, accepting a menu from the waitress and offering her his body. She laughed mechanically and recommended the Idaho trout. Eeeny adjusted his thick glasses and squinted at the entrées. "That Chris is just going to cause trouble, Emma," he continued, back to serious matters. "It was bad with Hector, for the whole Doukas tribe. It almost broke Hazel's heart. I can't tell you how many times she tried to go to Hawaii to see Margaret and that kid."

"Why didn't she do it?"

Eeeny looked at me as if I were dense. "Neeny wouldn't let her. That's why."

"Hazel Doukas must have been a wimp," I declared, trying in vain to imagine my own independent-minded mother knuckling under to my father in similar circumstances. Then I remembered the concessions I'd made to Neeny that very afternoon and gave Hazel a little mental slack.

Eeeny Moroni ordered cracked crab and a half bottle of Chardonnay. I excused myself, recalling that after a few drinks Eeeny's amorous words could turn into lecherous deeds. I'm not much of a flirt.

I got home just after seven, still stewing over *The Advocate*'s finances. The wind was up, making the stately evergreens sway and rattling the lid on my garbage can. I changed clothes, looked through *The Seattle Times*, heard somebody's dog howl at the brewing storm, and winced as the electricity flickered several times. I needed some business advice, so I called Dave Grogan, the newspaper broker who had handled the deal between Marius and me. He lived about a hundred miles away, in a small town not far from the ocean. After listening patiently to my tale of woe, he advised caution.

"You aren't going broke yet, Emma," he noted in his kindly voice. "Your repairs can wait. Take a look at those ledgers in January. Even Ed can't wipe out the Christmas spirit single-handedly."

"He'll probably try, though," I said, sounding almost as gloomy as Ed.

Dave Grogan, who knew virtually every small daily and weekly newspaper in western Washington inside and out, chuckled. "Have you ever considered that Ed may be using reverse psychology?"

"No," I said bluntly. "And if he is, I don't think it's working." I sighed. "I'm probably overreacting. But I want to make a go of this so much."

Dave paused, and I could hear the shuffling of papers over the miles. "You've got several options, Emma. One thing you might mull over is a partnership."

"No." I was emphatic. "The big attraction for me—or at least part of it—is being my own boss. I'm awfully independent, Dave."

"I don't mean an editor-publisher relationship per se," Dave said in his mild manner. "I'm talking about the kind of setup where a—I guess you could say silent partner—has a financial interest in the paper but no hands-on control. I've got a couple of people looking for that sort of a deal right now. They want an investment, but they don't want to get actively involved in the operation or else they don't want to live in a small town."

I frowned into the receiver. "What's the payoff?"

"For them? Money. That type of person is usually willing to sink a pretty good-sized amount of cash into expansion. Generally, they're interested in suburban weeklies, where the growth potential is obvious. But once in awhile you find someone who's a bit more adventuresome. Or farsighted."

I hesitated. "It's a thought." My ears caught the sound of a car outside. "I'll take your advice and hang tight until after the first of the year. If conditions look grim, maybe you can find me a pigeon." The car drove off; no one came to my door. A false alarm, I decided, figuring it was too early for Chris to come back anyway.

"I've got one right now," Dave said, accompanied by the sound of more paper shifting. "He's an old newspaper hand whose wife came into a lot of money a few years ago. He's bought into three weeklies in eastern Washington, four in Montana, one in Idaho, and has a deal in the making up in British Columbia."

I was impressed. "Who is this moneybags?"

At the other end, Dave's wife was calling to him. "What?" he said, momentarily distracted. "Oh, he used to work for *The Times*, 'way back. His name's Tom Cavanaugh."

By midnight, I was ready to give up waiting for Chris. Maybe he'd changed his mind and decided to stay with his relatives after all. It wouldn't be unusual for a kid that age not to call. Adam had always thought my rules about checking in with old Mom were arcane—and weird.

Besides, I was beat. It had been a busy, exceptionally long day. I marveled that I'd kept awake all evening, and figured I probably would have nodded off hours ago if it hadn't been for the jolt from Dave Grogan.

All I knew about Tom Cavanaugh was that he'd stayed on at *The Times* for another five years, had a second child with Sandra, and then moved to Los Angeles. After that, his history was a blank—except for a chance remark three years ago at a Sigma Delta Chi Journalism Awards banquet when a retired city editor had mentioned Tom's name, and added, "Poor guy." I pretended I didn't care and failed to ask for amplification. Of course I'd kicked myself ever since.

But *poor* apparently didn't describe Tom's financial state. I recalled that Sandra Cavanaugh came from a wealthy Bay Area family, and it would follow that she would end up rich in the wake of her parents' demise. So would Tom, since it appeared the couple had remained together. Good for them, I reflected grimly. I hoped Sandra had turned out to be every bit of the ditz she seemed to be. My better nature doesn't always win.

My back and my head both ached as I pushed the last of the logs into the cavernous stone fireplace. It dominated the room and provided enough space to roast a small ox. The wind was blowing down the chimney, sending the sparks flying against the smoke-blackened stones. I still had the poker in my hand when Chris came through the door. I must have looked menacing, because he actually jumped.

"I thought you'd be in bed," he said, his face not so much sullen as it was wary. His dark hair was windblown, and I suspected he hadn't shaved since yesterday morning in Honolulu.

"Almost," I admitted, setting the poker back in place. "How was dinner?"

Chris shrugged out of his jacket, which I noticed had suddenly turned from denim into leather. "Fine. They had steak."

"Were all your relatives there?" I had moved to the door to put the chain on for the night, a habit of my city days in Portland.

Chris was ambling around the living room, hands shoved in the pockets of his jeans. "Some of them."

I could see this was going to be the usual tooth-extraction sort of conversation I had grown accustomed to with most of Adam's friends and occasionally with Adam himself. "Not Neeny?"

"No." He had his back to me, apparently admiring a Monet print hanging above my recently reupholstered sofa.

I picked the leather jacket off the back of the rocker where he'd thrown it. "Where'd you get this?" I asked, trying not to sound like an inquisitor.

"Huh?" He shifted his weight, turning slightly to glance at me. His wiry frame seemed tense. "Oh, it's Mark's. He couldn't find it when he went out so he borrowed mine. Then I had to borrow his because it was so windy and stuff. I'll take his back tomorrow."

The explanation made as much sense as anything else at the end of a long, tiring day. I surrendered on eliciting further information from Chris. Maybe he'd talk more over ham and eggs at breakfast.

"I'm going to bed. Is there anything you need?" I inquired.

"No. Thanks," he added as an afterthought. His back was still turned. Maybe he was crazy about Monet. Certainly he was absorbed in something I couldn't fathom. His relatives, probably—seeing them again after all these years must have been a traumatic experience.

"Okay," I said, taking him at his word.

It wasn't the first mistake I ever made, but it was one of the worst.

I wasn't entirely surprised that Chris wasn't around when I got up at seven the next morning. I still felt a bit groggy, and it was raining like mad, a dark, wet September morning that could drain all but the hardiest native of enthusiasm for a new day.

Chris had slept in his bed—or maybe Adam really hadn't made it before he'd gone to Hawaii at the end of August. I didn't snoop in my son's room while he was away. I couldn't bear to; the disarray gave me the twitch. As long as there were no overpowering aromas and nothing slithered out from under the door, I figured everything else could wait until the Thanksgiving break.

Instead of ham and eggs, I ate two shredded wheat biscuits and drank a cup of coffee. By ten to eight, there was no sign of Chris, and I had to be on my way to the office. To my surprise, the Jag was parked in the carport. Deferring to the downpour and my new green suede shoes, I drove to *The Advocate*.

Ginny was in the front office, efficiently typing up the end-of-month statements. No one else had arrived yet. Carla was chronically late, Ed breakfasted with the Chamber on Thursdays, and Vida usually didn't come in until eight-thirty. I put the coffee on, checked the answering machine, and went over some notes I'd made on next week's editorial calling for the resurfacing of County Road 187 between Icicle Creek and the ranger station.

By the time Vida got in, I'd taken four phone calls, including two subscribers who were dead set against the public swimming pool, one who was for it, and a woman named Hilda Schmidt who wanted to take out a classified ad to sell her exercise bicycle. Instead of referring her to Ginny, I took the ad myself and felt like cheering her on.

I went out into the editorial office to greet Vida. She was shining her glasses and looking sly. I recognized that expression. "What's new?"

Vida stuck her glasses back on her nose but retained the smug look. "Phoebe Pratt did leave town—but only for a couple of days. Darlene Adcock says she went to Seattle to see an eye specialist. If she ever gets her vision fixed, she'll see how homely Neeny is and dump him."

"Not with all his money." I parked myself on Carla's desk.

"True," Vida conceded. "Phoebe always was one for the main chance." She rummaged around in her enormous purse and pulled out a tarnished gold compact. Flipping it open, she applied powder on a hit-and-miss basis. "According to Bill the Butcher, Cece Doukas bought enough New York steaks—not on sale—for six." She cocked her head to one side, the overhead light bouncing off her glasses. "Who do you think? Cece, Simon, Mark, Jennifer, Kent—and your Chris? No Neeny, right?"

"Right so far," I agreed. "Except I didn't know Jennifer and Kent MacDuff were there."

Vida sniffed at my ignorance. "Of course they were. Dot Parker saw them from her driveway. She was on her way to pick up Durwood. He fell off the barstool at Mugs Ahoy again." She paused to smear on bright pink lipstick. "Last but not least, Heather Bardeen has an appointment with Doc Dewey this afternoon. The *senior* Dewey," she added with a knowing look.

Since Dewey the son had been the recipient of Dewey the father's practice, with the exception of maternity cases and a few stubborn patients who refused to be tended by a young whippersnapper, Vida's meaning was clear: Heather must be pregnant. Or thought she was.

"Where did you hear that?" I asked, fascinated as always by Vida's sources.

She gave a careless shrug, powder flying from the ruffled, wrinkled collar of her blue blouse. "Marje Blatt. My niece. She works for old Doc Dewey." Vida obviously thought I had a faulty memory.

She was right. "I forgot." The phone rang, and I grinned at Vida as I reached to answer it. I stopped grinning immediately. It was Sheriff Milo Dodge. Mark Doukas had been murdered—and Christopher Albert Ramirez was wanted for questioning.

Chapter Five

ED AND CARLA entered the office just as I hung up the phone. I was in virtual shock. I stared at them open-mouthed, while they stared back. I'd had to ask Milo four times if he meant Mark Doukas rather than Neeny. He insisted he did. There was no mistaking the grandson for the grandfather.

"I've got to go down to the sheriff's office," I announced, pulling myself together and grabbing my handbag and raincoat.

Carla's cheeks had turned pink with excitement. "Should we put out a special edition?"

The idea hadn't crossed my mind. Although this was my first Alpine murder—if in fact that was what had happened—I knew the town didn't have a blameless track record. A drunken, jealous husband had strangled his wife two years ago. A pair of loggers had gotten into a brawl only months before that, and one had beaten the other to death. And going back almost a decade, there had been the Claymore family, some four miles out of town, with a brooding, schizophrenic father who had shot his wife and six kids before turning the .22-caliber rifle on himself. Murder was no stranger to Alpine. I decided this event didn't merit an extra.

The phone rang before I could get out the door. To my surprise—and relief—it was Chris. I started to tell him about his cousin, but for once he launched into a monologue.

"Hi, Mrs. Lord. This is Chris. Hey, thanks for picking

49

me up and stuff." His voice was perfectly natural. "I decided to split. Alpine isn't my kind of place. I hitched a ride into Seattle. I'd like to see the city and maybe go on a ferryboat. Then I think I'll head for L.A."

"Chris!" I couldn't keep the panic out of my voice. "Wait—don't go anywhere! Your cousin's been killed!"

"Huh?" He sounded understandably dumbfounded. "What did you say?"

"It was Mark," I said, clarifying my report. "Sheriff Dodge just called and said he'd been murdered."

Chris gave a short laugh. "That's lame. I just saw Mark last night."

Fragments of song and verse about Yesterday and Tomorrow skipped through my agitated brain. "I guess it must have happened after you saw him," I said somewhat stupidly. I took a deep breath; I had to convince him to stay put. "Chris, this probably sounds idiotic, but Sheriff Dodge would like to talk to you about Mark."

He hesitated. When he spoke again, a wary note had surfaced in his voice. "Why me? The whole family was there. Except Grandpa. They all know Mark a lot better than I do." He made a strange, muffled noise. "Hey, this is weird! All things considered, I don't ever want to see Alpine again."

"It's not that simple," I began, but an operator came on the line and told Chris his three minutes were up.

"Got to go," he said, and rang off.

I stood by Ed's desk, with the receiver in my hand. The city of Seattle was home to half a million people. I had no idea where Chris's ride had dropped him off. I dialed the operator and asked if the last call made to *The Advocate* could be traced. She said no. So much, I thought, for modern communications technology.

"Chris has gone to Seattle," I told my staff. "If he calls again, find out where he is."

Ed looked mildly puzzled. "I thought you said he was in Seattle."

I clamped my mouth shut and left the office. We have

no police chief in Alpine, since it's an unincorporated town, despite the best efforts of civic-minded citizens to change the status. The mayor and the city council have been empowered through a charter allegedly drawn up during World War II in an air raid shelter under Mugs Ahoy. But when it comes to law enforcement, we rely upon the state police and the sheriff, which works out well enough since Alpine is the county seat. The Skykomish County Sheriff's office is two blocks away, so despite the rain and my green suede shoes, I walked. I needed time to collect my thoughts. I couldn't imagine why Mark had been murdered. A drug-crazed vagrant passing through, maybe. Or someone who had taken the discovery of gold seriously. Mark was no gem, but he didn't seem like the type to inspire homicide. Of course there was always Heather Bardeen and her appointment with Doc Dewey Senior. Maybe her father had decided to take the notion of a shotgun wedding seriously.

But why, I wondered, nodding vaguely at the handful of passersby I knew only by sight, did the sheriff want to question Chris Ramirez? Just because he happened to come to town the same day—or night—that Mark had gotten himself killed? I heard the morning freight whistling in the distance. Traffic was heavy on Alpine's main street—by Alpine standards. There must have been at least a dozen cars. Life was going on, with or without Mark Doukas.

Sheriff Milo Dodge was a big, shambling man, well over six feet, with broad shoulders and pale graying blond hair. He had a long face, sharp hazel eyes, and a square chin. In appearance, he was totally unlike his predecessor, Eeeny Moroni. But in terms of efficiency, he more than matched his mentor and was considered one of the best law enforcement officials in the state.

Which, I must admit, was the main reason I was disturbed over his desire to question Chris. Milo Dodge didn't act precipitously. His intentions sounded serious.

Dodge looked up from the paperwork strewn all over the desk. His office was finished in knotty pine and a thirty-pound steelhead was mounted over his filing cabinet. He stood up and proffered his hand, which was long and strong. I winced a little as he ground my bones together.

"Where's the kid, Emma?" he asked without preamble.

"Seattle," I replied, knowing it was useless to try to hide the fact since Vida Runkel had probably spread the word in the five minutes since I'd left the office. I saw the speculative look in Dodge's hazel eyes and lifted my sore hand. "I don't know where. He had to hang up before he could tell me."

"Damn." Dodge sat down, making his faux leather chair creak. "Emma—this is urgent. A dead Doukas isn't just another stiff. You know that. Now I suppose I have to call the SPD and King County and the State Patrol. Couldn't you have kept an eye on the kid?"

"I can't keep an eye on my own," I confessed, sitting in the chair across the desk from Dodge. "Chris Ramirez was a guest. He's twenty years old. And how the hell was I to know he'd get involved in a murder case?"

Dodge picked up a roll of mints, offered me one, which I declined, and turned the package around in his fingers. "I've known you for a little over a year," he said thoughtfully. The hazel eyes fixed on my face. "How well do you know this boy?"

I lifted my shoulders. "I've met him a couple of times when I was in Honolulu with Adam."

He popped a mint in his mouth. "Are Chris and Adam pretty tight?"

"Yes." As far as I could tell, they were best friends. Adam is more gregarious than I am. He knows a lot of other students. But like me, he doesn't form close attachments easily. "He and Chris were roommates last year."

The door opened and Jack Mullins, one of Dodge's deputies, poked his shaggy red head inside. "You want to see Doc Dewey now, Sheriff?"

Dodge waved a hand. "In a minute." Mullins left. Milo turned back to me. "Old Doc Dewey's still the coroner, you know."

I did, of course. He was waiting until the next election to turn over the duties to his son. I was beginning to get my thoughts back in order. My presence in the sheriff's office wasn't confined to my roles as Chris's hostess and the mother of Chris's friend. But before I could start playing journalist, Dodge asked me a question:

"What do you make of Chris, Emma?"

"I told you, I don't know him very well." I searched my brain for any help from Adam. But twenty-year-old men aren't into character analysis, at least not into articulating the subject. "He seemed nice enough. Quiet, polite. He hadn't declared a major, so I don't know what kind of ambitions or interests he has. Adam mentioned that he had a bike." I gave another little shrug. "A motorcycle, I mean. His mother bought it for him." I paused, watching Dodge's mobile face take in my scant information. Clearly, he wasn't satisfied. "Look, Milo," I said, going on the offensive, "I need the facts. All I know is that Mark is dead and you want to question Chris. What actually happened?"

Milo leaned back in the chair and put his feet on the desk. His cowboy boots, which had recently been resoled, reached almost halfway across the littered surface. "You don't publish again until next Wednesday. What's the rush?"

"The outside media, for one thing," I replied. "The Seattle and Everett papers will be interested. So will the TV and radio stations. You said it—the Doukas family is rich enough and venerable enough to make news outside of Alpine."

Dodge looked pained. "I don't want a bunch of reporters nosing around town."

I gave him a flinty smile. "Then give me the story. I can be the media contact and save them all a trip."

Dodge cracked the mint with his teeth and swung his feet back onto the floor. He picked up a sheaf of papers and scanned them rapidly. "I got a call last night from Mark Doukas asking me to meet him up at Mineshaft Number Three at nine o'clock. I didn't take the call personally, because I was at an all-day meeting and a dinner in Monroe. I got to the mine right on the dot, and Eeeny Moroni was already there. It seems that Mark had called him, too." He leaned forward, resting his elbows on the desk and adjusting the expansion band of his watch. The hazel eyes were shadowy, and it dawned on me that unlike his counterparts in Portland's Multnomah County, dead bodies weren't a common occurrence for Milo. Especially bodies he was used to seeing on Front Street or in the bar at the Venison Inn.

"Eeeny was having a fit," Dodge continued in a quiet voice. "He'd found Mark with his head bashed in. He was lying near the old mineshaft. He was still warm. I doubt if he'd been dead for more than a few minutes."

I cringed a bit and allowed for an appropriate moment of silence. Dodge was now fidgeting with a small figure of a spotted owl around whose neck hung a sign: EAT ME—I'M YOURS. Logging humor often eludes me; any kind of humor was hard to come by at the moment. The significance of Dodge's words struck me: "His head was bashed in? How?"

Milo's gaze shifted to the opposite wall that was covered with maps of the county. "We aren't sure yet."

"But he was . . . uh, clobbered, right?"

"Right." Dodge stood up; he seemed to loom over me. "Emma, I've got to see Doc Dewey. I'll give you more later, okay? Meanwhile, you help us locate Chris. Deal?" He extended his hand.

I kept mine in my lap. I also remained seated. "Not until I know why you want to speak to him."

The pained expression returned. Milo Dodge knew I could be stubborn. On at least two occasions, he had compared me to his ex-wife, Tricia, whose nickname was Old Mulehide. In a perverse way, I was flattered. Generally, however, we got along, engaging in the symbiotic relationship that is inherent between the press and law enforcement. "You can keep your mouth shut," Milo conceded, more to himself than to me.

"It's part of the job description."

He nodded. "Right." He sighed, leaning one hand against the wall next to the steelhead's snout. "Chris Ramirez was going around town yesterday trying to buy a gun. He couldn't, of course, having just arrived in this state. But he didn't ask about a hunting license. So what should we make of that, Emma?"

"Not much," I answered. "Mark wasn't shot, was he?"

He eyed me with a smirk. "And if Chris wanted to whack somebody, he didn't have a gun. Mark and Chris had a big argument at dinner last night, according to Kent MacDuff." Suddenly, Dodge swung around the desk and stood next to my chair. He was definitely looming now. "Why did you keep asking me if I meant it was Neeny who'd gotten killed?"

The sheriff had caught me off-guard. Fleetingly, I wondered if this was a ploy he reserved for interrogation. "Because he's old," I said, hoping I hadn't missed more than one beat. I stared up at him with my best brown-eyed look of innocence. "I thought there might have been a mistake. Maybe Neeny had simply had a heart attack and somebody had jumped to conclusions."

Dodge cocked his head to one side. "Not bad," he remarked with a wry smile.

"Well?" I stood up rather awkwardly. "Are you absolutely certain Mark didn't fall?"

The wry expression intensified. "Oh, yes, we're sure of that."

"I still think you're nuts trying to direct suspicion at Chris. He didn't even know Mark."

Dodge ignored the comment. "What time did Chris get home last night?"

Damn, I thought. I was in the dark about so much when it came to Chris Ramirez. To make matters worse, I wasn't entirely certain why I was so eager to defend him. Except that he was Adam's friend, and a mother hates to admit her kid has lousy judgment when it comes to people. "Midnight," I answered weakly.

Dodge nodded. "He left Simon and Cece's a little before eight-thirty. I don't suppose he told you where he was for the rest of the evening?"

"I didn't ask."

For a long moment, Dodge was silent. At last, he loped toward the door and opened it. "Get him back here, Emma. Otherwise, I'll have to send out an APB."

I hoisted my handbag over my shoulder. "Then do it PDQ. I don't expect to see him again. He's going to California."

The hazel eyes bore down on me. "Like hell he is," Dodge said.

I brushed past him. "Don't call me. I'll call you."

"That's fine," the sheriff said to my back. "But don't call me dumb. I'm not."

I didn't reply. I already knew that.

I took Vida with me to the murder site. Carla had begged to come along, but this was a tricky story, dealing with the most powerful family in the county. Vida might have the tact of a bull elephant, but she knew the cast of characters, and they knew her. In a small town, that was crucial.

It was a mile from *The Advocate* to Mineshaft Number Three, just off the county road that wound up through the foothills to the ranger station and Icicle Creek Camp Ground. The wind had blown itself out against the mountains, and the rain was coming down in a straight, steady drizzle. In the older residential section of frame houses on the edge of downtown, smoke spiraled out of chimneys and many of the lights were on. Russet leaves drifted into gardens that still sported dahlias, roses, chrysanthemums, and marigolds. Yet the splashes of color in the gray morning seemed more brave than bright.

I followed the curve of the road past a tract of newer homes, mostly split level, almost all with some sort of recreational vehicle parked in the driveway or the two-car garage. These Apliners were outdoor people who spent their leisure time fishing and hunting, hiking and camping. I, too, have been known to do a little stream fishing. Unfortunately, since arriving in Alpine, all I've had to show for it are two small rainbow trout and an extremely ugly bullhead. Even this far from the urban center, I'm told the halcyon days of trout fishing are over.

At the edge of town, on the sidehill, the cemetery crept up into the evergreens. I glanced that way, thinking of the new grave that soon would be dug, no doubt near the final resting place of Hazel Doukas, Neeny's wife.

"Did Mark have any enemies?" I asked Vida, who would know if anyone did.

She was sewing a button on the cuff of her blouse, no easy task considering the ruts and curves in the road. "Dozens. He was a twerp."

Up ahead on the jutting bluff known as First Hill, I saw Neeny Doukas's big house, all gray stone and dark stucco, with a massive front porch. It stood on a full acre and was reached by a switchback driveway that wound above Icicle Creek and the woods around Mineshaft Number Three.

"I mean, *real* enemies," I said, slowing for the left-hand turn to the mine.

"Oh." Vida bit the thread. "Well, no. He's gotten into oodles of fights, usually when he's been drinking. But they don't count. He's never worked much, so he hasn't put a crimp in anybody's career. There have been a slew of girls, but most of them have dumped him, instead of the other way around. He had a bona-fide feud going with Josh Adcock, Harvey and Darlene's oldest boy, but Josh has a Fulbright to Cal Tech, so he's not around. Their quarrel had something to do with a high school football game. Mark fumbled one of Josh's handoffs in the league championship."

Alpine's grudges still amazed me. Mark Doukas and Josh Adcock had graduated from high school at least eight years earlier. Forgiving and forgetting weren't small-town virtues.

The mine was only about twenty feet from the main road, just off the turn into Neeny's long driveway. I pulled over when I saw two sheriff's cars and a van barring the

way. A half-dozen men were scrutinizing an area roped off
by yellow and black crime scene tape.

"In other words," I said to Vida as I turned off the engine, "you don't have a favorite suspect."

Vida shrugged. "Not off the top of my head."

"Gibb didn't like him," I noted, recalling the venom our
driver had exhibited the previous day. "How come?"

For once, Vida didn't have a ready answer. "Oh—lack
of respect, maybe. Gibb needs respect, especially since he
lost that leg." She took off her glasses and rubbed at her
eyes, always a sure sign that she was either agitated or lost
in rumination. "There was something about a hermit's
cache years ago. You know the sort of thing around this
part of the country—abandoned shacks or cabins in the
woods where recluses hole up."

I did. Often, they would bury their belongings, especially money. In the modern era, Sunday prospectors
would trot out their Geiger counters and go in search of
buried treasure. Once in a great while, somebody got lucky
and actually found some.

"Anyway, there was a story around town about—oh, ten
years ago, I guess—that Mark and Gibb got into a fight
over some valuable coins one of them had dug up. Mark
was just a teenager then, but he was always pigheaded.
Then again, so is Gibb. I think they split the loot down the
middle." She replaced her eyeglasses and stared out the
car window. "I suppose Gibb has never forgiven Mark.
But he wouldn't have waited this long to kill him."

I had to agree. "So who do you think murdered Mark?"

"Well." Vida buttoned up her serviceable brown wool
tweed coat. "I'd say Chris Ramirez is as good a pick as
anyone."

There was no arguing with Vida. There never was. "Are
you getting out?" I asked.

Always game, Vida unwound herself from the front
seat. We tromped across the muddy, leaf-strewn ground,
careful to avoid branches that had blown down in last
night's wind. My green shoes were a mess.

Bill Blatt, who had recently graduated from a two-year college in criminal justice and wasn't much older than Adam, broke away from the others to meet us.

"Hi, Aunt Vida, Mrs. Lord!" His round, freckled face beamed out from under his regulation cap. Bill was one of Vida's numerous nieces and nephews, an engaging young man with ash blond hair and deep-set blue eyes. "Isn't this something?" He stopped grinning, but the excitement remained in his voice. This was his first murder investigation, and he was clearly thrilled.

"It's wicked," Vida declared. "What are you boys doing, Billy?"

Bill Blatt glanced at the others who were crawling around on the sloping wet earth. We were surrounded by trees, with Icicle Creek tumbling downhill amid thick ferns and cattails. The road into the mine was no more than a dirt track that ended in a turnaround by a post marking the trailhead into Surprise Lake. "We're systematically going over the scene," Bill said, now very serious. "You'd be amazed at the stuff we're finding."

"No, I wouldn't," Vida replied. "Human beings are pigs." Her sensible shoes squelched in the mud as she pulled her hat down to her eyebrows. This morning she wore a black derby with a swatch of net. It was impossible to tell if she had it on frontward, backward, or sideways. "The point is, what have you found that's pertinent to Mark's murder?"

"Now, Aunt Vida," Bill began, looking nervous. "You know I can't divulge—"

"Rubbish!" Vida snapped her fingers. "I'm your own flesh and blood. Who used to take care of you when your crazy parents were gallivanting off to Reno every three months?"

Bill's heavy lids blinked over his blue eyes. "Well, it's not much anyway. Just a bunch of junk, like paper and gum wrappers and cigarette butts and a plastic fork." He gazed off in the direction of the creek, avoiding his aunt's keen stare.

"That's it?" Vida was incredulous.

Her nephew shuffled a bit. "Yes, ma'am. Except for the flashlight and the crowbar." Bill Blatt swallowed hard.

"Ah." Vida turned smug. "The crowbar was the weapon? Or was it the flashlight?"

"We aren't sure yet." Bill Blatt was virtually mumbling, his fresh, fair face downcast.

Discreetly, I had taken out my notebook but refrained from transcribing Bill's comments. I didn't want to intimidate him, though it was clear that he found his aunt more daunting than a sea of Camcorders. As for Vida, she never took notes. Her memory was extraordinary.

"Where did Eeeny Moroni find Mark?" I asked in my gentlest manner.

Bill perked up. "Over there." He pointed toward the mineshaft that had been sealed off very recently, no doubt to prevent curiosity seekers from getting inside and causing a cave-in. As far as I knew, the mine had been closed for decades, but apparently Milo Dodge was taking no chances. "We took a ton of pictures," Bill said, following my eye. "It's hard to draw an outline in the rain."

I nodded. "Hard to get footprints, too, I suppose."

"We got some," Bill said dubiously. "But you're right. Even though we made it here pretty fast, between the rain and Eeeny stomping around and carrying on, the ground's pretty chewed up. Same for tire tracks." He gestured back to the road, visible between the trees. "If the killer drove, he—or she—could have parked like you did, on the verge. That's all gravel."

Casually, I jotted down a few key words. "Where did Mark leave his car?"

"It was his Jeep," Bill replied. "He'd parked it in Neeny's drive halfway up. Mrs. Wunderlich found it when she came to work this morning."

I wondered how Neeny was taking his grandson's death. But that wasn't a question for Bill Blatt. I stuck to the basics. "What about dogs? Any scents?"

Bill swallowed hard, his Adam's apple bobbing above his crisply pressed tan shirt. "We did that already."

"And?" I kept my expression bland. The rain was pattering on the leaves, and my hair had gotten quite wet. I hate umbrellas, and I seldom wear a scarf. The air smelled of damp and decay. Only a foot away, a rotting log sprouted colorful clusters of red and brown toadstools.

Bill coughed into his fist. "I don't know exactly what conclusions Sheriff Dodge has come to." He sounded very formal.

"You'll find out, though." Vida thrust both chin and bust at her nephew.

With an anxious glance at his colleagues, Bill mumbled something in the way of reluctant assent.

I tried to bolster him with a smile. "Does anybody know why Mark wanted Dodge and Moroni to meet him up here?"

Bill considered the query. "He'd called the sheriff once or twice before, but Milo was out. I suppose it had to do with his prospecting. Maybe he really did strike gold."

"Was he working in the mineshaft?" I inquired.

Bill looked over toward the entrance, now covered with old moss and new two-by-fours. "He may have. But usually he panned in the streams."

Vida, who had meandered over to the quintet of deputies and specialists, turned back to us and sniffed. "That lazy lout didn't find gold." She swept a hand in a windmill gesture, encompassing the small clearing, the encroaching woods, and the steep hillside. "We're twenty feet from the road. This whole area has been gone over by every professional and amateur prospector in the Pacific Northwest, not to mention numerous unsavory Californians. Mark Doukas might have discovered a lost diamond ring or a stash of cash, but he didn't strike gold. Or silver, either. That mine is empty as the tomb."

Vida was right. Up to a point. But we didn't find out where she'd gone wrong until later.

Chapter Six

SIMON AND CECELIA Doukas's pseudo-Colonial house was situated west of town in a small but expensive development. Called The Pines by residents and real estate personnel, to everybody else the subdivision was known as Stump Hill—having been clear-cut during World War I, reforested in the 1920s, and partially hacked down again about ten years ago.

Neeny Doukas's father had bought Stump Hill early on and let some shirttail relation named Bump farm the land for about five years until he drank himself into a fit. The original house on what was known as Bump's Stump Ranch had burned down shortly thereafter. A couple of hobos who were passing through on the old Great Northern line stopped to spend the night and set the place—as well as themselves—on fire with the aid of old stogies and white lightning.

The neighborhood had definitely moved up in class since then, unless you prefer virgin forest to civilization. I suppose I do, except that trees don't buy newspapers. They just make them. I love trees for a lot of reasons.

There were several cars parked in the driveway of the Doukas house, including Simon's ecru Cadillac, Cece's silver Mercedes, Mark's Trans Am, and Kent MacDuff's blue Buick. I hesitated, but Vida gave me a whack on the arm.

"What's the matter? Are you going to let this bunch of goons scare you away? If nothing else, you can offer your condolences. I intend to, even if it chokes me."

In the newspaper business, being part voyeur, part ghoul, and all-around snoop is essential. But even after twenty years, once in awhile I get a twinge of guilt. Or an attack of good taste. This was one of those times. The white house with its pillars and green lawn and well-tended garden spoke not so much of Doukas wealth and power as it did of Cece's sweet nature. The woman could be cloying, but she was also decent. I didn't give much of a damn for the rest of the family, but I felt a genuine pang of sympathy for the mother of the murdered young man.

"Let's hit it," I said, getting out of the car.

Vida was already in the driveway, trudging toward the house with her peculiar flatfooted gait. I glanced at my watch; it was just after eleven-thirty. I hoped Cece wouldn't feel obligated to ask us to stay on for lunch. Just as we rang the doorbell, another car, bearing the Driggers Funeral Home logo, pulled into the drive. Our timing was awful. On the other hand, maybe I could talk Al Driggers into reverting to the weekly ad schedule.

Al, a suitably grave man of about fifty with gray hair, gray eyes, and gray skin, joined us on the long veranda just as Jennifer Doukas MacDuff opened the door. She was a pretty young woman, in her middle twenties, with her mother's honey-blond hair worn shoulder-length. Her pale blue eyes showed signs of fresh tears. Al put out a hand, but it was Vida who took over:

"Jenny, you look puny. It won't do for you to get sick right now. Your mother needs you to buck her up. Where is everybody?" Vida was already in the entry hall, darting glances into the study on the left, the living room on the right, and the kitchen down the hall. "Ah! There they are!" She wheeled into the living room, long coat flapping and hat askew.

The grouping included a very white Cece, a taut Simon, and a frowning Kent MacDuff. Cece, wearing black slacks and an off-white cashmere twin set, started to get up, but her husband laid a hand on her shoulder.

"Vida. Emma. Al," intoned Simon Doukas, as if he

were taking roll. He was of average height but seemed taller. His black hair, now graying at the temples, and his sharp beak of a nose gave him a melancholy mien. Had Simon Doukas smiled more often in less tragic circumstances, he would have been attractive. As it was, he verged on the alarming. His courtroom demeanor, which I had observed on various occasions, was dry, concise, and often sarcastic. He was, however, successful, for he came prepared. On this gray September morning, he was tight-lipped and high-strung. He was out of his element; life had not prepared him to face the loss of his son.

"Please sit," he said, after shaking hands with all of us and gesturing at the harmonious melding of comfortable beige and brown and sea-green furniture. "There's coffee. And tea. Unless," he added on a too-eager note, "anyone would like something stronger."

"Tea for me," said Vida, plopping down next to Kent MacDuff on a long brown sofa. "Cream, no sugar. Where's Neeny?"

Simon actually jumped. Kent scowled even more. Cece dabbed at her eyes with a flowered handkerchief. "Dad's taken to his bed. Doc Dewey Senior has gone up to see him." She placed a hand over her cashmere-layered breast. "It's his heart," she added in a faint voice.

"No wonder," remarked Vida, wrestling out of her coat. She glanced around the room, no doubt taking in every detail of decor and nuance of emotion. "You got new drapes. I think I like them."

Cece looked at the nearest panel as if she'd never seen them before. "What? Oh, yes, we had them made in Seattle."

Simon, aided by Jennifer, was pouring coffee and tea from a sterling silver tray on the glass-topped table. Kent MacDuff held his cup and saucer in his lap and put up a hand. "I'm over-coffeed," he said in the rather high voice that didn't fit his square shoulders and bulging biceps. Even in a subdued navy blazer the muscles seemed to ripple through the wool. Kent was close to thirty, with curly sandy hair and a florid complexion. He and Jennifer had been married for almost five years. So far, there were no children, and Jennifer had continued her job as a receptionist in her father's law office.

I had sat down in a striped armchair next to Al Driggers and across from Kent. "We owe you an apology," I said to Kent as Simon handed me a cup of coffee. "I think we misquoted your brother."

Kent MacDuff looked momentarily blank, then gave a little snort. "Oh, *Kevin*. He shot his face off about Mark and the gold, right? Dumb kid." He set the Royal Worcester cup and saucer down with a clatter and straightened his dark blue socks. "Does it matter now? I mean, with Mark gone and all. Or do you think somebody zapped him to get at the gold?"

Cece shuddered and Simon turned away. Kent seemed oblivious. He was lighting a cigarette with a sleek gold lighter that hadn't come off the rack at the local 7-Eleven.

"What did Mark really find?" I asked to break the awkward silence as much as to get the story straight.

Jennifer and Kent looked at each other, and both came up empty. "He never told us," Jennifer said at last in a listless manner.

I steeled myself and turned to Cece. "Neeny told me Mark was digging up maidenhair ferns for you."

Cece burst into tears. Simon leaped across the room and sank down beside her chair. "Dearest! Please! You're going to collapse!"

"But it's so like him!" Cece wailed. "Mark was so *thoughtful*!" She peered at me over the wrinkled handkerchief. "Especially of his mother. He always said I was his best girl." The sobs started up again, and this time, Simon pulled her to her feet.

"Come along, dearest. I'm putting you to bed. I'll talk to Al about the arrangements. Don't fret. We know what you would . . ." His voice trailed away as he led her out of the room and toward the spiral staircase.

"Well," said Vida, snatching a sugar cookie off a Wedg-

wood plate, "I don't suppose Mark would have called the
sheriff to tell him he couldn't find any maidenhair ferns,
would he?" She fixed her hawklike gaze on Kent and
Jennifer.

"What's that?" asked Kent. Even Al Driggers's carefully
composed face showed puzzlement.

Vida shrugged and munched. "Mark called the sheriff
two, three times to tell him something. He asked Milo—
and Eeeny Moroni, the old fool—to, meet him up at
Mineshaft Number Three. Now if that was all about a
bunch of ferns, I'll eat my hat." She touched the brim as
if to verify it was still there should the bet be called in.
"Well?"

"Well what?" Kent was getting annoyed. "Damn it,
Vida, what are you yakking about?"

Vida glared at Kent. "I'm yakking about the fact that
Mark must have found something pretty significant to send
for the sheriff. Maybe you'd better ask your little brother,
unless you want to go on being as dimwitted as you act,
Kent MacDuff. I remember when you had to repeat fourth
grade. Twice."

Kent turned crimson. He fairly bounced on the sofa. I
was reminded of a bantam rooster. "It was only *once*! And
that was because old Miss Grundle was too drunk to add
up the grades right!"

"Rubbish." Vida took a big swallow of tea, presumably
to wash down her cookie. "Grace Grundle doesn't drink.
She has an inner ear problem. That's why she staggers so
much."

I decided it was time to intervene before we got off onto
a tangent about public education in Alpine, chronic alcoholism of various inhabitants, insidious diseases, or any
combination thereof. "Jennifer, is it true that Mark and
Chris quarreled last night?"

Jennifer, who had been pleating the folds of her baggy
dress in her thin fingers, looked up with a mystified expression. "I don't think so." She turned to her husband.
"Did they, Kent? I forget."

"Hell, yes." Kent thrust out his chin in a pugnacious manner. "They had a hell of a row outside, just before Mark left."

"What about?" I asked.

Kent shrugged. "I don't know. I didn't stick around. None of my business." He started to drink from his cup, realized it was empty, and put it back down again. "Who knows? That Chris struck me as big trouble."

"I kind of liked him," Jennifer murmured.

"Where is he?" Al Driggers asked, and I was surprised to hear him speak. Somehow I was getting the impression that he'd filled himself with embalming fluid and was sitting there corpselike, waiting for his own eulogy.

I gazed unflinchingly into Al's somber gray eyes. "He left town."

"Oh, my." Al shook his head sadly.

"Skipped town, you mean," said Kent.

"Is he coming back?" asked Jennifer.

I opted for candor. "I doubt it."

Kent stood up, smoothing the creases in his rumpled slacks. "Don't worry. They'll haul his ass back. Old Neeny has sworn revenge."

"Phooey." Vida sniffed. "Old Neeny is full of it. What he needs is a good purge."

Jennifer looked shocked, Al Driggers winced, and Kent scowled even more ferociously than before. "That's none of your damned business, Vida. Neeny's a sick man."

"Maybe, maybe not." Vida was unruffled. "I think I'll go cheer him up."

"Please don't." It was Simon's ice-cold voice, emanating from the doorway. "Mrs. Pratt is looking in on him."

"Ha!" Vida sprang to her feet. "That old tart! Some nursemaid. She's got a terrific bedside manner, I'll give her that."

"*Please!*" Simon was holding up both hands. "Cece's trying to sleep." He motioned to Jennifer. "That casserole Mrs. Adcock sent over—why don't you put it in the oven for our lunch?"

The words seemed to be our exit cue, but Simon had come over to my chair. "Before you go, could we speak alone for a moment?" Not waiting for my assent, he glanced at Al Driggers. "We'll get down to business in about five minutes," Simon said. "It shouldn't take long." Apparently Al wasn't going to partake of the casserole either.

I followed Simon across the hall into his study. Like the rest of the house, the small room was tastefully appointed, with an unlighted fireplace, an antique oak desk, two chairs, and tall bookshelves boasting an eclectic collection. Unlike the comfortable living room, the study wore a stilted air. Perhaps it was the difference between Simon's occupancy and Cece's touch.

Simon Doukas sat behind the desk, looking like a coiled spring. "I have to ask about Chris," he said dryly.

I could hardly believe I'd seen this man less than twenty-four hours ago with tears in his eyes. If he had wept for Mark, he gave no sign.

"I have some questions of my own," I responded, sitting in the chair across from him.

He stiffened even more, if that were possible, and looked down his long nose at me. "I'll go first. What did he tell you about his relatives in Alpine?"

I felt as if I were in the witness box. "He didn't remember any of you very well. Except for Neeny."

Simon inclined his head. I guessed that he'd spent a lifetime being overlooked in favor of his father. "Didn't he speak of Mark?"

"No. Well, yes, once. Some prank when they were kids, I think."

"Oh." Simon seemed bored by pranks. "What else?"

"Nothing." I raised my palms. "Really, Simon, you were strangers to Chris as far as I could tell."

Simon put his hand to his head. "I don't understand any of this. Emma," he said in a plaintive voice, "do you think Chris killed my son?"

"No." It was the truth. I scarcely knew Chris Ramirez,

but despite the acrimony for his grandfather, I genuinely didn't believe he could commit murder.

Simon drummed his fingers on the desk. It was almost bare, except for a fresh blotter, a calendar, and a matching pen and pencil set. "If not Chris, then who?"

I shook my head. Outside, the rain continued to fall, spilling from the downspouts by the room's single window. "Who stands to gain from Mark's death?" I inquired.

"Gain?" Simon's heavy dark eyebrows lifted. "No one."

"He had no will?"

"No." He gave me what might have passed as a smile before warmth was invented. "Typical, eh? The lawyer's son without a will, the cobbler's children with no shoes. Oh, I tried talking to him about drawing one up, but it upset him. You know how young people are. They think they're immortal. They don't want to discuss death." Simon grimaced, his sad and empty gaze somewhere beyond my right shoulder.

"He had money, I take it?" It seemed the logical conclusion to draw. If he hadn't, then there would be no need for a will.

"Some." He clamped his mouth shut as if he'd been wildly indiscreet. But Simon Doukas must have had the need to talk. There was so much repressed within the man, and his wife wasn't very helpful at the moment. As for his daughter and her husband, I couldn't imagine Simon engaging either of them in meaningful conversation. "Fifteen years or so ago," Simon went on, "my father set up trusts for each of our children—two-hundred fifty thousand dollars apiece, to be turned over to them absolutely on their twenty-fifth birthdays. Naturally, the sums have grown considerably. Mark came into his money almost two years ago. Jenny will get hers next month." He fingered his sharp chin and waited for my response.

"So Mark's money will revert to you—or to Neeny?" I asked.

"To Cece and me, as his next of kin." He gave a pathetic little laugh. "You aren't thinking we killed our son to inherit his trust fund, are you?" His voice showed a trace of his well-known sarcasm.

Stranger things had happened, of course, but I knew Mark Doukas's nestegg couldn't compare to Simon's. I also assumed Mark had probably already blown a portion of the money. I ought to know; I'd done it myself.

I passed over Simon's comment. "What about this quarrel between Mark and Chris? What started it?"

Martin frowned. "I don't know. I didn't hear any of that."

"But they *did* quarrel?"

"Kent says so." His tone suggested that Kent wasn't the most reliable source in town. I tended to agree, but my own suspicions were based on something more concrete. The problem was, I couldn't remember exactly what.

"Simon," I began, taking another tack, "do you remember much about Chris as a little kid?"

A spark of life flickered in his black eyes. "He was a good-natured little fellow. Cute as a button. I used to try to make up to him, but he . . ." Simon paused, a catch in his voice. "He was a bit shy. And of course Margaret and Hector kept to themselves."

I tried to imagine Simon Doukas fifteen or twenty years ago, coaxing a small boy into a romp. The picture was out of focus. Even as a young attorney, Simon must have been stiff and intimidating, especially to a child. "Where did they live?" I asked, wondering how long it would take to wear out my welcome at this interview.

"East of town, by the golf course. It was one of my father's rentals." He gazed at the desk calendar; it hadn't been changed in a week. Simon carefully turned the pages. "Who would have thought . . ." he murmured, then placed his hand on today's date: Thursday, September 26. "Emma." Pushing back from the desk, he again looked down that long nose at me. "You don't intend to publish any of this, do you?"

"What?" I bolted forward in the chair.

Simon straightened his tie. "Over the years, we've been

very loyal to *The Advocate*. I presume you're willing to show your gratitude for our family's support. We certainly don't want the Doukas name smeared all over the newspaper."

I was aghast. Neeny's demand for a reprint was bad enough, but Simon's request was outrageous. And impossible. I leaned on the desk, suppressing an urge to pound my fist on the smooth oak surface. "Simon, you can't keep a story like this quiet. I'm surprised the met dailies haven't been up here. It might not make page one outside of Alpine, but it'll certainly find its way into the regional sections."

Simon's face had grown very tight, his shoulders rigid. "I think you're wrong. We haven't heard from anyone. And if we do, I know the phone numbers of some very important people in the media." He raised his head slightly, as if he were looking over a courtroom full of rabble, and I was the lowliest of the bunch.

I stood up. "Sorry, Simon. It won't work. You haven't got that big a Rolodex." I spoke with more confidence than I actually felt. There had been, alas, a couple of recent occasions when the local media had indeed suppressed stories. "You've got almost a week of peace as far as *The Advocate* is concerned. We'll be as careful and as tasteful as possible."

Simon had also risen to his feet. He was so angry he was shaking. "If you print this, I'll run you out of town! Do you hear me? You ... *whore*!"

My own temper was about to explode. But miraculously, I kept my wrath under control. "I was wondering who'd be the first one to call me that to my face," I said in a musing manner. "Funny," I went on, turning toward the study door, "I honestly didn't think I'd run into anyone that small, even in a small town. Until now."

I slammed the door behind me.

Chapter Seven

EXCEPT WHEN SHE was eating sugar cookies and chocolate truffles, Vida was always dieting. It wasn't easy coaxing her into driving down to Index for lunch. I didn't want to eat in Alpine, because I knew we'd be overheard. Index was just far enough away that we were guaranteed a certain amount of anonymity.

Naturally, Vida was wild-eyed when I told her about Simon's insistence that we not run the murder story. It took me most of the drive to calm her down. By the time we reached the little café just off the highway, she had stopped shrieking and rubbing her eyes long enough to look at the menu.

"I'm not hungry," she announced, and promptly ordered the hot turkey sandwich with gravy and cranberry jelly.

After raking Simon over the coals one more time, we finally moved on to Mark's murder. "Did you find out what happened at dinner last night?" I asked as an elderly waitress brought us each a small green salad.

Vida pitched into her lettuce. "Not much, from what I could tell. Of course I only had that idiot, Kent, and that ninny of a Jennifer to go by." She huffed a bit between mouthfuls of salad. "Simon and Cece and Chris sat around and visited before dinner. Since Kent and Jennifer weren't there yet, I haven't a clue as to what they talked about, but everybody seemed to be on good terms when the MacDuffs got there around six-thirty. Mark showed up a few minutes later, drank a beer, and then they all sat down to dinner. They finished up around seven forty-five. Chris talked quite a bit about Hawaii." Vida paused, noting my look of incredulity.

"Chris opened up?" I asked.

Vida shrugged and brushed a crouton off the front of her blouse. "He drank beer, too. Maybe it loosened his tongue. Anyway, about eight-fifteen, Mark said he had to go out. Which he did. Chris left about ten minutes later." She pursed her lips and gave me a shrewd look. "Simon dropped him off at your house. It was eight-thirty."

"At *my* house?" I almost dropped my fork. Then I remembered the car I'd heard while I was talking to Dave Grogan on the phone. "But Chris never came in. Where did he go?"

"You should have asked him," Vida said matter-of-factly. "As for Kent and Jennifer, they went home right after Chris and Simon left. Cece cleaned up from dinner, read the paper—both papers, ours and *The Times*—and went to bed." She gave me a significant look.

"So when did Simon get home after allegedly dropping Chris off?"

Vida paused as the waitress delivered her turkey and my BLT. "I'm not sure," she admitted. "I got most of this from Jennifer, so the part about Cece is second-hand. She never came back down, as you may have noticed when you flew out of Simon's study." She sprinkled her plate with lavish doses of salt and pepper. Across the aisle, three middle-aged fishermen eased into a booth, ragging each other about their abysmal luck. An elderly couple moved past us, the woman wheezing, the man shuffling. A Persian cat swished by, its plumelike tail exuding disdain.

"Cats!" Vida exclaimed, making a horrible face. "Dreadful animals. Have you ever dissected one of those things?"

I considered reminding Vida that we were eating, thought better of it, and replied that I had not. Luckily.

"It had to be the crowbar," she remarked, apparently apropos of nothing, except that I knew Vida well enough by now to follow her train of thought—which had led from dissecting cats to the autopsy on Mark Doukas. "Emma," she said in a more serious tone, "are you trying to cover this story—or solve the murder?"

Despite having raised three children, Vida wasn't particularly maternal. But she was old enough to be my mother, and once in awhile, she acted like it. I appreciated that. After all, I'd been an orphan for almost twenty years.

I mulled over the question. "Maybe I have to do one to do the other," I said.

But Vida shook her head, the derby slipping further down over her forehead. "No, no. That takes away your objectivity. Stick to the facts, Emma. That's your job. Don't try to play detective."

She was right, of course. Over the years, I'd covered a variety of murder investigations in Portland. Except for some random piecing together of information, I'd never concerned myself much with solving the cases themselves. But then I'd never had a personal stake in any of those homicides. The victims were all strangers; the killers, if indeed they were discovered, were just names.

"I feel responsible for Chris," I asserted. "He's my son's best friend. I may not need to find out who killed Mark, but I have an obligation to prove who didn't."

Vida chewed on her white meat and looked thoughtful. "Are you sure you just don't want to get back at Simon Doukas for being such a jackass?"

I hadn't told Vida exactly what Simon had said in dismissal, but she was shrewd enough to guess that it had something to do with my status as an unmarried mother. "The only way," I said slowly, "I could get back at him is if he did it. That may not be the case."

"It might be one of the other Doukases." Vida lifted her graying eyebrows, which met the brim of her derby. "Simon wouldn't like that."

I suppressed a smile. "But you would, Vida?"

She cut up her gravy-slathered bread with vigor. "You bet I would. If any family ever needed a comeuppance, it's that bunch."

The cat sidled past again, looking even snootier than before. Vida made another face, then she leaned closer, almost dipping her bust in her lunch. "All right, Emma, you've made up your mind. I'll do what I can to help, but you have to be candid with me. Why was Chris trying to buy a handgun from Harvey Adcock?"

I was wondering when Vida would get around to asking me that. I debated, but not for long. I not only like Vida, I trust her. She could tell the world about every scrap of gossip, but she could also keep a secret. It was one of the reasons she knew so much; I wasn't the only one in Alpine who trusted Vida Runkel. So I told her about Chris's animosity toward Neeny and the frightening conclusions I'd drawn.

Vida's reaction was typical. "Well, good for Chris. He's got some spunk. But that doesn't mean he intended to shoot his grandfather, tempting as the prospect may be. In fact, it doesn't mean much, since it was Mark and not Neeny Doukas who got killed."

I agreed. "The only reason I can think of for Chris trying to buy a gun is for self-defense. His mother may have told him some pretty hair-raising stories about her family."

Vida rolled her eyes. "As Margaret well might." Polishing off the cranberry jelly, she dabbed at her mouth with the paper napkin, then pitched it at the cat, which had parked its carcass next to our booth. The cat flinched but stayed put. "I wonder," she mused, rummaging in her purse for compact and lipstick, "whatever happened to Hector Ramirez?"

So did I, but at the time, it didn't seem pertinent.

This time Vida was right and I was wrong.

Vida took her own car up to see Neeny Doukas. I suggested joining her, but Vida was adamant. "Let me handle the old sap this time. If he's really sick, I may have to use tact. It's not a pretty sight."

Back at the office, Carla was agog about the murder, but Ed, who always expected the worst anyway, took it in stride. I fended off their questions as best I could before barricading myself in my office.

Predictably, a stack of phone messages had piled up. Ginny, Ed, and Carla had tried to intercept the ordinary snoops, but at least twenty callers had insisted on speaking personally to the editor and publisher. Before I could start dialing, Ginny Burmeister slipped into my office to complain that Gibb Frazier hadn't brought back the overage on the print run. She needed at least two dozen extra copies to mail for special requests, and we needed the rest for our files. I told her to give Gibb a call; it wasn't like him to be so absentminded.

For almost an hour, I wielded the phone, talking to the Methodist minister, the owner of the Venison Inn, two of the three county commissioners, the city's head librarian, and Cal of Cal's Texaco and Body Shop. All of them prefaced their inquiries with other, unrelated business, but the bottom line was Who Killed Mark Doukas? I kept repeating that Sheriff Dodge was working hard to solve the case. I certainly wished him luck, since I was baffled. None of the callers was satisfied, but at least they didn't cancel their subscriptions.

I had just hung up on Cal Vickers when Fuzzy Baugh, our current mayor, lumbered into my office. Fuzzy was the retired owner of Baugh's Fine Home Furnishings and Carpet, which had recently moved from Front Street to the new mall, causing a ruckus over whether or not downtown Alpine was dying. Since the entire commercial district was only eight blocks long and two blocks wide, the controversy struck my city-bred mentality as odd. But all things are relative, and when, two months later, Barton's Bootery also vacated Front Street, I actually asked Carla to poll the remaining downtown merchants and find out if they planned to stay put. As far as she could tell, they did. But with Carla, you could never be quite sure of her data.

Fuzzy was a tall, heavy-set man with curly blond hair, which I presumed was dyed. His face was nicely crinkled and his eyes were green and small. He had been mayor for

the past six years, though his first election back in '84 was
also steeped in controversy. It seemed that Fuzzy and
Irene, his wife of thirty years, had decided to split up.
Irene stayed at their house in town, and Fuzzy moved out
to a cabin he'd built on the Skykomish River, about ten
miles downstream. When Fuzzy announced he was running for office, the opposition declared he wasn't a resident and therefore was ineligible to stand for election.
Fuzzy moved back in with Irene, a gesture that was dismissed by his detractors as merely expedient, but the couple actually reconciled and went on a second honeymoon
to Mexico. Politics might make strange bedfellows, but in
this case, they had reunited a pair who probably should
never have stopped sleeping together in the first place.

"This is bad, Emma," Fuzzy announced, dropping into
the vacant chair on the other side of my desk. "Drugs, of
course."

"Drugs?" Though that was often a factor in homicides
I'd covered on *The Oregonian*, I hadn't seriously considered the issue. Not that we didn't have our share of substance abuse—but for all of Mark Doukas's failings, I'd
never heard him accused of taking or dealing drugs.
"What makes you say that, Fuzzy?"

Fuzzy leaned forward in the chair, trying to find a bare
spot to place his elbows. As usual, he was dressed impeccably in suit and tie, never having overcome his salesman's need to look his best. Perhaps he felt such formal
attire was worthy of his mayor's role, though his predecessor, Elbert Armbruster, had never been seen in anything
but overalls. "You haven't been here long, Emma," Fuzzy
said in a kindly tone that suggested it wasn't entirely my
fault. "This town was originally filled with Orientals.
That's why it was called Nippon. What do you suppose
those people brought with them?"

I resisted the urge to answer *tempura* and merely looked
curious. Fuzzy gave me his sage half smile. "Opium. I'll
bet dollars to doughnuts Mark found a stash of it at the old
mine. Other stuff, too, probably brought up there by

modern-day drug traffickers. The question is, who's the kingpin?"

Every first and third Tuesday, I sit in on the city council meetings, so I was used to Fuzzy Baugh's strange—and imaginative—hypotheses. Last spring, damage to one of the Burlington Northern spurs had, he insisted, been caused by neo-Nazis. The Fourth of July fireworks hadn't all gone off due to the devious machinations of the Monroe Elks Club, who were jealous of Alpine's display. The theft of a birdbath from young Doc Dewey's front yard was the plot of irate loggers who wanted to avenge their endangered livelihoods by getting back at all avian species, spotted owls or not.

Thus, I regarded Fuzzy's latest flight of fancy in context. "Mark might have found something up at the mine, Fuzzy," I allowed, "but I doubt it was drugs."

Fuzzy's small green eyes opened wide. "See here, Emma, you haven't thought this through like I have. I know human nature. I had to as a salesman. I still do, as mayor of this fine town. Mark was real anxious to get hold of Sheriff Dodge and get him up there to Icicle Creek. Now what could Mark have wanted to show Milo unless it was drugs?"

Fuzzy's conclusion might be off base, but his reasoning wasn't. Despite his lamebrained ideas, he was no dope. "Well, everybody agrees it wasn't gold or silver," I conceded. "As far as the mine goes, I understood it had been closed for years. Isn't it a safety hazard?"

"Definitely," Fuzzy agreed, sagely nodding his head. "There's a real danger of cave-ins. Plus, the springs can rise up and flood those shafts. That's one of the reasons they quit working the mines in the first place."

"You mean there was still ore?"

"Oh, maybe some. Not enough to risk lives over, though." Fuzzy made the statement with some authority, as if he had personally been in charge of the closure some seventy-five years ago. He sat up straight, turning so that I could catch his profile, which was still a fine one. "Mark my words. It's drugs. I intend to ask for a resolution at the city council meeting next Tuesday to open Mineshaft Number Three."

I tipped my head to one side. It didn't seem like a very helpful idea, but on the other hand, it couldn't do any harm. As long as nobody wandered inside and got hurt. "Who owns those old mines, Fuzzy?"

"Nobody. That is," he went on in his low, soft voice that still held just a hint of his native New Orleans even after twenty years, "the rights to the mines expired years ago. The Forest Service owns the land that Mineshafts One and Two are on, Number Four belongs to the railroad, Five is gone, and Three is on Neeny Doukas's property."

I lifted my eyebrows. "Do you have to get Neeny to approve of opening the shaft?"

A flicker of uncertainty passed over Fuzzy's crinkly face. "I hope not. But he'd do it, especially if it'll help find out who killed his grandson." Standing up, Fuzzy put out his hand. "I'm off, Emma. Nice as always visiting with you." He gave me his best marketing-mayoral smile. "You'll handle this with care, I'm sure."

"From now on," I replied with a smile of my own, "my middle name is *Alleged*."

Briefly, Fuzzy looked puzzled; then he nodded and let go of my hand. "Yes, that's right. Circumspection. That's the ticket." He started for the door, then turned back to face me. "In fact, it might be better to let matters sit for a time. There's no point in riling everybody up, is there?"

I feigned innocence. "How do you mean?"

Taking a step back toward my desk, Fuzzy assumed his best good-ole-boy air. "Well, the way I see it, if you run just an obituary on Mark this coming week, that pretty well covers it. The funeral will be over by then, I imagine. If Milo's arrested somebody, fine. If not, why upset folks?"

Neeny Doukas had Fuzzy Baugh, along with almost everybody else in town, tucked in his pocket. I wondered if Neeny, supposedly sick, had delegated his influence to Simon. I said as much to Fuzzy: "Have you been talking to Simon Doukas?"

Mild surprise registered on Fuzzy's face. "I offered him my condolences, of course. And to that fine wife of his, Cecelia." He gave a sad shake of his curly locks, reminding me of an aging cherub. "You realize how hard it is on the family, Emma." His voice had grown rather faint. "I know you'll want to spare them any further grief."

I decided to play the game. "Certainly. I have no intention of rubbing salt in their wounds, Fuzzy. You know better than that. Good journalism isn't cruel."

The green eyes turned cold, like agates. Fuzzy filled the doorway, and for the first time since I'd met him, I was aware of the menace of the man, seventy years and all.

When he spoke again, his voice was still very soft. "You behave now. There's no need to embarrass fine folks like the Doukases." He gave another shake of his head. "We sure don't want any more tragedies around Alpine, do we, Emma? I mean, you never know who could be next."

Giving me the most empathetic of looks, Fuzzy Baugh made his exit.

I tried not to let Fuzzy's thinly veiled threat bother me. Neither he nor Simon Doukas was the first in Alpine to attempt to scare me out of a story. There had been trouble with some of the loggers the previous winter. At least one irate taxpayer had promised to send me a bomb after I'd backed a school levy. And somebody had actually thrown a rock through the window of my office after I'd made the editorial comment that Alpine remained basically an unintegrated community because most of the residents weren't hospitable to people of other races. Threats were also part of the job description.

But the intimidation I'd faced twice in one day over Mark Doukas's murder unsettled me more than I liked to admit. It was no longer just a matter of Chris Ramirez's involvement, but of preserving my right to publish. I did not, however, intend to perish in the process. The more I thought about it, the more I became convinced that the only way to secure the story was to find the killer.

I put in a call to Adam. Nobody answered, but I wasn't surprised, since it was only one-thirty in Honolulu. I'd try again, after five, our time.

Meanwhile, Vida returned and reported on her visit to Neeny Doukas. She'd been gone for over two hours, and, given the sudden threatening atmosphere hanging over *The Advocate*, I'd begun to worry.

"Oooh—" she exclaimed impatiently, rubbing at her eyes, "you might know I was fine. I just nosed around a bit here and there after I left Neeny's. Not that it did me much good. People ought to pay more attention to what other people are doing."

"What about Neeny?" I asked, pulling a chair up to Vida's desk. Ed had left for the day, and Carla had gone to a hospital board meeting.

Vida breathed on her glasses, wiped the lenses on her slip, and settled the tortoise-shell stems over her ears. "I got lucky. Phoebe was just leaving to get her hair dyed."

"Neeny isn't at death's door, I gather."

Vida snorted. "Of course not! Oh, he's upset, I suppose he would be, he regarded Mark highly, which proves what an old fool he really is; but, except for gastritis, I don't think there's much wrong with him." She wagged a finger at me. "*He* says otherwise, but I don't believe him. He just wants to be babied."

Given the fact that Neeny had just lost his favorite grandchild, I felt Vida was being a bit harsh, but I didn't say so. "Had he seen Mark last night?" I inquired.

Vida took a sip from the hot water she always drank in the late afternoons. "No. He didn't realize Mark had parked that Jeep or whatever it is in the drive. Neeny said he heard sirens by the mine some time between nine and nine-thirty. He thought it was a wreck on the highway. Sheriff Dodge didn't tell him about Mark until this morning."

I gave Vida a quizzical look. "How come?"

The wry expression on her face told me she also thought the delay was strange. "Milo called around ten-thirty and talked to that idiot, Phoebe. She said Neeny was resting—I'll bet!—and shouldn't be disturbed. The sheriff should wait and give Neeny the bad news in the morning, after he'd had a good night's sleep. Ha!"

I reflected briefly on Vida's words. "So Phoebe knew?"

Vida rolled her eyes. "Taking a lot on herself, isn't she? Imagine Hazel Doukas making decisions like that for Neeny! Why, Hazel couldn't even decide for herself whether to broil or bake her pork chops!"

Not having known the late Hazel, I couldn't imagine much. But Vida's remark gave me an idea. "Phoebe doesn't live up there, does she?"

"She might as well," Vida huffed. "You should see her house over on Pine Street—I'll bet she hasn't washed her curtains in four years. And the yard—it's a mess. Nothing but a few ratty rose bushes and some poor bedraggled perennials. She spends most of her time up there at Neeny's, holding his—whatever." Vida's expression showed rampant distaste.

Out on Front Street, a car horn honked and somebody yelled a greeting to a passerby. Darkness was settling in over Alpine, but the rain had stopped shortly after my return to the office. I examined my sad suede shoes and considered heading home. I was anxious to get hold of Adam.

"Did Neeny say anything about Chris?" I asked.

Vida cocked her head at me. "Now that's odd. He didn't! At first, I expected him to launch into one of his diatribes about how Chris must have killed that nitwit, Mark, but he never let out a peep. I have to admit, Neeny was a little subdued. He figures Mark was murdered by bikers."

The theory was more plausible than Fuzzy Baugh's. About every four years, sort of like the Olympics, a horde of rough-and-tumble bikers descended on Alpine. They raised hell up and down Front Street and usually tried to smash up the bar at Mugs Ahoy. But on their last foray, the previous spring, they had taken on a bunch of disgruntled loggers at the Icicle Creek Tavern at the edge of town. The leader of the bikers had made the mistake of imitating a spotted owl. The final score had ended up something like Loggers 48, Bikers 3. Still, it wasn't impossible that they might have returned for revenge. But it was unlikely that they'd pick on Mark Doukas.

"I think it's odd that Neeny didn't mention Chris," I said.

"So do I." Vida raised her eyebrows above the rims of her glasses. "But what does it mean?"

I shook my head. "I don't know. Did he say anything about our running the story?"

Vida batted a hand at the air. "Oh, of course! I told him to go soak his head. I won't stand for that nonsense from Neeny Doukas or anybody else." She gave me a quick, shrewd look. "Who else has been trying to scare you?"

I told her about Fuzzy Baugh. Vida hooted in derision. "That nincompoop! He should have stuck to selling rugs! In fact, I'll bet he's wearing one. That mop can't be his real hair, and if it is, he ought to be ashamed of himself!"

In spite of my more serious concerns, I was amused. "What was his hair like when he was younger?"

Vida shrugged. "Fuzzy was never younger. Not by much. He came here only about twenty years ago and bought out my brother-in-law, Elmo, who owned the furniture store first. Elmo had to go away for a while, and the business had gone downhill. Fuzzy's wife was a Pratt whose first husband lived in Baton Rouge."

As ever, the intricate, inbred background of Alpine's citizenry never ceased to amaze me. But Vida, who apparently felt she'd finished dispensing all usable information, had begun pounding away at her old upright. I stood up and went back into my office to collect my gear and call it a day.

I was driving down Front Street when I realized that for the first time in years, I didn't much like heading home alone.

Chapter Eight

ADAM TOLD ME I was weird. "Chris wouldn't hurt a bug," he insisted after I'd explained the events of the last two days in Alpine. "Sure, he talked about having it out with old Neeny. It was his favorite subject after he'd had a couple of beers. But get violent? No way, Mom. You're too weird to even think it."

I assured Adam that I wasn't the one who thought Chris might be implicated in Mark's murder. Then, aware that I'd already used up over five minutes of long distance clock, I asked my son if he knew of any relatives or friends Chris had in Seattle. Adam didn't. The only family Chris had ever mentioned was the Alpine contingent. Margaret hadn't kept up with Hector's relations. She'd started a new iife in Hawaii, and all her real friends were still there.

I was coming to a dead end, but I had a sudden inspiration. "Adam, did Margaret have a boyfriend?"

"Huh?" He sounded shocked. Obviously, women in my peer group should not be allowed to date due to encroaching senility. "Gee, I don't think so. She was like you—sort of, like, well, you know, antisocial."

"I am not antisocial!" I bristled. "I'm choosy, damn it. Do you want a mother who's a tramp?"

My son gave out with a little laugh that was part sneer, part embarrassment. "You could go out with some guy once in awhile, Mom. You haven't done that since the Nutty Professor in Portland."

84

"Never mind my love life," I snapped. "How much money has Chris got with him?"

There was a pause. "I don't know," Adam finally answered. "He does okay. He got his mom's insurance and some attorney dude over here has rented out the house for him. He worked, too, at the Hilton."

No trust fund, I thought. Simon hadn't mentioned one for Chris, but there was always a chance that Neeny had kept his own counsel. Apparently Margaret had been completely cut out of the family money.

"Oh," Adam added as I mulled, "he has some plastic."

It sounded as if Chris could get by for a while without having to send back to Honolulu for more money. For the dozenth time that day, I wondered if Chris had stayed in Seattle or headed south. "Okay, Adam, I can't think of anything else to ask you. Is everything all right over there?"

"Sure," Adam replied. "Deloria and I are going to a movie tonight." I was about to pry when Adam continued: "Hey, what should I do with Chris's mail?"

"Hang on to it, I guess. Unless he settles some place." Like jail, I thought grimly.

"There isn't much," Adam noted, "except his *Sports Illustrated*, a couple of ads, and a letter."

In the past few years, I'd come to regard the writing of personal letters as dead as the dodo. My curiosity was piqued. "Who from?" Maybe it had something to do with the rental house; if so, Adam should attend to it in Chris's absence. It would help teach him responsibility, or so my unrealistic maternal mind-set ran.

"Let me see." Adam rummaged in the background. I reached over to click on the TV. I usually watch the early evening news, not just to keep informed, but to check out any possible local tie-ins. "It's postmarked Seattle," Adam was saying as the image of a sinking ship appeared on the screen. "That's weird," he remarked. "There's a printed return address from Alpine. Phoebe Pratt. Oh, I remember her. Isn't she the old bat with all the clown makeup and the hairdo that looks like a pineapple?"

I took in a sharp breath. "Open it," I commanded in my best breach-of-ethics tone.

"I can't do that," Adam protested. "It's addressed to Chris. That's *snooping*."

"That's my job. Come on, Adam," I coaxed, "just this once. It could be important. To Chris."

It was his turn to sigh. "Okay, hang on . . . It's dated September twenty-third. Jeez, I don't like this. . . . Why don't I just stick it in another envelope and send it to you so you can give it to Chris?"

"Why don't you just stick that idea in your ear? Phoebe is Neeny Doukas's girlfriend, get it?" I stopped just long enough to let that fact sink in on Adam. "It's very strange that she would write to Chris. Read me the blasted thing. Then you can mail it to me, okay?"

The stationery fluttered in my ear. I had visions of it being pale lavender and scented. I was probably wrong. No doubt it was typed on a word processor—but sometimes I cling to illusions.

" 'Dear Chris,' " Adam began. " 'This letter may come as a surprise to you. You probably don't remember me, but I certainly remember you as a little boy. You were such a handsome lad and so well-behaved.' " Adam paused. "This is a bunch of bilge, Mom. It'll make Chris puke."

"Go on." I gritted my teeth and gave only fleeting attention to the TV image of a North Seattle bank, the site, presumably, of an afternoon holdup.

"Where was I? Oh—'I'm sorry your poor mother passed away last year. You must feel her loss sorely. I should have written sooner to offer my sympathy, but time goes by so fast, even in Alpine.' What a crock!" exclaimed Adam. I could picture him shaking his head. Nevertheless, he went on reading: " 'I've been looking after your grandfather, and I hate to tell you this, but he's failing. I know he would love to see you, so if you could come over to the Mainland on your next college vacation, do consider it. Meanwhile, I stand ready to help you any way I can. Though bridges may be burned—' Get this, Mom. You're gonna blow chunks. '—the way home remains. Be assured, you still have one friend in Alpine. Sincerely yours, Phoebe Pratt.' Retch-making, huh?"

"Puzzle-making," I murmured. On Channel 4, a disabled Metro bus was blocking traffic on the freeway. I wished all the Doukases, plus Fuzzy Baugh, were trapped inside. "I think you had better send that to me. Overnight. I'll pay for it."

"It's just a bunch of birdcrap. What's it got to do with Mark Doukas getting whacked?"

"I don't know," I admitted. But deep down I had a feeling there might be a connection.

For the next minute or so, I listened to Adam try to weasel out of a trip to the post office. He was short of ready cash—of course. He had to study for a test—maybe. He didn't want to be late picking up Deloria—naturally. But eventually he gave in; the post office was only two blocks away. I figured he could throw the letter that far, which is how I assume the mail is often delivered anyway.

Still resisting the urge to ask more about Deloria, I poured myself a glass of English ale and sat back to catch the last fifteen minutes of news. Except for a feature on a couple in Kirkland who'd adopted a pair of aardvarks, the rest was weather and sports. Mark Doukas's murder hadn't made the Seattle television scene, and I didn't know whether to be glad or sad.

I turned off the set and realized I hadn't listened to my answering machine. I'd been too anxious to call Adam to notice the flashing red light. Luckily, there were only three calls: an old friend from Portland, Darlene Adcock asking if I could fill in for a sick bridge player Saturday night, and Sheriff Dodge. I dialed Milo first, hoping to catch him still at work.

He was. "The crowbar did it," he declared. "I tried to call you at the office, but Vida said you'd just left."

"Prints?" I asked, taking notes.

"Wiped clean except for some smudges we can't use. The weapon belongs to Simon Doukas—he thinks." Dodge sounded annoyed. "The flashlight was Mark's."

"What do you mean, Simon *thinks* it was his? Mark was trying to buy one from Harvey Adcock that afternoon."

"Seen one crowbar, seen 'em all. Simon said he had at least one, maybe two, but he couldn't find either of them," Dodge explained. "It sounds as if Mark had been trying to pry open the mine."

"Mayor Baugh wants to open it," I said in a casual voice.

"Jeez! That's great, we'll end up with fifty men trying to rescue some poor little kid who wandered in by mistake." Dodge's annoyance was turning into anger. "Why can't people leave well enough alone?" His tone changed quickly. "Have you heard from Chris again?"

"No. Are you looking for him?" I didn't sound quite so casual this time.

Dodge sighed. "I was hoping we wouldn't have to. By the way, did you know the story made the five o'clock news on the Everett radio stations?"

I gave a little gasp. Apparently, the Seattle media hadn't had the time—or the inclination—to pick up on the item yet. "No. Well, it's out in the open anyway."

"Simon's pitching a fit," Dodge said, not without a hint of pleasure. "Hey, you want to go get some dinner? How about that French place down the highway?"

In the past few months, Milo Dodge and I had shared a half-dozen meals, usually accidental luncheon encounters. This was the first time he'd issued a formal invitation. Rankled by my son's gibes, I accepted. Besides, what better way to ferret out more information than over boeuf Bourguignon and a glass of Beaujolais?

I was changing into a white crepe blouse and a black pleated skirt when Vida called.

"Can you swing a crowbar?" she demanded.

I allowed that I thought I could.

"So can anybody who's not feeble," she retorted. "So

where does that leave us? Did you hear about the Everett stations?" She was gleeful. "Let that moron Simon put that up his nose. As for Fuzzy, it'll make his hair fall off."

While trying to button my blouse and juggle the receiver, I told Vida about Phoebe's letter to Chris. She was flabbergasted.

"Well, if that doesn't beat all!" A teakettle whistled in the background and Vida's canary, Cupcake, competed with the sound. "Why would she do such a thing?"

"Sucking up, my son would say," I suggested, marveling that he hadn't. "How does Phoebe get along with the rest of the Doukases?"

"Like cat and dog," said Vida. "Except for Cece. Cece Doukas gets along with everybody, which is a sure sign that there's something wrong with her. Simon's never approved of his father carrying on with Phoebe, but he doesn't dare speak up, the little weasel, and Kent's been downright insulting. Jennifer sticks up her nose, and Mark—well, Mark considered Phoebe a world-class leech. Which she is, but I hate to admit to agreeing with Mark, even if he is dead."

I slipped into my sling-back black pumps. "You don't suppose Phoebe is angling to marry Neeny, do you?"

Vida scoffed. "After all these years? You know the old saying about the cow and the free milk—Phoebe's been a regular dairy farm for Neeny Doukas." She huffed a bit, then suddenly changed her tune. "Emma, people are *very* strange. Do you suppose that's why Phoebe dragged Neeny to Las Vegas?"

I'd forgotten about the trip the previous month. "Gee, it could be. At least it's something we could check out. Or Milo could. I'm going to dinner with him. I'll mention it."

"You're *what*?" Vida's voice exploded into my ear.

I cringed. I hadn't wanted to confess my date with the sheriff, but I knew that by tomorrow morning, it would be all over town. "We're going to discuss the case." It wasn't a lie: Given the circumstances, of course we'd talk about Mark's murder.

Vida huffed and puffed some more. "Ooooh—just be careful, Emma."

"Hey, I'm safe. I'll be with a law enforcement person."

Vida's tone turned dour. "Don't let him finagle any more out of you than you get from him. In *any* way," she added darkly.

"Don't worry, I'm a big girl," I insisted. But I sounded more confident than I felt. I had the feeling that Vida knew it.

The Café de Flore was run by a Frenchman who had married a Californian. Together, they had fled north with dreams of opening a restaurant that featured prime examples of cuisine from Paris, Brittany, and Normandy, with a dash of Beverly Hills.

The decor was as simple as it was predictable: one wall covered with wine racks, gleaming copper pots suspended from the ceiling, and bunches of dried wildflowers. The tables and chairs were an odd-lot collection that looked as if the owners had bought up kitchen donations to St. Vincent de Paul. But the food was excellent, and though the menu was small, the wine list was long. I chose the beef I'd envisioned, while Milo let me recommend the pork chops baked with apples. We didn't mention Mark until our entrées arrived.

"How did the radio people in Everett get the story?" I inquired after he'd raised the subject by remarking that murder investigations were exhausting.

"The usual way," he answered. Milo's shambling frame was decked out in what I guessed he considered semiformal attire—a brown corduroy sports coat, tan shirt, dark brown slacks. No tie. "They check our blotter over the phone every morning," Milo explained. "Then we got a couple of calls, so one of the deputies doled out the bare facts. We didn't know about the crowbar for sure at that time." He gave me a wry grin. "You'll be glad to hear they didn't mention Mark finding gold."

I was relieved. It's embarrassing to find yourself a

laughingstock among your peer group. "Are you still after Chris?" I asked bluntly.

Milo, who was trying to figure out the identity of his vegetable, gave a shrug. "We certainly need to question him, yes. I'm putting out an APB tomorrow if he hasn't shown up by tonight. I would have done it earlier, but Eeeny talked me out of it."

Inwardly, I thanked the former sheriff. "He doesn't think Chris is . . . involved?"

"He doesn't think we have any evidence." Milo surrendered and ate the unknown vegetable. My guess was that it was turnip; I had tiny brussels sprouts. "I think Eeeny's overly cautious."

Judging from that remark, I gathered that Milo Dodge did indeed have some sort of evidence. My appetite flagged. I approached the matter obliquely. "Have you figured out where Chris went last night?"

Milo nodded once. "Oh, yeah. We know quite a bit about that." He pushed aside the single candle that flickered between us. "Don't you?" His gaze was very level.

"I sure don't." I bristled a bit. "He was like a clam when he got back to my house. Where was he?"

Chewing on his pork chop, Milo shot me a disapproving glance. "I can't tell you that, Emma. Hell," he chuckled, "you won't even tell me what I'm eating. What's a *pomme*?"

"It's a walrus tusk," I snapped. "Okay, then I won't tell you about Phoebe Pratt eloping with Neeny Doukas."

Milo's sandy brows arched. "Where'd you hear that?"

"Never mind." I would have hummed a bit if we hadn't been sitting down to dinner. My mother had never allowed singing at the table. "If you don't believe me, check it out. Clark County, Nevada. August of this year."

To my satisfaction, Milo was hooked. "We will. Hell, Emma, this is a community property state. Neeny must have rewritten his will. If he hasn't, everything will go to Phoebe, should she outlive him."

"Simon would make sure it didn't," I pointed out. "Assuming he knows they got married."

Milo waved to a couple coming across the room. I didn't know them. In fact, I only recognized four of our fellow diners, both younger couples who lived on the fringes of Alpine. The rest of the two dozen customers had probably come up from Monroe, or even Seattle and Everett. The Café de Flore's reputation was growing beyond the boundary of Skykomish County.

"Whether or not Phoebe and Neeny eloped doesn't help us with Mark's murder," Milo noted. "It'd be more likely that somebody would have knocked off Phoebe. Or even Neeny."

I sipped my Beaujolais and tried to figure out the flaw in Milo's argument. I couldn't find one. I sighed. "What about Heather Bardeen?"

"Heather?" Milo looked puzzled. "She'd already broken up with Mark. Why would she want to bash his head in?"

"Maybe he done her wrong," I said lightly.

"I'm sure he did. More than once. But so what? When did you last meet a twenty-year-old girl who went gaga over her lost honor?"

Milo had a point. Even if Heather was pregnant, she wasn't likely to rush off to Icicle Creek and bust Mark's head with a crowbar. I savored my last mouthful of beef and wondered if the bikers had really returned.

Milo's plate was clean as a whistle, turnips and all. He took out a small spiral note pad with a ballpoint pen. "By the way, I'll need a description of Chris for that APB."

I grimaced, feeling like a traitor. But dissembling wouldn't serve any purpose. The Doukases, Harvey Adcock, and a dozen other people could provide the information Milo needed.

"Twenty years old, five-eleven, about a hundred and fifty pounds, straight black hair worn just a little too long, black eyes, straight nose, slight dimple in chin, no distinguishing marks." I hesitated, giving Milo time to finish writing. He was quick and looked up with approval. I went on: "Faded blue jeans, maybe Levi's, faded denim jacket, maybe ditto, Hard Rock Cafe—Honolulu T-shirt, Dodgers baseball cap, Reebok tennis shoes in white with black and green stripes. No, hold it."

Milo looked up again, pen poised over the pad. "What?"

"He'd changed his T-shirt." I shut my eyes, trying to picture Chris as I'd seen him last. "It was something about Hawaii—a cocktail, with SUCK 'EM UP! on it, I think. And . . . let me see . . . I can't . . . Oh!" I put a hand to my mouth. "He wasn't wearing that denim jacket. He'd loaned it to Mark. Chris had on Mark's leather bomber jacket."

Frowning, Milo flipped back through the pages of his note pad. "You're right. Mark had on a denim jacket, J. C. Penney issue." He regarded me very seriously. "Tell me more about the baseball cap."

"More? What can I say? That it was autographed by Tommy Lasorda?" I gave Milo a perplexed look. He didn't so much as flicker an eyelid. Then I saw Chris in my mind's eye again, standing in front of the Monet. "Chris wasn't wearing the cap when he came home. Is that what you mean?"

Milo nodded once and tapped the note pad with his pen. "Mark wore the cap. They found it next to his body. It's got his blood and his hair on it."

"Of course," I said slowly. "It was raining. Mark borrowed both the cap and the denim jacket. Chris's hair was wet when he came home. I remember that now." Struck by a sudden thought, I leaned eagerly across the table. "Now reconsider your suspicions regarding Chris—if he'd killed Mark, wouldn't he have taken back his own jacket?"

Milo looked at me as if I'd been sniffing Elmer's Glue. "I've never said Chris murdered Mark," he replied carefully. "What are you implying? First they swap clothes, then they try to kill each other? My sisters used to do that, but fortunately, nobody ever ended up dead."

The waitress came for our dessert order, but for once I abstained and ordered a King Alfonse. Milo settled for the café's version of burnt cream and a snifter of brandy.

There was something else about Chris and Mark and their jackets that bothered me, but my brain was numbed by the excellent meal. The fragmentary idea slipped away, and I changed the subject from violence to domesticity. "Where are your kids?" I asked Milo when the waitress had left.

"The youngest—Michelle—is living with Old Mulehide and her second husband, Peter the Snake, in Bellevue. Tanya is shacked up with some would-be sculptor in Seattle." He shook his head. "She supports him, and he makes erasers out of Play-Doh. I don't get it. My son, Brandon, is going to school in Oregon. Corvallis. He wants to be a vet."

"At least he has a goal."

Milo shrugged. "Of sorts. He wants to move to Kentucky and take care of million-dollar thoroughbreds. He'll be lucky to come back to Alpine and unruffle the feathers of Vida's canary."

I sympathized, briefly. Furtively, I glanced over at Milo, who was immersed in his burnt cream. He was attractive in his way, with regular, if unremarkable features, tall, solid, smart enough. He even had a sense of humor. So why did I feel about as thrilled by his presence as if I'd been dining with Vida? The truth was, I'd hoped the evening might provide a springboard for future intimacies. Maybe it was Adam's needling, or the thought of spending the night alone in the wake of a murder. Perhaps I was lonely and didn't know it. But whatever had spurred me into wishing for some sparks to fly with Milo Dodge, the truth was that nothing was happening. I fervently hoped it was the same with Milo.

I didn't get to find out. When we pulled up in front of my house half an hour later, Bill Blatt was waiting for the sheriff. Fuzzy Baugh had been rushed to Alpine Community Hospital with an apparent heart attack; he was listed in critical condition. Milo Dodge put the siren on and raced off toward Front Street, leaving me alone.

* * *

The last person I expected to see on my doorstep that night was Jennifer Doukas MacDuff. She knocked just before ten, about a half hour after I got home. Wearing another sack of a dress and with her long hair straggling over her shoulders, Jennifer was definitely waiflike. I took in a deep breath of fresh, pine-scented air and ushered her into the living room.

"Kent and I had a fight," she said, collapsing onto the sofa. "Over you."

"Me?" I had just changed into my bathrobe and was drinking a Pepsi. "Why?"

Jennifer slumped against the cushions, looking even more drab than usual by contrast with my emerald-green upholstery. "Kent thinks your story about the gold got Mark killed. He said you all but admitted it at my folks' house. And he also thinks you're hiding Chris Ramirez." She gave me a plaintive look. "Are you?"

"No. Want some pop?"

Jennifer did and opted for 7-Up. I returned from the kitchen to find her in tears.

"What's wrong? Are you crying for Mark?" I inquired gently, sitting next to her and putting the glass of soda on the coffee table.

Jennifer sobbed on but shook her head. "Mark was a jerk in a lot of ways," she said between sniffs. "I'll miss him, sure. But it's Chris I feel most sorry for."

"How come?" I shifted on the sofa while Jennifer tried to compose herself and sit up.

"I was the only one he'd make up to when he was little," Jennifer said. "Aunt Margaret had me baby-sit a couple of times. That was just before Hector disappeared. I never understood that. I was only a kid, about ten, but I liked Uncle Hector. He wasn't educated, but he was nice. He seemed to really like Aunt Margaret—and Chris, too. His running off has never made any sense to me. Maybe I was too young to take it all in."

"Tell me about Hector." It had occurred to me that in more ways than one, Hector Ramirez was the missing link in the Doukas family history. "What did he do for a living?"

Jennifer reached for her pop and looked vague, which I realized was typical. "Labor stuff. Not logging, but construction, maybe. My father said he was lazy. Hector didn't work all the time, but sort of off and on."

"Construction's like that," I remarked. Vida had said Hector had come to Alpine to help put in a sewer line. It would follow that he'd try to get work as a manual laborer; it would also follow that Neeny Doukas would try to prevent his despised son-in-law from getting employment. "Maybe Hector left town to find another job and something happened to him."

Lapping at her soda like a cat, Jennifer shook her head, the honey-blond hair swinging across her face. "If he had, wouldn't somebody have notified Aunt Margaret? He must have had an I.D. Besides, he and Margaret did go away for a while, when they were first married. In fact, Chris was born in Seattle. But I guess she got homesick. Or else she thought the rest of the family would change their minds. They didn't."

"Was Hector an American or a Mexican National?" I asked.

Jennifer considered. "I think he was from Los Angeles. He had kind of an accent but not much." She sat back, her shoulders hunched. The Doukas arrogance seemed to have been obliterated in Jennifer by Cecelia's self-effacing nature. In some ways, it was a pity. I wondered how Jennifer faced up to Kent MacDuff.

I finished my Pepsi and realized that the rich food and red wine had given me heartburn. A bit guiltily, I thought of Fuzzy Baugh, lying in the intensive care unit at Alpine Community Hospital. If his heart attack had been severe, he would be moved to Everett or Seattle. Alpine's medical facilities were limited.

I came back to the subject at hand. "Do you remember much about Hector's disappearance?"

Jennifer fiddled with her hair and squirmed a bit. "Not

really. Margaret didn't tell anybody at first. At least not the family. Then I guess she called the sheriff, but they didn't start looking for him right away. Grandpa interfered, I think, and told Eeeny Moroni not to bother."

Recalling that Vida had said there were rumors about Neeny paying Hector to hit the road, I decided to broach the topic. "Do you think your grandfather might have bribed Hector to leave town?"

Jennifer turned her pale blue eyes on me in astonishment. "Oh! I don't . . ." She swallowed hard, blinked and put her chin on her fist. "Gosh, I don't know. I never thought about it." For a few moments, she apparently did just that. Then she gave a tentative shake of her head. "I can imagine Grandpa trying it, but honestly, I don't see Hector going along with him. Like I said, Hector really loved Aunt Margaret and Chris."

The living room was silent while we each reflected on the life and times of Hector Ramirez. I hadn't built a fire, and there was a definite chill in the air. The wind was gentle tonight, a soft sigh in the trees that surrounded all but the front of my house. I heard a logging truck rumble down the street as someone came home, no doubt after a long stop at Mugs Ahoy or the Icicle Creek Tavern.

I was the first to break the silence. "I'm puzzled about Chris and Mark. Your brother borrowed Chris's cap and jacket, yet Kent says they had a fight. That doesn't make sense."

Suddenly edgy, Jennifer avoided my gaze, hiding behind her veil of fair hair. "There was no fight," she said in a mumble.

"I'm glad to hear it," I said, trying to sound cheerful. "Is Kent trying to cause trouble or is he always so full of bunk?" My guess was both, but I waited with a smile for Jennifer's reply.

She prefaced it with a deep sigh. "Oh, Kent can be such a pill! He doesn't mean to be, but I think he feels he has to act like a big shot because he married into the Doukas family. It's really very immature."

"It sure is. It's also harmful to people like Chris. It gave Sheriff Dodge the wrong impression. I'm very relieved to hear there was no quarrel."

Jennifer seemed to be brooding over her husband's faults. She looked up suddenly, pushing the long hair off her face. "I didn't say there was no quarrel. I just said there wasn't one between Chris and Mark." She thrust out her small chin in a surprisingly pugnacious manner. "Kent and Mark got into it, just before Mark left. Having him go off and get killed is enough to make me cry for him, too."

"Oh." I took note of the uncharacteristic spark in her eyes. "Yes, I can understand that. What did they fight about?"

Her shoulders slumped again. "Kevin. Mark was mad because Kent's brother had told your reporter about the gold. Except there wasn't any, of course. Mark blamed Kent for having such a dopey brother."

I'd meant to talk to Kevin but hadn't gotten a chance. By the time he was out of school, I was knee-deep in phone calls and Fuzzy Baugh's visit. Now it was too late to call a teenager who had to get up at seven in the morning. At least that's the way it had worked at our house.

I wondered how far I could push Jennifer. I sensed that her anger—or in her case, anguish was a better word—with Kent might temporarily overcome her protective instincts. "Was it a serious quarrel?"

"Well, they didn't hit each other this time. I heard some of it. They just yelled a lot, mostly about who had the stupidest relatives." A flash of alarm crossed her face. "Don't take this wrong, Ms. Lord—Mark and Kent were always on each other's case. It was some kind of macho deal. But they weren't enemies. They even partied together."

The kind of partying Mark and Kent had done depressed me. I could envision raucous nights with a half-dozen kegs, stale nachos, and bad jokes, culminating in ghastly trips to the bathroom. By comparison, my bathrobe and a can of Pepsi didn't look half so bad.

"But on that note, Mark left?" I asked innocently.

"I guess." Jennifer looked glum.

"Then I gather your dad gave Chris a ride home?"

She drank more soda. "Yes. A few minutes later, we went home, too."

"You didn't see Chris again?"

"No."

"You stayed home the rest of the evening?"

Jennifer looked faintly belligerent. "Sure. It was a work night."

"When did you hear about Mark?"

"We'd gone to bed. Around eleven, I guess." She glanced at her wrist, which was bare. Maybe she was confirming the fact that she didn't wear a watch. "Dad called. I got dressed and went over to be with him and Mom."

"Kent didn't go?" I was mildly surprised.

Jennifer shook her head. "No. He'd gone to see young Doc Dewey about a muscle pull. Kent was Dewey's last patient for the day, and he had to wait forever. That's why we were late getting to my folks' house for dinner. Kent had taken one of those muscle relaxant things before he went to bed, and he was out of it."

I couldn't think of anything else to ask Jennifer except how her grandfather was doing. Okay, she answered vaguely, all things considered.

"Look," I said, "tell Kent I'm sorry we ever ran that story in the first place. I'll tell him so myself if it'll help. But even if we hadn't printed it, rumors about Mark and the so-called gold find would have spread all over town." Jennifer didn't look convinced, but neither was I. While I didn't believe Mark had discovered gold, our black-and-white reporting job automatically gave authenticity. That's just the way it works with the media. We're supposed to be trusted to tell the truth. Fighting down regrets, I changed the subject. "Jennifer, are you going home?"

Her hair and shoulders drooped in unison. "I don't know. Maybe I'll go stay with Mom and Dad. They could use my help, I suppose."

Fleetingly, I considered asking her to stay with me. But my earlier fears of being alone had been tempered by good food and red wine. Besides, I wasn't having much luck with houseguests this week. I didn't want Kent MacDuff breaking down my knotty pine front door at three A.M. Then again, maybe he'd taken another muscle relaxant and was out for the count.

Jennifer got to her feet, the sacklike dress hanging unevenly. "I'm sorry I bothered you, but I was upset and I didn't want to go crying to my folks. Mom's pretty racked up. Mark was her favorite. She spoiled him something awful. It wasn't fair." The belligerence was back in her eyes.

"Lots of things aren't fair," I remarked, making one of those useless, if true, comments that serve no other purpose than to fill a void. "Feel free to drop in again."

Jennifer looked faintly surprised at the invitation. "Okay. Thanks for the pop."

I watched her go out into the overcast night, a bulky all-weather jacket thrown over her shoulders. Her white Japanese compact was parked at the edge of the short driveway.

Poor little rich girl, I thought—she was as unlikely an heiress as any I'd ever met. I'd known wealthy girls at Blanchet High School in Seattle; I'd rubbed elbows with their big sisters in Portland. They not only reeked of privilege, but they were often supremely self-confident. Jennifer, by contrast, could have been a gyppo logger's daughter. She'd married at twenty, stayed in Alpine, and seemed to have neither ambition nor curiosity. The Jennifer Doukas MacDuffs of this world bothered me.

Even after she'd driven away, I lingered on my small front porch, inhaling the fresh, cool mountain air. Tonight it was tinged with wood smoke, a sure sign that autumn had settled in. I peered around my front yard, still amazed that the dahlia tubers I'd planted last March had actually come up. There wasn't much lawn—just enough to separate the walk from the drive on one side and the narrow flower bed and the split-rail fence on the other. A big ma-

ple stood in one corner, by the street. In the back, where
the grass sloped gently upward, a half-dozen evergreens
protected me from the rest of the world.

The phone broke my reverie. To my surprise, it was
Chris, calling from Seattle. He sounded troubled.

"Hey, Mrs. Lord, I can't find your address. Maybe it
was in my denim jacket. I need to send back Mark's
leather jacket. I mean, I know he won't need it, but I don't
feel right keeping it, you know?"

Carefully, I gave him my address. "Chris, the sheriff really has to talk to you. I'll drive down and pick you up
first thing in the morning."

His reply was sharp: "No. I'm going to L.A." He
sounded not only incisive, but older.

"Why? What's wrong?" There was no mistaking the
sound of panic.

"I just want to get away from here," he said, trying to
keep his voice calm. "It . . . it rains too much. I miss the
sun."

"Okay," I said reasonably. "I'll buy that. Can I ask you
a question, just to set the record straight?"

"Sure." Despite the response, Chris didn't sound so positive.

"Where did you take my car last night after your uncle
dropped you off?"

"I just sort of drove around. I tried to find the house
where we lived when I was a kid." He hesitated, and I
heard a tapping sound, as if he were drumming his fingernails on the phone. Impatience or anxiety, I wondered.
Both, maybe. "Just for kicks, I went up to the ski lodge to
see Heather Bardeen. But she wasn't there. Not then. I ran
into her later, at the Burger Barn."

I kept my voice casual. "So you just cruised for over
three hours?"

"I guess." Apparently, it didn't strike Chris as strange.
For the moment, I gave up pressing him. "Where are you
right now?"

There was a faint pause. "In a motel, near downtown."

"Which one?"

"I don't know."

He could have been hedging. On the other hand, his lack of awareness was typical of his generation. "Have you got a view?" I asked.

Another pause. "Yeah. Of a parking lot. And the Space Needle. I went up there today." He definitely sounded more like himself, though I had the feeling it wasn't without effort.

"Forget about mailing the jacket," I counseled him. "I have to come into town tomorrow for a meeting." It was a lie, but made in a good cause. "I'll meet you for breakfast. Adam is sending your mail over. I talked to him today."

"Oh? Cool. Maybe I got my check."

I didn't disillusion him. "It should be here in a couple of days. Why don't you wait?"

"No way." The incisiveness returned. "I'll send you an address from California. Oh, hey, when you talk to Adam again, ask him to send my other denim jacket, okay? It's at the house. The people who rented it let me store a bunch of stuff in the garage."

I agreed to convey the message. In some ways, I was ambivalent about keeping Chris around, so I didn't try arguing with him further. But I was determined to see him before he left. "Is there a restaurant in the motel?"

"Yeah, I saw it when I checked in. But I want to catch the nine-thirty bus."

"No problem," I said easily, but inwardly groaning at the prospect of another early-morning run into the city. "I'll meet you in the restaurant at eight. Look on the table by the phone, Chris. There must be some advertising to give you the motel's name."

"There's some postcards and a sort of phone book thing—oh, yeah, here. It's a Ramada Inn. But I don't see an address."

"No problem," I repeated. "I know where it is. I'll see you in the restaurant at eight."

"Okay," he said a bit dubiously. "Mrs. Lord?"

"Yes?"

"You're not bringing anybody with you, are you?" The suspicion in his voice bounced off my ear.

I laughed. "Hardly. Do you think I'm a police dupe?"

"Well, it's all pretty strange, isn't it?" He sounded very young again.

"Yes, it is," I agreed. "Are you sure you're okay?"

"Huh? Yeah, I'm fine." He hesitated, then spoke with less certainty. "It's just that, well, like, this is really scary, you know?"

"Yes," I replied, grateful that Chris couldn't see my grim expression. "It's scary, all right. I've never been this close to a murder before."

"Me neither," said Chris. He sounded frightened. I wished I knew why.

Chapter Nine

THE SUN WAS trying to break through during the last half hour of my drive into Seattle. I'd given myself plenty of time and arrived at the Ramada Inn at seven forty-five. Fueled only by coffee, I was starving by the time I reached the restaurant. It was half full, a mixture of off-season tourists and business types. I drank more coffee but held off ordering breakfast until Chris came down. The pancakes tempted me, but so did the crab and cheese omelette. On the other hand, the ham and eggs special was appealing, too. I amused myself by playing my finely honed game of juggling the menu around in my head. It was a practice borne of countless hours of eating alone.

I'd picked up a morning paper in the lobby and scanned it for news of Mark Doukas's murder. Sure enough, the story was tucked away on an inside page. The brief, two-inch item stated that the body of Mark Doukas, twenty-six, had been found in Alpine, just off Stevens Pass. Sheriff Milo Dodge was investigating what was a probable homicide, since Doukas had apparently died from a blow to the head. There was no mention of gold. There was no allusion to the Doukas family's standing in the community. There was no information about leads or possible suspects. In other words, there was no real interest in the case outside of Alpine. That, I decided, was just as well.

I'm fairly adept at premonitions, so I was chagrined, but only mildly surprised when Chris didn't show. I gave him until eight-fifteen to be late, but by eight-thirty, I was worried. I stalled the waitress for the fourth time and went out to the desk.

A cheerful Vietnamese man told me there was no Chris Ramirez registered. It hadn't occurred to me that Chris would use a different name, but it made sense. Milo Dodge could have been already looking for him. In fact, it dawned on me that the sheriff might have sent out his APB at the crack of dawn.

I described Chris, and the round-faced clerk nodded in recognition. Mr. Jones had checked out early, around six A.M. Was I, by any chance, Mrs. Lord?

I told him I was. The clerk handed me a Ramada Inn dry-cleaning bag that contained Mark's leather jacket and a note with my name on it.

The waitress pounced as soon as I got back to my table. Although my appetite had dwindled in the past five minutes, I felt coerced into placing my order and asked for the special. Appeased, she scurried off, leaving me to peruse Chris's note.

He had surprisingly elegant handwriting, and his spelling was amazingly accurate for his generation. "Dear Mrs. Lord," the note on motel stationery read,

"I feel bad about taking off before you got here. The fact is, I should never have come back to Alpine. It was a mistake for a lot of reasons. I don't know how to explain this to you, but seeing the town and the people stirred up a lot of memories I'd tried to forget. I'm still not sure what's real and what isn't. Maybe if I go away, I can sort it out. Or else forget it all again. Thanks for everything. Yours truly, Chris Ramirez. P.S. Here's the jacket. Maybe Heather would like to have it."

I reread the note. The distress I'd heard on the phone last night was mirrored by the written words. I recalled how tense Chris had been when he came back to the house Wednesday night. I thought at the time it was because of his meeting with his relatives. Now I wasn't certain. A six-year-old isn't attuned to the nuances of adult behavior. As a child, Chris might have felt disturbed by the estrangement between his parents and the rest of the family, but he wouldn't have fought to keep the memory at bay. Indeed, it seemed that Margaret had done quite the opposite, and Chris had followed her lead. His hostility indicated that he wasn't suppressing his emotions.

So what was Chris trying to forget? Was it something ugly between his parents? That seemed the most likely, yet his mother must have been a constant reminder of any such incident. Chris spoke of the town and the people jarring his sleeping memories. Neeny? But Chris hadn't seen his grandfather. At least not as far as I knew. Now I wondered. There was that three-and-a-half-hour gap to account for. Milo Dodge knew something about that lost time, but he wasn't telling me. I'd have to find out for myself.

The waitress came with my order. I further frustrated her by immediately getting up and going back to the lobby. Sure enough, there was a Greyhound schedule in the tourist information rack. A bus left Seattle for L.A. at six twenty-five. Chris was already two and a half hours down the road. I couldn't possibly catch up with him, but the sheriff could. I went back into the restaurant and ate my breakfast. The waitress finally looked happy.

I did not.

Durwood Parker, a serious competitor with Eeeny Moroni for the Worst Driver in Alpine Sweepstakes, had run over a cow two miles east of Sultan. Debra Barton, of the Barton Bootery family, had announced her engagement to a Tacoma prelaw student. Averill Fairbanks reported a UFO hovering over his toolshed, his fifth sighting of the year. Francine Wells chalked up $350 worth of damages at Francine's Fine Apparel on Front Street when the wind blew over a bucket of blue paint being used to freshen the exterior, and spattered not only the display window, but the sidewalk and street. Bessie Griswold, up on Burl Creek Road, called the sheriff to report a prowler that turned out to be a cougar who mauled her Manx cat. Vida was pleased.

Those were the stories facing me when I got back to the office around eleven. I confided where I'd been only to Vida, who took the news of Chris's departure with a disapproving shake of her head. She was, however, glad to learn that I had not let Milo Dodge ravish me. So, of course, was I.

After giving Carla specific instructions on the handling of the morning's accumulation of news, I called to check on Fuzzy's condition. It was listed as stable. He would not, as far as they could tell, be shipped to a larger medical facility.

As for the homicide investigation, Milo Dodge reported no notable progress. The funeral was set for Monday in Seattle, since Alpine had no Greek Orthodox church. I designated Vida as the *Advocate*'s representative. The rest of us couldn't be spared, since Monday was always a hectic day in getting the paper ready for publication.

Just before noon, Milo called me back. Could I come down to the sheriff's office? Certainly. In fact, I could hardly wait, since I assumed he'd unearthed something newsworthy in the course of the investigation.

The sun was still peeking in and out from behind dirty white clouds, so I walked, taking a moment to admire the darkening red and gold of the trees that mingled with the evergreens on the hillside. Baldy was clear, looking comfortable above the town, its crest still free of snow.

Milo didn't seem much like the bemused man of the previous evening who'd relied on my sophistication to distinguish a turnip from a crocus bulb. He was sitting very straight in his leather swivel chair, his hazel eyes steely and his square jaw set. I felt like a criminal, which I supposed I was, having concealed the whereabouts of Chris Ramirez.

"Emma," he began, not bothering with small talk, "I have some questions to ask you."

"Go ahead," I responded, sitting down and trying to act unconcerned.

He consulted his notes. "You stated that Chris didn't say where he'd been during the time Simon dropped him off about eight-thirty and when he actually showed up at your house around midnight. Is that correct?"

"It is. I asked, but he didn't tell me." Why, I wondered fleetingly, if truth was such a great ally, did I feel so defenseless?

"Did you know Simon had dropped him off?" The hazel eyes were not only cool, but remote, as if he didn't want to make any personal contact.

"No. That is, I realized later that I'd heard a car pull up and then leave. But it might not have been them." I thought back to the night before last, which now seemed so long ago. "The wind was really blowing. It's a marvel I heard anything at all."

He flipped through some papers and pulled out a single sheet. "Did you leave your house at any time during the evening?"

My eyes widened. "No. I had dinner at the Venison Inn. In fact, I ran into Eeeny Moroni there. He can verify what time I left. It was about seven, I think. Anyway, I came straight home and stayed put. I was beat."

Deliberately, Milo shoved the paper toward me. "This is a lab report on the tire tracks in Neeny Doukas's driveway." He tapped at the page with his ballpoint pen. "One set belongs to your Jaguar."

I debated the merits of candor. But half the town had no doubt seen Chris driving my car Wednesday afternoon. In any event, Mark wasn't killed in Neeny's driveway. Still, Mineshaft Number Three was too close to the Doukas house for comfort.

"It wasn't me," I asserted. Annoyance had surfaced in my voice. Milo Dodge had picked up the check at the Café de Flore the previous night. Now he was grilling me like a felon on the FBI's Ten Most Wanted List. I felt like snatching up his roll of mints and sticking them in his nose. Carla had been right the first time: the sheriff was acting more like *Mildo* than Milo.

Milo seemed unmoved by my deteriorating temper. "I know it wasn't you. I saw the Jag coming from the opposite direction when I went up to meet Mark at Mineshaft Number Three." He fingered his chin while I absorbed that particular piece of information. "Could Chris have borrowed your car?"

There was no point in sheltering Chris over the issue. On the other hand, anybody could have figured out I kept that extra set of keys under the car. But somehow I didn't think they had. The simplest answers are usually the right ones. "He'd borrowed it earlier. I suppose he didn't think he had to ask again."

"But did he?" persisted Dodge.

"I don't know." The baldness of my reply seemed to sink in. "If he did, was it to go see his grandfather?"

Milo Dodge hesitated, then inclined his head. "Yes. He saw Neeny. It wasn't a successful reunion."

I'd hoped for better but expected worse. "Did they have a row?"

Milo was unbending a bit, extracting a mint and popping it in his mouth. He did not, however, go so far as to offer me one. "According to Neeny, it was pretty one-sided. Chris gave him some lip, and then the old man lit into him. The kid left with his tail between his legs."

"*According to Neeny,*" I quoted. Chris might have a different version. "When was that?"

"Around nine." Milo had glanced at his notes again. "Neeny isn't too accurate about time. The world turns on his schedule, not the other way around. It was before Phoebe made his cocoa, which usually transpires around nine-thirty." Milo looked a bit wry. "We haven't pressed Neeny much. He's not feeling too well, you know. He refused to discuss Chris at all at first. I stopped by for a minute yesterday to offer my condolences, and he admitted Chris had been there. Maybe later we can get more details."

"Like when Neeny isn't rich?" I knew Milo Dodge wasn't as likely as some to kowtow to the Doukases, but neither would he go out of his way to raise any hackles.

"Now Emma, the man's grieving," Milo admonished. "He was genuinely fond of Mark."

I ignored the comment. "Have you checked on Phoebe and Neeny?"

Milo couldn't restrain a little snort. "You were right about that, Emma. They were married by a J.P. in Vegas on August eighteen. Did Vida come up with that tidbit?"

I gave him a smug smile. "I can't reveal my sources. How does Neeny's will read?"

"How the hell do I know? That doesn't have anything to do with Mark's murder. Ask Simon."

"I will," I snapped, aware that my short chin was giving an imitation of jutting. "What if Neeny had a prenuptial agreement with Phoebe? What if she could only inherit if Mark and Jennifer and Simon died first? What if he figured out a way to circumvent the state community property laws?"

"Couldn't do it." Milo sat back, hands entwined behind his head. "Come on, Emma, can you see Phoebe Pratt whacking Mark Doukas over the head with a crowbar?"

"No. But I can see Phoebe *Doukas* doing it. As Neeny's wife, she might have more to gain." Indeed, Phoebe wasn't exactly a lightweight. She and Vida were the same age, about the same height, and though Vida probably outweighed Phoebe by a good twenty pounds, both women were solid citizens in more ways than one. I didn't know Phoebe very well, but Vida did, and that was good enough for me.

If Milo's more relaxed pose was designed to disarm me, this time it wasn't going to work. I was ready for him when he asked about Chris. And I was honest. Up to a point.

"You drove all the way into Seattle this morning?" the sheriff queried after I'd given my brief recitation. "Where did he go?"

"California, I guess." In truth, I couldn't swear that Chris had headed for L.A. In his present state of agitation, he might have changed his mind and gone up to British Columbia or back East. He might even have gone home to Hawaii.

Milo mulled over the situation. "It's no wonder he sounded scared. He ought to be. He might not have murdered Mark, but he hasn't been square with us."

"Oh, come on, Milo. He's twenty years old. Are your kids rational human beings yet? What about your daughter who's living with Gumby?"

"What?"

"Never mind. So what if Chris took my car and went to see Neeny? If anything, that gives him an alibi for Mark's murder. It sounds as if he was with his grandfather around the time Mark must have been killed."

Milo looked dour. "He could have done both. Chris was within spitting distance of the mineshaft when he was up at Neeny's."

"So was Neeny, if it comes to that. And Phoebe. No wonder Neeny hadn't been served his cocoa. Phoebe was probably too busy smashing Mark's skull to hear the tea kettle go off." I felt a bit proud of myself. At least I was coming up with theories that weren't any crazier than Milo's.

"You're too damned irreverent," Milo muttered.

I gave a little laugh. "That's part of the job description. I, like you, would have gone crazy a long time ago if I'd taken every godawful thing that came along too seriously." I paused, watching Milo mutely accept my appraisal of the occupational hazards we both faced. "By the way, it wasn't Chris and Mark who had words Wednesday night. It was Mark and Kent."

This time, the sheriff registered genuine surprise. I explained my visit from Jennifer. "Kent lied so he wouldn't invite suspicion. It may have been stupid—or maybe he has something to hide."

"At least he's got a motive," Milo admitted. "With

Mark out of the way, all of the money will eventually come to Jennifer. Which," he noted with a twist of his long mouth, "gives her a reason to get rid of Mark, too."

"True," I conceded, though somehow the image of Jennifer slamming a crowbar over her brother's head seemed more farfetched than most of our other wild ideas. "The only trouble with the money motive is that Neeny is still alive, and Simon is only about fifty. My guess is that Neeny's will is made out so that Simon inherits everything. I suspect that's why he set up those trust funds for Mark and Jennifer."

Milo didn't know about the trust funds. It occurred to me that from his point of view, the sheriff's office dealt only in hard evidence, not supposition or even motives. He did allow that maybe a check into the disposition of the Doukas fortune might be helpful.

Having dropped his interrogator's mask, Milo finally offered me a mint. This time, I accepted. The rigors of the past fifteen minutes had left my mouth dry. I was also hungry, since it was now well after noon. Before I could make my exit, Milo reached under the desk and hauled out a bundle of newspapers. "These belong to you?"

I stared at the papers, some fifty or so, tied with twine. "It's this week's *Advocate*, all right. Where did you get them?"

Milo didn't look too happy. "About twenty feet from Mineshaft Number Three." He waited for my reaction, but I didn't have one, other than puzzlement. "We also found an odd set of footprints—right one deep, the left a bare impression."

So Billy Blatt hadn't told his aunt all.

Now I was forced to respond. "Gibb Frazier?" Obviously, this stack of papers made up the missing overage. The bundle must have fallen off Gibb's truck. "Have you talked to him?"

Milo shook his head. "He's on a moving job for somebody in Snohomish. He won't be back in Alpine until Saturday night."

Vaguely disturbed, I left the sheriff to ponder his growing collection of evidence. Gibb could have driven up to Icicle Creek any time after he'd delivered the rest of the newspapers. But why he'd gone there baffled me. For the moment, I had to put that problem aside. Lunch would have to wait. Next on my schedule was a visit to Neeny Doukas. On my way out of the sheriff's office, I used the pay phone outside to call Vida and confirm the marriage between Phoebe and Neeny.

"Ooooh," she wailed, "doesn't that beat all! He finally made an honest woman out of the old tramp! Neeny's a bigger fool than I thought!"

"I'm going up there now. Shall I take them a wedding present in your name?" I asked, shielding my ear from the rumble of a passing truckload of logs.

"By all means," Vida replied. "The only trouble is, I don't know where you can buy a pair of jackasses on short notice."

Neither did I, so I arrived at the Doukas residence empty-handed. As I stood on the wide veranda with its ancient window boxes and rusty lawn swing, I was aware that I wouldn't be the most welcome of guests. The door was opened by Frieda Wunderlich, squat, square and toadlike. She had thick lips and protruding eyes the color of ripe huckleberries. I always thought of her as covered with warts, but that was only a figment of my imagination.

"His Royal Highness is resting," she announced with her usual lack of respect. "The Queen Bee went to Monroe."

Now I wished I had brought something with me—a bouquet, a casserole, even a sympathy card. "I just wanted to let him know I was very sorry about his loss," I said, getting a whiff of basil and oregano from the kitchen. "I spoke with him about Mark only a few hours before the tragedy."

The words were my ticket over the threshold. Frieda stepped aside with a mock bow. "He's in the living room, watching television. Make him turn down the sound."

I'd been in the elder Doukas's house on two or three previous occasions. The furnishings were massive and dark, remnants of the Victorian era. Heavy brown draperies shut out the autumn light, and the air was thick with the scent of hothouse flowers and those spices from a sunnier climate. The rooms were cluttered with too much furniture, too many paintings, classical sculptures, potted plants, and now, floral arrangements of sympathy.

Neeny Doukas sat in a big armchair that would have swallowed a smaller man. He was rugged of build, hairy of chest, with dark eyes and an olive complexion. His hair, which had once been black and wavy, was now streaked with white and receding from a forehead that was accented by slanting black eyebrows that matched a bristling mustache and full beard. Ensconced in the big gray mohair chair complete with antimacassars and with an afghan over his knees, Neeny Doukas looked for all the world like the King of Thrace.

"Emma." His voice boomed out as he beckoned to me with one crooked finger. "You got that story?"

"What story?" I said stupidly.

"The one correcting your screw-up. You said you'd show it to me." He waved in the direction of an occasional chair covered in faded red and black cut velvet.

Up close, Neeny looked haggard, older than when I'd seen him a week or two earlier. The flesh on his cheekbones sagged, the big hands trembled ever so slightly, the black eyes were a trifle cloudy. I sat. Next to Neeny was a tray with a half-eaten meal grown cold. A soap opera blared on TV.

"I haven't done it yet," I admitted, raising my voice in the hope that he'd take the hint and shut off the set. "I wasn't sure you'd want me to run it now that Mark's . . . dead."

Neeny reared back in the armchair, the afghan twitching on his knees. "Hell's bells, I sure do! All the more reason." Those extraordinary eyebrows drew together like a pair of black caterpillars. "You see what happened? Some greedy swine thought Mark had made a big strike and killed him over it! Pah!" He all but spat in the rest of his lunch.

The TV perils of a beautiful blonde and her handsome dark-haired lover were giving me a headache. I tried a different approach, this time lowering my voice so that Neeny couldn't possibly hear me without a Miracle Ear. "You don't really think that," I murmured.

Neeny took the hint, using the remote control to turn the sound off but left the picture on. "What?" He didn't wait for my response. "Hell, Emma, who else would wanna kill my grandson? Unless it was that no-good kid of Margaret's."

"Neeny, do you really think Chris Ramirez is a no-account?"

He snorted in disgust. "He's Hector's son, isn't he? Hector ran out on my daughter and the kid. Blood tells, Emma."

"Chris has your blood as well as Hector's," I pointed out. "Besides, half the town seems to think you bribed Hector to go away."

Neeny Doukas all but leaped out of the chair. The afghan fell to the floor. "That's a goddamned lie! Who told you that, old big-mouthed Vida? I wouldn't have given Hector Ramirez a plugged nickel!"

His vehemence exploded Vida's myth. Still, it had been a logical explanation. In general, people do not just disappear. Or if they do, there's usually a reason. In the matter of Hector Ramirez, I hadn't yet heard anything to convince me that he had cause to drop off the face of the earth.

"I'd hoped," I said, still keeping calm, "that you and Chris might have hit it off."

"Hell!" Neeny kicked at the afghan with his foot. I wondered if Hazel had made it for him. Phoebe didn't strike me as the domestic type. "He came in here the other night all full of bullcrap about the rough time I gave Margaret. Damn! Margaret made her own bed. She wanted to wallow in it with Hector. See where it got her. Right outta the family, that's where! She could have married ten other guys—lawyers, doctors, even a forestry professor from the university. They all were hot for Margaret. But oh, no, she had to run off with that greasy Mexican! It's a wonder she didn't go over to Hawaii and wind up with some Chinaman! Or a Jap!"

It was all I could do to keep from declaring my hope that Margaret had slept with every Oriental in the fiftieth state and had had the time of her life. But I'd been around prejudiced people enough to know that there was no changing them, especially when they were part of the older generation.

"Did Chris stay long?" I inquired innocently.

"Too long." Neeny bent down to retrieve the afghan. He looked up, the black eyes sharper now. "I don't wanna talk about it. You feeling around for an alibi for the kid?" His mouth twisted in the thick beard. "It won't work, Emma. He was here about twenty minutes. He could have killed Mark before he came or right after. The damned mineshaft is right over there." Neeny jerked his thumb toward one of the windows. "Imagine! My poor grandson died within shouting distance, and I didn't even know it! Do you wonder I won't discuss this Chris when he's alive and Mark's dead?" Neeny shook his head, and I actually felt sorry for him.

I said as much. Wordlessly, Neeny accepted my condolences. He didn't look ill, so much as devastated. I asked how he felt.

"How would you expect? I'm getting to be an old man. What's to look forward to at my age?"

I shrugged. "Lots of things. You could travel more. Didn't you enjoy your trip to Vegas with Phoebe?"

The black eyes narrowed, but before Neeny could respond, Phoebe Pratt Doukas glided into the room. As always, she was dressed expensively, if tastelessly. Today she sported bright green slacks and a matching blazer with enough gold chains to enhance a harem.

"Emma," she said, her usually languorous voice tense.

"How kind of you to call." She moved across the room, full hips swaying, her upswept hair plastered to her head. Phoebe was what you might call handsome, if artificial. Her attention was fixed on Neeny. "Doukums, did you eat?"

Neeny waved at the tray. "Swill. That Kraut can't cook Greek food. Fix me some soup. Chicken noodle."

Phoebe planted a kiss on the top of Neeny's head. "Of course, Doukums. Lots of crackers, too." She swayed away, leaving a scent of jasmine in the air and a sense of unease in the room.

"Hey," he shouted, "get me some cocoa, too, Big Bottom. Lots of sugar."

Phoebe's return from Monroe had thwarted my question about the trip to Las Vegas. In any event, I knew the answer. I decided it was time to leave Doukums and Big Bottom to their own devices.

It was Phoebe, however, who showed me to the door. She had put on a frilly apron that said RED HOT MOMMA and rattled her chains as she came down the hall from the kitchen. "I've a mind to take Doukums to Palm Springs for the winter," she announced with less than her usual aplomb. "The change would do him *soooo* much good."

"Phoebe, what did you think of Chris?"

Phoebe's gray eyes with their layered blue lids widened. She fiddled with her chains and avoided my gaze. "Chris? I didn't see him. I was upstairs watching TV." An uncertain hand smoothed the lacquered hair as she lowered both her head and her voice. "He sounds like a saucy boy, I'm afraid."

I couldn't help but make a face. "Don't believe everything you hear. Especially in this town."

Phoebe had the grace to look a trifle sheepish. "Well, I did hear he was quite handsome. My niece, Chaz, met him at the Burger Barn. Of course, he can't be as good-looking as Mark was." There was a slight catch in her voice as she shook her elaborately coiffed head. "I'd like to meet Chris, though. It's a shame he and Doukums didn't get on." She let out a nervous trill. "After all, Chris *is* family. I think it's *soooo* important to keep everybody close."

"Yes," I conceded, trying to envision a rollicking clan of Doukases, "but it helps if they don't hate one another." I gave her a bright smile and went out the door.

My Jag was wedged between Neeny's twenty-five-year old black Bentley and Phoebe's Lincoln Town Car. She had pulled in too close behind me, and I cursed her thoughtlessness. But as I was trying to figure out how to maneuver the Jag out into the open, I noticed that the red exterior of Phoebe's new car was dappled with blue spots. Curious, I thought, but I wasn't sure why the blemishes tugged at my brain. The real question I had for Phoebe was why she had written to Chris in Hawaii, but I wasn't going to broach the subject until I had the letter in hand. There were already too many unanswered questions about Alpine's extended First Family.

Chapter Ten

LUNCH WAS FISH and chips picked up at the Burger Barn and eaten at my desk. Vida, who was also running late, joined me with a hard-boiled egg, cottage cheese, carrot and celery sticks, and a water pistol.

"Roger shot me this morning," she said, speaking of her eldest grandson and looking annoyed. "He's supposed to be home sick with the flu, but he's running around like a savage. Amy and Ted don't know how to handle him."

A staunch fan of Louisa May Alcott, Vida had named her three daughters Amy, Meg, and Beth. Jo had never materialized. Amy was the only one of the trio to remain in Alpine, the other two having moved to Seattle and Bellingham. Roger, who was almost ten, seemed to devote his life to plaguing his grandmother. Naturally, Vida doted on him.

"Gibb's got some explaining to do," declared Vida, taking aim with the water pistol at the portrait of Marius Vandeventer that hung over my bookcase. "Maybe he went up to Icicle Creek to make sure there wasn't any gold after all. He never did trust Mark."

"That part of town sure was popular Wednesday. Between the mineshaft and Neeny's house, half of Alpine seems to have passed by."

"It's a small town, after all," Vida remarked while snapping off carrot sticks in rapid succession. "Everybody has to be somewhere."

I dipped a piece of too-dry cod into a small container of tartar sauce. "At any rate, Neeny says Mark didn't stop by

119

Wednesday night. And Phoebe didn't see Chris. She was watching TV."

Vida dug into her cottage cheese. "Maybe she was trying to figure out how to break the news of the elopement to Simon and Cecelia."

"I wouldn't think Neeny would care what his family thought," I said as the phone rang. It was Richie Magruder, acting mayor in Fuzzy Baugh's absence. He wanted to know if Carla could take a picture of the raccoon family that was setting up housekeeping at the base of Carl Clemans's statue in Old Mill Park. I told Richie I'd ask Carla when she got back from interviewing Darla Puckett about her two weeks in Samoa.

"Even Neeny would care about repercussions if he's changed his will," Vida said, not missing a beat. "Simon would raise more of a ruckus than a bear with a crosscut saw." She reached over to the bookcase and pulled out my Seattle phone directory. "I just thought of something."

"What?" The french fries were better than the fish. I washed them down with a swig of Pepsi.

"Why would Phoebe go all the way to Seattle to see an eye doctor? She only wears reading glasses." Vida glanced up from the Yellow Pages to wave a celery stick at me. "What if she went to see someone else?"

"Like?"

"Like a lawyer. Here." She tapped at the page. "Old Doc Dewey's daughter, Sybil, married an attorney who is in a big firm in One Union Square. Douglas Diffenbach. He specializes in estate planning. I think I'll give Sybil a call." Vida was wearing her smug expression.

"That's a long shot."

"Of course," agreed Vida, writing down the number and replacing the directory. "But Phoebe couldn't use Simon's firm. She wouldn't want him to know what she was up to. And Sybil's husband is the only attorney I know of in Seattle. I mean, personally. Phoebe wouldn't go to a stranger."

Of course she wouldn't, I thought. Small-town mentality

wouldn't permit such a digression. Vida might be right. "But what about client confidentiality?" I countered.

Vida shrugged. "It's no breach for Doug to say he's seen Phoebe. And he would say so. It isn't every day that someone from his wife's old hometown comes waltzing into One Union Square." She grabbed the phone and started dialing. As it turned out, she had called the law office, not the Diffenbach residence. Undeterred, Vida asked for Doug. I sat back, watching her operate. Vida was a lesson in subterfuge.

"Doug? yes, this is Vida Runkel in Alpine. . . . No, not since little Ian was christened . . . Four already? Oh, my! Again in January? How lovely! Phoebe didn't mention it. . . . Yes, she was too excited about being a bride, I suppose. . . . Oh, I know, but life's like that, marry and bury, laughter and tears. . . . No, but Milo Dodge is doing his best. . . . Phoebe was so impressed with your work. . . . True, she's easily impressed by a lot of things. . . . My daughter, Beth . . . Oh, that's all she'd want, too, but these things are necessary when you have children. . . . Yes, I'll have her call. . . . Thanks so much, Doug . . . My best to Sybil. 'Bye."

Vida took a deep breath. "Phoebe had her own will drawn up." She gave me a hawklike stare. "Who do you suppose she's left everything to?"

I knew Phoebe was childless; I also figured that even if Vida had drawn the bare facts out of Doug Diffenbach, she couldn't possibly have extracted the details. "I don't know. Who?"

Vida sat back, munching on her hard-boiled egg. "Really, Emma, I'm not an oracle. I just wish I knew."

So did I.

At three o'clock, I swung by Alpine High School and caught Kevin MacDuff climbing on his bicycle. He took one look at my car and turned away. I honked.

"You must be awful mad at me," he said as I got out of the car and hurried up to meet him. "Kent sure is."

"It's not your fault," I said with a smile. "All I want to know is what you actually told Carla."

Kevin hung his head. At fifteen, he was far more slender than his eldest brother, and his skin was comparatively pale except for a spot of color on each cheek. His hair was strawberry blond, very short, with a wispy pigtail in back. "I called Carla about the paper route and we got to talking, and I said I'd seen Mark and he acted like he'd found gold." Kevin's head bobbed up, his fingers clutching the handlebars of his mountain bike.

I nodded. "Mark *acted* like he found gold, right?"

Kevin nodded back. "Right."

"Exactly how did Mark act? Were you at the mineshaft?" I queried as an old beater without a muffler roared past.

Kevin screwed up his face. "Well, he was kind of excited. Out of breath, you know. I was going to see Eric Puckett up the road and Mark came down from the mineshaft just as I was going by. He said ..." Kevin paused, clearly trying to recall Mark's precise words. "Mark said he'd made a big discovery. I asked him what, but he just shook his head and got into his Jeep, so I rode off to Eric's."

Briefly, I considered Kevin's account. "But he didn't *say* he'd found gold."

"No."

"So Carla misinterpreted your remark." And, I thought, but didn't say so, that Kevin had misinterpreted Mark's reaction.

The entire student body seemed to be whizzing by us afoot, in cars, on bikes. The single-story high school, which had replaced the two-story red-brick building that had become the newly refurbished public library and senior citizen center, sprawled over a full city block, its playfield reaching to the edge of the forest.

Kevin screwed up his face. "Misinterpreted?"

"She took what you said literally," I said, still smiling.

"I guess." Kevin sighed.

I suspected he'd been taking considerable abuse from Kent. "Don't worry about it. I seriously doubt if that bit about the gold had anything to do with Mark's death."

Kevin didn't look convinced. "Kent was really pissed off. I guess so were all the Doukases."

"I don't know about that." I patted his arm. "Just be careful what you tell Carla next time, okay? She tends to go overboard."

"Yeah. Sure." He gave me a half smile. "I'd better go home and feed my snake."

"Kevin, what do you think Mark did find up at the mine?"

Balancing himself in mid-stride, Kevin turned to look back at me. "I don't know. Whatever it was, it must have been a big deal. He acted . . . weird." He gave a shake of his head.

"Scared?" I suggested.

"Maybe." His fingers clenched and unclenched the handlebars. "Yeah, maybe that was it. Scared." He gave me a curious look and pedaled off down the street.

I stared after Kevin. Mark Doukas didn't strike me as an easy person to scare. For a long moment, I stood next to the Jag, lost in thought. Maybe Fuzzy Baugh was right: the sheriff should open the mineshaft. I'd ask Milo what he thought, though I already knew he felt it would invite danger.

But Milo was out when I stopped by his office. Bill Blatt said he was paying a call on Neeny Doukas. That news buoyed me a bit. I hoped that Milo wasn't going to let the Doukases lead him around by the nose.

The sun was still out and the air felt crisp when I got back to *The Advocate*. Ginny was mailing out bills; Ed was at the Grocery Basket; Vida had gone to the drugstore; and Carla was taking a picture of the raccoons.

"Only four phone calls," Ginny said, handing me the slips of paper and showing off perfect white teeth in one of her rare smiles. "Some man is waiting to see you. He got here about ten minutes ago."

"Not Chris Ramirez?" I asked on a sharp intake of breath.

Ginny shook her head. "I never saw Chris, but it's not him. This guy's older."

I relaxed. Swinging my handbag over my shoulder, I strode through the editorial office and into my inner sanctum. The door was already open, and there was somebody sitting behind my desk.

It was Tom Cavanaugh.

Over the clutter of my desk and a chasm of twenty years, we shook hands. On the surface, we acted like civilized people who were mildly pleased to see each other. Tom was prepared for the encounter, but I was flabbergasted. A bit too quickly, I sat down, not in my own chair, where Tom was seated as if he owned the blasted place, but one of the pair reserved for visitors.

"Well, Tom," I remember saying in a voice about an octave too high, "how are you?" After that, I don't recall much except pleasantries. I suppose we spoke in clichés, acknowledgment of the years that had passed, the physical changes we had undergone, the quirks of fate that had brought us together in that tiny office in a small town on the slope of the Cascade Mountains.

Somewhere between noting the gray in Tom's black hair and his observation that I no longer looked as if I were starving to death, my brain began to take charge of my emotions. I nailed Tom down for the reason he had come to Alpine. Dave Grogan had contacted him, he said in that easy, mellow voice that also could have made a living in radio and television.

"Dave told me you were paddling a leaky canoe. Either you bail out or patch up the holes." He pointed to a bound volume that contained the first six months of my tenure. "I've been studying these. You'd have to be publishing out of a mud hut in the Third World not to make money with a weekly or a small daily these days."

My eyes narrowed. It was bad enough that he'd invaded

my life unannounced, stolen my chair, and forced me into a subservient role. But now he was lecturing me on how to run my freaking paper. I was getting angry, but the sight of him diluted my temper: Tom Cavanaugh was still handsome, whatever softness hammered out by life, leaving him sharp of feature and even sharper of eye. He was a tall man and had apparently kept fit. Tom looked so much like Adam that I wanted to cry.

"Except for Christmas and Easter and your loggers' festival, I don't think you've run a single promotion," Tom was saying. "You could do one a month—back-to-school, Halloween, Thanksgiving, you name it. Inserts are what make money, Emma. Chain stores, independents, co-op advertising. Who's your ad manager, Dopey the Dwarf?"

"Yes."

Tom lowered his head, looking at me in that dubious manner I recalled from twenty years ago. "That's what I figured. Dump him. Or her."

"Can't."

He started to look stern, then broke into that wonderful, charming, delicious grin. "Of course you can't. Old softhearted Emma. But you *could* hire someone to supervise him, a business manager, let's say, and . . ." He saw me start to argue and held up a hand. "In the long run, it would pay off. Unless you've had a personality transplant, you make a lousy boss, Emma. You couldn't even get the gofers at *The Times* to remember to put sugar in your coffee."

I shook my head emphatically. "Hold it. Listen, Tom, this is wonderful of you to offer advice. Really." I tempered my growing irritation with a thin smile. "But I'm in the middle of covering a murder investigation. It's big stuff, involving a very prominent old line family. I can't get sidetracked. Frankly, Tom, as usual, your timing stinks."

His eyes, which were so blue they were almost black, took on a hint of surprise, even hurt. "Dave Grogan painted a desperate plight. Leaky canoe, headed for the falls." His own smile was now a trifle limp, too.

I sighed. "Dave's right. But he probably didn't know about the murder." It crossed my mind that even as I had talked with Dave on the phone, Mark Doukas might have been meeting his killer. "Look," I went on, trying to sound more kindly, "come for dinner tonight. I'll have Ed Bronsky, the ad manager, and his wife, and Vida Runkel and Carla Steinmetz join us." If necessary, I'd ask the city council and the U.S. Forest Service, too. There was no way I'd share an evening alone with Tom Cavanaugh.

I'd risen, tired of Tom's advantage in my chair. Now he stood, too, and for one sharp, painful moment, it struck me that he looked as if he belonged behind that desk. But he didn't. I did.

He was still looking down at the back issues of *The Advocate*. His attire was casual, a navy blue sweater over a light blue shirt with gray slacks. He didn't look rich, just comfortable. Then, as I knew he would do eventually, he gestured at the framed photograph on the filing cabinet. "Adam?"

"Yes."

He stared at the picture. I suspected Tom had looked very much like that when he was in college at Northwestern. "Good-looking kid," he remarked. "Smart?"

"Fairly. Not motivated, though."

"Right. Nice?"

"Oh, yes."

"No big problems?"

In the context of today's teenagers, I knew what Tom meant. "No. Thank God."

"Not exactly," he said dryly. "Thanks to you, Emma. You've done well."

The dark blue eyes held mine just a moment too long. "So have you," I said lightly.

But Tom shook his head. "No, not really. Sandra did well. She was born into money. I just use it."

"How is Sandra?" I was trying to keep the light note in my voice, but it wasn't working very well.

"Bats." He shrugged.

"Define *bats*."

His expression was guarded. "She's unstable. Delusions. Paranoid. She also shoplifts. Fortunately, we can afford topnotch keepers."

"Is she at home?"

"Sometimes." He fingered a sheaf of papers in my in-basket. "If she undergoes a violent episode, her doctors and care givers recommend that I have her . . ." He stopped, apparently aware that he was reciting like a parrot. With a sheepish grin, he reverted to the irreverent candor I remembered so fondly: "I cart her off to the loony bin."

"Sounds like the place for her," I retorted, equally flippant. Now I understood the comment I'd heard about *poor Tom* at the Sigma Delta Chi banquet. "All the same, I'm terribly sorry."

He had sobered and shrugged again. "That's one reason I travel a lot. If I didn't get away, I'd go nuts, too. It's my version of a paper route."

"Only you buy them instead of deliver them," I noted. Fleetingly, I thought of Sandra Cavanaugh. I'd only met her twice, once at an office holiday party, and another time in a restaurant where she was lunching with other suitably well-heeled young matrons. She was a pale, pretty ash blonde, fine of feature, slim, and inclined to keep one eye on her handbag and the other on her conversational vis-à-vis. It not only made her look a little walleyed, but caused me to wonder if she thought the rest of the world was after her Big Bucks. Or maybe, it occurred to me now, after *her*.

Tom had come around to the other side of the desk, a scant two feet away. "Are you serious about dinner?"

I reflected. "Sure. Seven-thirty?" For safety's sake, could I possibly assemble another fifty people by then? I berated myself. What was I afraid of? Twenty years over the dam, and what was there still between us? Only Adam.

"Look," I said, lowering my voice as I heard Vida talking to Ginny in the outer office, "I may be able to use some advice, but I'm not a damsel in distress. Believe it or not, I've already come up with some ideas of my own for increasing revenue."

Tom's expression didn't change. "I'm sure you have. Like what? A Color-the-Pumpkin Contest?"

I, too, kept my face impassive. "Not quite. It's more like an Ask-the-Jackass-to-Dinner Party."

"Sounds like fun."

"We'll see."

"Who's the jackass?" asked Vida after Tom had left.

I explained, briefly. Since I'd never told Vida who had fathered my son, I felt there was no need to go into anything but the barest professional details. I invited her to dinner.

"With Ed and that fat, sad-sack wife of his?" Vida looked appalled. "And Carla? Don't feed that girl Jell-O. She'll giggle and jiggle all night! Ask Ginny instead."

I was looking at the pictures of the raccoons. Carl Clemans's bronze statue appeared to be feeding them. "Is that a yes or a no?"

Vida rubbed her eyes. "Ooooh—I'll come," she said grudgingly. "So will Ed and Shirley. That woman is so lazy she wouldn't get off a keg of dynamite if somebody lit the fuse."

As it turned out, everybody came, including Carla and Ginny. I left the office just before five, racing to the Grocery Basket before the commuters arrived. Luckily, sockeye salmon was in, if not exactly a bargain at $10.99 a pound. Local corn was still available, a new crop of Idaho bakers had arrived, and the bakery that supplied Café de Flore had made its semiweekly delivery to the store that morning. Dessert would be my lifesaving, timesaving, but not necessarily money-saving cherry cream cheesecake. Dodging Durwood Parker, who was driving down the wrong side of Front Street, I stopped at the liquor store before heading home.

It was when I was unloading the groceries that I saw the Ramada Inn laundry bag on the floor of the backseat. Mark's jacket, I thought with a pang. I should have given it to Milo Dodge. But I hadn't. Should I call and tell him where it was?

A glance at my watch told me it was almost six. My guests were due in an hour and a half. There wasn't time to spare. Or so I rationalized, as I tucked the motel bag into one of the grocery sacks.

I didn't want to admit that I could be afraid of what the sheriff might find on the jacket that Chris Ramirez had borrowed from Mark Doukas.

Chapter Eleven

Vida came early. "You need help," she announced, and without further ado, she put on an apron that displayed two pigs hunched over a trough. "My daughter, Meg, gave me this. It reminded me of Ed and Shirley. Where's your biggest kettle?"

I showed her. She shucked corn, and I greased potatoes.

"I went to see Fuzzy after work," Vida said. "That must be his real hair. It looked like it had died instead of him."

"How was he?" I asked, using a cooking fork to poke holes in the potatoes.

"Critical, my foot! He should be out of there tomorrow. Or Sunday, anyway." She filled the big cast-iron kettle with water from the tap. "At least I found out why he had the heart attack. *Spasm*, I should say. Or so young Doc Dewey told me. No wonder, Neeny is enough to give anybody a stroke. Or a spasm."

I closed the oven and eyed Vida curiously. She was dumping salt with one hand and sugar with the other into the kettle. I refrained from asking her why. Vida had been cooking a lot longer than I had, though, I knew from experience, not necessarily better. "What did Neeny do now?"

Vida looked at me over the rim of her glasses. "Fuzzy went up to see Neeny last night. He asked Neeny about opening up Mineshaft Number Three to see if it was filled with opium." She made a face. "Imagine! Fuzzy's such a dolt! Anyway, he had to ask Neeny because the mineshaft is on that old fool's property. And Neeny had a fit—not a

130

spasm—and threatened to have Fuzzy impeached if he did such a thing. So Fuzzy got all upset, and his ticker went kaflooey." She wiggled her eyebrows at me. "Well, what do you think?"

I wasn't sure. Obviously, Vida's suspicions didn't bode well for Neeny. "Neeny has hidden something in that mineshaft?" I asked. "How about Hazel?"

Vida sniffed. "I saw Hazel Doukas on view at Driggers Funeral Home in 1986. She looked almost pretty, considering that in real life, she reminded me of the back end of a Buick. No, it's one of two things: there really is gold in that mineshaft, or else Neeny is just being a stubborn old goat. I vote for Number Two."

I wasn't inclined to disagree. Hastily, I shoved the potatoes into the oven. "I forgot to check the mail," I said, running out of the kitchen, through the front room, and straight to the barn-red postal box that stood next to the road. Three bills, four circulars, and a cheese catalogue made up the sum of my correspondence. Nothing from Adam. I cursed him, imagining several scenarios, the most likely of which was that he hadn't gone to the post office until it was too late to make the overnight delivery. Maybe tomorrow I'd get the letter Phoebe had written to Chris. I said as much to Vida when I got back to the kitchen.

"You already know what it says," she pointed out. "What else? Invisible ink that will show up when you put the stationery over steam?"

Vida was right. It was the fact that the letter existed in the first place that bothered me. "Why?" I asked, as much of myself as of Vida. "Phoebe is not necessarily the tart with the heart of gold."

"Correct," said Vida crisply. With one sure, lethal motion, she slit the larger of the two salmon from head to tail. "Phoebe had a reason for writing to Chris. Especially since she sent that letter right after she eloped with Neeny." She pointed the knife at me. I was glad I didn't consider Vida a serious suspect. Otherwise, I might have been scared stiff. "Why indeed?" she demanded. "I don't see Phoebe as the kindly new wife, trying to make peace between the warring family factions."

"Me neither." I sighed in frustration and inadvertently managed to stop our speculations by turning on the hand mixer to whip up my cream cheesecake.

For the next three hours we put the murder of Mark Doukas aside. Tom arrived with a bottle of white wine from the Napa Valley; Ginny trotted out a bouquet from her parents' yard; Ed and Shirley brought their prodigious appetites; and Carla dragged in a dead squirrel she'd found next to the street.

"We ought to bury him in the yard," she said.

I hastily agreed, pointing her and Ginny toward my gardening shed out back. "Wash your hands after you're finished," I urged, turning on the porch light.

It was already dark, though the evening had turned mild. Maybe autumn had suffered a setback.

I served drinks, dispensing with appetizers, which I'd forgotten about, and, naturally, the talk immediately turned to newspapers. Carla and Ginny came back to the house with a couple of handfuls of trash they threw into the kitchen wastebasket. Ginny was violently antilitter, and I was mildly embarrassed that she had found any in my yard. I resolved to spend part of the weekend getting the garden ready for winter.

The evening was a pleasant interlude. In retrospect, it was an island of peace in a tempestuous week. Tom was the center of attention, always a master of anecdote, and delivered several witty stories about his career in journalism, both as editor and publisher. I began to feel like a rank amateur. It was partly Tom's fault, for making me feel like a semifailure. But I was damned if I'd let him rescue me. Not after twenty years, all of which I'd spent nurturing his son. To hell with him, I thought, after my third glass of pinot noir.

The topic of Mark Doukas's murder came up only at the door. It was Carla who mentioned it, asking who intended to go to the funeral. Vida had volunteered; so did Ed;

whose gloomy manner would fit right in at anybody's wake.

Since I had already decided that only one staff member should attend, I was just as pleased when Shirley Bronsky demurred: "I've so much to do, and I hardly knew Mark," she said in the squeaky voice that always sounded at odds with her bulk. "Cece Doukas is a nice woman, but Simon is too stuck on himself. Of course if Cece had raised five kids instead of just two, and if she didn't have help with that big house, and if I could afford to wear nice clothes like she does ... well, we'll just send a memorial to our favorite charity."

"It ought to be Weight Watchers," Vida muttered after the other guests had left. "But I'll bet it's the Bronsky family vacation fund."

I was too tired to quibble. And relieved. Vida had offered to stay on and help me clean up, which eliminated any prospect of being left alone with Tom. "Thanks, Vida," I said, emptying the first load of dishes while she scraped the dessert plates. "You're a good egg."

"Hard-boiled, some would say." She gave me an ironic glance. "Or gone bad." She shrugged. "We've got to ask the sheriff to open that mineshaft."

"Vida, you're the one who told me not to play detective."

"It's not the same thing. The mineshaft has become part of the story. It put our mayor in the hospital."

I didn't try to unravel her peculiar brand of logic. "Would Milo Dodge force the issue with Neeny?"

"He's the only one who can," Vida noted, rinsing silverware. "Unless Eeeny Moroni could talk Neeny into it." Before I could suggest that I talk to Milo and she should take on Eeeny, Vida eyed me over the butcher block counter in the middle of the kitchen. "He *seems* nice. Where's the wife?"

I feigned ignorance. "Whose? Milo's?"

Vida snorted and flapped the dishrag at me. "Don't act like an adolescent idiot, Emma. Tom Cavanaugh looks enough like Adam to be his father." She gave me her gimlet eye, then; to my surprise, turned away so abruptly that she almost knocked an empty wine bottle off the butcher block. "Never mind. It's none of my business."

I decided to leave it that way. For the moment. But something she had just said bothered me, and it had nothing to do with Tom Cavanaugh. Unfortunately, I was too tired to figure out exactly what it was. Maybe it was just as well, since a little knowledge can be a very dangerous thing.

Tom Cavanaugh was staying up at the ski lodge, which was still offering off-season rates. Not that the economy rate would matter much to Tom, but the lodge was a lot more plush than Alpine's two motels, neither of which rated more than two stars in the AAA travel guide. The old Alpine Hotel on Front Street wasn't recommended by anybody, except the retirees and occasional transients who lived there. But the lodge had four stars pending, due to the current remodeling. Rumors that a restaurant was to be added on to the mediocre coffee shop were yet to be confirmed.

I had thought about driving up to the lodge on Saturday to talk to Heather Bardeen but decided against it. With Tom in residence, it might look like a ploy to see him again. As it turned out, I didn't need to call on Heather. Vida was mining her extensive sources like a squirrel gathering nuts for winter.

"I talked to my niece, Marje Blatt, this morning," said Vida shortly before ten A.M. "She works for Doc Dewey, you know. Old Doc." She stopped and muttered something I couldn't hear. A noise that was a cross between a squeak and a squawk carried over the line. "That's Cupcake. She won't take her bath."

"I thought it was Shirley Bronsky." I tried to envision Vida's canary in a tiny tub full of bubbles. The idea struck me as funny. Then I thought of Shirley in a much larger tub, with many more bubbles. That was not so cute. "What did Marje say?"

Vida emitted a little gasp of incredulity. "I can't repeat it over the phone, Emma." There was reproof in her voice. "You don't know who's listening."

Since Alpine had been converted to a sophisticated automated electronic switching system the previous year, I doubted if anybody west of Denver could have overheard us. But I didn't say so to Vida. Instead, I invited her over for coffee.

"Fifteen minutes," she said. "I've got to fluff up Cupcake."

I made sure I had enough coffee for both of us before using the spare minutes to confirm the bridge date at Darlene Adcock's that night. Then I emptied the kitchen wastebasket into the fireplace where I burn most of my nonrecyclable junk. On the way into the living room, I stumbled over the vacuum cleaner cord. Several items in the wastebasket were jostled onto the carpet. With a mild curse, I retrieved them. A blurred scrap of paper caught my eye.

It was a note, addressed to Chris. Apparently, Ginny Burmeister had picked it up in the yard, along with a gum wrapper, a UPS delivery notice from the next door neighbor's, and a pop can some kid had tossed over the fence. Ginny must not have looked at the refuse or she would have commented on the note addressed to Chris.

Unfortunately, most of the words had been smeared by rain. All I could make out was "Urgent ... —me r—— away ... off CR 187 ... –eeny."

I was still trying to decipher the note when Vida banged on the door. She flew into the living room, her velvet beret cocked over one eye. "What's that?" she asked, jabbing at the piece of paper. "You look like somebody sent you a death threat."

I showed her the note. "Ginny must have picked this up when she and Carla were burying that squirrel. I'll bet it had been left on the porch or stuck to the front door. It must have blown off in that storm Wednesday night."

Frowning, Vida shoved the beret so far back on her head that I marveled it could stay put. "That must be: *come right away*. Is it signed Neeny or Eeeny?"

I considered. "Neeny's house is on County Road 187," I said. "But would he send Chris a note? Especially one that said *urgent*?"

"Not likely." Vida paced the room in her flatfooted manner. "But Eeeny Moroni wouldn't send Chris a note either. At least I can't think why." She stopped in front of the sofa, and we locked gazes. "That note is printed. Anybody could have sent it and signed Neeny's name. Everyone knows he'd never call himself *Gramps* or *Pop-pop Doukie*."

Vida's reasoning made sense. "I wonder if Chris saw the note," I said, taking it from the end table and putting it under a dictionary to flatten out the wrinkles. "He might have and then just dropped it." When Vida didn't say anything, I went right on conjecturing: "That would explain why he didn't come in. Simon dropped Chris off, Chris got the note, took my car, and drove up to Neeny's."

"Or," put in Vida, shrugging off her tweed coat, "he *didn't* see the note but headed straight out to visit Neeny anyway, because that was his plan all along." She scowled at me; I scowled back. "Yes, yes," she said testily, "*or* Chris went to the mineshaft and socked Mark over the head."

"You don't really believe Chris killed Mark, do you, Vida?"

Almost angrily, Vida hurled her coat onto the back of the sofa. "No, I don't, though I've only your word for his lack of homicidal intentions." She stared at me over the rims of her tortoise-shell glasses. "By faith alone, as Pastor Purebeck says in his oh-so-tedious Sunday sermons. Really, that man means well, and I suppose it's unchristian to say, but . . ."

I allowed Vida her customary diatribe about the First—

and only—Presbyterian Church's pastor. Meanwhile, I tried to figure out who had tiptoed onto my porch after I got home Wednesday night and left the note for Chris. Actually, tiptoes wouldn't have been required, not with the storm that had been raging at the time. But whoever it was probably hadn't bothered to knock. My car was parked outside, and the lights were on. The person who had summoned Chris to an unspecified spot on County Road 187 had not wanted to see me. Or more to the point, had not wanted to be seen by me.

". . . Wearing spats and nothing else!" Vida stopped to take a deep breath. "What do you think Pastor Purebeck did then?"

I didn't have the foggiest idea what she was talking about. "Um—offered to resign?"

Vida looked shocked. "Of course not! He came straight down out of the pulpit, took Crazy Eights Neffel by the arm, and led him outside. It was a genuine act of Christian charity."

"Oh." I was as accustomed to wild stories about Crazy Eights Neffel, Alpine's resident loony, as I was to harangues about Pastor Purebeck. Luckily, the phone rang, sparing me further embarrassment at my lack of attention. It was Tom Cavanaugh. I automatically turned my back on Vida.

"I was thinking that if you had some free time this afternoon, I could help you plot ad strategy," Tom said.

I was aware of Vida's eyes boring between my shoulder blades. Frantically, I sought an excuse. "I can't. I'm going to start writing up the murder story."

"What about tonight?" Tom was both a patient and a persistent man.

"I'm playing bridge."

I thought I heard him suppress a chuckle. No doubt he found it amusing that the one-time great love of his life was spending a Saturday night gobbling gumdrops and debating whether to bid one spade or two clubs. "And tomorrow?"

"I go to ten o'clock mass at St. Mildred's," I said, wildly casting about for whatever I could possibly be doing on a Sunday afternoon. "Then I really ought to work in the yard."

Persistence won out over patience. "I'll see you in church. We'll drive some place for brunch." He hung up the phone.

Turning around, I waited for Vida's comment. But none was forthcoming. In fact, she was stalking off to the kitchen, presumably to fetch us coffee. I followed her, like a kitten trailing a mother cat.

"Marje informs me that Heather Bardeen is not p.g.," said Vida, handing me a coffee-filled mug, sugar in place. I felt like calling Tom back and telling him I'd trained my staff better than those dimwitted gofers at *The Times*. "She had some sort of nasty infection and thought Mark had probably given it to her. Nothing serious, and according to Marje, he probably hadn't anyway." Vida sniffed. "Girls these days have no morals and less sense."

I wondered if Vida secretly said the same about me. But the very fact that she had made such a remark suggested that she did not. I was glad. But I was appalled at Marje Blatt's lack of professional ethics. "Does your niece blab everybody's case history around town?"

Vida looked faintly horrified. "Of course not! But I'm *family*!"

Since half of Alpine appeared to be related to Vida, I didn't quite see the difference. Still, a female is either pregnant or not, and given enough time, easy to prove one way or the other. I let the matter of Marje's big mouth rest. "So there's no help from Heather," I said, wondering if I should give Mark's jacket to her as Chris had suggested. Probably not—she didn't strike me as sentimental, and I supposed that if I didn't hand it over to Milo Dodge, I ought to deliver it to Cece and Simon Doukas.

"I didn't say that," Vida replied, and in my mental meanderings, it took me a moment to figure out what she meant. "Marje says—and this has nothing to do with patient confidentiality—that she heard from Dr. Starr's dental assistant, Jeannie Clay, who had talked to Chaz Phipps who said that Heather told her Mark wasn't the only Doukas in town." Vida wiggled her eyebrows.

I gaped. *"Simon?"*

Tapping her fingernails against her mug, Vida nodded. "It wouldn't be Neeny." She shuddered, sending ripples along the bustline of her floral print blouse. "Oh, God, I hope not! What a gruesome thought!"

It was indeed. But not as gruesome as murder.

After Vida left, I felt honor-bound to start putting together the story on Mark's death. I did the obituary first, after making a call to Al Driggers. Usually, he would bring obits by the office, but in this case, I didn't want to wait until Monday. I thought that maybe there would be some snatch of information in Mark's all-too-brief life story that would help solve the murder case. As far as I could tell, there wasn't: Mark had been born in Alpine in 1963; he'd graduated from the high school in 1981, where he'd lettered in football and baseball; he'd attended Everett Junior College for one year; he'd worked as a property manager for his grandfather and done a stint selling real estate. His hobbies were listed as prospecting, hunting, fishing, and watching sports.

I'm always amazed at how little obituaries tell about the deceased. I remember the first one I ever wrote while I was an intern at *The Times*. It was a woman whose name I forget, but the bare bones stated that she was a Seattle native, an enthusiastic gardener, a member of the First Church of Christ, was survived by her husband, four children, and eight grandchildren, and had "been beloved by all who knew her." I later learned that for twenty years, she had been the reigning madame in Seattle, with five previous husbands, and that she had also operated the highest-stake illegal poker game in Washington State. No wonder she had been beloved by all.

As for Mark, he sounded so ordinary. Even dull. Yet he

had incited someone to kill him. I started to organize the news story, listing the facts by hand.

Mark Doukas had been killed outside of Mineshaft Number Three on Wednesday night, around nine o'clock, his head bashed in by a crowbar. Something—or someone—had drawn him back to the mineshaft where he had exhibited some kind of excitement or fear that morning. Whatever had set him off was apparently unknown to anyone but him.

I paused, rubbing at the neck muscles which had grown stiff while I worked at my desk. The first time Tom had ever touched me was when he'd found me all tied up in knots over a complicated mutual fund story. It was late, almost midnight, and he took pity on me. I still remember the firm, yet gentle hands that relaxed my muscles but created other, more serious tensions. Damn the man, I thought, trying to chuck him out of my mind. I needed to concentrate on Mark Doukas. And the mine.

Despite Neeny Doukas, it had to be opened. I picked up the phone and dialed Milo Dodge's home number. He wasn't there. I tried the sheriff's office. Milo answered on the first ring. He sounded annoyed.

"Neeny and Simon are putting on the pressure," he admitted. "I've put out that APB on Chris Ramirez."

I suppressed a favorite four-letter word. "Chris could be anywhere," I said, hoping that wherever it was, the law enforcement officials wouldn't pay too much attention to the request of a small-town sheriff. Chris, after all, hadn't been charged with anything. I hoped.

"That's what Eeeny Moroni said," Milo replied, still testy. "He tried to talk me out of it, too."

Mentally, I thanked Eeeny for his caution. "Why?"

"Not enough evidence to require an APB." Milo sounded even more irked. "I know that, but if Chris didn't kill Mark—I'm saying, *if*, mind you, Emma—he may know something. Like what Mark and Kent were fighting about. Or some comment Mark may have made about somebody else."

"Or about the mine?" I ventured.

"Could be." The faint sound of paper shuffling reached my ear. "You going to the funeral?"

"No. Vida is, though." I wished we hadn't gotten off the subject of the mineshaft so fast. "Are you?"

"Yes. I shouldn't take the time away from the investigation, but I owe it to the family, personally, as well as professionally." His voice had lost its edge. This wasn't the sheriff talking now, but Milo Dodge, native Alpiner. "I went to high school with Simon, you know."

I didn't. "You aren't that old."

"I was three years behind him." Milo sounded as if he might be smiling. I decided to take advantage of his improving disposition.

"Milo, I think you'd better open up that mineshaft."

Silence. Then a sigh. "Neeny's dead-set against it."

"Why?"

"I don't know." I heard a clicking noise and figured Milo was lighting up one of his rare cigars. He exhaled into my ear. "With Neeny, he doesn't need a reason. Maybe it's because he's afraid somebody will get hurt and sue him. Maybe it's because Mark was killed there and he thinks of it as sacred ground. Maybe he just doesn't want the commotion. Hell, Emma, I don't know. The bottom line is, would forcing the issue be worth it?"

It was my turn to grow silent. I sat there at my desk, staring at my handwritten notes. "Yes," I finally said. "Think about it, Milo. Mark died on the spot where he seemed to discover something that made Kevin MacDuff believe he'd found gold. Obviously, Mark found *something*. Maybe if we knew what it was, we'd know who killed him."

Milo chuckled. "You sound like Fuzzy Baugh."

I ignored the remark. "Tell me this: do you know if Mark entered that mineshaft?"

"Not really. Have you ever looked it over? Up close?"

I'd never seen the blasted place until Thursday. Oh, I'd driven by it lots of times, but I'd never stopped. There was no reason for me to make a pilgrimage to an abandoned mine, especially on private property. "No," I confessed. "Vida gave it the once-over, though."

"Okay, then she might've noticed that somebody tried to open it up. Maybe with a crowbar." He paused to let that information sink in on what he no doubt considered was my thick skull. "But Gibb Frazier told me a long time ago that there was a second entrance, further up the creek. I'm waiting for him to get back from Snohomish to tell me where the hell it is."

I was suddenly exasperated. "Can't you and your deputies find the damned thing?"

"Sure we could," Milo snapped, his benign mood blown away, no doubt in a cloud of noxious cigar smoke. "Crank up your cranium, Emma. I've got five men for the whole county. One's on permanent traffic duty, one works nights, one's sick with the flu, and that leaves Jack Mullins and Bill Blatt. Jack's taken what little evidence we have into the lab in Seattle, and Bill is helping me at the office. In our spare time, we try to stop whatever other crimes may be going on in a four hundred square mile radius that includes some of the most rugged mountain terrain in North America. Any more dumbassed questions?"

"No," I said, hoping he'd swallow his cigar.

Chapter Twelve

IT WAS A beautiful fall day. I finished up the draft of my lead story, listened to the University of Washington Huskies trounce their hapless opponent of the week, and spent over two hours working in the yard. The letter to Chris did not come. I cursed Adam anew and considered calling him to see if he'd sent the blasted thing fourth class. But Vida was right. I knew the contents, and I couldn't see what bearing they had on Mark's death. I kept on weeding.

By five o'clock, I was bushed, the kind of tiredness that begets virtuous self-satisfaction. Mental and physical labor had refreshed my soul and let me feel at ease about running off for an evening of bridge.

Having grown up in a family of games players, I enjoy almost any kind of cards. Time is the problem. What little leisure I have, I prefer hogging for myself. Which, I suppose, is one reason Adam calls me antisocial. But playing bridge in Alpine is akin to doing research for the newspaper. I can learn as much in four rubbers of bridge as I can in four days of interviews.

Darlene and Harvey Adcock lived in an old but carefully restored house three blocks off Front Street, around the corner from Trinity Episcopal Church. Darlene's drapes were tightly closed, lest passersby peer in and observe some of Alpine's leading ladies sipping a glass of wine.

I didn't realize until I arrived that I was filling in for the bereaved Cece Doukas. Charlene Vickers insisted there was a madman on the loose and had forced her husband, Cal, to deliver her in his Texaco tow truck. Linda Grant,

143

the high school P.E. teacher, thought the murder must be drug-related, chalking up a point for Fuzzy Baugh. Betsy O'Toole, whose husband Jake owned the Grocery Basket, asserted that it was a suicide. She had once known a man in Gold Bar who had hit himself over the head with a hammer. Eight times.

"Poor Cece," said Darlene Adcock, a mite of a woman with enormous gray eyes and flawless skin. "Mark could be a pain in the neck, as our Josh always said, but he was the apple of his mother's eye."

Francine Wells, who felt a professional duty to be the best-dressed woman in Alpine, adjusted the big bow on the blouse that went with her Chanel suit. "Mark was a twit, dead or alive. Cece spoiled him rotten, and Simon has always been too busy to be a real father. It's Jennifer I feel sorry for. The poor girl has absolutely no fashion sense."

My glance took in the other women who made up the three tables for the monthly meeting of what had started out as the St. Mildred's Mission and Anti-Communist Guild back in 1949 but had evolved into an ecumenical group who sent their annual dues to an inner-city school in Newark. Some day I intended to do a feature story on the guild's history and find out how both their membership and goals had changed in the last forty-plus years. But this was not the time for it. Instead, I'd see if I could ferret out any information about Mark Doukas and his clan.

Alas, at the first table, I was faced with the Dithers sisters, Judy and Connie, who owned a horse farm up on Second Hill. Two of the silliest women I've ever met, they took only their horses seriously, and were said to allow some of the animals to join them at the dining room table on special occasions, such as Christmas, New Year's, and, I presumed, the Kentucky Derby. The Dithers sisters spoke in fragments, a strange sort of shorthand that was understood only by them—and maybe their horses. I didn't expect much help from that pair. My partner was Linda Grant, who is normally very outgoing but seemed subdued by the Dithers sisters' presence. An hour and a measly part score later, I was glad to move on, to Edna Mae Dalrymple, the exceedingly nervous but very accommodating head librarian; Janet Driggers, the funeral home director's vivacious, if blunt, wife; and Mary Lou Blatt, Vida's sister-in-law. Mary Lou is a CPA and the mother of Marje the Indiscreet Medical Receptionist. Mary Lou is at least ten years younger than Vida, and for one of those obscure internecine reasons, the in-laws have not spoken in five years. Vida has never offered an explanation. In fact, if it weren't for Marje Blatt, I wouldn't know that Vida and Mary Lou were connected.

Edna Mae opened with a spade, Janet passed, and I responded with two diamonds. Mary Lou Blatt doubled and, before Edna Mae could react, put her cards face down on the table. "What's going on with Phoebe Pratt and Neeny Doukas?" she whispered, darting a glance over her shoulder at Vivian Phipps, who was studying her partner's dummy. Vivian is Phoebe's sister, and the mother of Chaz, Heather Bardeen's chum. Both Vivian and Phoebe were Vickers before they married, the sisters of Cal who runs the Texaco station. There are times when I feel as if I should carry an Alpine genealogy tree around with me. This was one of them.

Edna Mae jumped, making the wineglasses jiggle. "What do you mean? They've been seeing each other for years." Alpine's head librarian nominally disapproved of gossip. She pursed her lips and gazed into her hand. "Pass."

Janet sighed eloquently. "Frig, now I'll have to bid. Oh, hell . . . let me think . . ." Her tongue clicked off points. "Two hearts." She leaned across the table. "Do you mean Neeny can't get it up anymore?"

Mary Lou rolled her eyes, reminding me of her sister-in-law. "Hardly. I heard a rumor that . . ." She took a deep breath and spoke from behind her fingers. "Phoebe and Neeny eloped!"

Janet's sea-green eyes goggled; Edna Mae's overbite clamped down on her lower lip; I looked up at the small Venetian chandelier.

"Well!" Edna Mae gasped, clutching the stem of her wineglass. "Well, well!" She frowned, then shook her frizzy salt-and-pepper head and fidgeted with her cards. "You all know what rumors are. At least that one would put some others to rest."

Janet Driggers looked down her pug nose at Edna Mae. "Such as? God, I love stories about screwing! It sure beats all those stiffs Al has to put up with."

Edna Mae squirmed and turned a shocked expression on Janet. "Really, Janet! I couldn't say what I heard, could I?" Edna Mae nodded jerkily at me. "What do you say to that, Emma?"

"I'd say if it's only a rumor, it's all *alleged*. That's newspaper talk." I tried to appear ingenuous.

"No, no, no," said Mary Lou. "Edna Mae means Janet's three hearts."

"Oh." I glanced back in my hand. I'd lost track of the bidding. "Pass." I turned to Mary Lou, awaiting her response.

"I didn't hear it from Vida," she declared, rather huffily. "Vida thinks she knows everything that goes on in this town, but she doesn't. My sister-in-law is just a big windbag." Mary Lou gave me an arch little smile. "Sorry, Emma, I know you have to work with her. But that's not your fault."

"Thanks, Mary Lou." I shoved a handful of bridge mix into my mouth and wondered what Tom Cavanaugh was doing on a Saturday night in Alpine.

"She must be a trial," said Mary Lou, apparently referring to Vida. "Four hearts."

Edna Mae practically passed out. "Oh! You jumped! That's *game*! But I opened! Oh!" Her frizzy hair seemed to fibrillate.

Janet took a big swig of wine and bounced in her chair. "Then double us, you goose. Or get some balls and bid four spades."

"Four spades!" Edna Mae twitched and rearranged her cards for about the fifth time. "Oh! *Pass*." She scooted around in her chair, eyeing Mary Lou Blatt suspiciously. "Where on earth did you hear that Phoebe and Neeny got married? That's the sort of story that ought to come from a reliable source."

Mary Lou lifted her chin and looked at Edna Mae over her half glasses. "It did. My nephew's in law enforcement, you know."

I had a vision of Billy Blatt, his arms and legs being pulled this way and that by his aunts, Mary Lou and Vida. The poor kid didn't have a chance. I wondered what his mother was like. As far as I knew, I hadn't yet met Vida's other sister-in-law.

Janet's green eyes widened. "Deputy Billy? Wow! He ought to know. Simon Doukas must be wilder than a three-peckered goat! Pass." She swiveled around to look at Edna Mae. "*What* rumors? Come on, Edna Mae, if you aren't going to double us, at least dish out the real dirt. Marrying and burying are damned dull. How about more screwing stuff?"

Edna Mae blanched. "Really, Janet ... It was nothing, just a silly story about Phoebe driving around town the other night." Her little round face crumpled. "Oh, my, I'm so confused! Who has the bid? Is it no trump?"

I was overcome with one of my perverse notions. "We're still bidding," I said with a sweet smile for my partner. "Five diamonds."

"*What?*" Mary Lou all but rocketed across the table. "Emma! How can you make an overcall like that!"

I couldn't, of course. Not with only seven points and five puny diamonds. "Where was Phoebe going?" I asked Edna Mae innocently.

"I don't know," Edna Mae said primly. "I worked late at the library Wednesday night, and I just happened to see that big red car of hers parked by the Clemans Building. That old truck with the wooden side panels was double-parked next to her. Isn't that illegal?" Still twitching, she cast a guileless look around the table.

Mary Lou arched her eyebrows. "Gibb Frazier! That's the old truck he uses to haul stuff in. What," she demanded, whipping off her glasses and putting her face in Edna Mae's, "are you implying, Ms. Dalrymple?" Mary Lou didn't budge as a single word fell from her lips: "Double."

Edna Mae jerked about in the chair, hair flying, hands shaking. "I'm not implying anything, Mary Lou Hinshaw Blatt! All I said was that I happened to see . . ." She stopped and looked at her cards. "Oh! She doubled us! Oh, no! I pass!"

Janet Driggers was chortling. "Me, too." She leered at all of us. "Phoebe and Gibb? That's hot. Then again, it might be a hoot to make love to a man with one leg." The leer intensified. "Think about it, girls."

Edna Mae shuddered, obviously not wanting to think about it at all. I considered redoubling, just to prove how truly perverse I could be, but decided that such a move might cause my partner to suffer an aneurism. I passed and waited for Edna Mae to lay down her cards.

"Poor Gibb," mused Mary Lou. "I wish he would find somebody. He's a nice guy, really. But of course Phoebe wouldn't do. Even if she hadn't gone off and eloped with Neeny."

"Yeah, Edna Mae," said Janet, "how about it? When was the last time you got laid?"

Valiantly, Edna Mae fumbled with her cards, getting the suits mixed up and blushing furiously. "Honestly, Janet, you say the most horrid things! Have you no decency?"

I grimaced at Edna Mae's dummy. She had no more right to open with one spade than I had to overcall with five diamonds. Doubled. We were up a stump.

To divert attention from what was going to be a slaughter, I posed what I thought was an innocuous question to Mary Lou. "I wasn't around when Gibb had his accident," I said, waiting for her to lead. "What actually happened?"

Mary Lou tossed out the ace of hearts. She turned suddenly sly, no doubt because she knew how badly they could set us. But that wasn't the entire reason. "Vida thinks she knows so much," Mary Lou breathed. "Let me tell you, she doesn't know what happened to Gibb, not even after all these years."

"Oh?" I kept my tone mild. "What did happen, Mary Lou?" I watched Janet scoop in the first trick.

Mary Lou was still smirking. "I used to keep the books for Simon Doukas when I was still working at home while the kids were young. I know this because I had to go over the medical expenses Simon paid out that year. Gibb and Mark Doukas got into a fight over some gold or something up above Second Hill, by those old cabins." She paused to lead the king of hearts. There went another trick. "Mark wasn't just a pain as a teenager. He was mean." She led the ace of clubs and exchanged knowing glances with Janet and Edna Mae. "He not only beat up Gibb, but after the poor guy was on the ground, Mark got into his car or whatever he was driving and ran over him." She led the ace of spades. "That's how Gibb lost his leg."

Of course I went set eight tricks and our opponents racked up several hundred points, but at least we weren't vulnerable. Gibb Frazier was, though, and the idea didn't make me very happy. I thought about that bundle of newspapers Milo Dodge had found by Mineshaft Number Three. I reflected upon Edna Mae's seeing Gibb and Phoebe downtown the night of the murder. That explained why Phoebe's car was splattered with blue paint. It had come from Francine Wells's store, blown about by the windstorm. Phoebe had lied about staying in that night. But what had Gibb been doing up at the mineshaft?

Shortly before midnight, we adjourned, walking out into the mild autumn air. The old moon sat above Baldy's black ridge, and the stars seemed so close, as if they were peeking over the mountains. About the time I polished off my third glass of wine and made a small slam to elude the booby prize, some of my fears had begun to ebb. It had been quite awhile since I'd strung together three nights of wine drinking. If, I thought with a giggle, I kept it up, I could be in the running with at least two dozen other people for the title of town sot. Waving good night to Vivian Phipps and the Dithers sisters, I reached my car and remembered to avoid the pothole on Cascade Avenue that I'd stepped in when I arrived. More resurfacing was needed, not just County Road 187, but on several streets in town. I must do some research for another editorial. I kept my eyes focused, more or less, on the dark pavement. Alpine could also use some new streetlights.

There was no pothole. I paused, giving myself a bracing shake. The fact was I hadn't drunk that much. Three glasses of chablis in a four-hour period had only given me the illusion of giddiness, perhaps a state I wished for to make my Saturday night more exciting than it might have been with Tom Cavanaugh.

The others were pulling out, including Charlene Vickers in Cal's tow truck. In the glare of Cal's lights, I saw the pothole just beyond my left front wheel. I was puzzled. Could I have been mistaken? My sense of well-being faded as I got into the Jag and drove home carefully. Maybe the murder case was getting to me. Maybe I was more worried about Chris Ramirez than I cared to admit. Maybe Tom Cavanaugh's arrival in Alpine had thrown me for a loop.

I pulled into my carport and scanned the front of my snug log house. The lights were on inside and over the front door. As ever, my home looked inviting, even reassuring. Yet I was nervous about getting out of the car. The night was very quiet. Through the trees, the neighbors' houses were dark.

Steeling my nerves, I slid across the seat and got out on the passenger side, nearer to the house. Dew glistened on the grass; a few leaves drifted off the maple. I hurried up the path, keeping watch over my shoulder. That was how I saw the dent in the Jag's right fender. Whirling around, I raced back to the car and swore aloud. Six inches across, deep grooves, paint scratched, my beautiful car was ravished. I'd have to call the insurance company in the morning, Sunday or not. A kid, no doubt, cruising on a Saturday night. I stomped into the house and threw my purse on the sofa. Then it dawned on me: the dent was on the *right* fender. I'd parked that side against the curb. Nobody could hit me at that angle. I thought about the pothole. It hadn't moved. But my Jag had. Someone had driven it off while I sat inside Darlene Adcock's closely curtained house, gulping bridge mix and glugging wine.

I called the insurance company first, then dialed Milo Dodge at home. It was shortly after eight A.M. "Somebody stole my car," I said, not caring that I'd probably awakened him from his much-needed sleep.

Milo sounded fuzzy. "Again?"

"Not again," I said crossly. "I loaned it to Chris." I explained what I thought had happened.

"Well," Milo said, yawning in my ear, "what's the big deal? You got it back."

"With a dent in the curbside fender." I was trying to be patient. "I suppose you blabbed to everybody that I had an extra set of keys under the car."

"Blabbed?" Now it was Milo who sounded testy. "Hell, Emma, you want me telling people Chris hot wired your damned car? Besides, I only told my men about it."

Visions of Billy Blatt getting a hot foot from Vida and Mary Lou flew across my mind's eye. "Look, Milo," I said, reining in my exasperation, "are you going to do something about this or not?"

Another yawn. "File a complaint. We'll check the car out this afternoon." Suddenly his tone became more brisk. "Say—do you think Chris is back in Alpine?"

Somehow, that had not occurred to me. I set my coffee mug down on the desk and winced. "No. Why should he do that?" Innocent or guilty, I couldn't think of any reason why Chris Ramirez would return to the town he insisted he despised. Unless, of course, he had unfinished business. . . .

I desperately wanted to ask Milo if Neeny Doukas was alive and well this morning, but I didn't dare. It took me a moment to realize that Milo, now sounding fully alert, was talking his head off:

". . . A baseball bat, or even a shovel. They were probably going for the headlights. We had a rash of that kind of vandalism a year or so ago."

"What?"

"I said . . . Emma, pay attention! Jeez, what's with you?" Milo was annoyed. "Kids. They go around banging up cars, especially snazzy ones. Your Jag probably never budged from where you left it. Or," he added slyly, "did you check the speedometer?"

Of course I hadn't. I started to tell him about the pothole, but knew he'd dismiss it as a flight of fancy.

"Go ahead," he was saying in a more amenable voice. "File the complaint. Then we'll see if any other folks got their cars smashed, okay?"

It was pointless to argue. I mumbled my thanks and hung up. My watch told me it was 8:15, 10:15 in Anguilla, Mississippi. Ben would be riding his Sunday circuit, saying masses at five mission churches on the delta. He had never left Mississippi, having come to love its black poor and its white poor, and even some of the middle class.

I missed my brother. Except for a few, too-rare visits, we'd been apart for over twenty years. Ben hadn't been out west since I'd moved to Alpine. I needed to hear his crackling voice, to feel his brotherly love, and, I admitted, to tell him that Tom Cavanaugh had shown up.

I dressed for church with more care than usual, in a red cowl-neck sweater and a black pleated skirt. It wasn't for Tom's benefit that I put on black heels and made a serious attempt at combing my hair, but because we were probably going somewhere nice for brunch. Everett, or maybe all the way to Seattle.

St. Mildred's is old, but not as old as its eighty-eight-year old pastor, Kiernan Fitzgerald, who is officially retired. Father Fitz retains his Irish brogue, is rail-thin, and is completely bald except for three wisps of white hair that tend to stand on end. His sermons have been recycled over the years, and as he is somewhat forgetful, we still occasionally suffer through a Sunday diatribe about the Red Menace. Younger parishioners are mystified.

But on this last day of September, Father Fitz chose his basic Christian charity homily, urging the congregation to put aside their cares in the mill (it closed in 1929), sacrifice their Sunday picnic to Burl Creek Park (now the mall), and take food baskets to the poor families on the wrong side of the railroad tracks (the golf course since 1961).

My mind began to wander somewhere between a cautionary note not to let your youngsters ride on the running board of your Model-A and the dangers of drinking unknown beverages from a certain still near Icicle Creek. It was too bad, I reflected, that Fuzzy Baugh wasn't a Catholic. He might change his mind and decide that Mark Doukas had found white lightning in Mineshaft Number Three.

Naturally, my eyes wandered along with my mind. I was sitting at the back of the white frame church, near a side altar dedicated to St. Anthony of Padua. At the end of the pew, I spotted Francine Wells, resplendent in an Escada ensemble. The O'Tooles were in front of me. Ed and Shirley Bronsky and their fat little brood squatted cross the aisle. Up ahead, in about the third row, I could see the back of Tom Cavanaugh's dark head. He was wearing a gray tweed sports jacket. I frowned. Those broad shoulders still had their power to make me twitter like a teenager. Damn.

On the way back from communion, Tom caught my eye and smiled. I remained solemn, seemingly wrapped up in fervent prayers of thanksgiving. The fervor that should have been reserved for my post-communion prayers rose up to smite me in a most unspiritual way.

After mass, Tom hailed me in the parking lot between the church and the school. He had a rental car, some kind of American compact I didn't recognize, though I envied its lack of dents.

"Would you like to show me how you can drive your Jag?" he asked with that big grin.

"You can drive it," I said in a petulant voice. "I'm mad at it. Look." I showed him the fender damage, and he commiserated. I'd explain my theory later. At the moment, I was anxious to be gone. Most of St. Mildred's parishioners were watching us, no doubt speculating on the stranger's identity. Since Ed had met Tom, the news would soon be out. By afternoon, most of Alpine would figure that *The Advocate* was going broke and was about to be sold to a newspaper magnate from San Francisco. Or worse yet, they'd note the resemblance between Tom and Adam. I didn't know which scenario upset me most.

I followed Tom up to the ski lodge where he left his rental. While he was parking the car, I spotted Heather Bardeen and waved. She didn't wave back. Maybe she really didn't see me. I gave a mental shrug. What could I say to her anyway? Is it true you're having an affair with your late boyfriend's father? Even for an aggressive journalist, that seemed too harsh. Besides, she might sock me.

Once Tom was behind the wheel of the Jag, I regretted my impulsive suggestion that he drive. First my chair, now my car. Maybe he'd like to move into my house. To my horror, the facetious thought didn't strike me as all that absurd.

I was surprised when we headed east, not west. "Where are we going?" I asked as he pointed the Jaguar up Stevens Pass. "Not Leavenworth, I hope. They're having the Oktoberfest this weekend. Too much bratwurst and too many tubas for my taste."

"I know," Tom said. It seemed as if he always knew everything. "Have you ever been to the Cougar Inn on Lake Wenatchee?"

I hadn't, though I'd heard about it and had even gone so far as to ask Ed Bronsky to see if they'd like to take out an ad. Ed told me the inn was too far away. As it turned out, it was less than an hour's drive, a short stretch beyond the summit, then twenty miles north of Leavenworth.

The Cougar Inn was built in 1890, a big farm house converted into a restaurant and hotel. The lavish buffet included ham, sausage, a baron of beef, eggs, pastries, vegetables, fruit, and just about every other imaginable food a brunch addict might desire. With plates piled high, we made our way to a table for two that looked out over the sparkling waters of Lake Wenatchee. The sun was out, but the wind ruffled the evergreens. It was a perfect autumn afternoon.

At first we spoke of trifles. Tom had gone fishing Saturday, somewhere around Gold Bar. No luck, though the salmon were due to come upriver to spawn soon. Living most of the time in the Bay Area, he missed fishing. There was a place he liked to go on the Sacramento River, but that was ruined because of the recent disastrous chemical spill at Dunsmuir.

I asked about his two children. Graham was at USC, studying cinema. Kelsey had just started her first year at Mills. It was just as well that they didn't spend much time at home. Sandra's condition had turned Kelsey into an introvert. Tom worried about his daughter. He wished she'd gone back East to school. "The farther the better, I think," he said, briefly letting his carefully cultivated mask of good cheer slip a notch. He gave me a wry grin. "Sometimes I wonder if mental instability isn't contagious."

We were on our second round of plates. I told Tom about my car, including the mobile pothole. Unlike Milo, he didn't scoff. "The sheriff may be right about one thing," he said, digging into a mound of crisp hash brown potatoes. "It was probably kids, going for a joy ride."

Tom could be right. The Jag was tempting, and if word had gotten out that I kept a spare set of keys under the car, some of Alpine's brasher punks might have succumbed. After all, several of the women at the bridge party had teenagers. The kids might know I'd be at the Adcocks' for several hours and figure they were safe to take off for a while. At least that's what I wanted to believe. I didn't much like the idea of Chris lurking around town in the shadows.

"Well?" Tom spoke, and I realized I'd missed a beat.

Before I could respond, he put a hand on my arm. "Hey, this murder really has you upset. Why? I gathered from what everybody said at dinner the other night that Mark was a jerk. Did you think otherwise?"

"No." I felt the light pressure on my arm and couldn't help but smile. "To be honest, I didn't know Mark Doukas very well. It's his cousin I'm stewing over."

As briefly as possible, I explained about Chris. Tom listened closely, devouring more hash browns, eggs benedict, croissants, and link sausages. I was finally full, surfeited with cinnamon rolls, ham, beef, scrambled eggs, blintzes, asparagus, and two kinds of juice. When I concluded my recital, Tom took a slice of cantaloupe off my plate. His appetite had always amazed me.

"I can't see why Chris would kill Mark," he said, obviously giving the matter his usual thorough consideration. "No fight, no motive. So who had a reason to get Mark out of the way?"

"Nobody. Not a *real* motive."

But Tom shook his head. Outside, the wind was growing stronger, whipping up the blue waters of the lake. "Unless you accept the theory of a nut on the loose, your killer has a motive. The question is: *what?* His sister would benefit from the standpoint of money. She'd get his share, and so would her husband—Kent?" He saw me nod. "But from what you say of Jennifer, she sounds meek as milk. Of course," he added on an almost wistful note, "you never know about people."

"And Kent did quarrel with Mark," I reminded Tom. "Although Jennifer insists it wasn't serious."

The waitress was removing our plates and bringing more coffee. Tom waited until she was done before he spoke again. "As for your driver, he had a grudge. But why wait all these years?"

"I know. It doesn't make sense. All the same, I'd like to find out when Gibb Frazier was up at the mineshaft. It had to be after he got back from Monroe, which would have been mid-afternoon."

"Have you asked him?"

"He's been in Snohomish the past couple of days. Milo was going to talk to him when he got back. Today, I suppose." Gibb had been due in Alpine last night. I wondered if Milo had already seen him. Maybe I'd call the sheriff again when I got home.

The bill appeared at our table. I made a feeble gesture, but Tom laughed. "I'm rich, remember? Besides, this is a write-off. We were talking newspaper revenue."

"We should do that, I guess." I sounded vague.

This time he put his hand on mine. "We should do a lot of things, Emma. But not right now. You're preoccupied."

I started to bridle, then made a funny little noise in my throat that wasn't exactly a squeak but came close. "Damn it, Tom. I can't believe you're here."

He still had his hand on mine; his smile washed over me like balm. "Well, I am."

"For how long?" I hated to ask the question.

He took his hand away and leaned back in the chair. "Oh—a few days. I have to be in San Diego at a publishers' meeting the second week of October. Look," he said, leaning forward again, "I've put some preliminary material together for you, but I left it at the lodge. I need some more background anyway—demographics, per capita income, property taxes. It'd bore you. But give me a day or so, and I'll impress the hell out of you, okay?"

"Wow." I laughed in spite of myself. "Do you do this for every poor publisher?"

"Yes," he replied, "I do. It's the only way I can make a decision about investing." He glanced over at the buffet, where the last of the brunchers were lining up. "There are lots of appealing weeklies and dailies out there, just like that smorgasbord. But you have to pick and choose, or you'll end up with the financial equivalent of a stomachache." He palmed his credit card and stood up. "What are you thinking, that I must miss the writing?"

"Yes," I said, though that wasn't what I'd been thinking

at all. I'd had an evil speculation about whether or not the inn had a room available for the night.

"I do miss it. In fact, it's not the writing so much as the editing." Ever the gentleman, Tom helped me with my chair. "My greatest love was making a good story even better."

It was a commendable emotion. I resisted the urge to ask Tom to name his second greatest love.

We walked along the lake for a while, but the wind was too brisk to linger. We reached Alpine about four. In the lodge's parking lot, I felt compelled to inquire after Tom's dinner plans.

"I've got a date," he said, opening the door of the car. Between the trees, I could see the steep roof and dormer windows of the ski lodge. A weather vane twirled in the breeze and smoke curled from one of the stone chimneys.

"Oh." I tried to sound casual. "Just as well. I don't think I could eat until tomorrow."

He stuck one long leg out of the car. "I'll manage. Anyway, my hostess swears she's not much of a cook."

"Oh."

"Well?"

"Well what?"

"Aren't you curious?"

I let out a hiss. "Sure I am. But I'll be damned if I'll ask."

He braced himself on the steering wheel and leaned across the well between the bucket seats to kiss my cheek. "It's Vida Runkel. Do you think she'll try to seduce me?"

"Vida!" I gasped. "I hope so!"

It would be better than having her bombard Tom with a litany of embarrassing questions.

Chapter Thirteen

AMONG THE MESSAGES waiting for me was the voice of Milo Dodge, inviting me to dinner at the Venison Inn. "Catch a bite," was the way he put it, "and have a look at your busted British car." I felt as if I were playing a role in a French farce, where all the wrong people run off with one another.

Although I still wasn't hungry after the monumental brunch, I called Milo back and told him I'd meet him at the restaurant at six-thirty. Even as we spoke, I snagged my panty hose on the leg of my chair. They were my last good pair, and I could have faked it by wearing slacks if the run hadn't gone all the way from toe to hip.

Parker's Drugs stayed open on Sunday until six. Originally owned by Durwood and Dot Parker, the store had been sold almost ten years ago to a young couple from Mount Vernon, Garth and Tara Wesley. They'd kept the name and remodeled the premises. Durwood had been a fine pharmacist but not much of a retailer. He retired about the same time he hit his first cow.

Tara was behind the counter when I breezed in at 5:55. No one else was around, and she was closing up the till, but she gave me a warm smile.

"Just ring up a three-pack of No Nonsense, petite to medium sheer reinforced nude toe," I called out, racing to the rack.

"Will do," Tara said, "but I've got to scan it first."

I zipped up to the checkout stand. Tara was a pretty brunette, mid-thirties, the mother of two small children, and, like her husband, a registered pharmacist. "Sorry I cut it so close. It was a last-minute disaster."

"That happens," Tara said, still smiling. "You're just the person I wanted to see. What's happening with the murder? There hasn't been a word on TV or in the weekend papers."

I told her there wasn't any substantive news. Sheriff Dodge was following up some leads, but he didn't have any serious suspects.

"That's scary," Tara said, no longer smiling as she gave me my change and receipt. "What if it's one of *us*?" Her big brown eyes widened with dread. "I'm always afraid of a holdup. Even in a small town, a drugstore is a sitting duck. Not the money so much as the drugs, I mean. That's why we came here. Mount Vernon was getting too big. We wouldn't have dreamed of going to Seattle or Everett or even Bellingham." With one wary eye on the street and the other on the cash pouch, she started removing checks from the till. "I'm here a lot at night because Garth works days so I can take care of the kids. I don't like being here alone." She took out the cash and stuffed it into the pouch. "I heard Mark was killed around nine last Wednesday. I was working by myself, and you know, I had the funniest feeling."

"Really?" Perfect hindsight always fascinates me.

Tara nodded twice. "I really did. It was so stormy. Nobody had come by in the last half hour. I had a mind to close up early and go home. Then Kent MacDuff stopped to pick up a prescription he'd had phoned in. I was sure glad I'd already made it up so I could get out of here."

I tried not to act surprised. "Kent came in so late? He's as bad as I am."

Tara lifted one shoulder in an offhand manner. "He'd hurt his shoulder. For such a macho man, Kent's a big baby. Unlike you, he didn't apologize for coming in at closing time."

"Jennifer said he was miserable," I remarked, wondering why I was making excuses for Kent MacDuff. To emphasize my superior manners, I thanked Tara and asked if she wanted me to wait and go out the door with her.

She laughed, albeit nervously. "Oh, no. It's only six. And there's the sheriff. I feel reasonably safe with him around."

Sure enough, Milo Dodge was just getting out of his four-wheel drive. I waved; he waved back. A minute later, I joined him on the sidewalk. "You're early," I said.

He was frowning, his shoulders hunched against the wind. "I stopped to see Gibb. He's not home yet." Milo's hair blew back from his forehead, but that wasn't what made his long face seem even longer. He was worried.

I decided to forget about stopping in the rest room to change my panty hose. Milo was in no mood to notice. "Do you think he's still in Snohomish?" I asked as we headed for the Venison Inn.

"No." Milo opened the door. He didn't speak to me again until after the hostess had greeted us and provided a table with a view of Front Street. I felt like a window display. "I checked. He finished the moving job about five yesterday and told the people he was working for that he had to go meet a steelhead."

"Maybe he caught one," I remarked, hoping to strike a light note. Steelheaders are a rare breed, inclined to suffer any hardship to catch their elusive prey.

Milo wasn't amused. "Even if he had, he'd be back by now. I sent Bill Blatt and Jack Mullins looking for him. I don't like this, Emma."

I debated about telling Milo what Mary Lou Blatt had said about Gibb Frazier at bridge club. I decided to hold back. "You think something's happened to Gibb?"

Impatiently, Milo pushed the unruly hair off his forehead. "I don't know. Gibb hated Mark's guts, but I wouldn't figure him for a murderer. Unless he got really pissed off."

Which, I reflected grimly, Gibb had a right to do. Next to Chris, Gibb was my least favorite suspect. Despite his rough edges, I liked him well enough, and he was my employee. I owed him a certain amount of loyalty.

Milo ordered Scotch; I opted for root beer. This was my day of total abstinence. Across the restaurant, the hostess was seating Jennifer and Kent MacDuff. Their arrival gave me the opportunity to change the subject.

"Kent's alibi won't wash," I said, trying not to look smug.

Milo stared at me. "How come?"

I explained about Kent's nine o'clock visit to the drugstore.

Milo looked thoughtful. "Kent never mentioned that. I suppose he was afraid to." He glanced over at Kent, who was haranguing their waitress while Jennifer hid behind her long blond hair. "But if Kent doesn't have an alibi, neither does Jennifer. They were supposed to be home together."

"True." I liked the idea of an alibiless Kent MacDuff. I wasn't as keen on the same status for his wife. But I was reminded of Phoebe. "According to Edna Mae Dalrymple, Phoebe was driving around downtown Wednesday night."

Milo's ears pricked up, like a hound on the scent. "What time?"

"I'm not sure," I admitted. "During the windstorm, though. She got Francine Wells's paint on her car."

The notepad came out. Milo wrote swiftly. Out of the corner of my eye, I saw that Kent MacDuff was on his feet, heading our way. So were the drinks.

"Hey, Sheriff," called Kent, oblivious to the stares from the other diners, "what's new with your dragnet for cousin Chris?"

Milo looked annoyed. "Nothing yet. That takes time."

Kent was blocking the waitress's path. She tried to get around him; he refused to budge. "Hell!" Kent waved an arm, narrowly missing the waitress. "Chris could kill ten other people while you guys screw around. Neeny's about to blow up. You'd better get Chris back here before the funeral tomorrow."

The chilly stare Milo gave Kent would have turned a more sensitive man to stone. "You'd better get your butt down to my office first thing tomorrow morning. Your wife, too."

"*What?*" Kent bellowed as more heads turned. The waitress executed as neat a step as I've ever seen outside of a chorus line and deposited our drinks. "We've got to leave early for Seattle. Are you nuts?"

Milo was unmoved. "Then show up as soon as you get back. I've got some questions for both of you."

"Oh, bull!" exclaimed Kent. He started to bluster but apparently realized the sheriff wasn't going to relent. "It may be pretty damned late," said Kent. "I hope you like overtime."

Milo shrugged. "I'm used to it."

Still belligerent, Kent wheeled away. Jennifer had been watching from over the top of her menu. Her blue eyes looked terrified.

"Dink," muttered Milo, taking a big swig of Scotch. "Why didn't somebody whack *him?*"

Before I could make a suitable rejoinder, Milo's beeper went off. He excused himself and went to the pay phone outside the rest rooms. I drank root beer and tried to avoid watching Kent and Jennifer MacDuff argue. Why weren't they with Simon and Cece? This must be a terrible night for the bereaved parents, with their son's funeral only hours away. Maybe the other Doukases had gathered at Neeny's. I hoped so. Even the most aggravating of families should cling together in a crisis.

Milo returned, looking downright dismal.

"What's wrong?" I asked brightly. "Did Durwood Parker mow down a herd of sheep?"

The sheriff didn't sit, but drained his Scotch in a gulp. "No." He drew a five-dollar bill out of his wallet and put it on the table, avoiding my stare. "Gibb Frazier's dead. Somebody shot him. I've got to go, Emma. Sorry."

* * *

After arguing all the way back to Milo's car, he finally relented and let me come with him. Out on the highway, he explained what had happened.

"Billy and Jack didn't find him. They were staying in our jurisdiction, this side of the Snohomish–Skykomish County line. But down by Gold Bar, some gun freaks stumbled across Gibb this morning in a gravel pit where they practice shooting. He didn't have any I.D., but somebody at the morgue in Everett recognized him."

I was still suffering from a mild case of shock. "I don't get it. Why would anybody kill Gibb?" My teeth were chattering, and my feet beat a tattoo on the floor of Milo's Cherokee Chief. It was his own car, and he'd had to put his temporary flashing lights on top of it before we left town.

Milo didn't have any answers, either. We covered the next fifteen miles in silence, whisking past the Sunday drivers heading for home. Outside of Gold Bar, Milo slowed down. "Over there, across the river—that's Reiter Ponds, a big fishing hole. Back off the road is the gravel pit."

It was dark; I couldn't see a thing. I knew about Reiter, though. Half of Alpine always seemed to be asking if there was any action there.

Milo accelerated. "The Snohomish County Medical Examiner said Gibb had been dead for at least twelve hours when they found him this morning around eleven."

"Poor Gibb." I held my head and tried to regain my composure. "Did he have any relatives? He never mentioned them."

"His wife died of leukemia almost twenty years ago. There was a boy about my age. He got married and moved to California—or was it the other way around? I forget." Milo was sailing past Startup, Sultan, the turnoff to Monroe. "Gibb and his son were never close, not even after Ruth died. There was a sister, too, but she moved to Portland a long time ago. I think Gibb went to see her when the spirit moved him, but she never came back to Alpine."

A lot of people seemed to leave and never come back. Was nothing left for them in their old hometown? Or, having moved on and maybe up, did they want to keep their roots well buried? I didn't know. But one thing I was sure of: I wished Chris Ramirez hadn't come back. And that Gibb Frazier's return to Alpine didn't have to be in a body bag.

The Snohomish County Coroner's office is fairly new but suitably drab, with metal and vinyl chairs, steel gray filing cabinets, and a framed front page of the Everett *Daily Herald*'s account of the 1916 I.W.W. massacre. The deputy coroner was anything but drab, however. A squat, rosy-cheeked cherub of a man, Neal Doke looked like he should be wearing a monk's robe instead of a white lab coat. Even his brown hair was balding like a tonsure.

Introductions were made, condolences were given, chairs were offered. Doke asked if we'd like to see the body. Milo said yes; I said no. I waited alone with a cup of weak coffee and the grisly reminder of what had happened to the radical Wobblies who tried to land in the Everett harbor seventy-five years ago.

Milo returned looking grim. He laid a hand on my shoulder, maybe for support as much as comfort. "It's Gibb, all right. Damn. I'm sorry, Emma."

"Me, too." I hate tears, and though I mourned Gibb, the loss didn't devastate me. More to the point, I was stunned and angered. Two deaths in less than a week were grounds for outrage.

Neal Doke was at his desk, leafing through papers. Jack Mullins and Billy Blatt had joined us. "Okay," said Doke, sounding too perky for the occasion. "Healthy white male, age fifty-eight, left leg amputated above the knee, small scars on forehead, both arms, left thigh, abdomen, etc. Time of death, approximately between five and eight P.M., Saturday, September twenty-eighth. Shot in chest, bullet passing through body, missing ribs. Probably from a distance of twenty feet, but that's guesswork." He looked up from his paperwork. "I did an autopsy on a giraffe once. Hell of a thing."

None of us commented, though it was clear from Neal Doke's expectant face that he had hopes of being asked. "I take it you didn't find the bullet?" Milo inquired, stony-faced.

Doke waved a pudgy hand. "Hell, no. That gravel pit is full of bullets, from all the gun people practicing. Oh, our deputies will come up with it eventually, but it'll take time."

As a journalist, I felt obliged to say something. Anything. "How will you know it's the bullet that killed Gibb?"

Doke was unwrapping a package of Ding Dongs. "It'll have blood on it. My guess is that the gun was a thirty-eight." He bit into one of the Ding Dongs. "Just a guess, mind you," he said with his mouth full. "You folks ever get any poison victims? I had one last year, woman from Mukilteo did her husband in with bleach. He must have been a real idiot." Doke shook his head and kept chewing.

We left as soon as Milo had called Al Driggers and asked him to drive the funeral hearse over to Everett. Billy Blatt and Jack Mullins finished filling out some forms, then took off in their sheriff's car. Milo and I stood outside of the county building and noticed that Everett didn't smell as bad as usual. Over the years, the paper mills have given the city an unfortunate reputation.

"You hungry?" Milo asked, zipping his down vest over his plaid shirt.

"I never was," I said. "I'm sure not now."

He gazed up at the dark sky that had grown partially overcast. "I feel like a jerk."

I looked up at him, the graying blond hair falling over his forehead, the long face glum, the hazel eyes shadowy. "Why?"

He kicked at a candy bar wrapper on the sidewalk. "Hell, this is my first real homicide. *Two* of them, god-damn it, and I'm getting nowhere fast. I've got an election coming up next year. The citizens of Alpine will burn my butt if I don't find the killer."

Casually, I linked my arm through his. "Oh, come on, Milo, it's only been four days since Mark was murdered. The poor guy isn't even buried yet. Let's go have a cup of coffee."

Traffic was heavy on Wall Street for a Sunday night. Milo scowled at the cars, as if he disapproved of so much coming and going. He gave a tug and pulled me along the sidewalk. "Come on, Emma, let's go home."

We did, driving in virtual silence along the black ribbon of highway. He didn't use the flashing lights on the way back but managed to exceed the speed limit most of the time.

"What happened to Gibb's I.D.?" I finally asked, somewhere east of Index.

"Damned if I know." Milo passed a big truck with British Columbia plates. "Maybe whoever killed him didn't want his identity known right away."

"Where's his truck?" I braced myself as Milo passed an R.V. from California.

"We'll find it," said Milo. "That's hard to hide."

I kept quiet for a while, trying to figure out any connection between Mark Doukas and Gibb Frazier. It was possible that the two men weren't killed by the same person. The weapons had been different. Yet I didn't really believe we had two murderers on the loose. I was about to spring a theory on Milo when he spoke:

"Who's the guy, Emma?"

I blinked. "What guy?"

"The big city type staying up at the lodge." Milo kept his eyes on the road.

"Oh." I cleared my throat. "He's a newspaper investor. He also gives advice." I felt the color rising in my face and was glad Milo wasn't watching me.

"You need advice?" Milo's voice was a little too casual.

"Of course I do. This is a tricky business. Marius Vandeventer was sort of old-fashioned. And Ed Bronsky isn't exactly a ball of advertising fire. I can use some help in terms of increasing revenues, expanding circulation, new marketing approaches. . . ." And making an ass of myself by babbling like an idiot, I thought. "It's very complicated." After that I lapsed into silence.

So did Milo, at least for the next five minutes. When he spoke again, he glanced over at me. "He's a good-looking guy."

"He's been very successful." I'd had time to regain my poise. My voice sounded natural. "The newspaper broker I bought *The Advocate* through recommended calling in a consultant." It wasn't exactly the strict truth, but it was close. "Listen, Milo," I went on, changing the subject as he swung out from behind a timorous driver in an old Honda, "you've got to open up that mineshaft. Why not do it tomorrow during the funeral when Neeny's not there?"

He shot another look in my direction. "I won't be there either. I'm going to the funeral, remember?"

"Oh. I forgot." I had. The conversation about Tom Cavanaugh had rattled me. I cringed as Milo took the Alpine turnoff too sharply. "Couldn't your deputies do it?"

"Maybe." Milo finally slowed to forty miles per hour. The road into town was deserted, dark, and unfriendly on this moonless night. "Why are you so set on opening that mine?"

I tried to state my case logically. "Mark's death occurred shortly after he showed interest in the mine. Gibb went there, too. That's how your men found the extra copies of *The Advocate*. Maybe Gibb made the same discovery that Mark did. At the very least, there's something strange about Mineshaft Number Three."

Milo didn't respond until we turned onto Front Street. "I'll sleep on it. You could be right. I'm sure as hell not getting anywhere otherwise."

Just as he was pulling into an empty parking space two cars down from my Jag, I remembered to tell him about

Mark's deliberate maiming of Gibb. With Gibb dead, the revelation couldn't matter now. Milo was shocked.

"So Gibb had a motive," he mused, awestruck.

"Of sorts. But it's ten years old."

Milo drummed his fingers on the steering wheel. "I don't suppose Gibb killed Mark, then somebody—like Simon—took out Gibb for revenge." He sounded faintly hopeful.

"It's not impossible," I said, but secretly I felt that it was unlikely. Still, I was trying to bolster Milo's spirits.

He was silent for a few moments, then threw open the door. "Hey—let me check your car. For the dent." He looked a trifle condescending.

It was still windy, but there was no sign of rain. Milo had gotten out a flashlight and was examining the Jag's damaged fender. "Kind of odd. I wonder what they hit it with? It doesn't look like a baseball bat or a tool. The dent's too big."

I was about to ask if he wanted me to reiterate my car damage theory when a big white Cadillac careened down Front Street, braked with a screech, and almost ran into a mailbox. Eeeny Moroni stepped out, leaving his car parked halfway up the curb.

"What the hell's going on, Milo?" Eeeny moved toward us with his quick, fluid step. He nodded vaguely at me. "Emma, *cara mia*," he said without his usual fervor. "I just saw Billy and Jack at the Burger Barn. They said Gibb was dead."

"That's right." Milo was suitably grave. "Shot. He was found down by Reiter."

Eeeny had pulled out a big red and white handkerchief and used it to mop his face. "Holy Mother of God! What did Gibb ever do except shoot his mouth off now and then?" He gazed quizzically at me. "You heard from Chris again?"

"No." I shifted my shoulder bag to the other arm. "I thought you didn't think Chris was guilty."

Eeeny gestured with his hands. "I never said that. I only

warned Milo here that he didn't have much to use against Chris. Making wrongful arrests isn't a good habit for sheriffs to get into." He paced a bit, rubbing the back of his head. "Damn it, this is getting ugly. In all the years I was sheriff, I never had anything like this happen." He gazed at Milo, dark eyes sympathetic. "Look, if there's anything I can do, let me know. This thing with Gibb has got me down."

"And me." Milo sighed, leaning against a lamp post and looking as if he'd like to disappear inside his orange down vest. "Emma thinks we should open the mineshaft. Do you agree, Eeeny?"

The ex-sheriff made an expressive gesture with his hands. "I think Neeny would sue us. He's dead-set against it, you know."

"We can get a warrant," said Milo with a touch of truculence. "Neeny doesn't own this damned town."

Eeeny wriggled his heavy eyebrows. "He used to. And he still has a pretty big chunk. What's the point, Milo? You don't really expect to find a six-inch vein of gold."

Milo sighed. "No." He glanced at me and looked away a bit too quickly. "I guess it was just a whim."

"It isn't a whim," I declared, getting a bit pugnacious. "As I explained to Milo, both Mark and Gibb were up at that mineshaft not long before they were killed. It's the one thing they have in common. So maybe there's something about it that . . ."

Eeeny was giving me a withering look. "Emma, *mio cor*, *dolce* Emma, you sound as pigheaded as Vida. That mineshaft has been closed off for fifty years. What could it be that would cause murder?" He turned to Milo. "Look for rational answers, concrete evidence, real motives. You need facts, not fancies. Hey, Milo, do your homework. You've got an election coming up next year."

"Don't remind me," Milo muttered, once again the picture of gloom.

Eeeny danced over to Milo and took him by the arm.

"Come on, *amico*, let's go to Mugs Ahoy and have a beer. Emma?"

I shook my head. "Thanks, Eeeny, but no, I quit drinking after a rowdy evening of bridge. Besides, I'm beat. You two go cry in your beer without me."

Eeeny shrugged and Milo uttered no protest. The past and present sheriffs moved off down the street while I got into my Jaguar to head for home. I wondered if Vida had heard the news about Gibb. I wanted very much to call her, but I was afraid Tom Cavanaugh would think I was checking up on him.

By the time I pulled into my carport, I realized I was being ridiculous. What Tom thought shouldn't make any difference. I was involved in a double homicide investigation. I strode into the house and dialed Vida's number. Nobody answered. I put the phone down with an uneasy feeling, triggered by various fears. It was after ten o'clock. I decided to wait and call Vida again in half an hour.

But it was six in the morning when I woke up on the sofa with the phone off the hook and a can of Pepsi spilled on the rug. I hadn't been lying when I told Eeeny Moroni that I was beat. Murder, it seemed, was an exhausting business.

Chapter Fourteen

BY THE TIME I put on the coffee, took a bath, got dressed, and ate some toast, it was almost seven. If Vida had to be in Seattle for the funeral at ten, she was probably up. To my relief, she answered on the first ring. I'd made up my mind not to ask any questions about her dinner guest. Not that I was jealous of Vida—she was older than Tom and not exactly my idea of a femme fatale. Besides, it was none of my business.

"Where the hell were you at ten o'clock last night?" I blurted.

There was a pause. Inwardly, I groaned at my lack of self-control. Then Vida's voice caromed off my ear. "At the Burger Barn, trying to get Billy to make sense about poor Gibb. Where were *you* at eleven?"

I laughed. I couldn't help it. Vida made a noise of exasperation. "Sorry, Vida," I apologized. "I'm kind of strung out. I fell asleep on the sofa and somehow knocked the receiver off."

I expected her to commiserate, but she was already off on another tangent. "I've already written up Gibb's obit. I'll drop it off on the way to Seattle. I called his sister last night, but she works and can't come up from Portland until the weekend. Al Driggers will have to wait till Saturday to hold the funeral."

It seemed that Vida had matters well in hand. I knew she was in a rush, so I told her I'd talk to her when she got back.

It was a busy morning at *The Advocate*, with the usual

Monday prepublication pressures and the added burden of at least thirty phone calls inquiring about Gibb Frazier. There could have been more, but it seemed that half the town had headed out for Mark Doukas's funeral in Seattle.

By two P.M., I had my share of the day's work in hand. I'd left some extra space for any late-breaking news on the homicides and reserved a small box on page three for an account of Mark's services. Vida could whip that out when she returned. I was just making some final corrections on a feature Carla had written about Linda Grant's personal fitness program when Tom Cavanaugh strolled in, looking resplendent in jogging togs.

Tom didn't sit down, saying he had to get back to the lodge because he'd asked for a lot of information to be faxed there. "I'll get back to you after I get a chance to go over it. I'd like to meet with Ed, too." He moved a step closer to my desk. "How are you doing? I couldn't believe the news when Vida got the call about Gibb last night."

"It's getting pretty grim around here," I admitted. "People are scared."

"It's not a random killer," Tom said. "Gibb Frazier must have been deliberately lured to that gravel pit. Vida's nephew said there was no I.D. on him."

"I agree." I tapped a half page of hard copy. "I wrote a short editorial to that effect this morning, urging Alpiners not to panic. At least four callers today insisted we've got a serial killer on the loose. That's nonsense. I think." Frankly, I wasn't sure which was worse—some sociopath indiscriminately knocking off the population, or a cold-blooded murderer with a motive. "How was dinner?" I couldn't resist the question.

Tom grinned. "Gruesome. Chicken and dumplings. The chicken was almost done and I could have used the dumplings in a softball game. Slow pitch. But Vida's a font of information. She ought to be your ad manager instead of Ed."

"Anybody ought to be instead of Ed," I moaned, glancing out into the news office to make sure he wasn't around. "Say, will you do me a favor?" Tom inclined his head, a mannerism I remembered as tacit assent. "I was just going to call Bill Blatt and ask him to get a warrant to open the mineshaft at Icicle Creek. If Vida isn't back by three, will you go up there with me?"

Tom glanced at his watch. "Okay. Shall I pick you up?"

Since the back road to Icicle Creek went past the ski lodge, and I also wanted to check the mail at my house, I told Tom I'd drive. As soon as he left, I called the sheriff's office. Bill Blatt hemmed and hawed, insisting that in Milo's absence, he didn't have the authority to issue a warrant. I figured he was hedging because he was scared of Neeny Doukas. But if we were going to have a look at that mineshaft, we'd better do it before Neeny got back to Alpine.

"To hell with Billy and the stupid warrant," I said, hurrying past Carla to the door.

Carla looked up from her portable makeup mirror where she was plucking her eyebrows. "What?"

"Never mind." I banged out of the office. Carla was almost as oblivious to the two murders as she was to everything else that qualified as news in Alpine. She'd also spelled the high school P.E. teacher's name as Linda *Grunt*. Some day I was going to ask to see Carla's diploma from the University of Washington.

There was nothing from Adam in my mailbox. I would have to call him after five, when the rates were down. In the present atmosphere of murder, I began to worry about him, too. He might be thousands of miles away, but I felt as if the danger in Alpine could somehow span the Pacific Ocean and menace my son. It was a silly notion, but it wouldn't go away.

The ski lodge was a classic structure, four stories of pine logs on the exterior, knotty pine interior, stone fireplaces, and snug little rooms with bright plaid curtains. The renovations that were being completed included plumbing and electrical updates, conversion of the basement pool room into a conference center, and expanded kitchen facilities. Perhaps there was still hope for a new restaurant after all.

I had purposely gotten to the lodge half an hour early because I wanted to talk to Heather Bardeen. As luck would have it, Monday was her day off. Disappointed, I went to the pay phone in the lobby to call Kip, the middle MacDuff, and ask if he would fill in for Gibb and use his pickup to take the paper into Monroe. Before I could find a quarter, Phoebe Pratt Doukas came through the main entrance with her niece, Chaz. I was startled. Did her return mean that Neeny was back, too? I greeted Phoebe with more warmth than I actually felt.

"I couldn't bear any more grief," said Phoebe in a broken voice. She was dressed in black crepe with lots of pearls and dangerously high heels. "I couldn't even go up to the casket. I'd rather remember Mark the way I last saw him, with those dark eyes looking out at me from under that baseball cap." Briefly, Phoebe turned away, lower lip quivering.

For all that my memories of Mark weren't so fond, I certainly mourned his untimely death and didn't have to feign sympathy. "He was too young," I said. "Violent death is always a waste." So were my words of comfort, I decided, but Phoebe seemed to drink them in like rare wine.

"Isn't that the truth?" She had turned back to me, tugging at her black kidskin gloves. "I was so glad to head back to Alpine. Seattle is too big. Neeny rode in Al Driggers's limo, but I took my own car." The statement seemed straightforward, but I wondered if there hadn't been a scene with Simon. Whether or not he now knew his father had married Phoebe, Simon Doukas would not have been keen on letting her join the family in what Vida termed Al's *Mourningmobile*.

"It was a wonderful service, but *soooo* long," Phoebe was saying as Chaz, apparently on break from her job at the desk, went back to work. "Greek, you know. Then there was a reception at the church, but the real wake will be at the house after they go to the cemetery."

I calculated. The funeral had probably been over between eleven and noon; the reception wouldn't go on for more than an hour unless the ouzo flowed like motor oil. If the mourners actually formed a cortege, they could hardly break the speed limit going up Stevens Pass. I figured I was safe at the mineshaft until almost four P.M.

"How is the family?" I inquired politely.

Phoebe's eyes got very round, and she tugged at her rope of pearls. "Poor dears! Doukums is such a strong old bear, but inside, his heart is breaking. I try to treat him like a china doll." The image she had conjured up was of a bearded Kewpie, watching daytime television. "Cece is ever so brave, and Simon is like a rock! Of course," she went on, lowering her voice and leaning down since her normal height and abnormal shoes gave her at least a six-inch advantage over me, "Cece must be gulping tranquilizers. And Simon never is one to show much emotion, is he?"

"That all depends," I replied, thinking of his tears upon seeing Chris and his anger upon meeting with me. No doubt he'd have apoplexy Wednesday when the paper came out. But my real concern wasn't centered on the grieving Doukases. I didn't have a lot of time to spare, and I wanted to steer the conversation to another topic. "You must make good time in that Town Car," I remarked, trying to sound casually congenial. "I had my Jag dented over the weekend. Have you gotten that blue paint off yet? Or will you have to have the whole car redone?"

Caught off guard, Phoebe teetered a bit on her high heels. "I really haven't had time to tend to it." She tucked a few stray curls under the wisp of black veiling atop her head. "There's been so many other things going on."

I gave a sympathetic nod. "How true. Edna Mae Dalrymple said it was so bizarre how that bucket of paint blew over just as you drove down Front Street Wednesday night." I gave her my blandest gaze and hoped Edna Mae would forgive me for misquoting her. She sure wasn't likely to forgive me for bidding five diamonds.

Phoebe doesn't have the quickest mind I've ever encountered, but the implication of my words eventually took hold. "Oh—well . . . that's right, I made a quick trip downtown the other night." I noticed she didn't refer to Wednesday as the night of the murder. Phoebe was virtually whispering now: "I wanted to see Simon about a legal matter, and Cece said on the phone that after he dropped his nephew off, he was stopping by the Clemans Building to pick up some papers. But he wasn't there."

"Gibb was, though," I said with feigned innocence.

Phoebe's carefully etched eyebrows lifted. "Gibb? Oh! Yes, poor Gibb! Isn't this all so *awful*? My, yes, it was the last time I saw him alive. He honked at me and told me the *naughtiest* story! I was *soooo* embarrassed, I couldn't laugh. But I had to giggle a bit on my way home." She gave me a meaningful look. Was it a question or a confirmation? I couldn't be sure. If *home* meant Neeny's house, maybe Phoebe was ready to acknowledge that they were man and wife. Was she just fishing? Or verifying that she'd gone nowhere else that night?

Tom was coming down the wide stairway, dressed in sweater and slacks.

I had one more comment for Phoebe in my arsenal: "It's too bad Chris never got that letter you sent to him in Hawaii. When he gets settled, do you want it forwarded?"

Phoebe pulled at a pearl earring. "Oh!" She was clearly marshaling her thoughts. "No, no, it was only my belated condolences on Margaret's passing. Though," she went on, looking over my shoulder to give Tom an inquisitive stare, "when you get an address for the boy, let me know." For a brief instant, her face sagged, and she gripped my wrist. "Emma, does the sheriff really think Chris killed Mark?"

Startled by the sudden shift in her emotions, my reply tumbled out mindlessly. "The sheriff doesn't know anything." Immediately I felt a pang of remorse. Milo Dodge had enough ₁ roblems without my picturing him as an imbecile.

Her composure restored, Phoebe gave Tom a coquettish smile and teetered off. I didn't waste any time but hurried Tom along to the parking lot. On the way to Icicle Creek, I told him about my conversation with Phoebe.

"Let me get this straight," said Tom as we drove past the high school football field. "Phoebe claimed earlier she hadn't left the Doukas house. Now she admits she did, but says she went to meet with Simon at his office. He wasn't there, right?"

"Which means Simon was out, Cece was alone, Phoebe was tooling around in the Town Car, joshing with Gibb, and since she was Neeny's alibi, that goes out the window, too." Why had Mark gone back to Mineshaft Number Three after dark? Why had he called both Milo Dodge and Eeeny Moroni? "Hey! Phoebe said something odd—about how she'd like to remember Mark the way she saw him last, wearing a baseball cap. But the only time I know of that he ever wore a baseball cap was when he borrowed Chris's—the night of the murder."

Tom gave me an indulgent look. "You may be reaching a bit on this one. Are you saying that Phoebe saw Mark just before he was killed?"

I braked for the blinker light at the three-way stop below First Hill. "That's right. Mark must have come to the house. There wouldn't have been time for him to go anywhere else after he left his parents' place. I doubt he would have come to see Phoebe, but why didn't Neeny see him? Or did she prevent Mark from talking to his grandfather? I honestly don't think Neeny saw Mark that night. Neeny has a passel of unpleasant traits, but he's not a liar."

I had sat through the passing of two cars, one van, and a logging truck. Tom gave me a gentle nudge. "If this were San Francisco, you'd have been arrested for erecting an illegal barricade by now. You'd better concentrate on your driving, Emma."

I did, or at least tried to, but I was convinced I was

right. Mark had gone to see Neeny; Phoebe had put him off; shortly afterward, she had left the house, supposedly to see Simon. Had Mark told her what he'd found at Mineshaft Number Three? It was possible.

It had taken us ten minutes to get to the turnaround by the mineshaft. The wind of the previous night had dwindled to a mere breeze, and the clouds had blown away. For the end of September, it was quite warm. Tom and I gazed at the entrance to the mineshaft in silence.

He was the first to speak. "Emma, nobody's been in this thing." He pointed to the moss-covered wooden doorway. "It looks as if somebody tried." He pointed to a half-dozen recent tears in the smooth green moss. "But that's as far as they got."

"Mark, maybe. With the crowbar." I made a face. "I could be wrong about this whole thing." My ears were pricked for the sound of any oncoming cars. We had skirted the cemetery but there had been no sign of Mark's funeral cortege. I glanced at my watch; it was bang-up three o'clock. The Doukases and the other half of Alpine could be arriving in town any minute.

My taupe flats pawed the ground like an anxious pony. "Somebody said—was it Gibb?—there was another entrance."

Tom walked up by the creek. I was pleased, if not exactly surprised, that he was being such a good sport about all this. Of course he was a journalist at heart and as curious as I was. Still, Alpine and its residents really had nothing to do with him.

He was about ten feet away, pushing at some vine maples. "Nothing here that I can see." He went around to the other side. I waited while he poked among some big boulders. "Say, Emma, these rocks have been moved recently."

I joined him. With a hefty heave, Tom displaced one of the boulders. We knelt down and peered into what must have been an offshoot of the main shaft. I let out a little shriek, and Tom swore under his breath.

Grinning back at us was a skull.

* * *

It took us at least a full minute to regain our mental equilibrium. Tom looked at me, and I looked at him. Leaves rustled above us. A chipmunk chattered somewhere close by. A blue jay called to its mate. The creek tumbled down the hill, rushing to the river. The amber and bronze vine maples bent low to form arches over our heads. It was all so peaceful, so natural, with the autumn sun filtering its golden light through the trees.

"Hell," breathed Tom, shaking his head. "When's the sheriff due back?"

I didn't feel like standing up just yet. "Any time," I murmured. I made a shaky gesture at the hole in the ground. "Is it just a skull, or . . ." I left the rest of the sentence unspoken.

Tom swiveled around and removed the other big boulder. He grimaced. "It's a whole skeleton." He put up his hand. "Don't look, Emma."

"A skeleton shouldn't scare me. After all, it's almost Halloween." My attempt at smiling failed.

"Seen one skeleton, seen 'em all, I suppose." Tom sat next to me and put an arm around my shoulders. "We'd better head back."

"Right." But I still wasn't ready to get on my feet. "How long has the . . . body been there, do you think?"

"I haven't any idea. It could even be some miner who got killed 'way back when." His dark blue eyes scanned my face. "Do you remember hearing anything about an accident?"

"No. But that doesn't mean there wasn't one. It's been—what? Seventy, eighty years ago." I tensed as a car approached and slowed down. "Damn. Somebody's coming."

We both stood up, Tom supporting me until I got my balance. A blue car had pulled in next to the Jag. I couldn't see the make of it from where we were. A moment later, Vida trudged across the little clearing, her black felt gaucho hat tipped over one ear.

"That knuckleheaded nephew of mine said you'd been calling about opening the mineshaft, so I figured you'd come up to—" She stopped as she took in the somber expressions on our faces. "Oh, Lord! What now?"

We told her. A mere skeleton held no terrors for Vida. She marched over to the open ground and bent down, exposing an inch of white slip under her black suit skirt. Clutching her hat to her head, she turned to face us. "I need a closer look. Tommy, can you get this out of here or will it crumble?"

Tommy, I thought. Had Vida adopted him? Tom didn't seem to notice; he was shaking his head. "I don't think I should try. What do you want to see?"

Vida jabbed a finger at the open ground. "There's a religious medal around the neck." She screwed up her face in the effort of recollection. "What do you Catholics call those things?"

I hazarded a guess. "Is it a St. Christopher Medal?"

"No, not that." Vida made more facial contortions. "Something marvelous." Her face lighted up, and she snapped her fingers. "That's it! A Miraculous Medal!"

"That's right," agreed Tom. He touched his chest. "I wear one myself."

Vida was brushing dirt off her black patent leather shoes. She gave us a sidelong look. "Yes. So did Hector Ramirez."

Vida and Tom stayed at the mineshaft while I went to get Milo. As I came to the intersection of CR 187 and Eighth Street, I saw the long funeral cortege wending its way into the cemetery. Vida had said Milo had left after the church service because he'd learned that Gibb Frazier's truck had been found at Reiter Ponds. Milo might have returned to Alpine by now.

He had, in fact, arriving about two minutes ahead of me. "Emma, we found—" Milo stopped, noting my wild-eyed appearance. "What's wrong? You seen a ghost?"

"Yes." I collapsed in the outer office's nearest chair.

Jack Mullins and Bill Blatt gaped at me from over the counter. In a garbled manner, I told them about the discovery Tom and I had made, along with the conclusions Vida had given.

"Jeez." Milo draped his big frame over a chair that was turned backward. He was wearing a rumpled gray suit, so outmoded that I suspected he had bought it for his wedding twenty-five years ago. "What makes Vida think it's Hector?" Milo's long face registered doubt.

Tom and I had been equally skeptical, but Vida had offered convincing arguments. "First," I recounted, "she remembered the medal Hector wore around his neck. Second, she swears she never discounted foul play. And third, she insists it couldn't be anybody else."

Milo hung his arms over the back of the chair. "I'll go along with reason number one, but I won't buy the rest of it." He paused as Jack Mullins passed out coffee in paper cups. "If Vida thought somebody killed Hector fourteen years ago, why didn't she speak up then?"

"She didn't want to believe it," I said, quoting her indirectly. "But the more she thought about it, the more likely it seemed. Vida kept quiet—" I raised a hand to fend off Milo's protest. "I know, I know, it doesn't sound like Vida, but she felt Neeny Doukas had Sheriff Moroni in his pocket and wouldn't press for an investigation."

Milo's head jerked up. "She thinks Neeny killed Hector?"

"She wouldn't put it past him," I allowed, trying to remember exactly how Vida had phrased it. "But mostly, she figured Neeny would say good riddance. He'd prefer that Hector not be found, dead or alive. If Hector had been killed, then he'd be some sort of martyr in Margaret's eyes, and Neeny couldn't go on saying what a rotter the guy was." There was still a glimmer of doubt in Milo's gaze. "Hey, you know these people better than I do. Vida's perception of Neeny hits home with me."

Milo was rubbing at his long chin. Bill Blatt looked

anxious, as if he didn't know whether to side with his aunt or his boss. Jack Mullins put on another pot of coffee.

"As for her third rationale," I went on when none of the men made a comment, "Vida will allow for a vagrant or an unknown prospector. But otherwise, she says nobody else has ever completely disappeared from Alpine."

Milo scoffed. "That's a crock of bull. I can think of three people in the last five years who—"

"So can Vida," I interrupted, my spirits restored and my need for action acute. I stood up. "But two of them were husbands escaping from impossible wives and one was a teenaged girl who ran off with her boyfriend from Index. Come on, Milo, let's get back there before the Doukases finish their graveside services."

Milo and his deputies led the way out to Icicle Creek. On the hillside in the cemetery, we could see at least a hundred people gathered under a green canopy. The line of parked cars reached almost back to the road.

At the mineshaft, Vida was sitting on a fallen log, a camera in her hand. Tom stood at the edge of the creek, probably watching for trout. I watched Milo as he shambled over to view the remains. His deputies followed him, somberly removing their regulation hats.

"I'll be damned," murmured Milo after an appropriate moment of silence. "It's *somebody*, all right."

"Of course it's somebody, you ninny," said Vida in annoyance. She had scrambled up from the log, damp earth clinging to her black skirt. "It's Hector Ramirez. Get Dr. Starr to dig out his dental charts."

Milo shot Vida a baleful look but didn't argue. "You three head out of here. There'll be all hell to pay when Neeny comes along and sees what's happening."

Vida glanced at me. "Do you have everything? I got some pictures. I had a couple of shots left over from the funeral."

I winced a bit at the gruesome tone *The Advocate* would be taking this week. "I'd like some positive I.D. before we send the paper into Monroe tomorrow," I told Milo.

He glared at me. "I can't promise that. What if Hector never went to the dentist?"

Vida pointed her camera at the sheriff. "Here, Milo, I want a picture of you so we can write a cutline saying 'Skykomish County sheriff Milo Dodge asserted today that Hector Ramirez never saw a dentist in his entire life.' Lift your chin, Milo. You look like you ate a bug."

Milo looked like he'd prefer eating Vida. A couple of cars passing by on CR 187 alerted me to the probability that the graveside services were concluded. "We're staying, Milo," I declared. "I wouldn't miss Neeny's reaction for the world." In my head, I was already rearranging the paper: Carla's feature on Linda Grant would have to be put on hold; maybe my piece on experimental logging practices would have to wait, too.

Milo gave me a fierce stare, then gestured impatiently at Jack Mullins. "Go get the van. We've got to move that skeleton out of here. See if you can bring Sam Heppner or Dwight Gould back with you. We could use some other deputies to help out." He turned back to me, fists on hips. "This isn't a tourist trap, Emma, it's law enforcement work. I want you people gone."

I set my jaw. "We're the press. We have a right to be here."

He jerked his hand at Tom. "He's not the press. He's a . . . *tourist*."

Tom strolled over to Milo, his engaging smile in place. "Actually, Sheriff, I'm the press, too. Would you like a list of my credentials?" He started to reach for his wallet.

Milo threw up his hands. "Never mind." Abruptly, he loped off to the open ground where the skeleton lay in blissful ignorance. At that moment, the Driggers Funeral Home car pulled up at the edge of the road. It was beginning to look like a parking lot out there.

Neeny Doukas, assisted by Simon, came tramping across the clearing. In contrast to his impeccably tailored son, Neeny was wearing a baggy black suit with a crooked knit tie. His olive complexion had a tinge of gray. "What the hell is going on here? This is private property!"

"It's a crime scene, Neeny," said Milo with commendable dignity. "We've found more remains."

"More?" Neeny's dark eyes bulged; a vein throbbed on his forehead. "Whaddaya mean, more? My grandson didn't come apart, did he? Whadda'd we bury? *Pieces?*"

Eeny Moroni's white Cadillac and Phoebe's red Lincoln had also pulled in. The limo was now disgorging Cecelia Doukas, Jennifer, and Kent MacDuff. Al Driggers tried to maintain his stately decorum as he came from the front seat to assist the women.

"Here," said Milo, taking Neeny by the arm that Simon released with reluctance, "we found a skeleton. You don't have to look."

"Look, schmook," said Neeny, waving Milo away. "Lemme go, you dinks." He glanced back at Simon, making sure his son didn't miss the point. "No skeleton's gonna shake me up. I've had enough crap in the last few days." He tramped past Milo and Vida. I stood between Tom and Simon, watching Neeny bend slightly at the waist. For a fleeting moment, I thought I saw him flinch. But when he straightened up and turned back to face us, he appeared as formidable as ever.

"What were you doing digging around here without my permission?" he demanded of the sheriff.

With an air of deference, Milo Dodge indicated the strips of yellow and black crime scene tape that fluttered in the breeze. "We have a right to be here, Neeny. You want your grandson's killer caught, don't you?"

"You think the killer buried hisself? Are you nuts, kid?" He gave a sudden shake of his head, then waved back at the skeleton. "Naw, I guess not. At least you found that."

I held my breath, waiting for Milo to reveal the truth. But whether he wanted to shield Tom and me or take credit for the discovery himself was unclear. In any event, he just stood there stoically, as the others approached the mineshaft. Simon tried to steer them away, especially the women.

"A tramp, from the Depression," soothed Simon, putting a protective arm around Cece. She was ashen and fragile, in simple, expensive black.

Kent MacDuff marched straight to the open ground. He stopped abruptly, almost lost his balance, and took a deep breath. "Hey," he said, his florid face suddenly pale, "at least we know that guy didn't kill Mark. He was too skinny."

Kent's attempt at bravado fell flat. Phoebe was clinging to Neeny; Jennifer had collapsed on the log abandoned by Vida; Al Driggers was looking for someone to comfort; and Eeeny Moroni was dancing around the mineshaft like a rooster gone berserk.

"Goddamn it, Milo, this used to be a quiet little town! What the hell is happening now? I feel like moving to L-Freaking-A!" The ex-sheriff gave Milo an ugly look.

I felt sorry for Milo. "Can it, Eeeny," I said. "It's not Milo's fault that there's a killer loose."

Vida chimed in. "It sure isn't, you old noodle," she said to Moroni. "In fact, that bunch of bones over there probably got killed while *you* were sheriff."

Moroni sneered at Vida who tipped her gaucho hat over one eye and sneered right back.

I intervened again. "Listen, all this wrangling isn't getting us anywhere. We're hindering, not helping, Sheriff Dodge. Does anyone here have any idea who this might be?" I made a stabbing gesture in the direction of the skeleton.

Judging from the shocked looks of my audience, most of them hadn't considered the possibility that the skeleton had once been a real person who had walked and talked among them.

"Oh, no!" gasped Phoebe.

"Hell," breathed Kent.

"Indeed," murmured Simon.

"Screw off," muttered Neeny.

Jennifer began to cry softly. Al Driggers, finally discovering an object for his professional sympathy, went over to the log.

To my surprise, Cece Doukas asked the first intelligent question of the impromptu gathering: "Are there any clothes or other objects that might be identifiable?" So stunned was everyone that she apparently mistook their blank faces for confusion. "I mean keys or jewelry or possibly credit cards. Even a hobo might carry something other than a little bag on a stick."

Again, I waited for Milo to make a revelation, this time about the Miraculous Medal. But Milo was proving remarkably reticent. "We'll have any information available after we've removed the remains." He looked past the little group to the road. "Here come my deputies now. I'd appreciate it if you'd all move on out of here. I'd like to have the van come in as close as possible." His voice was unusually formal.

To my amazement, the Doukas clan began to disperse. Only Eeeny Moroni stayed put, looking sheepish. "Hey, Milo, *amico*, I apologize a thousand times." He put a hand on Milo's rumpled suit sleeve. "I'm what you call, you know, distraught. Mark's funeral today, Gibb getting killed, now this . . . I spent my life chasing shoplifters and catching people breaking the speed limit. Maybe," he confessed with an off-center grin, "I'm jealous. This is bad stuff—but it's big stuff. And it's *your* stuff, not mine."

Milo shrugged. "Forget it." He glanced at Tom and Vida and me. "You coming or going?"

"I'll be at the office for quite a while. Will you let us know if you find anything else?" I inquired. "Like what Cece suggested?"

Milo gave me a ghostly smile. "Sure. Thanks, Emma."

I stared at Milo. "Huh?" But he had already turned away, to where Jack Mullins and Bill Blatt were taking pictures of the skeleton. Then it dawned on me: Milo had appreciated my support in front of the others. Somehow, I was touched. And inexplicably pleased.

* * *

"Do all doctors get rich?"

I held the phone out an inch from my ear; I wasn't sure I'd heard my son correctly. "What did you say, Adam?"

"I was thinking," he said, sounding vaguely muffled, "that maybe I'd like to go into medicine. Save lives and like that. How long does it take?"

"Many years and many dollars," I replied, vexed. This was not the time for Adam to discuss his life's goals with me. "Are you certain you mailed that material?"

"Yeah, like I told you. I guess I had too much to do to get to the post office the other day before it closed. Plus I had to look for Chris's denim jacket. It was under the bathroom sink. Then I found all those other letters and junk that belonged to Chris's mom. So I put everything in a box and shipped it off to you. The guy at the post office said it should get to Alpine in five days." Adam sounded as if he were talking to an imbecile.

I sighed. That meant tomorrow. If I were lucky. "Okay. Did it cost much?"

"About four bucks. There wasn't a lot, just letters and stuff. I kept the rest, it looked pretty useless."

I hadn't any idea what Adam was talking about. "The rest of *what*?"

A door banged across the Pacific, and I heard distant voices. Adam had company. "Papers, you know, like old bills and insurance policies and car registrations—stuff like that. Chris got the insurance, so he doesn't need that, and I thought it would be kind of grim to send him his mom's death certificate and all the hospital stuff."

"Probably," I agreed. "But don't toss it out. He may want all that some day. Especially the death certificate. They cost money."

Apparently, Adam had turned away from the receiver to say something to his friends. When he gave his full attention back to me, it was as if I hadn't spoken. "Like I was thinking—maybe not saving lives. I mean, if you can't, then you must feel rotten when a patient dies, right? So being a baby doctor would be better. What's a *live* birth?"

I screwed up my face. "What do you think it is, dopey?" I was in my editorial office, wishing Milo would pass on any new information he might have gleaned from the remains at the mineshaft. It was after six o'clock, and Vida was out in the front office, typing like mad. Tom was there, too, answering the phones that were now bringing us renewed interest from the outside media.

"Yeah, I know what live birth *sounds* like," said Adam as masculine laughter erupted in the background. "But it can't be what I think it is. See, I'm looking at Mrs. Ramirez's records from when Chris took her to the hospital when she got so sick with the cancer. It says right here on this form: *Live Births: None*. So what does it mean?"

I almost dropped the phone. "Say that again?"

Adam's sigh vibrated over the ocean cable. Then he repeated the information. "So if it means what it sounds like, did Mrs. Ramirez find Chris under a rock? Hey, Mom, you used to think you were really cool with your open-minded sex education. I think you missed something!"

I stared at my computer screen, which seemed to look very fuzzy. "I think I did, too. Adam, what hospital was that?"

"Huh? Oh, not that big one up on the hill. It's the other one: Kuakini. Hey, the guys want to know if you think Chris is in L.A."

"I have no idea." I wished I did, but there wasn't time to speculate about Chris's whereabouts just now. "Is there a doctor's name on that form?"

"I think so. . . . Yeah, here it is, Steven Furokawa. He's Chris's doctor, too. Nice guy." Adam responded away from the receiver to a comment about girls and Malibu.

I saw Vida shoot an inquiring glance through the open door, then plod back to her desk. "Have you got a number for Dr. Furokawa?"

The noise inside Adam's room was building. "What?

Oh—a telephone number? No, but there's a phone book here some place. . . ." At last, he came up with Steven Furokawa's business and residential listings. "Hey, Mom, what's this all about? I haven't made up my mind yet. I just thought that being a doctor might be—you know, like fulfilling. You don't have to start checking around for—"

"Put a sock in it," I said, then added on a gentler note: "I love you. Hang up."

He did, and I immediately dialed Steven Furokawa, M.D., at his Honolulu clinic. To my relief, he was in; to my amazement, his receptionist put me through. In my best professional voice, I identified myself. "I understand you treated the late Margaret Ramirez for cancer. Her nephew was murdered five days ago, and her husband's body may have been dug up from an abandoned mineshaft this afternoon. Over the weekend, there was another homicide. Margaret's son, Chris, is also a patient of yours. He's wanted for questioning." If all that didn't impress Dr. Furokawa, I couldn't think what would—except telling him there was five hundred pounds of TNT under his office chair. "Doctor, I don't want you to breach patient confidentiality, but can you tell me this: did Margaret Ramirez ever bear a child?"

Silence. Then a quick breath. "You said yourself she had a son, Ms. Lord." His voice was dry, almost humorous.

Obviously, I couldn't cut corners. I explained about the admitting form from Kuakini, implying that I had it sitting right in front of me.

More silence. Then Dr. Furokawa spoke in a brisker tone. "I don't recall. I have a very busy practice. Mrs. Ramirez's records aren't available right now. Even if they were, I couldn't tell you."

"Doctor, this is extremely important. Three people have already died. The county sheriff can get an order to send Mrs. Ramirez's records to Alpine. But that could take a couple of days, maybe more." Doggedly, I kept speaking. This wasn't the first time I'd had to pry material out of an unwilling source. "You must have treated Margaret for some time. *Think.* Had she borne a child?"

Now the silence seemed to fill the thousands of miles between us, creeping along the ocean floor, washing over the coast, rising up into the mountains.

"No." Dr. Furokawa uttered the word with reluctance. "That's all I can tell you."

It was enough.

Chapter Fifteen

"WE'VE GOT TO go into Seattle tomorrow," declared Vida, ripping her account of Mark's funeral out of the typewriter. "That's where Margaret supposedly had Chris, you know. His birth would be registered at the King County Courthouse."

I was pacing the office. "It's a long shot," I said for the fourth time. "But Chris looks too much like a Doukas to be anybody else."

"I can go to Seattle," volunteered Tom.

He struck me as a bit subdued, and I wondered if he would like to have talked to Adam. But that would not be a good idea. My son didn't know that his father was in Alpine. Indeed, my son knew only the barest facts about Tom Cavanaugh. I'd always felt it was better that way.

"There are a couple of people I should see while I'm in the area anyway," Tom went on. "You two have a paper to get out."

Vida and I exchanged glances. "True," I said. Tom had gotten us a pizza and some salad. I sat down at Ed's desk. "Okay, let's nail this down."

Tom nodded. "Remember, though—even if you're right, it may have nothing to do with these deaths."

I didn't argue the point. Just because Margaret and Hector Ramirez were not Chris's natural parents didn't solve the murder investigation. But I still wanted to know who he really was. I doubted very much that Chris himself was aware of his parents' identity. In this age of candor about such matters, I found that suspicious.

Vida, who had been leafing through the 1971 volume of *Advocates*, clapped her hands. "Here! Chris's birth announcement—'August twenty-one, 1971, to Hector and Margaret Ramirez, formerly of Alpine, a boy, seven pounds, ten ounces, at Seattle.'"

Tom jotted the information down in a small leather-bound notebook. "Do you know where Hector and Margaret lived while they were in Seattle?" The question was for Vida.

She took off her hat and vigorously scratched her head. "Ooooh—not really, Tommy. A rental, out in the south end, I think. Neeny might know, or Simon and Cece. But even if they'd tell you, I doubt they'd have an address after all this time."

The phone rang. It was Milo, and his voice sounded strained. "Doc Dewey's here. He says the bones are at least five and maybe fifty years old. But because the clothing was so decomposed—all that damp up there by the creek—it's impossible for him to pinpoint without lab work."

"What about Dr. Starr?" I asked.

"He's got Jeannie Clay checking their records." The sheriff spoke away from the phone, apparently to Doc Dewey Senior. "No papers, of course, but there was that medal, a belt buckle, a key chain, and a wedding ring. Kind of fancy, gold with a sort of scroll design."

"Are the bones the right size for Hector?" I was making notes of my own on Ed's memo pad.

"Doc says yes, as far as he can tell." Milo's tone was grudging.

I gave Vida and Tom a thumbs-up sign. "Can we quote you as saying this raises the possibility of the remains being those of Hector Ramirez?"

A heavy sigh fell on my ear. "I guess. Hell, Emma, it could be Elvis."

"Or Elvis. Thank you, Sheriff Dodge." I imagined Milo's expression and tried not to laugh. "What about foul play?"

"Doc can't tell yet. No sign of a blow to the head. Poison, strangulation, stabbing would all be hard to figure at this point. A bullet might leave some mark on the bone, but there's a lot of discoloration." Milo paused again as Doc Dewey spoke to him. "We're going to dig some more in that hole. If the victim was shot, the bullet may be in the ground. As the body decomposed, Doc says the shell would eventually work itself into the earth."

I grimaced at my pizza. "Right." Hastily, I tried to think of any other questions I should put to Milo while I had him on the line. Then I remembered to ask about Gibb's truck. That part of the investigation had gotten shunted aside in the wake of the discovery at the mineshaft.

Milo couldn't add much, however. "It was just sitting there at Reiter, where all the fishermen park. Gibb's I.D. was on the floor. So were his keys. Lots of prints, mostly smudged, but we may find something yet."

After I'd hung up, Vida and Tom mulled over the information I'd relayed from Milo. "I wish," said Vida, rubbing at her eyes, "I could remember what Margaret's wedding ring looked like. It just might have been a gold band. I doubt that Hector could have afforded a diamond set."

Tom polished off his third slice of pizza. "How long were they away from Alpine?" Again, he addressed Vida as the font of all knowledge.

Vida briskly stirred dressing into her salad. "A year, maybe. I know they missed one Christmas, because Cece told me she was glad they were gone so that she wouldn't have to host what could be an awkward family gathering. But they were back by the next holidays, because Fuzzy Baugh wanted to borrow Chris to be Baby New Year for the Kiwanis festivities in Old Mill Park. Margaret wouldn't hear of it, since we had three feet of snow on the ground."

Tom made more notes. I ate more pizza.

Vida stared off into space, glasses in her lap. At last she spoke. "We're assuming the bones belong to Hector," she began, obviously having given her theory careful thought.

"Then we must assume Hector was murdered." She looked at both of us for confirmation. We nodded in unison. "Mark may have found the body when he was prospecting. That could be what set him off. But who did he tell? Not Kevin MacDuff. Could he have given his story to the murderer? Did he know he was talking to the murderer? And Gibb—did he find the body, too, or was he killed because he knew there was another way into the mine?"

Tom was drinking a large Coke. "Could Gibb have killed Hector?"

Vida shook her head and sprinkled a tiny packet of salt onto her salad. "I doubt it. No known motive. Unless he was in love with Margaret. He was a widower by then. That's possible, though I don't recall any rumors."

In my opinion, if Vida couldn't remember them, they didn't exist.

She was still speaking: "Margaret was a beautiful girl. Half the men in Alpine were crazy about her. That's why Neeny was so put out when she married an outsider like Hector. But even if Gibb had killed his so-called rival, why would he murder Mark? And who would kill Gibb?" She gave an emphatic shake of her head. "Let's put that aside for now. We can rule out some of the others as Hector's killer because of age." Setting down her plastic fork, Vida began to eliminate suspects on her fingers. "Hector disappeared fourteen years ago. Cross off Kent and Jennifer. They were too young. And Chris, of course. Anybody under, say, thirty."

"Okay," I agreed. "But I don't get it. Milo says it's virtually impossible to tell how Hector died. Why, after all this time, would the killer care if the body was found? If Mark and Gibb hadn't been murdered, would we all jump to this conclusion about Hector? And even if we did, nothing seems to point to any specific person as his murderer."

Tom stood up, brushing crumbs from his tailored slacks. "Emma's right. The trail is decidedly cold. Either the killer panicked or isn't very bright. Unless we're missing something."

The phone jarred us from our mutual absorption. I reached over my shoulder and fumbled at the receiver. *"Advocate,"* I croaked, still juggling.

Jennifer Doukas MacDuff's uncertain voice came on the line. "Ms. Lord, you said I could come see you if I had a problem. Did you mean it?"

"Sure." I finally had the receiver under control. "Yes," I said, not wanting her to think I was being too breezy. "When do you want to talk?"

Jennifer's words were jerky. "Now. Alone. At your house. Don't tell anyone. *Please.*"

Vida and Tom were watching me. "In fifteen minutes," I said.

My first reaction was to shield Jennifer. But fragments of movies and books passed through my mind in which the hapless heroine falls into a trap and only the intrepid hero can show up in time to rescue her from the arch fiend. I didn't want to set myself up for further damsel-in-distress scenarios. I broke faith with Jennifer and ratted, reasoning that I wasn't betraying a source because she hadn't really told me anything yet.

"If I'm not back in half an hour, send for Milo," I said, heading out the door over protests from Tom and Vida.

It never occurred to me that Milo might like to be a hero, too.

Jennifer was already waiting for me, hunched over the wheel of her compact car at the edge of my driveway. I kept my apprehension at bay as I let us into the dark house. It was after seven-thirty, and the sun had long ago disappeared behind the mountains.

After I turned on the lights and went into the kitchen to get us each a can of soda, the house seemed as snug and safe as ever. Jennifer had flopped down on the sofa where she'd sat on her previous visit. She had changed from the plain black dress of the funeral into faded jeans and a floppy shirt.

"This is a bother," she began, twisting her hands and

turning red-rimmed blue eyes in my direction. "But except for the sheriff, I don't know who else to talk to."

"It's okay," I said. "What's wrong?"

Jennifer sighed, untwisted her hands long enough to fling a strand of hair over her shoulder, and eyed the can of pop as if it were a bomb. "Phoebe is taking my grandfather away tomorrow. I don't think that's right."

"Where?" I asked, knowing I should have said *why*? But the picture of a docile Neeny Doukas, being carted off against his will by anyone, threw me off balance.

"Palm Springs. In California," Jennifer added, in case my sense of geography didn't extend past the Columbia River. "She says all this has been too hard on him. He needs to get away, to be in the sunshine. But it scares me." Her chin quivered.

Now I asked the proper question. "Why?"

Jennifer finally picked up the can of soda and took a sip. "I'm afraid he won't come back. My dad is really mad. Even my mom thinks Phoebe shouldn't take him away."

I leaned forward in my armchair, noting how the light from the table lamp emphasized the contours of Jennifer's face and added character. "Have you talked to your grandfather about this?"

The blonde hair swung to and fro. "No. There wasn't a chance, with everybody arguing and yelling. I came straight from the house," she explained, and I knew she meant Neeny's, not her parents' home. "After the guests were gone, Phoebe made her announcement to the rest of us. Then they all got to fighting. Kent and I left, and then I called you."

"How does Kent feel about this?"

"He thinks Phoebe's up to something. He doesn't trust her an inch." She ran her forefinger about that far on my coffee table to underscore her point. "I don't, either."

I hesitated. But what I was about to say was a matter of public record. "Phoebe *is* your grandfather's wife," I said quietly.

Jennifer stared at me blankly. Then her mouth opened and she started to speak, but no words came out. Her hands clutched at the pop can; her blue eyes grew enormous.

"They eloped to Las Vegas awhile back. Remember the trip?" I smiled kindly.

"The old tart!" Jennifer exploded, showing more animation than I'd ever seen her display. She thrashed about on the sofa, spilling soda and beating at the cushions. Dust flew; I winced. But Jennifer wasn't about to notice my poor housekeeping. "I hate my family! They're a mess! I wish I were somebody else!"

"This is hard on everybody," I pointed out. Maybe, I thought, it was time to change the subject. "How's Kent's shoulder?"

Jennifer stopped flouncing around long enough to consider the question. "Better. He didn't have to take one of those pills last night."

I tried to keep my manner casual. "I don't suppose he saw Phoebe Wednesday night when he was downtown picking up that prescription?"

"Phoebe?" She spoke the name with disdain. "He didn't mention it." Obviously, it hadn't occurred to her that she was admitting her husband had left the house after all.

"Or your father?"

"No." Jennifer ran her fingers through her hair in an agitated manner. "Oh!" Enlightenment seemed to dawn on her. "You know," she said uneasily, "I forgot Kent went to Parker's to pick up that medicine. So much else happened afterward."

It could have been true. "I heard your father was going to his office after he dropped Mark off at my house."

Jennifer dismissed the idea with a slight shake of her head. "I doubt it. Kent said he parked in Dad's place. It's reserved in front of the Clemans Building for him, you know." Behind the veil of hair, her face contorted with distress. "Are you trying to tell me my dad went someplace else that night?"

"I have no idea." I felt as if I were pillorying the poor girl. "Look, maybe it's advantageous for your grandfather to get away. Phoebe's right. He's been through a lot, losing Mark. You've all suffered this past week. And Palm Springs isn't exactly the Amazon Jungle."

From the expression on Jennifer's face, they were one and the same to her. "My father says the sheriff won't let Neeny go. Not until they've caught my brother's killer."

That sounded like a strange—and suggestive—remark, coming from Simon Doukas. "Did Milo say that?"

Jennifer shrugged. "I don't know. Why don't you ask him? There he is now."

Sure enough, Milo Dodge's Cherokee Chief had pulled up out front. I could see the vehicle's outline under the light I'd put on in the carport. I glanced at my watch. It was 8:20. Tom had taken me at my word.

Jennifer didn't want to stick around to talk to Milo. She went out as he came in, and I was left on the porch, feeling inadequate. Not only had I failed to console Jennifer, I'd ended up sowing doubts and doling out more bad news. Jennifer Doukas MacDuff had shown poor judgment in choosing a confidante.

"What was that all about?" inquired Milo, still wearing his rumpled suit and looking bone tired.

"Come in. I'll tell you." I offered him Jennifer's place on the sofa and a fresh can of pop. He accepted both, and from out in the kitchen, I heard him utter a long sigh as he sat down.

"Did you think I'd been killed?" I asked with a grin as I handed him his soda.

"Your adviser thought so," replied Milo. "Or is he dating Vida?"

I gave Milo a steady look. "He's not dating anybody. He's been married for years."

Milo's hazel eyes were ironic. "Oh? Funny, he doesn't act married."

"Knock it off, Milo." My voice had a rough edge to it. "You ought to be grateful he's helping with the case." I stopped short of telling Milo everything, but I recounted Jennifer's concerns for her grandfather. Milo wasn't pleased about Phoebe's proposed trip.

"I can't stop them from going without causing a major war, but it would be better if they stuck around." Milo put his feet up on the coffee table. "They may be able to answer some questions. Like Chris."

"Are you hinting that Neeny may have killed Hector?" I asked.

"I don't *hint* things, Emma." He gave me a disapproving look. "If you're talking motive, Neeny had one for getting rid of Hector. But I still like the way Vida originally said he'd go about it—with money. Neeny could buy anybody off."

I tried to picture Hector Ramirez, Hispanic laborer, who had married into a wealthy small-town family. I didn't know what Hector looked like, but I had an inkling of how he felt. "Hector was proud, I think."

"But Neeny is stubborn." Milo made a slashing gesture with his hand. "And no way do I believe Neeny killed his grandson."

"Or Gibb?"

"Gibb's a different matter." Milo sank back against the cushions and yawned.

"Go home," I said. "You're tired. So am I." I gave him a feeble smile.

"Yeah." He took a swig of soda. "One thing, though." His high forehead furrowed as he regarded me across the space taken up by the coffee table. "We just got some tire tracks back from the road into Reiter and the gravel pit. Your Jag sure gets around, Emma." His expression was vaguely abject. "I guess you were right about your car getting swiped."

Right or wrong, it was still a shock. It made me a bit queasy to think that while I sat inside the Adcocks' living room, Gibb Frazier's murderer was using my car. Suddenly my Jag lost some of its charm. I was staring openmouthed at Milo.

"Can I have the keys?" he asked.

With an effort, I recovered my voice. "Why ask? Nobody else does."

"The extra set is gone," said Milo. "Whoever stole them probably wanted to make damned sure no prints showed up. I'd guess they've floated out to Puget Sound by now."

I'd never looked to see if the spare keys were still in place. "You're going to check the car now?" I asked.

He'd gotten up and had gone to the window. "Sam and Dwight just pulled up. They've got the gear. It shouldn't take long."

"Great." I waved at my purse which was at the end of the sofa. "My keys are in there, right on top."

Milo bent over, then straightened up abruptly. "What's this?" He was holding the Ramada Inn laundry bag with Mark's leather jacket. I'd left it there throughout the entire weekend.

"Take that, too," I said with a sigh of resignation. "I forgot I had it." It was true. Sort of.

Milo opened the front door and called to Dwight Gould who took the keys and the bag.

I glanced through the window, watching Sam Heppner open my car. "I wonder where you'll find the green paint."

"What?" Milo was still at the door. The cool air felt good. "Oh, you mean from the dent."

"Right." The phone rang; it was Tom.

"Are you all right? What's happening? Did Dodge show up?" Tom's voice was full of concern, and I could hear Vida yapping at him in the background.

I took a deep breath. My watch said it was after nine. No wonder Tom was worried. "Milo's here. Everything's fine. Listen, Tom," I said, wishing Milo wasn't watching me so closely, "I'm going to head for bed. You and Vida had better go home. It's been a long day."

There was a moment of silence. "Fine," said Tom. He clicked off.

Milo was still gazing at me. "Will you be all right alone?"

I lifted my chin. "Of course."

Milo raised a hand in salute and loped out the front
door. His deputies continued to subject my poor Jag to all
sorts of scientific humiliations. I considered going outside
to confer with them, but thought better of it. I'd had
enough crime for one day. Besides, other matters had
come home to roost for the night. I'd told Tom I was with
Milo, and I was going to bed. Tom had become quite terse.
Tomorrow, he would go into Seattle before I could explain. I could call him at the lodge, but it would be pre-
sumptuous of me to think an explanation was needed.
Why should Tom—a married man—care what I did? Why
should I care what he thought? Why should he think I was
doing anything wrong? And why wasn't I?

There were times when I thought the opposite sex was
not a good idea. This was definitely one of them.

Chapter Sixteen

THE FIRST CALL of the morning came from one of the last people I would have expected—Cecelia Doukas. At 7:35 A.M., just before I was about to leave for the office, she phoned to ask me over for a quick cup of coffee. While I was in a hurry to get to work, I could hardly refuse the invitation.

As I drove over to Stump Hill, I kept expecting the Jag to apologize to me for hauling a killer around. I squirmed a bit on the leather upholstery, trying to visualize who had sat in my place Saturday night. Maybe it was just as well I didn't know, or I might not have been able to drive the car at all.

The sheriff's deputies had left without telling me much. They'd have to wait for lab reports, Sam Heppner told me in his laconic manner. Obviously, they had not come up with the cliché cigarette butt or slip of paper bearing a mysterious phone number.

As I expected, Simon Doukas's car was gone from the driveway that led up to the Dutch Colonial in The Pines. I didn't think Cece would invite me over if Simon was around.

On this first morning after her son's burial, Cecelia Doukas appeared calm. I couldn't tell if her manner was induced by tranquilizers or an inner strength I'd never attributed to her. In any event, she was as well groomed as usual, in charcoal gray slacks and a light gray sweater. She led me into her big, airy kitchen, all white, with a few black accents. The only color in the room was a huge bouquet of autumn flowers, probably sent in memory of Mark.

"I know you're busy," Cecelia began, pouring us each a cup of coffee. "I'll be brief." She sat down across the dining counter from me on a matching stool. "Neeny and Phoebe are leaving tonight for Palm Springs. Jennifer says you told her they had gotten married. How on earth did you learn that?"

I reflected briefly on my need to protect sources. "We found out during the course of the investigation. Someone called the Clark County Court House in Las Vegas. They verified that there had been a marriage between the two parties back in August. You remember the trip?"

"Certainly." She offered sugar and cream. "I had no idea they'd gotten married. Neither did Simon." Cece's expression was melancholy. "I hope Neeny was sensible enough to have a prenuptial agreement drawn up. He didn't ask Simon to do it. That I know."

I could imagine Simon's fury when he learned of the elopement. And, if that is what it was, it occurred to me that Neeny probably hadn't bothered to consult a lawyer in Vegas. "Couldn't Neeny rectify any future unfairness by making a new will?"

"Perhaps." Cece gave me a wispy smile. "Isn't life peculiar? So often it blindsides us. I feel as if I'd been knocked down by a logging truck. Will I ever get up again?"

"You haven't any choice," I said frankly. "We have to get up if only so we can be knocked down the next time."

She saw the bitterness in my face and nodded. "Yes—I suppose you've had your share of trouble, too. It happens to everyone. But this all seems to have come at once." Her eyes brimmed with tears. "*All* of it."

I had the feeling she wasn't just talking about Mark's death and Neeny's marriage. "You mean Chris coming back?"

"Chris?" She seemed surprised. "Oh, well, I suppose, in

a way. It's funny, though—it seems as if he was here a long time ago. So much else has happened."

I studied her for a moment in silence. "I gather you don't think Chris killed Mark."

Cecelia picked up her mug and stared blindly at the glass-fronted cupboards behind me. "I don't want to think anybody killed him. If I knew who had, then I'd be forced to accept the fact that he's dead." Carefully putting the mug down, she gave me another tremulous smile, the tears still standing in her blue eyes. "That sounds silly, doesn't it?"

"Not at all." It had taken me weeks to grapple with the idea that I'd lost both parents. The call from the State Patrol, the visit to the funeral home, the memorial mass hadn't really sunk in. I was going through the motions. It wasn't really me. Those two dead people couldn't possibly be my mother and father. The realization hit me only when their birthdays, just four days apart, came along that September. "Did you know Phoebe was trying to see Simon last Wednesday night?"

"Yes. She called right after Simon left to take Chris back to your house. I told her my husband was going to stop by his office and she might catch him there." The blue eyes widened. "Oh! Do you think she intended to tell him she and Neeny had gotten married?"

I hadn't considered that possibility. "Wouldn't it have been better for Neeny to tell Simon? But Phoebe never found Simon." Again, I felt like the scourge of the Doukas women. "Your husband didn't show up at the Clemans Building."

Cece brushed at the tears with her fingertip. "No. He went somewhere else." She tilted her chin, looking both proud and vulnerable.

"I trust it was somewhere that gave him an alibi," I said, wanting to kick myself under the counter.

"It was." Her voice had turned cold. "But Simon would never use it."

I had to assume that Cecelia Doukas wasn't as naive as

she seemed. She must know about her husband's alleged affair with Heather Bardeen. It occurred to me that Heather might have tried to get revenge on Mark by sleeping with his father. No wonder Cece was so disillusioned with her life. "Do you think that skeleton could be Hector Ramirez?" I asked, going for a more neutral, if equally grim topic.

"It's possible. I'd hate to think so. I just want all this to end. It's not *nice*."

"Did you know Hector very well?"

She shook her head. "Margaret and Hector kept to themselves a lot. I saw him occasionally. He seemed well-mannered. But he didn't fit in, not with the family, not with the town. Neeny was quite unkind to him, and Simon felt the cultural differences were too great. It would have been better if he and Margaret had stayed in Seattle. People there are all rather different." She slid off the stool, going to get the coffeepot. I declined; I was already late. "By the way, I have no alibi for Wednesday night, if that's what you're trying to find out." She set the pot down and leaned on the counter, facing me. "Tell me, Emma—do you think I murdered my son?"

Impulsively, I put my hand on hers. It was ice cold. "No, Cecelia. I'm a mother, too, remember."

She gave her imitation of a smile. "Of course. Simon won't let me forget." She looked apologetic.

"You mean he won't let you forget I'm an *unmarried* mother."

Cecelia gave a sad shake of her head. I assumed it was not for me but for her husband.

Vida all but dragged me into the office. "Where've you been? I've got Chris on the phone!" She practically hurled me toward her desk. "Line two," she hissed.

"Chris? Where are you?" I was shouting into the earpiece. I turned the receiver around and repeated myself.

Chris's voice was calm. "I'm in Seattle. I never got to L.A."

Maybe that accounted for the fact that Milo's APB hadn't brought in any results. "Where have you been?"

"San Francisco. It's a cool place, but it costs too much to stay there. Everybody in San Francisco said L.A. had too much smog and too many nut cases. So I came back here." He sounded very matter-of-fact.

"Chris, let me ask you something." Even as I spoke, I scrawled a note to Vida, asking if Tom had left for Seattle. She didn't know. "Did you find a message at my house last Wednesday night?"

"What kind of a message?"

I explained to him about the piece of paper Ginny had found in my yard. "No," replied Chris. "I didn't see it. Neeny didn't send me a note. He wasn't that happy to have me come up to the house."

"Somebody signed his name and tried to lure you up there," I said. "Now listen, Chris, all hell has broken loose since you left. I want you to head back to Alpine." He started to argue, but I ran right over his words. "We think we know what happened to your father." I avoided telling him about the remains. That news shouldn't be delivered over the phone.

Chris let out a few obscene one-syllable words. "Won't the sheriff arrest me as soon as I come back?"

"No, of course not," I assured him, even though I wasn't certain. "Gibb Frazier, my driver, has been killed, too. You weren't around when that happened." At least Chris claimed he'd been in the Bay Area, but it suddenly dawned on me that he could be lying. After all, he was the one person who knew exactly where I kept that extra set of keys.

But I didn't want to think about that just now. The important thing was to get Chris back to Alpine. At Carla's desk, Vida was on line three, calling the ski lodge. She gave me a frantic nod and mouthed the single syllable, Tom.

"A friend of mine is coming to Seattle this morning," I told Chris, then went into details about the location of the county courthouse. Chris should plan on meeting Tom there at two o'clock. He would recognize him because I'd have him bring along a copy of last week's *Advocate*. "Where are you now?" I inquired, fearful that the rendezvous would never come off.

"The bus depot. I just got in." Chris was beginning to sound nervous.

With more admonitions to be sure to meet Tom, I finally hung up and pressed the button for line three. Tom was still distant, but he agreed to bring Chris back. "I assume I shouldn't tell him why I'm at the courthouse," Tom said in a formal voice.

Carla and Ed were coming through the door together. I tried to think of a way to ease the strain between Tom and me with most of my staff listening in. "By the way," I said to Tom, "Milo left right after you called, but his deputies stayed on to search my car. Gibb's killer drove it to Reiter."

Three faces registered surprise. But Tom's reaction was different. "Then I guess you really do like going it alone," he remarked. "I'll see you later."

Ed looked so downcast that I was sure the murders had hit him harder than I'd expected. But he had other matters on his mind. "I heard Safeway may be coming into town," he said morosely. "They want to build on the other side of the mall or maybe out by the golf course. God, what a mess that would be! Their media people like to use *color* inserts!" He made it sound as if their advertising department might ride into Alpine like the Four Horsemen of the Apocalypse.

Carla, of course, was much more upbeat. "Gee, I can't believe I missed more bodies! I knew I shouldn't have gone to Leavenworth for the weekend! But what a blast! I met this wonderful hunk who tried out for the Seahawks and he ..." Ginny Burmeister came into the office and Carla rattled on, driving me into my inner sanctum.

Five minutes later, Milo called to say that Dr. Starr had

confirmed that the remains from the mineshaft were those of Hector Ramirez. He had made only two visits to the dentist, both in 1975, after he'd chipped a tooth while working on the Pine Street L.I.D. project. But that, coupled with the X-rays, was enough for identification. I relayed the news to my staff. Carla put on a tragic face, Ginny remarked that violence was often triggered by untidiness, and Ed complained that dentists overcharged. Vida, however, grew thoughtful.

"Did they find a bullet yet?"

"Not that I know of," I said. "Milo would have told us, wouldn't he?"

Vida gave me an enigmatic look. "Maybe."

Thanks to the time I'd put in over the weekend, we had the paper well in hand by noon. Since there still might be late-breaking developments, I wasn't ready to call it a day. At ten after one, Tom phoned from Seattle. Vida and I were alone in the news office, with Carla out to lunch in more ways than one, Ed supposedly getting an ad from Stuart's Stereo, and Ginny paying bills in the front office.

Tom's voice sounded considerably warmer. I gestured for Vida to pick up her phone, too. He might as well relay any information he had found to both of us. "I hit pay dirt," he announced. "It took awhile, because there was nothing for August twenty-one, 1971. But I went through the whole month, then back into July. Here, I'll read from the copy I made." I held my breath; Vida's tongue plied her upper lip. " 'Born July twenty-one, 1971, Baby Boy Pratt, to Phoebe Phipps Pratt and Constantine Nikinos Doukas.' "

Vida put her hand over the receiver. "Neeny!" she gasped.

I could hear, if not see, Tom's grin of triumph. "Well, Emma? Is that what you wanted?"

I laughed. "I don't know what I wanted. But it fits. Phoebe had Neeny's baby and gave it up to Margaret and Hector. No wonder she wrote Chris that letter! Wow!"

Tom was chuckling, too. "I don't know how this fits in

with the murders, but we can sort that out when I get back. I'm going to get a sandwich and then wait for Chris." He paused, then lowered his voice. "Emma, I'm sorry I got upset about you and Milo. I never really believed you were sleeping with him. It's just that I thought if you were scared or didn't want to stay alone, you might have asked me to . . . oh, hell, Emma, we'll talk about it later. And Adam, too. See you."

I gripped the receiver tight and dared to dart a look at Vida. She was putting her own phone down and gazing straight ahead. "I wonder who handled the adoption," she said in an ordinary voice. "A Seattle attorney, I suppose."

I knew I was blushing like mad. "Margaret and Hector probably didn't get Chris until he was a month old. That's why the announcement gave his birthday as August instead of July."

"Lucky for Phoebe that the Ramirezes wanted him." She finally turned back in my direction. "No wonder he looks like a Doukas." She rummaged in her tote bag. "My, my, I seem to have forgotten my cottage cheese and carrot sticks. Want to go get a burger?"

I stood up. "Why not?" What I wanted most was to hug Vida.

Heather Bardeen and Chaz Phipps were just leaving when we got to the Burger Barn. Vida jabbed me with an elbow and then made her move, blocking the young women's exit.

"We need to have a word with you," she said in an imperious manner. "Where were you sitting?"

Despite their startled expressions, Heather and Chaz didn't argue but led us to a booth at the rear of the restaurant. The waitress, who wasn't Kimberly this time, was already clearing off the table. She pocketed her tip and left us in peace.

"This will be quick," said Vida, fixing her gaze on Heather. "If the sheriff asks you—and he probably will—

can you tell him where Simon Doukas was last Wednesday night between eight-thirty and nine-thirty?"

Heather drew back against the booth's plastic maroon upholstery. "What a dumb question! Even if I could tell the sheriff, why would I tell *you*?"

Vida was unperturbed. "Because the sheriff will tell us anyway." She glanced at me from under the brim of her veiled green fedora. "We have a deadline, you see." Clearly, Vida was counting on Heather's lack of curiosity as to how our journalistic endeavor might be tied to Milo Dodge's interrogation.

But Heather was on her feet, pulling Chaz along with her. "I don't give a rat's ass about your deadline. If you want to find out where Simon Doukas and I were Wednesday night, you'll have to hear it from the sheriff." She gave Vida a nasty look, ignored me, and hauled Chaz out of the booth.

"Well," said Vida, picking up a menu, "that takes care of that. Heather certainly gets around. But it doesn't let Simon off the hook as far as the murder is concerned."

"Vida," I said, motioning to the waitress, "you don't think Simon would kill his own son, do you?" I couldn't believe it of Cecelia, whom I rather liked; neither could I believe it of the less likable Simon.

"Stranger things have happened," murmured Vida in her cryptic manner. She threw down the menu and looked up at the waitress. "Oh, why bother with all those decisions about calories and fat and cholesterol? I'll have the bacon burger, fries, a small salad, and one of those pineapple malts. I hope the pineapple chunks aren't so big they plug up the straw this time."

Privacy wasn't ensured by the booth in which we sat, so Vida and I spoke of the case in whispers, pooling our information and drawing certain conclusions. It was, we agreed, possible that Hector, Mark, and Gibb had been killed by the same person. With Hector, it would be almost impossible after fourteen years to establish alibis—or the lack of them. Even Vida, with her encyclopedic memory, wasn't precisely sure when Hector had disappeared.

"Only Margaret would have been likely to remember the date," she said, dumping large pools of catsup on her fries. "A pity she's dead. Chris would have been too young to recall much."

Briefly, I thought about the note Chris had left for me at the motel. He had mentioned memories. Was his father's—or adoptive father's—disappearance one of them? Could we assume that Neeny was Chris's real father? Vida felt we could, since she asserted that Phoebe had been carrying on with Neeny long before the boy's birth.

"Nobody has an alibi," I said once more for the record. "The real problem is that nobody has a motive, at least not for killing Mark."

Vida wagged a finger at me. "Not true," she said around a mouthful of bacon burger. "Hector's killer had a motive if Mark had found the remains."

I didn't agree. "Hector's killer had no reason to think that finding a bunch of bones could trigger a fourteen-year-old murder investigation."

Under the brim of her green hat, Vida's expression wavered, but she wasn't quite ready to throw in the towel. "There's *got* to be a connection. Oh, I know, I know," she insisted, waving her fork and sending lettuce in the direction of the two men across the aisle. "You said you thought Phoebe had seen Mark the night he was killed." She swirled more lettuce around in her little plastic bowl. "Would he have come to tell Neeny about finding those remains?" As usual, Vida could best answer her own questions. "I think he would, they were on Neeny's property. Maybe he told Phoebe. It would be just like Mark to try to get a rise out of her with a ghoulish story—and for some reason, she didn't want Neeny to know."

"His health?" I suggested.

Vida gave an absent nod. "That would be my guess. So she put him off. And then went haring off to see Simon.

Why?" This time she had no answer. "We're missing something. Tommy thinks so, too."

Tommy. I refrained from giving Vida a look of reproach. "I wish he'd get back with Chris. My biggest fear is that Chris won't show."

"It's possible." Vida assaulted her malted milk, a noisy business at best. "Don't start worrying until after four. It's going to take them awhile to get to Alpine, especially if Tommy has to meet with those people he mentioned."

It was now almost two o'clock. I suggested that we get my car and go see if the mail had come to my home. When we arrived, there was a notice saying that since nobody was home, there would be a parcel from Honolulu waiting at the post office after five P.M. Vida and I decided it would be easier to chase down the mail truck. We found it at Fifth & Cascade, across from the middle school. Naturally, the driver was a Runkel once or twice removed.

We opened the package inside the car, just as the first contingent of prepubescent students charged out of the school. There was Chris's denim jacket and several piles of correspondence, mostly addressed to Margaret Ramirez. Judging from a cursory look at their varying rates of postage, they went back several years. The letter from Phoebe to Mark was on top.

Vida all but ripped it out of my hand. "You've heard it already," she said, whisking Phoebe's eggshell stationery from its matching envelope. Swiftly, Vida scanned the two handwritten pages. "Hrmph. If I didn't know that Phoebe is probably the poor boy's mother, I'd have lost my lunch." Thoughtfully, she refolded the letter and handed it to me. "Why did she write that, I wonder?"

I was about to speculate when Vida slapped at the dashboard. "Let's go ask her. Now."

"But Vida," I protested, "we've still got some last-minute details with the paper."

"So we work late. Let's go. To Neeny's," she added, sitting back and bracing herself as if she expected me to take off at ninety miles an hour.

I didn't think this was the best idea Vida had entertained lately, but if Phoebe and Neeny were about to leave for Palm Springs, this might be our only chance to talk to either of them for a long time.

Frieda Wunderlich, looking as sour as a leftover lemon, greeted us at the door. "The Queen Bee isn't here and Himself went to get a tune-up from Doc Dewey. You want them to call you before they take off?" She didn't wait for an answer, however, but shook her gray head. "Going to the *desert*! Can you imagine anybody leaving beautiful country like this to go look at *nothing*?"

"With Phoebe around, Neeny's always looking at nothing as far as I'm concerned," retorted Vida. "Where is the old cow?"

Frieda screwed up her homely face, reminding me of a gargoyle. "She's over at her own place, packing. I heard—not that I'd ask—she's putting it up for sale." Her inverted eyebrows lifted like a pair of apostrophes.

"How much?" asked Vida, getting right to the point.

Frieda leaned forward; the two women huddled like a couple of drug dealers on a street corner. "Eighty-five," said Frieda.

"Ridiculous!" snorted Vida.

"Lucky to get sixty," agreed Frieda.

They were probably right. Phoebe's post–World War II rambler needed paint, and the garden showed neglect. A few scraggly dahlias leaned against a fence with several missing pickets. Under a sparse rhododendron, a little stone gnome was covered with moss. The house's location wasn't noteworthy, either, just one block off Front Street, facing the rear of the Lumberjack Motel.

A frazzled Phoebe Pratt Doukas met us at the door. "Oh—what a surprise!" Her face indicated it wasn't a pleasant one. "I'm just packing a few things. My niece, Chaz, is going to take care of the rest while I'm gone. Oh!" She fluttered about in the small entryway where several half-filled cartons, three suitcases, and an old gas bar-

becue reposed. "Come in, sit down—if you can find a
spot." She sounded dubious.

The living room was also littered with cartons, mostly
empty, and there were piles of clothes on virtually every
piece of furniture. "I'll never get everything done in the
next three hours," Phoebe declared, making a valiant effort
at freeing up the Naugahyde sofa. Dust was thick on the
few surfaces showing, the windows were smudged with
dirt, and—as Vida had said—the curtains looked as if they
hadn't been washed in years. The room had a musty smell,
and the jade plant on the fireplace hearth looked dead as
a dodo. It was obvious that Phoebe spent very little time
in the home she had made with the late Clinton Pratt.

On the drive to Neeny's, Vida and I had discussed the
best way to approach Phoebe about her illegitimate child.
I had suggested that Vida's blunderbuss tactics could back-
fire. To my surprise, she had agreed. Vida and Phoebe had
a history spanning almost sixty years, whereas I was only
a casual acquaintance. And, as I readily volunteered,
Phoebe and I had something in common: our bastard sons.

Consequently, as we tried to get comfortable on the sofa's sagging springs, I was horrified when Vida unleashed
her barrage:

"See here, Phoebe, we know you're Chris's mother and
Neeny is his father. The only thing we want to know is
why, out of the blue, you wrote him a letter a couple of
weeks ago."

Phoebe, who for once wasn't plastered with cosmetics,
went white, then red. She began to shake, while tears
welled up in her eyes. "Vida!" she gasped, staring at the
other woman as if she'd been betrayed to the Gestapo.
"Oh, Vida!"

"Oh, bother!" huffed Vida. "This is the 1990s, and
Emma's an unmarried mother, too. All we're trying to do
is figure out who killed Mark and Gibb and maybe Hector
Ramirez." She turned to me. "Where's that letter?"

I extracted it from my handbag. "It's a very nice letter,"

I said, hoping to keep Phoebe from having a stroke. "Chris never got it, though. My son forwarded it to me."

The tears were coursing down Phoebe's crimson cheeks. She wiped at them with the sleeve of her green print blouse and gazed at the streaked front window. "He was all alone," she said at last in a thin voice. "Margaret had been a good mother, despite what Neeny said. For all I know, Hector may have been a good father, given his . . . limitations." Her head bobbed this way and that, presumably in search of a Kleenex or a handkerchief. I offered her a little packet of tissues from my purse.

"Thank you." Phoebe gave me a grateful look. I figured we were bonding, in some odd, pathetic way. "At the time he was born, Margaret and Hector were living in Seattle. Clinton had been dead for over a year, so there was no way I could convince people the baby was his. I went to Seattle, too, and got an apartment on Capitol Hill. Doukums didn't know. It was better that way since his old-fashioned sense of gallantry might have forced him to make an honest woman of me. And a divorce would have killed Hazel. So I let him think I was trying out my wings as a widow." Her lips quivered in a little smile. "I could have simply put the baby up for adoption, but I knew Margaret and Hector wanted a child so much. They went to Simon and had him make the arrangements. Neeny always assumed the baby was theirs. It was quite clever." Now Phoebe was really smiling, the tears finally staunched.

"Did they pay for him?" Vida asked on a somewhat sour note.

"Oh, no!" Phoebe's hands were at her breast. "They had nothing of their own, poor things. And there I was, not quite as young as I used to be, proud to be bearing Doukas fruit!"

I didn't dare look at Vida. To her credit, she didn't say anything but allowed Phoebe to continue: "It was so much better than giving little Chris up to strangers. And until Margaret moved away, I got to see him now and then." She sighed, her hands tearing at the tissue I'd given her. "I was heartbroken after they went to Hawaii. When Margaret died, I thought of writing immediately. But I kept putting it off—I didn't know what to say." She made a gesture at the letter I was still holding. "Does he know the truth?" She finally gazed directly at us, her eyes showing both hope and fear.

"No," I said. "But he's supposed to be back in Alpine today."

Phoebe clutched at the neckline of her blouse. "Oh! Dear Chris! Poor Doukums! Is ignorance really bliss? What to do, what to do?"

"What *did* you do?" inquired Vida. "About your will, I mean. After you and Neeny got married, did you leave everything to him, or to Chris?"

Phoebe had recovered a little of her natural color, but now it drained away as if Vida had pulled a plug. Instead of tears, however, Phoebe resorted to anger. "Vida Blatt, you are the biggest snoop in Skykomish County! No wonder they used to call you Goose Neck in high school!"

Vida smirked. "They used to call you other things, Phoebe Vickers. Like Freebie."

I thought it best to intervene. "Excuse me," I said, leaning between the two women like a referee, "but Vida's question may be valid." I hated to say what was coming next, but it couldn't be avoided. "If you intended to leave your estate to Chris, it might have a bearing on the murder case."

Phoebe was still glaring at Vida. "Of course I left everything to Chris," she said in a voice still choked with anger. "After Doukums, of course. And a little something for Chaz."

Again, my question came with reluctance. "Is it enough to kill for?"

The rage was beginning to ebb as Phoebe considered her financial state. "Doukums settled three million dollars on me when we got married. Simon doesn't know—we had Doc Dewey's son-in-law in Seattle handle it. Then there's some stock. Doukums always believed in buying into companies right around here. He's a great booster for people getting started. Besides," she noted guilelessly, "he gets some bargains that way." She gave us a big-eyed stare. "You know—local businesses. Like Microsoft. Nordstrom. Boeing. He's done quite well."

It sure beat my one stock investment—which involved making cat food out of bottom fish. The Japanese had violated about six fishing treaties and wiped out the fledgling company, along with my $200 stake. That was the last time I ever listened to a tip from *The Oregonian*'s business editor.

Having made an attempt at composing herself, Phoebe got to her feet. "Really, I must get busy. Our plane leaves at nine, so we're heading for the airport about six." Suddenly, she was picking up piles of clothing and dumping them into the empty cartons. "There's nothing more I can tell you. I wish I could, but—"

"You might let us know why you went to see Simon Wednesday night," Vida said, still sitting on the sofa.

Phoebe came to a dead halt, a stack of shoe boxes in her arms. "Oh! That!" She gazed around the cluttered room as if she expected to see an answer written on the faded striped wallpaper. "It wasn't anything important. Just something about selling the house."

Vida slowly but emphatically shook her head, the fedora listing from side to side. "Phoebe, Phoebe, that's a parcel of pigeon poop! You wouldn't go out at nine o'clock to track down Simon in his office when you could call him on the phone. Besides," she went on, yanking her skirt down over two inches of slip, "you didn't decide to sell this place until the last couple of days. I'd bet my last dime on it."

Phoebe dropped the shoe boxes, scattering several wedgies, high heels, and a pair of golf shoes. "Get out." Her voice was cold, with all nuances of the aging coquette vanished. I was already standing, halfway between the sofa and the entryway. To my amazement, Vida also rose. The two women faced each other, the same age, the same height, the same small-town background. Yet for one fleeting moment, they were titanic, a pair of Olympian goddesses facing each other not over a pile of shoe boxes but a chasm of memory.

Vida was the first to speak. "You're a fool, Phoebe Pratt." She dropped her voice a notch. "But maybe you mean well." In a flurry of tweed, she whirled around and stomped out of the living room.

I hesitated just long enough to give Phoebe a faint smile. Then I followed Vida out of the house, past the red Lincoln Town Car, and through the overgrown garden with its drooping dahlias and the moss-covered gnome that winked goodbye.

Chapter Seventeen

KIP MACDUFF HAD AGREED to take the paper into Monroe in the morning. We were running thirty-two tight pages, at roughly a sixty-forty ad-to-editorial ratio. It wasn't a bad proportion, but seventy-thirty would have been a lot better. Still, this was one week when we needed the news space. Unfortunately.

I'd finished calling the printer in Monroe to request an extra two hundred papers when I realized it was almost five o'clock. Carla and Ginny had just left. Ed was on the phone, and Vida was opening the box from Adam.

"Maybe we should go through these old letters," she suggested.

I didn't have much enthusiasm for the enterprise. "Go ahead. Just give me Chris's jacket." I looked at my watch again. "Damn it, Tom and Chris should be here by now."

Ed had hung up and was hauling himself into his plaid polyester sports coat. "Wouldn't you know it? Barton's Bootery is having a pre-Halloween sale. They want a half-page ad next week with pictures of *real* shoes. That means I can't use clip art!" He shot a forlorn look at the dog-eared volume of ready-to-print drawings that were his standby. Mentally, I thanked my lucky stars and lack of budget that I hadn't yet taken the plunge for the clip art computer program that would have made Ed's life easier while eliminating all advertising creativity.

The telephone spared me having to soothe Ed. To my relief, it was Tom, calling from the ski lodge. Yes, he had brought Chris back. They were going to get a quick bite in the coffee shop, then Chris would stop by the office or my house, whichever was more convenient. I said I intended to head for home in about fifteen minutes.

I did, leaving Vida to mull over Margaret's correspondence and Ed to wander away in a burdened state. As I drove up the hill that led to my home on Fir Street, the autumn sun was beginning to dip over Stevens Pass and a few clouds were scattered above the mountains. It was a perfect fall evening, cold enough to bronze the trees, but not to freeze the flowers. Yet I felt as if Alpine had been touched by a killing frost. I was glad that Chris was back in Alpine, but I realized that his presence might put him in danger. Surely he couldn't know about his real parents or that Phoebe had named him as her heir. But how would Milo Dodge react? I wanted to avoid the sheriff and to keep Chris away from him, too. It was impossible, of course. There was no place to hide in Alpine.

I had changed into slacks and a sweater when Chris came to the front door. Tom's rental car was parked in the drive. Now attired in a San Francisco Giants cap and an Oakland A's sweatshirt from the 1989 World Series, Chris somehow looked older, almost weary. On impulse, I hugged him.

"I was sure you were lost somewhere in Disneyland," I said, stepping aside to usher him in. "Where's your chauffeur?"

Chris strolled across the living room to stand by the fire I'd touched off as soon as I got home. "He had to make some long distance calls, so he let me borrow his car." He paused, giving me a wry smile. "I did ask."

I smiled back. My brain was whirling. Should I tell Chris about his real parents? But that wasn't up to me, it was Phoebe's responsibility. Yet I knew she and Neeny were probably already on the road to the airport.

The phone rang and I started to answer it, then stopped. It might be Milo, inquiring after Chris. No doubt he'd been sighted by the locals. I decided to let the machine take the call. Whoever it was would assume I was out to dinner. The thought triggered some nagging idea, but it fluttered away before I could grasp it.

"Mrs. Lord," Chris began, pacing the length of the hearth in long, uncertain strides, "is that really my father you and Mr. Cavanaugh found in the mineshaft?"

I hedged a bit as far as the definition of *father* was concerned. "Dr. Starr's dental records confirm that the remains belonged to Hector Ramirez." I sounded very formal.

Chris nodded once. "Okay." He stopped to finger the fireplace tools. "This is so crazy. . . ." His face crumpled, and for a moment, I thought he was going to cry. "You see," he said with a gulp, "I've been trying to remember things. I wrote that note, telling you how coming back to Alpine was such a bummer." He turned away, staring blindly at the mantel. "Could we drive up to the mineshaft?"

"Sure." I went to the front closet to get a jacket, then remembered to give Chris the one Adam had sent from Honolulu. I didn't know if we were making a pilgrimage to Icicle Creek or taking an exercise in memory. I thought it best not to ask.

The denim jacket brought a genuine smile to Chris's face. "Hey—that was nice of Adam to send this. He's a cool dude." Chris gave a little chuckle as we went out the door. "It's weird, but that Mr. Cavanaugh reminds me of Adam somehow. He's pretty cool, too."

"I like being around cool people," I remarked, unable to look Chris in the eye. Five minutes later we were turning off CR 187 at Icicle Creek. There was only one light burning in Neeny Doukas's house on First Hill as we drove by. The newlyweds were probably halfway to Monroe. It was getting dark, with only the sound of the creek breaking the evening silence.

Chris and I walked wordlessly up to Mineshaft Number Three. I'd brought along a flashlight. We could see the crime scene tape, now extended up the hill to the second entrance. Chris followed my lead, then stood staring down at the hole in the ground where Hector Ramirez's remains had been found. The excavation was much deeper than when I'd seen it the previous afternoon. I wondered if Milo and his deputies had uncovered any more evidence, such as a bullet.

"He was shot," Chris said, startling me with the baldness of his statement.

"How do you know?" I asked in a breathless voice.

Chris was staring at the deep hole that had been Hector Ramirez's grave. He was silent for so long that I wondered if he were praying. "I was there. *Here*," he added, making a sharp gesture.

"You saw Hector get shot?" I was so surprised that I almost stumbled over a root.

With his profile outlined by my flashlight, Chris stared straight ahead. "I remember it. For so long, I couldn't. But I do now." He sucked in his breath and bit his lip. "It was real grim. I never told my mom."

The flashlight wavered in my hand. "Did you tell anyone?" I asked, the horror of Chris's revelation sinking in.

Slowly, Chris shook his head. "I couldn't. And then . . ." He turned to face me, his features lost in the shadows. "I didn't remember anymore. Not until I came back to Alpine."

Frantically, I tried to think of words that might console Chris. It didn't matter that he really wasn't Hector's son— the slain man had been the only father Chris had known, just as Margaret had been his only mother. Feeling helpless, I watched Chris button up his denim jacket, then shove his hands in his pockets. He didn't weep. No doubt he'd shed all his tears a long time ago.

Except for the tumbling creek and the wind in the trees, it was too quiet. I wanted to get away from Mineshaft Number Three, to head into town with warm lights glowing from behind homely little windows. Tentatively, I put my hand on Chris's arm.

"Let's go back to the house," I said gently. "We can talk about it there. If you want to."

Chris looked down at me with sad dark eyes. "I have to, don't I?"

I wasn't sure what he meant. "You mean for your own sake? Or to tell the sheriff?"

"Both." He set his jaw, lifted his chin, and for the first time, I could see not just Mark, but Neeny, and Simon, too. We were still standing by the mineshaft, with the darkness enfolding us. My flashlight made a small circle of pale gold light on the forest floor. Chris was staring off into the trees again, shaking his head. "That's the part that mixed me up at the time. I thought my dad deserved to get shot. So I made myself not remember."

I tugged at his arm. "What are you talking about? What was he doing?"

Chris's gaze returned to rest on my anxious face. "He wasn't doing anything, except maybe talking or arguing. We lived on Eighth Avenue, before it turns off onto that road out there." He gestured with his free hand. "It was a little house by the golf course, but it's been torn down for a new development. That's why I couldn't find it the night I went driving around. We'd just finished dinner and somebody called my dad."

"Do you know who it was?" I asked, and that nagging little idea fretted at my brain. Dinner. Phone calls. Icicle Creek. But I couldn't get distracted.

"My dad didn't say who phoned. He went out, and I thought he was walking up to Neeny's, so I followed him. It was getting dark—I think it was spring, I know it was warm—but he came this way instead of going up my grandfather's driveway. I saw somebody else by the mineshaft, so I hid in the brush by the creek." At last, he freed his arm from my grasp and passed a hand over his dark hair. "The creek made a lot of noise, so I couldn't hear what they were saying. Then there was a shot, and my dad fell on the ground. I yelled and ran off." He paused, worrying his lower lip. "I don't know where I ran. I don't remember anything until my mother took me to Hawaii."

I was incredulous. "You don't remember the search for your father?"

"Not really. Maybe I thought he was still alive. Or maybe it was better if nobody knew he was dead." He gave me a pitiful look. "Like I said, I thought he deserved it. A kid's mind operates in black and white, I guess. There are good guys, and there are bad guys."

Somehow, in my shock at learning that Chris had seen Hector murdered, it didn't quite dawn on me that he would also know who had fired the fatal shot. Chris had been so young. The killer might have been a stranger, or someone who no longer lived in Alpine. Whoever it was would look far different to a young man of twenty than to a child of six.

"Who?" I asked, though I believed I knew. Unbidden, the nagging little fragment had clicked into place.

The car that had approached so quietly had not used lights. Its arrival was heralded by a soft thud, as if a bumper had made contact with a tree. As my Jag had done, I thought dully. Chris heard the noise, too, followed by the click of the car's door. Then a big flashlight switched on, momentarily blinding us.

I saw the white Cadillac's outline before I saw its owner's face. Steeling myself, I attempted a smile. "Hi, Eeeny, are we having a party?"

"Emma, *cara*," came the ex-sheriff's voice. His heartiness rang false. "Sure, why not? You, too, Chris? You like to party?"

I heard the catch in Chris's throat. Instinctively, I moved a couple of inches closer to him, as if I could shield him from his father's killer. From Mark's. And Gibb's. But Chris had been shielded too long, especially by himself. I saw the gun, a standard .38 service model, in Eeeny's hand.

"That's good," said Eeeny, his voice like olive oil. "You stand together. I can see you just fine, this close." He raised the gun, pointing it at me. "You tried to stop him from running away. He shot you. Then he saw there was

nowhere to run because I come along. So he shoots himself." Eeeny shook his head. "Sad. Very sad."

Next to me, I felt Chris tense. Would he, could he
spring at Eeeny? But the ex-sheriff was still quick on his
feet. I tried to think of words that would buy us time.
"Milo will figure it out, Eeeny. You made one very bad
mistake."

"Like what, *cara*?" He didn't sound as if he believed
me.

"You said Mark called you Wednesday night before
eight o'clock. He couldn't have. You were at the Venison
Inn, remember?" My mouth was dry; the words sounded
unnatural.

He gave a little grunt of a laugh. "No. And neither will
Milo, when you're not around to remind him." Eeeny
peered through his glasses down the end of the barrel.
"He's a nice kid, but not so smart. He'll get his speeders
and his shoplifters, though. Some day his pension." In the
artificial light, his smile was grotesque. "No pension for
you two, though." His finger squeezed the trigger, and I let
out a shrill cry.

The voice that boomed through the night startled the
birds from the trees and the animals from their lairs:
"Drop that gun—you're covered from all sides! Now!" A
great rustling followed, with twigs snapping and branches
crackling. Eeeny Moroni hesitated just long enough for me
to throw my flashlight at him while Chris leaped at the
hand that held the .38. I missed Eeeny but hit his glasses.
They fell to the ground, even as he and Chris struggled.
Chris had youth on his side, but Eeeny was strong as a
bull. Frantically, I looked around for the source of all the
commotion. Surely Milo and his deputies were just inches
away from rescuing us. But the figure emerging through
the trees was alone, carrying a megaphone—and a gun. It
was Vida, and for once, she was hatless.

"I said drop it!" she yelled, jabbing her weapon into
Eeeny's thick neck. Chris jumped back; Eeeny cursed but
complied.

"You old bitch!" he screamed at Vida, trying to writhe away from her.

"Oh, shut up, Eeeny!" Vida jammed the gun even deeper against Moroni's flesh. "I suppose you don't think I'd shoot you. Well, you're wrong. I think you're the most horrid man I ever met."

Dimly, I heard sirens. Chris was flexing his fingers, apparently injured while wrestling with Eeeny. I turned to him and asked the inevitable question: "Was it Sheriff Moroni who shot your father?"

"Yeah." He was breathing hard, staring at Eeeny with loathing. "That's what mixed me up. I thought my dad must be a criminal. Sheriffs are supposed to be the good guys, right?"

I gave Eeeny a disgusted look. "Right. But not this one."

Milo Dodge, Bill Blatt, and all the other deputies poured out of two sheriff's cars, guns at the ready. Eeeny seemed to shrivel with every step taken by his former comrades. I half expected him to turn into Rigoletto and announce that he was accursed.

Vida finally withdrew her weapon and all but recoiled from Eeeny. She turned not to Milo, but to Billy. "What took you so long?" she asked her nephew crossly. "I've been here for ages, tramping about in the dark like a mole. I even lost my favorite mauve pillbox."

Billy Blatt automatically removed his hat. "Well, you see, Aunt Vida, we had to rendezvous and make sure our guns were ready to fire and that we had a warrant and—"

"Oh, hush!" With her flatfooted walk, Vida headed back toward the road. I followed her, with Chris at my side. As a journalist, I should have stayed glued to Milo and Eeeny, but the arrest of one sheriff by another was not a pretty sight. Besides, I had more than enough news to fill up the extra inches.

"What on earth made you come here and bring the sheriff?" I asked, catching up with Vida at the edge of the road.

Vida gave me an impatient look. "Those letters, to Margaret. Half of them were full of mush from Eeeny. He was in love with her, too. But then I always said most of the men in Alpine were." She sighed. "I just didn't figure Eeeny was one of them. The old fool." She palmed her gun and waved the megaphone. "My car's parked in Neeny's driveway. We'd better get back to the office and get this story out."

"Wait a minute." I grabbed her sleeve. "Where did you get a gun?"

"What?" Vida looked blankly from behind her glasses. "Oh!" She held out her hand.

In it was Roger's water pistol.

The paper was put to bed, but the rest of us were still wide awake. Vida, Milo, Tom, and I were in the news office, drinking brandy out of paper cups and going over the extraordinary events of the past few hours. It was almost midnight. Milo had arrived only a few minutes earlier, looking exhausted. He was already into his second brandy.

"Where's Chris?" he asked, peering around as if he expected the young man to leap out of Ed Bronsky's desk drawer.

"I dropped him off at Jennifer and Kent's," I said. "What happens next is up to the family. He *is* a Doukas, after all."

Milo leaned back in Ed's chair and put his feet up on the desk. "I'm glad we caught Neeny and Phoebe at the airport. They're spending the night at a hotel and driving back in the morning. Neeny can't believe his old pal is guilty, but Phoebe will convince him." He laughed into his paper cup. "Damn, she thought Neeny killed Hector. When Mark came up to the house, he told her about digging up a body. He saw that medal, too, and remembered that Hector wore one like it. Phoebe wouldn't let Mark see his grandfather and she sent him away—to get killed, as it turned out. But she was in a stew, figuring that Neeny would have been the most likely person to have murdered

Hector. She went to see Simon, but she couldn't find him because he was out screwing Heather Bardeen." Milo laughed some more.

"Poor Cece," said Vida. "She'd better settle his hash, quick." The look she transmitted through her glasses should have melted the frames.

Tom was tapping a pencil on Carla's desk. "Jealousy and fear." He shook his head. "Ugly motives, when you think about it. Did Eeeny really think Margaret would marry him with Hector out of the way?" The question, as usual, was for Vida.

"How would I know, Tommy?" she replied. "He was certainly crazy about her. He didn't stop writing those letters until the postage rate went up to twenty-two cents. The sad thing is that he thought he had to kill again. Twice."

It occurred to me that I hadn't eaten since lunch. Along with that startling insight came another, one I'd been harboring ever since Chris Ramirez had walked in my door seven nights earlier. "The first one was the wrong person." I saw three stunned faces and clarified my statement. "With Mark, I mean. Eeeny thought it was Chris."

"Hey, Emma . . ." Milo began.

"Now, Emma," said Tom.

"Of course, Emma!" cried Vida. "Eeeny was blind as a bat! Mark was wearing Chris's cap and jacket!"

I nodded. "And they looked so much alike." I gave a little shake of my head. "Chris was really Mark's uncle, not his cousin. No wonder Simon cried when he saw Chris. He knew he was looking at his brother. I wonder how the Doukases will sort all that out?"

"Oh, they will, they will, knowing Neeny," said Vida impatiently. "But why kill Chris? Because he'd seen Eeeny shoot Hector?"

"Sure," I replied. "The return of Chris Ramirez spelled terrible trouble for Eeeny Moroni. The six-year-old boy who ran and hid was far different—and much less dangerous—than the twenty-year-old young man. You

see," I said, leaning on Carla's desk where I sat next to
Tom, "Eeeny never got a phone call from Mark. But he
left a note on my door for Chris. It blew away. Chris never
saw it. I don't know if he signed it *Eeeny* or *Neeny*. That
doesn't matter. It was a ploy to get Chris up to the
mineshaft. But of course Chris never went. Mark did, because he'd found Hector's remains. Maybe he actually told
Eeeny—or Eeeny guessed. That in itself was no serious
problem, but coupled with Chris's arrival, it spelled trouble. But when Eeeny went to meet Chris, there was Mark,
waiting for Milo—and wearing Chris's clothes. Eeeny may
have used Mark's crowbar or one of his own, but he was
light on his feet, and he probably sneaked up from behind.
I suspect Eeeny swung first and discovered later he'd gotten the wrong Doukas. But it was easy to say he'd been
called up there and found Mark already dead." I lifted my
hands like a conjurer. Brandy on an empty stomach had
magical effects.

Vida was nodding. "Yes, yes, then Gibb shot his face
off—as usual—about the second mineshaft opening, so
Eeeny had to lure him out of town, down to Reiter to
watch the salmon come upstream or some such blarney,
and then shoot him." She gazed at Milo. "Well?"

He gave her an off-center grin. "Same caliber bullet
killed Gibb, killed Hector. We found the old casing in the
dirt late yesterday afternoon. Fourteen years apart, but I'll
bet they were both fired from Eeeny's .38."

"No wonder," said Vida, "that Eeeny didn't want Chris
brought back to town, Milo. The farther away from Alpine, the better."

Milo turned solemn. "Damn. Eeeny was a good sheriff.
He had a fine reputation around the state." Slowly, he
swirled the brandy in his paper cup. "I might never have
gone into law enforcement if it hadn't been for him. He set
a hell of an example."

"Of what?" snapped Vida. "Homicidal mania? Honestly,
Milo, if you ever grow up, you'll turn into an old fool,

too!" She yanked off her glasses and rubbed her eyes with a vengeance.

Next to me, Tom was on his feet. "It's late, and I've got a plane to catch in the morning." He looked down at me. "Emma, I've got a lot of background for you at the lodge. Some suggestions, economic indicators, an overview and so on. I'll have Heather bring it by tomorrow."

I stood up, not too steadily. "You're leaving?"

He smiled. "You know what they say in news stories: personal reasons." Taking his navy blue blazer off the back of Carla's chair, he threw it over his shoulder. "Congratulations to all of you." The smile turned into a grin for me. "You not only caught a killer, but you got a terrific story. That should up circulation for a couple of weeks anyway." He paused to shake Milo's hand and give Vida a kiss on the cheek. I followed him out to his rental car, the brandy buffeting me against the cold night air.

"Tom . . ." I began, not certain of what I should say.

"Sandra took a jade penguin from Gump's this afternoon. It was worth eleven thousand dollars. She dropped it running up California Avenue." He looked less alarmed than bemused.

"Oh!" I felt terrible for him. I laughed. "Oh, Tom . . ."

He leaned down and kissed me, briefly, firmly. Then he turned away and looked over the top of his car, past the low-lying rooftops of Alpine, beyond the dense cluster of evergreens, up to the dark outline of Baldy with the moonlight bathing its contours. "You don't really need me, you know." He spoke so softly that I wasn't sure of his words.

My voice came out in a bit of a squeak. "I'm not the greatest publisher in the world."

He was still looking at Baldy. "I like this town." At last, he turned back to me. "Is it all right if I come back some day?"

I gave him a crooked smile. "Sure. Just don't wait twenty years."

"No," he said, opening the car door. "I don't want to

meet my son for the first time when he's middle-aged. Men get funny about that time."

"So," I said, "do women."

I watched the red taillights until they turned off on Alpine Way.

Kip MacDuff had driven the paper into Monroe. Vida was interviewing the mother of the bride about an upcoming wedding. Ed Bronsky was trying not to sell an ad to Stella's Styling Salon.

And Carla was chin-deep in reviewing the triple murder story. "I can't stand it!" she shrieked. "I didn't get to write a word about all these horrible things! Can I do the follow-up?"

"I tell you what," I said, stopping in the middle of the news office to take a handful of phone messages from Ginny Burmeister, "you can interview Chris Ramirez about his future plans. When he has some." For all I knew, Chris would be heading back to Hawaii in the next twenty-four hours. Unless, of course, Phoebe told Neeny Doukas the truth and he acknowledged the young man as his son.

Vida had put the phone down and was looking at me over the rims of her glasses. "She spelled it Al and Son."

"Who did what?" I tried to ignore Ed, who was telling Stella that he could solve all her problems with clip art.

"The mother of the bride," said Vida, shaking her head. "She submitted a description of her daughter's gown and spelled the lace on it as . . ."

"Oh," I said. "Alençon." That sort of thing happened a lot in Alpine.

"Exactly." Vida swiveled in her chair and began pounding her typewriter.

I paused in the doorway of my office to survey my domain: Ed was still on the phone, Carla and Ginny were arguing about the minutes of the county commissioners' meeting, and somewhere down the highway, the latest edition of *The Alpine Advocate* was going to press. Neeny

Doukas and Simon and Fuzzy Baugh and maybe a lot of other people might not like what they were going to read, but truth has a way of triumphing over human beings' petty emotions. Usually.

I smiled to myself. Another week, another paper. We were still in business. It was always a relief to make a deadline. And I'd done it on my own.

I strolled over to my desk. Something was not quite right. I looked around the crowded, cluttered office. Adam's picture was gone from the filing cabinet.

Maybe there are some things we can't do on our own.

THE
ALPINE
BETRAYAL

Chapter One

I WOULDN'T SET foot in Mugs Ahoy unless it was a matter of life and death. But finding my so-called advertising manager, Ed Bronsky, came close.

Ed is not given to hanging out in bars. Strong drink has a way of cheering him up—and Ed prefers walking on the gloomy side of life. But I knew he had to clear an ad for Mugs Ahoy's promotional tie-in with Alpine's Loggerama Days. Deadline was upon us, and so were the media representatives from the new Safeway that was opening west of the shopping mall. Ed had stood up the reps, and as editor and publisher of *The Alpine Advocate*, I had a right to be annoyed. I left the Safeway people in the capable hands of our office manager, Ginny Burmeister, while I ran the full block up to Pine Street to haul Ed back to the newspaper.

If they ever sweep the floor at Mugs Ahoy, they'll probably find a couple of patrons who have been lying there since the first Loggerama in 1946. The tavern is littered with bottle caps, peanut shells, cigarette butts, and crumpled napkins. At high noon on a summer day, the place is mercifully dark. No wonder the dart board with the curling edges looks otherwise unused; between the murky light and the bleary eyes, I doubt that most patrons can find it.

Ed was at the bar, drinking coffee and exchanging glum comments with the owner, Abe Loomis. A half-dozen other customers were hoisting glasses of beer and watching a soap opera. Their faces looked jaundiced; the air smelled stale. I began to feel as depressed as Ed.

Across the bar, Abe Loomis nudged Ed and nodded at

me. "Mrs. Lord. The boss." He mouthed the words, and looked as if he were announcing somebody's imminent death.

Ed swiveled his bulk slowly on the stool and peered at me through the gloom. "Hi, Emma. Can I buy you a cup of coffee?"

Ed's about as wide as he is square, but even sitting down he's taller than I am, and he weighs twice as much. As ever, when I upbraid my lugubrious ad manager, I feel like a gnat attacking a hippopotamus. This time around, I also felt a little foolish, since everyone in the tavern had turned curious, if befuddled, eyes away from the TV and onto me. After two years of small-town life, I'm getting used to being observed at close quarters.

"Ed," I began, trying to keep the exasperation out of my voice, "the Safeway reps are—"

Ed didn't exactly spring from the bar stool, but he landed with a thud that made the ancient floorboards creak. "Damn," he breathed, brushing crumbs off his plaid sport jacket, "I forgot! Sorry, Emma. I'll run right over there." He started to lumber toward the door, but stopped midway and turned back. "You don't suppose they want *color*, do you?" He asked the question as if it were immoral. Before I could answer, he waved a pudgy hand at Abe Loomis. "Oh, go ahead and check out that ad for Abe, will you? I didn't quite get around to it." Ed Bronsky creaked and squeaked his way out of Mugs Ahoy.

Gingerly, I sat down on the bar stool next to the one Ed had vacated. "Okay, Abe," I sighed, "let me have a look." Ed wasn't merely lazy, he seemed to have an aversion to selling advertising. If he hadn't been employed long before my tenure as owner of *The Advocate*, I would have gotten rid of him—or so I often told myself. The truth was I didn't have the heart to fire him.

Abe Loomis, a skinny man with deep-set eyes of no particular color, reached under the bar and produced a mock-up, two columns by six inches deep, featuring a busty blonde from Ed's clip art files. I winced at the illustration, then tried to concentrate on the copy.

Mugs Ahoy
proudly presents its
First Annual Boom & Bust
Wet T-shirt Contest and Chug-A-Lug Night
In honor of Alpine's Loggerama Days
Friday, July 31
Come meet Alpine's most up-front females!
Cheer them on with your favorite brew!
Listen up as a titter runs through the crowd!
Make this year's Loggerama a week to remember!

I'm all for equal rights, though I consider myself more of a humanist than a feminist. However, I am definitely a supporter of good taste. Even though Alpine may not be Seattle, and the First Amendment gives Abe the right to say what he wishes, I had to balk.

"Uh, Abe . . ." I pointed to the ad, careful not to let it get doused with coffee, beer, or God only knew what other liquid that might be stagnating on the bar at Mugs Ahoy. "I think this needs a little work."

Abe's eyes seemed to sink even deeper into his skull. "Like what?" he asked in a surprised voice.

"Like shorter," I suggested. "Or maybe more informative. Here, let's take out a couple of lines and put in something about the contest itself." I gave Abe what I hoped was an engaging smile. "Eligibility, for instance."

"You mean measurements?" inquired Abe, emptying Ed's coffee mug onto what appeared to be the floor.

I tried to avoid gnashing my teeth. "I was thinking more of age, maybe geography. You know, if they have to live within the city limits."

Abe furrowed his long forehead at the mock-up. For the next ten minutes, we rewrote the ad. He surrendered the two most offensive lines, while I let the artwork pass. As long as there were wet T-shirts and women willing to fill them, there really wasn't any other way to picture the contest.

"It should be a big year for Alpine," he said when we'd finally come to an agreement. "Especially with Dani Marsh coming back to be Loggerama queen and ride the donkey engine in the parade down Front Street."

"Right," I said, tucking the ad under my arm and slipping off the stool. "It was lucky for Alpine that her new movie is being shot on location at Mount Baldy."

"Lucky, my butt!" The hoarse female voice shot out of a darkened corner near the ancient jukebox. I turned, trying to recognize the figure sitting at the small round table. Although Alpine is made up of only four thousand persons and my job brings me into contact with the public, I still don't know half the population on sight. Abe, however, has owned Mugs Ahoy for over twenty years. He gazed at the woman with the indulgent expression typical of his trade.

"Aw, Patti, don't be so hard on the kid. She's made a name for herself, put Alpine on the map in Hollywood. You know darned well you'll be glad to see your daughter when she gets here."

"You're full of it, Abe," retorted Patti, shaking off the restraining effort of her companion, a lean, sinewy man in a red plaid flannel shirt. "I never want to see the little tramp again." She stubbed out her cigarette and got to her feet. "Come on, Jack, let's get out of here."

Patti and a man I recognized as owning a logging company, but whose full name eluded me, stalked out of the tavern. The remaining customers watched with interest while Abe made a pass at the bar with a dishrag.

I took a couple of steps back toward Abe. "That's Dani's mother?"

Abe looked up, grimacing. "Patti and Dani never got along. Patti thought Dani was a wild one." He rubbed his long jaw. "Case of heredity, if you ask me."

My cotton blouse was beginning to stick to my skin; it hadn't rained in over a month. Even the beer out of the tap looked warm. I needed to get outside. "Thanks, Abe," I said, waving the mock-up of his ad.

"Sure." He nodded absently, then lifted his head. "Say— who's your entry?"

I stopped on the threshold. "For what?"

He pointed to the banner that drooped over the bar. "The wet T-shirt contest. Most of the merchants are finding somebody to wear a shirt with their business' name on it. Then the girls can ride in the parade. Who you got from the paper?"

I made a real effort not to burst out laughing. The contest was serious business to Abe Loomis. My regular staff consisted of Ed Bronsky; Ginny Burmeister; Vida Runkel, the House and Home editor; and Carla Steinmetz, my solitary reporter. The idea of any of *The Advocate*'s female staff taking part in a wet T-shirt contest was laughable. Except maybe for Carla. It was hard to tell what Carla would do, except that she'd probably get it wrong the first time.

"I'll see," I said, trying to keep a straight face. "Maybe I'll ask Vida."

I'd expected Abe to guffaw at the image of my strapping sixtyish House and Home editor posing in a wet T-shirt, but Abe merely inclined his head. "She's a buxom one, all right."

"Right," I said, suddenly a little breathless, and scooted out the door.

"You *what?*" screeched Vida, rocketing back in her chair and snapping off her tortoiseshell glasses. Her summer straw hat flew off, landing in the wastebasket.

"I didn't really," I protested. "I was joking. But I thought I'd better tell you because I'm not sure how much of a sense of humor Abe Loomis has."

"Abe!" Vida rubbed frantically at her eyes, a gesture that always indicated she was annoyed or upset. "That man's dumb as a bag of dirt. If half this town weren't fueled by beer, he'd have been out of business a long time ago." She stopped trying to gouge out her eyeballs and glanced down at a half-dozen sheets of paper on her desk. "The whole thing is so silly. Vulgar, too. Here," she said, pushing the papers at me, "this is the background piece I just finished on Her Majesty, Queen Dani. Somebody called while you were out and said she and her entourage would be in around noon tomorrow. Do you want me or Carla to take pictures?"

I flipped through the story, noting the results of Vida's usual two-fingered, rapid-fire method of typing. Maybe it was time again to try to talk her into a word processor. I looked at the battered upright on the little table next to her desk and decided the right moment was probably a long way off, unless I smashed the typewriter with a sledgehammer. "If Dani and company don't get here until tomorrow noon, we won't have enough time to get a picture in Wednesday's edition. Let's just go with the studio head shot and run some new photos next week."

Having retrieved her hat and put her glasses back on her nose, Vida regarded me over the rims. "If everybody buys as much space as they promised, we may have room for a photo essay on Dani. You know—Dani arriving in Alpine, Dani on location, Dani at her old home, Dani getting ready for the parade. People love that sort of thing." Vida pulled a face and jammed her straw hat back on her head. Obviously, she didn't number herself among those people.

I considered her suggestion. Unless Ed somehow single-handedly managed to discourage Alpine's merchants from participating in the special Loggerama edition, we should be able to go at least forty-eight pages. Maybe even sixty. The sound of money jingled in my head. It was not a noise I'd heard much since buying *The Advocate*, but I liked it.

"Where *is* Ed?" Not in the newsroom; not in my editorial quarters. Nor had I seen him as I came through the front office.

Vida was putting a fresh piece of paper in the battered typewriter. "He and Ginny took the Safeway people to the Venison Inn for coffee. If you ask me, you ought to let Ginny handle this alone. Ed still thinks Safeway made a terrible mistake coming into Alpine and competing with the Grocery Basket."

I flipped through Vida's article on Dani Marsh. "That's only because he can't go on talking the Grocery Basket out of running big ads. Do you remember last Easter when he tried to convince Jake that he didn't need to advertise his hams because nobody else in town had any?"

"Oooooh!" Vida gave a tremendous shudder. "The man's impossible! Just this morning I overheard him telling Itsa Bitsa Pizza they shouldn't advertise their new special because that wife of his, who's built like a bathtub, is on a diet!"

I groaned, though it didn't do any good. All the badgering and coaxing in the world couldn't change Ed's attitude. But *The Advocate*'s balance sheets looked a little brighter now than when I'd taken over. The previous owner, Marius Vandeventer, had made a good living in the halcyon days of low paper costs and hot type job printing. But new technology had moved the printing business—including that of *The Advocate* itself—down the highway to Monroe. Even more ironically, in a town that once had been dependent on logging and mill operations, the price of trees had sent newsprint costs skyrocketing. But with the help of an old friend, I'd managed to pare down other expenses and somehow goad Ed into soliciting more advertising, however reluctantly. Circulation was up, too, a source of personal pride. I expected the Loggerama edition to be our biggest moneymaker of the year. Certainly the presence of a bona fide movie star would help.

"Vida," I said, now sitting at Carla's empty desk, "where did you get this stuff about Dani Marsh?"

She turned halfway in her chair. "What? Oh, the Hollywood bilge is from some press release. The early background is off the top of my head."

Most Alpine background comes from Vida's head. She is a walking encyclopedia of local lore. Vida knows so much about the town and its residents that usually the most interesting stories aren't fit to print. The piece on Dani Marsh, however, was bland in the extreme. "She was born, grew up, graduated from high school, got married, divorced, and moved to L.A." I tapped page one of the article with a fingernail. "Then you've got six hundred words of press kit. Couldn't we do more with the local angle? What about her mother?"

Vida gave another shudder, setting the paisley print of her summer dress aquiver. Fleetingly, I pictured her in a wet T-shirt. It was an awesome sight.

"Patti Marsh! Now there's a piece of work!" Vida yanked off her glasses again. "Do you know her?"

"I ran into her just now at Mugs Ahoy. She didn't seem real thrilled about her daughter's triumphal return."

Vida put out her hand. "Give me that story." I complied, and Vida put her glasses back on to scan it. "Dani was born—so far, so good. Ray Marsh allegedly knocked up Patti Erskine when they were in high school. They had to get married—or else. Ray walked out when Dani was a baby. Patti got divorced, went after Ray for child support, couldn't collect, took a job as a waitress in the old Loggers' Café, which is where the computer store is now. Patti had a string of men, but never married again. After the café closed, she went to work for Blackwell Timber. She's been seeing Jack Blackwell—or been seen with him—ever since his wife left him a couple of years ago."

I realized that it was Jack Blackwell I'd seen with Patti at Mugs Ahoy. "And?"

"And . . ." Vida ran a finger down the page. "Not a very stable upbringing, but I can't say that, can I?" She shuffled paper. "High school—let me think, Dani got suspended at least twice, for drinking and being naked during study hall. Not inside the school, I mean, but in somebody's pickup across the street. Still," she added grudgingly, "the girl graduated. Then she married Cody Graff."

That name rang a bell. Somehow, I connected him with Vida or one of her numerous kinfolk. Half of Alpine was related to the Runkels, her late husband's family, or her own branch of Blatts. I must have been looking curious, because Vida nodded. "That's right, Cody is engaged to my niece, Marje Blatt, the one who works for Doc Dewey. By coincidence, Cody is also employed by Blackwell Timber."

It was a coincidence, but not an amazing one. Although the original mill closed in 1929, logging had continued as a major enterprise, right up until the recent—and most serious—controversy over the spotted owl. The two smaller mills, located at opposite ends of the town and supplied by gyppo loggers, were outstripped by Blackwell's operation between Railroad Avenue and the Skykomish River. Jack Blackwell also owned some big parcels of land—on Mount Baldy, Beckler Peak, and along the east fork of the Foss River. It struck me as odd that I hadn't met Blackwell until today.

"Does Blackwell live here?" I asked.

"Part of the time. He's got operations in Oregon and Idaho. Timbuktu, for all I know." Vida spoke impatiently, going through the rest of her story. Jack Blackwell was obviously a side issue. "So Dani and Cody got married when they didn't have enough sense to skin a cat, and they had a baby—a full nine-month one, I might note—but the poor little thing died at about six weeks. Crib death, very sad. Then about two months later, the marriage blew up and Dani flew south. Five years later, with some big-shot director's backing, she's a star." Vida gave an eloquent shrug. "How much of that do you want me to put in?"

I accepted defeat gracefully. "I was hoping she'd starred in the senior play or something. How did the press kit cover her background?"

Vida waved a hand. "Oh, some tripe about how she came from a quaint Pacific Northwest logging town up in the mountains with snow on the ground half the year and deer sleeping at the foot of her trundle bed. You know—the sort of nonsense that makes us look like we've got moss growing around our ears and we're still wearing loincloths."

I inclined my head. Having spent all of my life in Seattle, Portland, and Alpine, I was accustomed to the attitudes of outsiders. Let them think we ate raw fish for dinner and held a potlatch instead of hosting cocktail parties. Maybe it would keep them away. I allowed Vida to put her story in the copyediting basket.

"What's the name of this picture Dani's doing?" I asked, feeling a bit passé. The life of a single mother running her own business didn't leave me with a lot of leisure time for moviegoing.

Vida, another single working mother, albeit with children out of the nest, had to look down at the press release on her desk. "Let me see . . . here it is. 'A film by Reid Hampton, starring Dani Marsh and Matt Tabor. *Blood Along the River.*' Ugh, what a stupid title."

I had to agree. Maybe they'd change it. It never occurred to me that it might be not only stupid, but prophetic.

Chapter Two

DURWOOD PARKER WAS under arrest. Again. Durwood, who had once been Alpine's pharmacist, was probably the worst driver I'd ever had the opportunity to avoid. Drunk or sober, Durwood could nail any mailbox, hit any phone pole, or careen down the sidewalk of any street in town. Since not all the streets in Alpine have sidewalks, Durwood often tore up flower beds instead. His latest act of motoring menace had been the demolition of Francine Wells' display window at Francine's Fine Apparel on Front Street. Francine was in a red-hot rage, but Durwood was stone-cold sober. For his own protection, Sheriff Milo Dodge had locked Durwood up overnight.

"We have to run it," Carla Steinmetz announced the following morning as she went over the blessedly short list of criminal activity for the past twenty-four hours. "It's a rule, isn't it? Any name on the blotter is a matter of public record, right?"

I sighed. "I'm afraid so. Poor Durwood. Poor Dot. His wife must be a saint."

"She's got her own car," put in Vida. "She'd be crazy to go anywhere with Durwood. Did you know he drove an ambulance in World War II?"

"Who for?" I asked. "The Nazis?"

Vida's response was stifled by Kip MacDuff, our part-time handyman and full-time driver. Kip was about twenty, with carrot red hair and cheerful blue eyes. He was, he asserted, working his way through college. Since I had never known him to leave the city limits of Alpine, I assumed he was enrolled in a correspondence school.

"Hey, get this!" Kip exclaimed. "Dani's coming in by helicopter! She's going to land on top of the mall! The high school band is coming out to meet her!"

I gazed at Vida. "I guess you'd better get a picture."

But Carla was on her feet, jumping up and down. "Let me! This is incredibly cool! When I was going to journalism school at the University of Washington, I never thought I'd get to meet a movie star in Alpine!"

And, I thought cruelly, her professors probably never thought she'd get a job in newspapers. But here was Carla, now in her second year as a reporter on *The Advocate*. Why, I asked myself for the fiftieth time, did all the good ones go into the electronic media? Or were there any good ones these days? Was I getting old and crotchety at forty-plus?

Vida was only too glad to let Carla take the assignment. "I've been looking at Dani Marsh since she was waddling around in diapers and plastic pants. Just make sure you load the camera this time, Carla. You remember what happened two weeks ago at Cass Pidduck's hundredth birthday party."

Carla, who usually bounces her way through life, looked crestfallen. "I left the film in the car."

Vida nodded. "At least you had it with you."

Carla's long dark hair swung in dismay. "So I went out to get it, but when I came back, Mr. Pidduck had died."

"Yes, I know," said Vida, "but his children liked that shot of him slumped forward in his birthday cake. They said it was just like old Grumps. Or whatever they called him," Vida added a bit testily. "Frankly, the Pidducks never did have much sense. Cass may have been long in the tooth, but he was short in the upper story."

Accustomed to Vida's less than charitable but often more than accurate appraisals of Alpine residents, I withdrew to my inner office. The usual phone messages had accumulated, including one from my son, Adam, in Ketchikan. After two years and no foreseeable major at the University of

Hawaii, my only child had decided to go north to Alaska. He was spending the summer working in a fish packing plant, and had a vague notion about enrolling for fall quarter at the state university in Fairbanks. I looked at Ginny Burmeister's phone memo with my customary sense of dread whenever my son called in prime time.

He was staying in a dormitory owned by the fish co-op, which meant that I was put on hold for a long time while somebody tried to determine if he was on or off the premises. For ten minutes, I counted the cost and perused the mail. Adam should be at work in the middle of the day. Maybe he'd had an accident. Or had gotten sick. I lost interest in the numerous bills, press releases, irate letters to the editor, advertising circulars, and exchange papers that jammed my in-basket—especially on Mondays. At last Adam's clear young voice reached my ear:

"Hey, Mom," he began, "guess what? Fairbanks is seven hundred miles away! I thought I could take the bus to campus."

Adam's sense of geography, or lack thereof, was astounding. Indeed, I had tried to explain the vastness of Alaska to him before he flew out of Sea-Tac Airport. I might as well have saved my breath.

"Is that why you're calling at two o'clock on a Monday afternoon when you ought to be at work?" I demanded. "Bear in mind, Fairbanks is so far away it's in another time zone, twice removed."

"I worked Sunday," Adam said, sounding defensive. "Didn't I tell you I'm on a different shift this month?"

He hadn't. Adam was well over six feet tall, weighed about a hundred and seventy pounds, was approaching his twenty-first birthday—and still qualified as my addled baby. One of these days, I'd turn around and find him gainfully employed, happily married, and the father of a couple of kids. And maybe one of these days I'd fly to Mars on a plastic raft.

"So you just discovered you couldn't commute to Fairbanks?" I said, wondering whether to be amused or dismayed. At least he'd never suggested taking a degree in transportation.

"Well, yeah, but that's okay. I'll just move there next month. I can take a plane." His voice dropped a notch. "If you can advance me the price of a ticket."

"So why are you working? I thought you made big bucks in Alaska."

"I got tuition, room and board, you know—I didn't count on having to pay for an airline ticket." He sounded faintly indignant, as if it were my fault that Alaska was so spread out.

"I'll see what I can do." I didn't have the remotest notion how much it cost to fly from Ketchikan to Fairbanks. It appeared I'd have to dip into savings. At least I still had some, thanks to a fluke of an inheritance that had allowed me to buy both *The Advocate* and my green Jaguar. Still, it crossed my mind that this was one of those times when it would have been nice to have Adam's father around, instead of off raising his own kids and taking care of his nutty wife.

"Thanks, Mom." My son spoke as if the ticket purchase was a *fait accompli*. "Hey, I just talked to some guy who's leaving for Seattle this afternoon and then going on to Alpine. Curtis Graff. You know him? He works here in the cannery as a foreman."

The name rang a bell, but it was off-key. "Cody Graff I know. At least I know who he is. His name just came up a few minutes ago." There was no point in boring Adam with details. "How old is Curtis?"

"Oh—thirty, maybe. He went to Alpine High, worked in the woods, was a volunteer fireman, and went out with the daughter of the guy who owns the Texaco station."

Adam's thorough account amazed me. Usually, I was lucky to get the last name of his acquaintances. But I still couldn't place Curtis Graff, unless he was Cody's brother. Vida would know. "What's he bringing down?" I inquired. Surely Adam couldn't pass up the chance to have somebody hand-carry videos that were six weeks overdue, a broken CD player, or a torn jacket that only Mother could mend.

"Nothing," my son replied, sounding affronted. "I just thought it was kind of strange that there was somebody else up here from Alpine. It's not exactly the big city."

"True," I agreed, thinking wistfully of the metropolitan vitality I still missed since moving to Alpine. But my years on *The Oregonian* in Portland and my upbringing in Seattle seemed far away. I had committed my bank account to *The Advocate* and my soul to Alpine. My heart was another matter.

We chatted briefly of mundane concerns before Adam announced he had to race off and help somebody fix an outboard motor. I turned my attention back to the other phone messages, the mail, and the print order for the weekly press run in Monroe. It was after one o'clock when I realized I'd skipped lunch. I said as much to Vida, who had already consumed her diet special of cottage cheese, carrot and celery sticks, and a hard-boiled egg.

"You eat alone too much," she announced, depositing two wedding stories with accompanying pictures on my desk. "I'll come with you. I could use a cup of hot tea."

"Good." I started to sign the print order just as Carla returned, bubbling like a brook.

"Dani Marsh isn't much taller than I am," Carla declared, dancing into my office. "She's in terrific shape though, works out for two hours a day, and drinks nothing but cabbage extract. Her skin is *amazing!* But you ought to see Matt Tabor! What a hunk! He's six-two, with the greenest eyes ever, and muscles that ripple and bulge and—"

Happily, the phone rang, cutting short Carla's bicep recital. The mayor, Fuzzy Baugh, was on the line, his native New Orleans drawl characteristically unctuous. He wanted to make sure we included an article about the celebrity bartenders who were going to be on duty at the Icicle Creek Tavern during Loggerama. He and Doc Dewey Senior; Dr. Starr, the dentist; and Sheriff Milo Dodge would make up the star-studded cast of mixologists, unless they got lucky and enticed somebody from the movie crew to take part. That struck me as dubious, since the Icicle Creek Tavern makes Mugs Ahoy look like the Polo Lounge. Located at the edge of town, the rival watering hole is famous for its Saturday night brawls which usually involve raucous loggers hurling each other through the windows. I frankly couldn't imagine Fuzzy or any of our other more dignified citizens having a beer at the place, let alone serving the rough-and-tumble clientele. But this was Loggerama, and apparently a truce was in effect.

I was still listening to the mayor's long-winded description of how he planned to give civic-minded names to his libations (*citizen schooner, mayor's mug, political pitcher*—I didn't take notes) when Ed Bronsky staggered in, looking as if he'd been attacked by wild beasts.

"Inserts!" he wailed, clutching at the doorjamb. "In color! Every week! It's worse than I expected!"

Inwardly, I was elated. Enough color inserts might pay for Adam's ticket from Ketchikan to Fairbanks. But between Fuzzy yammering about his Beer à la Baugh, the star-struck Carla still twittering to Vida, and Ed now threatening to have an aneurism over Safeway's advertising temerity, I was anxious to escape. Hastily, I shoved the print order at Vida to sign for me while I relented and took down the dates and times that the various so-called celebrities would be at the Icicle Creek Tavern. At last I was able to hang up, console Ed, listen to Carla, and get out the door before some other obstacle rolled my way.

"Burger Barn," I said, feeling the full impact of the sun overhead. *The Advocate* wasn't air-conditioned, but its proximity to the Skykomish River gave an illusion of cold water and fresh air. Outside, I could see the dry foothills of the Cascade Mountains. Even the evergreens seemed to droop. To the north, Mount Baldy was bare of snow, with wild heather blazing under the blank blue sky. The forest fire danger was extreme, and all logging operations had been curtailed. After over a month without rain, we natives were beginning to feel as if our own roots were drying up and withering our souls.

The Burger Barn is both restaurant and drive-in, located two blocks west on Front Street, across from Parker's Pharmacy, once owned by the wayward Durwood. Fleetingly, I wondered how he was managing in jail. In Alpine, the county prison consists of six cells in the building that houses the sheriff's office. Usually, the only inhabitants are drunk drivers, transients, and the occasional spouse batterer. Durwood probably had the place to himself. I mentioned the fact to Vida, who snorted loudly.

"He'll probably ask to stay an extra day. Dot Parker talks like a cement mixer. Non-stop, just grinding her jaws away." She took a stutter step, then waved, a windmill gesture that might have stopped traffic had there been more than three cars on Front Street. "Marje! Yoo-hoo!"

At the entrance to the Burger Barn, Vida's niece, Marje Blatt, returned the wave. She was accompanied by a lanky young man wearing cutoffs and a tank top. As coincidence would have it, he was Marje's fiancé, Cody Graff. Introductions were made, but before I could inquire about Curtis Graff, Vida whisked us inside the Burger Barn.

"We might as well sit together," said Vida, heading for an empty booth that looked out toward the bank across the street. "I'm just having tea."

Marje and Cody looked a little reluctant, but docilely sat down. "I'm on my lunch hour," said Marje. She was in her mid-twenties, with short auburn hair, bright blue eyes, and a piquant face. Unlike her more casual counterparts in many big city medical offices, Marje wore a crisp white uniform. She scanned the menu as if it were an X-ray. "Why am I looking at this?" she asked, pitching the single plastic-encased sheet behind the napkin holder. "I'm having the Cobb salad."

The waitress, a pudgy middle-aged woman named Jessie Lott, stood with order pad in hand, blowing wisps of hair off her damp forehead. Cody asked for the double cheeseburger, fries, and coffee. I opted for a hamburger dip au jus, a small salad, and a Pepsi. Vida requested her tea. The waitress started to wheel away, but Vida called her back:

"There's a minimum per table setting, right?"

Jessie Lott shrugged. "Really, that's just when nobody else orders more than—"

"In that case," Vida interrupted, "I'll have the chicken basket with fries, tartar sauce on the side, and a small green salad with Roquefort." She threw Jessie a challenging look and deep-sixed the menu. "Well," Vida said, eyeing her niece and Cody, "when's the wedding? I heard you ordered the invitations last week."

"October nineteenth," replied Marje in her brisk voice. She didn't look at all like her aunt, but some of their mannerisms were similar. Both were no-nonsense women, devoid of sentiment, but not without compassion. "We're going to Acapulco for our honeymoon." She turned her bright blue eyes on Cody, as if daring him to differ. "We'll love it."

Cody, who had been toying with the salt and pepper shakers, gazed ironically at his beloved. "Yeah, sure we will, Marje. Especially the part where we both get the Aztec two-step."

"Don't believe everything you hear," Marje retorted. "You just don't drink water out of the tap, that's all. Or eat in strange places. Good Lord, Cody, don't be such a wimp!"

Cody drew back in the booth. He was sharp-featured, with straw-colored hair, restless gray eyes, and a sulky cast to his long mouth. Though he was narrow of shoulder, his bare upper arms were muscular, and I supposed that younger women would find him attractive, especially with that petulant air. He struck me as spoiled, but I hoped—for Marje's sake—that I was wrong. Certainly she seemed to be getting her way about the honeymoon.

"You just wanted to go fishing in Montana or Wyoming or some godforsaken place," Marje was saying. "As if you don't hotfoot it out to the river every chance you get around here."

"Fishing stinks in this state," declared Cody. "There isn't a river in Washington that isn't fished out. I haven't caught a trout bigger than eight inches since I was sixteen. And steelheading is a joke. You're lucky if you get one of those babies every season."

Cody wasn't exaggerating, but I kept quiet, not wanting to take sides. But Cody wasn't finished with his griping: "Everything stinks around here these days," he proclaimed, flexing his biceps for emphasis. "Take all these wimpy environmentalists trying to wipe out the logging business. How does a guy like me live in this state? I don't know how to do anything but work in the woods. Do they want me sitting on a street corner with a tin cup and a sign that says WILL WORK FOR FOOD? Work at *what*? It pisses me off."

It was pissing off an increasing number of people in the forest products industry, though I noticed that Cody seemed to take the environmentalists' concerns very personally. I supposed I couldn't blame him, but I had an urge to point out that there were two sides to the story, and that while I sympathized with him, he was not alone in his outrage. Vida, however, intervened.

"Just be glad you can afford a honeymoon at all," she admonished them. "And the time. How long will you be gone?"

"A week," replied Marje. "That's all I can take off at once from Doc Dewey's office. It's too hard to get anybody to fill in for me in this town. In fact, he'd rather I went next week because he's going to be gone." She pulled a face at her aunt. "Frankly, I don't think he wants me to go at all. Doc's been real cranky lately."

"We ought to elope," said Cody, his ruffled feathers apparently smoothed. "With the logging operation shut down and that bunch of dorks making a movie up there on Baldy, this would be a good time for me to take off." He jostled Marje's arm. "What do you say, honey, want to slip off to a J.P. and forget about all those flowers and champagne glasses and ten pounds of gooey cake?"

"I sure don't," Marje countered crossly. "Between Doc's

constant advice and your weak dose of enthusiasm, I wonder why we're getting married in the first place. It may be old stuff to you, but I've never had a wedding before. Besides, I don't know how long Doc's going to be away this time."

Vida leaned across the table, scenting gossip. "Where's he going?"

Marje lifted her slim shoulders. "Seattle, I think. Frankly, he's been sort of vague. Mrs. Dewey's going with him, though. Maybe it's just a getaway. He could use it—that's probably why he's such a crab. Doc doesn't take much time off for a guy his age, especially when he's got his son to rely on to back him up."

Vida sniffed. "His son has too many peculiar ideas, if you ask me." She paused as Jessie showed up with our order. "Last Friday, Amy took Roger in to see young Doc Dewey," she went on, referring to her daughter and grandson. "Amy and Ted think Roger is hyper." Vida rolled her eyes and pounced on her chicken. "Hyper what, I asked? He's just a typical spirited nine year old. But young Doc Dewey is putting him on some kind of medication. Doesn't that beat all?" She bit into her chicken with a vengeance.

Marje looked as if she were trying to keep from smiling. "Well, Roger *is* pretty lively. Amy told me how he tried to microwave Mrs. Grundle's cat. And put a garter snake in the bank's night depository."

"Kid stuff," asserted Vida. "Roger has an active imagination, that's all."

The truth was that Roger was a terror, but Vida doted on him all the same. Although her three daughters had provided her with a running total of five grandchildren, only Roger lived in Alpine. Familiarity did not breed contempt, as well it might, given Roger's proclivity for mischief.

"Somebody," said Cody, who had seemed temporarily lost in his world of double cheese and fries, "ought to smack that kid. At the family Fourth of July picnic, I caught him putting cherry bombs in the barbecue pit. Remember those big explosions?"

Marje nodded, but Vida gave Cody her most severe expression. Before she could defend the errant Roger, however, the sound of honking horns blasted our ears. We all craned our necks to look out toward Front Street.

"What is it?" asked Marje, whose vision was blocked.

Cody had gotten to his feet, dropping a couple of french fries in the process. "Jeez." He turned pale under his summer tan as the honking grew louder, competing with the whistle of the Burlington Northern, heading east. "It's that ballbuster Dani."

I was sticking to my clothes and my clothes were sticking to the booth. I leaned out as far as possible, but could see only the rear end of a big white car, no doubt a demo on loan from the local General Motors dealership. "They got in about noon," I said in what I hoped was a neutral voice.

Cody sat down, looking more sulky than ever. He picked up his napkin, crumpled it into a ball, and threw it in the direction of the empty booth opposite us. "That bitch is going to be here for two weeks!" He gave a violent shake of his head, straw-colored hair quivering. "Why couldn't she go away and stay away? What's the point of coming back just to get everybody riled up?"

Marje gave Cody a cool look. "As far as I can tell, you're the only one who's riled up. Ignore her, Cody. All that was five years ago." She pushed at his plate. "Eat up, I've got to get back to the office."

But Cody wasn't so easily mollified. With one furious gesture, he swept the plate off the table, sending it crashing to the floor. I jumped and Vida tensed. Marje opened her mouth to protest, but Cody was on his feet, yelling at her:

"You don't know squat about that slut! She's not fit to set foot in this town! Wait and see. She'll be lucky to get out alive!" He started to heel around, slipped in a puddle of catsup, and caught himself on the edge of the table. The gray eyes glittered like cold steel. "If ever a woman deserved to get herself wasted, it's Dani Marsh! Don't be surprised if I kill her with my bare hands!" Having steadied himself, Cody Graff stood up straight and looked down at his clutching fingers.

They looked as if they'd fit neatly around Dani Marsh's throat.

Chapter Three

CARLA INSISTED THAT I go with her to Mount Baldy and check out the movie company. Despite some confusion about the print order, the press run was underway in Monroe. Ordinarily, I should have had my weekly bit of slack time on a Wednesday, but the extra work caused by Loggerama was interfering with our routine. I demurred, but Carla was adamant.

"Come on, Emma, you got your sixty pages," Carla argued. "Ed came through for once. Celebrate. How often do you get to see real movie stars?"

How often do I want to? was the retort that almost crossed my lips. But Carla was so enthusiastic that I finally gave in. It wasn't that I didn't admire actors—I am actually a devoted film buff—but the idea of seeing them in the flesh has never thrilled me. Maybe I don't want my illusions spoiled. Maybe I want to keep the on-screen magic untarnished. Or maybe I figure those celluloid gods and goddesses will turn out to be every bit as human as the tabloids insist they are. Why make a pilgrimage to meet somebody who is just as flawed as I am?

But I went, piloting my precious green Jaguar across the Skykomish River and down to the highway and veering off onto a switchback logging road leading up the side of Mount Baldy. I noticed that what was known as Forest Service Road 6610 had been recently resurfaced, perhaps even widened. When we stopped at about the three thousand-foot level, I saw why: four enormous truck-trailers rested at the edge of a meadow miraculously covered with snow. Even under the afternoon sun, I marveled at how much cooler I felt. Phony or not, the delusion seemed to lower the actual temperature by at least ten degrees.

Carla was hopping about, looking for someone she recognized. Although there must have been thirty people milling around, I saw no sign of either Dani Marsh or Matt Tabor. But Carla had zeroed in on a lion-maned man wearing a straw hat, cowboy boots, and faded blue jeans.

"Mr. Hampton!" she called. "It's me, the press!"

Mr. Hampton's teeth sparkled in his tawny beard. "Carla, my favorite media personality! Are you here to do a behind-the-scenes feature? Maybe you'll get it picked up by the wire service."

Carla's petite body jiggled with pleasure. Proudly, she introduced me to Reid Hampton, a director whose work I've sometimes admired but rarely enjoyed. Hampton's pictures tend to be gloomy, not so much film noir as Kafkaesque. Come to think of it, Ed Bronsky would love them—if he ever stopped watching *Mister Ed* reruns long enough to see a movie.

"*Road Weary* was very provocative," I said, knowing it was his most recent directorial effort. In truth I had seen only the trailer. Two hours of watching three derelicts beat each other over the head with tokay bottles had not impressed me as entertainment. But Reid Hampton was still holding my hand and beaming that dazzling smile.

"It was a statement," he said in as modest a tone as his deep, rumbling voice would permit. "I hope George Bush saw it."

Personally, I hoped the president had better things to do, but I, too, kept smiling. "Is this picture a statement?" I inquired, feeling my fingers shrivel.

He finally let go and made a sweeping gesture. "*All* my pictures are statements. Poverty, politics, sex, violence—the whole human condition. The camera not only conveys truth; it demands a response from the audience. What did you think of Little Louie?"

"Ah ..." Little Louie, Big Louie, even Medium Louie

were all outside my frame of reference. Whoever Louie was, he probably had been one of the three grubs in *Road Weary.* "Vulnerable," I said, taking a guess. "Strong, though, in many ways. Under the surface," I added hastily.

Still grinning, Reid Hampton slapped his hands together. "Exactly! It isn't every cocker spaniel you can get to put those emotions across. Cockers in particular aren't too bright. I should have used a collie, but then everybody thinks *Lassie* and all that sentimental crap. On screen, animals always have a—" He stopped and looked over my head. I turned to see Carla outside one of the big trailers talking to a slim blonde who had to be Dani Marsh. Hampton took my arm. "Come on, you must meet our star, your own hometown heroine. Dani's great, a real talent, absolutely catches fire in front of the camera. And Matt Tabor—together they'll scorch the screen. I've been trying to put this package together for over two years."

Dani Marsh was one of the most beautiful women I've ever seen. She had honey blonde hair, limpid brown eyes, and not-quite-perfect features with a mouth too wide and brows too thick, but the overall effect was stunning. I realized I had never seen her in a movie, but according to Vida's reworking of the studio press release, Dani had zoomed to the top of the heap with only three major roles, two of them in pictures directed by Reid Hampton.

Dani was almost as expansive as her director. She shot out a hand and gave me a dazzling smile. "Ms. Lord! Carla has told me all about you! I think it's wonderful that a woman has taken over from that old curmudgeon, Marius Whatsisname. Is he dead?"

"No," I answered, finding her forthright manner irresistible. "Just retired and moved away. Marius Vandeventer is indestructible."

Dani laughed, a lovely, tinkling sound that made Carla's frequent bouts of giggling sound like a car crash. "I've so much catching up to do in Alpine. Five years! And it *has* changed. I'm so glad I talked Reid into doing some location shooting up here." She threw back her head and looked up toward the twin, flat crests of Mount Baldy. "I used to go berry-picking up there. My mother and I would make pies and jam."

From what I'd seen of Patti Marsh, making book would have been more like it. Fleetingly, I wondered if Dani had attempted a reunion with her mother yet. I tried to see any resemblance between Dani and Patti, but my recollection of the senior Marsh was fogged by the dark smoky interior of Mugs Ahoy.

At the edge of the meadow, activity was suddenly underway. Cameras were being moved into position, equipment was being set up, a background—which looked to me like a replica of the view I was looking at—had even been dropped in the middle of the fake snow.

"Excuse me," said Dani, "I have to get into my costume." At the moment, she was wearing a dark green leotard that displayed finely toned and roundly contoured body parts. I had an insane—and fleeting—urge to exercise. "Believe it or not," she laughed, "I have to put on a parka and ski pants. I may melt before this picture is wrapped!" With a graceful little wave, she climbed the four portable stairs that led to the trailer that housed her dressing room.

Reid Hampton was off consulting with his assistant director; Carla was hobnobbing with a bald man behind the camera; and descending from the cab of the trailer was Matt Tabor, carrying a can of diet soda. I allowed myself to stare. I have seen Matt Tabor in at least four films, and although his acting range may be limited, his sexual attraction is not. Matt had been cast in the heroic mold, with chiseled features, wavy black hair, a terrific torso, and those seductive green eyes that had earned rave reviews from Carla and fifty million other females. Indeed, Matt Tabor was so incredibly good-looking that I not only stared, but laughed out loud.

He shot me a curious glance, and I actually flushed. I felt fourteen instead of forty-two. As he strolled in my direction, I seriously considered bolting. Then I remembered how unimpressed I was by movie stars and that I was a newspaper publisher and that I had once met Gerald Ford. Somehow, the comparison was inadequate, especially since Ford had seemed far more at a loss for words than I had been.

"Are you from the logging company?" Matt Tabor's famous baritone echoed off the evergreens.

It was the last question I expected. "What?" I sobered quickly. "No, I own the local newspaper. Do you mean Blackwell Timber?"

"Right." He was wearing some sort of black vest over his bare chest and had on a pair of very tight black pants. I tried not to notice. "Those jackasses can't make up their minds," Matt remarked, not necessarily to me. He was wearing his brooding look, which had served him so well in *Beau Savage*.

"Oh?" I pretended we were having a conversation. "You mean Jack Blackwell and his crew?"

He nodded, the black forelock somehow staying in place. "I guess that's his name. He tells us we can use this place for the location shoot, extorts twenty grand for the privilege, then pitches a fit because we cut down eight lousy trees." Matt Tabor sneered. I remembered the expression from *No Mercy at Midnight*. "What the hell, he can't log anyway because his workers get too hot. Or something like that." He gave a contemptuous shrug of his broad shoulders, just the way he did when he walked out on the heroine at the end of *Jericho in Jersey*.

"It's because it's too dry," I said, trying to keep my eyes on Reid Hampton and a tall redhead with what looked like a script in her manicured hands. "There's a danger of forest fire."

"Hell." Matt Tabor reached inside his vest and pulled out a pack of cigarettes. "Where's Smokey the Bear when we really need him, huh?" For the first time, he looked directly at me as if I were really there. I looked at his cigarettes. Even after three years of not smoking, I hadn't lost my craving. But maybe it was safer to lust after Matt Tabor's tobacco than the rest of him. "Who are you?" he asked, in a tone that implied I might not know.

"Emma Lord. I own *The Alpine Advocate*." Matt was puffing away, and I resolutely returned my gaze to the preparations in the meadow. I decided I must be seeing double. Two people who looked exactly like Matt and Dani Marsh were standing knee-deep in snow while several others peered, prodded, and conferred. It dawned on me that the man and woman were the actors' stand-ins, helping the crew get ready for the actual shooting.

Reid Hampton was coming toward us, a copy of the script under his arm. "Bundle up, Matt. We're almost ready."

"Hell." Matt Tabor dropped his half-smoked cigarette but didn't bother to stomp it out. I watched it nervously and as soon as he turned away, I pounced.

"Is it true," I asked, hoping Hampton would find my safety zeal contagious rather than laughable, "that Matt Tabor and Dani Marsh plan to marry?"

Hampton's smile seemed to stick, rather than merely stay in place. "So I hear. We'll see if they survive the picture." He tipped his cowboy hat, then moved off to speak with his cinematographer. Carla had settled into a folding chair, obviously keen on watching the filming. I strolled around the meadow's edge, looking for wildflowers.

The mating of Dani Marsh and Matt Tabor struck a discordant note. Visually, they were a perfect pair: beautiful blond Venus; dark and handsome Adonis. But Matt Tabor seemed like a first-run version of Cody Graff. Surely five years and dazzling success in Hollywood should have changed Dani's taste in men.

Standing next to an old-growth Douglas fir and hearing the cedar waxwings chatter among its branches, I could believe they were talking about me. Who was I to criticize Dani Marsh's love life? In over twenty years, I not only didn't have a new man in my life, but I'd never gotten over the one who got away.

Out in the snow, under the bright, hot sun, the two people who so resembled Matt and Dani were embracing. In their heavy parkas and ski pants, they didn't look like they were having much fun. All the same, the idea of embracing appealed to me. A lot. Maybe it was time to call the sheriff.

Milo Dodge was too busy with Loggerama to have dinner with me. Or so he began, speaking in his laconic voice from the sheriff's office just before five o'clock. Carla had endured a bee sting and I had fought off boredom to see less than thirty seconds of film finally ready to go into the can. It had taken almost three hours, with Reid Hampton no longer so genial, Matt Tabor cursing a blue streak, and even Dani Marsh beginning to show signs of impatience under her fur-lined hood.

"If we went about eight o'clock, I could do it," Milo finally allowed. "I've got to check on Durwood on the way home. I let him out this morning if he promised not to drive for a month."

Whatever spark of passion I'd felt igniting in the meadow had been doused by Milo's lack of enthusiasm for my company. To be fair, Milo and I weren't exactly an item. We were friends, comfortable together, mature adults who didn't feel the need to leap into the sack to keep close. At least that was the theory.

"I could fix dinner here," I offered. Occasionally, within the past year, Milo and I had traded home-cooked meals. He was good with the basics, but God forbid he should have higher aspirations. After five months, his beef tournedos were still a bad memory.

"What?" asked Milo.

"Whatever. I can stop at the Grocery Basket on the way home." It occurred to me that after this weekend's grand opening, I could stop at Safeway. Maybe they wouldn't have gray meat.

"I feel like chops," said Milo.

"Pork or lamb?"

"Lamb. Wait—which one is the real little kind?"

"Lamb." I winced. According to the Grocery Basket's

ad, which even now lay before me in the new edition of *The Advocate*, pork chops were on special. Lamb would cost me about three times as much. "Say, Milo—who is Curtis Graff? I meant to ask Vida, but I forgot."

"Curtis? He's the older Graff kid. You know, Cody's brother. I think he went to Alaska." In the background, voices erupted. Milo apparently had visitors. "I've got to go, Emma. Mrs. Whipp just broke her Mixmaster over Mr. Whipp's head up at the retirement home. See you around eight."

The Whipps had recently celebrated their sixtieth wedding anniversary at the VFW Hall. Vida's account had omitted the part about Mr. Whipp trying to drown Mrs. Whipp in the punch bowl.

Maybe it was just as well that Milo and I weren't madly in love.

Ten minutes later, I was about to head for the Grocery Basket when Carla and Ginny Burmeister flew into my office. To my amazement, Carla's eyes were red-rimmed and Ginny was showing signs of deep distress.

"Carla's poisoned," Ginny declared, her usual composure in disarray. A tall, thin girl whose thick auburn hair was her best feature, Ginny was an ardent adherent of order and routine. Carla was adroit at ruining both. "Look!" Ginny grabbed Carla's left arm and thrust it at me as if it were a haunch of meat. Irreverently, I wondered how much it would cost a pound at the Grocery Basket.

"It's that bee," gasped Carla. "I must be allergic."

Sure enough, Carla's forearm was flaming red and swollen twice its normal size. Lightly, I touched the bright flesh. "It's hot, all right. Have you ever been stung before?"

"Sure," gulped Carla. "Lots. At least when I was little."

"Maybe it wasn't a bee," I said, flipping through my Rolodex for Doc Dewey's number. "It may have been a wasp or a yellowjacket, especially at that elevation."

To my relief, Marje Blatt answered. Obviously, at least one of the Deweys was still around. Young Doc was at the hospital, waiting for Mr. Whipp and his concussion, but Doc Senior was just getting ready to go home. Could we come right away?

We could and did, all three of us jamming into the Jaguar. Carla moaned a lot as we drove the four blocks from the newspaper to the medical-dental clinic. Since Alpine is built on a sidehill, most of the streets going away from the downtown area are fairly steep. I geared down as I approached the intersection at Third and Cedar; a logging truck, minus its rig, had the right of way and was going much too fast for town driving. BLACKWELL TIMBER was painted in bold black letters on the cab's door. I recognized Jack Blackwell in the driver's seat, with Patti Marsh at his side. From this angle, Patti didn't look much like her famous daughter. One of these days maybe I'd get a close-up in good light.

I hadn't seen Doc Dewey Senior since the high school commencement exercises in June. He had always been a small but robust man of about seventy, with a brusque bedside manner masking a gentle soul. Yet as I watched him tend to Carla, he looked as if he had shrunk. His white hair seemed more sparse and the sparkle had gone out of his blue eyes. Doc's expertise was intact, however, as he administered a shot of adrenaline to Carla.

"Yellowjacket, that's my guess," Doc Dewey announced while Carla flinched and moaned some more. "I'll write you a prescription for an antihistamine. Don't cheat on it, girlie."

Doc, whose first name was Cecil, always referred to female patients, regardless of age, as *girlie*. Males were addressed as *young man*. I wasn't sure if there was sexism involved, since his overriding attitude was that all his patients were idiots, regardless of gender.

Doc was at his desk, scribbling away. "Where'd you get that, girlie?" he asked, looking back at Carla over his glasses.

Breathlessly, Carla explained. "I didn't notice much at

the time," she concluded. "I was so caught up in the cinematic experience."

"The what?" Doc had gotten to his feet and was looking at Carla as if she were delirious. "You mean those Hollywood people?" He all but spat. "Stupid, just stupid! Dani ought to know better than to come back to Alpine. What's that poor girlie thinking of?"

Ginny, who had been holding Carla's hand, eyed Doc curiously. "What do you mean, Doc? Carla says she's very sweet."

Doc made a whistling sound through the excellent dentures constructed for him by his fellow tenant, Dr. Starr. "Never mind. Let's just say some things are better left alone. It would take God Almighty Himself to sort out that mess, though it makes a body feel guilty not to lend a hand. Here, take this over to Parker's Pharmacy. They don't close until nine." He thrust the prescription not at Carla, but at Ginny. I guessed that Doc knew instinctively which of them was more reliable.

At the moment, I wished I knew what Doc was talking about. It seemed to me that Carla was right—Dani Marsh was a very genuine, pleasant person. But a lot of Alpiners didn't seem to agree. Maybe Dani was acting. It was, after all, her profession. In the two weeks that she would be in Alpine, I might be able to find out what the real Dani Marsh was like.

It didn't occur to me then that there might be reasons why I wouldn't want to know.

Chapter Four

EXCEPT FOR AN occasional Clint Eastwood video, I don't think Milo Dodge has seen a movie since his wife left him for another man. The location shooting up at Baldy held no fascination for the sheriff of Skykomish County. Milo loved his lamb chops, but he wasn't much interested in the return of Dani Marsh.

"She was in school with one of my kids. I think," he added a bit doubtfully.

If Milo was right, Dani had probably been a classmate of his oldest daughter, Tanya. I'd met only one of his three children—Brandon, who had spent most of July with Milo before going to Bellevue to stay with his mother and her second husband. Tanya lived in Seattle with an aspiring sculptor Milo referred to as Flake Nuts. The youngest of the Dodge offspring was still in high school. Milo usually went to Bellevue once a month to see her and to avoid Old Mulehide, the mother of his brood.

"Dani's twenty-four, according to her press release." I noted, shoveling out more green beans for Milo. "Tanya's the same age, right?"

"I guess so," Milo replied vaguely. Birthdays were more of a mystery to the sheriff than was the criminal mind. He was polishing off his third lamb chop and eyeing the empty platter wistfully. A big, shambling man with sandy hair and hazel eyes, Milo Dodge did a pretty good imitation of a bottomless pit.

Since dessert didn't exist, I offered him more bread. Obviously, I wasn't going to get anywhere interrogating him

269

about Dani Marsh. Vida, as usual, would have to be my primary source. I changed the subject to Loggerama and saw Milo's long face grow longer.

"Let's just hope we don't get a bunch of tourists overrunning the town," he said, slapping much butter and a lot of jelly onto his bread. "The ski lodge is already full, what with the movie people staying there, and both motels have been booked for a month. I wish they'd hurry the hotel renovation along. We could use some extra space in the summers."

Milo referred to the restoration of the old Alpine Hotel, which until this past winter had housed a few elderly tenants and an occasional transient who could afford the twenty dollar minimum. A California consortium had bought the property, however, with intentions of restoring it to its former Edwardian glory. They were taking their time about it, perhaps somewhat daunted by the discovery that the hotel's glory days were a figment of some glib realtor's imagination. The Alpine Hotel had never been anything more than a boarding house with a lobby.

"I'd like to have a lot more than five deputies," Milo grumbled. "I'm thinking of scouting around for some volunteers."

"What are you expecting? A riot at the base of the Carl Clemans statue?" My tone was dour; old Carl was not likely to incite pandemonium. As the town's founder and owner of the original mill, he was always described as a benevolent, if shrewd, human being. "This will be my third Loggerama. I don't recall any big problems the last two years."

Milo's plate was now bare, except for three bones. I halfway expected he'd grind them up with his teeth. Pushing away from the table, he stretched out his long legs. "Maybe I'm just nervous because I've got an election coming up this fall. I hear that Averill Fairbanks is thinking of running against me."

I got up to fetch the coffeepot. "Averill is gaga. He reports a UFO sighting about once a month. Nobody would take him seriously."

"That's not necessarily so. Crazy Eights Neffel runs for the legislature every two years, and even though he's certifiable, he's never gotten less than ten percent of the vote in this district. Back in '64, Dolph Swecker ran his goat for city council and beat A. J. Iverson by thirty votes."

I glanced back into the little dining room to see if Milo was joking. He didn't look like it. Small towns are strange places, hell-bent on preserving their individuality. It wouldn't have surprised me to find that the goat had been impeached for embezzling. It wouldn't be any stranger than the man up on Burl Creek Road who had gone through a wedding ceremony last May with a deer named Cora.

"I wouldn't worry about Averill," I said, pouring us both more coffee. It was beginning to cool off inside the house. I had both doors open and several of the windows, too. My two-bedroom home is built of logs at the edge of the forest. Tonight, no breeze stirred the tall evergreens, but their sheltering branches helped protect me from the sun. Feeling guilty over the lack of dessert, I suggested a brandy with coffee. Milo looked at his watch.

"Better not, Emma," he said. "It's after nine. I've got to be up at the crack of dawn to help with the parade route."

"What do you mean, parade route? They start at one end of Front Street and stop at the other. This isn't Macy's Thanksgiving extravaganza, you know."

Milo took three quick gulps of coffee and stood up. "All the same, I'd better run." He avoided my gaze. "Did I have a jacket?"

"In eighty-five degree weather?" I was following him into the living room. "Gosh, Milo, you're jumpy tonight. You shouldn't let Loggerama get to you. It's supposed to be fun." Casually, I placed a hand on his arm. Maybe it really was the upcoming election that was bothering him. But Milo was already finishing his second term. I hadn't been in Alpine when he'd run for office before, but I knew he'd won handily. "Who is it?" I asked, looking up at him.

Surely there had to be another, more credible candidate in the offing than Averill Fairbanks and his UFOs.

Milo's reply rocked me: "Honoria Whitman. She's a potteress in Startup." Milo was looking miserable as he put a big hand over mine. "I meant to tell you about her, Emma, but I didn't have the nerve."

I was gaping at him. "A *potteress*? You mean you're seeing someone?" My voice sounded shrill. I pulled my hand away and stepped back.

Milo swallowed hard. "I met her last June when I was fishing down on the Skykomish River. She owns a place just off the back road that hooks up into the Sultan Basin. I guess she's been there about a year, up from California."

"California!" It figured. Even though I knew all Californians didn't have horns and forked tails, I wasn't reassured. The Pacific Northwest had been invaded by Californians for the last two decades, jamming our cities, crowding our highways, polluting our air, and even daring to introduce a work ethic. Honoria Whitman, with her crude clay pots and organic compost heap, was no doubt lounging around in Startup wearing flowing ethnic garments and hoping to improve the lot of the pitiful natives.

"Your private life is your own business," I told Milo frostily. My brown eyes shot daggers. "Are you bringing Honoria to Loggerama, or would she find it too vulgar?"

"I told you: I'm working the whole damned time," Milo replied, his annoyance as plain as my own. "In fact, this might be the only night I'll be able to see her until Loggerama is over."

"Then," I demanded, as he edged toward the door and I stalked him with arms folded across my breast, "why the hell didn't you have her feed you? Or don't you like Tofu Helper?"

Milo gazed at the beamed ceiling. "Wednesday nights Honoria teaches a class in pottery at Everett Junior College. She doesn't get home until almost ten." He seemed to be talking through gritted teeth.

My rational self told me to calm down. There was no

reason for me to be angry with Milo. His private life was indeed his own. We had never exchanged so much as a kiss. Why then did I feel betrayed? Was it only my ego and not my heart which was wounded?

I threw up my hands. "It must be the lamp chops," I confessed sheepishly. "They set me back fourteen bucks. If you'd asked for hot dogs, I'd have told you to bring Honoria along."

Milo appeared partially convinced. Or else he was just anxious to make his peace and be gone. "You'd like her, Emma. She's very soothing company."

On drugs was the evil thought that flickered through my mind. But I tried to smile. "Go on, have a good time. I'll see you at the Loggerama kickoff banquet tomorrow night."

If Milo hadn't already been wearing his cotton sports shirt open at the neck, I swear he would have run his finger inside his collar. Instead, he gave me a lopsided grin and an awkward wave, then loped out the front door. With a sigh, I went out on the porch, conscious as ever of the fresh scent of pine on the clear mountain air. Milo was climbing into his Cherokee Chief. He was a nice man, and I ought to wish him well. Certainly he wasn't the sort I'd want to spend the rest of my life with. He was too rough around the edges, too small-town in his outlook, too anti-intellectual and too unsophisticated.

But even more than what he was, there was what he wasn't: Milo Dodge wasn't Tom Cavanaugh, and that was that.

Front Street was lined with bunting and banners, looking more festive than the Fourth of July, more colorful than Christmas. Just as Milo had feared, tourists were beginning to arrive in Alpine. Traffic on Front Street was unusually heavy, which meant there were cars in both lanes. I made a mental note to have Carla do a story on the visitors, with perhaps two or three interviews included.

Having walked to work, as I often did in the summer, I greeted Ginny Burmeister, who informed me that Carla wasn't coming in. The yellowjacket sting was less swollen, but the reaction had upset her stomach. She hoped to be back to work tomorrow.

Vida hadn't yet arrived, and Ed was at a Kiwanis breakfast meeting. I went into my editorial office and made a haphazard attempt to clear my desk. Among the leftovers from this week's edition were several glossy photos of the movie crew—Dani Marsh, Matt Tabor, even Reid Hampton. I started to pitch them into the wastebasket, but it occurred to me that there might be some fans around town who'd appreciate having the pictures as souvenirs. I left them to one side, then sorted through the notes Ginny had left on my desk. As always on a Thursday, there were repercussions from the previous day's paper. Several people had responded—unfavorably—to my article on the danger of flooding caused by clear-cutting timber. Never mind that I'd tried to balance the piece. In a town that leaned on lumber for much of its economic stability, it was hard to present any other point of view.

Most of the criticism, however, had to do with the historical pieces we had run in the special Loggerama section. The turn-of-the-century silver mines had been worked by Chinese, not Japanese. The Japanese and possibly some Koreans had worked on the Great Northern Railroad because the Chinese had been excluded by a federal act in 1882. That, asserted Grace Grundle, was why Alpine had originally been named Nippon. The largest steelhead ever caught in the Skykomish River was thirty-two pounds, three ounces, not thirty-three pounds, two ounces. And the year was 1925, not 1924, insisted Vida's eldest brother, Ralph Blatt. The correct spelling of the name of the Norwegian emigrant who had helped Rufus Runkel found the ski lodge was Olav Lanritsen, with just one *n*, not two, said Henry Bardeen, the current resort manager.

No matter how certain a reader may be, it doesn't pay to accept criticism on faith alone. I would check and recheck each correction. I never ran a retraction, never suppressed a story, never allowed anyone to censor the news—but I always owned up to mistakes.

I was verifying the spelling of Olav the Obese's surname when I heard the newsroom door open. Vida, I thought, without looking up. But it was Patti Marsh, tramping purposefully toward my inner sanctum.

"You bitch!" she flared, leaning on my desk and showing her teeth like a she-wolf. "You defamed me! I'll sue your butt off!"

Being threatened by furious readers wasn't a novelty to me. Usually, however, they resorted to the telephone, being timid about facing me in person. But Patti Marsh was bold as brass tacks, glaring at me from about three feet away.

"What's the problem?" I asked, turning slightly in my swivel chair and staring right back.

She jabbed at a copy of *The Advocate* that lay on my desk. "That's the problem, right there on page four! You said my husband left me! That's a lie, I threw the bastard out! Nobody leaves Patti Erskine Marsh!"

Calmly, I pulled the paper out from under her hand and opened it to the offending page. I read Vida's copy aloud:

" 'When Dani was less than a year old, her father left Alpine. Patti Marsh raised her only daughter alone, working at the Loggers' Café. After Dani's graduation from Alpine High School in 1985, she married . . .' " I stopped and shrugged. "Excuse me, Ms. Marsh, it doesn't say he left *you*; it says he left *Alpine*. That's not exactly the same."

"The hell it isn't!" Patti Marsh waved a sunburned arm in repudiation. Up close, in the daylight, I could see a faint resemblance to Dani. The brown eyes were similar; so was the aquiline nose. But the bad perm and the tinted blond hair didn't do much to enhance her features. I judged her to be about my age, but there was a lot more mileage in her face than mine. She was short, like her daughter, but carried an extra twenty pounds. The polka dot halter top and the skintight white pants showed that most of the added weight was well-distributed. It was too bad that her head seemed to be empty.

"Look," I said, standing up but staying behind the desk which I always thought of as the moat that kept my public at bay, "you're trying to interpret the sentence. Why? It just says that Dani's father left town. Some other reader might figure that you chased him off with a two-by-four. Did you?"

Patti was still wild-eyed, but she was beginning to lose steam. I gauged that she was the sort of person who can bulldoze her way through life as long as there's nothing very substantial in her path. In my guise as editor and publisher of *The Advocate*, I always felt fairly substantial. It was in my other roles that I sometimes felt like a will-o'-the-wisp.

"This town's full of gossipy old bitches—the men, too." Her brown eyes raked over my small cluttered office. Patti Marsh had a skittish, nervous gaze, as if her emotions were in charge of her vision. "How many calls have you had?"

My own stare turned blank. "About what?"

She pointed again at the paper. "About me. And . . . Dani." It seemed she could hardly get her daughter's name out.

"None. It's a pretty tame story, Ms. Marsh."

The expression of scorn she bestowed on me might have withered a person who wasn't used to letters that started "Dear Knucklehead." Or worse. "Hey, kiddo, you don't know the half of it," asserted Patti, with a toss of her bleached hair. "This whole ball of wax is anything but tame." She started to heel around on her black thongs, then her mouth twisted into a nasty little smile. "If you ask me, we'll all be lucky if somebody doesn't end up killed." Her eyes dropped to the stack of glossy photos at the side of my desk. "Who's that?" she demanded, looking startled.

I glanced down. Reid Hampton's picture was on top of the pile. "The director. Why?"

Patti Marsh gave herself a vigorous shake. "Hunh. So he's the one who's been pushing Dani. I wonder why." There was a sneer in her voice, then she strutted out of the office, almost colliding with Vida, who was just coming in.

I didn't hear the exchange between them; I was too busy trying to figure out what on earth Patti Marsh was talking about. Whatever it was, I assumed it had nothing to do with Loggerama.

Vida surged through the newsroom, heading straight for my office. Her sailor hat was tipped over one ear. At least she didn't have it on backward, as often happen with Vida's headgear. Behind the tortoiseshell glasses, her eyes were afire. "If I didn't think all you Catholics were a bunch of smug hidebound hypocrites, I'd convert so I could be eligible for sainthood. Any normal person would have put Patti Marsh's nose in her navel."

Accustomed to Vida's fulminations against any religion but her own Presbyterian sect, I merely grinned. "Got you riled, huh? What's really eating that woman?"

"Woman!" sniffed Vida, plopping down into one of the two chairs on the other side of my desk. "Patti doesn't qualify. Real women aren't so hare-brained." She stopped fuming, then cocked her head to one side. "You're right, Emma. What *is* wrong with Patti? Oh, she and Dani were always at sixes and sevens, but that doesn't make for such bitterness. Patti's the type who'd hitch her wagon to a star, especially if the star's her daughter. Five years have gone by, and it sounds as if Dani has grown up considerably. I can't help but think they ought to have worked through their differences by now."

Not knowing either mother or daughter, I was in no position to speculate. Admitting as much, I let Vida continue her mulling out in the newsroom while I answered another rash of post-publication calls. By ten o'clock, I was mired in conversation with Alpine's oldest rational citizen, Elmer Kemp, 101 years old, who had come to town as a teenager to work in the sawmill. Elmer had a laundry list of omissions from the historical coverage, and paid no heed to my attempts to remind him that we were limited in terms of space. He didn't much like the implication that clear-cutting was bad; he objected to a reference to the Lumber Trust of the post-World War I era, claiming there never was such a thing; he asserted that the big price hike back in 1919 was due solely to an unprecedented demand for lumber in the mysterious East—i.e., New York, Boston, and Philadelphia.

I was taking desultory notes for a possible feature when Ginny Burmeister signaled from the outer office, mouthing something I couldn't understand. At last, she whipped out a piece of paper and scrawled her message in red pen:

"Reid Hampton on line two."

Getting rid of Elmer was no mean feat, and I was finally forced to resort to the promise of an interview, perhaps in early September. "I should live so long," huffed Elmer. He finally hung up, giving me no opportunity to point out that having already reached 101, his chances of being around in another month might be better than mine.

The telephone only served to amplify Reid Hampton's booming voice. "You're a busy woman," he remarked in what I took to be a chiding tone. It was likely that Reid Hampton was rarely put on hold.

"The paper came out yesterday," I explained, holding the phone a half-inch from my ear. "We always get a lot of feedback. Like a movie premiere."

His hearty laugh rumbled along the line. "But unlike the picture business, it's too late for you to make any changes."

"Yes. Journalism is real life." I felt my voice tense.

"And movies are *reel* life," Reid Hampton noted with a deep chuckle.

At least he hadn't condescended to spell *reel*. We were making small talk, and I couldn't see the point.

Reid Hampton went straight to it: "Are you free for dinner tonight?" The question was posed on a softer note.

"Why—yes." Taken by surprise, I blurted out the truth.

"Where can we get a decent meal within a fifty-mile radius?" He sounded pleased with himself.

I was nervously shuffling papers on my desk. I didn't particularly want to have dinner with Reid Hampton. But how often would Emma Lord, small-town newspaper publisher, have a chance to go out with a famous Hollywood director? How often would old Emma have a chance to go out at all? Alpine wasn't exactly a hotbed of eligible middle-aged men who were sufficiently sophisticated to know they were supposed to sniff, not chew, the wine cork.

"There's a good French restaurant just a few miles down the highway," I said, gathering courage. "It's run by a Californian and a Provençois," I added, hoping to give the place credibility.

"French food via Rodeo Drive? That sounds fine to me."

We settled on seven o'clock, and I gave him directions to my home. Then Reid Hampton was off, presumably to tell Dani Marsh how to shiver in eighty-six-degree weather. I had regained my poise and was smiling, a bit wryly. Take that, Milo Dodge, I said to myself. I, too, can strike California gold.

It was busier than usual Thursday, with all the Loggerama doings. I filled in for Carla at the Miss Alpine pageant rehearsal in the high school gym, stopped by the football field to catch the trials for the timber sports competition, and checked out the parade floats being assembled in an empty warehouse by the river.

Since I was afoot, I was hot and tired by the time I dropped off four rolls of film at Bayard's Picture-Perfect Photo Studio, where we do most of our developing work. Buddy Bayard is efficient, competent, and contrary. He will argue any issue, any time, choosing any side you're not on. I cut my stay at his studio short and dragged myself the last two blocks along Front Street to the *Advocate* office.

Vida was already gone, leaving a note atop a pile of copy. Ed was going over an ad with Francine Wells for Francine's Fine Apparel. Francine was set on buying half a page to show the first of her new fall line; Ed was determined to cut the ad by half.

I stopped at his desk, greeted Francine, and admired the sketches she'd brought along. "Terrific separates," I gushed, wondering how anyone could contemplate woolens in July. "What are the colors this season?"

Francine brightened; Ed blanched. No doubt he had visions of Francine wanting a special four-color insert. But before Francine could respond, a tall, lean young man with sun-streaked blond hair came through the door, carrying a bouquet of tiger lilies, gladioli, and asparagus fern. He looked vaguely familiar, but I couldn't immediately place him.

"Excuse me," he said in a soft, diffident voice. "Could someone tell me where I could find the movie people?"

My first reaction was that the film crew probably preferred not to be found. But perhaps this self-effacing young man had a reason for going to the location shoot, such as delivering his flowers. "Do you have some connection with the company?" I asked, making an effort to sound friendly.

"Hey," said Ed, looking up from Francine's ad dummy, "aren't you Curtis Graff?" He rose awkwardly from his chair, lumbering across the room to shake the newcomer's hand. "I remember you from the fire department. You rescued a couple of kids from a burning house out on Burl Creek Road."

Curtis Graff smiled in a modest manner. "I had help." His smile grew wider. "I don't think those kids wanted to come out, though. They'd been playing with matches and were more afraid of their parents than the fire."

I backed off, allowing Curtis and Ed to get reacquainted. Francine sidled up to me, her carefully styled hair and her white sleeveless dress somehow keeping unruffled in the heat of the day. "He's better-looking than Cody," she whispered. "Maybe Dani should have married him instead."

Francine was right. The weaknesses in Cody Graff's features weren't evident in those of his older brother. Perhaps it was a matter of character. Curtis Graff struck me as more serious, with a touch of melancholy. At any rate, he didn't look as if he were prone to pouting.

"I just got in from Alaska," Curtis was saying. "I'm staying with some friends." He turned to me and his dark blond eyebrows lifted. "Say—are you Adam Lord's mother? He asked me to have you send him a few things when I go back up north."

"Surprise, surprise," I murmured. "Just let me know what and when. Are you looking for anyone in particular with the movie or did you just want to watch the filming?"

Curtis, who was wearing knee-length shorts and a T-shirt, shifted from one foot to the other. "I know someone who's making the movie. I just didn't know how to get hold of anybody. Do they stay around here at night?"

"They're all up at the ski lodge," I said without further hesitation. The movie company's lodgings were no secret. Indeed, a lot of locals—and maybe a few tourists, too—had probably made their way by now to the location site.

"Great," said Curtis Graff. He offered us his diffident smile. "Thanks. I'll get back to you in a couple of days, Mrs. Lord. Adam gave me a list, but he said he might call you about some other stuff he forgot."

I inclined my head. Curtis Graff moved quickly out of the office, giving the impression that he was making an escape. "That's odd," I remarked, more to myself than to Ed and Francine. "I wonder why he isn't staying with Cody." My ad manager didn't pay any attention, but Francine's bright blue eyes fastened on me.

"If my memory hasn't failed," said Francine, "there's no love lost between the brothers. Their parents retired to the San Juan Islands about the same time Curtis went up to Alaska. I never knew the boys very well, but Hetty Graff was always hanging around the sale rack. She never bought anything unless it was at least forty percent off."

Ed's head shot up. "Forty percent off? Gosh, Francine, don't tell me you're having a clearance sale!"

Francine's carefully plucked eyebrows lifted slightly. "Not yet, Ed." She gave him her sweetest smile. "I thought about having a renovation sale after Durwood wiped out my front window, but I'll wait until September. Do you think I should take out a *full page* ad?"

Ed reeled against the desk. Trying not to laugh aloud, I crept into my office.

* * *

My walk home was uphill. I arrived at my cozy log house in a weary, wilted state, hoping that the shelter of the evergreen trees had kept the interior cool. Clutching the mail I had retrieved from my box by the road, I went inside and discovered that though there was no breeze, the temperature in the living room seemed at least ten degrees below the heat outdoors.

I got a Pepsi out of the refrigerator and poured it over a tall glass of ice. Collapsing on the sofa, I scanned the mail. The usual bills, ads, catalogues—and a single letter. The return address put my heart in my mouth: a well-heeled residential street in San Francisco. Hurriedly, I ripped open the plain beige envelope.

This was the third letter I had received from Tom Cavanaugh since he had visited Alpine the previous autumn. He had come to town to give me advice on running the newspaper. He had also expressed an interest in investing in *The Advocate*, since buying into newspapers was one of the ways he had built up the considerable fortune his wife had inherited. I had not been keen on a partnership, no matter how silent, and Tom had respected my wishes. But he and I were already partners in another far different enterprise: Tom was Adam's father, and in this letter, he was insisting on playing a bigger role in our son's life.

"With my other children virtually raised and on their own, I feel honor-bound to help you with Adam," Tom wrote on his word processor. "I haven't pressed you about this because I know how hell-bent you are on being independent. If you don't want to tell Adam about me, you don't have to, but in good conscience, I can't go on ignoring my responsibilities. It's not fair to Adam, and it's not fair to me."

Bull, I thought to myself angrily. None of it was ever fair to anybody. It wasn't fair that Tom had married a wealthy heiress before I met him. It wasn't fair that we had fallen in love and that his wife and I had gotten pregnant about the same time. And it certainly wasn't fair that Sandra Cavanaugh had turned out to be a raving loony.

"I can see you wadding this letter up and throwing it across the room while you swear like a sailor," Tom went on in his usual wry—and perceptive—manner. "But I'd like you to at least think about this. I may be coming up your way in the early fall again, so maybe we can have dinner. Meanwhile, there are a couple of recent developments that came out of a publishers' meeting last month in Tampa . . ."

He went on to enlighten me about a new way of billing advertisers and how small newspapers could become the middlemen in job printing. I didn't pay much attention. All I noticed was that he signed the letter, "Love, Tom."

And I still did.

Perhaps I'd give his proposal some thought. After Loggerama. I might even consider his suggestions about the paper. Certainly I would think about having dinner with him if he came up from the Bay Area in the fall.

One thing I would not do: I wouldn't crumple up the letter and throw it across the room. But I did swear like a sailor.

Chapter Five

MY DINNER WITH Reid Hampton was a dud. The food at the Café de Flore was excellent as always, the wine list was extensive and impressive, and the service was superb. But the company was definitely second-rate.

To be fair, I suppose a lot of women would find Reid Hampton fascinating. Certainly he had traveled a lot, read widely if not deeply, and knew everyone who had graced the covers of *People* magazine in the past year. But by the time the main course arrived, I was already full—at least of Reid Hampton, who was so full of himself. It's an occupational hazard of journalism that much of one's career is spent listening to other people tell you the stories of their lives. So maybe just once, I was hoping that in my off-hours, I'd find someone who might want to hear mine. As it turned out, Reid Hampton didn't. He didn't even ask any questions about Alpine, which struck me as strange—certainly a director who was setting a film in a small town should want to know what life was really like. But I gathered that Reid Hampton preferred to make up his own version.

It was no wonder that he didn't ask to come in when he brought me home or that he made no romantic advances. I suspected that he was as glad to park me on my doorstep as I was to see him drive away. Most of the time he had talked about himself, his films, his ambitions, his philosophy. My efforts at steering him away from his ego and onto his coworkers came to naught. He remarked that the camera loved Dani Marsh, and that she was like an empty bottle, just waiting for him to fill her up with emotions. He appeared to know next to nothing about her background, except that she came from Alpine. "Cute little town," he had commented. "We'll do a couple of street scenes after all this Loggerama crap is out of the way. I should have some of those buildings repainted along the main drag. They're not right for this picture. I need more blue, some green, maybe even a splash of red. Say, Emma, how would you like to have your newspaper office take on a coat of canary yellow?"

The Advocate badly needed a make-over, but *yellow* coupled with *journalism* did not strike me as a suitable visual message. Somehow, I'd avoided a direct answer. Reid had waxed a bit more eloquently on the subject of Matt Tabor, praising the actor's "brooding presence" and "unquenchable masculinity." Matt was from Kansas and had started out as a dancer. I had refrained from asking if he'd worn ruby slippers or had owned a dog named Toto. My only revenge had been dessert, a marvelous confection of meringue and apricots and whipped cream topped with crystalized sugar.

If I had not turned Reid Hampton into a slathering beast, he had not stirred me to pulse-throbbing excitement either. It was strange, perhaps, since he was good-looking in his lion-maned, broad-shouldered way, and certainly had the trappings of power and success to provide the necessary aphrodisiac. As I slipped out of my plain black linen sheath, it occurred to me that the evening might have gone better if I hadn't received the letter from Tom Cavanaugh just over an hour before Reid had picked me up. To my addled heart, Tom would have made Erich von Stroheim seem bland.

It was not yet ten. I put on my summer-weight cotton bathrobe and went back to the living room to check my messages. Carla had called to say she'd definitely be in on Friday. Francine Wells wanted to know if I'd like to look over her new stock when it came in the second week of August. Henry Bardeen had phoned from the ski lodge to tell me they had found a family of raccoons living in the little house where they stored their firewood. Did I want a picture?

I supposed I did. Raccoons always make good pictures. I called Henry to tell him I'd send Carla up in the morning.

"I'm afraid we can't wait," said Henry, sounding unusually testy for a man whose job as resort manager required endless patience and perennial good will. "One of our guests suffers from raccoon-phobia. If we don't get those animals out of the wood house tonight Matt Tabor says he'll drive into Seattle and stay at the Four Seasons Olympic."

"Oh, for heavens' sake!" I didn't know whether to laugh or be annoyed. "Okay, Henry, I'll be up in ten minutes."

While changing into slacks and a blouse, I decided I was definitely annoyed. I didn't want to bother Vida this late, and Carla needed a good night's sleep to complete her recovery. Fortunately, I had an extra camera at home. The drive to the ski lodge would take less than five minutes, since my house was on the edge of town. But the idea of the aggressively masculine Matt Tabor being afraid of a bunch of big-eyed bandits with four legs was irksome. I wished that Henry Bardeen had at least cornered a grizzly bear.

Mama, Papa, and four babies posed graciously for my camera. Then Mama wanted to borrow the camera. I back-pedaled out of the wood house and was grateful for Henry's assistance. He had brought some cooked hamburger and peeled oranges to lure the raccoon family out of its self-styled lair. A van with open back doors waited a few yards away, to transport the raccoons to the other side of Alpine.

"Having these Hollywood people here is no picnic," Henry sighed as the van headed down the road. "Oh, they're paying a pretty penny, which is always welcome in off-season; but I tell you, Emma, it's one aggravation after another." Henry Bardeen shook his head, which was topped by an artfully graying toupee.

"Like what?" I asked guilelessly.

"Like diet." Henry's thin mouth twisted. He was a slim man of medium height, with an aquiline nose and fine gray eyes. Unlike most professional men in Alpine, who tended to go in for more casual attire, Henry always wore a suit and tie. "They have the strangest eating habits. And schedules. In bed by ten, maybe even nine, then up at the crack of dawn, which means the kitchen help has to come in early. Not only to fix breakfast, but to pack up the hampers for their lunch up on Baldy. I've had to hire extra people. Tonight, Dani Marsh wanted some sort of cabbage drink sent up to her room. We had no idea how to make it, and when we finally got through to somebody in Everett, Dani was gone. Now she's a local, wouldn't you think she wouldn't be as queer as the rest of them?"

"She hasn't lived here for five years," I pointed out, wondering if there was a feature story in *The Peculiar Palates of Picture People*. Probably not, I decided. It would annoy most of the locals as much as it irked Henry Bardeen.

"She's been gone from the lodge for three hours," said Henry, looking even more aggravated. "That Hampton fellow is about to call the sheriff."

"Good," I said, hoping Reid Hampton would catch Milo Dodge in the sack with Honoria Whitman. It would serve all of them right.

"Good?" Henry stared at me. He may have possessed a gracious manner—usually—but he had absolutely no sense of humor. "What's good about having Reid Hampton roar around the lobby while Matt Tabor is cringing in a corner because some of our furry friends are living outside his window? What's good about Dani Marsh being gone for several hours? She has a wake-up call scheduled for five A.M.!"

"As you pointed out," I said in a soothing voice, "Dani *is* a native. She probably has some old friends here. And her mother, of course."

Henry's stare grew hypnotic. "Patti?" He shook his head, breaking the spell. "I know for a fact that Dani has tried to call Patti at least three times, but either she isn't in or she hangs up on Dani." Suddenly he turned sheepish. "My daughter, Heather, should be more discreet. But I'm afraid she's star-struck."

I knew Heather Bardeen, a pretty, self-contained young woman who worked for her father in various capacities, including that of PBX operator. Somehow, his description didn't sound right. "Aren't Heather and Dani the same age? They would have gone to school together."

Henry grew tight-lipped. "They did. Heather was a year behind Dani. They weren't really friends, but they knew each other. I suppose that's why Heather is so curious. In fact, Heather says that by the time Dani left Alpine, she didn't have any friends. Maybe that's why she went away."

"She'll show up," I said hopefully. "Did she take a car?"

"She may have," Henry replied, looking pessimistic. "The crew rented a whole fleet of them. They're all a white Lexus model. They got them from a dealership in Seattle, except for some custom-built job that belongs to Matt Tabor, and Reid Hampton's Cadillac. He got that here."

The Cadillac had served to take me to dinner at the Café de Flore. I gave Henry an absent nod, then glanced up at the ski lodge. Except for the main floor, most of the lights were already out. It was my understanding that the movie crew had taken up at least three of the lodge's four floors.

"You've got only a little more than a week to go," I said encouragingly. "Think of this as free promotion. It can't help but bring in more visitors next year."

"*Normal* visitors, I trust." Henry was looking very glum.

I gave up trying to cheer him, said good night, and headed for my Jaguar. Sundown had brought cooler temperatures, and a faint breeze stirred the trees. I didn't trouble to turn on the air-conditioning.

At the bottom of the road that led to the ski lodge, I noticed a white car pull up on the verge. My headlights caught a man getting out on the passenger's side. He came around to speak to the driver, who had apparently rolled down the window. As I stopped to watch for any oncoming cars from Alpine Way, I recognized Curtis Graff. And, just as I stepped on the accelerator, I realized that the woman behind the wheel was Dani Marsh.

An odd couple, I thought. Unless Francine Wells hadn't been talking off the top of her carefully coiffed head.

My intention was to tell Vida first thing about seeing Curtis Graff with Dani Marsh. Her reaction would prove interesting. But when I arrived at the office Friday morning, Vida was screaming at the top of her ample lungs and browbeating Abe Loomis. Ed Bronsky watched in dismay while Carla twittered in the vicinity of the coffeepot.

"You're crazier than a bear on a bee farm, Abe Loomis!" cried Vida, waving a sheet of paper at the shocked owner of Mugs Ahoy. "I wouldn't enter your ridiculous contest in a million years! I ought to have you horsewhipped!"

"But Vida," protested Abe, pointing a bony finger at the piece of paper, "you signed the entry form. See for yourself."

Vida glared through her glasses. Her jaw dropped. "Oooooh . . ." She yanked the glasses off and rubbed furiously at her eyes. "I couldn't have! It's a forgery!"

I took the sheet of paper from Abe. Vida's unmistakably flamboyant signature was emblazoned in the space marked for *Entrant*. Someone might have signed her name, but I doubted that anyone would go to the trouble—or have the expertise—to render such a perfect facsimile of her handwriting. It seemed to me that there was another more logical explanation. But I didn't want to mention it in front of Abe Loomis.

Finally, Vida stopped grinding her eyeballs. She sat up very straight, fists on hips, bust thrust out as if she were auditioning for Abe's contest. "All right. I'll do it. What time?"

Abe didn't exactly smile, but at least he moved his mouth. "That's wonderful, Vida. It's tonight, nine o'clock . . ."

I rolled my eyes at Ed, who was shaking his head. Carla

was bouncing up and down, trying to get Vida's attention. But Vida was jotting the specifics on a notepad. At last, Abe finished relaying information, nodded to the rest of us, and left the office.

"Vida!" shrieked Carla. "You can't do this! It's demeaning! You'll give journalists a bad name!"

Vida gave Carla the gimlet eye. "A lot of journalists do that every time they get their byline on a story. Put a sock in it, Carla, I won't go back on my word. Though how my name got on that silly form, I'll never—"

I sprang around Carla to face Vida. "I think I know. You signed the entry form instead of the print order. They called from Monroe Wednesday to say we didn't have an authorized signature this week, but they'd go ahead and print without one."

"Oh!" Vida blanched. "That's right! There was a lot of hubbub about then. Oh dear!" She whipped off her glasses again and started a renewed attack on her poor eyes. "Then I'm glad I gave in to that idiot Abe. I have no excuse."

In his typically lugubrious fashion, Ed had come around to Vida's desk. "It'll be just fine, Vida. We'll all come and root for you. I'll bring Shirley. Say," Ed exclaimed, showing signs of actual animation, "maybe Shirley ought to enter, too. She's pretty buxom."

Buxom wasn't the word I'd have chosen to describe Ed Bronsky's wife. *Barrel* usually came to mind. I shuddered at the thought, but left the lecture to Carla. She did not disappoint me, rattling off at least a half-dozen reasons why Shirley Bronsky should not engage in such a sexist competition. For once, Ed seemed to pay attention.

By mid-morning, Carla had gone off to talk to the Chamber of Commerce about the influx of tourists, and Ed had left to confer about an ad at the Toyota dealership. Their departure gave me the chance to tell Vida about seeing Dani Marsh with Curtis Graff.

Vida turned contemplative. "How very odd," she remarked, chewing on the tortoiseshell earpiece of her glasses.

"Why?" I inquired, perching on the edge of her desk. "Didn't Dani get along with her brother-in-law?"

Vida squinted up at me. "No, no, that isn't what I mean. Curtis and Dani were on amicable terms, as far as I know. I meant that it's strange for Curtis to show up after all these years at the same time that Dani comes back to town. This is his first trip to Alpine since he went to Alaska."

"Well," I said, as Ginny Burmeister came into the office with the morning mail, "there hasn't been much to draw him here if his parents are in the San Juans and he and Cody weren't close."

"Exactly." Vida gave a single, sharp nod of her head. "The brothers were always scrapping. But Dani makes an appearance and here comes Curtis." She snapped her fingers. "Don't you find that curious?"

"I had a crush on Curtis when I was thirteen," said Ginny, distributing stacks of mail in each of the three in-baskets in the news office. "He was almost ten years older than I was, but I used to hide behind our hedge and watch him go down the street. The Graffs lived at the other end of the block, on Cedar. I'd gotten over him by the time he went to Alaska, but I still felt sort of sad."

"Everyone felt sad for the Graffs and the Marshes," said Vida. "That was the first case of Sudden Infant Death Syndrome in this town in several years. We've only had one SIDS tragedy since, thank heavens."

I accepted the pile of bills, news releases, and letters to the editor from Ginny. "It sounds to me as if the death of that poor baby changed a lot of lives. Dani and Cody broke up, Dani left town, the Graffs moved away, Curtis went to Alaska, and Patti Marsh doesn't want anything to do with her daughter."

"Exactly," agreed Vida, fingering a couple of wedding announcements she'd just received. "And Art Fremstad committed suicide. It was an awful year for Alpine."

I blinked at Vida, who was ripping open one of the envelopes, pink stationery with a gilded edge. "Who's Art Fremstad?" In two years, I'd never heard of the man.

Vida scanned the announcement. "Michelle Lynn Carmichael and Jeremy Allan Prescott. A have-to. Marje says she's six months along." Vida tossed the pink and gilt announcement into the box by her typewriter. "What? Oh— Art. He was a deputy sheriff, not yet thirty, and seemed to have good sense. But he was found in the river, about a mile from Alpine Falls. His family insisted it had to be an accident, but later they found a note. He was despondent, or depressed, or whatever claptrap people use to disguise the fact that they have no self-discipline."

I winced a little at Vida's harsh pronouncement. "What did Milo Dodge think?"

Vida had turned to her typewriter, obviously ready to roll. "Milo?" She gave a little shrug. "He was pretty upset. He was sure it was an accident, too, until that note turned up." The typewriter keys began to clickety-clack at about a hundred words a minute.

I looked at Ginny. "Do you remember the incident?"

Ginny ran a hand through her auburn hair. "Sure. Not that many people kill themselves in Alpine. I suppose," she added musingly, "because there aren't that many people to begin with." Her gaze was ironic.

"I suppose," I said, and wondered why I suddenly had a feeling of unease.

To my amazement, Milo Dodge called me in the late afternoon and asked if I'd like to go with him to the Mugs Ahoy wet T-shirt contest. "I heard about Vida," he said, obviously trying not to sound too amused. "You and your staff could probably use some moral support."

"Moral?" I snorted into the phone. "I don't know whether it will help or hinder Vida to have us there. In some ways, I think we should spare her the embarrassment."

Milo laughed outright. "Vida? Embarrassed? She'll love it. What did Abe say in the ad about sticking *more* than your neck out? Vida's been doing that with her nose for years."

"We're not talking about Vida's nose," I snapped, unhappily recalling one of the changes I'd allowed Abe Loomis to make. "This whole carny show is offensive, and you know it, Milo Dodge. What does Honoria Whitman think about it?"

There was a faint pause. Apparently, Honoria had declined to attend. "She finds small towns amusing. Not that she's a big city girl," he added hastily. "She's from Carmel. She says it's getting too crowded."

"Tut," I remarked, but decided it might be prudent to drop the subjects of Honoria and the wet T-shirt contest. "Milo, why did Art Fremstad kill himself?"

This time, the pause was longer. "Jesus," breathed Milo at last, "why are you bringing that up? I was finally beginning to forget about poor Art. At least a little."

"His name was mentioned today," I said. "How was he connected with the death of Dani and Cody's baby?"

"Dani called Doc Dewey, who told her to send for the firemen and the sheriff," said Milo carefully. "I was out of town—it was during the time that Old Mulehide and I were wrangling over custody and all that. Art Fremstad covered for me while I was in Bellevue. He went to the trailer park where Dani and Cody were living, out there past the fish hatchery where those new townhouses went up last year. He and his wife had a new baby of their own. I think the Graff kid's death unhinged him somehow. At least that's what his note indicated."

"He was distraught, you mean? Or depressed?"

"All of the above," replied Milo, sounding very unhappy. "Muddled, too, judging from the way he wrote. Hell, Emma, it wasn't at all like Art. If we hadn't found that note, I'd have sworn it was an accident. Or worse."

Involuntarily, I pushed myself and my chair away from the desk. "What do you mean? Foul play?"

"We considered that at the time. But three days after Art was found—in fact, it was the day of his funeral—this note turned up at his home. His wife discovered it when she got back from the Lutheran church. Case closed."

And, I thought to myself, with good reason. Art was a young man with a wife and a new baby. The trauma of finding a baby dead from the most inexplicable of causes must have shaken his very soul. Even thinking about it upset me. Art Fremstead must have been a sensitive man, as yet unhardened to the realities of the world.

"Pick me up at eight," I told Milo. There was no point in distressing him further. His recollections were obviously painful. My own emotions were unsettled.

Oddly enough, I would be very glad to see Milo Dodge.

Chapter Six

MUGS AHOY WAS jammed. The noise level was deafening; the cigarette smoke weakened my resolve to abstain; the lack of air-conditioning made the interior uncomfortably warm, even at sundown; and the usually murky interior was intermittently lighted up by some sort of revolving lamp above the bar. Even Abe Loomis looked brighter than usual, his long face teetering on the edge of enthusiasm.

If I hadn't been escorted by the sheriff, I would have ended up standing by the door. But Milo pushed his way through the crowd, dragging me by the hand. We stopped at a table near the front where Carla, Ginny, and the Bronskys were already seated. Somehow, Milo commandeered two more chairs, and I squeezed in next to Shirley Bronsky while Milo draped his lanky frame in the chair beside Carla.

Our attempts at small talk failed. It was too loud for normal conversation; the jukebox was playing the Judds and Randy Travis at ear-splitting volume. Milo had ordered a pitcher and a bowl of complimentary thin pretzels. Shirley Bronsky was shoveling mixed nuts into her round mouth, and Carla was drinking white wine. If it was Abe Loomis's house vintage, I figured it probably tasted like paint thinner, but Carla was smiling all over the place. To my amazement, she leaped right out of her seat when Jack Blackwell picked up the microphone and announced that the contest was about to begin.

Jack, who had been seated in front with Patti Marsh and two couples I recognized but didn't know by name, was wearing a silk sportcoat and a string tie. For all the money he had allegedly made in the timber business, I had never seen him dressed up. He didn't exactly rival a Wall Street banker, but at least he looked presentable. Patti glowed up at him, her rhinestone earrings swinging almost to her shoulders.

Jack's first words were indecipherable, mainly because nobody had thought to turn Garth Brooks off on the jukebox. Finally, someone had the sense to pull the plug. Jack grinned at the crowd, revealing very white, if uneven, teeth.

"This is it," he began, clutching the mike to his chest as if he were about to serenade a honeymoon couple in the Poconos. "You've all been waiting for the great moment, the biggest beer bust of them all. Here we go, it's time for Mugs Ahoy's Jugs Ahoy!"

I sighed, Ed chuckled, Ginny grimaced, and Shirley giggled. Milo, thankfully, remained impassive, but to my horror, Carla clapped like crazy. It appeared that her principles had evaporated in a bottle of Yosemite Sam.

The contestants came out from the ladies' room, mounted four temporary stairs to the bar, and to the relatively subdued strains of Waylon Jennings's "Sweet Caroline," paraded above the crowd, strutting and straining in their remarkable wet T-shirts. Jack, meanwhile, shouted each contestant's name and occupation. First in line was Chaz Phipps from the ski lodge, wearing neon green with blinking earrings that must have been on batteries. I wished I'd been on drugs. The catcalls were obnoxious. But Chaz and the three young women who followed her didn't seem to mind in the least.

Milo squeezed my elbow. "You could do that," he remarked, more seriously than I would have wished. "You have a nice chest, Emma."

It was the first personal observation Milo had ever directed at me in the two years I had known him. I didn't know whether to slug him or smile in gratitude. Deciding that he meant well, but couldn't help being an inarticulate boob, I settled for a noncommittal shrug. Then I realized that *boob* was probably inappropriate. I had to stifle a laugh, lest I encourage Carla to further mayhem.

There were twelve contestants in all, and either by accident or design, Vida was last—but certainly not least. She stomped up the stairs to Johnny Cash's classic "Ring of Fire," her head held high, her glasses almost at the end of her nose. She wore a pair of dark gray slacks I'd seen fifty times at work, but her T-shirt was a sight to behold: Vida's impressive bust was adorned with the front page of *The Advocate*'s Loggerama edition, and in each hand she held a small pennant. The left said SUBSCRIBE NOW!; the right said READ BOOKS! Carla jumped onto the table and lead the applause. Naturally, I joined in. Vida sailed off the bar and down the ramp at the far end to join her fellow contestants in the men's room, which was temporarily off-limits. I noticed that Patti Marsh was no longer seated at the first-row table. Maybe she was having regrets about not having taken part in the competition.

I was never sure who the official judges were, though when I had gone in, I had assumed them to be Abe's favorite local drunks. Whoever they were, they deliberated for over five minutes before announcing that the winner was Vida Runkel. Amid a thunderous ovation, marred by only a few boos, Vida reappeared, still waving her little flags and thrusting her bosom in various directions. Jack Blackwell shoved the microphone in her face.

"Thank you," Vida said after the crowd had begun to quiet down. "The judges' decision proves that older is better. Abe Loomis's idea to hold this contest proves that he's dumb as a rope, but we all knew that before there ever was a Loggerama." She pushed her glasses back up on her nose and gave Abe a flinty look. "The fact that you're all here proves that you're no smarter than Abe. That doesn't say much for Alpine. So two weeks from tonight, at this same time and same place, I want to see all of you back here. Your ticket in the door is a book. The drinks will be on me." Vida pasted the microphone on Jack's chest and moved majestically toward the ladies' room.

The crowd had gone very quiet, but as she made her exit, more applause began to break out. Carla had climbed down from the tabletop, but was now back up on her chair, shrieking and clapping. "I'm going to read *War and Peace!*" she yelled after Vida. "I cheated and rented the movie for Russian lit at UW! Oh, yeah, Vida! Go, go, *go!*"

Vida went. I had hoped she'd exchange her wet T-shirt for one of her more modest—if gaudy—blouses and join us, but she didn't. Apparently, Vida had had enough of Mugs Ahoy. I had, too, and it didn't take Milo more than half an hour to realize it, especially after I asked him four times to take me home.

Sheriff or not, Milo had been forced to park his Chero-kee Chief two blocks away, in back of the Clemans Building. As we walked along Pine Street with the night air feeling like a tonic, Milo remarked that Vida had certainly been a good sport. I agreed. He said he felt that her challenge about reading books was very appropriate. I said I thought so, too. He allowed that it had been a while since he'd read anything except newspapers. I told him he was missing a lot.

"I used to read more," he said, pulling out from the curb. "Of course I have to go over loads of stuff at work. Some days I get sick of words." Stopping at the Pine Street arterial across from the Alpine Medical and Dental Clinic, Milo suddenly whistled and leaned into the steering wheel. "Look at that!"

The pearl gray car cruising past us was unlike any automobile I'd ever seen, except on a visit to Beverly Hills six years earlier. I, too, stared. "What is it?" I asked in a breathless voice.

"Damned if I know," said Milo, shaking his head as the sleek two-door coupe disappeared past the hospital. "Custom job. Did you see who was driving it?"

I'd gotten a glimpse of the profile behind the wheel. "Henry Bardeen said Matt Tabor brought a customized make to Alpine. But that wasn't Matt driving."

Milo grinned at me before making his right-hand turn. "No, it sure wasn't. That was Dani Marsh, right?"

I gave a faint nod. "Along with Patti Marsh and somebody else."

Milo and I exchanged puzzled looks.

Saturday should have been a day of rest, but journalists are never assured of having weekends off. Vida was going to cover the Miss Alpine pageant in the evening, Carla was assigned to the kiddy parade in the late morning, and I was taking on the timber sports competition in the afternoon.

The event was scheduled for the high school football field, which is less than two blocks from my home. Carrying a camera and a notebook, I walked over under the noonday sun to find a large crowd gathered in the stands. At one end zone, ALPINE was spelled out in fresh white letters; at the other was BUCKERS, the team nickname, which referred to millworkers who specialized in the sawhorse. Or something to do with the old mill—I was never quite clear; but the mascot depicted a big lug with a big grin and an even bigger saw. It seemed to fit the town's image, though there were grumbles that it was sexist. My feeling was that it was traditional, and at least the Bucker wasn't using the saw to cut a woman in two.

While Alpine's annual event is not on the official Timber Sports circuit, a number of the regular professional competitors usually show up.

Many of the Loggerama contests are not part of the usual circuit, but are steeped in local lore. One of these is Shoot the Duck, in which a decoy is perched high among the branches of a portable Douglas fir and the contestants attempt to hit the target with a catapult. Since I couldn't figure out what this event had to do with timber, logging, and other woodsy work, I questioned Vida about the connection. She informed me that her father-in-law, Rufus Runkel, was responsible. Back in 1927, his wife had promised visitors from Seattle that they would have roast duck for dinner. Armed with a shotgun, Rufus had headed into the woods, but after hiking for over three miles, he discovered he'd forgotten his buckshot. To ensure his honor as a hunter and his wife's reputation as a cook, Rufus had used a rope and a rock to fling at the unsuspecting ducks. Somehow, he bagged three of them, proudly carried them home, and earned not only the thanks of his wife, but an epigram as well:

"I figured Rufus has been shooting blanks for years, but I'm sure glad he still has rocks in his head," said Mrs. Runkel. The trophy for the event was named in his memory.

Due to my status as a member of the press, I was allowed on the sidelines. It was probably even warmer on the field than in the stands, and after the first two hours of sweating, heaving, grunting lumberjacks, I scoured the program in an effort to figure out how much longer I would have to stick around to write an adequate story. I had at least a half-dozen decent photos already and could always get the final results from Harvey Adcock, the hardware store owner who was one of the officials. There were probably close to six hundred people on hand, virtually filling both sides of the stadium. To my surprise, Dani Marsh arrived with Matt Tabor and Reid Hampton shortly after intermission. They were ushered to folding chairs just below the stands and a few yards away from my vantage point. Dani and Reid waved; Matt ignored my existence. Indeed, Matt Tabor seemed to be ignoring the entire occasion. His handsome face looked blotchy, and even at a distance, his eyes seemed unfocused. I thought again about seeing Patti Marsh in the custom-built car. If it belonged to Matt, her presence there seemed very peculiar.

Having suffered through shaving hunks of wood with an axe, log-rolling on a makeshift pond at midfield, and numerous bouts with chain saws, I decided to leave after the Standing Block Chop competition. Kneeling on the dry grass with my camera at the ready, I watched as ten contestants, including Cody Graff, confronted three-foot blocks of wood set in four-legged iron stands on blocks of concrete.

As Harvey Adcock blew his horn to start the competition, I kept my eye on Cody Graff. Like most of his rivals, he was bare to the waist. The muscles of his back and upper arms rippled as he flailed away at the block of wood. His narrow shoulders prevented him from having a physique as imposing as several of the other young men, but he seemed to wield his axe with great authority. I glanced up into the crowd to see if I could find Marje Blatt. She was probably on hand to watch her fiancé, but I couldn't pick her out in the stands.

It was while my back was turned that the axe flew past me. It sailed within two feet of my head and landed with a loud thud at the feet of Dani Marsh. The onlookers uttered a collective gasp. I let out a little cry of my own and whirled around. Cody Graff was standing with his empty hands at his side, while his malevolent expression was fixed on the trio of Hollywood visitors.

Harvey Adcock, Jack Blackwell, and Henry Bardeen were out on the field. The other contestants were still hacking away, though all eyes in the audience were glued on Cody or his axe. Matt Tabor was yelling obscenities, while Reid Hampton picked up the sharp-edged tool and shot a furious look at Cody Graff. Dani Marsh was on her feet, shifting nervously in front of her folding chair.

I moved closer to Harvey, who was now talking to Cody. Harvey seemed very earnest, but I couldn't make out his words without crossing the sideline marker. Cody was shrugging, then nodding. Jack Blackwell retrieved the axe from Reid Hampton, but he didn't give it back to Cody. Instead, Cody jogged off the field, his head down, his face impassive.

I grabbed Harvey as he came over to where I was standing. "What happened? My back was turned."

Harvey, who is no taller than I am, looked at me with troubled green eyes. "Cody says it was an accident. The axe slipped." His graying eyebrows lifted slightly.

"What do you think?" I asked as the crowd began to settle back into the rhythm of the contest.

Harvey shook his balding head. "I can't say, Emma. It just seems odd that the axe landed right in front of Dani and her friends." With one of his typically quicksilver movements, Harvey started down the sidelines. "The heat's over. I've got to go be an official."

It seemed to me that there was more news—if you define the concept as public interest—in the flying axe than in any further description of the competition. I headed off the field and under the stands to try to find Cody. But by the time I reached the cramped, dank-smelling area that was used mostly for halftime pep talks during football season, Cody was nowhere to be seen. Having come this far, I kept going, out the back way, and into the dirt parking lot.

Cody Graff and Marje Blatt were getting into his pickup truck. They drove away without seeing me.

Two nights in a barroom were two too many for my taste, but Carla and Ginny insisted I join them at the Icicle Creek Tavern to take part in the Celebrity Bartender festivities.

"Doc Dewey's on hand for the first two hours," said Carla as we drove in my Jaguar out Mill Street to the edge of town.

At least we would avoid Fuzzy Baugh and his civic-minded libations. I pulled into the parking lot which was only half full, probably because most of the local residents were attending the Miss Alpine pageant at the high school. No doubt they would pour in later, griping about the winner's deficiencies or extolling her virtues, depending on who was related to whom.

The Icicle Creek Tavern has been controversial in the past few years, not only for its reputation as a site of weekend brawls, but because the area south of the railroad tracks has been built up with new solid middle class homes. In addition, several more expensive residences now sit just across the creek above the river. And the golf course is situated on hilly, tree-shaded grounds a few hundred yards down the road. Naturally, the neighborhood does not approve of the ramshackle old tavern with its boarded-up windows and raucous clientele. They're not even too fond of the gas station which sits next to the tavern, though they will admit it's convenient.

At one time, probably just after Prohibition ended and before the loggers started pitching each other through unmarked exits, perhaps the tavern had its share of charm. The paint has faded from its shake exterior; the cedar shingles on the roof have weathered to a dull gray; and the corroded metal sign that stands in the parking lot is virtually unreadable.

The interior is even worse. So many of the chairs have been used to bash heads that in recent years the management has simply brought in apple boxes and other relatively sturdy crates as replacements. The tables are splintering, the floor is uneven, and the long mirror behind the bar has cracked in the form of a spider. Yet on this muggy Saturday night of Loggerama, there was the suggestion of a festive air. Bunting hung from the ceiling along with the cobwebs; a montage of old logging pictures had been mounted over the bar to cover up the shattered mirror; and the pool table had been turned into a display of logging tools from the early part of the century. Most of them were rusty and broken, but it was still a nice idea.

Carla insisted on sitting at the bar. Checking the stool for slivers, I sat down and greeted Doc Dewey who, surprisingly, looked as at home in his white bartender's apron as he did in his white medical coat.

"What will you girlies have?" he inquired, giving the bar a professional swipe with a wet cloth. He looked over his half glasses at Carla. "How's that sting? Any reaction?"

"Not to the antihistamine," replied Carla, crossing her legs and swinging her feet like some barfly out of a Forties second feature. "Only to the stupid bee. Or wasp."

"Good, good," said Doc. "You're over the danger now. It can have a lot of different symptoms, though. Everything from drowsiness to heart palpitations." He patted his apron-covered chest, causing something to click in his shirt pocket. An extra set of dentures, I mused, just in case some of the patrons weren't on their best Loggerama behavior and tried to knock out his teeth.

Ginny and I both ordered beer, but Carla again opted for white wine. I shuddered, hoping it wouldn't have the same effect on her tonight as it had during the wet T-shirt contest. Taking the schooner from Doc, I swiveled on the stool to check out the rest of the customers. There were a few regulars, mostly loggers, but there was also a sprinkling of people I figured didn't usually hang out at the Icicle Creek Tavern: Cal Vickers, who owned the Texaco station on the other side of town, had come with his wife, Charlene; Heather Bardeen and her buddy, Chaz Phipps from the ski lodge; Jack Blackwell and Patti Marsh; Marje Blatt and Cody Graff.

I considered going over to Cody and asking him about the incident with the axe, but Marje seemed to be deep into a one-sided lecture and Cody was well into his cups. I decided this wasn't the time or place. Just as I was about to turn back to the bar, the door opened. Milo Dodge came in with Honoria Whitman. At least I assumed that the woman in the pale yellow painter's smock shirt and the black tights was Honoria. Her face was a perfect oval, with short ash blond hair and wide-set gray eyes. She had an air of serenity about her, as if nothing could go wrong in her world as long as she was on hand to prevent it.

Except that something obviously had: To my dismay, Honoria Whitman was in a wheelchair. I tried not to let my jaw drop.

Milo nodded in my direction. A bit awkwardly, I descended from the bar stool and went over to greet him and his companion. Milo made the introductions. Honoria extended her hand. It was long, slim, and milk white. She did not fit my preconceived notions of a transplanted Californian in the least.

"Milo speaks so well of you," she said in a cultured, husky voice. "He says you're every inch the professional, a real addition to this community."

"Oh—that's kind of him." I glanced up at Milo, who was flushing. So was I.

More people were coming into the tavern, including Al Driggers, the undertaker, and his spunky wife, Janet. Right behind them, a contingent from the high school faculty trooped in. I recognized Steve Wickstrom, who taught math, and his wife, Donna, along with Coach Rip Ridley and Mrs. Ridley, whose first name I seemed to remember was Dixie. Schoolteachers who drank in public were frowned upon in Alpine, but Loggerama was obviously an exception. The faculty could get as drunk and stupid as the rest of the residents without being hauled up before the school board.

Milo pushed Honoria's chair over to an empty table near the rest room doors. I returned to the bar, where Carla and Ginny were head-to-head, obviously speculating about Milo and Honoria.

"The sheriff has a *girlfriend*?" Carla shook me by the arm. "Emma, I thought you and Milo Dodge were—"

"We weren't," I cut in tersely. "Milo and I are friends, period. Honoria seems quite charming." It was, I thought, unfortunately true. Swiftly, I changed the subject, trying to draw Doc Dewey into a conversation about Art Fremstad's suicide. But Doc had suddenly become very busy. He didn't have time for chitchat. I nursed my beer and sat back to listen to Carla exchange gossip with Ginny about the latest Alpine romances. Since most of the people involved were young enough to be my children—though I was awfully glad they weren't—I didn't pay much attention. Instead, I studied the growing crowd, watching an animated Janet Driggers use lots of hand gestures to describe something to Charlene Vickers. Patti Marsh and Jack Blackwell were snuggling near the pool table. The Wickstroms and the Ridleys were still trying to find some vacant boxes to use for seats. Milo Dodge was demonstrating concern for Honoria Whitman's comfort. I sighed. If it had been me instead of Honoria, I could have been sitting on a six-inch spike and Milo wouldn't have noticed.

Another dozen people had entered the tavern in the past half hour. Jack Blackwell had abandoned Patti Marsh to help Doc behind the bar. I had no idea who the regular bartender was, but the owner was an old curmudgeon who lived way up on Icicle Creek not far from the ranger station. I debated about ordering another beer, but before I could get Doc's attention Dani Marsh came in with Reid Hampton and Matt Tabor. A hush fell over the gathering, then scattered applause broke out. Dani bobbed a curtsy and flashed her beautiful smile. Across the room, her mother curled her lip. I couldn't see Cody Graff from my angle on the bar stool, but I suddenly felt uneasy. If the axe incident had been unintentional, would Cody apologize to Dani and her coworkers? Or had he done so already? Somehow, I doubted it.

And I was right. While Dani Marsh and Reid Hampton moved straight for the bar, Matt Tabor angled over to Cody and Marje's table. I twisted around for a better view. The crowd had quieted down. There probably wasn't a person in the room who didn't know about that axe.

Carla was nudging me in the ribs. "Emma—are you going to write up what Cody did at the stadium? How close did that axe come to Dani?"

"Within inches," I replied soberly. "He was just damned lucky he missed all three of them. And me, for that matter. It flew within a couple of feet of my head."

Carla's dark eyes grew very wide. "Wow! I didn't know that! Everybody's been talking about what a close call Dani had! I wonder what Marje Blatt thinks. Hey," she went on, giving me another jab, "I've got a headline for you—CODY GRAFF AND MOVIE STAR EX-WIFE: WAS IT REALLY AN AXE-CIDENT?" Carla let loose with her high-pitched giggle.

I didn't bother to tell Carla that headline writing wasn't her strong suit. Come to think of it, I wasn't sure what was. Carla was deficient in a lot of areas, except for enthusiasm.

The conversation between Matt Tabor and Cody Graff was getting heated. Cody had gotten to his feet, despite Marje's efforts to restrain him. By now, all of the customers were staring, and except for the blur of background music over the tavern's antiquated sound system, silence dominated the room like an unwanted guest.

Cody was unsteady on his feet. Matt braced himself against the table with his knees. "You ever pull a stunt like that again and I'll kill you, you son of a bitch!" roared Matt in his trained movie voice.

"Go screw yourself!" shouted Cody, though the words weren't quite as distinct as he'd intended. He lunged across the table, but Matt Tabor was too quick for him. Matt's fist struck Cody square on the jaw, sending him slumping against the wall. The apple box beneath him crashed to one side. Marje and several others screamed. Milo Dodge was on his feet, wrestling his way around Honoria's wheelchair.

Matt backed off, while Cody wallowed around on the floor. Marje, having made sure her beloved was still alive, sprang at Matt. "Listen, you two-bit Hollywood jerk, we don't need your type around this town! Why don't you take yourself and that hotshot movie star tramp of yours back to California where you belong?"

Milo had a hand on Matt's arm, but his words were directed at Marje. "Sit down, Marje. Or better yet, take Cody home. I think he's had enough already. In a lot of ways."

Marje shot Milo an outraged look. "He's had two crummy beers! Big deal! If he were really drunk, would Doc serve him again? Hey, Sheriff, is this Loggerama or what?"

Matt was trying to shake loose of Milo, but the sheriff was holding fast. "Then you'd better drive, Marje. And keep Cody under control, okay?" He shook a warning finger at her, then pulled Matt Tabor back to a safe distance.

"Watch it, Badge Man," said Matt in a surly tone, as Milo finally let go. "I'm under contract to Gemini Productions. You want to get your butt sued?"

"My butt's covered, buster," retorted Milo, wheeling around to lope back to Honoria. He stopped short as he realized that war had broken out on yet another front at the

Icicle Creek Tavern. Jack Blackwell was refusing to serve Reid Hampton.

"This is the bastard that cut down my trees! To hell with him!" He hurled the bar towel onto the floor and spit into the nut dish. "He owes me eighty grand! He's outta here, or else I am!"

Reid Hampton, who was wearing a snakeskin vest and an array of Indian jewelry, threw his fawn-colored felt hat across the bar. "Don't be a jackass, Blackwell! We've got an iron-clad contract and you know it!"

"And you've got iron-clad pants!" roared Blackwell. "Just show me where it says in that freaking contract that you got any right to saw up my valuable timber."

From three stools down, I watched Dani Marsh watch Hampton and Blackwell. She looked vaguely alarmed, but not exactly upset. More to my surprise, she had made no move to console Matt Tabor, who was drinking thirstily from a mug poured by Doc Dewey. It was only when Patti Marsh charged up to the bar that Dani shrank back.

"Look here, Doc," yelled Patti in her hoarse voice as she elbowed Reid Hampton out of the way, "have you got a right to serve or not serve whoever you want in this dump or not?" Before Doc could answer, she pointed a painted fingernail at her daughter. "Let's start with her. She doesn't have a right to mix with decent people like the rest of us! How about dumping her out in the gutter where she belongs?"

Doc's mouth set in a rigid line, the type of expression he used on patients who wouldn't take their medicine. "Button it up, Patti. You don't know your backside from a hole in the ground."

"Yes, she does," said Janet Driggers, who had come up to the bar to get a new pitcher and some snacks. "It's the one on the left, obviously."

Doc broke into a grin, and Patti whirled around, her anger diverted. But Janet was so outrageously blunt that only the most mean-minded Alpiner could be annoyed by her. Patti started to say something, then saw that Reid Hampton was heading back to his table. "Hey, you!" shouted Patti. "Come here! I want a word with you, Mr. so-called-movie producer-director-whatever-the-hell-you-are!"

But Reid Hampton ignored her. Patti started after him, but Milo again resorted to his strong-arm technique. "Come on, Patti, sit down, go eat some of that popcorn with the Driggers. Let's not turn Loggerama into a war zone. I had more peaceful evenings in Nam."

Patti glared at Milo, then realized that his hand was on her waist and gave him a coquettish look. "Hey, sheriff," she cooed in a sudden shift of gears, "did anybody ever tell you you got terrific eyes? Soulful, or something like that."

Milo didn't flush this time, but he steered Patti away from the bar and into the care of a bemused Al and Janet Driggers. If Al was at a loss, his wife wasn't: "Sit down, Patti. Tell us if it's true about you and Jack doing it on the donkey engine up at Carroll Creek."

Cody was back on his box, looking like a floppy doll. Marje fussed over him, checking his bruised chin and offering him a fresh beer. Dani Marsh had finally joined Matt Tabor at the other end of the bar. Reid Hampton was allowing Doc Dewey to pour him a beer while a fuming Jack Blackwell served Milo. Patti had settled in with Al and Janet Driggers. I had to wonder why Patti and Dani had been driving around in Matt Tabor's fancy car Thursday night. How had they not managed to gouge out each other's eyes? I gave myself a shake, feeling as if I'd been involved in an old-fashioned Hollywood Western barroom brawl.

Back at the sheriff's table, Honoria looked composed, her head moving on her graceful neck as her serene gray eyes surveyed the aftermath of the mayhem. She caught me looking at her and gave me a conspiratorial smile. *Drat,* I thought, *I might get to like this woman.*

"This is fun," exclaimed Carla to Ginny. "We should come here more often. It's a lot more exciting than the Venison Inn."

"So is gang warfare," I remarked, wondering how much longer I could hold out.

Luckily, Ginny wasn't as taken with the Icicle Creek Tavern's floor show. "Frankly, I've got a headache from all this noise. Why don't we grab a pizza and then head home?"

Carla's face fell, but she rebounded quickly. "Double cheese, pepperoni, mushrooms, anchovies, and onions? Okay, we can eat it at my place. Want to get a video or catch the end of the Miss Alpine pageant? Emma?"

I shook my head. "Count me out. I've got a whole weekend to cram into half of tomorrow. Don't forget the parade and the banquet and the fireworks." Fortunately, my presence was required only at the banquet. Carla would cover the parade; Ed had volunteered to take pictures of the fireworks.

Carla finished her wine, and Ginny took a last sip of beer. My schooner had been empty for a long time. I asked Doc for our tab and insisted on treating my employees.

"Quite a night, eh, girlies?" asked Doc with a shake of his head. He was looking extremely tired, and I couldn't say that I blamed him. "I wonder when the loggers will start trying to kill each other?"

"I thought they signed a truce for Loggerama," I said with a grin. "When do you get done with your shift?"

He looked above the bar at the old clock featuring the Hamm's beer bear. "Ten minutes," he said with a grateful expression. "This seems like the longest two hours of my life. It wears me down, girlie. I'd rather do surgery. Dr. Starr should be along any minute." His lined face became unwontedly grim.

I led the way to the door, but halfway across the room I paused to greet the Driggers and the Vickers. Patti Marsh had returned to her table where she sat alone, sending malevolent glances in her daughter's direction. After an exchange of pleasantries, I began to pick my way through the tables again. I saw Cody and Marje leaving just ahead of us, about a minute after Curtis Graff had come into the tavern. The brothers ignored each other. Or, more likely, Cody was too bleary-eyed to recognize Curtis. Marje had her fiancé by the arm, propping him up. Milo had been right: Cody Graff hadn't needed a third beer. He looked as if he could barely make it to the parking lot.

It was fortunate that Marje Blatt was going to do the driving. At least Cody would get home alive and in one piece.

I couldn't guess that I was only half right.

I allowed myself the luxury of sleeping in until nine-fifteen on Sunday morning. Mass at St. Mildred's was at ten, and I could shower, dress, grab a cup of coffee, and get to church in under three-quarters of an hour. I was just about to struggle out of bed when the phone rang. Shielding my eyes against the bright morning sun, I groped for the receiver. It was Milo Dodge.

"Emma," he said, sounding tense. "I've got some bad news."

My brain wasn't quite on track yet. "What?"

Outside, I could hear the blare of trumpets. The high school band was assembling just a block and a half away, practicing for the big parade.

"There's been an accident," said Milo, with the sound of male voices in the background. "Durwood Parker ran over Cody Graff last night. Cody's dead and Durwood's back in jail."

I fell back on the bed, one hand on my head. Sunday wasn't going to be a day of rest, either. Except, of course, for Cody Graff.

Chapter Seven

CODY GRAFF HAD been struck down out on Mill Street, just west of the turnoff for Burl Creek Road. A weeping Durwood had turned himself in shortly after six A.M. He knew he wasn't supposed to drive, he told Milo, but he figured that if he took just a little spin on a quiet Sunday morning, nobody would be out on the road.

"We'll have to charge him with vehicular manslaughter," Milo told me after I got to the sheriff's office two blocks up from *The Advocate* on Front Street. I'd gone straight from mass, which Father Fitzgerald had cut short due to Loggerama.

"You know the prayers," he'd announced from the pulpit, so it's at home ye'll be saying them." His parishioners were grateful, since the little wooden church was already unmercifully hot. We were also spared Father Fitz's meandering sermon of the week, which frequently came out of a time warp and often featured The Hun and The Red Menace.

"Poor Durwood," I sighed. "How's his wife doing?"

Milo shrugged. "Dot's pretty upset. She said she knew this would happen some day. I told her to get a good lawyer, somebody from Seattle maybe."

"Can't you release him on his own recognizance?"

Milo sat down heavily in his imitation leather chair. "It's Sunday. He can't post bail until tomorrow. What can I do?" He gave a helpless lift of his shoulders.

A silence fell between us. I was the first to break it, suddenly aware that we seemed to have forgotten about the dead man. "What on earth was Cody Graff doing out by

312

Burl Creek Road at six in the morning? The last time I saw him, he looked as if he'd sleep for a week."

"Beats me." Milo gazed at the ceiling of his small no-nonsense office. As usual, his desk was cluttered and his in-basket piled high. He was in uniform, because he was due to ride in the parade with a couple of his deputies. "Cody lived in those apartments between Pine and Cedar, across from the medical-dental clinic. How he ended up out at the edge of town at that time of day, I don't know. Maybe Marje Blatt could tell us."

"Have you told Curtis?" I asked.

"I don't know where he is," replied Milo, taking a roll of mints out of his pocket and offering me one. "We called up to the San Juans to let Cody's parents know. They're coming down this afternoon, if they can get on a ferry. You know what traffic is like between the islands and the mainland this time of year on a Sunday."

I did. Despite the frequent ferry runs, car passengers were often forced to wait in line overnight on summer weekends. "Maybe Curtis is staying in a motel," I suggested, tasting spearmint on my tongue.

"We're checking," said Milo. "Damn, this is a hell of a thing to happen during Loggerama. And I've got an election coming up." He gave a rueful shake of his head.

"It's not your fault," I said in what I hoped was an encouraging tone. "Durwood shouldn't have been driving. And the thought of Cody wandering along on a country road at dawn is pretty bizarre. In fact, it's just plain inexplicable." I gazed straight into Milo's hazel eyes, waiting for him to agree with me.

But Milo's thoughts were going off in another direction. He stood up. "I've got to go get my horse from the Dithers sisters' farm. Fuzzy Baugh insisted we ride like some Wild West posse, instead of in our squad cars. Jeez!" He made a disparaging gesture with his hand. "I haven't been on a horse in ten years."

I wished Milo well and headed for my car. I had no desire to watch the parade, which was scheduled for one o'clock. It was now after eleven-thirty, and I hadn't had any breakfast. The Venison Inn and the Burger Barn both looked crowded. I stopped by the office to call Vida and asked if she'd like to drive with me down to Index, where we could get some brunch.

"Do you want to eat or have a powwow?" Vida demanded. "What's this gruesome business with Cody Graff? Marje has been bleating in my ear for the last hour." Vida didn't sound too sympathetic toward her niece.

We agreed that we could eat and discuss Cody's demise in Index as well as we could in Alpine. Five minutes later, I picked Vida up at her neat white frame cottage on Cascade Street, and we headed for the main highway. The town of Index is located some twenty-five miles down Stevens Pass on the north fork of the Skykomish River. The Bush House Country Inn is old, architecturally interesting, and serves an exceptional buffet brunch. We had to wait fifteen minutes for a table, but at last, with our plates piled high, we seated ourselves and tackled not only our food, but also Cody Graff's death.

"You're right," Vida agreed, buttering a fluffy blueberry muffin. "Durwood's an old fool, but Cody shouldn't have been out on that road so early in the morning. Marje says she dropped him off at his apartment right after she took him home from the Icicle Creek Tavern. She took his pickup to her place. So how did he get to the Burl Creek Road?"

"You mean she's still got Cody's truck?"

Vida gave a jerky nod. "That's right. It's parked in front of her house. Or rather her parents' house, but then you know what I think of her mother and father. Nincompoops, both of them, even if Ennis is my own brother. But Marje is sensible, all things considered. I just never thought Cody was suitable for her. Still," she added virtuously, "I kept out of it. Now, I can't say I'm sorry she won't be marrying him. It's a shame he's dead, but it may save Marje a lot of grief later on."

How Vida managed to say all this while consuming two

link sausages, half a muffin, and a great quantity of scrambled eggs, I'll never know. But she did. "This is beginning to sound stranger by the minute. I didn't ask Milo—was Doc Dewey called in to do his medical examiner's act?"

Vida attacked a small container of marionberry jam. "Doc and Mrs. Dewey headed for Seattle early this morning. Young Doc Dewey was in emergency, setting some fool of a tourist's broken leg. I suppose he was going to view the body after he got done, but Marje says he's pretty busy with all the visitors in town. They don't have enough sense not to keep hurting themselves while they're trying to have fun. One idiot from Idaho fell out the window of the Tall Timber Inn last night."

Visions of lawsuits and tricky news stories danced through my head. But that lay in the future. Cody Graff's death had occurred in the last few hours. "There's something about this whole thing that bothers me," I confessed. "I saw Cody leave the tavern around ten o'clock last night with Marje. I know how drunk he was. He probably passed out as soon as he got back to his apartment. So he wakes up at five or even earlier this morning and *walks* two miles out to the Burl Creek Road? It doesn't make sense."

Vida didn't seem at all unsettled by my pronouncement. Indeed, it was obvious she'd already come to the same conclusion. After waiting for a busboy to clear the table next to us, she leaned closer: "Of course it doesn't, Emma. That's why I don't think Durwood killed Cody."

I hadn't gotten quite that far in my thinking. I gaped at Vida over a forkful of ham. "You mean he was already dead when Durwood hit him?"

Vida's gaze was steady. "That's right. Dot told me on the phone that Durwood swore he didn't see Cody. Now Durwood couldn't see an elephant on an escalator, but it *is* fairly light at six in the morning this time of year, and according to Dot, Durwood was just going around that little bend by the Overholt farm. The road dips down. If Cody had been walking on the pavement—or even close to it, Durwood doesn't exactly keep to the road—he would have seen *something*. But if Cody had been lying there, not moving, that might explain it." She waved a spoon at me. "So we're back to the original question. Dead or alive, what was Cody Graff doing out there in the early morning dew?"

I stared at her thoughtfully for some moments. "I suppose we'll have to wait for young Doc Dewey to tell us what really happened."

"Of course." Vida poured a lavish dose of syrup over her stack of pancakes. "I told Dot to insist on an autopsy. I'm not for letting Durwood loose in that rattletrap of his, but I'd hate to see the poor old fool get sent to prison for something he really didn't do."

As ever, I marveled at Vida's communication network. Already, she'd been in touch with two of the major figures involved in Cody Graff's death, Marje Blatt and Dot Parker. For all I knew, she'd been receiving messages from Durwood in a bottle sent floating down the Skykomish River.

For the rest of the lengthy meal—Vida went back for seconds and thirds—we discussed some of the other incidents of the past twenty-four hours, including the flying axe at the timber sports competition, the row between Cody Graff and Matt Tabor, the face-off featuring Jack Blackwell and Reid Hampton, and Patti Marsh's defamation of her daughter's character in front of the Icicle Creek Tavern patrons—even though Milo and I had seen the two of them drive off in Matt Tabor's custom-built car the previous night. It was only when we were paying the bill that I remembered to tell her about seeing Curtis Graff show up at the tavern just before Cody and Marje left.

"Do you know where Curtis is staying?" I asked.

But for once, Vida had to confess ignorance. She had not seen Curtis since he returned to Alpine. "A nice boy," she allowed. "Much more character than Cody. Smart, too, but not terribly quick." She tapped her temple.

We returned to Alpine just as the parade was ending. For the first time since I'd moved to town, I became embroiled in a genuine traffic jam. As soon as we turned off the main highway, we found ourselves backed up on the bridge over the Skykomish River. Some of the parade participants had taken the wrong route after leaving Front Street, and a float featuring a giant fried egg, as well as a girls' drill team from Monroe, had ended up on the bridge instead of going in the opposite direction on Alpine Way to the football field. It was after three o'clock when I got Vida home. I decided to drive back downtown and see if Milo had survived his horseback ride.

He had—barely. Looking as if he were in pain, Milo was sitting gingerly in his chair, sipping ice water. I commiserated briefly, then asked if Dot Parker had requested an autopsy on Cody Graff. Milo eyed me curiously.

"Yes, she has. How'd you know that, Emma?"

I tried to look enigmatic. "It's my job to know all things."

Milo pulled a face, enlightenment dawning. "Vida." He sighed wearily. "We'll have to get somebody from Snohomish County to do it. Young Doc Dewey is all tied up. You heard what happened to the Three Little Pigs?"

I wasn't sure I wanted to, but Milo told me anyway. The Three Little Pigs, whose job it was to promote homeowners' insurance for the local independent agent, had been the victim of the Big Bad Wolf, who had huffed and puffed so energetically that he'd gone right through the flooring of the float, sending the driver into a Skykomish Public Utility District pole at the corner of Fifth and Front. The Big Bad Wolf had managed to keep his balance, but the Three Little Pigs had tumbled into the crowd, causing several lacerations, abrasions, and contusions. No one was seriously hurt, but the mending, patching, and stitching would keep young Doc Dewey busy for the next few hours. It was a driving mishap that would have made Durwood proud—if he could have seen it from his jail cell.

"When will the autopsy be done?" I asked, after I had emitted the appropriate chuckles and expressed the suitable regrets.

"Tomorrow, maybe. It depends," said Milo, once again

showing signs of discomfort. "They'll be doing us a favor in Everett, so we can't push them. It's a bunch of bull, but I suppose the Parkers have their rights. As I said, this was bound to happen to Durwood eventually."

I decided not to let Milo in on Vida's theory. He would dismiss it out of hand. But if the autopsy proved that Cody was already dead when Durwood's car hit him, then Milo would have to consider other uglier possibilities.

I was on my feet, wishing Milo would install air-conditioning in his office. "I'll see you at the banquet tonight. Are you bringing Honoria?" I tried to keep my voice light.

"No," he said with a laconic shake of his head. "She's going to some gallery deal in Seattle." He looked up. "You want a lift?"

The Loggerama banquet was going to be held in the Lutheran Church hall, the only adequate facility for such a large gathering. The Lutherans also owned the retirement home in the same block. Due to Alpine's large Scandinavian population, the members of their faith outnumbered any other flock by at least a two-to-one ratio.

"Sure," I said, wanting to be a good sport. "By the way, I thought Honoria seemed like a lovely person."

For a brief moment, Milo's face lighted up. "Really? Well, yes, she's pretty nice. Determined, too. She drives— she's got a specially rigged car—and goes everywhere on her own. But then she's had a lot of practice."

I leaned on Milo's desk. "What happened?" I wasn't going to pry unless Milo gave me an opportunity. Now he had.

Milo's face tightened. "She married very young. Her husband beat the crap out of her. On her twenty-first birthday, he threw her down a flight of stairs."

I winced. "That's awful! Did she leave him?"

Again, Milo gave a mournful shake of his head. "Her brother shot him. And got ten years for it. He should have had a medal."

I didn't argue.

* * *

To my relief, the banquet had gone off without incident. Pastor Nielsen had asked us to bow our heads in memory of Cody Graff. Fuzzy Baugh had introduced the new Miss Alpine, a shy redhead who was a checker at the Grocery Basket. Dani Marsh had been invited, but had bowed out of both the parade and the banquet, apparently owing to the death of her ex-husband. Harvey Adcock, as the current Chamber of Commerce president, read a brief note from Dani, expressing her regrets for not attending. I wondered if she had some other regrets as well.

Monday was a wild day at work. We were going to have another jam-packed issue, but this week we wouldn't have the extra Loggerama ads to support so many pages. I decided to hold off writing the story about Cody's death until we got the autopsy report. I hoped it would come in before our late Tuesday deadline. I also chose not to run anything about the axe incident. Now that Cody was dead and couldn't defend himself, it didn't seem right to carry an article that would, by its very existence, imply that he'd been trying to injure his ex-wife or her companions.

Meanwhile, Durwood no longer languished in jail. Dot had posted bond and taken him home in the early afternoon. I didn't talk to Milo all day, since I was too busy putting the paper together. Vida, however, had stopped in at the sheriff's office and said that he had told her he hoped the autopsy would be completed before five o'clock. Meanwhile, Cody's parents were at the Lumberjack Motel, waiting for the body to be released. Curtis Graff was with them.

Out on Front Street, a small crew of city employees and several merchants were dismantling the Loggerama decorations. Down came the bunting, the banners, and the bigger-than-life-sized model of a woodsman that Fuzzy Baugh insisted on referring to as "an erection." I don't think the mayor ever stops to listen to what he's saying, but I suppose that's all right, because none of the rest of us do either. Fuzzy, in his native New Orleans fashion, does tend to run on.

Hot, tired, and feeling a headache coming on, I drove home shortly before six. This time, the mail held no surprises. But it reminded me that I had yet to deal with Tom Cavanaugh's letter. Tomorrow night, perhaps, I told myself as I fell onto the sofa and kicked off my shoes. I needed one more day to recover from the rigors of Loggerama.

I was in the kitchen cleaning up from my meager supper of creamed shrimp on toast when the phone rang. It was Milo Dodge.

"We got the autopsy report from Everett about an hour ago," he said, sounding as weary as I felt. "It's the damnedest thing you ever heard."

"So what am I hearing?" My voice was a little breathless.

Milo cleared his throat. "Cody Graff had been dead for several hours by the time Durwood hit him. The extent of rigor—" He stopped, obviously reading his notes. "Anyway, we'll have to dismiss the charges against Durwood." Milo sounded almost sorry. I'm sure he had visions of Durwood immediately leaping into his old beater and wiping out a whole herd of cows.

"Go on," I urged. "Who did run over him?"

"Nobody," replied Milo. "The medical examiner says he didn't die from getting hit by a car. Cody Graff was murdered. Somebody poisoned the poor bastard. What do you think of that?"

Chapter Eight

MILO AND I were having drinks at the Venison Eat Inn and Take Out. We were both relieved to note that most of the tourists had departed from Alpine, leaving our streets and restaurants and shops back under our control. Even though Pacific Northwest politicians and Chamber of Commerce types may work hard to promote tourism and thus beef up the economy, the truth is that most people, merchants included, aren't fond of visitors. Worse yet, some of the tourists may decide to move in. Growth is not good. Money is suspect. Space is much better.

"What kind of poison?" I asked after the cocktail waitress had glided away. I didn't want her to think I was talking about the Venison Inn's beverages.

"Haloperidol," said Milo, emphasizing each syllable. "A central nervous system depressant. It's especially lethal with alcohol. It also produces symptoms that are very similar to drunkenness. Marje Blatt insisted that Cody had only two beers when I told him he ought to go home. They'd had an early supper at the Loggerama fast food stand in Old Mill Park because Cody was hungry from all that action with the axe at the high school field. Then they went to see some of the Miss Alpine competition. They got to the Icicle Creek Tavern about half an hour or forty-five minutes before I did."

"So how did he ingest this stuff?" I asked, reconstructing Marje's account of their evening to see if it made sense. As far as I could tell, it did. If she wasn't lying.

"The M.E. in Everett says it was probably in the beer.

Marje says they ate around five-thirty. If it had been in Cody's food or his coffee, it would have started to act much sooner, maybe even by six o'clock. There's no sign that he had anything to eat or drink after he left the Icicle Creek Tavern shortly before ten. Maybe Marje was right about how much—or how little—he had to drink. I just thought she was covering for him."

"How long does this stuff usually take to act?" I asked, unable to keep from looking at my bourbon without a certain amount of suspicion.

"That depends, according to the M.E. If Cody had been some old guy in poor health and was drinking shots of gin, he could have been a goner within fifteen minutes. But Cody was young and in good shape. He'd only had a couple of beers. The M.E. says it might take up to two hours before he died."

I shuddered. "Poor Cody. But how on earth did he end up dead by the Burl Creek Road?"

Milo lifted his shoulders and hoisted his Scotch. "Nobody's come forward to say they carted him off. What I'm trying to figure out is why somebody would poison him, then drive him off and dump him on the road. It's crazy."

"Marje doesn't know anything, I take it?"

"No. She said it was just after ten when they got to his apartment. There's no elevator, so she had to help him up the stairs to the second floor. She left him on the couch."

"Had he passed out?" I asked.

"No. She said he was muttering about his brother Curtis, and Dani, and Matt Tabor. He was sort of incoherent, but still conscious." Milo nodded to a young couple I knew only from seeing them at church. They sat down at a table near the unlighted fireplace. I gave a little wave. It wouldn't hurt for me to help Milo woo his constituents.

"Where would anybody get that . . ." I reached down for my purse and took out a notepad. "Spell it, will you Milo?"

He did, and I jotted the unfamiliar word down. Haloperidol. I'd never heard of it. I repeated my question.

Milo gave a wry little laugh. "Five, six years ago, Durwood would have been the prime suspect, being a pharmacist. But nowadays, who knows where drugs, legal and otherwise, come from around here? The only thing I can say for sure is that somebody planned ahead."

"Premeditated," I murmured. It was an ugly thought. "Why? Who? And how?"

Milo's smile became more genuine. "Ever the reporter, huh, Emma? I sure as hell don't know who or why. But how? If it was in his beer, somebody slipped it to him when nobody was looking. Even Marje couldn't be watching every minute. Unless," he added, the smile fading, "it was Marje who did it."

My eyes widened at Milo. "Marje? No, that's crazy. If she wanted to get rid of Cody, all she had to do was break the engagement. Besides, I think she genuinely loved the guy."

Milo nodded. "Could be. But there was so much commotion going on that anybody could have dumped this stuff into his schooner. It can come in several forms, including a syrup. Cody wasn't the sharpest tool in the shed. He liked to guzzle. And frankly, if something tasted funny at the Icicle Creek Tavern, I'm not sure I'd notice. I'd half expect to find a trace of ugly in my brew."

Milo was only half-kidding. I mulled over his words, then had a sudden flashback. "Hey, Milo—Cody had *three* beers the other night. He got another one after you warned him off. Would that make the poison work faster?"

Milo said it probably would. But he cautioned that the M.E. was cagey about fixing the time of death. "Somewhere between ten and midnight is as close as he'll come."

Somebody had seen Cody during those two hours. But it suddenly dawned on me that that mysterious blank face didn't necessarily belong to the killer.

Selfishly, I wished the autopsy hadn't been concluded so soon. The old-fashioned concept of a newspaper *scoop* had all but died out with the advent of the electronic media. In a small town like Alpine, a scoop had never had a chance: the grapevine was always faster and more effective. Everybody from Burl Creek to Stump Hill would know that Cody Graff had been poisoned before we could get the paper to Monroe to be printed.

I spent most of Tuesday tying up loose ends. I wrote the story of Cody's death, careful to stick to the facts and quote strictly from Milo and the Snohomish County Medical Examiner. For the time being, I avoided contacting Cody's parents, his brother, or his ex-wife. Their comments could come later, for next week's edition, when I had more room and the sheriff had more results.

Vida did the obituary, noting that the funeral was set for Thursday. It would not be held in Alpine, but up at Friday Harbor, with burial in the cemetery on the San Juan Islands.

"Marje thinks that's a shame," said Vida, yanking the article out of her typewriter. "She said she thought Cody would want to be buried here, next to his baby. But I suppose his folks have a plot up at Friday Harbor."

I looked up from the headline Carla had written about the wet T-shirt contest. I hadn't seen it until just now and was dismayed: NO FALSE FRONT FOR ADVOCATE ENTRY; RUNKEL BUSTS UP COMPETITION. It wouldn't do. What had become of Carla's high-minded principles?

RUNKEL WINS T-SHIRT CONTEST; ASKS BOOKS FOR BEER. My revision was deadly dull, but it would keep Vida from blowing up—and prevent a stack of letters from irate readers.

"Is Marje going to attend the funeral?" I inquired.

"She doesn't know yet," Vida replied, looking up from the finished version of her House & Home page. "With Doc Dewey Senior gone, there's not as much for her to do, but young Doc has been so busy she may have to help cover. They only have the two nurses and Marje at the clinic, you know."

I did. But it seemed strange that Marje wouldn't attend Cody's services. Of course, it wasn't easy to get up to the San Juans this time of year. "How's she taking it?" I asked.

Vida handed her completed page over to me. "Oh—she's upset, of course. But Marje isn't an emotional type. Crying her eyes out won't bring Cody back. Maybe she hasn't taken it all in yet. She certainly refuses to consider that Cody was murdered."

"Really?" Milo had officially announced that Cody Graff's death had been caused by foul play. Luckily, the sheriff hadn't made a formal announcement of accidental death. Otherwise, he would have to go through all the legal rigmarole regarding corpus delicti. Perhaps he had also saved himself from getting sued by Durwood Parker. Milo had a right to throw Durwood in jail just for breaking the thirty-day ban on driving.

Vida was pushing up the window above her desk. The midday heat was bringing unwelcome humidity. "Marje insists that nobody would want to kill Cody." Vida brushed tendrils of damp gray hair off her high forehead. "I suppose she has a point. I have to admit I'm flummoxed over this whole mess."

So was I. Worse yet, I had the feeling that Milo Dodge was as baffled as we were. If Cody Graff had been poisoned at the Icicle Creek Tavern, Milo and I had both been eyewitnesses. Yet neither of us had seen anything suspicious. Milo probably would question everybody he could find who had been in the tavern Saturday night, but it was doubtful that they would be able to shed any light on the matter. Not only had there been too much confusion, but many of the patrons probably had been too far gone with drink to be observant or reliable witnesses.

Vida was sorting through some handouts on late summer garden care. She uttered a contemptuous snort and dumped the whole batch into her wastebasket. "What do these promotional people think we are, *idiots*? Who wouldn't know when to cut back old growth and prune fruit trees?" Vida wasn't the best gardener in town; she worked only in spurts, but with great energy. Still, she was knowledgeable. I was about to ask her when I should put in my spring bulbs, but she had already moved on to another topic: "You never told me about your date." There was a hint of reproof in her tone.

"Some date." I made a deprecating gesture. "At least the food was good."

"Reid Hampton's not your type. Shallow. Pretentious. Stuck on himself." Vida was dead-on.

I decided to get her opinion of Milo's new friend. "What did you think of Honoria Whitman?"

"Pleasant. Smart. Dull. Milo needs somebody with more pep."

"She's very gutsy," I pointed out.

Vida pushed her glasses back on her nose and frowned at me. "What has courage got to do with *pep*? Milo does his job well enough, but he's on cruise control when it comes to his personal life. If you ask me, that's what went wrong with his first marriage. It's too bad you're so hung up on Tommy."

I winced for various reasons: Vida had met Tom Cavanaugh on his visit to Alpine the previous autumn. She had liked him a lot. She also knew the rest of the story, and passed no judgment on either of us. But she was the only person I knew who ever called him Tommy.

I was going to tell her about Tom's letter when Marje Blatt walked into the newsroom. Marje's piquant face was sunburned, yet somehow lifeless. Her white uniform didn't seem quite so crisp. The bright blue eyes had lost their luster. Yet there was no indication she had been crying. Marje said hello to me, then went straight to the point:

"Aunt Vida, have you had lunch?"

Aunt Vida had, varying her customary diet lunch with Rye Krisp instead of cottage cheese. "Yes, it's after one. But if you want company . . ." Vida was already springing toward the door.

I wanted to talk to Marje, too, but I couldn't intrude. Besides, the fish and chips basket I'd brought over from the Burger Barn would do me until dinner. Unlike Vida, I wouldn't be able to sit down and consume an entire meal with all the trimmings.

Instead, I finished working on the paper, then gave Milo a call, using the need to find out if there had been any further developments as my excuse for bothering him. We wouldn't want to send *The Advocate* off to Monroe without the latest news.

"There's nothing new," admitted Milo, unhappily. "Our forensics guy is checking fibers and such. We've been talking to some of the other customers who were at the tavern Saturday night. Janet Driggers says Cody probably poisoned himself, but that's only because she and Al are miffed that the funeral is being held up at Friday Harbor—Al won't get his usual fat undertaking fee. Cal Vickers said something kind of interesting, though."

"Such as?" I asked, wondering what the owner of Cal's Texaco & Body Shop might have to add.

"Well, he and Charlene stayed on for about an hour. It was their twenty-fourth wedding anniversary, so I guess they got sort of sentimental and decided to drive out to Burl Creek, where he proposed. They were coming back down around midnight when they saw a strange-looking car parked across from the Overholt farm. Cal had seen it around town this past week and said it was a Zimmer. You know how interested he is in unusual cars."

"Was it the same one we saw the other night?" I inquired.

"Sounds like it. It's definitely Matt Tabor's car—he drove it up from California, but he had it made out south of Seattle, in Des Moines. They're only three places in the country that hand-build these things. They must cost a shitload, but they sure are beautiful."

I wasn't paying much attention to Milo's car commentary, which had no doubt been inspired by Cal Vickers. I was more interested in why the custom-built Zimmer had been parked in the vicinity of Cody Graff's body. "Did Cal or Charlene notice if anyone was in the car?"

Milo sighed. "No, they were either too moonstruck or concentrating just on the car itself. The Zimmer's headlights were off, though. Cal did notice that."

"Hmmmm." I mulled over Milo's information while one of his deputies asked him a question in the background.

"We know it wasn't necessarily Matt Tabor driving, don't we?" I finally remarked after Milo had finished talking to his subordinate.

"I'm going to ask Dani—or Matt—about that," said Milo. "If I had a car like that, I sure wouldn't let just anybody drive it."

I agreed. But Dani and Matt were hardly strangers; they were engaged to be married. Still, I wondered what the Zimmer was doing parked out by the Burl Creek Road at midnight on Saturday. It was such a conspicuous vehicle—somebody was bound to see it.

And somebody had. But the real question was whether or not the murderer was at the wheel.

As I drove up to the ski lodge after dinner, I had to scrutinize my motives. Was I going to see Dani Marsh because I thought there was a real news story in her reaction to Cody Graff's death? Or was I insinuating myself into her life because I wanted to help Milo find her ex-husband's killer?

Or, I asked myself with a grimace, was I trying to put off replying to Tom Cavanaugh's letter?

I couldn't answer any of my own questions. I'm a great one for rationalizing my actions, and rarely will one clear-cut explanation serve. I must have at least two or more reasons for anything I do that might be on shaky ethical ground. By the time I reached the lodge, I'd convinced myself that I was also calling on Dani to offer my condolences. Judging from a lot of comments about her return, she might not have a local shoulder to cry on. Certainly not her mother's.

Henry Bardeen informed me that Dani was in her room, but that all visitors had to be screened by some flunky who was eating dinner at the Venison Inn.

"Half the town has tried to get in here in the past few days to see the movie stars," Henry said crossly. "Fortunately, the company makes its own rules. We're off the

hook. But it's been a real nuisance all the same. Even Patti
Marsh came storming in here this afternoon."

"She did? To see Dani?"

Henry shook his head. "No—Reid Hampton. I had to get
very firm with her. Patti has no manners."

Apparently, Henry Bardeen was going to be very firm
with me as well. He had the grace to look ill-at-ease, however, as he suggested I call the Venison Inn and ask for the
flunky to come to the phone. I was considering just that
when Reid Hampton strolled through the lobby.

Hampton greeted me heartily, practically squeezing the
blood out of my hand. Relieved to have someone from the
film company present, Henry slipped away toward his office. I informed the movie director that I would like to see
Dani.

Hampton's hearty manner changed instantly, shifting into
appropriately mournful gear. He gazed up into the vast ceiling of the lodge with its rough-hewn rafters and knotty pine
walls. "Dani's really distraught," he said at last, lowering
his booming voice to a mere rumble. "She and Cody . . .
what was his name? Grass?" He seemed to be reading from
a cue card on the Indian blanket suspended from a cross-
beam. "Graff, that's it. They may have been divorced, but
it's still a shock."

"It must have been a shock when Cody threw that axe
and practically chopped off her feet," I remarked.

Reid Hampton's gaze deigned to drop down to earth and
meet mine. "That was strange," he admitted. "An accident,
though, I'm sure. Would you like to have a drink in the bar,
Emma?"

I considered my options: I could decline the invitation
and renew my efforts to see Dani. But Reid Hampton
would probably refuse permission, and I might not fare any
better with the flunky who was eating chicken-fried steak at
the Venison Inn. If I accepted Reid's offer, he might mellow
and let me talk to his star.

"Sure," I responded, with a smile meant to flatter.

Hampton nodded, then swaggered off toward the bar on

the other side of the lobby. The Après-Ski Room had recently been remodeled, a tasteful job that featured the best appointments of the original hole-in-the-wall watering place. More warm wood, rustic lamps with cedar bark bases, and some handsome sketches by Pacific Northwest Indian artists gave the room a comfortable native flavor.

After ordering us each a brandy, Reid Hampton leaned across the polished pine table and gave me a seductive smile, capped teeth flashing in his tawny beard. The man must be close to fifty and there wasn't a gray hair in sight. I suspected that not only did Reid Hampton dye his hair—and beard—but that the lionlike shade wasn't natural. It certainly didn't match the darker hairs on his arms and chest.

"I've been meaning to tell you I had a wonderful time at dinner the other night," said Hampton, at his most suave. "I hope we can do it again before I leave town, Emma."

I don't think I managed to hide my surprise. Reid Hampton had to be kidding. I was certain he'd had as crummy an outing as I had. But maybe he felt compelled to say otherwise. Accepting his gallantry at face value, I stopped looking startled and smiled politely.

"Thanks, Reid. When do you wind up the shoot?"

"Early next week." He twirled the brandy snifter under his nose and inhaled. "We finish up at Baldy Wednesday. Are you ready for the paint job?"

Again, I was evasive. Surely Reid Hampton really didn't want to colorize Front Street. "Has Dani been able to work the past couple of days?"

"She's a trooper. I was afraid she might want to go up to the San Juans for the funeral, but she hasn't insisted. That relieves my mind—it would have put us off schedule. We can't shoot around her with the way the script is written." He took a sip of brandy and savored it slowly. "It's lucky she's had Cody's brother to lean on."

"Curtis?" Again, I had to guard my reaction. "I didn't realize they were close. I've only lived in Alpine a couple of years."

Hampton lifted one of his broad shoulders. "He came to see her as soon as he heard Cody was dead. Say, Emma," he continued in a different, more intimate tone, "you aren't going to play this as a homicide, are you? In the newspaper, I mean?"

"But that's what it is," I replied, dumbfounded.

Hampton lifted his hands in an expressive gesture. "Crazy! Who knows what that guy was taking? He has a lot of beer and then he overdoses. It happens all the time in L.A. Nobody goes around shouting, 'Help, Murder!' Your sheriff must be very naive."

Cody Graff had his faults, but taking drugs wasn't one of them, as far as I knew. If he had been a user, Marje would have known, and thus so would Vida. I gave a definite shake of my head. "Sorry, Reid, the sheriff is right. Somebody deliberately poisoned Cody Graff. Have you got any ideas who?"

The question was off the top of my head, and Reid Hampton looked as if I were out of my mind. "Hell! That's rot, Emma! No, I don't have—Why would I know who'd kill some small-town loser?" He looked genuinely offended. He also looked as if he'd define anybody who lived in a small town as a loser. Including me.

I began to feel irritated. "You certainly made Jack Blackwell angry by cutting down those trees. Cody worked for Blackwell. If you want to start scratching for motives, I could count you in." I gave him my most ingenuous smile.

Hampton was not amused. "More rot," he muttered. "My lawyers are better than Blackwell's lawyers. I don't need to waste some punk over a pile of logs. All this poison crap is ridiculous."

I realized it was useless to argue with Reid Hampton. It was also counter-productive. I had probably already ruined my chances of using him to get to Dani Marsh. I drank some brandy and tried to think of a different, more conciliatory approach.

But I didn't need it. Dani Marsh floated into the bar at

that moment, smiling sweetly at a middle-aged couple in
the corner and a couple of men I recognized as grips or gaf-
fers or some such technical workers from the movie location. She headed straight for us. Reid Hampton grimaced.

"Dani," he began, standing up, "Emma and I were just
leaving. I'll see you upstairs in half an hour, okay?"

Dani had already sat down in the chair next to me.
"Oh—Reid, I don't want to drink alone. In fact, I only want
some mineral water. Don't rush off." Her limpid brown
eyes appealed to both of us.

"That's okay, Reid," I said, with a little wave. "You go
do whatever a big director has to do, and I'll keep Dani
company. I haven't finished my brandy yet."

Reid Hampton did not look pleased. He gave Dani a
glance that might have been a warning, tossed a ten dollar
bill on the table, and left the bar. Dani gave me a conspiratorial smile.

"Reid can be a twit, but he's wonderful to work with,"
she said with a wave to the cocktail waitress. Dani ordered
a gin and tonic. I wondered what had happened to the cabbage extract.

After Dani was served, I offered my condolences on
Cody's death. She assumed a mournful expression which
seemed genuine enough, though I reminded myself she was
an actress. "It's terrible," she said with a sigh. "When
somebody dies young, it's such a waste. Even with Cody."

I wasn't precisely sure how to take her qualifying remark. Instead, I asked about Curtis. "Was he very upset?"

Dani turned thoughtful. "Yes, I think so. Curtis won't
miss Cody, since they hadn't seen each other in almost five
years. I don't think Cody had seen his parents since they
moved up to the San Juans. Still, they've got to be feeling
blue."

Unbridled grief wasn't the watchword of the week. I said
as much. "I take it Cody didn't have a lot of other family
or a wide circle of friends."

"There were some relatives in Spokane," Dani said.
"Cousins, aunt and uncle. But I don't think they kept in

touch. He had his beer-drinking buddies. And of course there was that girl he was going to marry."

I thought of Marje Blatt as I had seen her earlier in the day. Maybe she was still in shock, and great gushes of grief would come later. "Reid Hampton doesn't think Cody was murdered," I said, watching closely for Dani's reaction.

"I don't think so either," said Dani Marsh flatly. "Why would anyone kill Cody? He didn't have any money. He wasn't involved in a triangle, at least that I know of. And I doubt that he'd turn to blackmail. What other motives are there besides monetary gain, jealousy, and fear?"

"Knowledge," I replied promptly. "People have been killed for knowing too much."

Dani emitted a lame little laugh. "Knowledge doesn't suit Cody. He wasn't exactly stupid, but he wouldn't be interested enough in anybody to invite their secrets. No, Ms. Lord, I don't buy into this murder business either. It's so . . . so melodramatic. Oh, Cody may have ingested some strange drug, but he probably did it himself."

My eyes widened. "You mean suicide?" Maybe Janet Driggers's idea wasn't so wild after all.

"No, no," replied Dani, after a gulp of her gin and tonic. "He'd never do that. But he might have been experimenting, or taking some kind of medication. Surely the sheriff has checked into that?"

Surely Milo had, I thought. As the Deweys' medical receptionist, Marje was in a position to know if Cody was taking prescription drugs. If so, she would have told the sheriff. Or Vida. I had to wonder why Dani and Reid were so determined on insisting that Cody had not been murdered. Maybe they didn't want the adverse publicity.

"As far as I know, Cody wasn't on this stuff." I wished I could pronounce the name of the drug more easily. "If I may be blunt, Cody Graff struck me as the kind of person who might incite someone to violence. He appeared to be a very sulky, perhaps even selfish young man."

Dani Marsh threw back her head and laughed, that rarified musical sound that reminded me of tinkling crystal chandeliers. "If every sulking, selfish man I know in the movie business got killed, Hollywood would have to fold."

I was faintly miffed by her dismissal of my theory. "You couldn't get along with him," I pointed out. "At least that's why I assume you got divorced."

Dani's gaze wandered around the Après-Ski Room. "Oh—I don't know. We were so young, immature, impatient. I wanted more out of life than Alpine could offer. I think we both saw that we'd made a mistake. After the baby died, we realized there wasn't any future for us." She still wasn't looking at me, but rather at the totem pole that stood between the tall windows at the far end of the bar.

Dani didn't seem to be helping me much in terms of information. I'd finally finished my brandy and she was over halfway through her gin and tonic. "You've got Matt Tabor now," I said, hoping to sound more congenial. "You can make a fresh start."

Dani took another swallow from her tall glass. "Right. Matt's a good guy." Her eyes were still wandering around the bar.

"When's the wedding?" I felt as if I were prying. Was it because Dani was a celebrity? Yet the question was as natural as asking a chicken farmer how his eggs were doing.

Dani finally met my gaze. "We haven't set a date. Next summer, maybe. We both have commitments through June."

I decided it was time to throw in the towel. Getting to my feet, I started to make my farewell, but had a sudden thought. "I understand you've seen your mother." The statement tripped off my tongue, and I waited for Dani to look startled.

"Mom's such a hard-nosed person," she said, then laughed again. "Honestly, she has never forgiven me for getting crummy grades in high school. Somehow, going to Hollywood and breaking into the movie business doesn't make up for it. I think she hates me because I didn't enroll in the University of Washington and get a degree in education." She ran a hand through her honey blond hair. "I shouldn't say that. She doesn't hate me, she's just resentful. And I understand why. Some day, I hope she'll get over it. We used to be great pals."

"The two of you must have made up enough that she'd let you drive her around in Matt's Zimmer," I remarked, hoisting my handbag over my shoulder. "I saw you the other night in that gorgeous car."

For just an instant, a strange look passed over Dani Marsh's beautiful face. Surprise? Fear? Anger? I couldn't tell. She composed herself quickly and gave a little shrug. "Matt likes to show off that Zimmer. He let me drive it to go see Mom. She couldn't resist taking a spin around town. I suppose nobody up here has ever seen a car like that. There aren't that many even in L.A., not at all like sighting a Rolls or a Lamborghini—*they're* a dime a dozen."

Not on my salary they weren't. But I merely smiled and left Dani to lap up her gin and tonic. She might look like an angel, but she acted like a clam. My trip to the ski lodge had been a washout.

It was only later that I realized Dani—and Reid Hampton—had told me almost everything I needed to know.

Chapter Nine

HAVING FLUNKED WITH Dani Marsh, I decided to make a complete fool of myself and call on her mother. Patti Marsh lived in a small frame house above the cemetery, between Spruce and Tyee Streets. It was almost dark when I arrived, but I could see that the yard was overgrown, the lawn needed mowing, and the house itself begged for fresh paint. I assumed this was where Dani Marsh had been raised. It was a far cry from Benedict Canyon.

Patti came to the door in tight black pants and a green halter top. She had a drink in one hand and a cigarette in the other. "What do you want?" she asked in her hoarse, hostile voice.

I gave her my most winning smile. "I just wanted to make sure that our article didn't cause you any problems. The more I thought about it, the more I realized that you had a right to be upset." The truth was, I hadn't thought about it at all. But I needed some excuse to get my foot in the door.

Patti gave a little snort. "You're damned lucky so much other crap was going on around here. Otherwise, half the town would have been sniping behind my back. No, I got no problem with it. Now."

"Good." I tried to look relieved. And lied some more. "It occurred to me after you left that we hadn't told the whole story. After all, we never got your feelings about what it's like to have a famous movie star for a daughter. Let's face it: Dani is what you made her."

Obviously, that idea had never occurred to Patti. She

threw back her shoulders, looking like a candidate for Abe Loomis's next wet T-shirt contest. "Well now," she said with a toss of her bleached hair, "when you put it like that . . . Sure, I did what I could for the kid. Role model, isn't that what they call it?" She seemed to realize that we were conducting our conversation both inside and outside her house. "Come in, Mrs. Lord. Want a drink?"

I calculated: I was five blocks from home and not feeling much effect from the brandy. "Sure," I said, following her into the living room. It was small, with aging Italian provincial furniture that would have made a gypsy wince. Reds, greens, and yellows predominated. The sagging drapes were drawn, making the house not only too warm, but oppressive. Half-naked gods and goddesses stood on the mantel, skin-by-fin with several carved trout. The walls boasted Harlequin masks, a watercolor of Mount Baldy, and a bas-relief of Bacchus doing what looked like the bop with a lot of unclothed nymphs.

Anxiously, I searched for a place to sit down. The green and gold sofa was covered with celebrity magazines and tabloids; the chairs were piled high with old *TV Guides* and *Soap Opera Digests*.

"Here," said Patti, whisking a foot-high stack of tabloids topped by *The Globe* from the end of the sofa. "What'll you have?"

"Bourbon? Canadian?" I sat down gingerly, putting my feet under the big coffee table that covered most of the floor space between the sofa and the TV across the room. More magazines, several romance novels, three dirty glasses, and a full ashtray shaped like a big leaf stared back at me. The house smelled of smoke, onions, and a perfume I'd once been trapped with in a Portland high-rise elevator. I'd almost gotten carsick.

Patti was at the bar, which was actually a counter between the living room and kitchen. "I was a bit of an actress myself," she said, shoveling ice out of a mock leather-covered bucket. "In high school, we did *Our Town* and something about a bunch of Pilgrims."

"Oh?" I was wondering if the change in Patti Marsh's attitude had been engendered by my soft soap or her previous highballs. She wasn't drunk, but she wasn't exactly sober. I tried to pay attention. "Pilgrims?"

"Yeah, right." She handed me a hefty bourbon on the rocks. Her own drink was fresh, either vodka or gin. "They had this thing about witches. All the women were called Goody something-or-other. They ganged up on people." Patti sat down in the faded red cut-velvet chair next to the TV. "Imagine, saying all this guff about innocent men and women! What kind of a small town was that, I wonder?" Patti rolled her eyes.

"The Crucible?" I offered, thinking that Salem, Massachusetts could easily be substituted for Alpine, Washington any day.

"Right!" Patti laughed and held out her glass as if toasting me for my fabulous wit. "I wanted to say *Cubicle*. Oh, well. Cheers."

"Cheers." I sipped slowly. "So you encouraged Dani with her acting?"

"Oh—no." Patti seemed to have gulped a fourth of her drink already. She set the glass down long enough to light another cigarette. "Dani wasn't interested in acting back then. I just sort of set the stage, if you know what I mean." She clapped a hand to her cleavage. "The stage! That's good! Get it?"

I smiled appreciatively. Patti kept going. "Dani was more interested in boys and clothes and boys and hair and boys and makeup—and boys." She stopped to see if I'd gotten the point. "So she got married right out of high school to Cody, and I could have told her it wouldn't work. Just a couple of kids, playing house. I should have told them to live together for a while. Everybody does that nowadays, no harm, no foul. But she wanted a wedding with a long white dress and a veil, so off they went to the Methodist Church and tied the knot." Patti puffed and guzzled. I waited for her to continue. "Then along came the baby. A little girl, named Scarlett. Dani'd just seen *Gone with the Wind*. If they'd had a boy, he would have been Rhett."

Patti was losing steam. She stared into her glass while the cigarette burned down in the overflowing ashtray. "Of course she didn't look like Scarlett. She was blond, blue-eyed, so sweet." Tears welled up in Patti's eyes. "Then she was gone." She made an ineffectual snap of her fingers. "Like that. Dani was a rotten mother."

"But SIDS isn't caused by anything," I protested. "At least that they know of. It just happens."

Patti didn't seem to hear me. She was crying noisily, her face on her forearm. "Dani wanted to go dancing and do the malls and party. She didn't give a damn about taking care of that baby! I couldn't even get her to use cloth diapers! No wonder Scarlett died! She was neglected!"

I waited for the storm to pass. Patti had my sympathy, a grandmother robbed of her grandchild. But somehow I had the feeling she was being too hard on Dani. Her tears seemed to flow out of an excess, either from a pent-up reserve of self-pity or too many glasses of vodka. It was quite possible that at nineteen, Dani Marsh Graff hadn't wanted the responsibility of parenthood. Still, the infant's death could not be blamed on Dani's desire to have a good time. After five years, I figured I didn't have a prayer of getting through to Patti Marsh.

"Dani's older now," I finally said when Patti showed signs of composing herself. "She and Matt Tabor will probably have children of their own. They'll be able to afford nannies and the best of care. You'll have another grandchild, maybe soon."

Patti made a slashing movement with her hand. "Bull! Dani won't sacrifice her career for a kid! And I wouldn't want Matt to be the father if she did!" Another wild gesture, this time almost toppling her half-filled glass.

"You've met Matt?" It was a guess; there had been a third person in the Zimmer last Friday night.

Patti wiped her eyes with her hand. She sniffed several times, then put out her cigarette and picked up her drink.

"Naw. I seen him, at the tavern. Another loser. Dani don't know how to pick 'em. If I want to meet a drunk, I can go down to Mugs Ahoy and pick out somebody I know."

I didn't argue. In fact, Patti was getting to the point that she could meet a drunk by staggering to her feet and walking over to the gilded mirror above the fireplace. I took another sip of bourbon and decided to take my leave. But before I could say anything, the doorbell rang.

"Who's that?" asked Patti, as if I should know.

"I can get it," I volunteered.

But Patti yelled for her visitor to come in. A moment later, Jack Blackwell was in the living room, looking surprised at my presence, but undismayed by Patti's efforts to drink herself under the coffee table.

"What's this?" he asked in a contentious manner. "You being grilled by the press, Pats? You don't know anything about Cody. Or so you told me."

" 'Course I don't," growled Patti. "Get a drink. Lord here and me are talking about how I made Dani a star."

Suddenly I had the feeling I'd taken the wrong tack with Patti Marsh. Or at least a detour. "A lot of people don't think Cody was poisoned," I said calmly. "How do you two feel about it?"

Blackwell turned away from the makeshift bar to scowl at me. "It doesn't matter one way or the other. Cody hadn't worked for me long enough to get vested. He missed death benefits by six months."

"Timely of him, wasn't it?" I smiled sweetly. Probably sappily, too, but the irony was lost on Jack Blackwell, who was making himself a powerful Scotch, no ice, a splash of soda.

"Cody came on with us right after he split with Dani," Blackwell said, turning around and looking not at me, but at Patti, who was studying her empty glass. At least she still had enough sense to realize there was a decision to make about a refill. "He was a decent worker. Loading and hauling, mostly. At the rate things are going in this crazy business, I'd probably have had to lay him off anyway. If it isn't the weather, it's the chicken-shit environment experts." Blackwell looked fit to spit.

Pattie learned forward in the red chair and held her glass out to Jack. "Gimme half," she muttered. "I'm gettin' sleepy."

Blackwell took the glass but made no move to fill it. "I thought you wanted to go down to Skykomish and do some dancing."

Patti slumped in the chair, her head resting against a crooked antimacassar. "Naw. Not tonight, Jack. I'm beat."

Blackwell put the glass on the counter. Apparently he had made Patti's decision for her. "Poison is a weird way to go. I mean, for a murderer. How can you be sure it'll work?" Blackwell belched.

"You've got to know what you're doing," I said. "Whoever killed Cody must have planned his death very carefully."

Blackwell raised his dark eyebrows. "That right? Jeez!" He seemed more bemused than dismayed. "With all the ruckus going on at Icicle Creek, the wrong bastard might have got poisoned."

Patti's eyes were slits. "Maybe he did." The words were almost incoherent. But that didn't make them any less credible. I was about to ask her why she thought so when I realized that she'd passed out.

"I'd better go," I said, resolutely getting up.

Blackwell followed me to the door. "Patti's smashed," he said. "It was Cody, all right. Milo Dodge won't have to look far to find the killer."

I gazed up at Blackwell, who was looking faintly smug and drinking his Scotch. There was a saturnine quality about the man that made me feel uncomfortable. "What do you mean?"

Jack Blackwell took a package of long thin cigars out of his shirt pocket. "That actor guy—Matt Tabor. Who else?" He shrugged, jiggled the packet, and caught a cigar in his mouth. "Bad blood between them. You saw what happened with the axe, you were at the tavern. Maybe this Tabor guy

figured Dani still had the hots for Cody." Blackwell produced a slim silver lighter and touched off his cigar. The
little flame made shadows on his face, emphasizing the hol-
lows under his cheekbones, the sharp angle of his nose, the
thin line of his lips.

"Could be," I said lightly, not wanting to argue with Jack
Blackwell. Avoiding his gaze, my eyes traveled to the
chipped Bombay chest that stood in the narrow entry hall. A
wilted bouquet drooped in a green glass vase. Tiger lilies,
gladioli, and asparagus ferns: the same arrangement I'd seen
Curtis Graff carrying when he'd stopped by *The Advocate*.
Had he brought them to Patti? I hadn't noticed the flowers
when I'd come in.

I sketched a wave at Blackwell and started down the
three steps that led from the tiny porch. From inside the
house, a hoarse, strangled voice followed me onto the overgrown walk:

"Could not!" growled Patti Marsh. "Jack, you don't
know the half of it!"

Apparently, neither did I.

Milo Dodge was sitting on my doorstep, looking like a
rejected suitor. It was almost nine o'clock, and I couldn't
imagine what he was doing. I was so surprised to see him
that I almost nicked his Cherokee Chief with my Jaguar as
I made the turn into the driveway.

"You got a beer?" he asked, unfolding himself and standing up.

"I think so," I said. "If Adam didn't drink it all the last
time he was home."

He waited for me to open the door, then trooped along
behind me into the blessedly cool living room. My log
house smelled like pine needles and sink cleanser. It was a
definite improvement over the atmosphere at Patti Marsh's
place.

"What's up?" I asked, handing Milo his beer and opening a Pepsi for me.

Milo loped out of the kitchen and planted his long shambling frame on the sofa. "This is the damnedest homicide case. If that's what it is." He let out a weary sigh, then drank thirstily.

I waited as patiently as possible. Milo was gazing at the fireplace, which had accumulated a lot of trash in the past few days. Maybe I could set it off tonight if the house stayed cool.

"Billy Blatt talked to Marje today," he finally said, referring to one of his deputies who also happened to be Marje's first cousin. "She told him Cody was taking that suff, Haloperidol. It's a tranquilizer, and he was having some weird mood swings."

"Oh." I felt deflated, and wasn't sure why. Was it disappointment that Cody's death had been an accident after all? Or did I get a thrill out of homicide? If so, my only consolation was that Milo was looking as dejected as I felt. "Well, Marje would know," I said. "She works for the Deweys."

Milo's hazel eyes were still troubled. "Right, except that when we checked the prescription out with Garth Wesley at the drug store, he couldn't find one. So Billy went back to Marje, and she said that was because she'd been able to give him some pharmaceutical samples." Milo gave me an inquiring look.

I, too, grew puzzled. "Hmmmm. That's probably not ethical. Do you know if either of the Deweys had treated Cody for his mood swings?"

Having unburdened himself, Milo stretched out his long legs under my coffee table and relaxed a bit. "Marje told Billy that Cody hadn't seen a doctor. She'd noticed how moody he was and had told him he ought to make an appointment, but he wouldn't, so she got him the samples."

"Of syrup?" I asked.

Milo stared at me. "That's right. It wasn't pills." He sat up straight, pounding his fist into his palm. "Damn! Marje Blatt is lying! Why?"

"No," I said slowly, "she may not be lying. Perhaps she just doesn't know the whole truth. Cody might have gotten hooked on the stuff and got it from somebody else in another form. Or someone knew he was taking Haloperidol"—I uttered the word carefully—"and slipped him an extra dose."

Milo was shaking his head. "I don't see how we'll ever figure this one out. I can't get a handle on it. None of it seems quite real to me."

I was forced to agree. We sat in silence for a few moments, Milo drinking his beer while I sipped my Pepsi. "Any report from your forensics fellow?" I asked.

Milo gave a little jump. "Yeah, I almost forgot. He found some fibers that match the upholstery in Matt Tabor's Zimmer."

That seemed like big—if not unexpected—news to me. Milo, however, wasn't exactly elated. "So? Cody rode out to the Burl Creek Road in Matt Tabor's car," I mused. "Who drove him? Was Cody dead or alive at the time?"

"I don't know the answers to either of your questions," Milo replied glumly. "Matt Tabor says he didn't take his car out at all Saturday night. He rode with Dani and Reid Hampton to the tavern. Henry Bardeen isn't sure if the Zimmer left the ski lodge that night because he was up at the high school, helping judge the Miss Alpine contest. But we know somebody had that car out by the Burl Creek Road, and we know that Cody was in it."

I was sitting in the easy chair across from the sofa, my chin resting on my hands. "You're right, Milo—this is a real mess. On the one hand, we've got several people who refuse to accept the fact that Cody was murdered. Then we've got some others—some of them the same ones—who refuse to tell us anything helpful."

"*Us?*" Milo gave me a crooked grin. "Jeez, Emma, when did I slap a badge on your chest?"

"Let's leave my chest out of this," I snapped, recalling his comment at Mugs Ahoy. "Don't you want me to help? It seems you could use a little assistance." To strengthen my case, I told him about my visits to the ski lodge and

Patti Marsh's house. Milo didn't look terribly impressed, but at least he seemed mildly interested.

"Dani insists there's no motive to kill Cody," I pointed out. "On the face of it, she's right. But I think Cody knew something about somebody. I don't mean he was a black-mailer, but I'll bet he had some knowledge that was danger-ous. And it can't be a coincidence that he was killed right after Dani and the rest of the movie people came to town."

Milo's expression was skeptical. "I don't see it that way. The only one of those people that Cody knew was Dani. I've got another angle on the timing—it was Loggerama, and emotions were running high, they always do. Whatever it was that spurred the killer into action was probably triggered by all the excitement."

I suppose I haven't experienced enough of small-town life yet to go gaga over a three-day celebration of tree-chopping. Still, I had to allow for the differences in back-ground. Loggerama definitely changed the ebb and flow of Alpine's life. It wasn't every day that we had an erection, as our mayor would put it, in the middle of Front Street. At least I hoped not.

"I don't know, Milo . . ." I began, but he was crushing his empty beer can in his hands and shaking his head at me.

"Look at all the tourists and locals who got themselves banged up over the weekend," he said with uncharacteristic heat. "Look at the hordes of people who crowded into town. Look at Cody himself, throwing that axe at Dani and her friends. I wasn't there, you were, but now that Cody's been killed, I'll bet my boots he did it on purpose."

"If he did, it was a dumb stunt," I said. "Even if he'd ac-tually hurt one of them, there were several hundred wit-nesses."

"And he could claim it was an accident." Milo was still wringing the beer can. I gathered he wanted a new one.

"He hated Dani," I remarked, heading into the kitchen. "He said some awful things about her the day she came to town. Oddly enough, Dani doesn't seem to hate Cody. Or else she hides it better. I have to keep telling myself she *is* an actress." I returned to the living room and gave Milo his fresh beer.

He took a deep swig, feet now flat on the floor, arms resting on his knees. "Hell, Emma, this isn't getting us anywhere."

Somewhere between the refrigerator and Milo's outstretched hand, I'd had a thought: "Milo, if somebody brought that Haloperidol to the Icicle Creek Tavern, what was it in?" I noted the sheriff's blank look and clarified my question. "If it was a syrup, it had to come in some kind of container. A bottle, a vial, a ten-gallon jug. Did your deputies go through the tavern's trash?"

"Hell, no," replied Milo, faintly belligerent. "By the time we got the autopsy report, everything had been hauled away. Shoot, Emma, whoever brought the stuff—assuming somebody did—could have walked right out the door with the bottles or whatever. It took two days before we realized Cody had been poisoned."

Milo was right. "I suppose the risk was minimal," I allowed, now back in the easy chair, with my legs tucked under me. "Your forensics guy must have found something in the Zimmer. Who else has been driving it besides Matt Tabor and Patti Marsh?"

"Patti's hair, Dani's hair, Hampton's hair, lots of stuff," said Milo with another sigh. "You'd think they'd all gone bald in that car."

They hadn't, of course. But Cody Graff might have lost more than his hair in the Zimmer. In the elegant, hand-crafted, meticulously detailed setting of the custom-built automobile, he very likely had lost his life.

Chapter Ten

"MARJE IS *NOT* a liar." Vida was emphatic. She tipped the straw hat over one eye and gave me a cold stare. "She may be confused, but she wouldn't lie. In fact, I find it hard to believe she admitted passing out purloined pills to Cody. She certainly never told *me* he was on medication."

"They were samples," I reminded her. "I had a friend in Portland who was a nurse. She was always handing out free samples. What else can they do with them?"

Vida wasn't appeased. She was, however, disturbed. It appeared that her own arguments had created misgivings. "There's something very wrong here," she pointed out. "I had lunch with Marje yesterday. She hadn't talked to Billy yet. She was upset, mostly about Cody, and the fact that she couldn't believe anyone would have a reason to kill him. Marje actually got quite inarticulate—most unlike her. But she never once mentioned that he was taking that Haloperidol. And even though Cody had a bad temper and could be mean as cat dirt, she didn't complain about him being moody. Now why did she suddenly give her cousin all this blather?"

If Vida didn't know, I couldn't even guess. We were in the news office, waiting for the paper to come back from Monroe. Vida was at her desk, and I had borrowed Ed's chair.

"I suppose," I ventured, "because Billy is a deputy sheriff and Marje felt she had to be candid with him. Let's face it, Vida, we're not out of the Dark Ages yet when it comes to attitudes on mental problems. Would Marje want to go around town telling everybody that her fiancé was taking tranquilizers because he couldn't control his moods?"

Vida shook her head so hard that she had to hold onto her hat. "I'm not talking about telling *everybody*. I'm talking about telling *me*. Marje and I are very close. Her mother, Mary Lou, is a pinhead."

Ed lumbered into the office just then, with Curtis Graff in tow. I hid my surprise and gave Curtis a pleasant smile. He was leaving in a few hours for the San Juans, and wanted to clip Cody's obituary. Did we have copies of the newspaper yet?

We didn't, but I told Curtis he could wait for Kip MacDuff who ought to be getting in from Monroe very soon. Curtis sat down at Carla's desk, I vacated Ed's chair, and Vida fixed our visitor with a shrewd gaze.

"Curtis," she began without any bothersome preamble, "who do you think killed your brother? Or do you think he may have accidentally killed himself?"

Curtis did not return Vida's gaze. "I haven't had anything to do with Cody for five years. Don't ask me how he died. I just wish I hadn't been around when it happened."

"But you were," Vida noted, never one to let a squirming fish off the hook. "Didn't you talk to Cody before he died?"

"I sure didn't," said Curtis with fervor. He was now looking at Vida, matching stare for stare. "Why would I want to talk to that jerk?"

Ed looked up from his clip art and I gave a little jump from my place by the coffeepot, but Vida was unmoved. "I never did know what you and Cody had your falling-out over," she said, implying that someone had been remiss by not telling her. "But it must have been a pip. What was it, Curtis—a girl?"

Curtis stood up abruptly, glaring at Vida. Then he uttered a lame little laugh, and shoved his hands into his pockets. "Yeah—you could say that. A girl." He made a half-hearted effort to kick Carla's desk. "I'm heading out. I don't want to miss the Anacortes ferry. I'll pick up those papers when

I get back to Alpine in a couple of days." He moved swiftly to the door and let it swing shut with a loud bang.

Vida was bristling. "Well! I was right. The Graff boys did have a real set-to. Now I wonder why?"

We all did. But at the time, we couldn't begin to understand what had caused the rift. And we certainly didn't see the connection with Cody's death. Given the circumstances, we couldn't blame ourselves.

When I got home that evening, there was a call from Adam on my machine. He had a few more items for Curtis Graff to bring back to Alaska. His fleece-lined denim jacket. His navy blue ribbed knit sweater. His leather driving gloves. His ten-speed bike. And, if I had time to go shopping, could I throw in some crew socks, a half-dozen boxer shorts, a pair of Nikes, and olive green Dockers with one-inch belt loops? Oh—and a seven-eights of an inch woven black belt?

Grimly, I dialed the cannery's dormitory. But Adam wasn't there. He had a couple of days off and was on an overnight rock climbing expedition. My son had neglected to tell me about that, obviously being too caught up in the size of his belt—which was considerably larger than the size of his brain.

Or so I decided as I banged down the phone. It rang under my hand, and I answered in a vexed voice.

"Emma, you sound as if some outraged reader put a bomb under your desk," said Tom Cavanaugh, in that easy, resonant voice that always made me tingle. "What's wrong?"

I was about to say "My son," then realized that would get us off on the wrong foot. "We had another homicide. I don't suppose it was in the San Francisco papers."

"No, we have too many of our own," said Tom. "Who got killed?"

I explained, as briefly as possible. The account gave me time to catch my breath and regain my temper. It also allowed me to recover from the surprise of hearing Tom's voice. Even though I'd spoken with him as recently as early June, I had the feeling that he could call me every day and I'd still get a little breathless. *Sap*, I chided myself, and concluded my recitation with Milo's frustration over the complexities of the case.

"Dodge is a good man," said Tom, "but he's not much for subtleties. I agree with you, I don't think this Loggerama business is what set the killer off. Assuming there *is* a killer. Your theory about Dani Marsh's return makes more sense. Given that, though, it would work better if Dani, not Cody, had been the victim."

"Well, she wasn't," I said. "Cody was a bit of a drip, but he wasn't worth murdering. If you know what I mean," I added hastily, aware that I sounded crass.

"Right." Tom spoke absently. "Did you get my letter?"

I bit my lip. "Yes. I was going to answer it . . . tonight. I just got home. We've been so busy with Loggerama and then Cody's death . . ."

"And you didn't know how to fob me off." Tom chuckled. "Emma, I'm going to do *something* for Adam, and that's that. But it would be better if we agreed on what it would be."

"Okay," I said. "Pay for his tuition to the University of Alaska. Throw in room and board." I smirked into the phone, figuring I'd hoisted Tom on his own petard.

I was wrong. "Fine, when does he have to register? Are they on a quarter or a semester system? Has he declared a major?"

I was virtually speechless. "Tom—"

He trampled my protest. "I don't know much about the state university system up there, but he ought to make sure his courses are transferable to the lower forty-eight. How many credits does he have from Hawaii?"

Tom had to stop asking me questions I couldn't answer. Adam's transcripts looked like Egyptian hieroglyphics. "Adam has saved up to go to school. That's why he's working in Ketchikan. I think he needs the responsibility of earning most of his own money. But you could give him the price of an airline ticket to Fairbanks."

Tom was silent for a moment. "Stanford would be closer."

"To who? You?" The words tumbled out unbidden.

"Emma." Tom was a patient man, but he sounded faintly exasperated. "To both of us, if you put it like that. But I was only thinking in terms of Stanford because of its reputation. What does Adam want to do with his life?"

I laughed. "Adam has planned his life only as far as his next party. Give me a break, Tom, do your kids know what they're doing?"

"My *other* kids?" Tom with the needle was a new experience for me. "Graham still likes taking cinema at USC, but he doesn't know if he wants to be a director, a cinematographer, or sell Milk Duds at the Tenplex in Beverly Center. Kelsey says she's not going back to Mills. She wants to see Europe and meet Alberto Tomba on the ski slopes." He paused, but not long enough to let me interrupt. "Okay, airline tickets it is. I'll send enough so Adam can come home for the holidays."

I was about to ask how his mentally unstable wife, Sandra, was doing when he turned away from the phone. "Terrific," I heard him say. "I always said green was your color."

A woman's voice answered in the background. Sandra's voice. She sounded almost normal, which meant she wasn't cackling like a chicken or howling like a loon. I glanced at my watch—it was almost six-thirty. I guessed that they were going out to dinner. Together. I put my hand to my head and fought down a terrible urge to cry.

"Thanks, Chuck," Tom said into the phone. "I'll get back to you in a few days. Good-bye."

Chuck. Chuck who? Chuck what? I felt my mouth twist into a bitter little smile. I should have chucked my emotions out the window a long time ago. Unfortunately, feelings aren't as easy to dump as old clothes.

But, I thought, getting up off the sofa and moving briskly into the kitchen, I'd just saved the price of an airline ticket.

I tried out Tom's theory on Vida. She didn't discount the idea. "Tommy's no dope," she said. "So where does it lead us? Back to Dani and Cody five years ago?"

"Maybe." We were driving in my Jag out to the Burl Creek Road. It was a muggy Thursday morning, and we wanted to have a look at the spot where Durwood had mistakenly thought he'd run down Cody Graff. "Vida, what do you remember about Cody and Dani?"

Vida leaned back against the leather upholstery, her flower-strewn fedora slipping down almost to the rim of her glasses. "Not much," she admitted. "That was the year my three daughters insisted I go to Europe. They'd been nagging me to use their father's insurance money for a long time, and after they were all married and settled down, I finally gave in. I was gone three months, so I missed the wedding."

I stopped for the arterial onto Alpine Way. Across the street, I could see Old Mill Park with its statue of Carl Clemans, the town's official founder, and despite the discrepancy in spelling, kin to Samuel Clemens. A family of tourists was going into the museum that housed logging memorabilia. On the tennis courts, a half-dozen people were energetically lobbing balls back and forth across the nets. It was too early in the day for the picnickers to show up with their jugs of Kool-Aid and containers of potato salad and raw hamburger patties. In my mind's eye, I tried to recreate the original mill, which had stood next to the railroad tracks. Old photographs usually showed it under a lot of snow, with lumber piled high on the loading dock and great puffs of smoke pouring out of slim steel stacks.

"They had a baby shower for Dani at Darlene Adcock's," Vida went on. "I didn't go, but I wrote a little story about it. Darlene said Dani was very excited, thrilled to pieces over every gift she got. Then the baby came—and went." Vida shook her head, tipping the fedora even farther down on her forehead.

"Patti told me Dani was a rotten mother," I remarked, following the railroad tracks past the sign advertising the new Safeway.

Vida adjusted her hat. "I don't think that's true. I saw Dani a couple of times downtown with little Scarlett—what a terrible name to give a child, no wonder she died, probably of mortification—but Dani was proud as punch. She had the baby all dressed up in the sweetest little things—which is a lot more than I can say for Patti when Dani was a baby. She just threw a bunch of hand-me-downs on her and stuffed her into a stroller."

"I take it Dani never knew her father?"

"Ray Marsh? No. Patti couldn't track him down to get any child support, which made her wild. I think he went to California. They often do," Vida said, as if there were big signs at the Agricultural Inspection Stations on the state line that read WELCOME IRRESPONSIBLE MEN OF THE WEST.

At the little dip in the road, I applied the brake. "It must have been right about here," I noted. The Burl Creek Road was to our left, the Overholt farm just across the intersection. Vine maple, cottonwoods, and a few firs lined the other side of the road, concealing the train tracks and the river. We pulled over and got out of the car. "The Zimmer must have been parked where we are, at least according to Cal and Charlene Vickers."

"Yes," said Vida, walking slowly around the Jaguar. "I suppose Milo and his deputies scoured this area thoroughly."

"No doubt." I watched Vida bend down, her lack of confidence in Milo and his men apparent. "Do you think they missed something?"

Vida shot me a wry look. "Did you ever know a man who didn't? Remember, Emma, men aren't like other people. My late husband could never find his hunting shirt, right there in front of him in the closet. It was *red plaid*. Imagine!"

I joined Vida in her search. Three full days had passed since Milo had decided that Cody Graff had been murdered. Maybe. Careless passersby had already littered the roadside with the usual beer cans, gum wrappers, and Styrofoam cups. Vida clucked at the vandals' leavings, even as she checked each item to make sure it couldn't possibly be a clue. She was well off into the brush now, up to her knees in fiddlehead ferns.

"Ah!" she cried, holding up an object that looked like a pen. "See this!" Triumphantly, she charged up through the ferns and presented me with an eyeliner pencil. "It's almost new, obviously expensive. What do you bet it belongs to Dani Marsh?"

I turned the eyeliner over in my hand. It was a brand I'd seen only in high fashion magazine advertisements. No store in Alpine carried the line, and it would probably be hard to find even in Seattle. "Could be," I said. "So what?"

Vida was gesturing in the vicinity of my car. "Let's say the Zimmer was parked the way we are now, heading out of town. The driver's side is next to the road. Dani has Cody with her, he passes out, maybe dies right there, she panics and pushes him out of the car. The eyeliner rolls out, too, and goes down that little bank. Got it?"

I wasn't sure. "Then how did Cody get onto the road? If he'd been on that side of the car, he would have gone down the bank, too. And Durwood would never have thought he'd hit him."

Vida frowned. "If Cody acted so tipsy, there's no way he could have driven. So to put him on the passenger side next to the road, they had to be coming *from* somewhere. But where? And why?"

"We can't be sure Dani was driving," I objected. "An expensive eyeliner doesn't prove she was in the Zimmer."

"It does if it's hers." Vida was once again combing the underbrush, without much success this time. "Let's return it. Are they still up on Baldy?"

"I don't think so. They were going to film on Front Street today, remember?"

Vida did, but pointed out that the movie company hadn't been in evidence when we left the *Advocate* office at eight-thirty. "There was some action down by the taco place, but no lights or cameras," she informed me, tramping back to the Jag.

We decided to head for the ski lodge, which could be reached by taking the Burl Creek Road. Henry Bardeen's attempt to enforce the film personnel's screening process fell flat with Vida.

"Who started this lodge, Henry?" she demanded, using her height and her hat to tower over the unfortunate manager. "Rufus Runkel, my father-in-law, that's who. Where did your most glowing reference come from when you applied for this job, Henry? This old girl, that's who. Now turn your back and pretend you never saw us. We're going upstairs."

"Wait," I hissed, trotting after Vida, who was already inside the small elevator. "How do you know which room Dani is in?"

Vida gave me a patronizing look. "The FDR suite, what else? The old fool stayed here back in 'forty-two when he came West for the Grand Coulee Dam opening. Then that busybody wife of his came here in 'forty-three. What a pair! It's a wonder this country didn't lose the war. Or maybe it did." She tromped out of the elevator on the fourth floor and headed down the hall to the last door, which was set in an alcove. Vida's knock was anything but timid: It could have raised FDR's ghost. If he'd had the nerve.

But Dani Marsh didn't respond. Vida tried again, then pressed her ear to the pine door. "It's quiet," she whispered. "Oh, well. We can wait." She started retracing her steps down the hall.

"We can't wait forever," I said to her back. "I've got to get to work. So do you."

Vida stopped so unexpectedly that I almost fell over her. She froze, then pointed to the room on our right. The words ALPINE SUITE were burnt into a slab of cedar. We could hear voices on the other side of the door. Or one voice, at least. Matt Tabor sounded very loud and extremely angry.

Though the walls were thick and sturdy, we could catch snatches of his furious words:

"... faithless as they come ... You used me! ... You don't know the meaning of love! To think I cared about you so damned much. ..."

Vida and I exchanged startled glances. Down the hall, the elevator opened. The young woman I'd seen with the script up at the location on Baldy now emerged carrying a big manila envelope. She gave us a curious glance.

Undaunted, Vida yanked at the collar of my cotton blouse. "There! Now you're presentable. Let's go see Henry Bardeen."

The ruse apparently worked. The young woman walked off in the opposite direction. Vida and I made for the elevator. We were in luck, catching it before the doors closed all the way.

"My, my," said Vida, leaning against the frosted glass at the rear of the car, "true love isn't running smoothly. Maybe it's a mercy that Matt and Dani haven't set a date for the wedding."

"Hollywood romances must be especially rough," I remarked, though I would be willing to match my own true love against any of them. "All those egos and temptations and ambition."

"Ambition." Vida breathed the word and gave me a puzzled look as we got out of the elevator. "Now that's something I would never connect with Dani. Whatever else she was when she was growing up, ambition played no part in it."

We were in the lobby, where several guests were checking out at the front desk. Heather Bardeen was looking very professional this morning in her desk clerk's navy blazer and silk crimson scarf.

"We can check with Dani about the eyeliner later," I said, looking at my watch. "It's going on ten. The mail will be in any minute and Ginny will wonder what happened to us. If they're going to film on Front Street, we may be able to catch Dani this afternoon."

Reluctantly, Vida agreed. But in the parking lot, she grabbed my arm. "We can catch Dani now," she whispered in my ear. "Look!"

In a specially reserved slot next to the lodge, Dani Marsh was getting out of a brand-new Lexus. She had obviously just arrived. My jaw dropped; Vida stared over the rims of her glasses. Then she charged after her prey.

"Dani! Yoo-hoo! Over here!" Vida waved her fedora.

Dani squinted at us against the sun, then smiled pleasantly. "Yes?" She was obviously in a hurry.

Vida whipped around the other parked cars like a halfback breaking tackles. "Here, Dani," she said, handing over the eyeliner. "We found this."

Dani glanced down at the proffered object. "Oh! Thank you. I was wondering what I'd done with it." She gave Vida her dazzling smile.

I had moved a few steps so that I could see both of the women's profiles. Vida was gazing down at Dani, the tortoiseshell glasses catching the sun. "You lost it out by the turnoff to the Burl Creek Road."

Dani blinked a couple of times. "Oh? That's odd—I thought I lent it to my mother." She took the eyeliner and dropped it in her Sharif handbag. "I'm glad to get it back. I always prefer using my own cosmetics, rather than the makeup crew's." The smile remained fixed as she turned to head into the ski lodge.

Vida was standing with her hands on her hips. "Well, if that doesn't beat all!"

I had sidled up next to her. "Yes?"

Vida looked down her nose at me. "Dani and Patti trading makeup? Punches would be more like it. And who was Matt Tabor quarreling with, if not Dani Marsh? What's going on here?"

I hadn't the slightest idea. My only hope was that Milo Dodge had a better grasp of the investigation than we did.

But, unfortunately, that was not so.

Chapter Eleven

CARLA HAD GONE in to see young Doc Dewey and find out if she needed a refill on her antihistamine. She didn't, but when she got back from the clinic, her dark eyes were huge and her cheeks were flushed.

"Patti Marsh was there, all black and blue," gasped Carla, leaning on Vida's desk. "She said she'd fallen off her porch."

I was standing in the doorway to my office, holding the mail that Ginny Burmeister had just brought in. "Porch or perch?" I responded. "Or neither one?"

Carla nodded vigorously. Vida sniffed. "Jack Blackwell. He probably beat her up. I'd guess it wasn't the first time."

"Creep," remarked Ginny, who was dumping Ed's mail in his already overflowing in-basket. "Maybe that's why his first wife left him."

Irrationally, I felt a twinge of guilt. "It must have happened last night, after I left Patti's. Jack seemed okay, and Patti was practically on her ear."

But Carla shook her head, long black hair swinging over her shoulders. "No, it was this morning, I'm sure. She had a cut over her eye, and it was still bleeding."

"Men!" huffed Vida, glancing at Ed's vacant chair as if he were responsible for the entire sex. "I've been tempted to deck Patti a few times myself, but that's different. I'm a woman."

"Now Vida," Ginny began, "violence doesn't have a gender. You really shouldn't say things like that."

Vida had turned back to her typewriter. She veered

around in her chair, giving Ginny a vexed look. "Hush! I'm old enough to be your grandmother! Do you want to get *spanked*?" The typewriter rattled and shook as Vida launched into her latest article. Before any of the rest of us could say anything further, a knob flew off, a couple of screws clattered to the floor, and Vida's typewriter was dead in the water. "Oh, blast!" she cried. "Now what?"

"Vida," I began, tossing the mail onto my desk and re-entering the news office, "it's time to upgrade yourself. Let's go buy you a word processor."

"No!" Vida recoiled as if I'd threatened to burn her at the stake. "It just needs fixing, that's all!" She groped with one foot, retrieving the knob. "Get me a screwdriver. I can do it myself."

"Ed borrowed it to fix his front door," said Ginny. "That was three weeks ago."

"Great," I muttered. Ed had a habit of borrowing items from the office and never returning them. "I'll run over to the hardware store and get another one."

"I can go," offered Ginny.

"You need to answer the phones," I said, already halfway to the door. "It's Thursday. I don't want to talk to every crackpot with a complaint about the latest edition of the paper."

Harvey Adcock's Hardware and Sporting Goods Store was only a block and a half away, and coincidentally in the same building as the local florist. I hurried up Front Street, trying to pretend that at eleven o'clock in the morning it wasn't already stifling. Compared with the previous week, the tempo of the town seemed to have slowed to a snail's pace.

Across the street, a middle-aged couple looked longingly at the Whistling Marmot movie theatre's air-conditioning sign. In the next block, three teenagers stood close together in the shade of the Venison Inn's entrance. At the corner of Fifth Street, the bookstore's cat had decamped from its usual place in the front window to sit among the leafy greenery of a sidewalk planter. The air, which in other sea-

sons smells of evergreens and damp and woodsmoke, was
tinged with gasoline fumes and cooking grease. The smoke-
stacks at the mill were moribund; the ski lodge catered only
to the traveler. In summer, there was a fallow feeling to Alpine, despite the number of tourists and the presence of the
movie company. It was as if we were on hold, waiting for
the rain and the real business of the community to begin
anew.

Harvey's store, with its high ceilings and two separate
showrooms, seemed cool by comparison to the outdoors.
He was behind the counter, sorting faucets. His pixie-like
face brightened when he saw me.

"Emma! What broke?"

I explained, asking him for a cordless screwdriver, just
like the one I had at home. Ed would probably walk off
with it eventually, but I might as well facilitate matters for
now.

"Regular or bendable?" asked Harvey, coming around
the counter to a display rack on the other side of the store.

"They bend now, too?" I was impressed. "Sure, why
not?"

Harvey sprinted back behind the counter, ringing up the
sale. "That's $43.27, with tax."

My jaw dropped. I had only twenty-five dollars in cash,
about twice that much in my checking account, which
hadn't been balanced in two weeks, and payday wasn't until tomorrow. I dug into my wallet for my emergency fund,
a hundred dollar bill I kept tucked away for dire necessities.
Like bendable cordless screwdrivers.

"Can you change this?" I asked, almost hoping Harvey
couldn't and thus I would be let off the hook. An ordinary
screwdriver probably went for under five bucks.

"Sure can," said Harvey cheerfully. "I went to the bank
when they opened at nine-thirty." He took my hundred; I
hoped he didn't notice how my hand lingered on the bill.
"There I was waiting for them to open up, and who comes
along but Patti Marsh, sassy as you please." The cash reg-

ister jingled and Harvey made change. "She must have won the lottery."

I frowned at Harvey as he counted the money into my hand. "What do you mean?"

Harvey's pointed little ears seemed to move up and down. "What? I mean she was pleased with herself. She had a big deposit, or so I gathered standing next to her in the bank. You should have heard her and that MacAvoy kid carry on! 'Shall I get a gunny sack for it, Mrs. Marsh?' he asked her. They were laughing themselves sick. Of course Richie MacAvoy is new at the teller's job and probably should be a mite more discreet."

"Wait a minute, Harvey," I said, leaning on the counter and lowering my voice as an elderly man I didn't recognize ambled into the store. "Patti Marsh was just treated by young Doc Dewey for . . . cuts and abrasions," I said quickly, not sure I should spread gossip any faster than the rest of Alpine. "How did she look?"

Harvey gave a shrug of his slender shoulders. "Fine. You know Patti—lots of goo on her face, even in the morning. I suppose she was on break from work."

From work at Blackwell Timber, I thought to myself. "Well." I tried to act unconcerned. "She must have taken that spill after she went to the bank."

"Maybe so." Harvey was handing me the paper bag with the screwdriver, but he was looking at the elderly man who was bringing a box of washers up to the counter. "Hi, Marco. What've you got?"

Thanking Harvey Adcock, I left the store and scooted around the corner to Posies Unlimited. The owner, Delphine Corson, was a flabby blonde of fifty with high color and a low neckline. She greeted me with a throaty laugh.

"You're too late," she announced, slapping the empty plant stand next to the refrigerated case. "I can't get any more flowers up to the San Juans in time for the funeral, not even by wire or phone."

To my dismay, I realized that while Cody Graff's death was never far from my mind, I had completely forgotten about his services, which were scheduled for today. Hastily, I explained that I didn't know the family and had only met Cody a couple of times.

Delphine moved with a graceless tread to the bench, where she was arranging red and yellow roses in a wicker basket. "It's mostly friends of his parents who've sent flowers," she said. "I don't think Cody had a lot of pals." She picked up a handful of maidenhair fern and clipped an inch off the stems. "Funny, though—you'd think his fiancée would have had me do a spray for his casket."

"Marje?" I fanned myself with my hand. It was very warm in the small shop, and the heady scent of flowers was almost overpowering. "Maybe she had something sent from Friday Harbor."

"Oh, no," said Delphine with certainty. "The Blatts always use me. Marje had already been in to discuss the flowers for her wedding. That's off now, so there goes a nice chunk of change. She wanted four hundred gardenias."

I didn't comment on the canceled ceremony or Delphine's unrealized profits. Instead, I steered the conversation back to the Graffs. "I gather Curtis was in the other day. Those tiger lilies were gorgeous."

Delphine plucked out a red rose that wasn't up to snuff and put it in her cleavage. "Curtis? The older Graff kid? Oh, right, he's back from Alaska. He sure had lousy timing. Isn't your kid in Ketchikan, too?"

"Yes," I said, trying not to get sidetracked. "I couldn't figure out why Curtis was taking flowers to Patti Marsh. What's the connection?"

My blatant probing didn't seem to bother Delphine. That's one advantage of being a journalist: other people figure you have a right to know. It rarely occurs to them that you may be just plain nosy.

Delphine gazed at me with cornflower blue eyes. "It was July 30."

My face must have been a blank. "So?"

"Oh, that's right," said Delphine with a little grimace. "I forgot. You're a newcomer."

I had the feeling that I would still be a newcomer if I stayed in Alpine until I died. Native Alpiners were not only wary of strangers, but were loath to embrace anyone who hadn't spent at least a couple of decades in their town.

Delphine had finished with the arrangement and was gathering up leftover leaves and stems. "Five years ago on July 30, the Graff baby died. Curtis was taking a bouquet to Grandma Patti. Nice of him, considering."

"Considering what?"

Delphine shrugged. "Considering that he's been gone for so long. And that he and Cody were on the outs. As for Dani, I don't know—it seems to me he should have taken her a bouquet, too. I suggested it, but he didn't seem to hear me. So I lost a fifteen dollar sale on that one." She looked disappointed.

"What about Cody? Did he buy flowers, too?"

"He never has, not in all the years since little Scarlett died." Disapproval was etched on Delphine's face, though I couldn't tell whether it was motivated by Cody's lack of sentiment or the loss of another order.

"Say, Delphine," I said, suddenly reminded of another tragedy, "do you remember when Art Fremstad killed himself?"

Delphine's heavy jowls sagged. "You bet. What a nice guy. Talk about flowers! I made enough off of that one to send myself to Palm Springs for a week! I even had to hire extra help to deliver. Poor Art. Poor Donna."

I assumed Donna was Art's widow. "Did she remarry?"

"Yeah, about two years ago. You know Steve Wickstrom from the high school? Trig and geometry teacher."

I remembered seeing Steve and Donna Wickstrom at the Icicle Creek Tavern with Coach Ridley and his wife. In the spring, Carla had done a piece about Steve's contribution to a math text. She'd called him *Stove*. Carla's proofreading wasn't any better than her typing.

Thanking Delphine for her time, I started to leave but felt her blue eyes boring into my back. "Oh," I said a trifle giddily, "I forgot. I wanted to get a bouquet." I cast around the flower shop. Everything looked as if it would cost at least twenty dollars a dozen. "Or maybe a plant. Yes, how about a nice cyclamen?"

With a grunt, Delphine bent down and picked up a bright pink specimen. "This is a beauty. That'll be $17.58 with tax. After it finishes blooming, keep it in the dark."

That figured, I thought to myself. We all seemed to be in the dark when it came to Cody Graff's death. But I was the only one who was going broke. If I hurried, maybe I could still get back to the office while I had enough money for lunch.

But as I carted the plant and the cordless screwdriver over to *The Advocate*, I decided I could put the cyclamen to good use. The Jaguar was parked around the corner. I jumped in and drove the five blocks down Railroad Avenue to Blackwell Timber.

Patti Marsh wasn't there. The fresh-faced young woman at the receptionist's desk said Ms. Marsh had gone home early. Sick, she gathered. Maybe the heat. It was really too warm for Alpine.

It was almost noon. Maybe it was just as well if I skipped lunch. I got back in the car and drove up to Patti's house. In the midday sun, the tired little house didn't look any more hospitable than it had last night. Although Patti's black compact car was in the drive, the door was closed and the drapes were still drawn. I hesitated, then knocked loudly.

On my second effort, Patti called from inside, asking my identity. I told her. Warily, she opened the door a couple of inches.

"I heard you'd had an accident," I said, feeling a bit foolish as I tried to wedge the cyclamen inside the door. "Isn't this a pretty shade of pink?"

"What is it?" she asked, opening the door all the way. "Some kind of orchid?"

"It's a cyclamen, from Posies Unlimited." I had a fixed smile on my face as I crossed the threshold. The bouquet on the Bombay chest was shedding petals. Patti looked as if she'd lost all her bloom, too. Her face was swollen, and there was a small bandage above her right eye. "How do you feel?"

Patti took the plant and limped into the living room. The house was still dreary and airless. She went over to the TV and turned off a soap opera.

"I feel like crap," said Patti, indicating that I should sit down on the cluttered sofa. "I decided to take the rest of the day off."

"How'd it happen?" I asked in what I hoped was a guileless voice.

Patti eased herself into the cut-velvet chair and lighted a cigarette. She still wore a wary expression. "Hey, Mrs. Lord, cut the bullshit. Since when were we buddies? What do you really want?"

I allowed the smile to die. "Okay. I don't like seeing women get knocked around. You didn't fall off your front porch, Patti. You looked just fine when Harvey Adcock saw you at the bank this morning. If somebody's beating you up, why don't you file a complaint?"

"Sheesh!" Patti rolled her brown eyes and looked at me as if I were the original babe in the woods. "Where'd you grow up, in a bird cage? Hey, people—like men—get pissed off. They start swinging. That's how they handle stuff. They don't mean anything by it, they just don't know what else to do. Then they're sorry, and they come crawling back, full of apologies, and maybe a present or two. It's the way of the world, honey."

"Not my world." I spoke firmly, perhaps even primly, judging from the amused expression on Patti's face. Before she could contradict me, I leaned toward her, careful not to knock any of the items off the coffee table with my knees. "Beating up women is a coward's way of dealing with problems. It's also stupid, and men who do it are stupid. What kind of woman wants to hang out with a stupid coward? I can't think of any present that's worth the price, and that includes a terrific night in the sack."

No longer amused, Patti stiffened, apparently surprised at

my candor. Maybe she didn't expect it from me. "So how do you change a man?" she asked with a sneer.

"I'm not sure you can change a man. But you can change men. Find somebody who doesn't think with his fists. They don't all go around beating women senseless. Jeez, Patti, that can get out of hand pretty fast. You could end up dead." I stared straight into her eyes, which were so like Dani's, except for being bloodshot and a bit puffy.

Patti recoiled as if I'd decided to use her for a punching bag. "Shut your mouth!" she gasped, clearly shaken. "Here!" She struggled to her feet and grabbed the plant from on top of the TV set. "Take this cycling thing and get out!"

I didn't budge. "No, I won't." If Patti needed a lesson in being firm, I was about to give it. "I'm not done." I waited for her to sit down, pitch a fit, or throw the cyclamen at my head. Instead, she cradled the plant against her bosom and narrowed her eyes.

"You're nervy," she said. The anger still sparked in her eyes, but she also looked frightened. "What now?"

I had been sure of my moral ground when I'd lectured Patti about allowing herself to be beaten. But I had absolutely no reason to inquire about her bank deposit. Not even my credentials as a journalist gave me the right to ask such a question.

I stuck with candor as my best weapon. "I heard you had some good luck today. Then I heard you were at the clinic, all banged up. It didn't make sense, and maybe I thought there was a story in it, especially since Cody Graff was murdered. Violence breeds violence. I was following my reporter's instincts, I guess." My attitude was self-deprecating; I was relying on Patti's sympathy. If she had any. "After all, we've got a murderer loose in this town."

Her response startled me. Patti Marsh threw back her head and laughed, a hoarse, unsettling sound that turned into a cough. She stubbed out her cigarette, wiped her mouth, and leaned against the back of the cut-velvet chair.

"No, we don't. Stick to your movie star stories and your
raccoon pictures, Emma Lord. You don't know siccum."

I left the cyclamen, convinced that it, too, would wither
and die in the sunless, stifling atmosphere of Patti's house.
I didn't understand a woman like Patti, who seemed content
to live off the leavings of an ill-tempered man like Jack
Blackwell. Then again, I didn't understand myself, hanging
on to a twenty-year-old dream. Maybe Patti and I weren't
so different after all.

"Well," said Vida, when I returned to the office, "you
look like a dying duck in a thunderstorm. What happened?
I thought you went out for a screwdriver."

I recounted my adventures of the last hour and a half
while Vida sipped iced tea. "I'm only guessing it was Jack
who beat her up," I said in conclusion, "but I can't figure
out why she hooted with laughter when I told her there was
a murderer on the loose."

Vida was looking thoughtful, her floppy pink linen hat
shoved back on her head. "Why do so many people not
want to believe Cody was killed? Isn't that what it comes
to?" Vida peered at me through her glasses.

"Is it?" I was sitting in Ed's vacant chair. He had gone
to a Rotary Club luncheon; Carla was out getting a story at
the fish hatchery. "Vida, do you know Donna Fremstad
Wickstrom?"

"Of course." Vida looked at me as if I were losing my
mind, which I felt wasn't far from the truth. "Donna
Erlandson Fremstad Wickstrom. A four-point student in
high school, two years at Skagit Valley Community College, Associate Arts degree, worked in the library, married
Art Fremstad, one child, a girl, widowed, remarried Steve
Wickstrom about three years ago. She runs a day care in
their home, has another baby, a boy, ten months, she jogs,
belongs to the Alpine Book Club, is an excellent baker,
does their own plumbing. What else do you want to
know?"

I was about to say I couldn't possibly imagine when I

saw an odd movement outside the window above Vida's desk. Somebody was putting a ladder against the building. "What's that?"

"What?" Vida eyed me curiously, then followed my startled gaze. "Oh! Good grief! Public Utility District workers? No—there's no PUD truck. I've no idea."

We both went outside. Three men in coveralls were hooking up a spray painter. One of them, a short stocky youth with black eyes and dark brown hair, smiled broadly.

"I hear you like yellow," he said, revealing lots of white teeth.

"Says who?" I gaped as one of the other men began to assault *The Advocate*'s outer walls with a blast of sun-bright color. "Hey! Stop that!"

The stocky young man was still grinning. "We've got permission. It'll look great on film. You'll love it."

"The hell I will!" I glanced up Front Street. Half the buildings, from Francine's Fine Apparel to Adcock's Hardware, wore new coats of paint. I had returned to the newspaper office from the other direction and hadn't noticed the change. "Oh, damn! Is this for the movie?"

It was. I asked who in the name of heaven and earth had given permission to turn *The Advocate* the color of a giant canary.

The stocky young man gestured at the entrance to the newspaper. "Your advertising guy. Burnski? Bronsti? We gave him a check for five hundred bucks."

I held my head. Vida was standing with her hands on her hips, watching *The Advocate* take on a jaundiced hue. Ed Bronsky had sold me out for five bills. If somebody had offered to buy that much advertising, he would have fought them tooth and toenail. I didn't know whether to throttle Ed—or Reid Hampton.

As I took another look down Front Street, I could see not only the newly painted red, blue, and green facades, but a barricade at the corner of Fifth, by the Venison Inn and the Whistling Marmot Theatre. Ironically, the Marmot needed some work, as its owner, Oscar Nyquist, hadn't fixed up the exterior since 1967, when an outraged member of a Pentecostal sect had set fire to a life-size cutout of Mrs. Robinson's stocking-clad leg in a promotion for *The Graduate*. Further along Front, cameras were perched on big dollies and bright lights shown down on the main drag. As far as *The Advocate* was concerned, it was too late to do more than groan.

"This is hopeless," I muttered to Vida. "Let's go see Donna Wickstrom."

Vida had screwed up her face, observing the paint job in process. "Donna? What for?"

I was already heading for my car. If nothing else, I wanted to keep its green exterior from getting splattered with yellow dots. "We need to stop another murder," I yelled over the sound of the spraying machine.

Vida, with her flat-footed step, hurried to join me. "Who?" she asked, startled.

I opened the door for her on the passenger's side. "Ed. If I don't get out of here, I think I'm going to strangle him."

Chapter Twelve

VIDA'S FURTHER LACK of curiosity about my insistence on seeing Donna Fremstad Wickstrom puzzled me. As we made a detour to avoid the film company's barricade, she was unusually quiet. At last, as we approached the Wickstrom home in the Icicle Creek Development, I asked her what she was thinking.

"I'm thinking about what you're thinking about," she said very soberly. "You're trying to tie Cody's murder into something that happened between him and Dani, that something being little Scarlett and the effect of her death. At least that's the only incident we know about. And somehow, Art Fremstad fits into it. Maybe."

I was trying to concentrate on finding Wickstrom's address while listening to Vida. "That's right." I remarked. "The only common topic in regard to Dani and Cody is their baby. They haven't been in touch for five years. Curtis has been gone for five years. His parents moved away five years ago. Art Fremstad has been dead for five years. Everything points backwards. If there's any link between Cody's death and Dani's return, it has to be the baby. I don't know if Milo is on the same wavelength."

"Milo is doing fibers and fingerprints and tire tracks," said Vida, with a shake of her head. "That's how he works."

"Well?" I had turned into Dogwood Lane. "Do you think Art Fremstad was a suicidal type?"

Vida had taken off her floppy hat and was mopping her brow. "No. He had too much sense. But I'm not a mind

370

reader. If there's one facet of human behavior I've learned in over sixty years, it's that you can never be completely certain what anybody else is thinking."

I spotted the address on my right. Donna and Steve Wickstrom lived in one of the more modest homes in the new development, a two-story version of a Swiss chalet with a single-car garage. There were no goats on the lawn, but there was a tricycle, a sandbox, and a plastic wading pool.

Donna Wickstrom came to the front door with three small children attached to her legs. She was a pretty young woman with short brown hair and long curling eyelashes. Her unruffled expression indicated that not only was she unfazed by our unexpected arrival, but that there was very little in life that amazed her.

"Mrs. Runkel," she said, extending a hand. "How nice! I haven't seen you since the shower for Angie Fairbanks last May."

Vida introduced me to Donna, who somehow managed to lead us into the living room without disengaging herself from the trio of toddlers. Two more children were playing on the floor, pounding colored pegs into a sturdy wooden bench. The room was filled with sunshine, bright colors, and soft furniture. Donna Wickstrom was only a mile from Patti Marsh, but their dwellings were worlds apart.

I allowed Vida to broach the subject of our visit. She did so with remarkable tact—at least for Vida.

"This town is in a mess," she said, after we refused Donna's offer of tea or coffee. "First Cody Graff's baby dies. Now Cody is dead, too. Nobody, including the sheriff, knows why. I'm wondering, Donna, do you think Art would know if he were still alive?"

If Vida's words upset our hostess, she gave no sign. Donna Fremstad Wickstrom looked very grave, but didn't seem to find Vida's line of inquiry peculiar. She glanced into the dining room, where all of the children, including a girl of about five who looked remarkably like Donna, were dumping a pile of toys out of a big cardboard box.

"Do you mean that Art knew something so awful he killed himself?" she asked in a low voice.

"Exactly." Vida, as ever, was brisk. "Has that thought ever occurred to you?"

Again, Donna appeared undismayed. "Frankly, yes." She gave a quick look into the dining room to make sure that all was well, then folded her hands in her lap. "I was visiting my sister in Seattle when the Graff baby died. I came back to Alpine three days later, and Art was very upset. *Upset*, not distraught." She gave us each a hard look to make sure we understood. "For a long time, I kicked myself for being so caught up in restoring order after my visit out of town. You know how it is when you're gone, even for a short time. It takes forever to get everything back on track. Anyway, when Art disappeared two days later, I was stunned." For the first time, emotion showed in Donna's hazel eyes.

"Where did you think he'd gone?" Vida asked, giving Donna a chance to collect herself.

"He was on the night shift, five to midnight. It was just this time of year, and at first I figured he'd arrested some tourist or picked up a drunk driver. But about two in the morning, Jack Mullins called and asked if Art had come home instead of checking in at the sheriff's office. Of course he hadn't. That was when Jack and Milo and Sam Heppner went looking for him." She turned away, not toward the dining room this time, but to the front door, as if she still expected Art Fremstad to come home.

Vida, who was sitting next to Donna on the sectional sofa, placed a hand on the younger woman's arm. "They found him in the late morning, down past the falls. I remember that very well. His patrol car was parked off the highway on a dead-end logging road, about a hundred yards from the river." Vida glanced over at me. "We were all sure it was an accident. Especially Milo."

Donna's head jerked up. "And me. There was no way I would ever have thought Art would kill himself. I still wouldn't believe it if he hadn't left that note." In her fervor, she had raised her voice. Donna turned swiftly to see if the children were listening. They weren't. Toys were sailing in various directions, and several squeals erupted from small lungs.

I decided it was my turn to ask a question: "What did the note say, Donna?"

But Donna was on her feet, moving swiftly to intervene with the squabbling youngsters. Gently but firmly, she set matters straight and returned to the living room. "It said . . ." She paused to swallow hard. " 'Life is too tough. I hate being a deputy and arresting people. I can't go on.' Then he signed his name—'Art.' That was it." She raised a limp hand, as if her late husband's last words had not only summed up his suicide, but a lifetime of events that had led up to it.

We were silent for a moment, as if acting out our own commemoration. Then Vida tapped Donna's wrist. "Wait a minute—he *signed* his name? I never heard that part. Do you mean he typed the note itself?"

Donna nodded. "We had an electric typewriter then. Steve and I have a word processor now—he uses it for school."

Under her floppy pink hat, Vida was frowning. "Art typed a note that ran about four lines? Donna, does that make sense to you?"

"He must have been under a lot of stress. People behave strangely." Donna smoothed the wrinkles in her olive walking shorts.

"Was he under stress? Did he seem depressed?" Vida wasn't giving up.

"No, not really. I told you, he was upset by that Graff baby's death." Donna ran a hand through her short brown hair. "Art didn't talk a lot about his feelings. I wish he had. You know how most men are. They keep their emotions bottled up."

I looked at Vida. "Did Art talk to Milo?"

Vida was chewing her lower lip. "No. Not that I know

of." She turned back to Donna. "Where did you find the note?"

"Under the telephone. I'd invited everyone back here after the funeral, and I noticed this piece of paper sticking out when I went to call Delphine Corson and ask who sent the big basket of begonias while we were gone. There wasn't any card. Then I read the note . . ." She stopped, her shoulders slumping. "I showed it to Sheriff Dodge. He couldn't believe it, either. But of course we had to. It was a terrible shock."

Again we were silent, the little ones providing a background of innocent vigor. Vida's next question surprised me as well as Donna.

"Who did send the begonias?"

Donna stared at Vida. "Why—I don't know. I was so stunned by the note that I never called Delphine." She shook herself. "Isn't that awful of me—somebody didn't get a thank-you note."

I looked at Vida. Judging from the flash of her eyes, she was thinking about something far more dreadful than a lapse of etiquette. But she didn't say so to Donna. Maybe that was just as well.

There was a story in the dispute over the movie company's alleged unauthorized cutting of Jack Blackwell's trees. It wasn't the kind of article I usually ran before formal charges or lawsuits were filed, but it gave me an excuse to talk to Blackwell. After taking care of the most urgent messages that had accumulated on my desk, I returned to the timber company. Filming was underway in the vicinity of the Lumberjack Motel. The bright lights seemed blinding in the middle of the afternoon. Even from a distance, they looked hot. As for *The Advocate*, its bright new coat of yellow paint was drying quickly in the August sun.

The same young woman who had told me Patti Marsh wasn't in led the way into Jack Blackwell's office. His desk was an oval of mahogany, highly polished and fairly tidy. A salmon, in the neighborhood of sixty pounds, was

mounted on one paneled wall, and a moose head stared
blankly above a glass-fronted bookcase. The decor didn't
suit my taste, but in general, the room had more class than
its owner.

Jack looked up from a computer printout. "No, I haven't
any idea when the logging ban will be lifted. The fire danger is still higher than a kite. I'm losing money hand over
fist. And in the meantime, all those do-gooders in D.C.
work overtime trying to figure out how to screw me and
the rest of the timber industry."

I sat down in a curved chair that matched the desk. "Actually, that isn't why I'm here. I wanted to find out if
you're going to file a civil suit against the movie company
for chopping down your trees."

Blackwell's forehead creased, and his thin mouth formed
a firm, tight line. "I will if I have to, but I'm thinking criminal, not civil, charges. How'd you get wind of this?"

"I was at the Icicle Creek Tavern the other night," I explained, feeling somewhat puzzled. "You and Reid
Hampton had words, practically under my nose."

Jack Blackwell made an angry gesture with one hand,
sweeping the computer printout onto the floor. "I don't
mean that crap. I mean about the payoff. Has Patti been
shooting her face off?"

Enlightenment was beginning to dawn. I decided to play
it close to my chest. "It's hard for her say much of anything, with her face so swollen." It wasn't exactly the truth,
but I took the chance that Blackwell wouldn't know any
better. "She sure made the people at the bank happy,
though."

"Goddamn!" Blackwell pounded his fist on the desk, rattling pens, a stapler, an ashtray. "That bitch! What kind of
games is she playing now?"

Although I knew the question wasn't meant for me, I
hazarded an answer: "Why would the movie people make
a check out to Patti and not to you or Blackwell Timber?"

Jack Blackwell turned an angry, baffled face on me.
"That's what I want to know. That Hampton is one real

dumb bastard. Patti's not an officer of this company; she's a secretary. And then she lies about it, the cheating little tramp!" He jackknifed out of his chair, whirling around and looking as if he were about to assault the stuffed salmon. " 'Get your own money, Jack,' she told me, laughing in my face! 'I got mine.' Bullshit! Why does Reid Hampton owe *her* money? Those were *my* goddamned trees!"

"So you smacked her," I said calmly. "I don't imagine that got any money out of her."

Blackwell was facing me again, his saturnine face dark with rage and frustration. It dawned on me that I might get smacked, too. "So what? She's a thief!"

I got to my feet, forcing myself to remain casual. "Then you ought to tell Milo Dodge. Maybe you can get Patti *and* Reid Hampton arrested."

Blackwell's mouth twisted, not so much in anger, as in confusion. Maybe the idea hadn't occurred to him. He stared at me as if I had become an ally. "You think so? Ah hell, I don't want to put Patti in the slammer. She'll pony up. I just don't like her laughing in my face."

"That can be annoying," I allowed, inching toward the door. "Have you ever heard of friendly persuasion?"

Blackwell wasn't impressed by the suggestion. "Patti's already friendly enough. She can wear a man out. Are you saying she's too friendly with that Hampton prick?"

I wasn't, but it was a thought. Yet it didn't ring true. Or did it? Vida was right—you never really knew what went on in other people's heads. "She hardly knows him," I said, aware that the remark didn't necessarily exonerate Patti.

"Oh, yeah?" countered Blackwell. "He's been over to her place a couple of times. And she sure as hell knows him well enough to get fifty grand out of him."

That, I thought, was well enough for me.

Milo was going to bring Honoria Whitman over for a drink after dinner. I had issued the invitation when I checked in with Milo before I left the office. There was nothing new to report on the investigation, he told me, but

they were working on the source of the Haloperidol. They
were also trying to prove that Dani Marsh and Cody Graff
were in the Zimmer at the time of his death. Dani had been
unreachable all afternoon, because she was filming on Front
Street. Milo would try to see her before he brought Honoria
to my place.

But Milo showed up alone. Honoria had unexpected
company from Carmel, old friends touring Washington
State. I had to smirk. A recent arrival, and already Honoria
was suffering from a virulent Pacific Northwest disease: the
surprise guest with a complete ignorance of the motel and
hotel industry. I hadn't had anybody drop in for three
months, except for my brother, who had spent a week with
me in June. Ben had come to visit before going on to his
new assignment as a parish priest in northern Arizona. After over twenty years in the home missions of Mississippi,
he was feeling both sad about leaving the people he loved
and excited at the prospect of working with the Navajos.
Ben wasn't company; he was my other self.

Milo entered my house looking downhearted. "Honoria
asked me to drive down and have dinner with her and this
other couple, but I was too beat to go all the way into
Startup. You got any Scotch, Emma?"

"You're the only one who drinks it here," I said, going
to the bottom shelf of the bookcase where I kept my limited
liquor supply. "Why don't you just strap it to your leg?"

Milo didn't respond to my feeble effort at humor. "I
might as well resign," he said in a doleful voice. "If I don't
arrest somebody pretty soon, my chances of getting re-
elected are down the drain."

"Oh, shut up, Milo," I said testily. "Here, have a drink.
Shall I make some popcorn?"

Milo brightened. I was heading for the kitchen when a
voice trumpeted from the porch. It was Vida. "Well." She
stalked into the living room, wearing her gardening clothes,
which consisted of red culottes and a white blouse. "Here
you are. Where's Delphine?"

Milo and I both stared. "Delphine Corson?" I finally said, sounding stupid.

Vida threw her floppy pink hat onto the sofa. "Yes, yes, Delphine Corson. She was going to come over and tell us who delivered those blasted begonias. She had to go through her records. The woman isn't computerized."

"Neither are you, Vida." I couldn't resist the barb.

"Never mind," said Vida, going to the phone and punching in a series of numbers.

Milo clutched his Scotch as if it were an antidote. "What's all this about?"

I explained while Vida talked to Delphine. Vida finished first. "She just found it. I was right—Cody Graff delivered those flowers to the Fremstad house. He volunteered. In fact, he paid for them."

"How did he get in?" I asked.

Vida plopped down on the sofa next to Milo, narrowly missing her hat. "The door wasn't locked, I suppose. This isn't the big city, Emma. Especially five years ago." She looked very smug.

Milo, however, was still looking mystified. "Will you two please tell me—"

"Yes, yes, just pay attention," said Vida. "Really, Milo, you ought to have been more aware five years ago. Do you want some idiot like Averill Fairbanks to beat you when the primary election comes 'round next month?"

Milo groaned. Vida ignored him and continued: "I'm betting dollars to doughnuts that Art Fremstad didn't commit suicide. Nobody ever thought he did. Cody Graff brought those begonias over to Art and Donna's house during the funeral, when he knew no one would be around. He also left a phony suicide note. It was typewritten, badly worded, not up to Art's style, in my opinion. And how hard is it to sign a name like *Art*?"

Milo's face was working in an effort at comprehension. "But . . . Vida, why?"

"Oh, Milo!" Vida gave him a little kick with her blue canvas shoes. "Because Cody killed Art, that's why!"

* * *

It took another Scotch and a lot of fast talking by Vida
to convince Milo that Art Fremstad had died at the hands
of Cody Graff.

"Of course you can't prove it," huffed Vida. "And what
good would it do if you could? Cody's dead, too. The important thing is to figure out *why* Cody killed your deputy."

In his usual deliberate, thorough manner, Milo was sift-
ing through the possibilities. "Cody must have asked Art to
meet him near Alpine Falls. Somehow, he must have
caught him by surprise—hit him over the head maybe.
There was a blow to the skull, but at the time we figured
it was from jumping off the cliff and hitting those big
rocks. We checked for tire tracks, but there were too
many—plenty of tourists stop there in the summer." With a
somber expression, Milo made some notes on a little pad.
"Damn it! This is really terrible. Why would Cody kill poor
Art?"

Vida took a big gulp of her ice water. "If we knew why
Cody killed Art, we might know who killed Cody." Her
eyes were hard, like those of a canny gray wolf catching
the scent. "Get up," she snapped at Milo. "We've got
things to do and people to see."

Milo looked up at Vida, abashed by her command. "It's
after eight o'clock, I've had two drinks, I don't want to go
around smelling like a distillery. I'm running for office."

"Oooooh!" Vida waved her floppy hat. "You're running
away from a five-year crime wave, you idiot! All right, all
right." She turned to me. "We'll go, Emma. Get your shoes
on. Really, how you girls can go around barefoot without
ruining your arches . . ."

Having both been chastened by Vida, Milo and I decided
he should take his Scotch-tainted breath to his office and
look up the official reports of Art Fremstad's death while
Vida and I called on Dani Marsh.

But Dani wasn't at the ski lodge. Henry Bardeen claimed
he didn't know where she'd gone, but that Reid Hampton

did. Hampton, however, wasn't around either, having driven over to Lake Wenatchee for dinner at the Cougar Inn.

Vida announced that we were stuck with Patti Marsh. "There's nobody else," she explained as we headed back into town. "Curtis Graff is still up in the San Juans, Doc Dewey is in Seattle, and no Dani." She sighed. "Poor Marje."

The remark caught me off guard. "Marje?"

"Of course. She almost married a murderer. And I thought she had more sense." Vida shook her head sadly. "Well, she's out of it now."

Is she? I wondered. But I wasn't sure what I meant. It wouldn't be tactful to mention to Vida that her niece was embroiled in an ugly murder investigation. But Vida, of all people, knew that. At the arterial on Alpine Way, I shot Vida a sidelong glance. Her expression was inscrutable. That wasn't like Vida.

To my relief, there was no sign of Jack Blackwell's presence at Patti Marsh's house. I steeled myself for another foray into that stuffy, dismal dwelling, which seemed so rife with bitterness.

But Patti wasn't home. Her car was parked in the driveway, but the house was dark. We figured she might be watching TV with the lights off, since the sun had set only a few minutes earlier. I fought down an ominous feeling as Vida and I descended the three steps from the front porch.

"She may be with Dani," Vida said in an uncharacteristically uncertain voice.

"Should we get Milo to check?"

Vida stood in the middle of the overgrown cement path. "Yes. Let's do that." She turned around, once again animated. "We'll help him."

"Vida, he'd need a warrant for us to go snooping through Patti's place."

Vida wasn't concerned with the niceties of a warrant. We drove downtown, where we found Milo in his office, drinking instant coffee and going through a file folder. We expressed our apprehension about Patti. To Vida's chagrin,

Milo said he'd send his deputy, Jack Mullins, to check out the situation.

"She's probably out drinking with Jack Blackwell," said Milo. "Let's piece this together. Vida, you've got a memory like an elephant. Help me out."

The one window in Milo's office was open halfway, its screen dotted with moths seeking the light. The overhead tube fixtures made all three of us look as if we had jaundice. A big fan stood on the floor, whirring around at low speed. Vida and I sat down in front of Milo's desk. He picked up a sheet of paper on which he'd made some notes.

"There's not much from the reports on Art's death that we don't already know," said Milo. "Everything here is consistent with suicide or homicide. Did Donna Fremstad keep Art's note?"

"*Alleged* note," corrected Vida. "I've no idea. She repeated it from memory, I'm sure. But you might ask her."

Milo nodded. "Okay—so I've made a chronology of what happened, going back to Art's disappearance."

"No, no," interrupted Vida. "Go back to little Scarlett's death. Really, Milo, if Art was killed by Cody, then we have to tie the two of them into the event that brought them together in the first place."

Milo regarded Vida with skepticism. "You don't know that it had anything to do with the baby."

Vida, who had taken off her hat, ran her fingers through her short gray hair in an impatient manner. "Of course I don't *know* it. But it's the obvious situation. It's the one event we *do* know that ties Cody, Dani, Curtis, and Art together. Where's your file on that?"

"There isn't one." Milo gave a shrug. "Dani called the sheriff because Doc Dewey told her to. And the fire department. But there was no criminal activity, so Art didn't file a report, except for the log."

Vida cocked her head to one side, her thick curls looking more disheveled than usual. "I did the story. Not that I put anything in it except that little Scarlett died,of SIDS, survivors blah-blah, services set for etcetera, memorials to Alpine Volunteer Firefighters—Oh!" She clapped a hand to her cheek. "How very strange! Why didn't I think of that before?"

"Before what?" asked Milo dryly.

Vida gave Milo a severe look. "The firefighters. Why didn't Dani and Cody ask that the memorials be sent to the SIDS foundation?"

Milo had flipped to an empty page in his legal-sized tablet. "In shock, probably. People don't think straight. Okay, so what happened?"

Vida appeared to be lost in thought. She gave a little jump, then rallied. "Dani had been out somewhere—the grocery store maybe. Cody was with the baby. Dani came home and went to check because it was time for a feeding, or whatever. Little Scarlett was dead. Dani called Doc Dewey who said he'd be over, but to call the sheriff and the fire department. They came first, I have no idea in which order. Then Doc came and Al Driggers was sent for, and they took the baby away to the funeral parlor." She lifted her hands in a helpless gesture. "That was that. The funeral was three days later, the same day Art Fremstad disappeared. Dani was gone by the end of the week. It turned out she'd filed divorce papers at Simon Doukas's law office before leaving town."

I stared at Vida. "That fast?"

"Yes. There was trouble from the start," said Vida. "Nobody expected it to last. The death of little Scarlett merely sealed the fate of the marriage."

Milo was laboriously writing everything down. "A week after the baby died?" He was also having trouble keeping up with Vida's rapid-fire delivery.

"That's right," said Vida. "Dani left the day of Art's funeral. Oh, dear." She took off her glasses and rubbed her eyes. "So many tragedies all at once. Life's like that. But could they really be a coincidence?"

I knew Vida didn't think so, and I was beginning to agree with her. "So when did Curtis and his parents go away?"

"Well, now," mused Vida, putting her glasses back on and blinking several times, "my guess is a week or two later. I know he left Alpine before his parents did, and they moved out over the Labor Day weekend. Curtis said—or so I was told—he wanted to get in on the late summer salmon run in Alaska. We thought he was going for just a few weeks. But he never came back. Until now." She looked first at me, then at Milo. "That's what I mean—everybody suddenly shows up. And Cody Graff dies. Why?"

Chapter Thirteen

IT WAS UNSPEAKABLE, but not unthinkable. Indeed, I couldn't keep it out of my mind. Had Cody Graff killed his tiny daughter? If he had, why didn't Dani turn him in? Perhaps the answer lay not with Dani Marsh, but Patti Marsh: the inexplicable mixture of fear and acceptance at the hands of a violent man. Like mother, like daughter, I thought as I undressed for bed. Dani had taken the easy way out. She'd run away. But she'd left behind a legacy of hate, much of it directed toward herself.

Unless, of course, it was not Cody who had killed that little baby. I pictured Dani Marsh, with her beautiful face and dazzling smile, acting out a scene of violence more tragic than any part she had ever played on the screen. It didn't fit. But Dani was an actress. I felt as if I were immersed in a drama where the script made no effort to search for truth.

I didn't sleep well and I awoke to bright sunlight and more heat. While the rest of the world may welcome cloudless skies and rainless days, unrelieved sunshine depresses the true Pacific Northwest native. Like the Douglas fir and the wild rhododendron, we too need our roots watered. After about two weeks of hot weather, tempers grow testy and dispositions turn glum. My soul was beginning to feel parched, my brain withered. I drank three cups of coffee, choked down a piece of toast, and drove to work.

Carla, being young and therefore resilient, had not lost her edge on enthusiasm. But she did feel that the atmosphere was getting dreary.

384

"All that stuff on Loggerama was okay," she announced, hopping around my office, "but I'll bet anything that what readers remember most about that issue was Cody Graff dying. *Downer*. I've got this terrific idea to get a really romantic piece about Dani Marsh and Matt Tabor. Pictures, quotes, the whole nine yards. It'll be like an antidote to death." She looked suddenly wistful. "Gee, I wish I could call it that."

"Gee, I'm glad you can't." I gave her a baleful look. "But go ahead, see if you can get Dani and Matt to talk about their love life. They probably wouldn't mind some positive publicity."

"I'm sure Mr. Hampton would like it," said Carla, hopping around some more. "I just read in *Premiere* magazine that he's financially troubled." She stopped long enough to arch her thick black eyebrows at me.

"Who isn't?" I responded as the phone rang. Carla danced away, presumably to line up Dani and Matt with a cutout of Cupid. Putting the receiver to my ear, I was half-relieved, half-annoyed to hear Patti Marsh yelling at me.

"Can't you keep your mouth shut? Why don't you just run my frigging bankbook in the paper? Everybody in town knows how much I put in my account yesterday! It's nobody's goddamned business, and I can't even walk into the 7-Eleven without four people asking me how I struck it rich!"

I waited for her to run down. "It wasn't me, Patti. Hey, you've lived here all your life—you know how gossip travels around this town. Start with the teller, the bank manager, the rest of the customers who were there. And don't forget Jack Blackwell. How do you feel today?"

"Fine. And leave Jack out of this." She had stopped shouting, but still sounded angry. "If I had any sense, I'd take that money and blow this town. Seattle, maybe, or some place on the Oregon Coast. I went there once with Ray. He liked the ocean."

It took me a minute to recall Ray Marsh, Patti's ex-husband. "Is that where he ended up?"

"Huh?" She sounded surprised at the question. "No."
Patti laughed, a harsh sound that jangled in my ear. "Ray.
That's funny." She hung up.

In the outer office, Ed Bronsky was trying to find a picture of a chicken in his clip art. "Whole-bodied fryers,
eighty-nine cents a pound," he said into the phone. "What
about lettuce? I got a picture of lettuce."

Vida was late, and when she came in the door five minutes later I realized why: she had her grandson Roger in
tow. I shuddered. The last time she had allowed Roger to
spend the day with her at work he had sat on Ginny's copy
machine and made a Xerox of his rear end. It was a wonder
Ed hadn't tried to include it in his clip art.

"Roger's going to help me today," Vida said with a big
smile for her grandson, who was eyeing me as if I ought to
be wearing a tall pointy hat and straddling a broom. "He's
going to organize my files."

I was speechless. Vida's files consisted of five drawers
stuffed with wedding invitations, birth and graduation announcements, death notices, recipes, gardening tips, household hints, and all manner of articles culled from other
publications. She almost never referred to these wrinkled
bits and pieces, but carried everything she—and her
readers—needed to know inside her head.

"Amy and Ted had to go to Vancouver for the weekend,"
Vida explained, yanking out a drawer bulging with paper.
"They left Roger with me. He has an eleven o'clock appointment with Doc Dewey, so we'll be gone for about an
hour. In fact," she beamed at Roger, who had discovered
my new cordless screwdriver and was trying to take Carla's
desk apart, "I'm treating him to lunch so we won't be back
until after one."

Two hours of peace, I reflected, then asked Roger to give
me the screwdriver. To my amazement, he did. He even
smiled. "Young Doc Dewey?" I asked as an afterthought.

"No," replied Vida, putting the drawer on the floor. "Doc
Dewey Senior. He got back from Seattle late last night."

She gave me a meaningful glance. Obviously, Vida had some questions for Doc.

Roger was ignoring Vida's so-called file drawer. Instead, he had crawled under Ed's desk. Ed was still on the phone, now trying to talk the Grocery Basket out of a double-truck ad. "Why go two pages when you've always done just one? People around here aren't going to change to Safeway overnight. Alpiners are loyal. Hey!" Ed jumped, almost dropping the phone. He ducked under the desk. "Knock it off, Roger! I don't want paste all over the floor. I'll get stuck."

"Right," said Roger, emerging on all fours. "Hey, Grams, can I go down to the 7-Eleven and get a Slurpee? I'm bored."

Roger, with money in hand, went out the door just as Carla came in. There was a blight on her bounce. "They won't do it," she pouted. "They're too busy *filming*." She made it sound illegal.

"Maybe later," I soothed. "They're supposed to wind up shooting in a few days. What about tonight?"

Carla collapsed into her chair, sinking her elbows onto the desk. Something clattered to the floor. "Hey—the knob fell off my drawer! How'd that happen?"

Vida didn't look up from her typewriter, where she was now ripping away at a story. I took the cordless screwdriver over to Carla's desk, searched for the screw, and put it back in. "Never mind," I sighed, keeping one eye on Ed who, judging from the puce color of his face, was giving in to the Grocery Basket's wild whim to go to two pages. "Carla, talk to Reid Hampton. If he needs publicity for this picture, he may be able to get Dani and Matt's cooperation. You could get a wire story out of it. Hampton would have to like that."

Carla, however, was still pouting. "No. Dani was very obstinate. In fact, she was almost rude. Matt Tabor sneered. I think they're both stuck up. And Dani seemed so nice! She's a two-faced Hollywood snot!"

Carla's original idea had struck me as good copy, though I hadn't been foaming at the mouth over it. Now, in the face of adversity, and with a building painted the color of egg yolk, I felt *The Advocate* should be treated with more respect.

"I'll see Reid Hampton," I said. "They're right down the street." Putting on my publisher's face, I headed out into the bright overbearing morning sun. The camera crew had advanced up Front Street to the Venison Inn, where the sidewalk was covered with fake snow. I had a frantic desire to cross the barricade and wallow in it. Instead I paused, watching Matt Tabor, in parka and ski goggles, approach the restaurant's entrance.

"Cut!" yelled Reid Hampton, who was aloft on a crane. "Matt, you're not out for a morning stroll! The woman you love is inside with another man! Purpose, purpose, *purpose*! She's yours! Claim her!"

It took six more takes before Matt appeared to be full of purpose and ready to claim his ladylove. The shot, which couldn't have lasted more than five seconds, was pronounced ready to go into the can. Several onlookers applauded. Feeling hot and sweaty, I waited for Reid Hampton to come down off his perch.

"Emma! I was going to call you," he said, ventilating his wide-open denim shirt with tugs of his hands. "How about dinner before we leave town?"

I hesitated. "Saturday?" I suggested.

"Damn!" He smacked a fist into his palm. "I can't. I'm going into Seattle tomorrow to meet with some film lab people. I was thinking maybe Monday, if everything goes along on schedule."

I was about as anxious for a rematch with Reid Hampton as I was to get a tetanus shot, but I realized he might have some pieces of the murder puzzle tucked away inside his tawny mane. At the very least, there was probably a story in it. I should have taken notes the night we ate at the Café de Flore.

Agreeing to the possibility of Monday, I tried to exhibit enthusiasm. I also tried to put the arm on him for Carla's sake. "She's been very much entranced by Dani and Matt,"

I gushed. "I'm sure she'd do a wonderful article on them. She takes pretty good pictures, too." That much was true, as long as she remembered to put film in the camera. And remove the lens cap.

Hampton, momentarily distracted by a query from his assistant director, ran a hand through his thick tawny hair. "It *sounds* good," he said in his deep voice which was tinged with regret, "but Dani and Matt are very private people. This business with Dani's ex, Dody? Tody? Cody, right?" He gave me a quick, brilliant smile. "It's made her skittish. Understandably. Besides, I think she's committed to *People* or *Good Housekeeping* or *Esquire*. Tell your little reporter we'll send her some stills from this picture. Steamy clinches. Then she can do a memory piece, you know, 'I Watched Dani and Matt Make Love in Alpine.' That approach. Your readers will go nuts."

I had the impression that he thought they already were. Frustrated, I tried to think of an argument that would sway Reid Hampton. Glancing around the street, I realized that Dani wasn't present. "Where's your star?" I asked.

Hampton looked puzzled, then nodded at Matt Tabor, who was complaining volubly to the assistant director about his ski boots. I gathered they hurt. "Matt's right there. Isn't he something? If only he could act!" Hampton caught himself. "I mean, if he'd only had formal training. He could be an American Olivier. You wait; he'll be bigger than Gibson, Costner, Schwarzenegger."

"And Dani?" I spoke quietly, not quite sure what motivated me to ask.

Reid Hampton stared, then broke into a huge smile that didn't quite reach his eyes. "Oh, Dani! She's luminous! I've been in her corner all along. Major talent, major star. This is a breakthrough picture for both of them. If *Blood* doesn't encourage Dani to go on, nothing ever will."

He turned away abruptly, his attention drawn by his cinematographer, who appeared to be verging on an aneurism. I waited for at least two minutes; then, as Matt Tabor started shouting about the inadequacies of wardrobe and the assistant director announced that the stunt man was missing, I gave up and headed back to *The Advocate*.

I was startled to find Dani Marsh waiting for me, her cheeks stained with tears. Closing the door to my office, I sat down and offered Dani coffee. She declined.

"I'm being persecuted," she sniffed, using a Kleenex to wipe her eyes. "My mother warned me not to come back to Alpine. I should have listened."

"Who's doing the persecuting?" I asked, noting that even with smeared makeup and reddened eyes, Dani still looked beautiful.

"The sheriff. He came to see me this morning at the ski lodge, but I'd already gone down to Front Street to start shooting. Reid didn't need me for a while, so I went over to Dodge's office." She gestured in the direction of Milo's headquarters, two blocks away from *The Advocate*. "Why is he raking up the past? What has that got to do with Cody overdosing?" She was perilously close to shedding more tears.

My initial reaction was to utter a disclaimer on her theory about Cody's manner of death, but I didn't see any point in arguing. Yet. "Did Sheriff Dodge ask you about Art Fremstad?"

Dani shifted in the chair, obviously trying to compose herself. "Yes. I don't know anything about Art. I mean, I knew him, I'd seen him around town, but he graduated from high school before I got there. The first time I really talked to him was . . . when . . . when he came to our place after I called for help." The thick lashes dipped over the big brown eyes. Dani didn't seem to be able to say the words out loud: *when my baby died.* I didn't blame her.

"Did the sheriff ask what Art did or said while he was at your house?"

"It was a trailer, out where those new town houses are now. I don't remember a thing," Dani asserted, her voice cracking. "How could I? It was all so horrible!"

Posing tough questions is part of my job. But I either

lack the nerve or am too softhearted to always go for the jugular. My editor on *The Oregonian* used to tell me I was gutless. I preferred to think of myself as kind. But this was one of those nasty situations where I knew I had to seize the moment or very likely never know the truth.

"Dani," I began, keeping my voice firm and determined, "are you absolutely certain your baby died from SIDS?"

Her head jerked up, the honey blond hair floating like a soft cloud around her shoulders. "Of course! What are you saying?" The agony was back in her eyes, her voice, every fiber of her body. "Why? Why? You, the sheriff, everybody ... I can't take this!" To prove her point, she flew out of the chair and ran from my office.

Vida gaped from behind her desk, Ed stumbled on his way back from the coffeemaker, and Roger put the straw from his Slurpee up his nose.

"What was that all about?" demanded Vida.

I started to explain, but Vida suddenly noted the time. "Oh! It's five to! We're going to be late. Come along, Roger."

Roger expelled the straw into the coffee mug Carla had left on her desk. After grandmother and grandson left, I took the mug out to Ginny Burmeister who was in charge of coffee.

"Roger's a caution," she remarked, finishing up the particulars for a new classified ad.

"Actually, he seemed a little subdued today," I said. "He hasn't tried to set any fires or blow anybody up. For Roger, that's good." I paused, glancing at the list of classifieds Ginny had taken for the next issue. It wasn't impressive, but that was typical for early August. Many people were on vacation, it was too soon for end-of-summer garage sales, and the housing market wouldn't move for at least another week. "Say, Ginny, you don't recall talking to Curtis Graff before he left Alpine five years ago, do you?"

Ginny, in her conscientious manner, frowned in recollection. "I did, as a matter of fact. I ran into him one morning on my way to the Burger Barn. I bused tables there that summer. He said he was going to Ketchikan and get rich fishing."

"That's it?"

Ginny was still frowning. "I think so. He seemed kind of nervous. No, not nervous, just ill at ease. I remember, because I'd had that crush on him and he'd been broken up with Laurie Vickers for a while. So I suddenly thought, hey, what if after all this time Curtis has a crush on *me*? But he didn't. I suppose he was just in a hurry, getting everything ready to leave for Alaska. He took off kind of quick. I mean, one day he was here, and the next day, he was gone. Almost."

"He didn't mention anything about Cody and Dani Graff's baby?"

"No." Ginny slowly shook her head. "No, though it had to be on his mind. It was certainly on everybody else's since it had just happened."

"Did he bring up his brother?" I marveled at the lack of curiosity Ginny displayed at my questioning. But Ginny has absolutely no imagination.

"No. All he said was what I told you. At least that's all I remember." She looked faintly apologetic.

I was considering a tactful explanation for my inquisitiveness when Vida stormed into the front office. Her car wouldn't start; could I drive them up to the clinic?

Doc Dewey's office was only four blocks away. Vida was a notorious walker. She saw the puzzlement on my face and made an exasperated gesture. "Roger doesn't feel like hoofing it. Please, Emma, we're going to be late."

I didn't argue, though I knew that Roger had already hiked twice the distance and back to the 7-Eleven to get his Slurpee. But Roger was looking mulish and Vida was growing frantic. We hurried to the Jaguar, which Roger appraised with an expert eye.

"Buff," he said, presumably in approval, and scrambled into the backseat.

Ten minutes later I returned to the office, having agreed to collect Vida and Roger at eleven-thirty. I called Milo to ask about his interview with Dani Marsh, but he was out. For a long time, I sat with my arms folded on my desk, trying to figure out why so many people were still denying that Cody Graff had been murdered. And why Dani Marsh had become so distraught over my suggestion that her baby hadn't died of SIDS.

My reverie was broken by the telephone. It was Milo. Curtis Graff had returned to Alpine. He was staying with Patti Marsh.

"I think he stayed with her before," said Milo. "Hey, Emma, why do I feel as if I'm running around like a hamster in a big maze?"

"Swell," I responded. "You're supposed to know all the tricks of the homicide trade. I already feel as if I've got the second female lead in a B movie. Milo, do you or do you not think Cody Graff may have killed little Scarlett?"

I heard Milo suck in his breath before he answered. "Why don't you ask his brother? Curtis is just pulling up in front of your cute yellow building. I saw him drive by in Patti's car."

But Curtis wasn't calling on me. When I got outside, he was at the barricade, talking to Matt Tabor. Neither man looked very happy, and before I could make up my mind about approaching them, they disappeared inside the Venison Inn.

Just as well, I thought: it was smack on eleven-thirty. I drove up to the clinic and parked across the street by the gift shop. Marje Blatt was behind the desk, her face thinner and her uniform less crisp.

"Doc's running late," she said without preamble. "Aunt Vida and Roger will be out in a few minutes."

I sat down in one of the venerable chairs that had served two generations of Dewey patients. The only other person in the waiting room was an elderly man with a cane who was reading a well-thumbed copy of *Business Week*.

"How are you doing, Marje?" I asked infusing my voice with sympathy.

Marje looked up from her appointment book. "Okay. How are you?"

Somehow, it didn't seem an appropriate rejoinder. "Have you talked to Cody's parents?" I wasn't letting Marje off the hook, though I knew she must have already been thoroughly grilled by Vida.

"Only on Sunday." She set the appointment book aside and scooted her chair over to a tall metal filing cabinet. "Curtis says they're doing okay. Considering."

The elderly man wore a hearing aid. I wondered if it was turned off; he didn't seem to be paying any attention to us. I got up and walked over to the reception desk, lowering my voice.

"Marje, did you have any premonition about Cody?"

She glanced up from the open file drawer. It was as neat as her aunt's was untidy. "No. Why should I?" Marje flipped through the folders, pulling a chart. "Look," she said, meeting my gaze head-on, "you and Aunt Vida get a kick out of playing detective. Cody had his faults, like everybody else. Maybe he had more than I knew about—we never lived together. He was moody, he could fly off the handle. I don't like ups and downs. So I thought some medication might make him more steady. That's what you really want in a husband, isn't it?"

How would I know? I thought. "Wasn't that a little risky?"

Marje shrugged. "I know what both Deweys prescribe for people with Cody's problems. I only gave Cody a couple of sample packets."

"But they were pills, not syrup," I pointed out.

A flicker of emotion passed over Marje's face, then she gave another shrug. "I suppose he got the syrup somewhere else. It's terrible how easy it is for people to get hold of drugs these days. Young Doc Dewey is going to start a drug education class at the high school this fall. Really, it amazes me how even a small town like Alpine can have so many people who are hooked on something. I wish big cities like Seattle would keep their vices to themselves." She had grown quite heated, causing the elderly man to look up from his magazine. He nodded once, then resumed reading.

I was about to say that I knew Alpine had its share of drug-related problems, though I wasn't aware of any epidemic. But the words never came out. Vida and Roger emerged from the examining room area with Doc Dewey bringing up the rear.

"You're not keeping pace, Vida," warned Doc Dewey. "You know darned well I'm a cautious man. Too cautious, my son would say, and he's the one who should be seeing Roger today. But we're doing right by your grandson, believe me."

"It's ridiculous," Vida declared, her hand on Roger's shoulder. "I expected better of you than of Gerry—your son never did have as much sense as he should have. But you're as pigheaded as he is. I'm telling you once and for all, I won't take this prescription into the pharmacy." She waved a white slip of paper in Doc Dewey's face.

"Amy and Ted will when they get back." Doc spoke matter-of-factly, though his expression indicated he wished Vida would shut up and go away. Indeed, he brightened a bit when he recognized me. "Hello there, girlie. How's your little reporter doing with her allergy reaction?"

"Carla's fine," I assured him. Doc was looking less haggard than when I'd seen him at the Icicle Creek Tavern almost a week earlier. But the fragile air remained. Perhaps he'd earned it. The man must be over seventy, and he'd devoted a half-century to healing Alpine's sick. "How was your trip?"

"Hot," replied Doc, turning to greet the elderly man who was struggling to his feet with the aid of the cane. "The air-conditioning doesn't work most of the time. Well, young man," he said to his next patient, "how's that knee?"

Vida and I bade Marje farewell, then let Roger lead the way outside. "Doc's daffy," said Vida. "It's bad enough that his son's pouring medicine down Roger's throat, but after only a week, they're changing the prescription. If you ask me, the Deweys are experimenting on poor Roger. You'd think the child was a gerbil."

Since Roger was now climbing onto the roof of my Jaguar, I wasn't inclined to argue. "What's he taking?" I asked, trying to show an interest in Roger's problems, which seemed to stem from a complete lack of discipline rather than any chemical cause. But I didn't dare say so. Besides, I had to assume that Doc knew what he was doing. Or, it dawned on me, he'd gotten absolutely nowhere with a diagnosis similar to mine.

Vida glanced at the slip of paper while I gave Roger a frozen smile which I hoped would coax him off the car roof. "Thorazine. Roger can't drink juice with it. Doesn't that beat all?" She crushed the prescription and threw it into her purse. "Three freshly squeezed oranges a day is what he gets for breakfast when he stays with me. If Amy and Ted want to be such silly fools, that's up to them."

Roger finally dismounted, badgering his grandmother about what he wanted for lunch, which sounded like great quantities of deep-fried grease. Inside the car, I asked Vida if she knew why Doc had gone to Seattle.

"I never got a chance to ask," she said, still grumpy. "I was too busy trying to talk sense into the old fool. But he told Marje it was for a tune-up. Every year or so I guess he checks himself into the Mason Clinic or one of those places and gets an overhaul. If you ask me, he should have his brain replaced. Maybe I should take Roger into Seattle myself and see what they think. I'll bet they'd find out he's just too bright for his age."

I glanced in the rearview mirror at Roger. His eyes were rolled back in his head and he was drooling. "Hey, Grams," he said in a gurgling voice, "I'm having a fit. Double fries'll cure me."

Vida smiled fondly at Roger, then turned to me. "You see, Emma, the boy knows what he needs. Maybe he'll grow up to be a doctor."

Maybe, I thought to myself, he'll grow up. *Maybe.*

* * *

I'd assigned myself the task of taking a picture of the new baseball diamond, which was being put in at the high school field now that Loggerama was over. Coming down Seventh Street, between Spruce and Tyee, I saw Patti Marsh's house. The front door was open and the drapes were pulled back. A white Lexus stood in the driveway, looking as out of place as a tiara on a bag lady.

I stopped and got out. Sure enough, Dani Marsh came to the door. I expected her to be annoyed by my unannounced arrival, but instead, she looked embarrassed.

"Ms. Lord! Are you here to see my mother? She's at work."

In the golden glow of afternoon, Dani looked very different than she had in the harsh morning sun. Her eyes were no longer red; her hair was pulled back and tucked into a knot at the nape of her neck; and she wore a mint green leotard that suggested she'd been working out.

"You're not shooting?" I inquired.

"I finished for the day about an hour ago. Do you want to come in?"

I did, if only to get out of the sun that was beating down on the little porch. Entering the house, I noticed that someone had finally removed the wilted bouquet from the hall. My cyclamen reposed there and looked as if it had been recently watered. Indeed, the whole house looked different, more welcoming. Not only were the drapes open, but so were two of the windows, bringing in badly needed fresh air. Some of the clutter had been cleared away, and the ashtray on the coffee table was empty. Was this Dani's handiwork, or had Patti used her day off to clean house? It didn't seem right to ask.

"I'm sorry I was so upset this morning," Dani said, giving me a penitent smile. "Sometimes I can't seem to separate my emotions off and on the set. I realize that Sheriff Dodge was only trying to do his job. But it seems to me that he's going off on a tangent. Poor Cody simply made a terrible mistake. It happens all the time, mixing drugs and alcohol."

"You really think that's what happened?"

"Yes, I do." Her voice was firm, but she avoided my eyes. "Two more days, then I'm done with this stupid picture," Dani said, going over to the makeshift bar. "Would you like something to drink?"

I requested pop, which she produced from the refrigerator along with a seltzer for herself. "You don't like the movie?" I asked, sitting on the sofa, which was marred only by a cookbook and a *TV Guide*. It seemed as useless to pursue the manner of Cody's death with Dani Marsh as it had been with Marje Blatt.

"It's trash," she said simply. "They should have brought in a script doctor, but Reid's too cheap. Oh, it'll have big grosses the first week or so, but word of mouth will kill it. Still, Reid should make money with all the ancillary rights. It's hard not to these days, as long as your budget isn't out of control."

I marveled at her candor. Didn't she realize she was talking to a newspaper person? "I thought stars were supposed to ballyhoo all their movies, no matter how lousy."

Dani sat down, not in the cut-velvet chair her mother favored, but in a blue-and-green-striped lounger that looked as if a cat had used it for a scratching post. "We are. *They* are," she amended. "I'm thinking of changing careers. I'd rather dance."

I was startled. "Can't you do both? I mean, act and dance? Like musicals?"

"Musicals aren't really in," said Dani, sipping at her seltzer. "Reid told me that. He thinks I'm crazy. To quit acting, I mean." The brown eyes caught and held mine, as if she expected me to side with her director.

I was, in fact, tempted to agree with Hampton. Dani Marsh was just beginning to emerge as a bona fide star. At twenty-four, she seemed too old to start a dance career. But it was none of my business. "What does Matt think?"

Dani's wide-eyed gaze glistened with amusement. "Matt? I've no idea. I haven't asked him."

I may never have been a wife, but I've certainly been a

mother. My maternal instincts took over, suddenly lending me wisdom for the daughter I'd never had. "I'm all for independence, Dani, but husbands and wives—lovers, engaged couples, what have you—should talk things over. You don't want Matt to feel left out. He thinks he's marrying a movie actress. Will it change his feelings if he discovers his wife is a would-be dancer?"

Dani laughed. The wondrous sound filled the room, making it suddenly a happy place. "Oh, Emma," she said, tucking in a strand of hair that had come loose from the knot at her neck, "*Blood Along the River* is almost in the can. I want to stop the charade, at least when I'm off-camera. Matt and I aren't going to get married."

Recalling the heated argument Vida and I had overheard at the ski lodge, I wasn't completely surprised. "I've wondered," I said vaguely. "Somehow, you never seemed . . . devoted." It was an old-fashioned word, worthy of Vida, but I suddenly felt like a fogey. "I figured there might be someone else."

Dani had picked up a videotape that pictured an athletic young woman in a dance rehearsal costume doing something strenuous in a room with big skylights. Dani studied the cassette, then turned her gaze back to me. "There is someone else. There always was." She put the videotape down on top of the TV and laughed again. This time the musical sound was a trifle discordant. "Matt's in love, but not with me. I'd tell you who, but you'd print it in your paper. That wouldn't be right, I guess."

I was literally on the edge of my seat. "You could always go off the record."

Dani's gaze wandered around the room, to the mediocre watercolor of Mount Baldy, the half-naked gods and goddesses, the Harlequin masks, the carved trout, and the one good piece I hadn't noticed before: a small silver dancing girl, sweetly graceful, realistically posed.

Dani saw that I had followed her eyes. "I got that for my mother when I was in Rome last year on location. Isn't it pretty? She loves it."

It occurred to me that perhaps I had missed the little fig-
urine because it hadn't been there earlier. If Dani wasn't
going to talk about Matt Tabor's defection, perhaps she'd
unload about her mother.

"Dani, what's with you and Patti? She's behaved as if
you were the worst daughter who ever lived, yet here you
are, in her house, talking about sending her gifts. What's
going on? It's not fair to you for everybody in Alpine to
think she hates your guts."

To my surprise, Dani opened a drawer in the end table
next to her chair and pulled out a pack of cigarettes. "Do
you mind?" she inquired. "I don't do this often."

"I don't do it at all. Any more." I made a face. "I wish
I did sometimes. Go ahead."

Dani lighted up, her awkwardness with the cigarette indicating that she was telling the truth about her amateur
smoker's status. "For a long time, Mom blamed me for
what happened to Scarlett. She was convinced I'd been a
rotten mother. It preyed on her mind, maybe because she'd
lost her grandchild—" Dani paused and bit her lip, the
words not coming so easily now "—and, in a way, her
daughter at the same time. I was no comfort to her, I
couldn't be, I needed too much comfort myself. So she cast
me as the villainess, and it was only after I came home to
Alpine and we talked and talked that she realized I wasn't
at fault. Now things are much better." Dani smiled, a bit
tremulously. "We're almost back to where we were six
years ago, before I married Cody."

"She wasn't in favor of your marriage?"

"Oh, God, no!" Dani exhaled a thick cloud of smoke.
"She tried to talk me out of it, said he was as bad as my
father. Maybe worse. But I was young and headstrong and
wouldn't listen. Why," she asked plaintively, "do we know
so much more at eighteen than we do at twenty-four?"

I had to smile. "It goes with being a teenager. My son's
out of that stage now, and one of these days, I'm going to
become really smart. I hope."

Dani smiled, too. "I'll bet I'd like your son. I wish he

were a little older. Maybe I could fall in love with him. I haven't done that yet." She made it sound like an item she was anxious to check off on her list of life.

"You didn't love Cody?"

Her smile was wry, seen through the fog of her cigarette. "No, it was a typical adolescent crush. All heat and hormones. For both of us."

I gripped my Coke and slipped farther back onto the sofa. "You realize that the sheriff thinks you're the last person to see Cody alive?" I didn't know if Milo really believed that, but it made sense to me. Dani's jaw dropped and she began to shake her head in denial, but I gave her no opportunity to contradict: "You were seen, out by the turnoff to the Burl Creek Road. That's where you lost your eyeliner. What on earth were you and Cody doing out there that night?"

Dani scanned the ceiling: left, right, right, left. I had the impression she was looking for answers, the way she'd study a frame of film for dramatic composition. "I had to see him, just once. Not because I cared about him—but to tie up some loose ends."

"Did you?"

"No. Not really. He was too drunk." She fiddled with the cigarette, moving it from one hand to the other.

I waited for her to say more, and when she didn't, I posed another question. "Why did you drive out to the edge of town?" I knew I was pushing my luck with my prying, but Dani seemed more uneasy than annoyed.

"I didn't want to go up to his apartment," she replied, her voice steady. "It might have given him the wrong idea, especially since he'd been drinking. I picked him up in Matt's Zimmer and I drove without thinking." She waved away the cloud of smoke, the better to meet my gaze. "We used to live out that way, past the reservoir and the fish hatchery. I guess it was an automatic reflex on my part."

"Was he alive when you left him?"

"Yes." Her unblinking stare challenged me to disbelieve her.

"Then why didn't you drive him back to town?"

Dani touched the soft coil of hair at her neck. "He wanted to get out. He was being obnoxious. I figured the fresh air would do him good. And I was by the Burl Creek Road, so I could zip straight up to the ski lodge."

I studied Dani's face carefully. She seemed to be telling the truth, but her acting skills could probably convince me if she said there was a blizzard going on outside. It was hard for me to conceive of leaving an extremely drunk man out on a lonely road at midnight. But the man was Cody Graff, and if what I believed about him was true, he would not have invited common courtesy.

I was casting about for other, more pointed questions concerning Cody's death when I heard a car pull up outside. Dani looked down at her watch which was lying on the coffee table. "It's after three. Mom said she'd be home early. She was beat."

In more ways than one, I thought, watching Dani stub out her cigarette. I wondered what the daughter felt about the mother's passive resistance to Jack Blackwell's fists. But there was no chance to ask. Patti Marsh came into the house with a sack of groceries. From Safeway. I had a sudden urge to call Ed Bronsky.

"Hi, Dani," she said, then saw me sitting on the sofa. "What's this, more news you can get wrong in your paper? Or are you going through my checkbook?"

I started to make a rejoinder, but Dani merely smiled. "Don't have a tizzy, Mom. Emma and I were just philosophizing. Life, love, career choices. What did you get for dinner?"

Patti appeared appeased. "Beef ribs. Macaroni salad. Jojo potatoes. Safeway's got a great deli. I don't have to cook, all I have to do is pay a lot of money. But I've got that now, haven't I, chicken?" Despite the bruises, Patti looked quite smug.

"Right, Mom." Dani exchanged a conspiratorial glance with her mother. "Let's go to Paris. I'll show you how people really eat."

Suddenly, I felt like the original third wheel. All this mother-daughter camaraderie was making me oddly uncomfortable. Was it real? Maybe. Yet thus far so little about the Marshes and the Graffs and the rest of them seemed genuine. I stood up, making ready to leave.

"Hey," exclaimed Patti, doing a typical about-face, "don't run off. Have a drink. What have you got there?"

"Coke," I said. "But I have to drop a roll of film off at the photographer's—"

"Buddy Bayard's open until six," cut in Patti. "Have a real drink. Gin? Scotch? Bourbon? Vodka? Rum?"

I felt contrary enough to ask for tequila, but settled for bourbon. The truth was, I didn't like drinking strong alcohol during the day in summertime. But I decided to humor Patti Marsh. Her mood change made me think I might learn something. She had set the groceries on the counter in the kitchen and was now at the makeshift bar, mixing tonic with vodka and pouring me a bourbon over ice.

"Here, kiddo," she said, handing me my drink. "Has mild-mannered Milo given up yet?"

I was taken aback. "What?"

"The sheriff." Patti sat down in the cut-velvet chair and lighted a cigarette. "Hey, Dani—you cleaned this place! It looks like a frigging motel. You deserve a husband when you get married."

Dani smiled. "I deserve a man I can love. You should be so lucky, Mom."

"So should we all," I murmured, deciding that the bourbon didn't taste so unpalatable with the windows open and the living room feeling not quite like a mausoleum.

After a deep swig, Patti Marsh set her drink down on the coffee table. "Men. I could write a book on that subject." She gazed at me through a haze of smoke. "Can you use *asshole* in a title?"

I uttered a wry laugh. "Probably not."

Patti nodded. "I didn't think so. But you could say it in the book. On the pages inside, I mean." She took another gulp of vodka and settled back into the cut-velvet chair, the smoke from her cigarette swirling around her like a snake. "Twenty-four years. I waited twenty-four years." She glanced at Dani who looked faintly alarmed. "Oh, screw it, honey! What do we care? I already told Jack."

Dani gave a little jump, then reached for the package of cigarettes in the drawer. "You did?" She sounded incredulous.

"You bet. I didn't mind having a laugh at his expense, but I don't want a broken jaw." Gingerly, she touched her cheek. "He was still pissed this morning, so I told him. God, I thought he'd have a heart attack!" She drank some more and laughed uproariously.

Dani cradled her almost-empty seltzer bottle in her slim hands. "Oh, Mom . . ." She sounded disapproving.

"Oh, hell!" Patti drank, smoked, waved her hand. "The bastard owed me! And you! Never mind!" She shot a finger in her daughter's direction. "Sure, sure, he's helped you with your career and all that crap. But that's now, not then, when we really needed it. Stop looking so prissy, kiddo." Patti turned to me; I knew I wore an utterly mystified expression. Who was she talking about? Blackwell? Or someone else? "Reid Hampton didn't pay me fifty grand because he cut down a bunch of frigging trees," Patti declared. "He owed me that money from way back. Reid Hampton's real name is Ray Marsh. The son of a bitch is Dani's father."

Chapter Fourteen

VIDA WAS INCREDULOUS. She slammed the carriage of her typewriter so hard that I thought I'd have to do some more repair work.

"Reid Hampton is Ray Marsh? Oooooh ... that's ... *silly!*"

"It's true." I eased into Ed's chair. He and Carla had both left for the day, since it was now nearing five o'clock. Roger was out in the front office, driving Ginny Burmeister crazy. Or so I guessed. "You said yourself Ray went to California. He did, he'd always been fascinated by movies and he got a job as a gofer at Paramount. He changed his name—Reid, as in r-e-e-d, apparently being derived from Marsh and the Hampton coming from the side of the family that was related to the two Wades, American Revolution and Civil War generals."

"Oh, nonsense! Ray's family didn't have any distinguished ancestors hanging on their family tree. They were the sort who'd have been related to camp followers." Vida uttered a deep, impatient sigh. "Honestly, Emma, I can't believe I wouldn't have recognized him. I think Patti is pulling your leg."

"Not for fifty grand, she isn't," I countered. "Reid—Ray—gave her that check to make up for all the years he missed paying child support. Listen, Vida, you haven't seen Ray Marsh in almost twenty-five years. He's gotten older, grown a beard, dyed his hair. He worked his way up in the business, through the ranks. Then he launched his own production company about eight years ago. When he discov-

ered that Dani had come to Hollywood, he must have felt
a pang of conscience. He helped launch her career. He's
been a patron and a father to Dani, at least in the last few
years."

"Did she know who he was all along?" Vida was still
looking skeptical.

"No. It was Patti who figured it out. She *did* recognize
Reid. I remember how she looked at his photograph on my
desk the day she came in to complain about the article on
Dani. I suppose it was the eyes, because he wasn't wearing
sunglasses in that picture. Then she went after him, threatening to reveal all if he didn't pony up."

Vida's forehead creased in a frown as she considered my
explanation. "I'm slipping," she murmured. She gave me a
look that bordered on the pathetic. "I'm turning into an old
fool, just like everybody else. Do you want to put me out
to pasture?"

"Vida!" I laughed, though more in exasperation than
amusement. "Have you *seen* Reid Hampton up close since
he came to Alpine?"

Vida rested her chin on her fist and thought for a moment. "No. But I did glance at those pictures."

"Big deal." I waved a hand in dismissal of Vida's nonexistent senility. "The problem is, I don't know what to do
about using the information as a story. Patti blabbed everything to Jack Blackwell so he'd stop slapping her around
and realize that she wasn't taking a payoff for his blasted
trees. Jack won't keep quiet. And I'll bet Patti won't stop
with Jack."

"So Ray—Reid—paid in vain. At least as far as Patti's
silence is concerned. That's very ironic." Perplexity crossed
Vida's face, but she appeared to be growing resigned to
Reid Hampton's true identity. "How did Dani react to all
this?"

"I guess she was shocked when Patti told her a few days
ago. But she seems to be comfortable with it now. After all,
she's known Reid for quite a while, and he's always been
in her corner. Just like a father. In fact, she said she could

never understand why he didn't make the obligatory pass at
her.'"

As usual, Vida went straight to the heart of the matter:
"That's nice, family reunion, dues paid, all that. But what
has it got to do with Cody's murder?"

I gave a little shake of my head. "I don't know. Reid's
never been at the top of my list as a suspect. The only motive I could think of was something to do with the trees, but
it would have made more sense if he'd killed Jack, instead
of one of Blackwell's underlings. Now I'm wondering if he
might have killed Cody because he mistreated Dani—or the
baby. You know, sort of expiating his own sins for walking
out on Patti and Dani."

Vida didn't look impressed by my theory. "I don't hold
with all this psychological claptrap. It's too convoluted.
Whatever happened to financial gain, jealousy, revenge, and
all those horrible secrets that only one person knows, at
least in books?"

"Half of Alpine probably knows Reid's secret by now,"
I said dryly. "Maybe I can do a feature, 'From Alpine to
L.A.—Father and Daughter Reunited on Sunset Boule-
vard.' "

"Oh, good grief, you sound like Carla!" Vida rolled her
eyes. She put the plastic cover on her typewriter, tugging it
over the machine like a dressmaker trying to fit a size eight
sheath on a size fourteen figure. "Let's talk motive."

I didn't answer right away. My personal apprehensions
about the case still appalled me. "I don't think we can talk
motive until we deal with what happened to little Scarlett."

"You mean whether or not Cody killed her." Vida spoke
briskly. "He did, of course. That's why Art Fremstad had to
die. Brother or not, Curtis Graff would have been next, if
he hadn't left town. As for Doc Dewey . . ." She slowly
shook her head. "Maybe some people are still sacred. Or
maybe Cody lost his nerve."

I dragged Ed's chair closer to Vida's desk. "Are you saying that Art, Curtis and Doc all knew that Cody murdered
his baby? Oh, Vida!"

"Knew, or suspected. Dani, too—perhaps." Vida removed her glasses, but instead of the usual vigorous rubbing of her eyes, she gently massaged the lids. "Emma, some things are so awful. You don't want to believe them, your instinct is to turn away and pretend they couldn't possibly have happened. I wonder if that isn't what went on with Dani and some of the others as well. We humans are such a terrible mix of good and evil. Yet we must pretend that evil doesn't exist—or we'd go quite crazy."

For some moments, I gazed at Vida, moved by her little soliloquy. "If," I said at last, in a quiet voice, "we accept the fact that Cody caused that baby's death, we don't need any other motive. There's Dani, Patti, Curtis, even Reid. Or Jack Blackwell, acting on Patti's behalf."

"What about Matt Tabor? He's engaged to Dani."

I explained that the engagement was off, if indeed it had ever really been on. Vida took the news in stride. "A publicity romance. Oh, well." She gave a start. "So who was Matt quarreling with up at the ski lodge?"

I admitted I didn't know. We were mulling over the possibilities when Roger charged into the news office, carrying a fake snake.

"Ginny went home," Roger announced. "She ran. I guess she doesn't like snakes." He put the wiggly creature next to me on Ed's desk. I gave Roger a half-smile. The snake moved. I let out a shriek and leaped from the chair.

"Damn it, Roger, that's real! Get that sucker out of here!" I was flat against the wall, while Vida gaped at the snake.

Roger's round face was wreathed in a cherubic smile. "It's just a little ol' garter snake, Mrs. Lord. They don't bite. Here, pick it up." He made as if to shove the snake in my direction.

"Out! Now!"

Roger took my measure, then darted a look at his grandmother, who was trying very hard not to laugh. "Do as Ms. Lord says, Roger. It's *her* office." Vida didn't sound too pleased with the concession.

With a heave of great reluctance, Roger grabbed the snake and exited. I hoped he would take the damned thing down the street, across Railroad Avenue, and leave it by the river. Which, I presumed, was where he'd found it in the first place. But knowing Roger, I suspected he would put the garter snake in one of the concrete planters that lined Front Street. Or, I thought with alarm, *in my car.*

I leaped across the office. "Vida, I've got to run. I'll call you tonight." Gathering up my belongings, I raced outside, but Roger was nowhere to be seen. The Jaguar appeared safe, devoid of snakes. I drove to Cal Vickers's Texaco station to get gas. Cal, who used to do business across from the General Motors dealership down the street, had moved last year to Alpine Way, directly in front of the shopping mall. He looked busy, with activity inside the garage; three cars, an RV, and a van lined up at the pumps; and a pickup parked in front of the snack shop that Cal had added at his new location. The pickup didn't strike any chords, but the young man who was standing by it did: Curtis Graff was waiting for Cal Vickers to finish with a customer.

Pulling the Jag up near the car wash, I got out and strolled over to Curtis. He was wearing stone-washed jeans and a T-shirt with the sleeves cut out. When I called a greeting, he looked puzzled, then shaded his eyes against the western sun, and gave me a half-smile.

"Mrs. Lord," he said, "I didn't recognize you at first. I forgot to come in and get those newspapers. Are you closed?"

"Yes, but I can send them to you. Or your parents." I nodded at the pickup. "Is that your brother's?" It seemed a logical guess.

"Right." He patted a rusty red fender. "I'm selling it. But I thought Cal ought to give it a once-over. It's pretty beat-up, but I might as well get something out of it and use the money to pay off Cody's bills."

I nodded. "I suppose he had his share of debts like the rest of us."

"The usual." Curtis didn't seem too interested in his brother's financial obligations.

"I'm glad he and Marje didn't get themselves in too deep," I remarked, angling for an opening. "She strikes me as a sensible soul." The statement implied her fiancé was not.

"Marje is a good kid," said Curtis, pulling a pack of gum out of his back pocket and unwrapping a stick. As an afterthought, he offered me a piece.

"No, thanks," I said, recalling the last time I'd tried a wad of bubble gum and had ended up at Dr. Starr's with a shiny gold crown, a large dent in my savings account, and the happiest dentist in Skykomish County. "Marje seems to be coping," I noted, still at a loss in my effort to get Curtis to open up.

"She's tough." Curtis chewed with vigor.

"I saw Dani and her mother today." Cal was coming our way, his wide, florid face beaming at us under his billed cap. "I suppose you can't blame her for dumping Cody off by the side of the road the night he died."

Curtis, who had been turning toward Cal, rocked slightly on his heels. "She told you that?"

I acted nonchalant. "Sure. Cal and Charlene saw them. Right, Cal?"

"What's that?" Cal took off his cap, used his forearm to wipe the perspiration from his brow, and grimaced into the sun.

"You and Char—you saw Dani Marsh and Cody Graff in that Zimmer last Saturday night." I ignored Curtis's scowl, which was uncannily reminiscent of that of his dead brother.

"We saw somebody," replied Cal, smoothing back the fringe of black hair that curled around his ears.

Curtis shot me a belligerent look. "What did Dani say?"

I gave a little shrug, shifting around to avoid the sun in its downward path over the mall. "She said he was too drunk to talk to. So she let him out of the car. I suppose she thought the fresh night air might revive him. It didn't." My own gaze was as harsh as his.

Under the sawed-off T-shirt, Curtis's shoulders relaxed. "He was smashed, all right. On drugs, too. It doesn't surprise me."

I was about to protest, but Cal spared me the effort. "Aw, Curt, Cody had his problems, but he wasn't mixed up with drugs. He'd come in here, once, twice a week, and josh around with me and the guys. I never saw him look squirrely. And I check eyes, just in case somebody is about to gas up and go off goofy. I've called Dodge half a dozen times to let him know I thought we had a druggie on the road."

Curtis made a disaparaging gesture with his hand. "You're no expert, Cal. Believe me, I knew my brother. I'm surprised nobody found out he was taking stuff before this."

"But he wasn't," I protested. "His death was caused by an antidepressant, not some illegal substance."

"Whatever," said Curtis, turning to Cal. "Hey, can you look over this pickup? I think the fuel pump . . ."

Feeling snubbed, I started to walk away. I also felt frustrated. What had happened to my journalist's right to ask and the public's need to know? Or was I treading on ground so private that my lingering status as an outsider created a conspiracy of silence? Feeling the perspiration drip down my neck, I considered going through the car wash. Without the car. But Milo Dodge was pulling up in his Cherokee Chief. I ran over to meet him.

"Milo," I hissed, leaning into his open window, "get off your duff and go over and ask Curtis if he thinks Cody killed his little daughter."

From behind his sunglasses, Milo gaped at me. "Emma, are you nuts? I can't ask Curtis something like that!"

"If you don't, I will." I gave his regulation shirt collar a tug. "The trouble is, he won't tell me. But he might tell you. Come on, Milo, you're the sheriff. Do you want to get beat by Averill Fairbanks and his UFOs?"

Milo's long face worked in consternation. At last he uttered a sigh, presumably of surrender. "I've got to pick Honoria up by six-thirty ... Oh, hell, I'll take Curtis out for a quick beer. This is no place to interrogate anybody." Milo got out of his Cherokee Chief, long legs unwinding onto the gas-stained tarmac.

Satisfied, I got back into the Jag and wheeled it in behind the RV, which was about to leave. Curtis, Cal, and the sheriff now formed a tight little trio, hovering around the open hood of the pickup. My victory over Milo had proved almost too easy.

Five minutes later, I was on my way to the Grocery Basket, proving my loyalty to a home-grown merchant. I lingered in the frozen food section, feeling blissfully cool, and wondering if the forecast for ninety the next day was accurate. I hoped not.

I was tossing frozen chicken pies in my cart when I saw Donna Fremstad Wickstrom approaching. Her manner was frazzled, her attention riveted on the orange juice section. I reversed directions and came up alongside of Donna. To my surprise, she looked as if she'd been crying. A rumpled Kleenex was stuffed in the top of her polka dotted sundress.

"Heat got you down?" I asked guilelessly.

Donna didn't look fooled by my feigned innocence. "It's all this Cody Graff business that's got me down," she snapped. "First you and Vida, now the sheriff. I'm so upset I don't know what to do."

Feeling repentant, I put a hand on her arm. "I'm sorry, Donna, I know this is rough on you. What did Milo want?" My triumph with the sheriff now seemed easier to understand; maybe he wasn't as slow of wit as I sometimes thought him.

Donna lowered her head, chin almost resting on her breastbone. "It should make it easier ... but it doesn't, not in a way," she murmured. Slowly, she raised her face to meet my gaze. "Sheriff Dodge thinks Art may have been murdered, maybe by Cody Graff. I'd rather believe that than think Art killed himself. But it makes me so *angry* . . ." She literally gnashed her teeth. "I wish Cody was still alive. I swear I'd kill him!"

I blinked. Had she? Donna and Steve Wickstrom had been at the Icicle Creek Tavern Saturday night. Had Donna, who must have known her late husband better than anyone, suspected that the suicide note was written by somebody else? I shivered, and not from the blast of cold air that poured out of the freezer as an elderly woman reached for a bag of frozen peas.

"Why do you think Cody killed Art?" I asked, keeping my voice low.

Donna rolled her cart back and forth, the wheels grating on the floor. "I don't know!" she whispered, the tears back in her eyes. "Art never did anything to Cody. That's what makes it so awful! It's like one of those gang stories you read in the Seattle papers, where somebody shoots somebody just to see what it's like. It doesn't make sense!"

It did, though, to me. Fleetingly, I wondered if I should say as much to Donna. Perhaps it would help. The irrational taking of a life is harder to bear than death with a reason. At least that's how my mind works.

"Donna," I said in a level voice, "I think Cody murdered his own baby. I also think Art knew that but didn't quite know what to do about it. Or if he did, he never had a chance. Cody killed him first."

As the words came out, Donna's face stiffened and her eyes grew huge. The knuckles clutching the grocery cart turned white. But the tears didn't fall. "Shit," breathed Donna. The cart rocked back and forth, but more gently now, as if she were rocking a baby. Hers, maybe. Or even little Scarlett, forever small, always ready to be soothed.

I waited. If Art had ever hinted his knowledge, or even suspicion, to his wife, perhaps she would remember it now. But Donna kept shaking her head and rocking the cart. "Shit," she said again, her voice leaden.

"He never said anything?" I asked quietly.

"No." She tucked the Kleenex farther down between her small breasts. "But he was worried. Or troubled." Donna looked straight at me. "That's why I could accept that note, even though it made me feel like such a failure, a wife who wasn't there for her husband. He couldn't talk to me, he couldn't tell me how his job bothered him, he couldn't share his troubles, so he . . ." She lifted a hand, then let it flutter to her side, like a crippled bird.

"But that wasn't it," I said firmly.

Donna's chin shot up. "No. It wasn't. He was probably just mulling over what he should do. Art was like that, he never did anything on impulse. If only Sheriff Dodge had been in town, if only Art had talked to me, if only . . ." She sniffed hard, swallowing her tears.

"If only Cody Graff hadn't been a killer," I murmured.

Donna squared her slim shoulders. "But he was. And by God, I'd like to shake the hand of whoever killed him." With a tremulous, brave smile, she gave the cart an aggressive push and headed off down the aisle—to frozen vegetables, past whole grain waffles, and beyond ice cream, on special at $2.89 a half gallon.

I stood for a few moments, resting my fingers on the boneless ham I'd picked up in the meat department. Donna Fremstad Wickstrom was a courageous woman. Or a very clever one. Either way, it struck me how life and death could mingle with broccoli spears and party pizzas. We humans did not live by bread alone, but sometimes we died in the most unexpected ways. At the hands of a stranger. In the arms of a lover. Under the evil eye of a parent.

For the first time in days, I was too cold. I moved on, into the fresh, fragrant realm of produce.

I was still too cold.

Saturday brought the ninety-degree temperatures I'd dreaded. It also brought a phone call from my brother.

"Quit bitching," said Ben in his crackling voice. "It's almost a hundred and twenty in Tuba City. I'm thinking of saying mass tomorrow in the nude."

I laughed, then insisted he hang up. I wanted to pour out my troubles, but not on his long distance bill. He refused, saying that he'd been in Vegas the previous week and had won $500 at craps. "I found a shooter," he said. "I even hit boxcars."

For ten minutes, I regaled him with the Cody Graff murder; for two more I told him about Tom Cavanaugh. Ben addressed the latter first:

"Don't reject Tom's generosity. As a priest, I'm telling you that's selfishness and pride. As your brother, I'm telling you you're too damned stubborn. Tom can afford it, he wants to do it, let him. And listen, Emma, one of these days you're going to have to let him meet Adam. I've met Tom. He's a hell of a guy. Are you ashamed of him?"

"I'm ashamed that he's married," I said.

"So's he, probably. But that's a fact, and you have to admire him for sticking by Fruit Loops, or whatever her name is. I admire him for wanting to help you and Adam. Give the guy a break. After all, he's half Tom's. Adam looks more like his father than he does like you, Sluggly." The old nickname came from our extreme youth, a cross between Sluggo and Ugly. I'd always called him Stench. Fortunately, we had not lived up to our childhood monikers.

I mumbled something that was akin to agreement, then waited for his words of wisdom regarding the murder investigation. This time, his counsel came more slowly.

"It sounds to me as if nobody wants to admit this Cody guy got himself murdered. Why is that? Not because he didn't deserve it, right?"

"Right," I echoed into the receiver. "So what are you saying?"

I heard Ben speak away from the phone, presumably to a parishioner who had just arrived at the rectory he had described as about the size of a recycling bin. "I'm saying that everybody really does know Cody Graff was murdered." He paused, waiting for his slow little sister to let his words sink into her brain. "But nobody wants to let on who did it."

I caught my breath. "Ben, do you mean somebody—maybe several somebodies—know who killed Cody?"

"That's what it sounds like to me." He paused, again speaking to another party. "Hey, Emma, I've got to run. I forgot I was hearing confessions this morning. It gets too damned hot to sit in that booth come late afternoon. Call me when you find out whodunit."

Chapter Fifteen

VIDA WAS TAKING Roger to the Science Center in Seattle for the day. I considered it a wasted trip, since Roger didn't need any more ideas about how to wreak havoc. But her absence meant I couldn't confer with her about my encounters with Curtis Graff and Donna Wickstrom. As for Milo, I didn't know what his sleeping arrangements were, if any, with Honoria Whitman. I preferred not to call him and discover that maybe he hadn't yet gotten back from Startup.

The mail arrived early, before noon. Along with my Visa, Texaco, and Skykomish PUD bills, I received a manila envelope from Tom. Inside was an Alaska Airlines schedule, a cashier's check for $2500, and a short note.

"Dear Emma," the note read in Tom's sprawling, not always decipherable hand, "this should cover Adam's flight to Fairbanks, plus enough to bring him home before school starts or for the holidays. I'm sending you the schedule because I suspect (from what you've told me) that Adam may not always be specific about matters like time, place, etc. Your Loggerama edition looks good. What did you do— threaten Ed Bronsky with a chain saw? Love, Tom."

I was smiling as I tucked the note in my desk. The check seemed too generous, but I decided to take my brother's advice and not quibble. As for Tom's comment on *The Advocate*: he was on our mailing list. I wondered if he went through every issue. Probably not, but it made me feel good to know that at least he looked at the paper once in a while. And approved. I told myself that I didn't need any green lights from Tom for personal reasons, but that I respected

417

his professional opinion. Maybe that wasn't quite true, but I knew it should be.

I wrote to Tom at once, thanking him for his generosity. The first paragraph sounded stiff; I tried to loosen up in graf two, telling him about Roger. I mentioned the murder investigation, the progress of the location shoot, the interminable hot, dry spell. I thanked him again, on Adam's behalf, on my own. I signed "Love, Emma," slipped the stationery into a matching envelope, and stuck on a stamp. Then I sat back to try and figure out what to tell my son. *Our* son.

Adam knew I'd had some contact with Tom over the years, but he'd shown a remarkable lack of curiosity about the relationship. When Adam was small, I rarely mentioned Tom. About the time Adam started school in Portland, he began to ask more questions. I was honest, if reserved. Kindergartners cannot understand the adult human heart. Ph.D.s can't either, but at least they like to talk about it. I merely told Adam that his father was a very good man who couldn't marry me and who didn't live close to us. Adam, growing up in an era of single parents, hadn't found his situation unique. Eventually, I told Adam what his father's name was, what he did for a living, that he had a wife and family in California. But it wasn't until he turned seventeen that he expressed a desire to meet Tom. I discouraged Adam; I hadn't heard anything of Tom in years. *Wait,* I cautioned.

And Adam had. It wasn't until he came home from Hawaii on Christmas break that I told him Tom Cavanaugh had been in Alpine. To my amazement, Adam sank into uncharacteristic gloom for three days. On Christmas Eve he came to himself and asked some pointed questions. Why had Tom come? Had he asked about Adam? Who were his other kids? Was he coming back?

I explained how Tom had visited on business, to advise me about the running of the newspaper, possibly even to make an investment. He had two other children: a boy Adam's age and a girl a couple of years younger. Yes, he'd not only asked about Adam, but he'd taken his picture with him. And some day, he might be back.

Oddly, Adam expressed no immediate desire to meet Tom, but he cheered up and the rest of the holiday went by happily. Now I had the cashier's check in hand, made out to me. I would cash it and put it in my savings, to parcel out to Adam as needed. But I would have to tell my son about it, because if he wanted to fly home before the semester started, he'd have to make his reservations soon.

I was sitting in the backyard under the evergreens, mulling over the best approach, when I heard Milo call my name. I shouted that I was outside. Milo loped around the corner of the house, carrying a small box.

"Here," he said, handing me the box and slipping onto the matching deck chair. "Honoria thought you might like it."

I carefully opened the box and searched through crumpled tissue paper. My hand touched something round and smooth. It was about the size of a tennis ball, and when I removed it from the box, I saw there was a hole about half an inch in diameter. The object itself was dark green with just a hint of white in the glaze. I held it out in front of me.

"Well!"

"Isn't that something?" said Milo, leaning forward and smiling in admiration.

"It sure is," I agreed, wishing I knew what that something was.

Milo must have noticed my puzzlement. "It's a vase," he asserted. "For a single flower, like a rose, or a daisy. You stick the stem in that hole. With water, of course."

I studied the would-be vase, rolling it on my palm. It was very heavy. "I like the color. But how do you keep it from tipping over?"

"What?" Milo frowned. "Oh, that's up to you to figure out. Honoria likes to think of her work as . . . how does she put it? *Involving* people. Art shouldn't just sit there, it should *do* something. Or make *you* do something. Isn't that fine?"

"It's very thoughtful." Which, I had to admit, it was. But short of floating the blasted thing in a mixing bowl full of water, I hadn't the foggiest notion what to do with Honoria's gift. "I'll drop her a note. Or call her." I gave Milo my brightest smile, not wanting him to think me ungrateful.

"She made me a pet cock." Milo looked very pleased.

"A *what*?" The heat must be getting to me. Surely I couldn't have heard Milo correctly.

"You know," he said, very seriously. "A pet cock is a kind of valve. For releasing pressure."

I kept a straight face. "I think I'd rather have this," I said, hoisting the glazed ball-cum-vase. "I wouldn't know what to do with a pet cock."

I'd expected Milo to tumble to the double entendre, but it seemed his mind had wandered off to other matters. "Emma, I'm worried. Time's running out. The movie crew is going to leave Tuesday or Wednesday. Curtis Graff will probably take off tomorrow. I've got no reason to hold any of them."

"You haven't found any physical evidence?" Overhead, a pair of chipmunks chattered in the Douglas fir.

Milo shook his head. "Matt Tabor pitched a fit, but we went all over that fancy car of his a second time. All we could find besides those hairs was a thread that may or may not have come from Cody's jeans."

I made an appropriately sympathetic remark before offering Milo a beer. I took Honoria's gift into the house and returned with two cold bottles of Samuel Smith ale I'd found at the back of the refrigerator. For half an hour, Milo and I sipped and talked, getting nowhere. He was, however, intrigued by Ben's theory.

"Your brother must know people pretty well," he said, "being a priest and all." I allowed that was fairly accurate. Priest or not, Ben had his blind spots. "Now why," mused Milo, "would somebody know who the killer was and not say so?"

"The most obvious reason is that whoever knows wants

to protect the person who killed Cody. That could be Dani and Patti, or Reid and Dani, or various combinations of people who care about each other." I moved my chair back a few inches as the sun rose high over the treetops. "It could also be fear. Cody's murderer might not stop there. Take Jack Blackwell, for example—I don't believe he poisoned Cody, but if he did, I think he's the type who would kill again to save himself. There's a ruthless quality about that man."

Milo gave a grunt of assent. "Hampton, too. Hell, I remember Ray Marsh—we went to high school together. He was a wrestler. I played basketball."

"But you didn't recognize him?" I asked.

"No. He was kind of scrawny then, wrestled at a hundred and twenty-six pounds. His hair was about the color of mine, only more washed-out." Milo brushed at his sandy forelock, a few strands of gray glinting in the sun. "By the time he walked out on Patti, he'd put on some weight, but he was still more boy than man."

I made a murmur of acknowledgment. The flutter of bird's wings, the shadows cast by the evergreens, the heavy heat of midday were all conspiring to make me sleepy. My mind didn't want to dwell on murder. Yet Milo was right—we were running out of time. I was trying to stir myself into some kind of mental action when Milo's beeper went off.

"Damn," he mumbled, getting up and going into the house to use the phone. I leaned back in the deck chair, craning my neck to look out toward the street. I caught the rear end of Milo's Cherokee Chief. So far, he had resisted efforts to have a cellular phone installed in his off-duty vehicle.

He returned with two more bottles of beer. They were warm. I knew he must have rummaged around under the sink to find them. "That was Bill Blatt," he said, sinking back into his deck chair. "There's some sort of ruckus going on up at the ski lodge. I told him and Sam Heppner to see what it was, and if it looked serious, to call me back.

I suppose Henry Bardeen has a guest who tried to skip without paying the bill."

I eyed Milo curiously. Hadn't it dawned on him that trouble at the ski lodge might involve the movie crew? But of course there were other guests, perhaps half again as many non-Hollywood types. Milo must know his own business. I kept quiet.

"This theory about Art," he was saying, cradling the bottle of ale against his chest as he stretched out in the chair, "really threw me. I stopped to see Doc Dewey about it this morning, but he wasn't around. Or," he added with a wry glance in my direction, "if he was, Mrs. Dewey wasn't going to let me talk to him. She's pretty thick with Dot Parker, and I don't think Mrs. D. has forgiven me for arresting Durwood."

"Did Doc ever say anything to you about the Graff baby's death?" I was still trying to fight off my feeling of inertia.

"Never." Milo took a long drink of the warm ale. My own bottle rested on the grass, unopened. He sat up abruptly, an awkward jangle of long arms and legs. "You know, that's strange, Emma. If that baby had been murdered by Cody, wouldn't Doc have guessed? I mean, if Art was suspicious, Doc sure would have been."

"That's true." I gave him an accusing look. "You never told me what Curtis said last night."

"Curtis turned into a damned clam. He refused to talk about it, said it was too painful to bring up." Milo's face was rueful. "Maybe so, but it's driving me nuts with everybody pulling this hush-hush act. The only thing Curtis would say was that his brother was scum, that Marje Blatt was blind if she intended to marry him, and that Dani was misunderstood by a lot of people."

The beeper went off again. Milo swore and returned to the house. He emerged in less than a minute. "Goddamn, that tears it!" He started to drain his ale, thought better of it, and handed the bottle to me. "Billy and Sam had to arrest Matt Tabor. They're bringing him down to the office."

I struggled to my feet, my lethargy gone. "Why?"

Milo was already taking long hurried strides across the grass. I ran to keep up. "Assault with a deadly weapon," he called back over his shoulder. "Matt took a fireplace shovel to Reid Hampton. Reid's on his way to emergency. Maybe that'll get Doc Dewey away from his baseball game on TV."

I was torn between following Milo down to the sheriff's office and going to Alpine Community Hospital. Halfway from the front door to the carport, I made up my mind to head for the emergency room. Milo would tell me what went on with the booking of Matt Tabor, but I needed a first-hand report of what had happened to Reid Hampton.

The waiting room for Emergency was small, spartan, and air-conditioned. By the time I arrived, Reid Hampton had already been wheeled into an examining room. The nurse behind the reception desk was short, red-haired, and had a face that reminded me of a Pekingese. Her plastic name tag identified her as Ruth Sharp, R.N.

I told her who I was, which didn't seem to impress her in the least. "I'm checking on Mr. Hampton's condition," I said, trying to sound official.

Ruth Sharp arched her finely penciled eyebrows at me. "His condition? He just arrived. Why don't you call back later this afternoon." The suggestion was clearly intended as a dismissal.

"Where's Doc Dewey?" I asked, digging my heels into the gray-and-white-flecked carpet.

"Dr. Cecil Dewey or Dr. Gerald Dewey?" The nurse's pug nose twitched a bit, probably in disapproval.

"Either one," I replied, my patience on the wane. Behind her, a young woman carried a howling infant through the double doors.

Ruth Sharp looked down at some papers on her desk. She appeared to be debating whether or not to tell me anything. "Dr. Gerald Dewey isn't on call this weekend. Dr. Cecil Dewey isn't here yet. He's on his way, I believe. Perhaps you'd like to speak to Dr. Simon Katz. He's up here from Monroe." She glanced at her watch, which looked as if it should have adorned the wrist of a railroad conductor. "Dr. Katz will be free in an hour or two."

I decided to wait for Doc Dewey. Stepping aside for the woman with the screaming child, I began to roam around the little waiting room. Ruth Sharp and the beleaguered mother had to shout to be heard over the youngster's cries. I had just sat down when the young woman approached and set the child next to me. It was a boy, about three, with very bright red cheeks, curly brown hair and a runny nose. I tried to smile; the boy let out another howl. I buried myself in a year-old copy of *National Geographic*. The child suddenly stopped crying, hopped off the chair, and began to run full tilt in circles around the waiting room. *Another miracle cure*, I thought, remembering the times I'd hauled Adam off to the doctor's, usually in the dead of night with the threat of snow, and had been certain he was near death. On virtually every occasion, it had taken him less than three minutes to recover his usual form and raise hell until we got into the examining room. On one particularly harrowing night, he had run away while I was filling out an admittance form. I had chased him all over Portland's Good Samaritan Hospital and through a side door, where he had jumped into a reflecting pool. It turned out that he had gas. It was a wonder I didn't have a stroke.

Twenty minutes passed before I saw Doc Dewey behind the window of the doors that led into the emergency area. I got up, careful not to trip over the whirling dervish who apparently was still awaiting the ministrations of Dr. Katz. Crossing the small room, I rapped softly on the glass. Doc turned, giving me a quizzical look.

"What is it, girlie?" he asked, opening the door a couple of inches. "You sick?"

I explained that I was performing in my professional capacity. "Reid Hampton's famous. It's a news story. What happened?"

Doc expelled a gruff little breath. "Reid Hampton, Ray

Marsh, what a crock! Give me five minutes, we'll catch a cup of coffee." He nudged the door shut.

It was actually ten minutes before Doc Dewey shuffled into the vending machine area that served as the hospital cafeteria. I noticed that his hand shook as he carried his paper cup over to the table where I was sitting. Crock or not, his experience with Reid/Ray had seemingly unnerved him.

"Slight concussion," said Doc, easing himself into an orange vinyl chair. "He'll have to stay overnight, but he should be all right. It's a good thing that Tabor fellow's got a swing like a bear with a crosscut saw."

"He really attacked Reid?" I realized I shouldn't be incredulous; movie people were known to be excitable. Still, I hated relying on clichés.

Doc drank his coffee as if he were parched. "Seems like it, all right. Reid—oh, hell, I'm going to call him Ray, I brought the kid into the world over forty years ago—said there was a row. Heather Bardeen was doing something upstairs outside their rooms and heard all the commotion, so she called her dad, who called the sheriff. I didn't ask Ray a lot of questions, because he has to keep quiet." Doc shook his head, the sparse white hairs looking limp. "Damned fools, all of 'em. What's this world coming to, Emma?" He looked at me as if I should know.

"Frankly, it's a miracle Matt didn't do some serious damage," I noted. "Reid—or Ray, if you will—is in terrific shape, but so's Matt and he's several years younger. They must have been going at it a while before the sheriff's deputies got there."

"Oh, yeah?" Doc eyed me inquisitively. "What are you trying to say, girlie?"

I considered. It wasn't advisable to toss irrational answers back at Doc. His shrewd blue eyes demanded judicious thinking. "I mean that if Matt really wanted to brain Reid, he could have done it. Or if they were going at it tooth and toenail, they'd both be here in the hospital."

Doc nodded once. "Good point. Makes you wonder, doesn't it?" He polished off his coffee and stood up, lifting himself out of the chair by hanging onto the table. "I'd better go see if Katz needs any more help. If not, I'll go home and watch some golf. The Red Sox won again—what do you think about that?"

I thought that was fine. On the way out we talked of Fenway Park, of the Green Monster, of Boggs and Clark and Clemens. "No relation to Carl or Samuel," remarked Doc as we passed through the now-empty waiting room. "Roger, I mean. At least that I know of. Carl and Samuel spelled it different from each other, but they were related all the same. Did you know that?"

I said I did. "Speaking of Roger, do you really think Vida's grandson needs medication, or just a good swift kick?"

For a fleeting instant, Doc looked appalled, then he broke into a grin. "If it were me, I'd prescribe the medication for his parents. Tranquilizers, heavy-duty. But I can't argue with Gerry. It wouldn't be right. My son knows what he's doing. And nowadays, you can't tell a parent to give their kid a good licking. That's child abuse."

I glanced over at the reception desk. Ruth Sharp, R.N., appeared absorbed in charts, but I doubted it. She struck me as a world-class eavesdropper. I lowered my voice:

"Was Cody Graff a child abuser?"

Doc's body gave off a tiny tremor, but his blue eyes were steadfast. "Yes."

I couldn't suppress a little gasp. The confirmation of my private beliefs came as a shock. Even when you fear the worst, you still hope for the best. "Did you know it at the time?" My voice was barely audible.

Doc nodded slowly. "I was pretty sure. The trouble was, I didn't know who did it. Then."

The soft thrum of a telephone sounded in the background. I put a hand on Doc's arm. "You mean you thought it might have been Dani?"

Doc was looking very grim. "Maybe. It wasn't obvious who it was. If you're going to ruin somebody's life, you want to be damned sure you got the right one."

Ruth Sharp was standing, leaning across the reception desk. "Dr. Dewey, a Mrs. Whipp is on her way in. She fell out of a lawn swing. Possible wrist fracture."

Doc rolled his eyes. "The Whipps are at it again." He adjusted his stethoscope and turned toward the emergency receiving area. "There goes the golf," he muttered. "A good thing it bores the bejeesus out of me." Doc disappeared behind the swinging doors.

"I had to let him go," Milo asserted in a peevish tone. "We have to wait to see if Reid Hampton presses charges."

I was sitting across from Milo in his little office, angling my chair to get the full benefit of the fan that was whirling at high speed on the floor. According to Milo, the quarrel had started over Reid's refusal to take Matt with him to Seattle to meet the film lab people.

"Sounds silly," said Milo, fingering a round blue object on his desk, "but I've known men to fight over dumber things."

"Was Matt penitent?" I asked.

Milo stuck his finger through the middle of the blue object. It was smaller than a doughnut, but basically the same shape. "Actually, he was. Not at first—he was pretty belligerent. But then he simmered down and seemed worried about Hampton. I had to talk him out of going over to the hospital on his way back to the ski lodge."

"Alone?"

Milo stared, wearing the blue object like a big ring. "Yeah, why?"

I tilted my head to one side. "If Matt is in love with somebody other than Dani, who is it? It's got to be a woman who is here in town, because Vida and I heard them quarreling. Who?"

Milo's hazel eyes wandered around the room. "Hell, I don't know, Emma. There are several other women on that movie crew. Are you sure you heard two voices? Maybe he was talking on the phone."

I reflected. "I thought we heard someone else, but I

couldn't make out who it was. Matt was doing all the shouting."

"I'll bet he was on the phone," said Milo.

"Find out," I said. "I can give you the day and the time. Have Heather check it and see if Matt was making a call then."

"Why?" Milo was regarding me skeptically.

I had no rational answer. But unlike my exchange with Doc Dewey, I didn't feel the need for logic with Milo. "Just do it. Don't you believe in hunches?"

The disparaging expression on Milo's face told me he didn't. But I knew he'd do it anyway. I got up to leave, but paused in the doorway.

"Say, Milo, what's that blue thing you're fiddling with?"

Glancing down at his hand, Milo's long mouth twitched in a dry smile. "This? It's my pet cock. Want to play with it?"

I giggled. "No, thanks."

Sometimes Milo wasn't as dense as I thought he was.

I hoped Vida wouldn't be too late getting back from Seattle. It was too hot to do yard work, or clean house, or get a head start on the next issue of *The Advocate*. I flopped on the sofa and read for an hour, then took a chance and called Adam. He wasn't in, but I suddenly realized I hadn't collected all the items on his wish list. If Curtis Graff was leaving for Ketchikan the next day, I had to get cracking. In less than an hour, the mall would be closed. At least the stores were air-conditioned. The idea should have come to me sooner.

By six P.M., I had finished my shopping, coming as close as I could to Adam's specific desires. I stopped at the Venison Inn for dinner and was surprised to see Matt Tabor sitting alone at a window table. He wore his brooding look, and a feeble attempt by two young women seeking an autograph was rejected with a surly remark. My initial instinct to say hello died aborning. Matt was obviously in no mood for company.

But I was wrong. Five minutes later, Marje Blatt came into the restaurant and walked straight to Matt's table. He looked up and gave her a tight smile. It appeared Matt was expecting Marje.

As I ate my London broil, I watched the couple surreptitiously. Could Marje be the love of Matt's life? It didn't seem possible. How would they know each other? He'd been in Alpine for less than two weeks. She had been engaged to Cody Graff until his death. I chewed very slowly on my buttered carrots. But if somehow they were lovers, what would be more convenient than that Cody should die? I chewed some more, turning the carrots to pap. Matt apparently had a terrible temper and wasn't adverse to beating people up with a fireplace shovel. Marje, however, seemed of a more peaceable nature. But poison was said to be a woman's weapon. . . .

I tried to read the signals they gave off between them. Earnest conversation, a serious discussion, no physical contact, not so much as a smoldering glance. Their meal outlasted mine. I dawdled over my lemonade, wished I could smoke about six cigarettes, and finally left while they were still finishing their entrée.

The phone was ringing when I got in the house. I caught it just before it switched over to the answering machine. It was Milo.

"You were right, Emma. Or were you wrong?" He sounded vague. "Whatever. No call was made from Matt Tabor's room that morning. Whoever he was talking to was with him."

I told him about Matt and Marje. "I have to be honest, though," I cautioned. "I didn't see any sparks fly."

"Hmmmm." Milo was musing, and I could see him fingering his long chin. Or his pet cock. "Marje would have been at work that time of day, right?"

"Probably." My hunch was teasing me. "Are you keeping an eye on Matt?"

"Not really, why?"

"I just wondered." There was something I had to say, to

tell Milo, to keep the hazily evolving idea alive in my mind. "How's Reid?"

"I haven't heard. What's up, Emma? You sound antsy."

"I am," I admitted. "Say, where's Curtis Graff staying? I've got to see him before he goes back to Alaska."

"He was at Patti's, but he may be at Cody's apartment, clearing stuff out. That's my guess. The number's in the book."

I found Cody Graff's listing before Milo did and I rang off. Curtis answered on the first ring. To my surprise, he offered to come up and collect Adam's parcels.

He arrived half an hour later, just as I felt the first breath of fresh air filter through the evergreens. Curtis was wearing a dress shirt, no tie, but tailored slacks. I couldn't help but stare.

"You look sharp," I said, showing him into the living room. "I don't have the gumption to get dressed up in this kind of weather."

He gave me a diffident smile. "I've got a dinner reservation in less than an hour at Café de Flore." His eyes roamed the living room, taking in my Monet and Turner prints, the stone fireplace, the braided rug my great-grandmother had made almost a century earlier. I expected him to comment on the decor, but instead he shoved his hands in his pockets and looked at me sideways. "I'm taking Dani to dinner. She could use an evening out."

"Well!" I cleared my throat. "That's nice, Curtis. She's been through hell." I collected myself and turned a level gaze on him. "Now—and a long time ago."

To my further surprise, Curtis sat down on the sofa. "I'm getting the idea that a lot of people know the truth about what happened—a long time ago. Maybe that's good."

I seated myself in the armchair opposite him. "You don't sound positive."

"I'm not." He was now looking away, in the direction of the tall oak cabinet that housed my alphabet soup collection of audio-visual pleasures: TV, VCR, CD player. Curtis's gray eyes had the same restless quality as his brother's, but there was no sign of Cody's sulkiness. "It's tough," Curtis said, after a long pause, "to know when you've done the right thing, isn't it? I mean, even if you've pondered long and hard, and you know it's the only way, you still don't feel easy in your mind."

Curtis's remarkable, if cryptic, little speech caught me off guard. "Life is very complicated," I said, falling back on a platitude. "Are you talking about dealing with other people or making independent choices?"

For some reason, my query brought a faint smile to Curtis's face. "Not independent. No, not at all. Let's just say it's about people." He rested one leg over the other knee, careful of the crease in his slacks. "I must sound weird. Coming back to Alpine after all these years has been an unreal experience."

"I should think so. It would feel odd under any circumstances, but with Cody getting killed, it must almost make you sorry you came."

"I had to come." His face had turned very earnest; the words almost sounded desperate. "But I'll be real glad to leave tomorrow night."

"Curtis," I said, hoping to strike a balance between friendly curiosity and professional interrogation, "why *did* you come?" I hoped my tone would imply that I had a right to know and that he had a duty to tell me.

His response came slowly. Curtis's teeth worried his lower lip and his fingers thrummed on his knee. "I wanted to see Dani."

"You care for her that much?"

Above the shake rooftop, I could hear the cawing of crows. A car took the corner too fast on Fir Street, causing the wheels to screech. On the other side of town, a Burlington Northern freight whistled as it slowed on its ascent into the mountains.

"Dani's special," Curtis said at last. "I don't mean because she's a movie star. She was always that way. Even when she was a kid, there was something different about her. She didn't *act* different, she just *was* different. It's hard to explain."

I had an inkling of what Curtis meant: Reid Hampton had described her as *luminous*; but the word was too extravagant. Dani Marsh struck me as more down-to-earth. "She seems like a very decent person. Vulnerable, too, the kind you'd want to protect."

Curtis nodded energetically. "That's it. She's tough in some ways, but not in others. Her mother is the other way around. I mean, Patti talks tough, but she really isn't. Dani's the opposite. And she's decent, all right. You got it." He seemed pleased with my analysis.

"I'm guessing that you weren't pleased when Dani married your brother."

"I sure wasn't." Curtis scowled at the memory. "Anybody could have told her it was a bad idea. I don't think it took her more than two weeks to figure it out for herself."

I was searching for another roundabout way to ask the obvious. It's not easy for a journalist to avoid direct questions. But unlike Vida, I couldn't be so blunt in casual conversation.

"Yet they stayed together for over a year," I remarked, "and went ahead and had a baby."

Curtis put both feet on the floor and stood up. "They stayed together for over a year. That's right." He moved in a semicircle, one hand ruffling the hair at the back of his neck.

Curtis didn't seem inclined to elaborate. "The baby's death must have sealed the fate of that marriage," I said. "How did Cody take it?"

Curtis gave me an odd look, part puzzled, part scornful. "He acted all broken up. He blamed Dani for going out."

"But Cody was with the baby," I pointed out.

Scorn vanquished puzzlement. "That's right." Curtis bit off the words.

"What happened that night, Curtis?" I'd finally managed to ask the direct question.

Curtis looked as if he were going to sit down again, but

instead he wandered to the end of the sofa. Deep in thought, he gazed at the end table—at the telephone, answering machine, pen, notepad, and my prized Tiffany lily lamp. "Dani called the fire department. She was hysterical, almost impossible to understand. I was on active status, so I answered the phone. All I could figure out was that something terrible had happened." He was speaking dispassionately, divorcing himself from his memories. "A couple of other guys and I went out to their trailer home, ready for anything. Art Fremstad was already there. Dani was a little calmer, but still a mess. Cody was blubbering into his beer, trying to drink himself stupid. Little Scarlett was dead, probably had been for almost an hour."

He stopped, presumably gathering courage. Curtis moved the length of the coffee table, pausing by the floor lamp with its shade of geometric stained glass. "I got sick. I threw up in their bathroom." He hung his head. "Then Doc Dewey came. He asked Art and me a lot of questions. It dawned on me what he was getting at. But he never said anything. He just sort of looked at us, and at Dani and Cody, and said to send for Al Driggers and the hearse."

"But you knew then that the baby's death wasn't natural?"

Cody's face had darkened, his features looking sharp in the shadow cast by the lamp. "Not for sure. There were some marks on her face, but Cody said he'd tried to revive her. You don't want to think about the other possibility."

"No," I breathed. "Of course not. Especially when it's your own brother and his child."

Curtis wrapped his fingers around the lamp's slim column and stared straight at me. "But," he said softly, "it wasn't his child."

I sucked in my breath. My jaw must have dropped, and I knew I was gaping stupidly at Curtis. "What . . ." I began, but Curtis's face had closed up, as if he had given everything he had, and the larder was empty. Judging from the blank look in his gray eyes, his soul was empty, too.

"I'd better go meet Dani," he said in his normal voice.

"It takes a while to drive down to Café de Flore if there's heavy traffic coming over the pass on a Saturday night. You got Adam's stuff?"

I did, having hastily packed everything into a large cardboard box just before Curtis arrived. I thanked him, wished him well, and hoped he enjoyed his dinner. It was almost dark when I watched him go down the walk to the street where Cody's pickup was parked. I wondered if Curtis intended to drive it to Café de Flore or if Dani was going to borrow Matt's Zimmer.

Most of all, I wondered about little Scarlett's father. Perhaps Curtis had been suffering from grief as well as shock when he'd thrown up in his brother's bathroom. It struck me as very likely that Curtis Graff hadn't lost a niece that summer night, but a daughter.

It was after ten o'clock when Vida called. "Did you have a good time?" I asked, envisioning the Pacific Science Center in ruins.

"Yes, yes, never mind that," she said in a voice that sounded as if her engine was racing. "Listen, Emma, I just tucked Roger in and went through his belongings to get his dirty clothes. I found the medicine young Doc Dewey gave him. Amy had sent it along, but Roger forgot to tell me." Vida took a deep breath while I waited for her to launch a new attack on the modern approach to child-rearing. "Emma, it's Haloperidol. *Doesn't that beat all?*"

Chapter Sixteen

I DROVE OVER to Vida's in my bathrobe. She couldn't leave Roger, of course, lest he parboil a burglar or engage in some other childish prank. Insisting that I see for myself, and convinced that despite modern electronic switching equipment in the telephone company's central office, our words could be overheard, Vida had asked me to come to her house.

I arrived just as she was putting a green-edged cloth over the cage of her canary, Cupcake. "Roger's asleep," she said in a whisper. "The poor little fellow is all worn out. He had no idea those security guards could run so fast at the Center."

I decided not to ask why Roger was being chased, and could only hope that he also had been chastened. At the sound of the tea kettle, Vida whisked into the kitchen. I followed her while she made tea.

"Here's the stuff," she said, pointing to an innocent-looking bottle on the counter. "It's also called Haldol."

I read the label, with its usual cautions. "Okay," I said, sitting down at her Formica-covered kitchen table, "so we know the drug existed in this form in this town. So what?"

Vida, unlike most people I know, actually serves tea in teacups. She carried a Radford's yellow rose pattern for me and an English garden scene by Royal Albert for herself. "Emma—look at that label." She blew on her tea and waited for my reaction.

I started to read aloud, but Vida gave a vigorous shake of her head. "I'm not talking about what's there—I'm talking about what's not." Her eyebrows arched above the tortoiseshell frames. "No pharmacy label. Young Doc Dewey took it right off the shelf in his office."

"Oh!" I sighed at my obtuseness. But I still didn't see Vida's point. I admitted as much.

"It means," said Vida, "that this stuff—which was what Cody ingested—was available at the clinic. Someone could have gone in to see either of the Deweys and made off with a bottle of it and poisoned Cody."

The theory fell flat with me. "No, Vida. They lock up drugs. You know that."

Vida's chin jutted. "I know they don't. They're really rather careless. Back by the lab, they have a room which is part dispensary, part supply closet. It's never locked. I walked right in once and helped myself to one of those travel-sized boxes of Kleenex for the car. I think we should check with Marje and see who had appointments in the week or two before Cody died."

"I suppose." I fingered the little bottle as if it could give me inspiration, then set it back down on the table, accidentally knocking it against Vida's cut-glass sugar bowl. The small sound triggered a random thought in my brain, but I couldn't grasp it quickly enough. "There are other sources," I suggested. "Parker's Pharmacy. The hospital."

"Certainly," agreed Vida. "But I daresay either of those places is more secure. I still opt for the clinic."

I rested my chin on my hand, mulling over the idea. Certainly there was one person involved with Cody who had access to the clinic's supply of Haloperidol: Marje Blatt. But maybe it wasn't wise to say so to Vida.

In the end, after we had hashed over the doings of the day in Alpine, I hinted to Vida that Marje couldn't be dismissed as a suspect.

"We can't leave anyone out," I said. "That's what Milo and I were discussing this afternoon—how somebody may be protecting somebody else."

Vida, who was still exclaiming over Matt Tabor's attack on Reid Hampton, frowned at me. "Are you making too much of Marje having dinner with Matt? Really, I admit it's a bit odd, but I'm sure Marje will explain it to her old auntie. After all, Matt may be a movie star, but basically he's probably just a young man who enjoys the company of a pretty girl."

"When he isn't out creaming his director with a shovel?" I threw Vida a caustic look. "Come on, Vida, who do you think Matt was arguing with the other morning up at the lodge?" I watched her roll her eyes, but didn't wait for her answer. "It wasn't Marje, I'll admit. I don't know why your niece was being wined and dined by Matt Tabor, but I doubt it had anything to do with her feminine charms. Am I right?"

"Probably." Vida looked exasperated.

"So who was the other half of the lovers' quarrel?"

Setting her teacup in its matching saucer, Vida drew herself up in her customary majestic style. "Really, it's so galling. It shouldn't be, of course, but it is, because I'm a woman. I suppose I hate to see good men go to waste." She pursed her lips, glanced into her now empty cup as if she were going to read the dregs, and gave a little shudder. "Obviously, the great love of Matt Tabor's life is Reid Hampton."

It made sense that when Reid Hampton found himself up against a double exposure, he chose the lesser revelation of the two secrets. Patti Marsh knew her husband. Perhaps Reid's homosexuality had caused the breakup of their marriage, rather than his unwillingness to take on the responsibility of a wife and child. Reid Hampton, or Ray Marsh, had paid $50,000 to Patti Marsh not to keep his real identity a secret, but to guard his sexual preference.

Vida and I both doubted that Reid was ashamed of being gay. Instead, we figured that he didn't want his hot new protégé, Matt Tabor, to be labeled anything but a raging macho man. Box office was the bottom line, and a hero who called his male director Honey wouldn't bring in the paying customers. And if the trade reports were accurate,

Reid Hampton's production company desperately needed a hot ticket.

Just before midnight, I pleaded exhaustion, more from the heat than any stress or strain. Naturally, Vida was tired, but she seemed too involved in the murder case to wind down. She was particularly fascinated by the notion that Curtis Graff might have been little Scarlett's father, a lapse on Dani's part that Vida found not only excusable, but commendable.

As Vida escorted me to the front door, she gave the sleeve of my bathrobe a little shake. "We're getting close, Emma. I can feel it."

I offered a weary smile. "What you're feeling is polished cotton, Vida. And I feel as if my head is full of cotton wool. Good night."

"I mean it," she shouted, heedless of her sleeping neighbors. "We're hot on the heels of that killer!"

I got into the Jaguar and locked the doors. I only hoped that the killer wasn't hot on our heels as well.

Father Fitz was on vacation, replaced by a young priest from Wenatchee who was into social justice. With my own quest for justice nibbling at my attention, I caught only the high points of his sermon. Everyone is equal. Christianity is not a passive state. Taking action is better than not taking action. Society is upside down. Purify your soul, but if you can't handle that, clean up the water. At least it was better than listening to Father Fitz rant about fast young women with shingled hair or the atrocities of the Bataan Death March.

After mass, I strolled out into the parking lot. Beyond Mount Baldy, a few wispy clouds teased the land with the promise of better things to come, such as rain. Ninety again today, with no break in sight. No precipitation in the five-day forecast, fire danger in the extreme. I slumped into the Jaguar and headed home.

I was pulling into the driveway when the young priest's sermon hit me like a punch in the stomach. With a squeal of tires, I put the car into reverse and headed straight for Vida.

Vida's first reaction was that I was crazy. Ten minutes later, over tall glasses of iced tea, she began to accept my inspired theory.

"I don't see how you can prove it, though," she remarked, keeping one eye on me and the other on Roger, who was out in the front yard catching bugs in a jar.

"I'm going to have to rely on Milo. I thought of asking everybody who was at the Icicle Creek Tavern, but I've covered too many court cases to not know how much conflicting testimony eyewitnesses can come up with. I'm afraid it would be a waste of time." I gave Vida a semireproachful look. "I wish you'd been there."

Vida lifted her chin. "I did my duty at Mugs Ahoy. You can't expect me to be everywhere."

"I know." My smile was meant to placate. "It's just that you're a better observer than Milo is, for all of his law enforcement experience."

"That's because he's only a man," said Vida, pouring more iced tea from a fat green pitcher. "They don't notice things the way other people do, Emma. Their vision is limited, as if they're wearing blinders. They rarely see the whole picture."

"True," I agreed in a vague voice, wishing I could lay claim to seeing more than I had. The bar stools on which Carla, Ginny, and I had been seated hadn't given us a particularly good vantage point except for the immediate vicinity. There were too many bobbing heads and moving bodies blocking our view. As for Carla, she was a hopeless witness. I might expect better of Ginny, but in cursory conversations during the past few days, she hadn't been able to tell me any more than I already knew. The tavern had been such a jumble of people, noise, and movement that isolated incidents were hard to recall. After more than a week, I could barely keep a coherent account in my own mind.

Vida had gotten up to call to Roger through the screen door. "No bees, dear. Just grasshoppers." She paused as

Roger responded in a voice I couldn't hear. Vida gave a shake of her head. "I can't tell which are boys and which are girls, either, Roger." She turned to her chair, still shaking her head. "He wants to dress the grasshoppers, according to sex. Isn't he the one?"

Resisting the urge to ask *one what?* I started to steer the conversation back to the topic at hand. But despite the distraction, Vida was already there. "You're forgetting someone," she said, pushing her glasses farther up on her nose. "I have a feeling that one of those people at the tavern would make an exemplary witness."

I winced as I saw Roger go from A to Z in a single bound, trampling a bed of asters and zinnias. "Who?"

"The sort of person who isn't as physically active as most people." The glasses slipped a notch. Vida regarded me over their rims. "Honoria Whitman."

Vida couldn't come to Startup with me because she wasn't sure when her daughter and son-in-law would be back. I almost suggested we take Roger along, stopped long enough to question my sanity, and said I might give Milo a call. But Vida informed me that Milo had gone to Seattle to take his son to the Mariners' game. Briefly, I cursed Milo for appearing to regard Cody Graff's murder less seriously than I did.

There was heavy traffic going both ways on Stevens Pass. The sun beat down on the broad highway; the south fork of the Skykomish River was so low you could walk across it; and I had to search to find patches of snow in the mountains that lined both sides of the road. My directions to Honoria's house had been divined from Milo's description. Feeling guilty because I hadn't phoned ahead, I stopped in Gold Bar to call Honoria.

To my relief, she was in; to my surprise, she sounded genuinely glad that I was coming. I took the turn she had given me and wound my way a quarter of a mile on a dirt road through overhanging vine maples.

Honoria's house probably had once been a summer cottage. But somewhere between the need for indoor plumbing and rising real estate prices, the cedar shake dwelling had been renovated. Tucked among the trees near a sluggish creek inching through ferns and cattails, the little house possessed a certain charm.

Honoria was sitting in her wheelchair on the front porch, which spanned the width of the cottage. "I made separators," she said as I trudged up the ramp to join her. "Kahlua, brandy, and milk. Not really a hot weather drink, but somehow it sounded wholesome."

"It does at that," I agreed, sitting in a rough-hewn chair that was surprisingly comfortable. For the first quarter of an hour, we sipped our separators and made polite if congenial conversation. I thanked Honoria for her gift, emphasizing that I intended to find one perfect rose to set in the hole.

Honoria laughed, a delightful, husky sound. "Oh, Emma! Did Milo tell you it was a *vase*?" She laughed some more, shaking her head on her graceful neck. "It's nothing! It's just a . . . *thing*. But Milo is so practical, I had to tell him it was . . . useful." Her laughter subsided into a rich giggle.

I laughed, too, but not quite as heartily. "And I thought it was a small bowling ball for a one-fingered amateur," I murmured. "Oh, dear."

Honoria giggled again and tucked her linen shirt into her neatly pressed slacks. "It's the shapes and the textures I like," she explained, growing more serious. "I don't see why pottery always has to be useful. It's like any other art. It can be whatever you want it to be, which in this case, is really nothing but a blob. Except to the Milos of this world, bless them. They're so *practical*, they can fix dripping faucets and replace fuel pumps and shingle your roof. We'd be lost without them."

I had visions of Milo with a ladder, scrambling about on Honoria's roof in the middle of a winter windstorm. I tried to refocus, with Milo on my roof, but all I saw was him asking me to move the ladder and help him get down. Just the same, I admired Honoria's candor. Indeed, I admired

Honoria. Only in the most perverse corner of my often per-verse soul did I wish I didn't.

It was time to get down to business. My curiosity was rampant, not only on a professional level, but because I sensed that I was on the right track in discovering the kill-er's identity. If only Honoria were as keen an observer as Vida thought she was . . .

I began by asking Honoria if Milo had questioned her—in his official capacity—about the Icicle Creek Tav-ern. He had, she assured me, but there had been very little she could tell him. As a newcomer, she didn't know most of the people involved. It was only after the fact that she had discovered their identities.

"Dani Marsh and Matt Tabor, of course," she said, re-filling my glass from a green and yellow carafe I presumed she had created. "I recognized them from their movies. But the others . . ." She gave a simple shrug. "They were new to me."

"You were sitting near the bar, and fairly close to Cody and Marje," I pointed out. "Do you remember anything about Cody being served that last beer?"

Honoria paid me the compliment of pausing long enough to consider my question seriously. "Milo asked me that, too. At the time, I told him I didn't. But the more I tried to remember . . ." Her oval face puckered in concentration. "So much was going on, with those angry exchanges be-tween all sorts of people, including Matt Tabor and Cody Graff . . . Dani's mother, that was easy to figure out, there *is* a resemblance . . . And Reid Hampton—I'm sure I've seen his picture in some film magazine or the newspa-pers—and the timber company fellow . . . It was all so dis-tracting, and yet predictable." Honoria gave me a helpless look. "Do you know what I mean? It was almost like a movie, the cliché barroom brawl scene."

Recalling that my reaction had been similar, I tipped my head in assent. "Do you mean *phony*?" I asked.

Again, Honoria stopped to consider my query. "Phony . . . not that, but not exactly genuine, either. It was as if everyone was playing a part, not staged in that sense, not rehearsed, but doing what was expected of them." She made a sudden impatient wave of her hand. "I can't quite get a fix on it. I do know, however, that I was quite fascinated, and in watching all the action, I didn't pay strict attention to where the beer was going."

"That," I said, "may have been intentional."

Honoria's gray eyes locked with mine. "I see." She ran her tongue over her upper lip. "Why?"

"I'm not sure," I admitted. "Maybe as cover for the murder."

The gray eyes grew very wide. "But ... that would mean that somebody else—other than the killer—was involved."

My gaze kept a steady pace with Honoria's. "That's right. At least I'm guessing it is." I leaned forward on my rough-planked chair. It was very quiet at Honoria's place, the highway sounds muffled by the trees, the slow-winding creek making barely a gurgle, the leaves unruffled by the still, warm air. Only the occasional chatter of a chipmunk or caw of a crow broke the silence. "Beyond all the fuss and furor, what else did you see, Honoria?"

She slumped slightly in the wheelchair, her eyes following a shaft of sunlight between the vine maples and the cottonwood trees. "That's what I've been trying to remember. I don't think I saw anything. Except," she went on, more slowly and with great care, "there was that awkward moment—for me, that is—when Patti got playful with Milo. You understand," said Honoria, returning her gaze to my attentive face, "that I wasn't reacting in a possessive way. It was more as if I were watching Milo take a test— how would he handle the situation? He passed beautifully."

Momentarily sidetracked by Honoria's apparent concern for my feelings about Milo, assuming I had any, I smiled wryly. "He palmed her off on Janet and Al Driggers, knowing full well that if anybody was up to the task, it would be Janet."

"Yes, and it raised him a notch in my esteem." Honoria

paused to sip from her drink and watch a pair of blue jays hop around a slim cedar tree just off the porch. "But I didn't want him to catch me staring at him like a teacher watching a pupil, so I made myself look the other way. You may recall that we were sitting at the far end of the bar, near the rest rooms and fairly close to Cody and his fiancée."

I nodded. I remembered that part well enough. "Most of the time, my view of you was blocked by all the action. But I remember catching your eye when things seemed to simmer down."

"Exactly," agreed Honoria. "But before that, while Milo was getting rid of Patti, I kept my eyes on the bar itself. That timber fellow—Blackwell?—was serving the service station man a beer, I think, and the doctor poured one for somebody else. Dani took it off the bar and handed it to Marje Blatt who carried it over to Cody. I suppose he drank it." Her gaze was meaningful, yet it conveyed a question.

"I suppose he did," I replied, wishing that Honoria could have arrived at the Icicle Creek Tavern earlier. She had confirmed some of my suspicions, but not quite all of them. For a full minute, we let the silence wrap around us, feeling the heat of the day and the tension of the moment. "That's it?" I finally asked.

Honoria made a rueful face. "I'm afraid so. I didn't see Dani or Marje slip anything into that beer mug. And I didn't notice if anyone went up to Cody after that. Milo came back and the next thing I knew, Cody and Marje had left the tavern." With a helpless gesture of her graceful hands, Honoria gave me an apologetic look. "I'm not much help, am I?"

I tried to make my expression encouraging. "Every tiny bit helps. This is Milo's job, after all." Maybe it was wrong of me to meddle; certainly it wasn't fair to criticize the sheriff's handling of a difficult case.

Honoria raised her glass. "To Milo, then."

I nodded as we clicked glasses. Something clicked in my brain as well.

"I think you just showed me a missing link," I asserted, noting the puzzled expression on Honoria's face. "Now we'll let Milo take over. Let's hope he passes this test as well as he did the one at the Icicle Creek Tavern."

Chapter Seventeen

MY HANDS WERE tied until evening, when Milo returned from Seattle. By then, Vida should be free of Roger, though I realized she would not regard his departure with the same enthusiasm I would. Meanwhile, I made another attempt to call my son in Ketchikan. He was working, I was told, and wouldn't be back until ten, my time. Maybe, I thought, I should set aside some of Tom's $2500 to help defray the cost of long distance.

I spent what was left of the afternoon piecing together the evidence, most of which was circumstantial, as well as guesswork. Much of what I'd learned had nothing to do with Cody Graff's murder. At least not on the surface. The relationship between Patti Marsh and Jack Blackwell was, alas, what it was: an abusive man and a woman who could defend herself only against those who meant her no serious harm. I didn't know if Reid Hampton had abused Patti, but their daughter apparently had carried on the family tradition by marrying Cody Graff. And Cody, fueled by jealously or maybe just a vicious streak, had smothered little Scarlett, and then killed Art Fremstad. For five years, Cody Graff must have figured he'd gotten away with murder.

Dani must have realized early on in her marriage that Cody was a nasty piece of work. My guess was that she'd sought consolation from his brother, who had been more than willing to give her his all. Curtis had said he and Cody had fallen out over a girl. Had he meant Dani? Or Scarlett? Or both? Dani had run away to Los Angeles; Curtis had fled to Alaska. No doubt both had been horrified as well as grief-stricken. And probably afraid.

In California, Dani had found not only a mentor but a father. I couldn't help but speculate that the lure of Hollywood had been in their blood, sending each of them from the evergreens of Alpine to the palm trees of L.A. As for Reid Hampton, the revelation of his real identity didn't perturb him as much as any hint of his relationship with Matt Tabor. But I didn't think that their feelings for each other had anything to do with Cody's death. Reid had tried to cover up his sexual preference for professional, not personal, reasons. He had promoted a nonexistent romance between Dani and Matt while dating women—such as me—casually but publicly. Who better to ask out for an evening than the local newspaper publisher? Nor did I think that Matt's jealous rage was aimed in my direction—if Reid Hampton was straying, the object of his affections could be anybody, and probably another man. Again, I felt that episode had very little to do with Cody's murder.

I could also dismiss the ruckus between Jack Blackwell and Reid Hampton. Strictly business, to be settled by their lawyers, not with their fists. Matt might make a show of defending Reid's rights, and Jack had certainly pitched a fit over Patti's fifty grand, but nobody was going to kill one of Blackwell Timber's employees because of financial gain or loss.

The key, I kept telling myself, was what Marje Blatt and Dani Marsh and so many others had told me all along: that Cody Graff had not been murdered, that his death was accidental, that he had overdosed. I didn't believe that for a minute.

The problem was that the tighter I pulled the pieces together, the less I liked my conclusions. There is a truism in the news business that as long as a journalist is on the scent of a story, real emotions are held at bay. Once all the facts are gathered, personal reaction sets in. On this oppressive, humid evening in August, I had reached that point. I was almost sure I knew who the killer was, and I didn't like the answer one bit. I didn't even much like myself for coming up with such a terrible solution. The combination of too much heat and too little wisdom was making me feel depressed and faintly nauseous. Maybe I was hungry. Food, which can usually sustain me through almost any crisis, is not quite as appealing when the temperature nudges ninety.

As I got up from my writing desk to forage in the kitchen, I realized I was dizzy. I stumbled over the phone cord and went down hard. The wind was knocked out of me, but it was my left foot that hurt badly. Writhing about, I regained my breath and tried to pull myself up.

The foot did not want to bear my weight. I knelt on my right knee, feeling tears of pain sting my eyes. It had been a few minutes after seven when I'd last looked at my watch. Would Milo be home? Would Vida have bade Roger good-bye? Should I call the hospital?

Feeling foolish as well as awkward, I stretched for the phone. It rang in my hand. My voice was feeble as I said hello.

"Mom? Hey, you sound weird. Did I screw up the time change again? I got off early and somebody told me you'd called a couple of times."

For once, my son's voice was not the most welcome sound in the world. "Oh, Adam," I began dismally, "I just fell flat on my face."

"What did you do, break your beak?" He sounded more amused than alarmed. "Hey, if you knocked out your front teeth, you can probably use the dental insurance to get caps."

In spite of my pain, I laughed. "It's my foot. Or ankle. Not nearly so mirth-making as the prizefighter or jack-o-lantern look."

"No, that's pretty boring," Adam agreed, beginning to show a bit of concern. "Can you walk?"

"I can't even get up." I was, however, edging my way onto the sofa. "It's okay, I'll get somebody to check it out for me tonight. How are you?" God forbid, I didn't want

my son to worry about his mother. God give me reason—
would Adam really spare me a pang?

To my amazement—and probably God's as well—he did.
"You better have it X-rayed, Mom. Remember the time I
fell out of that old pear tree next door to our house in Portland and I crawled around for two days before you decided
it wasn't just a sprain?"

"Right," I said in a guilty voice. "It was your third crash-
and-burn in less than a month. I was getting blasé. Adam,
I got a letter from your father." Wincing as I pulled myself
onto the sofa, I waited for my son's reaction.

"No kidding." His voice had dropped an octave. "What
about?"

I explained, in as businesslike a tone as I could, caught
as I was in a web of pain and a wash of uncertainty. "So,"
I concluded, "this is your father's way of making a contribution to your education. I haven't yet checked on what the
airfare is between Ketchikan and Fairbanks, but—"

"I have," Adam put in, again amazing me. "Jeez, Mom,
that $2500 will pay for a ton of trips. Maybe I can come
home before school starts. Or go to Japan."

"Japan!" For just an instant, my foot didn't hurt any
more. My son's irresponsibility had obliterated my suffering. "Adam! Don't be an idiot! That isn't what Tom intended." I tried to simmer down and lower my voice. "Why
would you want to go to Japan anyway? Now, I mean."

"Don't you remember Miko Nagakawa, that major babe
I met just before I moved from Honolulu? She lives in
Kyoto. I called her last week and she said it would be cool
for me to come over any time."

"It's not cool," I said sternly. The foot was throbbing
again, so hard I was sure I could hear it. "Let her come
over here. As I recall, her father owns about six corpora-
tions and a couple of third world countries."

Eventually, it seemed that I had talked Adam out of his
notion to fly to Japan. As a veteran of the motherhood
wars, I've learned never to be certain of anything. But he
was definite—as definite as any young person his age—

about flying home for the Labor Day weekend. I didn't argue that one. I'd be too glad to see him.

"You go take care of your knee," he said, obviously no longer obsessed with my dilemma. "But give me his address, okay?"

"What?" I stopped, aware that Adam never called Tom by name, almost never referred to him as *father*. "Oh—you mean . . ." I faltered, feeling the moment's awkwardness.

"That's right." Adam suddenly sounded older. "I want to write a thank-you letter. To . . . *him*."

When I hung up, the tears in my eyes weren't just from pain.

Vida drove me to Doc Dewey's, half-carrying me to her car. She is literally a tower of strength, and I thanked her profusely.

"Don't be silly," she snapped. "If I didn't know better, I'd think you did this on purpose."

I gave her a sidelong look as we drove down Fourth Street in the twilight. "Maybe I did." Vida merely snorted.

Doc had directed us to go to the clinic, rather than the emergency room of the hospital. Young Doc was on duty and the father didn't want the son to think he was usurping patients. Or so Doc informed Vida when she made the call from my house.

"I can run an X-ray machine as well as any whippersnapper," Doc said, pushing a wheelchair toward us. "It's all these damned specialists who can't do anything but tend to one part of your anatomy. Take a bone man: he'd be out of luck trying to tell you what to do with a sore throat. Or a urologist—now there's a fellow who may know an asshole when he sees one on the examining table, but can't deal with one in real life. Specialists—no sense of a patient's overall well-being, girlies. Take my word for it."

Vida had wheeled me into the room which contained the portable X-ray unit while Doc lectured us and adjusted the equipment. He was wearing a faded cotton sports shirt and baggy suntan pants. His face was drawn and his color

seemed off, especially since we'd had so much sun in recent weeks.

With Vida's help, I got up on the examining table. Doc
was still griping about certain segments of the medical profession, interspersed with directions on how I should hold
my battered body.

"A first-year resident can make between twenty-five and
thirty thousand these days," he was saying as he clicked on
the X-ray machine. "Hell, I didn't make that much in the
first five years I was in practice. Try to turn your ankle to
the right, girlie. Oh, I know, everybody talks about infla-
tion, but I still say—no, no, a little more to the right . . .
That's better—the problem is, these young people are
spoiled today, they've been given everything . . ."

Doc rambled on. I realized Vida had slipped out of the
room. Gritting my teeth, I tried to keep the ankle from flop-
ping over into a less painful position.

"Just one more," Doc was saying. "Straight. Point that
toe, girlie."

I winced some more, but Doc was quick. He took the
films into the little darkroom while I tried to relax. I was
beginning to recover from the shock of the fall, which I felt
should be a good sign. But even as I collected my wits and
stared at the ceiling, my nerves became unraveled for different, more tragic reasons. By the time Doc emerged from
the darkroom, I was feeling giddy.

"No break," he said, plastering the three X-rays up
against the wall under a strong light. His thin fingers trailed
the outline of my foot bones. "It's a bad sprain, though,
girlie. Keep off it for about three days. You want crutches?"

My mind, which had been wandering in circles over
Cody Graff's corpse, snapped back to earth with a thud.
"Oh, Lord! I never could manage crutches!"

Doc eyed me sharply. "Can you stay home from work
for three days?"

"No," I admitted with a heavy sigh as he helped me sit
up. "I'd better get the damned crutches." At least there
were no stairs at *The Advocate* or inside my house.

Doc pushed me back into the waiting room just as Vida
came out of the supply closet. I was too preoccupied with
figuring out how to avoid getting blisters under my arms to
notice that she was holding something in her hand.

"Here, Doc," she said, unfolding her fingers. A small
glass bottle caught the overhead light. "I found some more
Haloperidol syrup. Do we congratulate you or call the sheriff?"

What little color Doc had retained was sapped by Vida's
words. His drawn face turned haggard and his hands shook
as he groped for the back of the nearest vinyl chair. He
seemed to shrivel up inside his shirt and pants. I realized
that his clothes weren't baggy so much as they were ill-
fitting. Doc had lost a considerable amount of weight. My
heart sank even deeper. "Call 'em," he replied. "And don't
forget Al Driggers. I don't want to cheat him out of an undertaking job."

We sat in Doc's office for close to an hour, with the
night enfolding the clinic like a shroud and the wind finally
blowing up through the river valley between the mountains.
Doc was behind his desk. Vida had the patient's seat. And
I languished in the wheelchair.

I'd interviewed murderers before. Some were sullen;
some were self-righteous; some were scared to death. There
had been a few I'd felt sorry for, but there had never been
one I'd admired. Until now. Doc might not have acted in
self-defense, but he'd killed Cody to save others. In effect,
he'd defended the community. Cecil Dewey had devoted a
lifetime to saving lives. Now he'd taken one, but only to
spare others. The earnest young priest, with his call for justice, had jolted my mind. It was Doc himself who had said
only God could straighten out the Marsh family's problems.
But Doc had decided not to wait for divine intervention.

"I couldn't let Cody marry Marje," Doc said flatly, after
he'd recovered from the shock of being discovered and ushered us into his private office. "She's been like a daughter
to me and she wouldn't listen to reason. But I knew that

what happened to Dani and little Scarlett could happen to
Marje and her baby some day. Cody was a vicious spoiled
brat with no conscience."

"He had charm," Vida put in. "*I* couldn't see it, but those
girls could. Girls can be so silly."

Doc nodded, a gesture that seemed to tax him. "Dani and
Marje may seem unalike, but they're not. Basically, they're
small-town girlies who figure they can reform the Cody
Graffs of this world." He gave a sad shake of his head. "No
woman can do that with any man, let alone a bad apple like
Cody."

Silence filled the room for a few moments, while the
three of us contemplated the futility of trying to improve on
nature. It was Vida who spoke next, her elbow resting on
Doc's desk and looking for all the world like a patient giving advice to her doctor.

"It was the denials that gave you away," she said.
"Nobody—at least among the people who could be considered suspects—would admit it was murder. When Emma
and I finally discovered that little Scarlett hadn't died of
SIDS, we assumed that either Dani or Cody had killed her.
Then we figured that Art Fremstad must have realized the
truth, so he was pushed over the falls. That didn't seem like
the work of a woman, especially a little thing like Dani. So
it had to be Cody, and of course it was Cody who was poisoned."

Doc inclined his head. His eyelids seemed very heavy,
but when he looked up at us, his gaze was as shrewd as
ever. "I knew, too. I went around looking over my shoulder
for almost a year. And Curtis—I think he guessed, but he
didn't want to turn in his own brother, and he was in love
with Dani."

"Was the baby his?" I asked.

Doc frowned. "I've never been sure, but I think so.
Which may be why Cody killed the poor little thing. But I
wouldn't have put it past him to do it to his own. God help
us, it happens. My problem was that I wasn't positive who
had smothered that tyke. And maybe I was wrong. It's not

the kind of thing you run around asking people to help you
make up your mind. If it had been Dani, she'd left town
and there was nothing I could do about her. As for Cody,
as long as he wasn't remarried or living with some woman
who had kids, I figured it was best to let sleeping dogs lie.
I could have done an autopsy, but I didn't have the heart for
it. And somehow, knowing that one of the parents—maybe
both, as it turned out, if Curtis was Scarlett's father—were
innocent, I couldn't put them through that. It was a mistake,
of course."

I gave Doc a sympathetic look. "But it didn't happen
again, and that was the main thing."

Doc turned very grave. "It might have saved Art
Fremstad, if I'd acted fast enough."

Vida's jaw thrust out. "You and Curtis and even Dani
might have ended up dead, too, Doc. You can't look at it
like that."

Doc shrugged. I scooted the chair forward a few inches.
"All along I kept feeling as if I were watching scenes from
a movie," I said, unable to keep from wondering how long
it would be before I could get some painkiller inside my
aching body. "How much of all that was make-believe?"

Doc scratched his bald spot. "Not as much as you'd
think. Patti always blamed Dani, and Dani was never sure
what had happened. But when Curtis came back to town
and told Dani and Patti what he thought was true, they
joined forces. Then Reid and that actor fellow got into the
act, too. After all, Scarlett was Reid's granddaughter as
much as Patti's. They came to me one evening and asked
what I thought. Then they asked what ought to be done
about it." He stared at his hands which were lying flat on
the desk. "I'd already tried to talk Marje out of marrying
Cody. Now it seemed that I was being asked to administer
justice. I considered going to Milo, but what could we
prove? It never occurred to me that Art Fremstad had been
murdered, at least not by anyone around here. Maybe I
didn't want to believe it. Art wasn't the suicidal type, that's
for sure. But," Doc went on and his words were meant for

me, rather than Vida, "a small town is the center of the universe to the people who live there. Even though we know better, we like to believe that its imperfections aren't as bad as other places'."

I tried to give Doc a thin smile of understanding. "So you and the others formed a sort of pact?"

"There was never much said out loud." Doc leaned back in his chair and let out a weary sigh. "The rest of them had somehow designated me as their avenging angel. They tried to create a smokescreen by carrying on as if they were all still mad at each other—at least Dani and Patti did—but the only one who was really disturbed by Dani's return to Alpine was Cody. He may have hated her, but mostly I think he was afraid of her. I'd bet my bottom dollar he would have liked to have landed that axe right in her gizzard."

"I was never in favor of Marje marrying Cody, either," sniffed Vida. "I said something to her parents once, which wasn't enough, because my brother and his wife are both dumb as a brick wall. And Marje thought I was being an old fogey."

"But," I noted quietly, "Marje knew, didn't she?"

Doc again nodded. "I told her. After he was dead. She carried on something fierce when she heard he'd been hit by a car. She called me at the hotel in Seattle that Sunday, all upset. I didn't let on then, I hoped maybe the whole thing would actually be passed off as an accident. But after Cody's autopsy, I called her back a couple of days later and told her what Cody had done to little Scarlett. She cried some more. But she thanked me."

"For what?" The question fell out of my mouth.

Doc gave a little grunt. "For saving her, I guess." He glanced at Vida, then looked back at me. "If I'd told her earlier what I thought Cody had done to that baby, she might not have believed me. Even if she had, there would have been another foolish girl and another innocent baby. Nobody—not Dani, not Patti, not Curtis, not me, by God— wanted that. I think Marje guessed . . . what I'd done to Cody."

Vida nodded vigorously. "Of course she did. Marje tried to divert Billy Blatt and Milo by saying Cody was taking Haloperidol. But he wasn't. You and Marje were really the only ones who could have put the stuff into Cody's beer. In fact, you put it in all three of his beers, didn't you, Doc?"

He gave a little grunt of assent. "I had to be sure. Nobody can calculate an individual's tolerance."

"I guessed that," I put in. "Cody was already showing signs of drunkenness when I got to the tavern with Carla and Ginny. You were the only one on duty behind the bar and you'd been there the whole time, doing your two-hour stint. I wondered about the bottles of Haloperidol, then I remembered that clicking sound in your pocket. Although it didn't register at the time, it was glass striking glass. I finally realized that when Honoria and I toasted Milo."

Vida shot me a sidelong glance, but this was no time to get distracted. "I thought the person with the poison"—I was careful to avoid the word *killer*, which seemed so ill-suited to Doc—"might be taking a risk by bringing the stuff into the tavern, but if you were found with it, no one would think twice. You're a doctor. Still, I had to wonder if you were concerned about being found out."

Letting out a disdainful breath, Doc scowled at me. "I sure was! My family, my reputation, the whole works, would—will—be hurt. I didn't want that to happen. I may have killed somebody, but I'm not nuts."

"Of course not," Vida agreed. "You carried it off beautifully. This is all conjecture, Doc. I doubt that a serious case could be made against you."

"Oh, I don't know," mused Doc. "It could be done if we had a decent prosecutor in this county." He seemed quite untroubled, however, his clinical air intact.

"Witnesses are so unreliable," Vida remarked. "Dani passed the mug along, but someone might have seen her tamper with it."

"Actually," I noted, "Jack Blackwell could have done it, since he was behind the bar. He had no motive, unless he was acting on behalf of Patti. But I ruled him out when

Honoria Whitman told me he hadn't touched Cody's beer. Neither did Reid or Matt or Patti herself. Honoria never mentioned Donna Fremstad Wickstrom. I doubt she knew who Donna was, but I never seriously considered her anyway because I honestly don't think she knew Cody killed Art until the last few days. If she did, and had wanted revenge, she would have acted much sooner." I paused, my voice tired and my ankle making my ears ring with pain. "Curtis Graff was there, but he was nowhere near his brother. That left you and Marje, Doc. And I had to believe Honoria would have seen Marje if she'd been the one with the Haloperidol." Oddly enough, the once-unfamiliar word slipped easily off my tongue. I was beginning to know its name all too well. "But Vida's right. Conflicting testimony, no concrete evidence—it's all circumstantial."

Vida was making stabbing gestures on Doc's desk with her forefinger. "Tell me this, Doc—was it planned that Dani would drive Cody out and dump him by the Burl Creek Road?"

Doc's tired face wrinkled up, then sagged again. "No. There was no plan, as such. But I think Dani knew what I'd done and she hoped to make it look like an accident, so she borrowed Matt's car—more smokescreen, maybe—and went over to Cody's. I'm surprised he could get as far as the street, but he must have, unless she had help."

"Maybe she did," I suggested. "Maybe there were two cars." Had Dani lost her eyeliner while she was trying to get Cody out of the car? Or had Patti, perhaps with Reid Hampton in tow, actually dropped it? The point was now moot. "Reid or Matt or even Curtis might have been driving the other one."

"Could be." Doc looked as if not only the subject at hand, but the world itself had gotten very tiresome. "When are you going to call Milo?" The question was put to Vida.

For once, she actually squirmed. "Ooooh . . . I don't know—he may not be back from Seattle yet." Her hand went to her glasses, then her hair, and finally came to rest

on the edge of the desk. "Doc, what did they tell you in Seattle?"

He lifted his hands, which still trembled slightly. "Three
months, six at most. It's lymphatic. I diagnosed myself, you
know."

"I should think so," Vida retorted, bridling a bit at the
mere suggestion that Doc would allow some big city specialist to figure out his condition.

Doc was on his feet, moving toward the door. "Parker's
is closed," he said. "I'll get something out of the supply
closet for you, girlie."

"Okay," I said, much relieved. I had the good sense not
to tell him to skip the Haloperidol.

Chapter Eighteen

MILO SHOWED ME how to shift my body and thus keep my weight on my hands rather than my armpits. I thanked my lucky stars I only weighed a hundred and twenty-five pounds. I cursed the Fates that had made every ounce so clumsy.

"Damn," said Milo, after he'd finished his demonstration and was lapping up a beer, "what do I do now?"

"That," I replied, lying on the sofa like a nineteenth-century tubercular heroine, with a bowl of popcorn as an unlikely prop, "is up to you."

"Hell." Milo was staring at Honoria's ceramic blob which I had put on the coffee table for want of a better venue. "This puts me in a terrible spot," he muttered. "If I arrest Doc, the whole town will hate me and I could lose the election to Hitler. If I don't make an arrest, I'm a goner, too."

I moved my ankle, complete with tightly wrapped Ace bandage, slightly to the left. "You have to see that justice is done, Milo." I put absolutely no emotion into my words. The truth was, I didn't have much left.

"Yeah, sure, right . . ." Milo's annoyance could have been with me or with the concept. Maybe both. Finally it dawned on him that he wasn't the only professional who was on the hook. Since it was almost midnight and we'd been hashing Cody Graff's death over since ten-thirty, it was about time. But as Vida says: *men aren't like other people.* I could hardly have expected him to consider anybody's position but his own so quickly.

459

"Say, Emma," he said, rolling the beer can between his hands. "What are you going to do about this? You've got one hell of a story."

I gave him my most innocent gaze. "Only if you make an arrest, Sheriff. Otherwise, I've got hearsay and a libel suit." It was a non-story, and I mustn't beat myself over the head for suppressing the news.

"Oh." Milo slumped with disappointment. I didn't add that if I were back in Portland, working on *The Oregonian*, I would have used the information I had to rock City Hall. If some doctor had poisoned somebody else, no matter how benign the killer or how malignant the victim, I would have seen it as my professional duty to bring the culprit to justice. But that was Portland, and this was Alpine. I knew Doc Dewey. I knew Cody Graff. I knew what had gone before, and what might have been. I would rather burn *The Advocate* to the ground than sully Doc's reputation.

"Cancer, huh?" murmured Milo. I nodded. Milo swore. "What'll we do without Doc?" There was a plaintive note in the sheriff's voice.

"There's young Doc, and I suppose he'll get somebody new. It would have happened eventually. Doc must be seventy, at least."

"Seventy-four," said Milo, into his beer can. The words echoed; the can must be empty.

"Go get another beer," I urged. "And bring me some milk instead of Pepsi this time. I'm getting high enough on Percodan."

Milo complied, loping back with a glass of milk and a Miller. The ale was gone. Reclining in the rocker, Milo closed his eyes. "Everybody says it was an accident. An overdose maybe." He spoke musingly. "It's Art I'm thinking of . . ."

"Donna knows the truth," I put in. "Isn't that enough?"
Milo's eyes flickered open. "It is if she tells it."
"She'll only have to tell it once."
"True."
We lapsed into silence. In the distance, I could hear the

midnight train, followed by a roll of thunder. I smiled to myself. Perhaps the heat wave was breaking, at least for a day or so. All up and down the Cascades, I could imagine rain beginning to fall, up on the mountain crests, down into the foothills, onto the hillsides, and eventually, with luck, all over Alpine.

"I could stall." Milo lifted his head from the back of the rocker.

"For six months? A year?"

"People forget."

"In Alpine?"

Milo gave me a twisted grin. "No. But they get sidetracked. And sometimes even when they don't forget, they forgive."

I smiled back at Milo. "Go for it."

Milo's grin widened, then he sobered abruptly. "Go for what, Emma?"

Our gazes locked. I heard myself let out a little gasp. Then I started to giggle. "Oh, Milo, you dope, you know what I mean! Besides, right now, I'm a helpless cripple. What about Honoria?"

Milo turned sheepish. "She's a helpless cripple, too."

"Oh, dear. You know the strangest women!" My giggles were verging on hysteria, the result of emotion, pain, and Percodan. "I should go to bed."

A bit clumsily, Milo got to his feet. He loomed over me. "How are you going to get there?"

"Damned if I know," I admitted.

Milo sighed. "I'll help. Then I'll sleep on the couch. Don't argue. Nobody's waiting up for me at home. Damn it, Emma, why can't we be as sexually irresponsible as our children?"

"We weren't raised that way," I replied. And wondered what that said about the likes of Milo and me as parents. By the time I put my head on the pillow in my bed and Milo had settled down in the living room, I decided that maybe our children were smarter than we were. Or was it that our own parents had been wiser? Again, maybe it was the Percodan. . . .

" 'Robert Cohn was once middleweight boxing champion of Princeton. Cal Vickers paused to clear his throat, take a sip of beer from his mug, and receive a glance of approval from Vida. Do not think that I am very much impressed by that as a boxing title, but it meant a lot to Cohn.' "

Cal's monotone droned on, as he read the opening chapter of Ernest Hemingway's *The Sun Also Rises*. I sat back on my orange crate, while the crowd of customers at the Icicle Creek Tavern listened to the fourth reader of the evening.

Vida's brainstorm had been a success. Over fifty patrons had brought an eclectic array of books to the Saturday night gathering. New paperbacks from the drugstore rack, old novels culled from boxes in dusty attics, books checked out on seldom used or often abused library cards, even a collection of Latvian recipes, rested on the tavern's rough tabletops and blemished bar.

During the past six days, we had had a rainstorm that lasted less than an hour, a minor earthquake with the epicenter just south of the Canadian border in Whatcom County, and the resumption of our hot, dry summer. Reid Hampton had been released from the hospital, had apparently made up with Matt Tabor, and *Blood Along the River* was proclaimed a wrap about the same time *The Advocate* hit the street on Wednesday. Our building was still the color of Vida's canary, but we were promised it would be repainted in thirty days. I disposed of my crutches on Thursday, though I still walked with a limp that Doc Dewey informed me would last until Labor Day. But it was mid-August, and if I peeked at the calendar, autumn would officially commence in just a little over a month. But I didn't peek. I never do—for fear that somehow I will jinx the change of seasons.

Milo was sitting between Honoria and me, wedged in at

the same table the two of them had shared the night Cody Graff had been poisoned. Two weeks had passed since Cody had staggered out the door on Marje Blatt's arm. It seemed like a lifetime. On Monday, Milo had announced that the investigation of Cody's death was closed. He and Doc Dewey, who was the county coroner, after all, had come to the conclusion that Cody had accidentally overdosed. I wrote the story for Wednesday's front page, but kept it to under two inches of copy, buried in the lower left corner. No one called or wrote to question the article. Maybe that was because the much longer piece that surrounded the Graff announcement had dealt with Tacoma City Light's desire to build a dam on the Skykomish River. Since such a project might threaten the already meager number of fish in the river, Alpiners took umbrage and personally blamed me for such a harebrained scheme. The locals knew their priorities, and Cody Graff was no longer numbered among them.

Fuzzy Baugh was now reading a Tennessee Williams play, changing his voice up and down, depending upon the speaker's sex. The relic of a New Orleans accent that remained in Fuzzy's voice lent authenticity, which was a blessing—because he couldn't act worth a hoot. Vida, seated on a tall stool behind the bar, kept a poker face; I tried not to snicker when I caught her eye.

Feeling a jab in my shoulder, I craned my neck, careful not to upset my orange crate. Patti Marsh and Jack Blackwell stood behind me. She carried a Jackie Collins paperback; he held a hardcover Elmore Leonard.

Patti leaned over to whisper in my ear. "Dani called from L.A. this afternoon. She's decided to make at least one more movie."

"For Reid?"

Patti's laugh was on the wry side. "Yeah. Co-starring Matt. Reid—Ray—thinks they're *hot*."

"They certainly looked hot in all those winter clothes," I replied, forgetting to whisper. Fuzzy Baugh frowned at me in his most mayoral manner, then resumed reading Maggie the Cat's impassioned lines to her husband Brick.

Patti started to edge away, but Blackwell stayed put. He addressed his words not to me, however, but to Milo. "It looks like you're unopposed, Dodge. You feeling comfortable?"

Fuzzy had concluded his scene, so Milo was able to speak in his normal voice. "I do now. Averill Fairbanks had me worried for a minute there."

Blackwell snorted in disdain. "Averill! He's nuts." When Milo didn't argue, Jack slapped the sheriff's shoulder. "Don't get too cozy under that badge, pal." His grin wasn't exactly sinister, but it would have gone well with a curling mustache and a flowing black cape. Jack Blackwell might not be as evil as he seemed, but I still didn't like him much. I was betting he always rooted for Leonard's sleaziest characters. "I'm going to the courthouse Monday and file for sheriff myself."

Milo choked on a mouthful of small pretzels. *"You . . ."* It was hard to tell if the word was a question or an accusation.

"Why not?" said Blackwell, as Vida introduced the local dentist, Dr. Bob Starr, who had brought along Lawrence Sanders's latest deadly sin. "It's not that hard to run a timber company when the woods are shut down for two to three months at a time with this lousy hot weather. Who knows? The way things are going, it could be curtains for the whole frigging industry. It might be smart to have a sideline." He gave Patti a light slap on the behind. "Let's go, babe. Milo wants to play games with his pair under the table. His guns, I mean." Blackwell leered at Honoria, then at me, and sauntered off in the wake of Patti's swaying hips.

"Damn," breathed Milo.

Honoria surveyed him over the rim of her plastic wine glass. "He won't beat you." Her tone brooked no argument.

"It's still a pain," said Milo. But he gave Honoria a grateful smile.

"It's a democracy," I noted, trying to keep my voice down so that Dr. Starr's audience could hear him say something other than "Wider."

"Maybe Blackwell's kidding," said Milo as the dentist stepped down to polite applause.

"Maybe," I allowed. Honoria said nothing.

Vida was standing up, thanking all those who had participated in the reading and everyone who had brought a book. Of our trio, only Honoria had read aloud, leading off the program with Anne Lindbergh's *Gift from the Sea*. Milo had brought a book on fly-fishing, which he admitted he'd never opened. I toted a much-worn, two generations-old copy of *Winnie-the-Pooh*.

". . . to continue reading, not because you have to, but because you want to," Vida was saying. "If you think back to the early days of Alpine, what did those first settlers do in the long winter evenings?"

"Screw!" It was, of course, Janet Driggers.

Vida gave her a flinty smile. "Besides that. We are, after all, a small town, so they must have done something else. They read. And they did it by Coleman lantern for the first twenty years or more. Alpine was always a remarkably literate town. I'd hate to see that reputation lost." She paused, turning to her left. "To end this fine evening of books and beer, I'd like to present one of our most beloved and distinguished citizens. Ladies and gentlemen, I give you Dr. Cecil Dewey."

Doc was wearing a suit and tie with a white dress shirt. He looked shrunken, yet undaunted. His hands no longer shook as he held them up to quiet the raucous ovation. I glanced at Milo, whose long face was wistful. Did Honoria know? Probably not. She was wearing her most serene expression as Doc read from Samuel Clemens's speech delivered on the occassion of his seventieth birthday. Doc spoke in a clear, strong voice:

" '. . . This is my swan-song . . . Threescore years and ten! It is the Scriptural statute of limitations . . . You have served your term, well or less well, and you are mustered

out . . . you are emancipated, compulsions are not for you
. . . You pay the time-worn duty bills if you choose, or decline if your prefer—and without prejudice—for they are
not legally collectable.

" '. . . Keep me in your remembrance, and . . . wishing
you well in all affection, and that when you . . . shall arrive
at Pier No. 70 you may step aboard your waiting ship with
a reconciled spirit, and lay your course toward the sinking
sun with a contented heart.' "

Until then, I'd never seen Vida with tears in her eyes.

Doc's funeral was held on the Saturday after Thanksgiving at Trinity Episcopal Church. The rector, the gaunt-faced
Regis Bartleby, whose ascetic appearance belied his horse-
like appetite, gave a fine eulogy. Fuzzy Baugh's words
were fulsome, and Young Doc's reminiscences were suitably personal. But the truth was, I thought Doc had given
himself a better send-off at the Icicle Creek Tavern on that
August evening three months earlier.

There was snow on the ground, almost six inches of it,
and the forecast called for more throughout the weekend.
Indeed, it had started snowing in early November, typical
for Alpine. We might not see bare earth until April.

Though in fact, we were seeing it now, as we stood
around Doc's grave and waited for the casket to be lowered. I had one hand on Vida's tweed coat sleeve, and
Adam draped an arm around my shoulders. He had gotten
in from Fairbanks Wednesday afternoon, his second trip
home in three months.

The rector intoned the final prayers as a few flakes of
new snow drifted down over the cemetery. The church had
been packed, and at least a hundred brave souls had ventured up the hill for the burial service. Milo, newly re-
elected in a walk over Jack Blackwell, had been one of the
pallbearers, along with Dr. Starr, Fuzzy Baugh, and
Durwood Parker, who, thankfully, had not been required to
drive. At the head of the grave, Doc's widow was leaning
on her son, clutching a rumpled handkerchief in her gloved

hand and looking very brave. When Regis Bartleby presented the American flag to Mrs. Dewey, Young Doc kissed his mother's cheek.

"Medical Corps, Army Air Force, World War II," whispered Vida. "Stationed in England, 1943 to 1945."

"I know," I whispered back. "I read your obit."

Under her black felt bowler, Vida frowned at me. "It's not finished."

Out of the corner of my eye, I saw Donna Fremstad Wickstrom approach the grave. She hesitated, teetering on her high heeled calfskin boots, then dropped a single white rose onto the casket. I turned back to Vida.

"Yes, it is," I said.

Vida gazed at Mrs. Dewey and Young Doc. Marje Blatt had joined them. She hugged Mrs. Dewey and glanced in her aunt's direction. Marje smiled.

"You're right," said Vida. "It's finished."

Adam wanted to get a tan. "Two days at Malibu," he said for the fifth time. "That's all. Hey, Mom, I've got mucho money. I can come home for Christmas, then Easter, maybe even a midwinter break. But, man, I've got to catch some rays."

"You're not a native; you're a changeling," I accused. We had just dropped Vida off after the reception at the Dewey house. Adam was driving, having developed a love as great as mine for the green Jaguar. "If you fly to L.A. tomorrow, even for two days, you'll miss Monday and Tuesday classes. Wait until Christmas break. You'll have over three weeks of freedom."

To my surprise, Adam seemed to be considering my suggestion. Surreptitiously, I watched his profile. As he matured and the angles sharpened, the likeness to his father grew even more apparent. Except for his eyes and twenty years of bills, there was nothing to show my claim on this son of mine.

"Okay," he finally agreed, leaning back into the leather bucket seat as he maneuvered the slippery corner onto Fir

Street. The snow was coming down harder now. With a sinking feeling, it occurred to me that by tomorrow afternoon, the pass might be closed.

"It's not snowing in Seattle," I said suddenly. "Do you want to drive in tonight, catch a Sonics game if they're in town, and stay over?"

Adam eased into my driveway. "Sonics—or Warriors?"

I started to make a face of noncomprehension before his meaning dawned on me. "The sun doesn't shine in the Bay Area this time of year, not even where the Golden State Warriors play. At least not much. Were you talking L.A. or S.F.?"

"L.A.," he answered, his brown-eyed gaze level with mine. "But now I'm thinking S.F. I could fly down there and be back in Fairbanks Monday morning."

I kept my voice steady. "Is that what you want to do?"

Adam looked away, to the windshield, which was already almost covered with thick flakes of snow. "I'm not sure. I'd call first."

"Good thinking." I should be giving him advice, I told myself. Or encouragement. Or something. Instead, I waited.

"Would he pitch a four-star fit?" Adam continued to stare at the white windshield.

"Probably not. As long as it wasn't awkward for Mrs. Cavanaugh."

Now he turned again to face me. "Do you want to come?"

"No." I gave a single shake of my head. "Not this time."

"It's the first time," Adam pointed out.

Let's hope it's not the only time, I thought, and was astonished at my reaction. "That's okay."

Adam opened the car door. "I'll call now, then check the flights," he said into a flurry blowing out of the north.

"I'll get the number," I responded, careful to watch my footing on the surface of newly fallen snow. There were times when my ankle still hurt.

Inside the house, I busied myself while Adam took up the phone. On my knees, I shoved crumpled newspaper under the grate, piled up kindling, and dumped a couple of logs on top. Striking a match, I tensed as I heard Adam's voice, tentative but clear.

"Hi, this is Adam Lord. Your son."

I caught my breath. How like Adam to be so direct! What must Tom be thinking? I tried to picture him at the other end, gripping the receiver and chewing on his lower lip.

Adam was laughing. "Right, I'm in Alpine ... Yeah, well, I've got all this money. . . . Huh? Right, she's fine, she's here playing with matches. . . . No, not till Monday, so I thought maybe I'd fly down to—okay, sure, right. . . . No, I haven't checked with the airlines yet." Still grinning, Adam glanced over at me and gave a thumbs-up sign. "I'll call you when I land. What? Call ahead from Sea-Tac? Okay. Thanks ... sir."

I struck a match and set off the fire. But it was Adam who had lighted up the world.

THE
ALPINE
CHRISTMAS

Chapter One

FATHER FITZ HAD lost it. That didn't come as a surprise to those of us who were his regular parishioners, but it knocked the socks off my brother, Ben. Luckily, Ben has enough poise as a person and experience as a priest that he didn't fall off the altar.

On holy days of obligation, Father Kiernan Fitzgerald always managed to keep mass under forty minutes. Since December 8 commemorates the Immaculate Conception of the Blessed Virgin, I attended the eight o'clock service on my way to work at *The Alpine Advocate*. Ben was concelebrating the liturgy while on vacation from his job as pastor to the Navajos in Tuba City, Arizona.

It is always with a sense of pride that I watch Ben say mass. Like me, he is dark and brown-eyed; he has the same round face (but more nose), and an extra six inches of height. He is not handsome and I am not beautiful, yet—as our late parents used to say—we make a very presentable pair. When we try. Certainly Ben looks most impressive in the vestments that some of his female parishioners made for him, complete with Navajo symbols of sun, earth, and sky.

The fifty parishioners and one hundred schoolchildren from St. Mildred's sat huddled together in winter coats and heavy-duty footgear. At the left of the altar, two purple candles burned in an Advent wreath fashioned from fir, cedar, and pine. The remaining candles, one pink and the other

473

purple, would be lighted on the last two Sundays before Christmas.

Outside, three feet of snow covered the ground. As usual, winter had arrived early in Alpine. At over two thousand feet above sea level, we were not only in the mountains, we were part of them. I turned my attention to Father Fitz as he stood to give the final blessing.

"I have some announcements," he said in his low, mellifluous voice with its trace of County Cork. Father Fitz's legs might be crippled by arthritis, his hearing may be poor, but there is nothing wrong with the way he speaks. "Last week's Christmas bazaar brought in $1,185.37. Half we'll be giving to the school, the other half to the families of unemployed loggers. God bless you for your generosity and hard work." He paused, peering at his notes through thick trifocals. "The school Nativity pageant, *Elvis Meets the Three Wise Men*, will take place Thursday, December 17th, in the school hall at seven P.M." He gave the principal, Mrs. Monica Vancich, a glance of disapproval. Mrs. Vancich smiled serenely, then tweaked the white shirt collar of Joey Bronsky, a notorious fidgeter and my ad manager's son. Joey snapped to.

Father Fitz continued: "Finally, we ask you all to pray for the repose of the souls of the thousands of brave Americans who died in yesterday's attack on Pearl Harbor in the Hawaiian Islands. Monstrous cruel it was, and our president will be needing your prayers as well. May Almighty God keep Mr. Roosevelt." Father Fitz turned to his breviary. "The Lord be with you."

"And also with you." The congregation's response was a little wobbly. I caught Ben's eye. He was staring stonily ahead, his face tight. It was a sure sign that he was trying not to laugh.

Father Fitz bestowed the last blessing and dismissed us. Annie Jeanne Dupré pumped away at the old organ as the congregation launched into an off-key rendition of "Immaculate Mary.'' Father Fitz and Ben left the altar, the school-children began to file out in a disorderly fashion, and little clutches of worshippers buzzed in the aisles, presumably about Father Fitz's unfortunate lapse. I edged off to a side altar where the statue of St. Joseph seemed to wear a bemused air. I was waiting for Ben and didn't want to get caught up in controversy just yet. I faced enough of that every day in my job as editor and publisher of *The Advocate*.

It wasn't unusual for our officially retired pastor to operate in a time warp. His sermons often reflected an era of bootleg liquor, creeping Communism, or family life lived only by Andy Hardy. This, however, was the first time he'd enlisted his parishioners' prayers for a event long past.

Except for Mrs. Patricelli, who was lighting enough votive candles to bake a ham, the church had grown empty. I could feel the cold come through the stained glass windows and hear the wind stir in the belfry. It was going on nine in the morning and very gloomy outside. The heavy gray clouds had been hanging over Alpine since early November. We might glimpse the sun before May, but we wouldn't see the ground. Only seven miles from the summit of Stevens Pass in the Cascade Mountains, the four thousand residents of Alpine knew winter far better than most Pacific Northwesterners. Eighty miles away in Seattle, I suspected it was fifty degrees with a seventy percent chance of rain.

Ben came from the sacristy just as Mrs. Patricelli ran out of matches. On her way out, she beamed at my brother, a gap-toothed, maternal smile, befitting the mother of nine and grandmother of eighteen. Maybe they were the reason for all the candles. The last I'd heard, her oldest was president of a bank in Yakima and her youngest was doing time for embezzling. Not, I guessed, from his brother's bank.

Ben had planned on taking himself to breakfast at the Venison Eat Inn and Take Out after mass. "I'd better skip the ride downtown," he said in his crackling voice that could keep even the sleepiest parishioner awake during a sermon. "Father Fitz is pretty shaky and the housekeeper is upset."

"Mrs. McHale? Really?" Teresa McHale had been the housekeeper at the rectory for a little over a year, but she struck me as having a cast-iron disposition. "Is Father Fitz sick or just daffy?"

"He went through his usual routine this morning: up at six, got dressed and showered, devotions in his room, heard confessions at seven-thirty for the holy day, then readied for mass. He seemed fine, but Mrs. McHale wants to call Doc Dewey." Ben steered me down the aisle toward the main entrance. "She thinks Father may have had a little stroke."

"Oh, dear." I pulled on my driving gloves as we stood in the vestibule. At eighty-nine, a stroke couldn't be a surprise. Still, in the second week of Advent, Father Fitz's timing was lousy. Or, I thought, glancing up at Ben, maybe not. "Could you take over?"

Ben rolled his eyes. He was back in his street clothes, thick navy sweater, blue jeans, and knee-high boots. He was very tan from his assignment in the desert. "So there goes twenty days of my twenty-one day vacation? Hell, Emma, I just got here day before yesterday."

"Ben . . ." I sounded reproachful. "You're a priest, after all. . . ."

"A *tired* priest," he put in, looking unwontedly grim. "After twenty years, I finally got things halfway organized down on the Mississippi Delta, then I get shipped to the Navajo reservation a year ago and have to start all over. To make matters worse, the Mormons got to Tuba City first— over a hundred years ago. And the Hopis have been plucked right down in the middle of the Navajos. No wonder they hate each other. The federal government's relocation in the Seventies still causes hard feelings. Now D.C.'s got a new plan, but who knows if it'll work. It's rough out there on the fringes of the Painted Desert. I'm almost forty-five, Emma.

I have this dream of a well-heeled, well-oiled parish in the suburbs. Alpine ain't it, Sluggly."

I grinned at the old nickname, a cross between Sluggo and Ugly. "You'd last about two weeks in the suburbs, Stench," I asserted, retaliating with my childhood moniker for him. "You thrive on adversity and you know it. Besides, it may be only a few days. Think not of your vacation, but of your vocation."

"The parishioners might resent my stepping in." Ben rubbed the thatch of brown hair that he combed off a side part. "On the other hand, I *am* here. . . ." One of Ben's flaws is his indecisiveness. He always sees six sides of any issue. I have a similar tendency, which I regard as journalistic objectivity. But with deadlines to meet, I can't often indulge myself. Conversely, Ben's propensity for equivocation has grown more pronounced over the years, perhaps as a result of two decades spent in the slow lane along the Mississippi Delta.

We argued briefly, and at last he gave in as I knew he would. "I'll have to check with the arch," he said, referring to the archbishop in Seattle. "But first we'd better see how bad Father Fitz really is. I don't want to usurp his authority. You know how proprietary these old pastors can be, especially the ones from Ireland."

I was about to concur when Teresa McHale entered the vestibule from the church proper. She gave me the briefest of nods, murmured "Mrs. Lord," and then addressed Ben: "I called young Doc Dewey. He's in surgery, but that new man, Peyton Flake, will be over as soon as he finishes cleaning his guns."

Teresa McHale had replaced Edna McPhail, who had served in the rectory for over thirty years. Edna had died the previous year, suffering a heart attack while cleaning the bathtub. Since Edna was some ten years younger than Father Fitz, he had presumed she would outlive him. When she didn't, he had a tizzy and put an ad not only in the church bulletin but *The Advocate* as well. Except for a well-known alcoholic and a woman whose wits could be most kindly described as lacking, there were no takers.

Alpine is predominantly Scandinavian, and there are only about seven hundred registered Catholic parishioners in the vicinity. Since half of these are either too young or too old, and half of the rest are men, that doesn't leave a large labor pool of would-be housekeepers on which to draw. Father Fitz had called the Chancery in Seattle for help. He got it, in the form of Teresa McHale. I suspected he viewed the replacement of McPhail by McHale as a minor miracle.

Teresa did not look like a typical parish housekeeper, being rather chic, at least for Alpine, sporting dyed red hair, considerable makeup, and a plump, unbridled figure. She had strong features and shrewd green eyes adorned with long false lashes. Yet from all accounts, she was very efficient, and Father Fitz had not been heard to complain, though naturally some of the parishioners did.

"I'll go sit with Father," said Ben, giving me a punch in the upper arm. "Later, Sluggly."

I took my cue and headed out into a world of white. My green Jaguar was the only car in the lot between the church and the school. St. Mildred's had been built shortly after World War I, a white frame structure that would have been right at home in New England. The rectory, which was connected to the church by a covered walk, was of the same vintage, a one-story frame house with a basement, and enough room for two priests as well as a housekeeper. The parochial school was much newer, from the early Fifties, with a beige brick facade, an even newer gymnasium, and a school hall that also served as a lunchroom. The convent had stood behind the church, approximately where my car was now parked. About twenty years ago, when the shortage of nuns forced the school to hire lay teachers, vexed parishioners refused to pay for renovation of the convent. The archbishop had gotten a bit vexed as well, and had ordered the convent razed. Any nuns who taught at St. Mildred's were forced to live elsewhere. At present, there were two, Sister Clare and Sister Mary Joan, who shared an apartment in a three-story building across the street.

The Jag started immediately, and I drove carefully into the drifting flakes, hearing my chains grind and crunch. Alpine is built on a mountainside, which makes for very dicey driving in the winter. I eased my way down Fourth Street, past the Baptist Church, Mugs Ahoy, the local bank, and finally, the intersection at Front Street. The newspaper office was across the street, repainted a tasteful light blue after its brief passage of egg-yolk yellow during a film crew's location shoot the previous summer.

Ed Bronsky's station wagon was pulled up to the curb, as was the white Buick sedan that belonged to my House & Home editor, Vida Runkel. My sole reporter, Carla Steinmetz, had probably walked to work, as had our office manager, Ginny Burmeister. Carla had owned a car of sorts when she first arrived in Alpine after graduating from the University of Washington a year and a half ago, but she had turned it in last September for a motor scooter. Naturally, it didn't work very well in the snow, but neither did Carla. In fact, Carla didn't work very well under any conditions, but at least she was enthusiastic.

Vida was playing the trombone. Badly. I winced and put my gloved hands over my ears. "Stop!" I shrieked. "Why are you doing that?"

Vida gave one last toot and put the trombone down on the empty chair next to her desk. "It was stolen from the high school last night. Somebody broke into the band room. My nephew Billy found it this morning at the base of Carl Clemans's statue in Old Mill Park." She rummaged under her desk. "There's a piccolo, too. And a pair of drumsticks."

Bill Blatt was not only Vida's nephew—as I sometimes thought half of Alpine was—but also a deputy sheriff. "So why didn't Billy take the instruments back to the high school?''

Vida, who is in her early sixties, and exudes an aura of rumpled majesty, shrugged her wide, multilayered shoulders. ''He intended to, but he got a call from the sheriff, so he left them here. For the time being.''

''Milo was having a cow,'' said Carla, bouncing up from her chair and looking like a Christmas elf in her red parka. ''He raised his voice on the phone. I actually *heard* him.''

I gazed at Carla. Excitement did not become Sheriff Dodge. Carla, I felt, must be exaggerating. ''I thought Milo was taking the morning off to go steelheading.''

Ed looked up from a dummy ad for Barton's Bootery. He was wearing an old overcoat that was two sizes too small for his ever-expanding girth. ''Why bother? Fishing's terrible around here these days. I haven't gone out in five years.''

An eternal pessimist, Ed probably wouldn't have hit the Skykomish River if a twenty-pound steelhead had flopped onto his desk. ''Milo caught two last winter,'' I remarked, taking off my purple car coat and discovering that the news office was freezing. ''What happened to our heat?''

Ed gave me a doleful look. ''It broke. The Public Utility District's having problems. They're going to try to fix it by this afternoon.''

''Great.'' I gazed down at the baseboard that ordinarily would be emitting comfortable waves of warmth. Stubbornly, I refused to put my car coat back on. I might not be a native Alpiner, but I wasn't going to give in to a spate of twenty-degree weather. ''Okay, so what's with Milo?'' I inquired, getting back to the sheriff's uncustomary state of excitement.

But Ed was picking up the phone, Carla was rocketing off to the front office, and Vida was typing sixty-to-the-dozen on her battered old upright. Vida, however, had the courtesy to eye me over the rims of her tortoiseshell glasses. ''Milo was disturbed. He didn't tell Billy why." She kept right on typing.

A car wreck, I decided, and no wonder, what with the compact ice under the fresh snow. Even with four-wheel drive or chains, there were plenty of accidents not only in town, but out on the pass. I went into my office, which felt like a deep freezer. Trying not to let my teeth chatter, I wished for once that I didn't have a fear of portable heating units. But my career as a reporter on *The Oregonian* had included too many gruesome stories about people who had died in fires caused by plug-in heaters. I'd rather watch my breath come and go in little puffs while my knees knocked together under my desk.

The best cure for freezing, I decided, was work. It was Tuesday, after all, and our deadline for the weekly edition of *The Advocate*. Despite a sagging economy and Ed Bronsky's best efforts to discourage advertisers, we were putting out a thirty-six-page paper, crammed with holiday specials. It was a good thing, since we were running light on real news. This was the season for Vida to shine, with plenty of party coverage, charity functions, and how-to holiday articles. I'd allotted her six pages this week, but of course they were all inside. The front page was unusually bland; Carla's lead story recounted the city council's decision to allow a ten-foot plastic Santa Claus to tower over Old Mill Park.

"It will blow away," said council president and ski lodge manager Henry Bardeen.

"It will detract from the memorial to our town's founder, Carl Clemans," said council secretary and apparel-shop owner Francine Wells.

"It will be the target of every snowballer and potshot artist in town," said council member and building contractor Arnold Nyquist.

"It will be an appropriate seasonal reminder, and a compromise in response to criticism of the manger scene that has stood in Old Mill Park every Christmas since 1946," said

Mayor Fuzzy Baugh. "Let it not be said that the City of Alpine is insensitive to those who do not share basic Christian beliefs. No matter how misguided, these fine folks still vote." Fuzzy was your basic Baptist.

He was also a savvy politician, but his quote needed pruning. I was about to exercise my editor's pencil when the phone rang. It was Milo Dodge. He didn't sound excited so much as disturbed.

"Emma, can you come over for a minute?"

I started to fabricate an excuse, then realized that Milo's office might have heat, and said I could. The Skykomish County Sheriff's office was only two blocks away, after all. "Shall I pick up some doughnuts?" The Upper Crust Bakery had recently moved into the space formerly occupied by the hobby and toy shop, which had graduated to the Alpine Mall. The town's original source of baked goods had dried up three years earlier when its current owner had left Alpine to dry out and had never come back. The Upper Crust was owned by a pair of upstarts from Seattle who had a yen for the wide open spaces—and cheap real estate prices. Their baked goods were fabulous.

But Milo declined. "Just come over, quick as you can," he said, then hastily added a word of warning: "Be careful— it's slippery out there."

I agreed not to turn cartwheels on Front Street. After putting on my car coat, I trudged over to the bakery, which was closed. No heat, I supposed. No ovens, no doughnuts. The marzipan reindeer in the window display looked as if they were seeking shelter in the gingerbread house. Next door, Parker's Pharmacy was open, but I noticed that the clerks were wearing heavy sweaters and the fluorescent lighting had taken on a jaundiced tinge. Across the street, the Burger Barn was completely dark.

Luckily, Milo isn't afraid of space heaters. He had a large one going full tilt next to his desk. I sat down opposite him and cozied up to the glowing coils. Milo asked Bill Blatt to bring me a cup of coffee.

"At least the lights work," I noted, though they gave an ominous flicker even as I spoke. "What happened?"

Milo thought I meant him, rather than the PUD. He shook his head slowly, incredulously. "Emma, it was the damnedest thing. I hit the river above Anthracite Creek, six miles down the highway. I got there just before first light. Jack Mullins got a twelve-pounder in that hole Saturday morning," he went on, referring to another of his deputies. "Within the first fifteen minutes, I had a couple of bumps. I was sure it was going to be my lucky day."

Milo paused as Bill Blatt brought my coffee. I could visualize the scene, the river rushing among big boulders, the leaden sky overhead, the freezing air, the wind cutting to the bone, the snow swirling everywhere. Perfect steelheading weather. Only a true masochist could love the sport.

"And?" I encouraged Milo after Bill had made his exit.

Milo leaned on his elbows. He was a big shambling man in his mid-forties, with sharp hazel eyes, graying sandy hair, and a long face with a square jaw. It was a nice face, even an attractive face, though I made a point of not usually acknowledging the fact. When it came to the male-female thing, Milo and I had our own agendas. Or so it seemed.

"Then something really hit," Milo continued, his high forehead creasing. "It didn't feel like a fish, but it didn't seem like a snag, either. I let the line play out a little, but there wasn't any fight. So I started to reel in. I damned near died when I saw what I had." Milo gulped, blanched, and gave a shudder. Impatient, I stared at his stricken expression. He'd been the sheriff of Skykomish County for over eight years. Surely he'd seen it all.

"Well, what was it?" I demanded.

He passed a big hand over his face. "It was a leg, Emma. A human leg. And it was still wearing a tennis shoe. With no sock."

Chapter Two

I FELT A bit pale, too. For a long moment, Milo and I stared at each other across the desk. Finally, I spoke, my voice a trifle weak: "What did you do with it?" I clutched at my Styrofoam cup, feeling the warmth, but not benefitting from it.

Having related his grisly tale, Milo sat back in his chair. His color was returning, but he was shaking his head again. "I had a big garbage bag in the Cherokee Chief, so I got it and put the thing in it. Then I came back here and called Bill and Jack to come over quick. Doc Dewey will do the rest. I tell you, Emma, it's the damnedest thing I've ever seen in twenty-five years of law enforcement."

I sipped my coffee and reflected. We could get the story on page one, but it wouldn't run more than a couple of inches. Later, when and if we knew more, we could do a detailed article. Over the past two or three years, several body parts had been hauled out of rivers in Snohomish and King counties. This, however, was a first for Skykomish.

"So it's all up to Doc?" I inquired. Gerald Dewey, M.D., known locally as young Doc, had recently taken over not only his late father's practice, but old Doc's coroner's duties as well.

Milo nodded. "It's pretty routine. Try to make an ID, figure out time and cause of death. If foul play is suspected, then we go to work." Draining his mug with its NRA emblem, Milo seemed to have regained his composure. He actually chuckled. "Weird, huh? Except for a couple of those Snohomish County cases, nobody's been able to figure out if we've got another serial killer or a lot of accident-prone people in western Washington."

"Or too many nuts living in the woods and playing with their Skilsaws," I remarked.

"Always a possibility," agreed Milo. "City people don't realize how many goofballs take to the high country. Recluses who were strange to start with and keep getting stranger."

"Transients, too," I pointed out. "Either as victim or as hermit. Or both. Do you figure this was a man?"

Milo turned serious again. "My guess is that it was a woman, or maybe a kid. It had been in the river a long time. I'll spare you the decomposition details, but judging from the sockless tennis shoe alone, I'd say maybe two or three months."

I was grateful to be spared. One of my flaws as a journalist is my squeamish stomach. "Will you check out a list of missing persons?"

Milo gave a grunt of assent. "It won't do much good. Nobody I know of is missing around here, except for the usual wandering husband or fed-up wife. If it's a juvenile, we'd have a better chance—most of them are on the National Crime Information Center computer. After the Green River killer investigation, there was a move to report missing prostitutes on a national basis, but the truth is that the people who first miss them usually aren't anxious to get tangled up with the law."

I had taken my notebook out of my handbag and was writing swiftly. Maybe the story could run at least six inches if I included the background Milo was giving me. I could dump all of Carla's quotes about the plastic Santa and cut the last two grafs of my latest spotted owl piece, which was merely a rehash of the most recent plan to resolve the environment-logging industry controversy.

"Let me know if you find out anything more," I requested as I stood up, loath to leave the space heater. "We've got the rest of the day to get the story in this week's edition."

Milo grimaced. "Don't make me look like a damned fool."

I cocked my head to one side. "Have I ever?"

The sheriff looked the other way. "No—I can probably manage that on my own."

"Can't we all?" I gave him a wave and headed out through the reception area where Arnold Nyquist was pounding his fist on the counter and griping at Jack Mullins. Nyquist was a large, bluff man in his fifties, with a fringe of gray hair and a ruddy complexion. Known to most Alpiners as Arnie, but to some as Tinker Toy, he was the biggest building contractor in Alpine. The nickname had been coined by some wag who didn't consider Nyquist's residential dwellings up to snuff. Since three of the thirty homes in the Ptarmigan Tract west of town had collapsed during the early 1980s, the criticism might have been justified. Of late, Nyquist was concentrating on commercial construction.

". . . couldn't find a two-by-four up your butt!" Nyquist was saying to Jack Mullins.

Mullins, who had a reputation for drollery, turned his head to look down at his backside. "Golly, I don't see anything. Do you?"

Nyquist banged his fist again, causing ballpoint pens to jump and papers to flutter. "Don't be a wiseass, Mullins! That stuff cost close to a grand. And the fountain pen belonged to my granddad. He brought it over from Norway in oh-seven."

Standing at the bulletin board, I pretended to scan the various announcements and notices. Arnie Nyquist stormed out, with a parting shot for Jack: "This isn't the first time I've had problems with theft and vandalism. That moron of a sheriff and the rest of you dumbbells couldn't arrest anybody if they broke into the county jail. I'll expect to hear from you or Dodge by five o'clock this afternoon. You got that?''

Jack nodded his shaggy red head. "I'll put it with the two-by-four," he said after Nyquist had made his exit. "Hey, Mrs. Lord, isn't old Tinker Toy a world-class jerk?''

"He can be," I conceded. Luckily, I hadn't dealt much with Arnie Nyquist. The kind of news he generated usually came through cut-and-dried building permit or zoning council stories. I had, however, dealt with his father, Oscar, who owned The Whistling Marmot Movie Theatre. At one time, in the 1920s, Oscar and his father had owned the entire Alpine block where the theatre was located, kitty-corner from *The Advocate*. Although Lars Nyquist had chosen *Gösta Berling's Saga* with Greta Garbo for the opening of his new picture palace in 1924, his son had refused to show foreign films for decades. Oscar asserted that they were all obscene, obscure, and anti-American. He had been tricked into presenting *Wild Strawberries* because he thought the Bergman involved was Ingrid, not Ingmar. According to Vida, at least four people in Alpine noted the irony of one Norwegian getting confused by two Swedes.

"What's the problem?" I asked of Jack, sensing another late-breaking, if minor, story.

Mullins pushed the official log my way. "Somebody got into Nyquist's van last night and stole a bunch of stuff. Portable CD player, half a dozen CDs, some tools, a box of Jamaican cigars, a couple of fancy photographs . . . whatever. Nyquist left the van unlocked. It serves him right."

It probably did, but people in Alpine still have a tendency to trust each other, at least with their belongings, if not with their spouses. "Could it be the same thief who stole the band equipment up at the high school?"

Jack shrugged. "Maybe. But Nyquist's van was parked at his son's place on Stump Hill. That's a good mile or so from the high school." The implication was that Alpine's crooks were too lazy to cross town to commit a second burglary. Especially in the snow.

I jotted down some more notes, just in case Carla had forgotten to check the log. I recalled some other incidents involving Arnold Nyquist. Last December, a display of Christmas lights at his home on First Hill had been swiped; his second floor office in the Alpine Building was egged in the spring; a load of garbage had been dumped on his front lawn in July; a small fire was started at his construction site for the new bowling alley across the river. Nyquist was right about one thing, though—if memory served, no one had been apprehended for any of the mischief. I supposed it was only natural that Arnie would take it more seriously than the law enforcement officials did. Indeed, the family's string of minor bad luck was ongoing.

"How is Travis?" I asked, referring to Nyquist's son, who was recovering from a broken ankle suffered in a skiing accident over the Thanksgiving weekend. Until the theft of last night, Travis's mishap on Tonga Ridge had been the most recent Nyquist calamity.

Jack grinned, which always seemed to make his teeth sparkle and his freckles dance. "If I had that wife of his to take care of me, I'd break a leg three times a year. Trav's doing fine, and why shouldn't he? There's a guy who's got it all."

On the surface, at least, Travis Nyquist had attained many a young man's dreams before he was thirty. A graduate of Pacific Lutheran University in Tacoma, he had gotten his M.A. in finance at the University of Washington, gone to work for a big brokerage house in Seattle, met his future bride, Bridget, and moved back to Alpine to mull over his stock options. The young Nyquists had been married for a little over a year. They now lived in a handsome Pacific Northwest version of a Cape Cod on Stump Hill, otherwise known as The Pines. The house had been built six years earlier by Arnie Nyquist on speculation, but this time he'd spared no expense. When the well-to-do commuter family from Everett had gotten fed up driving back and forth on Stevens Pass, Arnie put earnest money down and held onto the place until his son carried his bride over the threshold.

"Trav and I went to high school together," Jack was musing, his freckled face now wistful. "He never seemed to work that hard, but he always got good grades. The other guys and I used to say that he charmed his teachers, at least the women, but I guess Trav is really smart. He must have gotten his brains from Mrs. Nyquist. Old Tinker Toy's IQ isn't so hot, if you ask me. My dad says it's a wonder Arnie didn't flunk out of UDUB in his freshman year."

Briefly, I considered Arnie Nyquist's wife, Louise, a meek ex-schoolteacher who had reputedly jumped out the window of her seventh-grade classroom during a particularly arduous social studies session. Fortunately, she was on the first floor at the time and landed virtually unharmed in a rhododendron bush.

With some reluctance, I left Jack Mullins to his musings about The Life and Times of Travis Nyquist, and headed out into the snow, which had turned fairly heavy. Through the curtain of white, I could barely make out the Christmas decorations along Front Street: golden strands of tinsel, big red shiny bows, and tall amber candles that covered the regular streetlights.

Back in the office, I found Ginny Burmeister distributing the mail. There was nothing much of interest: only the usual press releases, bills, promotions, and a couple of letters to the editor and/or publisher. The first missive was in response to our front-page article about cutting Christmas trees on state lands, an activity that was permitted in certain areas every year from the last week of November until mid-December. The irate correspondent, Ruth Rydholm, asserted that such plundering of the forests was unnecessary and even dangerous. Since Mrs. Rydholm's son Cliff owned a Christmas tree farm in Snohomish County, I figured she was a bit biased.

The other letter, also tree-oriented, chided me for my previous spotted owl story. A week without a spotted owl letter was like a week without a Monday. Alpiners, except for the recycled Californians, were generally anti-owl and pro-logger, which befitted a town founded on the timber industry. Even though the original mill had closed in 1929, logging was still an important, if severely jeopardized, source of income. Most of the locals viewed efforts to protect the endangered spotted owl as no more necessary than saving the pterodactyl. The longer I lived in Alpine, the more I tended to agree, but I hoped, in my fair-minded journalist's way, that a compromise could be reached.

What I could not reach was my son. Adam was taking a final. He was due to arrive at Sea-Tac Airport Saturday from the University of Alaska in Fairbanks. Although I'd spoken to him by phone, I hadn't seen him since he'd spent two days with his father, Tom Cavanaugh, in San Francisco. It was the first time Adam had met his dad. My son indicated that all had gone well. Young men—most men—aren't much for relating intimate details. Wish I'd been there. Wish Tom were here. Wish my life away. That's what I'd done for over twenty years. . . .

Just as I was entering Milo's fishing incident on my word processor, the phone rang. I hoped it was Adam, returning my call, but the voice at the other end of the line was equally pleasing to me.

"Hi, Sluggly," said my brother. "I'm at the hospital. Mrs. McHale was right: Father Fitz has had a small stroke. Dr. Flake wants to keep him for a couple of days. I'm wondering if I should move into the rectory."

I was torn: Ben was currently staying in Adam's room, but had insisted he'd take up residence on the living-room sofa once my son got to Alpine. I had argued that I would sleep on the sofa—Ben was on vacation. But maybe the rectory was a good idea. Someone besides the housekeeper should be there during Advent.

"Have you called the Chancery?" I asked. Ben had. The archbishop—or an underling—had given my brother a green light. Priests were scarce; priests were needed. The Chancery office was only too glad for someone who had actually taken holy orders to run St. Mildred's. Otherwise, we might have been stuck with liturgical services conducted by Helga Wenzler, parish council president and manic-depressive—or worse yet, Ed Bronsky, eucharistic minister, who would immediately change the Good News to the Bad News. Or no news at all . . . Such was Ed's morbid style.

I made the proper sisterly noises about having Ben sleep away from my cozy log house, but ultimately we agreed that he ought to stay at the rectory, if only until Father Fitz was released from the hospital. I thought of telling him about Milo's dreaded catch, decided to wait, and said I'd see him for dinner around six.

"Make it eight," said Ben, sounding apologetic. "I've got to say a seven o'clock mass for the Immaculate Conception."

Having done my duty at eight A.M., I'd forgotten about the extra mass for a holy day. "No problem. We'll have T-bone steaks."

"Maybe I should stick around at the rectory," Ben mused. "Somebody might wander in after mass."

This time, I made up Ben's mind for him. "Tell Mrs. McHale to make an appointment for the lost soul. You want your steak medium rare, don't you?"

Ben did. Shivering from the cold, I hung up and returned to Milo's account of the leg. Now that I had recovered from the ghastliness of the incident, I began to wonder where the rest of the body was. Halfway through the story, I dialed Milo's number.

"Hey, Milo," I said, my fingers on the keyboard and the phone propped between my shoulder and my left ear, "will you and your deputies go looking for the missing pieces?"

Milo uttered a heavy sigh. "With the river up the way it

is? Hell, Emma, I'd be lucky to catch a steelhead, let alone find a spare arm. What's the point?''

I made a little face of exasperation into the receiver. How typical of Milo, to be only as curious as circumstances permitted. On the other hand, it wasn't up to me to tell him his business. ''Just curious,'' I said. ''Bye.''

''Emma—wait. What are you saying in the paper?'' Milo sounded faintly alarmed.

I almost never offered copy on approval. My readers had to trust me, while I, in turn, worked hard to earn that trust. But Milo was a friend as well as a news source. ''What's it worth to you, Dodge?''

There was a slight pause. ''Dinner at King Olav's?''

I'd had worse offers. The lights flickered; so did my computer screen. ''What would Honoria think?'' Milo's current lady love was Honoria Whitman, a transplanted Carmel potteress who lived in Startup and got around in a wheelchair.

''Honoria wouldn't mind,'' said Milo. ''She likes you.''

The feeling was mutual. Still, I was a bit chagrined. Milo's trust was fine when it came to my writing efforts. Honoria's trust was an insult when it came to my feminine wiles. I read the three paragraphs I'd written aloud to Milo. He quibbled over a couple of words, but I ignored him. The sheriff wasn't any more qualified to meddle in my business than I was in his.

I'd just finished the piece when Henry Bardeen made his brisk way through the newsroom. Trim, slim, and ever-dapper, Henry ran the ski lodge with great efficiency. His brown toupee, gracefully etched with just a touch of silver, rested naturally on his well-shaped head. Henry had come to confer with Ed Bronsky, and was not pleased to learn that Ed was out.

''I wanted a final look at that ad about the sleigh ride to the restaurant,'' said Henry in his dry monotone voice. ''We've decided to keep doing it after New Year's, maybe until ski season is over.''

"I can find it for you." I led Henry back into the larger office. Ed was more organized than either Carla or Vida. Under a double-truck ad for Safeway, I found the mock-up Ed had created for Henry. It was tastefully done, with an original illustration of a horse-drawn sleigh going through snow-tipped evergreens. "This is very nice," I remarked. "How did you talk Ed out of using his odious clip art file?"

Henry was mulling over the copy. The promotion had its charm and was practical to boot. Diners heading for the new King Olav's restaurant could park on the far side of the bridge near the highway and ride a horse-drawn sleigh for two miles up to the ski lodge. While the gimmick was primarily an advertising promotion, it was also aimed at out-of-towners who didn't mind traversing the pass in winter weather but weren't keen on making the final leg up a steep, narrow, winding stretch of road. The last quarter-mile was through trees decorated with fairy lights, and ended in front of a Christmas scene straight out of Dickens. Like many Alpiners, I was anxious to take the sleigh ride, too.

"Can we say *through February* instead of *until January 3*?" Henry inquired. I told him we could, and made the appropriate changes on both the dummy and Ed's computer. Henry, who had left his sense of humor in the nursery, was actually smiling, albeit thinly. "That's Evan Singer's art work. He's the one who drives the sleigh."

The name rang no bells, sleigh or otherwise. After almost three years in Alpine, I was still lost in the maze of names. Small-town residents love to toss out names, as if testing newcomers. They assume everybody knows everybody else. It's a form of snobbism, making the new arrival feel even more like an outsider. As the editor and publisher of the local newspaper, I was supposed to know all—but names were still my nemesis.

Henry noted my blank expression.

"Evan's new in town, what you might call a free spirit." He wrinkled his aquiline nose. "As a rule, I'm not in favor of hiring that sort of person, but this sleigh driver's job was hard to fill. The Dithers Sisters volunteered to take turns since we're using their horses, but you know what *they're* like.'' This time, Henry not only wrinkled his nose, but wiggled his eyebrows. The Dithers Sisters were a pair of middle-aged horse owners who had been left a considerable amount of money by their parents. It was probably the greatest misfortune ever to befall them, since neither had ever had to work, except to keep the farm going. That should have been sufficient to instill a sense of responsibility, but they'd had enough wealth to hire help. Judy and Connie Dithers spent their days pampering their horses and their nights watching TV. They were said to be eccentric, miserly, reclusive lesbians. As far as I could tell, they were none of the above. Occasionally, they played bridge in the same group I did, and the worst that could be said of Judy and Connie was that they were unmotivated and dizzy. Still, I had to agree with Henry—I wouldn't want them pulling my sleigh, either.

''. . . how fussy some people can be,'' Henry was saying in his flat delivery. I realized I was wool-gathering, thinking not only of the Dithers Sisters, but admiring Evan Singer's art work. ''And don't I know it, running a resort. But what I say is that Video-to-Go's loss is my gain.''

Hastily, I tried to reconstruct the conversation. ''Evan was there . . . how long?'' I took a wild guess.

''Just a month,'' said Henry, initialing the mock-up with his silver ballpoint pen. ''He came to Alpine in October, one of those city boys who thinks the grass is greener in a small town.'' The glance Henry shot me implied that such beliefs were quite right. I could have argued the point, but didn't.

''Dutch Bamberg fired Evan, but he gave him a recommendation anyway,'' Henry went on earnestly, as if he needed to justify the hired help with me. ''Dutch said Evan not only knew movies backwards and forwards, but that he'd waited tables, driven a cab, done some retail, and worked at a riding stable near Issaquah. That was good enough for me. Then I found out he could draw, too.''

I gave Henry an encouraging smile. "Evan sounds like a real Renaissance man. Who did Dutch get to replace him at Video-to-Go?''

"He hasn't found anybody yet," replied Henry, looking troubled. Even though it appeared that Evan Singer had been dismissed for reasons I hadn't quite grasped, Henry, in his typical self-flagellating manner, seemed to blame himself. "By the time Dutch let Evan go, most of the folks around here had taken seasonal jobs. The only people out of work right now are loggers, and they wouldn't fit in at Video-to-Go." Henry looked very somber, as if the idea of a former logger discerning between Woody Allen and Woody Woodpecker was impossible.

Henry lingered long enough to grouse about the Forest Service's recent decision to reject expansion plans for the White Pass ski area near Mount Rainier. Supposedly, the project would endanger the habitat of the spotted owl, the grizzly bear, and the gray wolf. "I've been considering adding two downhill runs and a warming hut below Mount Sawyer, but I'll never get approval now. If one of those grizzlies ate a couple of environmentalists, I wonder if they'd change their tune?''

Still grumbling, Henry left just as Vida returned with Bridget Nyquist in tow. It might seem coincidental that I could run into two Nyquists in less than two hours, but Alpine was small enough to make such occurrences unremarkable. Indeed, I had seen Bridget the previous afternoon at the Grocery Basket, and on Sunday she had passed me in her cream-colored Mercedes on the bridge over the Skykomish River as I headed for Sea-Tac to meet Ben.

Vida shrugged out of her tweed coat, yanked off her kidskin gloves, and adjusted the ties of her black gaucho hat. "Bridget has volunteered to be Santa's Little Helper for the Lutheran Retirement Home's Christmas party," said Vida, shoving her spare chair at our visitor. "Fuzzy Baugh is going to be Santa."

Gingerly sitting down, Bridget gave me a charming smile. She was in her early twenties, tall, slim, auburn-haired and blue-eyed. Her skin was flawless and her clothes were expensive, if casual. A russet fox-lined raincoat was worn over a cashmere sweater and wool slacks. Her hand-tooled boots came almost to the knee and matched her shoulder bag.

"This will be fun," said Bridget in a breathy little voice. "I used to visit old folks' homes when I was a Girl Scout in Seattle."

"Then you've had lots of practice," said Vida, whipping out a ballpoint pen. "Just remember: you'll never run out of old people, but someday you'll be one of them. Now—give me the program, in order of events."

As usual, Vida seemed to have the situation well in hand. I returned to my office just as the phone rang. This time it was Teresa McHale, the parish housekeeper. She went straight to the point, expressing her displeasure over Ben's decision to move into the rectory.

"It was one thing with Father Fitz being almost ninety," she asserted. "But this is quite different. People will talk. Your brother is very close to my age."

I figured Ben was probably a good ten years younger than Teresa McHale, but if she wanted to kid herself, that was okay with me. It wasn't okay for her to interfere with the clergy, however.

"Sorry, Mrs. McHale," I said cheerfully, "but this isn't the Chancery. Ben's a big boy, and while I'd just as soon have him stay on with me, I understand why there ought to be a priest available at the rectory. As I'm sure you realize, people undergo more spiritual crises at this time of year. They need to know somebody's there to help."

Teresa McHale emitted a snort of contempt, probably aimed at me rather than the spiritually depressed. "So what if he's six blocks away? You live on Fir Street, don't you?"

I acknowledged that I did, then started to say that the distance between my home and St. Mildred's was beside the point.

Teresa interrupted: "Have it your way." She huffed as if I were indeed a Chancery official rather than merely the sister of a visiting priest. "But don't blame me if something happens."

I gave a little sniff of my own as she banged down the phone. *Dream on, kiddo,* I thought to myself. If anything happened, it wouldn't be Ben's fault. Women weren't a weakness with my brother, at least not one that he hadn't been able to overcome. Teresa McHale was looking for trouble that didn't exist.

But of course it was already there.

Chapter Three

BEN HAD BORROWED Father Fitz's aging but still reliable Volvo to transport his few belongings up to the rectory. He had come and gone while I was at work, but left a message on my answering machine asking me to pick him up after seven o'clock mass. It seemed that Teresa McHale, who had no car of her own, had commandeered the Volvo so that she could visit Father Fitz in the hospital.

Ben and I had a leisurely dinner, prefaced with two bourbons apiece. The steaks were excellent, the conversation mellow, and the Viennese torte divine. The Upper Crust, along with the rest of downtown Alpine, had gotten its power restored just after lunch.

Ben talked at length about the challenges of his assignment in Tuba City, how tough it was for the Navajos to keep their pride, to pass on their culture, to not lose their children to the wider world while at the same time preventing them from falling into poverty and alcoholism. I talked about the differences between general assignment reporting in a metropolitan area such as Portland and running a weekly in an isolated community like Alpine. My problems seemed trifling compared to Ben's. As usual, I came away from our one-on-one session feeling as if his role in life far surpassed my own. He, of course, always insisted that this was not so.

"You're the community's conscience," he told me over coffee. "You not only inform, you serve by example. A newspaper is a watchdog, a catalyst. Especially in a small town. Don't shortchange yourself, Sluggly.''

I appreciated his words. Indeed, they were mine, too. But I still felt trivial by comparison. Circulation was up by a small percentage in Alpine, yet elsewhere it was generally down, and newspapers were dying across the country. People didn't read any more; they relied on TV. The print media might go the way of the dinosaur, but there would always be souls to save. If I hadn't had to drive Ben back to the rectory, I'd have poured us a double brandy.

Ironically, the only business that is more precarious than print journalism is logging. While Alpine hasn't been a one-industry town since Carl Clemans's original mill closed in 1929, forest products still provide a major source of income. There are three mills, two of them on the small side, and several independent logging companies. The threat of the spotted owl looms large over the entire Pacific Northwest, but nowhere does it flap its wings more ominously than in towns like Alpine. Ironically, the ski lodge, which had saved the local economy during the Depression, was beginning to suffer from the endangered species fallout. Sooner or later, I had to come to editorial grips with the issue. As a city girl, I tended to side with the environmentalists. But since moving to Alpine, I was beginning to realize that simplistic solutions don't solve multifaceted questions. Ben agreed, citing the differences he had discovered not only on the Delta, but also on the reservation. Issues, like people, were never simple. And, as my brother pointed out, I was the community's conscience.

By morning, we had another six inches of snow. The plows were out early, while a sanding crew blemished the pristine new fall along Front Street, Alpine Way, and the third main artery in town, Highway 187. I crept down Fir Street to Alpine Way, taking the long route to work. The current issue of *The Advocate* had been hauled off to the printer in Monroe, but there was a good chance it would come out late. Our driver, Kip MacDuff, had broken his chains on the newly-laid gravel and had gotten off to a bad start.

Vida, however, was beginning the day with a burst of creative energy. "I think I'll do a feature on Bridget Nyquist," she announced after I'd poured a cup of coffee. "For a young bride, she's done oodles of charitable work since she came to Alpine. I doubt that she has a brain in her head, but I ought to give her credit for a kind heart. Besides, this old folks' home story is a dud unless I perk it up with something personal. I'll be a sap six times over if I write another word about that old blowhard, Fuzzy Baugh. He refused to carry a pack because of his lumbago and wouldn't pad his stomach because he wanted to show off the ten pounds he lost at TOPS. Take Off Pounds Sensibly, my foot! They should have drained Fuzzy's brain!"

Having dismissed our mayor's role as Santa with a slashing gesture of one hand, Vida turned to her battered typewriter. "I got the impression you weren't wildly warm about Bridget," I commented, perching on Carla's desk.

Vida shot me a look over her shoulder. "I'm not, but you know I like to be fair. The girl hasn't had an easy time of it, I gather. Don't you remember the wedding?"

I didn't. Vida swiveled around, took off her glasses, and rubbed furiously at her eyes. "Of course you don't, you weren't here. It was last November—a year ago, I mean—when you went to Portland for the weekend to visit your friends."

I recalled the trip, to a former *Oregonian* colleague's home in suburban Tigard. Mavis Marley Fulkerston had worked on the editorial page while I toiled as a reporter. She had married a sportswriter from the paper, given birth to three children, won a Pulitzer, survived cancer of the cervix, and retired early. I had attended her fiftieth birthday party the previous November, a gala affair at the Benson Hotel.

"Bridget didn't have anybody on her side." Vida was gazing at me without her glasses. Her face always looked so naked, yet never really vulnerable, without those big tortoiseshell frames. "Doesn't that beat all?"

"You mean—no family or friends of the bride?" In Alpine, wedding etiquette was still observed to the letter.

Vida nodded solemnly. "That's right. Oh, the Lutheran church was packed—the Nyquists know everybody in Skykomish County—but there was nobody there for Bridget."

Ed was lumbering into the office, shaking snow off his overcoat. "There's no end to it," he grumbled. "Some of those dopey merchants in the mall want to have a pre-Christmas sale. Imagine!" Under the brim of his wool cap, Ed rolled his eyes.

"I guess there's no stopping them," I noted in mock sympathy. It was a wonder Ed hadn't tried to persuade the local retailers that they didn't need to advertise in the paper because people would shop for Christmas anyway. As Ed heaved himself out of his overcoat and muttered under his breath, I turned back to Vida. "I thought Bridget was from Seattle. Why didn't anybody come up for the wedding?"

Vida gave a shrug of wide shoulders covered with a print blouse, a suede vest, and a plaid muffler. Apparently she wasn't taking any chances on the heat going out again. "There wasn't anybody to come. That's why they had the wedding in Alpine, instead of Seattle. She's an only child," Vida continued, settling into one of her favorite sports, Family History. "Her father died about six years ago of a heart attack. He owned a small trucking company. Her mother committed suicide shortly before the wedding. As for friends, I couldn't say." Vida made a little face, as if she were disowning responsibility for Bridget's lack of sociability.

"Poor Bridget," I remarked, watching Ed discover we were out of coffee. His galoshes made dark marks on the floor as he went out to give Ginny the bad news. "Has she made friends since she got to Alpine?"

"I don't know," Vida admitted. "She's trying, I'd guess. I think that's why she does so much charity work. But let's face it, Emma, there aren't very many young women in her age group who have much in common with her. More to the point, she'd make them feel inferior with her lovely home and beautiful clothes. I suppose that's why I feel sorry for her.''

It was, I reflected, typical of Vida to lament the plight of someone who appeared to have everything. A successful husband, material possessions, financial security—on the surface, envy would be the emotion Bridget would elicit in most people. But Vida would go straight to the heart of the matter and see that somebody like Bridget was lacking a lot.

"Why did her mother commit suicide?" I had worked with Vida long enough not to question her sources. Bridget's background could have come from any number of Vida's friends or relations.

"She had cancer, poor thing," Vida replied as Ginny tended to the coffee maker while Ed watched. "I heard that she didn't want to do something embarrassing—like die—about the same time Bridget got married. So she threw herself off the Bainbridge Island ferry."

I winced. "Poor Bridget!"

Vida inclined her head, then flipped open her phone book. "I think I'll set up an interview at her house. I wonder how they've decorated the place. The Lovells went Amish."

The Lovells were, of course, the previous owners of the house on Stump Hill. I suppressed a smile, wondering if Vida's desire to do the story on Bridget wasn't motivated as much by curiosity as by sympathy. It didn't matter; Vida would turn out a first-rate profile. In the process of talking to her subject, she'd also dig up material that she wouldn't be able to use in the paper. Vida had a knack for unearthing the darkest secrets, which she usually kept to herself.

Hearing my phone ring, I went into my office and grabbed the receiver. Milo Dodge had Doc Dewey's report.

"This is pretty sketchy," he warned me. "Subject was female, aged fifteen to twenty-five, about five foot six, a hundred and twenty pounds, probably Caucasian, reasonably well-nourished, dismembered after death. Oh, and the tennis shoe is a Reebok, size seven and a half.''

"It doesn't sound so sketchy to me,'' I said, making notes. "What's this *dismembered after death* bit?''

I heard Milo's sigh. "You don't like gory details, right?''

"Right. Oh, dear.'' I steeled myself for the worst. "You mean . . . ?''

"Sawed up. Just like you said.''

Somehow, it sounded worse coming from Milo than it had from me. But maybe that was because I had been guessing. Milo's verdict—or rather Doc Dewey's—was official. "Foul play?'' I asked in a faint voice.

"We can't rule it out,'' said Milo. "That's obvious. Right now, we're checking the missing persons file, but as I told you . . .''

"What about the tennis shoe?'' I didn't care to hear Milo's missing persons lecture a second time.

"It's pretty ordinary,'' he replied. "It'd take forever to track it down. In fact, we probably never could.''

I fiddled with my ballpoint pen. It would be almost a full week before we'd publish again. Maybe Milo would learn something else by that time. If he didn't, I might as well relegate the item to next week's back page. In this case, no news wasn't good news, but it was no more than a follow-up.

After I hung up from talking to Milo, it occurred to me that Evan Singer, Jack of All Trades, Master of Some, might be worth a feature. I went into the newsroom and offered Carla the assignment. She balked.

"Evan is weird,'' she declared. "I was in Video-to-Go a few times while he worked there. He was always trying to push X-rated films off on me. All I wanted to do was chill out with Mel Gibson or Dennis Quaid.''

Since Carla rarely balks at anything and enthusiasm is her major asset, I capitulated. "I'll do it myself. I need to keep in practice." It was true—I hadn't done a feature in six months. My last interviewee had been a U. S. Senate candidate who'd made a swing through Alpine. The quotes were platitudes, the pictures were dull, the background was bland. The would-be senator had lost in the primary. It served him right for making such lousy copy. Yet it had occurred to me that maybe I was losing my touch as an interviewer. I would try to do better by Evan Singer.

But I had another task slated for that afternoon. It was December 9, the traditional day I bring home my Christmas tree. When Adam and I had lived in Portland, we'd always bought one from a lot, made a two-inch cut off the trunk, and stuck it in a bucket of water outside for a week. Sometimes the trees stayed fresh and fragrant through New Year's; other times, their branches drooped and needles dropped by Christmas Day. Since coming to Alpine, I had cut my own trees, not on designated forest service lands, but wherever I happened to find the perfect Douglas fir during the course of the year. Last June, I had discovered my tree, eight feet tall, bushy, virtually symmetrical, just below Alpine Falls. As always, I'd checked with Milo to make sure I wasn't trespassing or poaching or whatever I might be doing if caught in the act of hacking down a tree with somebody else's name on it.

"That's state land, so don't tell me about it," Milo had said as he did every year. "It's not strictly legal, and if you get caught, I've never seen you before in my life."

About eleven-thirty, I called Ben at the rectory to see if he wanted to have lunch and accompany me to Alpine Falls. Teresa McHale answered the phone and sounded pained when I asked for my brother.

"I thought he'd be spending the days with you," she said in an irritated voice. "I don't see any need for him to go through yesterday's collection. Father Fitzgerald can handle that when he feels better."

"It's probably wise to get the cash to the bank," I said in a mild tone. "It may be a few days before Father can cope."

"He's coming home tomorrow, Friday at the latest," Teresa went on in her irritable manner. "Knowing him the way I do, he'll want to get right back to work. Speaking of which, why doesn't the city get off its lazy backside and plow Cedar Street or Cascade? It's very hard for our older parishioners to get to mass in all this snow."

I sympathized, though I was confident that most of Alpine's senior citizens had probably been dealing with snow all of their lives. Maybe it was Teresa who was having problems. I made commiserative murmurs, then asked if the Volvo had four-wheel drive. It did, she assured me.

"That's not the point," Teresa went on, sounding increasingly cranky. "I've been here over a year and I can't believe how backward this place is. Half the streets don't have sidewalks; the power is unpredictable, you can't get decent TV reception without one of those ugly satellite dishes, the growing season lasts about four months, the Seattle Sunday paper has to be trucked in on Saturday. There's only one dress shop, two decent restaurants, no public swimming pool, no espresso carts, no live entertainment unless you count the drunken loggers throwing each other through the windows at the Icicle Creek Tavern. I feel marooned in this town!"

Again, Teresa McHale struck a sympathetic chord. After almost three years, I often felt the same way—cut off, isolated, cast adrift. I, too, missed the opera, the theatre, major-league sports, vast shopping malls, and high-rises. But most of all, I missed the energy of the city. Despite the demons that drive urban dwellers to despair, there is no other atmosphere that has such vitality. But I wasn't about to say so to Teresa McHale.

"Dear me," I sighed in mock anguish, "why ever did you move up here from Seattle?"

There was a faint pause. When Teresa spoke again, I heard a defensive note in her voice. "I wanted a change. I thought

I'd be doing some good, taking this job. I never figured I'd be bored to tears in the bargain.''

"I wouldn't think you'd be bored, what with all the help you could give Father Fitz in the parish,'' I pointed out, genuinely trying to exercise compassion.

"He's got plenty of lay people to do all that,'' asserted Mrs. McHale. "That's another thing: this town has more busybodies than we had in the whole north end of Seattle. I'm talking about spare time activities. Instead of passing that bond issue for the new swimming pool in the last election, these backwoods dodos voted it down because they're getting a bowling alley. Now who in their right mind would rather bowl than swim? No wonder everybody is about fifty pounds overweight!''

Again, Teresa had a point. Alpine, like many other small towns, seemed to churn out a greater proportion of people with greater proportions. On the other hand, Teresa wasn't exactly wasting away. "There is a gym,'' I said, a bit sharply. Teresa and her gripes were spoiling my festive tree-cutting mood. "Has my brother shown up yet?'' *Like in the last ten minutes while you were bitching my ear off,* I wanted to say.

"He just walked in.'' Mrs. McHale was obviously not appeased by my suggestion of working out at the gym.

The next voice I heard was Ben's, faintly amused. "I haven't cut down a Christmas tree since we were kids,'' he said in response to my invitation. "The parish council meets tonight. I wonder if I should prepare for it.''

"Why? It's not your parish.'' Exasperation tainted my voice.

"True.'' He hesitated. "Father Fitz probably doesn't hear half of what goes on anyway. He's pretty deaf. Do you want me to bring the axe from the rectory woodshed?''

"I've got Dad's old Swede saw already in the trunk,'' I said. "And some ropes and clippers, in case we see any good greens for a swatch.''

Ben emitted a little sigh. "Dad's old Swede . . . I didn't know you kept that, Emma."

I knew Ben was picturing our dad sawing up the cord of wood we had delivered every fall to our home in Seattle's Wallingford district. Dad never started cutting the wood until it had stayed on the parking strip for at least three days. Mom would nag at him, insisting that it would rain, or that somebody would trip over it and sue us, or that kids would steal it. I still remembered the smell of the freshly cut wood, usually hemlock with just enough cedar to provide some snap, fourteen-inch chunks, to fit our small fireplace.

"I wonder if the big maple is still there," I said, my mind staying in a tree mode. "We used to rake leaves until we dropped."

"Mom and Dad made us take down our tree house," recalled Ben. "We never should have dropped water balloons on Mr. and Mrs. Peabody."

"That wasn't so bad," I noted. "What really riled Mom and Dad was when we threw Brewster Baxter out of the tree."

"It was Baxter Brewster," corrected Ben. "Hell, he landed in one of those big piles of leaves. He wasn't hurt—just rustled around and got dog poop in his hair."

We both laughed. I wondered if Teresa McHale was lurking in the rectory, listening to our reminiscences. I told Ben I'd pick him up in fifteen minutes. Nostalgia is best when shared, but it's sometimes painful. The memories Ben and I had of our parents were wonderful, but there weren't enough of them. They had died together, when a semitrailer jackknifed in front of them on the way home from Ben's ordination. Dad was fifty-two; Mom was forty-nine. In the usual scheme of life expectancy, we could have had another thirty years to make memories.

After lunch at the Burger Barn, it took us only five minutes to get to Alpine Falls, which is just up the highway from the town. The tree I had selected was about twenty yards from the river's final cascade—far enough not to get drenched, though close enough to impair our hearing. The snow had stopped, but the air was chill and damp. I struggled over the rough ground in my boots, gesturing for Ben to watch his footing.

"Here!" I yelled, pointing at the stately Douglas fir I'd adopted half a year ago.

Ben sawed, while I clutched the trunk. When he finished, I sniffed euphorically at the cut he'd made. But before he could hoist the fir and carry it up the bank to the car, I motioned at a couple of small cedars. Ben waited while I attacked them with my clippers. There was no pine in sight, but I could pick up a couple of branches off the Christmas tree lot in town. Maybe some holly, too, I decided, and even a bit of blue spruce. That always made a cheery combination for a swatch.

Gathering up a half-dozen branches, I saw Ben at the river's edge. The waters roiled past him, the churning falls at his left, the snow-covered ground under foot, the great stands of evergreen marching up the mountainside. How different this must be for him from the hot, dry plateau in Arizona. Or the humid, lethargic delta of the Mississippi. How much did Ben really miss his roots here in the Pacific Northwest? My brother and I were city children, but never far from the forests and mountains and rivers and sea.

Ben was bending over, presumably digging around in the rocks at the river's edge. I smiled fondly. When we were young, he was always looking for a flat pebble that he could skip across whichever body of water we were visiting. I waited, expecting him to reach back and pitch. Instead, he turned to look at me, and his face had gone pale under its all-year tan.

"Don't come any closer, Emma," he yelled. "Go up to the car."

Puzzled, I stared at him. But his stunned expression, more than his words, urged me to flee. Clutching the greens and the clippers to my breast, I scurried up the bank. I slipped twice, swore, dropped the clippers, retrieved them, and finally reached the Jaguar. A minute later, Ben appeared, dragging my beautiful Douglas fir.

"What's wrong?" I gasped, out of breath.

Ben righted the tree, shaking snow from its branches. His color was beginning to return, but his face was very grim. Suddenly, I thought of Milo and let out a little squeal. "Ben—what did you see down there?"

He shoved the tree into the trunk of my car. "Shit." His gloved hands dangled at his sides. "It was an arm. I swear to God, Emma, it was an *arm*." He gazed at me as if he didn't expect to be believed. Along with my shock came the realization that Ben didn't know about Milo's ghastly catch. The paper wasn't out and I hadn't thought to tell him.

I stuffed the greens into the trunk and began to wrestle with the ropes. "We have to tell the sheriff," I said, hearing my voice crack. Abruptly, I began to laugh. Ben stared at me, the horror on his face replaced by mystification at my reaction. I waved a weak hand at him. "It's okay," I gasped. "It's just that . . . somebody has gone to pieces!"

Ben didn't laugh. There was nothing indecisive about my brother as he pushed me into the passenger side of the car and took the wheel. I was still semi-hysterical when we crossed the bridge into Alpine.

Chapter Four

FOR OVER TWENTY years, I had relied on nobody but myself. I took great pride in my independence, my resourcefulness, my competence. On the short ride into Alpine, I chided myself for falling apart. Was it because I had Ben at my side, the older brother who had shielded me from all harm unless he was the one perpetrating it? Or was I genuinely shattered by the discovery of various body parts along the Skykomish River? I didn't know. But I wasn't about to go on being such a weak sister, as my mother would have put it. Giving one last sniffle, I showed Ben where the sheriff's office was located. He pulled the Jaguar into the slush at the curb just as Milo came down the street, presumably from lunch.

After listening to our recital, Milo looked as if his lunch had rebelled. "Damn," he breathed, then gave Ben an apologetic nod. "Sorry, Father. I didn't mean to offend you."

"Shit," said Ben, "I didn't know that you'd already found a leg. What the hell is going on around here?"

Milo looked askance at Ben, apparently shocked by my brother's salty language. Milo had been brought up a Congregationalist, which explained his amazement, as well as a few other matters. Milo said he'd get Sam Heppner, then take his deputy and Ben up to the falls in a county vehicle. Having regained my composure, I insisted that I should go along, too. After all, I was the press.

"Here comes more of the press," said Milo, indicating Vida, who was marching briskly down the street, her tweed

510

coat flapping around her boots. "Why don't the two of you have a press conference?"

"What is all this?" demanded Vida, forthright as ever, but testier than usual. Her boots crunched on the rock salt the city had used to melt the ice and snow on the downtown pedestrian walkways. "Well? Did you find the other leg?"

Milo had gone into his office to get Sam Heppner. "It was actually an arm," said Ben, reaching out to hug Vida. He knew how fond I was of my House & Home editor, and although he had met her on a previous visit to Alpine, this was the first time he had seen her on this trip. "How are you, Mrs. Runkel? I hear you're converting from Presbyterianism."

"Aaaaargh!" Vida shuddered in Ben's embrace, then stepped back a pace. "I'd rather be burned at the stake! Or have you people stopped doing that by now?" She didn't wait for an answer, but jabbed Ben in the front of his down jacket. "Don't you ever wear a collar, Father Lord? That old fool of a pastor up at St. Mildred's has been seen in long underwear."

"He was wearing *pants*," I pointed out. "Anyway, that was a stupid story from Grace Grundle. She also reported that the Episcopal rector was seen kissing a woman. Which he was, but it happened to be his wife."

"Never mind." Vida retreated, almost stepping in the slush. Obviously, she didn't want to hear any more scandal spawned by a fellow Presbyterian. "An arm? What sort of arm?" Again, she didn't wait for an answer, but turned to me. "Shall I get a camera?"

I started to tell Vida that I wasn't sure we were wanted. Just then my Christmas tree fell out of the trunk. In his haste, Ben apparently hadn't secured it very well. The ride home must have jarred it loose. At that moment, Milo reappeared with the dour Sam Heppner. A small crowd was beginning to gather in front of the sheriff's office: Cal Vickers from the Texaco station; Dr. Bob Starr, the dentist; Heather Bardeen, who worked for her father, Henry, at the ski lodge; and a half dozen other people I recognized but couldn't name.

"All right, everybody," ordered Milo, as if he were dispersing an unruly mob, "let's move along. If you want a show, go down the street to the Whistling Marmot." Somehow, he'd managed to include Vida and me with the riffraff. Before Vida could do more than shriek at Milo over Cal Vickers's head, the sheriff, the deputy, and my brother were off in the squad car, lights flashing, siren squealing.

"Well!" Vida was miffed. "Doesn't that beat all!" She gave me a dark glare. "You're the newspaper publisher. Don't you have any clout?"

"If you want to know the truth, I'd rather rescue my Christmas tree." I pointed to the Jaguar.

Vida started to join me at the curb, but the little crowd surged around her, asking questions. Typical, I thought, they would seek out Vida as the font of all knowledge. Even after almost three years in Alpine, I was still regarded as a newcomer. I tugged and hauled at the Douglas fir, finally managing to get it back in the trunk.

"Let's go," Vida shouted, at last making her way to the Jag. She got in on the passenger's side, grumbling all the while.

I turned on the ignition. "I'm not sure we should follow . . ."

Vida heaved a sigh of annoyance. "I don't mean Milo; I mean your house. You'd better get that tree home before you ruin it."

Vida was right, though her attitude struck me as wrong. It wasn't like her to abandon the trail of a juicy story. But it would take only a few minutes to deposit the Douglas fir. I shifted into first gear and waited for a UPS truck to pass before I pulled out.

"I don't like all these spare parts floating around," Vida declared as we headed up Fourth Street. "Milo's got trouble on his hands."

"Is that why you didn't want to go to the falls? Are you afraid he might screw up and we'd have to report it?"

"Oh, no! He and Sam and your brother will dig and delve and measure and put samples of this and that into little plastic bags and well nigh freeze to death in the process. Men like to do stupid things like that, but the rest of us have more sense. We'll find out everything in good time and have hot cocoa while we do it." Vida paused, pointing at the windshield. "Be careful, Emma, there's Averill Fairbanks, skiing across Cedar Street."

Alpine residents on skis in town weren't a rarity. On certain days, Seventh Street was barricaded from Spruce to Front to provide a free ski run. Henry Bardeen didn't approve, but the lodge made plenty of money off the tourists.

"On your left," Vida noted. "Mother with child on sled." She took a quick breath. "Meter reader, the Whipps' grandson, not looking where he's going. Dunce."

"Stop!" I braked for a school bus that was heading out to collect its afternoon load of middle-school children. "Vida, what's wrong with you? You're driving me nuts."

From under the brim of her knitted cloche, she shot me a penitent look. "I'm annoyed. It makes me edgy."

I was passing St. Mildred's. "Annoyed about what?"

Vida heaved another sigh. "Bridget Nyquist. I set up an interview with her for one forty-five, but when I got to the house, she'd changed her mind."

"Why?" It was starting to snow again.

Wriggling in the bucket seat, Vida mimicked Bridget's wispy voice: " 'I don't think it's right to draw attention to myself. I like to help others. It's the way my mamma raised me. Tee-hee, simper, simper.' *Ugh!*" Vida's lip curled.

I turned onto Fir Street. "Don't worry about it. Say—what happened to that idea you had about an anniversary story for the Whistling Marmot? Isn't that coming up January first?"

Vida emitted a snort. "Oscar had the wrong year. His father started showing movies in the old social hall during

World War I. So either we've missed the seventy-fifth anniversary, or we'll have to wait a couple of years for the official opening of the theatre commemoration. Personally, I don't care. Oscar probably won't talk to me, either. Even when he does, he never has much to say. He told me once that when he was young he thought silent pictures had to be that way because people in California hadn't yet learned how to speak. Moron.''

I turned into the driveway. My log house looked particularly charming with snow on the roof and icicles hanging over the little porch. It would be wonderful to have a painting of the house as it looked in December and another to show the way it was in June. I'd had a hanging fuchsia then and window boxes full of red geraniums, white alyssum, and purple ageratum. If Evan Singer could draw, maybe he could also paint. I'd ask him when we did the interview.

Vida helped me haul the tree out back, where I put it in a bucket of water. Maybe it wouldn't freeze if I kept the tree close to the house. Vida recommended the carport, but there wasn't room.

Fifteen minutes later, we were back in the office. Vida was still grousing about Bridget Nyquist. I asked Ginny and Carla, who were about the same age as Bridget, if they knew her very well.

"I met her once during Loggerama," Carla said. "She seemed okay, but too much into herself."

"The first time I saw her," Ginny explained in her usual carefree manner, "was at Dr. Starr's. She was coming out just as I was going in. We said hi." Ginny's fair brow furrowed under wisps of auburn hair. "I've seen her a couple of times at the Grocery Basket and once at the Venison Inn, but we didn't speak. They only other time I saw her up close was about a month ago when I picked up some pictures for the paper at Buddy Bayard's Picture-Perfect Photo Studio. Bridget was there with Travis. They were having a first-anniversary portrait taken. Travis was friendly—he usually is—but Bridget sort of hung back.''

Carla flounced around her desk, long black hair flying. ''Low self-esteem. Imagine, with her money and looks. Maybe she's dumb.''

Vida eyed Carla over the rims of her glasses. ''She behaves as if she might be. But I doubt it. Travis Nyquist wouldn't marry a *nincompoop*.'' She uttered the word with emphasis on all three syllables, still looking meaningfully at Carla. Vida and I were at odds in assessing *The Advocate*'s reporter. My House & Home editor thought Carla was definitely stupid; I felt she was merely dizzy. Unfortunately, the result was often the same.

When my phone rang, I figured it was Milo or Ben. But it was neither. Adam was on the line, calling from Fairbanks.

''Hi, Mom,'' he shouted over a bad connection. ''You okay?''

''Sure,'' I shouted back. ''How are finals?''

''I could do them in my sleep,'' said my son so breezily that I assumed he had. ''Hey, I may not get in until Tuesday or so. To Alpine, I mean.''

''Why not?'' I felt a pang of disappointment pierce my maternal breast.

''What? Wow, is this phone screwed up or what?''

I heard a clicking sound which might have been the cable but more likely was the drumming of my son's nails on the mouthpiece at his end. ''Why not?'' I repeated.

''Wow, I can't hear you—we've got about a hundred feet of snow. I'll call you when I get to Seattle.''

''Hold it!'' Vida, Ginny, and Carla were all watching me. I'd taken the call at Ed's desk. I tried to ignore my staff members. It was impossible. ''Adam, where are you going if not to Alpine?''

''Erin asked me to spend a couple of days in Kirkland.'' Though Adam had lowered his voice and semi-mumbled, I still managed to catch the words.

"Erin who?" Or was it Aaron? Either way, I didn't know the name.

"Erin Kowalski. She lives in Kirkland. With her family. Right on Lake Washington. She's into animals." Now Adam was speaking more clearly. I could never keep up with his girlfriends. They seemed to exist on a monthly rotation. Even as he spoke, I was rummaging through Ed's out-of-town phone directories. I found Seattle, but that wouldn't do. The suburbs east of the lake had their own phone books. I rummaged some more. "We're going skiing," he added.

"You can ski in Alpine. Right in town, as a matter of fact," I pointed out.

"That's for pussies, Mom. We're going up to Crystal Mountain. I'll call you from Kirkland, okay? How's Uncle Ben?"

I'd finally found the Kirkland listings. There were two Kowalskis, a Leonard C. and a Douglas L. Kirkland, like the rest of Seattle's Eastside, had grown so much so fast that the addresses didn't mean anything to me. "Ben's fine," I replied, deciding to give Adam a dose of his own medicine. "Right now, he's out on a limb."

"Huh?"

"Call me as soon as you get in. Bye." With a smirk, I hung up the phone. My staff applauded me.

Ben, Milo, and Sam Heppner still weren't back at four o'clock. Worried, I called the sheriff's office, but Dwight Gould, another deputy, informed me that he'd been in touch with Milo as recently as three-thirty. They were heading back into town with the ambulance, stopping first at Doc Dewey's.

"Ambulance?" It didn't make sense.

"Right," said Dwight in his rumbling bass. "For the body. Young Doc'll do an autopsy."

"On . . . what?" I had an awful feeling I knew.

"The body," repeated Dwight. "It wasn't just an arm, Mrs. Lord. It was a whole body."

I put a hand to my forehead, for some irrational reason thinking of Safeway's ad in today's paper: WHOLE BODY FRYERS, 89 CENTS A LB. Maybe that was better than thinking of the previous week's CUT-UP FRYERS, $1.19 A LB. But of course I thought of both and feared my hysteria was returning.

I got a grip on myself. "Do you mean that literally? About being whole? Nothing missing—like a leg?" I winced as I spoke.

"Nope," rumbled Dwight. "All of a piece, at least near as I can tell from over the radio phone. Excuse me, Mrs. Lord, Bill Blatt and I are here all alone. Arnie Nyquist just came in, steamin' like a smokestack."

I passed the news on to Vida. She, too, was shaken, albeit briefly. "That means two dead bodies. My, my." Her face was grim as she looked up to see Kip MacDuff come through the door with the latest edition of *The Advocate*. He was only two hours late, which wasn't bad, considering car troubles and the weather.

By five o'clock, I'd had six phone calls inquiring about the leg item. Three asked if there was any further identification. Two reported they thought they'd hooked onto something strange, maybe an arm or a torso, maybe near Anthracite Creek, then again, maybe closer to Sultan or Index or Gold Bar or in their dreams. The last caller wanted to know if Milo got any fish.

All my staff had left by ten after five. Vida had been reluctant to go, but was committed to her round of festive holiday parties, this particular gala sponsored by the Burl Creek Thimble Club at the Grange Hall. Just before five-thirty, I closed up shop and walked over to the sheriff's office.

Milo, Ben, and Sam had just returned, not directly from Doc Dewey's, but from Mugs Ahoy. None of them were feeling any pain.

Exasperated, I turned my ire on my brother: "You jerks! I've been stewing and squirming all afternoon! You might have at least called!"

Ben grinned lopsidedly and punched me in the arm. The crackle in his voice had turned into a cackle. "Knock it off, Sluggly. You sound like Mom. Why didn't you get off your duff and look for us? We were a whole block away."

Sam Heppner had managed to slip off quietly, but Milo was lounging against the front counter, looking vaguely sheepish. "Ben's right, Emma. We just went into Mugs Ahoy to steady our nerves. You think it's fun freezing your unit off while you try to thaw out a stiff? Hey, that's good—frozen stiff!" He glanced at Ben, and they both broke into unbridled laughter.

I was grinding my teeth. I hadn't been this mad at Ben since he filled my strapless bra with Elmer's Glue the night of the Blanchet High School winter ball. I'd never been this mad at Milo, period. Where was Vida when I needed her? And the hot cocoa? If I'd had some, I would have poured it over Ben and Milo's heads.

"I need news, not a pair of drunken sots!" I railed. "What's this about a body? A *whole* body?" The image of a chicken hopped through my mind. I started to laugh, too. "Oh, good grief!" I collapsed onto a chair, shaking my head, but still laughing.

"Hey, Emma," said Milo, trying to lean his elbow on the counter, but missing, "your brother's okay, especially for a priest. And I'm okay, too. I'm off-duty. It's after five."

I stopped laughing. "A priest is never off-duty," I said, but my voice didn't convey much indignation. "What will Mrs. McHale think?"

It was Milo, not Ben, who answered: "That old broad? Who cares? She tried to put the make on me at the Labor Day picnic. Maybe she's the one who gave Father Fitz his heart attack."

"It was a stroke, you boob," I replied. "Do either of you two rollicking goofballs know how Father is doing?"

"As well as can be expected." It was Ben, this time,

giving me a skewed look. "We saw Doc Dewey, remember?"

I narrowed my eyes at my brother. "I sure do. But do you remember *why* you saw Doc Dewey?"

Ben ran both hands through his thatch of hair and turned around in a little circle. "Oh, yes. We remember. Why do you think we were drinking to forget?"

"But we didn't," put in Milo. He was patting himself down, as if searching a suspect for weapons. "Hey, where's my beeper? Did I leave it at Mugs Ahoy? Shit!"

I realized that Ben couldn't return to the rectory in his inebriated condition, nor could Milo drive home. I wasn't making much progress in getting to the facts, but if I stuffed them both with food, they should be able to tell me what I wanted to know. With the lure of beef stroganoff, I led them out of the sheriff's office to my car. The snow was coming down quite hard, with another two inches on the ground since mid-afternoon. I drove home cautiously, while Ben and Milo told each other perfectly dreadful jokes.

"I'm divorced," Milo announced to Ben as I pulled into my driveway. "Do you care?"

Ben responded with more laughter. "Joke's on you, Dodge. In my church, you were never married. Ha, ha!"

Milo's jaw dropped. "You mean . . . my kids are . . . Whoa! That's great! If I turn Catholic, can I stop paying child support for the little bastards?"

"You're only paying for one of them as it is," I said, pushing the car door open. "The other two are over eighteen. Besides, we're talking church, not state. Get out of the car, you two bozos. The first thing I'm going to do is make coffee."

My beef stroganoff takes only about twenty minutes to cook. By the time I was ready to serve, Ben and Milo had downed three mugs of coffee apiece and were almost themselves again. I suspected that neither of them—or Sam Heppner, for that matter—had drunk as much as it appeared.

There hadn't been time for them to down more than two or three beers apiece. Rather, I surmised, my brother and the sheriff were reacting to the horror of their find down by the falls.

My guess was verified when Milo announced that we'd wait until after we finished eating to discuss the afternoon's occurrences. Ben agreed, but almost blew it by saying grace and offering a prayer for the repose of the soul ". . . of the unfortunate young woman who met a violent end in Alpine." My curiosity further piqued, I ate very fast.

Clearing away the remnants of stroganoff, rice, and green beans, I offered Ben and Milo the rest of the Viennese torte with more coffee. I love food, but am not a big sweets freak. While they tackled the torte, I remembered Vida's words and heated some cocoa.

Milo was the first to broach the subject that held our minds hostage. "The body apparently had been dumped in the river, but the current had pushed it toward the bank. Snow had drifted onto some big boulders where the body was wedged. All you could see was the arm." He paused, looking at Ben for confirmation. "When we got there, we realized there was more than just an arm. It took us some time to dig her out. She probably hadn't been there very long." Milo's voice had grown subdued. Ben's mouth twisted at the memory.

"Was she naked?" I asked, and wondered why the question had sprung into my mind. I hadn't seen the arm, but if it had been clothed, surely Ben would have said so.

"Right," nodded Milo. "She was young, early twenties, pretty, I'd guess, hair about the color of yours, but longer. She had a tattoo."

I arched my eyebrows. "Where? What?"

Milo touched his backside. "Here. It spelled C-A-R-O-L, then B-A-S or something like that, then I-O-B-F, all in small letters. It was hard to read."

Finally, I was managing to set aside personal feelings and follow the story. "Not a last name?"

"I don't think so." Again, Milo turned to Ben. "You agree, Father?"

Ben inclined his head. "The B-A-S or whatever it is was under the name Carol, but smaller and centered. Then the I-O-B-F beneath that, also centered and even a little smaller."

"I-O-B-F doesn't spell anything," I said, getting up to put another log on the fire, "unless it stands for something like International Order of whatever. Are you sure that's what it said?"

"No," Milo replied flatly. "Doc Dewey will use one of his high-powered microscopes on it. We'll get a full report tomorrow."

I sat back down on the sofa next to Ben. The living room was cozy, with its comfortable, eclectic furniture, stone fireplace, forest green draperies, and the wonderfully warm, stained log walls. So far, the only Christmas decorations I'd put up were the first ten pieces of my Nativity set—one for every day of Advent. It was a tradition I'd started when Adam was a toddler. Tonight I would add another sheep.

"I suppose," I mused, "there's no way to connect this corpse with the leg?"

Milo gave me a wry glance. I made a face. There didn't seem to be any way to discuss this case without uttering something that sounded like a bad joke. "No. Two different parts of the river, probably a time frame of three or four months' difference. It's probably just a coincidence."

"Probably." I had to agree, yet I wasn't much of a believer in coincidences that didn't mean anything. "But you've got to admit that there *could* be. What about foul play?"

Before Milo could answer, the phone rang. It was Vida. "I'm almost out the door," she said in a rush, "but Marje Blatt just called from Doc Dewey's office." Marje was Vida's niece and Gerald Dewey's receptionist. As such, Marje walked a fine line between strict patient confidentiality and her aunt's mighty badgering. Her aunt usually had the edge. "Marje worked late tonight, so she was still around when young Doc started the autopsy. He practically had a fit—that body Milo and your brother dug out of the snowbank had been frozen!''

I pulled back, staring at the receiver. Had Vida lost it, along with Father Fitz? "I should think so," I said calmly. "It's been getting down to about ten above zero the last few nights. You'd be frozen, too, if you were lying under a snow-bank in the Skykomish River."

Vida's tone was not only rushed, but impatient. "I mean frozen beforehand. She'd thawed a bit, maybe the other af-ternoon when it got up to thirty-six. Monday, wasn't it? Think about it—I've got to head out to the Grange Hall. By the way, Doc can't find Milo. He doesn't answer his beeper."

Milo called young Doc right away. Yes, Doc figured the victim had been left to freeze, judging from the internal or-gans, then somehow had been partially thawed. Definitely, foul play: signs of trauma, a blow to the head. Blunt instru-ment, no idea what, brick, bat, or bowling trophy—that was Milo's department. When? Hard to tell, given the frozen state of the corpse. Maybe, said young Doc, four or five days, possibly longer. No, there was no sign of sexual assault or of recent intercourse. As for the tattoo, Doc hadn't gotten around to that yet. Ever the man of science, young Doc was more interested in the medical post-mortem than in such superfluous details as who he was performing it on. Milo looked very unhappy when he hung up.

"Now the rest is up to us," he sighed after relaying Doc Dewey's multiple messages. "You wait and see, everybody will jump on that spare leg and figure we've got a serial killer loose. Damn."

The Burlington Northern whistled in the distance, a mournful sound. Outside the window, I could see snow pil-ing up, drifting against the small panes, obscuring the rest of the world. The train whistled again. Irrelevantly, I thought of the avalanche, over eighty years ago, that had caved in the Great Northern Railroad tunnel on the second switchback up the line at Tyee. Ninety people had died, buried under a mass of snow. There had been only a handful of miners and loggers living in Alpine at that time. The disaster had served as a reminder that death lurked even in the most remote, beautiful settings.

Trying to shake off such grim thoughts, I made an attempt to encourage Milo. "You ought to be able to find a match with missing persons. If this poor young woman has been dead for going on a week, she'd be reported by now."

Milo refused to be consoled. "Not if she was a prostitute. Or if she's from out-of-state. Or on the run from some guy who was trying to beat the crap out of her. You'd be surprised. People can lose themselves pretty easily. At least on a temporary basis."

Ben had gotten to his feet and was toying with my manger scene. He set the three shepherds in a row, as if they were queuing up to get into the small wooden shed. "She must have worn clothes. What happened to them?"

Looking mildly affronted that Ben would raise such a point, Milo shrugged. "How do I know? According to Doc, it wasn't a sex crime. At least not rape. Maybe the killer is trying to hide the victim's identity."

Putting the two sheep in line behind the shepherds, Ben turned to Milo. "Do you mean she had her name stitched in her clothes?"

"Not necessarily," replied Milo. "Labels, maybe, that would narrow down where the clothes came from. You know, like some fancy designer store." He glanced at me. "Isn't that right, Emma?"

I nodded. "Some boutiques put their own labels in their merchandise. But it seems a little strange to me that the killer would check something like that." I played the scenario through in my head: violent murderer bashes in skull of victim, then calmly looks to see if clothing came from other than off the rack. It didn't make much sense, and I was sure that Vida would agree with me. It also didn't strike me as likely that a young woman with a tattoo on her rear end would buy her apparel at an exclusive shop. But people were unpredictable.

The discussion wound down. Ben finished putting the cow and the ox on the top of the stable roof, then announced that he had better get back to the rectory. I volunteered to drive both men, but they insisted on walking. St. Mildred's was half a mile from my home; Milo's house in the Icicle Creek development was about twice as far. I didn't press either of them, figuring the cold air would do them both good.

After they left, I cleared away the remnants of our meal and played around with possible ways of handling coverage of the latest murder victim. I had almost six days to write the story. A lot could happen between now and then. Still, it was a mental reflex on my part to take any news item and run with it. Two decades on daily newspapers was habit-forming. Often, I still found myself unable to adjust completely to the slower pace of a small town. I also found it impossible to adjust to murder.

I rearranged my Nativity set, added the new sheep, and tried to focus on other, more pleasant concerns. It was Advent, my favorite liturgical season. Hope. Joy. Peace. Those were the emotions I should be experiencing. Year after year, I had vowed to seek more quiet in the weeks before Christmas. But as a single working mother, there had been little time for anything but my son and the job. As Adam grew older, I figured I'd have extra hours to myself. Yet every December had brought a new, unexpected crisis: for example, the gingerbread house for German class which Adam had wanted to resemble Mad Ludvig's castle in Bavaria, but which, after forty-eight hours of shared toil, looked more like an overturned Dumpster. Adam knew he wouldn't get extra credit when his teacher had to ask, *"What is it?"*

When Adam went off to college, I was already an editor-publisher. Free time, let alone quiet time, was hard to come by. This year was proving no different. In a flurry of activity,

I hauled out a half dozen boxes from the storage room off the kitchen. Candles, wreaths, figurines, garlands, colored lights, ornaments, tinsel—it was all there, most of it mine, some of it my parents', and a few treasured items passed on from my grandparents. I set aside all the decorations for the tree with the remainder of the nativity pieces, then began to drape artificial pine over the doorways. I arranged candles on the mantel, hung a trio of wreaths, and put the rest of the Santas, Madonnas, angels, reindeer, and elves on whatever spare places I could find. Weary, but content, I surveyed my handiwork. My log house looked festive, warm, welcoming. When the tree was up, it would become sheer magic. I smiled with pleasure.

The tree. I had thought about it in the abstract, almost as if it were the same tree, from year to year, as artificial as the pine garlands. But the perfect Douglas fir that stood in a bucket next to the house had been witness to a murder. Or at least to a murder victim.

It was not a thought that brought hope or joy or peace. In fact, it was a damned rotten thing to happen to me during Advent.

But of course it was even worse for the victim.

Chapter Five

OSCAR NYQUIST, OWNER of the Whistling Marmot, had started going bald in his early twenties. He was, like so many older people in Alpine, a living legend. One of my favorite bits of Oscarana, as I called it, concerned Alexander Pantages, famed West Coast theatre entrepreneur. When the great man took his final curtain call in 1936, Oscar wanted to pay homage to a fellow impresario. Either out of respect for this icon or vanity for himself, Oscar was compelled to cover his half-bald head. His neighbor, Millard O'Toole, had butchered a cow that very morning. In a fit of inspiration, Oscar had cut off enough hide to make a toupee. It didn't match his remaining hair; it didn't fit his large head; and it wouldn't stay put—but Oscar wore it anyway. He drove off to Seattle in his Model-A Ford feeling respectable and looking ridiculous. When he bent over Pantages's coffin, the makeshift hairpiece fell off. Humiliated, Oscar left it there, and all Alpine assumed that the famed impresario was spending eternity with a little bit of local lore.

At eighty-two, Oscar had long since become completely bald. He was still a big man, an inch taller than his son Arnie, and probably thirty pounds heavier. On Thursday morning, he lumbered into the *Advocate* office behind his grandson, Travis, who had graduated to a walking cast, but still leaned on a pair of metal crutches.

"I want publicity!" boomed Oscar, standing in the middle of the room and somehow making the walls suddenly appear to close in on all of us. Ed looked up from his copy of the *Seattle Post-Intelligencer*. Ginny pivoted in the act of handing me some phone messages. Carla jumped so violently that she spilled latte on her desk. And Vida gave the newcomer a tight-lipped glare.

"Oscar, you old fool," she railed, "how many times do I have to tell you—and fifty other idiots in this town—that we don't do *publicity*. We do news or ads. After sixty years of running that movie theatre, you ought to know the difference. Either get yourself arrested or plunk out some money. Which is it you want?" She stopped long enough to cock her head to one side and smile warmly at Travis. "You're up and about, I see. How's your leg?"

"Dr. Flake put the walking cast on this morning and it feels . . ."

"Like hell!" interrupted Oscar, barging in front of his grandson. "If I say publicity, I *mean* publicity! Isn't this a newspaper? Isn't it printed for the public?"

"Oooooh . . . !" Vida whipped off her glasses and frantically rubbed at her eyes, the telltale gesture that indicated she was highly agitated. "I give up! Emma, you deal with this crazy old coot. He's impossible!"

So far, my dealings with Oscar Nyquist had been limited. Ed handled his weekly ads; Ginny did the billing; Carla had written a little news story the previous spring when a new Dolby sound system had been installed; and Vida, of course, covered any social events connected with the Nyquists. I knew Oscar only by sight—and sound, since his presence in the office was always unmistakable. To get my further acquaintance off on the right foot, I invited Oscar and his grandson into my inner office. Travis, however, demurred and sat down at Carla's desk. With a shrug, I followed Oscar and closed the door. It wouldn't prevent the others from hearing him, but at least it might muffle the roar.

"Have you seen my marquee?" he demanded, sitting across from me with his elbows on my desk.

"I saw it yesterday, I guess. You have your special annual showing of *It's A Wonderful Life*. I'd like to see it again. . . ."

"Today!" He pounded on the desktop, rattling objects and shivering timbers. "Yesterday I was showing *It's A Wonderful Life*, this morning I'm showing *It's A Wonderful File*! Who's the culprit, I ask you? Who's persecuting the Nyquists? That stupid sheriff of ours does nothing! We want you to help us. It's your duty, right?"

My brain was still dealing with the switch of letters on the marquee. It was simple enough, no doubt the nocturnal effort of some kids. It was also kind of funny, but I didn't dare say so to Oscar.

"Frankly, Mr. Nyquist," I said in a serious voice, "I'm not sure *publicity* would suit your purpose. That only calls attention to this sort of thing and invites more trouble. As long as there's no damage to your . . . ."

"Not yet," bristled Oscar, taking a briar pipe out of his lumber jacket. "Not to the Marmot, I mean. But damage, yes, oh, yes, we've had plenty of that. Theft, vandalism, passion pits—what next? Where does it end when there's no police protection in this town?"

Oscar Nyquist was shaking his pipe. He had gotten very red in the face, which in his case meant all over his skull as well. His jaw jutted, and there were deep furrows in his forehead. Fleetingly, I wondered if he were about to have a stroke, like Father Fitz.

"Wait a minute," I urged, keeping calm. "Back up a bit. I heard about the theft and some of the vandalism. That's happened mostly to your son, Arnie, right?" I saw Oscar give a jerky nod. "What's this passion pit business? That's news to me. Are you talking about necking in the movie theatre?" I phrased the question in the old-fashioned terms Oscar understood.

"Sheesh!" breathed Oscar, arching his eyebrows far up into his dome. He settled down enough to extract an oilskin pouch of tobacco from his jacket. "Not in *my* theatre, you don't. I still got ushers, remember? But I can't say exactly in mixed company," he murmured, lowering his voice as well as his head. "It's the new bowling alley site. Immoral acts. You know what I mean? My son has proof of it. That's not all, either." His voice began to rise again. "Somebody punctured the tires of two of Arnie's construction trucks. And then there's that Peeping Tom at my grandson's place."

"Has all this been reported to Sheriff Dodge?" I asked, still trying to keep my tone mild.

"Why bother?" exploded Oscar. "I tell you, he hasn't done anything! Oh, Arnie went to see him about the break-in the other day, but this new stuff—what's the use? That's why I'm here."

A single knock sounded on my door. I called out.

Travis Nyquist poked his head in. His words were for his grandfather: "Popsy, what did I tell you?" Travis's blue eyes narrowed slightly, distorting his otherwise appealing, all-American face.

Oscar turned slightly, then banged the desk again. "You're soft, boy! This is persecution, I tell you!"

Travis, however, stood firm, if slightly unbalanced on his new walking cast. "For Bridget's sake, Popsy. Come on, she asked nicely, didn't she?"

"Nyaaah!" Oscar made a scornful gesture, taking a swipe at the framed Sigma Delta Chi Award from my days at *The Oregonian*. "She's a baby, still wet behind the ears. . . ." But he caught the warning stare from Travis and began to simmer down. "Okay, okay, but those tires—do you know what they cost?"

"The tires don't bother me," agreed Travis, his face regaining its usual pleasant aspect. "Just remember what you promised." He winked, then closed the door.

"Maybe," I suggested, having racked my brain for a way out of this awkward situation, "what we need to do is look into the matter of the sheriff's office. That's what you're really

complaining about, right?'' I saw Oscar give a little shudder
that passed for assent. ''Perhaps I could assign one of my
staff to investigate how the sheriff handles complaints. We
might do a series, you know, in-depth, and in the process,
goad Dodge and his deputies into taking complaints such as
yours more seriously.'' It sounded exemplary, even though I
had absolutely no intention of following through. Over the
years, however, I have learned that most unreasonable requests made to journalists can be put off by the promise of
in-depth. The average layman is impressed by the idea, and
when nothing comes of it, the explanation is easy: *in-depth*
takes time. Most people's attention span is only slightly
longer than that of a bug's, so eventually the crisis dries up
and blows away.

Oscar, however, was looking dubious. Instead of protesting, however, he set aside his pipe and pouch, reached for
my notepad, and picked up a ballpoint pen. Apparently, Oscar was incapable of whispering. His handwriting was large
and overblown, like the man himself: *Someone is trying to
kill my grandson's wife. Help us*.

I blinked at the message, then stared at Oscar. He motioned for me not to speak out loud. *Who?* I scribbled.

Don't know, he scrawled in reply.

With a sigh, I leaned back in my swivel chair. It would do
me no good to urge Oscar or any other Nyquist to go to the
sheriff. Rapidly, I considered the previous problems the family had encountered. All of them were petty, probably pranks.
Young people in Alpine didn't have enough to do, especially
in the winter. None of the Nyquist complaints would lead
me to think that they could be connected with a killer. My
initial reaction was to dismiss Oscar's fears as part of a persecution complex.

Except that we already had two dead young women. Was
it possible that Bridget Nyquist might become number three?

I found a fresh piece of paper and invited Oscar to come
over to my house around six. He mulled over the request,

fidgeted with his pipe, then gave a nod of assent. "Okay," he said out loud. "You promise to help?"

"Of course." It felt like an empty vow, but at least I could hear the man out. He was on his feet, heavy shoes tramping on the floor. "What about Travis?" I murmured. "Would he like to come?"

The bald head gave a sharp shake. "No." Oscar started for the door. "He needs to rest." The remark was an afterthought.

Out in the news office, Vida and Ed were gone, Ginny had returned to the front desk, and Carla was deep in conversation with Travis. She giggled, which Carla often does, a decidedly unmusical sound. Travis was laughing, too. They were head-to-head, and I noticed that Oscar stiffened at the sight of them.

"Let's go, boy!" bellowed Oscar, barreling through the newsroom like a tank. Startled, Travis looked up from his tête-à-tête.

"Sure, Popsy," he said, appearing to struggle with the crutches. He slipped, caught himself on the desk, then allowed a wide-eyed Carla to brace him. "Thanks, I needed that." Travis beamed down on Carla, who actually blushed. I was refreshed and at the same time annoyed. Carla's private life was none of my business, but flirting with married men was dumb. After all, look where it had gotten me. . . .

I waited by the window to make sure Oscar and Travis had taken off in a brown Range Rover. Throwing my purple car coat over my shoulders, I turned to Carla. "What's with the bridegroom? I thought he had a nurse at home."

Carla giggled and blushed, blushed and giggled. "Travis Nyquist is just a friendly kind of guy. You know, the type who makes you feel like a *woman*."

"So how come you're acting like an idiot?" The response was more cutting than I'd intended. Immediate remorse set in, and I gave Carla a crooked smile. "Sorry, Carla, but

someday I'll tell you the story of my life. It'll cure you of
friendly men who wear wedding rings."

Carla sobered suddenly, and her complexion returned to
its usual smooth olive hue. "Do you mean Adam's dad?" If
nothing else, Carla was direct.

With a resigned sigh, I perched on her desk. "Yeah, that's
right." So far, I'd confided only in Vida about my ill-starred
love affair with Tom Cavanaugh. But with Adam due home
for Christmas break and no doubt headed back to the Bay
Area to visit his father over the holidays, my secret was about
to come out. "It wasn't just a flirtation, though. It was the
real McCoy. But that hasn't made it any easier for the past
twenty-plus years." I lifted my chin, attempting dignity.
Carla frowned. "Hey," I went on, shaking her arm, "I don't
mean to deliver a lecture. I'm overreacting. But Travis reminds me of Adam's dad—on the surface, that is. Smart,
good-looking, charming, ambitious, talented—and married.
Seeing the two of you together at your desk brought back
those days at *The Seattle Times* when I was an intern and
Adam's father was a copy editor. I was just about your age,
maybe a year or so younger. Do I sound sappy?"

Carla considered. "A little. Gosh, Emma, it's tough up
here in Alpine. Most of the unmarried guys have grease under their fingernails or have lost a few digits in the woods.
Where do you find a guy who isn't married and who uses
good grammar?"

My brown-eyed gaze met her black-eyed stare. "Good
question. Where, Carla? Where?"

Carla giggled. But she didn't blush.

The one man in Alpine who might have qualified, as far
as I was concerned, was sitting in his office with the phone
propped up against his ear and his long legs stretched out on
his desk. The problem with Milo Dodge was that there was
no chemistry between us. Then there was Honoria Whitman,
his current woman of choice. Also, he was divorced, and I

was Catholic. But most of all, there was Tom Cavanaugh. As long as I remained stupidly, stubbornly in love with Tom, Milo's flaws and virtues counted for naught.

Milo gestured for me to sit down, then went on with his monosyllabic side of the conversation. Whoever was at the other end was monopolizing the call. With a promise to see to it ASAP, Milo rung off.

"Dot Parker," said Milo with a sigh. "Durwood bought a snowmobile."

Durwood Parker, retired pharmacist, and unarguably the worst driver in Skykomish County, had been grounded by Milo for six months. Obviously, he was chafing at the bit and had discovered a new way to make mayhem. I clapped a hand to my head and gave Milo an incredulous look.

"Where is he?" I inquired, hoping it was nowhere near civilization.

"Somewhere up the Icicle Creek Road," replied Milo, rubbing his temples. "He got Averill Fairbanks to give him a lift as far as the ranger station. Ave saw a UFO land near the campground up there this morning."

"Oh." I marveled that Ave hadn't called the paper to report his latest sighting. He usually did. In fact, we could have kept a standing headline for Averill Fairbanks and his alien spacecraft. "Is Dot worried?"

"Yeah, a little. She wants Jack or Bill or somebody to go check on him if he's not back by mid-afternoon. You had lunch?"

Since it was only eleven-thirty, I hadn't. But breakfast had been meager: cinnamon toast and coffee. Tired out from my decorating efforts, I'd slept in, almost twenty minutes later than usual. I decided that if we could find a discreet table at the Venison Inn, it would be as appropriate a place as any to tell Milo about Oscar Nyquist's concerns.

Since we had beaten the usual lunch crowd to the restaurant, we had our choice of seating. I steered Milo to a back booth, next to a window. Red paper bells hung from the

ceiling, with silver tinsel looped wall-to-wall. Springs of holly
stood in slim white vases and red felt stockings were hung
over the fireplace at the rear of the main dining room. "Rudolph the Red-nosed Reindeer" was prancing along the restaurant's music track.

"What's up?" Milo inquired after he'd ordered a steak
sandwich medium-well and I'd opted for the beef dip because
I could get it rare this early in the lunch hour.

I relayed Oscar's complaints, as well as my empty promise. Milo looked mildly exasperated. "Jesus, those Nyquists
think they own the damned town. Old Lars used to face off
with Carl Clemans about once a month. Luckily, Carl usually won," said Milo, referring to the fair-minded mill owner
who had been Alpine's unofficial founder. "Oscar followed
in his father's footsteps, then Arnie, and now Travis, I suppose. I wouldn't bother myself with that marquee crap—kids
have been doing that for years around here. Remember *The
Mail and Louse*? Then there was *Lethal Peon 2*. We found
the extra letters in the litter can. Same with *The Prince of
Ties*. My favorite, though, was *Silence of the Lamps*—they
turned the *b* upside down . . ."

"Yes, yes," I interrupted, for Milo was starting to chuckle
himself into a small fit. "But that's definitely kid stuff. Stealing isn't."

"Arnie didn't lock the damned van. . . ."

"It's still stealing. Did you even bother to get prints?"

Having recovered from his bout of mirth, Milo gave me
an irked stare. "Sure. We got a bunch of smudges. In this
weather, who isn't wearing gloves?"

I paused as the waitress brought our salads and poured
more coffee. "Okay, let's skip the silly stuff," I said, a trifle
tight-lipped. Reaching into my purse, I took out the note
Oscar had written to me. Milo's long face twisted in what
might have been dismay, but more likely was disbelief.

"Hunh. So the old fart thinks he can get us moving by

making a claim like that?'' Milo tossed the sheet of notepaper back.

"Can you disregard it entirely?'' I asked. "Especially with dead bodies floating down the Sky?''

With a wave of his fork, Milo guffawed. "Now how the hell can you tie in one spare leg and an unidentified girl with the Nyquists? If the body was one of ours, okay. But nobody's missing from Alpine. I've checked. The only person unaccounted for as of this morning is Durwood.''

"Okay, okay,'' I said hastily. "But I promised I'd talk to Oscar about it tonight after work. I think I'll ask Vida to come over, too.''

Milo rolled his eyes, then stuffed his face with salad. "Don't you have enough to do with Ben in town and Adam on his way and the paper and all?'' At least that's what his remark sounded like through the lettuce.

"Oscar Nyquist isn't exactly the fanciful sort. And he's far from senile.'' I speared a piece of tomato and gave Milo what I hoped was a steely stare. "I'll hear him out. Vida thinks Bridget is behaving a bit oddly. Maybe the reason is because she feels her life is threatened.''

"Vida!'' Milo chuckled again, though he spoke the name with affection as well as scorn. "By the way, those weren't letters on that dead woman's body.''

"What?'' I held my coffee cup poised in mid-sip. "What do you mean?''

"They were numbers. One-Nine-Eight-Seven. The year, maybe, 1987. And it was B-H-S, not B-H-F, or whatever we thought it was at first. Doc Dewey used his microscope.''

"BHS?'' I gave a little start, spilling some of my coffee. Quickly, I mopped it up with my napkin. "That means Blanchet High School to me. I went there. The *1987* could be the year she graduated. Well, Milo?''

An unsettled look came over Milo's long face. "Is that right? In my line of work, it stands for Bushy-Haired Stranger. You know, the suspect who wasn't there,'' he said in an unusually tentative voice. His gaze fixed on the remainder of his salad. "You're right, it could be a high school. But why Blanchet? What about Bellevue? That's where my kids have gone since Old Mulehide and I split up. Or Ballard or Bremerton or Bellingham or . . . hell, any place in the country with a high school that starts with the letter B."

"That's true. It's just that those initials mean Blanchet to me," I pointed out. "Had you figured that it might stand for a high school?"

Milo looked a trifle sheepish. "No. I was thinking more of a person. A guy, maybe." He finished his salad, shoved the plate to one side, and nodded at a couple of loggers who were going into the bar. "There are about six missing women in the state who fit her description, but none of them are named Carol. If we could access a data base for high schools beginning with a B, then we could narrow it down to any Carols from the 1987 class. At least we'd have some place to start."

"Then what?" I asked as the waitress removed the salad plates.

Milo lifted his hands in a helpless gesture. "Then we'd try to find out if any of them are missing. That's assuming the dead woman's name is Carol. It would be one hell of a job. I doubt that we could do it out of this office. If we found out that there are no missing Carols from Blanchet, Ballard, Bellevue, or any of the other *B* high schools in the state, then maybe we could get the FBI to come in."

"For starters, I could call Blanchet," I offered. "Mrs. Hoffman is still in the tuition office. She's very helpful."

"I could get my kids to check out the Bellevue annuals," said Milo. "In fact, my oldest daughter graduated in 'eighty-seven."

The waitress returned with our entrees and more coffee. There was still no one sitting directly across from us, though I'd seen four men move into the booth at my back. I couldn't hear them, so I assumed they couldn't hear us. I decided it was time to reopen the subject of Oscar Nyquist's biggest worry, but I'd do it in a roundabout way. I started by asking Milo if any of the Nyquists had reported a Peeping Tom incident.

"Not officially," said Milo, drenching his meat with steak sauce. "But Arnie mentioned it when he was in with one of his numerous other complaints. Bridget Nyquist is a knock-out. It's no wonder some guy felt an urge to watch her undress. She should have pulled the shades."

"Do you know who it was?"

"Hell, no. Sam Heppner tried to pin Arnie down, but he suddenly became vague. It makes me wonder if Bridget didn't know damned well who the peeker was, but got skittish about saying so." Milo wiggled his sandy eyebrows at me.

"You mean she knew the guy?"

"I mean she sure did, and maybe he thought he had a right to be there, but her husband wouldn't have agreed." Milo chewed his steak complacently.

"But they're still newlyweds," I protested. Then I thought of Travis, apparently flirting with Carla. I also remembered Travis's warning to his grandfather. Had Travis been trying to keep Oscar from saying anything more about the Peeping Tom? I tried a different tack. "So you wouldn't tie this peeker in with a threat on Bridget's life?"

Milo gave a little grunt of a laugh. "If it's what I think it is, the only danger she's in is from Travis. In fact, the most likely victim would be the peeker. But if there's something going on between this guy and Bridget, Travis is the type who'd want to save face. He's got a big reputation in this town as an all-around success story. Four years on the job and he retires. Hell, why couldn't I have found a boondoggle like that?"

"Luck," I noted. "In my opinion, playing the stock market isn't much different from betting on the horse races. You might as well pick out the corporate logo you like best, just like choosing a horse by the jockey's colors."

"He sure knew how to pick them," said Milo. "Travis knew how to pick women, too, or so I thought until the so-called Peeping Tom showed up. If she's playing around on him, he's not so lucky after all."

I wasn't as ready as Milo to dismiss the peeker as a love-struck suitor waiting for Bridget to give the all-clear. In fact, I was beginning to get the uneasy feeling that the Nyquists weren't entirely wrong in their criticism of the sheriff's department. I was getting anxious to hear what Oscar would have to say when he came to my house.

"How's Saturday?" Milo was watching me expectantly. I'd been wool-gathering, and hadn't heard the first part of the question. Judging from Milo's quirky smile, he knew he'd caught me unawares. "For dinner at King Olav's? Paging Emma Lord, paging Emma Lord . . ."

"It's fine," I said hastily. "Adam won't be in until early next week. Ben will have the Saturday evening mass. What about Honoria?"

"She's going to spend Christmas with her family in Walnut Creek," said Milo. "She leaves Saturday morning." His expression grew wistful.

"Do you want to have Christmas dinner at my place?" I asked.

"I'll have the kids." Milo didn't seem thrilled by the prospect.

"So bring them." His son, Brandon, was almost the same age as Adam; Tanya was a couple of years older, and Michelle was a high school senior. My brother related beautifully to young people. We could have a real family gathering. I rocked a little in my seat, excited at the idea.

"I don't know. . . ." Milo was still looking uncertain. "They'll be driving up from Bellevue Christmas morning. Tanya is probably bringing that five-star jerk she lives with. It'd be a lot of bother, Emma."

"No, it won't. I'd love to have you. The jerk, too. Honest." Impulsively, I put my hand on Milo's. "I'll get a twenty-five pound turkey. Stuffing, mashed potatoes, gravy, cranberry sauce, green beans, and mince pie. Oh, rolls, too—I've got the Clemans family's potato roll recipe. Vida gave it to me." As far as I was concerned the matter was settled.

"It sounds good." Milo was weakening, enticed by the vision of a groaning sideboard. "I could bring some wine."

"Ben's doing that. You can get sparkling cider or pop. And maybe some rum so I can make Tom and Jerrys." I was very pleased. It would be the first big holiday dinner I'd fixed in years. In Portland, Adam and I had spent the first three Christmases by ourselves. I had been absolutely miserable.

Putting his free hand over mine, Milo gave me a surprisingly diffident smile. "It could be fun, huh?"

"It *will* be fun," I assured him. "We can play board games and act goofy. We can have a snowball fight. We can eat ourselves into a big fat fit."

"It's been a while since I've done that," Milo mused. "Had a big family-style Christmas, I mean. Last year the kids and I ate at the Venison Inn."

"Vida asked you to come to her house," I reminded him. Adam and I had gone there, joining Vida's three daughters, their husbands and children, and Carla. It had been lively, it had been lovely—but it hadn't been my own.

"It would have been too crowded," Milo asserted. Slowly, he removed his hand. I did the same. Our gazes locked, just for a moment, then fell away. "How about those Seahawks?" said Milo.

We returned to the outside world, once again firmly closing the door on our inner emotions. If we had any. I could never be quite sure.

". . . So it could be Blanchet or Bothell or Burnaby, up in B.C., or any—"

Vida stared at me, her eyes wide behind the big round lenses. "Don't you remember my wedding story?" She gave a swift shake of her head. "No, probably not, you weren't here, you were out of town. Bridget Nyquist went to Blanchet. And if memory serves, she was in the class of 'eighty-seven."

Chapter Six

I HAVE SEEN the mountains scarred by logging; I have seen the loggers scarred from living. The great gouges along Mount Baldy and Tonga Ridge speak to me. But so do the men who made them, and their voices keep me awake at night. I have heard the cry of the spotted owl. I have seen tears in the eyes of rough-and-ready human beings whose pride has been destroyed along with their livelihood.

In early September, when newly restricted logging activities were further curtailed by the danger of forest fires, I'd interviewed several loggers and their families. The image I'd carried in Seattle and Portland of two-fisted, hard-drinking, poorly educated louts armed with chain saws and no brains had begun to change. In its place, a new portrait began to emerge, not in bright red and green plaid, but in more somber colors. Despair, discouragement, depression were etched in the worried faces of the men, women, and children who depended upon the woods to make their living. A logger is a logger, and can't—not won't—think of himself as anything else. In Alpine, as many as four generations in one family had worked in the timber industry. Some had lost a leg or an arm, many were missing fingers and toes, a few were paralyzed, and the death toll was too high for any business. But the risks didn't scare off these gutsy woodland knights. What frightened them was the possibility of losing their livelihood—and their pride. The threat of shutting down the for-

541

ests hovered over these people like an axe. I decided it was time to take my stand.

Culling my research from a number of sources, I started to outline my piece for next week's issue. After returning from lunch with Milo, I had called Blanchet High School in Seattle, but Mrs. Hoffman wasn't in. Supposedly, she would call me back.

"Look," Vida said, not exactly appearing out of nowhere, since I could hear her coming from a mile away. "I put together a Nyquist family tree."

Sure enough, Vida had scrawled a genealogy of sorts on a sheet of typing paper. Lars, the Norwegian emigrant and founder of the dynasty as well as of the Whistling Marmot Theatre, had married Inga Fremstad in 1909. Oscar was born a year later; his sister Karen came along in 1917. Oscar had taken Astrid Petersen as his bride in 1932. Karen had become Mrs. Trygve Hansen in 1938. Astrid Nyquist had passed away three years ago. Two children had been born of that union—Thelma, who married a man named Peter Nordoff and moved to Spokane, and Arnold, whose wife, Louise, had been born a Bergstrom. Their son, Travis, was an only child.

"I've met Louise Nyquist but I honestly don't remember the woman," I mused. "What does she look like?"

Vida was scanning my owl editorial on the computer screen. "Good for you, you're taking a stand. You've got spunk, Emma. I've always said as much. Which," she went on without missing a beat, "is more than I can say for Louise Nyquist. No wonder you don't remember her. She fades into the woodwork, like an unnecessary coat of varnish. Mousy creature, your height, plump as a pigeon, and about the same coloration—gray and more gray. She's never stood up to Arnie, but how many people have where the Nyquist men are concerned? They don't even stand up to each other."

I couldn't place my encounter with Louise Nyquist. Not at bridge club, not from the library, not in passing at the grocery store, not as a member of any of the civic groups I came into contact with through the newspaper. "Does she ever leave the house?"

Vida gave me a scathing look. "Well, of course! She's not a recluse, and she's no dope—she's just a mouse. She still occasionally substitutes as a teacher. She taught all the time Travis was in high school. Then she decided to get her M.A. about three years ago. Now that was something, I'll admit. She had the gumption to live in Seattle and take classes at the UDUB and come home every other weekend. I heard Arnie was fit to be tied."

I admired Louise Nyquist's determination. "At least she's tried to establish her own identity," I remarked.

Vida nodded. "It's taken some doing. But when she isn't subbing, Louise keeps busy as a homemaker and does her share for the Lutheran church. She and Arnie take trips now and then. Arnie's always asking me to write them up, but they never go anywhere interesting. Arizona, Palm Springs, Hawaii—you know, all the places that everybody else goes and is sick to death of hearing about. Do you really think we need to run a photo of Louise Nyquist standing next to a cactus? Or Arnie cavorting around Konopali Beach in Bermuda shorts? Ugh!"

I smiled agreement, then again studied the Nyquist family tree. "They sure stick to their own," I noted. "These are all Scandinavian names except for Bridget. I see she was a Dunne." Irish, maybe. And, if she had graduated from Blanchet, possibly Catholic.

Vida picked up on my wavelength. "If Bridget was R.C., she gave it up. She married Travis in the Lutheran church, remember? Don't think the Nyquists would permit anything else. In college, Arnie was crazy about some Catholic girl. Oscar put a stop to that, I can tell you!" To my dismay, Vida didn't look entirely disapproving. I was still having trouble adjusting to the narrow-mindedness of Alpiners when it came to people of different races and creeds. Alpine might be only seventy miles from Seattle, but it was seventy years behind the times in terms of social integration.

"So he got stuck with the mouse?" I remarked innocently. "Or is Louise a pigeon? I forget."

"She's both," Vida replied, a bit testily. "So was Arnie's first love, for all I know. I never met her. He wanted to bring her home from the University of Washington to meet his family, but you can imagine how Oscar reacted to that. And old Lars, too. He was still alive then. Karen's first husband was killed early on in World War II. She married again," Vida noted, pointing to Oscar's sister on the makeshift genealogy. "He was Jewish. You can imagine how *that* stuck in the family's craw!"

Vida exited my office just as Ben came through the outer door. He greeted my House & Home editor warmly, but I could tell from the drawn expression on his face that he was upset. Either as a measure of trust in Vida or an acknowledgment of my friendship with her, Ben didn't bother to shut the door behind him. Vida, however, appeared to be absorbed in her typing. I knew better. Vida could have overheard whispers on game day in the Kingdome.

"Dr. Flake is sending Father Fitz to Everett for tests," Ben announced, sitting down in one of my two visitors' chairs. "He's not responding as well as he should. His speech is impaired and he's partially paralyzed on one side. Flake thinks he may have had a second stroke."

"Oh, dear." I wasn't sure who I felt more sorry for—my pastor or my brother. "Are you stuck at St. Mildred's for the duration?"

Ben grimaced. "I can't be. I've got my own parish. I have to be back in Tuba City on January second. You know that."

"I mean are you going to have to take over for the holidays?" I gave Ben a look of genuine sympathy.

He sighed, reached into his pocket, and pulled out a huge cigar. "I suppose so. Dr. Flake went over to Everett to see Father Fitz. The poor old guy has been trying to give Flake instructions to pass on to me. He's sure St. Mildred's will collapse without his guidance, I guess. He can't speak very well and he can't write, so it's very frustrating. All I can do is have Flake tell him everything is under control. Technically, I'm not under this archdiocese's jurisdiction, but my conscience wouldn't let me walk away. With the shortage of priests, I doubt very much if the arch can spare anybody, especially during Advent and Christmas.''

For a moment, we were silent. Ben was lighting the cigar; I was trying to make the best of a disruption. St. Mildred's was a self-sustaining entity. The parish council, the school faculty, the various committees would hold the parochial fabric together. Given Father Fitz's advanced age, he wasn't the most active priest in the archdiocese. Ben would be stuck for daily and weekend masses, a couple of weddings, maybe a baptism, and, if he had time, visits to the sick. Except for the fact that he'd probably have to stay on at the rectory, he'd still have plenty of free hours to spend with Adam and me.

''Where'd you get that cigar?'' I inquired as my office grew hazy with smoke. ''Your old drinking buddy, Milo?''

Ben shook his head. ''Peyton Flake. He says they taste even better over a fifth of Wild Turkey. Ever see a Desert Eagle?''

''I've got enough problems with the spotted owl. Does the Desert Eagle hang out with the Wild Turkey?''

''You got it, Sluggly.'' Ben grinned, clenching the cigar in his teeth. Apparently, he'd faced up to his unexpected responsibilities, acknowledged his pastoral duties, and made peace with himself. Ben was like that—he went through agonies of indecision, but once he'd made up his mind, he put all doubts behind him. ''A Desert Eagle is a gun, in this case, a .357 Magnum. They're made in Israel. Dr. Flake just bought one. He may be able to solve the spotted owl controversy single-handedly. Right now he's threatening to practice on the religious statuary up at St. Mildred's. I told him he'd.

better not, or I wouldn't lend him my Browning high-power nine-millimeter semiautomatic.''

"You've got a *gun*?" I shrieked. Vida, I noticed, paused in her typing, but briefly.

Ben gave me a disgusted look. "Of course I've got a gun. Do you think I'd wander all over the Mississippi Delta or the Arizona desert without a gun?''

I was flabbergasted. Of course our dad had owned guns, and had done some hunting before he decided that too many of his fellow hunters couldn't tell a cow from a deer—or each other. "What are you afraid of," I demanded, "the Ku Klux Klan and the Mormons going after your parishioners?''

"I'm more afraid of my parishioners." Ben chuckled, then shook his head. "No, it's not people that worry me so much as animals. Snakes, mainly, in Arizona. Anyway, Dr. Flake asked me to go shooting with him. He's quite a guy. Not what I'd expect to find in Alpine.''

I'd met Peyton Flake twice, and had to agree with Ben. The new doctor in town was not much over thirty, and a graduate of the University of Chicago's medical school. Flake was a lanky six foot three with a ponytail, rimless glasses, and a careless beard. His professional uniform seemed to consist of faded blue jeans and a rumpled denim work shirt. His untidy appearance, not to mention his somewhat flamboyant personal habits, had aroused a good deal of criticism, but his medical expertise was slowly starting to win people over. Doc Dewey sang his new partner's praises.

I was still reeling from my brother's revelation that he roamed the reservation with a cocked and loaded handgun when I saw Ginny and Carla come into the outer office carrying a couple of cartons. I recognized them as containing *The Advocate*'s official Christmas decorations. They were, I recalled from my previous Alpine Yuletides, a pathetic lot. Marius Vandeventer, who had founded the newspaper almost sixty years ago, had been many things. Most of them were admirable, but he hadn't been overly keen on Christmas. I cringed as Ginny pulled out a two-foot-high tree made from aluminum foil.

The phone rang. It was Mrs. Hoffman, calling from the Blanchet attendance office in Seattle. As we caught up with each other over a gap of almost twenty-five years, I scrawled a note to Ben.

He nodded, then made a notation of his own: *BHS chaplain—Bill Crowley—fellow seminarian.*

Mrs. Hoffman and I finally got down to business. Offhand, she recalled two or three Carols in the class of '87. I could hear pages turning. Maybe it was easier to look through the yearbook than to rely on computer records.

"Here's Carol Addams, tall, blond girl—it helps to look at their senior pictures—got a scholarship to some school back east, graduated in biology, got married last summer, and lives in Maine. Or is it Vermont? It's so hard to keep track of these kids, but her youngest brother is a junior this year. . . ."

It occurred to me that—at least as far as Blanchet High School was concerned—Clarice Hoffman was almost as valuable a resource as Vida was for Alpine. But of course it was Mrs. Hoffman's job to keep track of students, at least while they were attending the school. It was she who took the calls from parents reporting on sick, tardy, or otherwise absent teenagers, and she who had read—and heard—every excuse in the book.

"Janovitz," she was saying, "but she spelled it Carole, with an *e*. You said this one doesn't?"

"Uh . . . right." I hadn't told Mrs. Hoffman why I was trying to track down a 1987 graduate named Carol. If there was no connection between Blanchet and the body by the river, then there was no need to unduly alarm the attendance office or the rest of the faculty and staff.

"Neal," she said. "Let me think . . . Carol Neal . . . Her parents weren't as well-off as some." Which, I assumed, meant that they were often behind in their tuition payments.

"St. John's? Or St. Catherine's? I can never remember home parishes. North end, though—she took the bus. That is, until she got a car in her junior year." The sound of more pages being riffled came over the line. "Winters, but that's Carolyn." Mrs. Hoffman paused, presumably finishing up the alphabetical listings. "That's it, Emma. Do you think you're looking for Carol Neal or Carol Addams?"

"Neal," I replied. "Addams doesn't live around here, right? By the way, was that the same year Bridget Dunne graduated?"

"Bridget!" Mrs. Hoffman's voice took on an edge. "Now there was a piece of work! I could never figure that kid out. Say, didn't she marry somebody from up your way?"

"She did. A local named Travis Nyquist." Ben was watching me closely through a cloud of cigar smoke. Ginny and Carla were putting cheap plastic ornaments on the aluminum-foil tree. Vida had given up all pretense of typing and was standing in the doorway of my office.

"Funny girl," mused Mrs. Hoffman. "You never knew where you were with her. One minute, she'd be sweet as candy; the next, she'd be a real little snip. Of course she lost her father when she was a sophomore. And I heard Mrs. Dunne committed suicide. I guess I'd better go dig into my bag of Christian charity and spare a bit for Bridget."

"Do you remember if Bridget and Carol Neal were friends?" I asked innocently.

Mrs. Hoffman hesitated. "That whole class was even more cliquish than some of the others. I'm not sure. They may have been. But it seems to me that Bridget in particular palled around with girls from other private schools. Holy Names. Forest Ridge. Even some of the non-Catholic ones. I told you: she was odd."

I didn't know if Mrs. Hoffman's judgment of Bridget was based on the girl's unpredictable personality or her choice of companions. It didn't matter. I had a link between Bridget

Dunne Nyquist and Carol Neal. If, of course, that was Carol Neal's body lying in Al Driggers's mortuary.

"Have you got a mailing address for Carol Neal?" I asked, giving Vida and Ben a high sign.

"The alum office would have it. Should I transfer you?"

Briefly, Mrs. Hoffman exchanged pleasantries about our reunion via telephone. Just before she rang off, she wished me luck in finding Carol Neal. I mumbled my thanks.

I didn't recognize the female voice that answered for the alumni association. She sounded young, eager, and efficient. Maybe she thought I wanted to give money. But she met my request with a buoyant spirit. As I waited for her to look up Carol Neal's address, my gaze shifted from Ben to Vida and back again. Vida was waving both hands, not at me, but in an attempt to disperse Ben's cigar smoke.

"Filthy," she muttered. "What kind of vices do you priests have?"

The lively voice came back on the line. "We have an address for Carol Neal in the University District, on Fifteenth Northeast. But that was four years ago. She moved after that and apparently left no forwarding address. We have her listed as inactive."

That, I thought, was an understatement.

Chapter Seven

THE ALUMINUM-FOIL TREE with its plastic ornaments, the ragged red and green paper streamers, and the Styrofoam snowman with his missing nose and mangled top hat didn't do much to cheer up the editorial office. I flinched when I remembered what Ginny had to work with in the reception area: three cardboard Magi, a Star of Bethlehem that had lost half of its pasted-on gold glitter, and a Holy Family fashioned from bread dough. The array was depressing.

"Nice decorations," Ed Bronsky commented as he lumbered through the office. "I really like the tree. It's like the one we have at home, only smaller. We put homemade stuff on it, like cranberries and popcorn and hard candy."

Ben had left for the rectory and Vida had returned to her desk. "What a stupid idea," she declared, narrowing her eyes at Ed. "I've seen your tree. By the day after Christmas, it's bare. Your children have eaten all the decorations." The accusing stare she gave Ed indicated that she thought he and his wife had probably helped.

I didn't give Ed time to defend himself. "Here," I said to Ginny and Carla. "I'm writing a check to Harvey's Hardware and Sporting Goods Store. Go get something decent, and keep it under fifty bucks."

Ed stopped removing his heavy overcoat. "Harvey Adcock! I was supposed to see him fifteen minutes ago! Wouldn't you know it! He wants to double the size of his usual ad next week just because he thinks men like to get tools and sports stuff for Christmas! Why can't they be happy with a tie? I am.'' He plodded out of the office behind Ginny and Carla.

Vida rolled her eyes. "Honestly," she breathed. "It isn't just that people are jackasses, Emma. It's that there are so many *kinds* of jackasses!''

"I'm afraid so." I poured a cup of coffee and sat down in Ed's chair. "I've got to go see Milo and tell him about Carol Neal. Then he can start tracking her down and find out if she's really missing.'' I paused, waiting for Vida to respond. But Vida was doodling on a notepad. "If she's the same Carol," I went on, "then she must have known Bridget. Blanchet's not that big—under a thousand students at the time, I'd guess.'' Vida kept doodling. "I should have asked Mrs. Hoffman who Carol's friends were, assuming she and Bridget weren't buddies. Maybe Ben can call Bill Crowley. He's been the chaplain there for almost ten years.''

At last, Vida looked up. "Who was your best friend in high school, Emma?''

I blinked. "I had two. Chris Sullivan and Ursula Guy.''

"When was the last time you saw them?''

My brow furrowed under bangs that needed a trim. "I had lunch in Seattle with Chris last summer. The Fourth of July weekend. Ursula lives in Houston. I owe her a letter. She sent me a Thanksgiving card and enclosed a note.''

Vida nodded slowly, while I gazed at her in puzzlement. "You keep up. Even though you live a whole county or half a continent away. Now if you and Tommy''—I made a face as Vida called Tom Cavanaugh by the nickname only she dared to use—"had taken the trouble to get married, I imagine you would have invited these dear high school chums to your wedding. Oh, stop looking like you swallowed a dill pickle! I know it wasn't your fault you didn't get married, and he may be Tom to you, but he's Tommy to me. And he's a very fine man, not nearly as big a lunkhead as most. But don't get me started on *that*. What I'm saying is that it's very strange Bridget had no friends at her wedding. She's only twenty-two or twenty-three. At that age, they couldn't possibly have all moved to Timbuktu. So what is wrong with Bridget Dunne Nyquist?''

I was taken aback by Vida's question. "How do I know? More to the point, what's Bridget's lack of social expertise got to do with Carol Neal's dead body? If, that is, the corpse turns out to be Carol?'' I saw Vida's expression of exasperation and grabbed the phone. "That does it! I'm not waiting to go over to Milo's office; I'm going to call him right now!''

As I vigorously punched in the sheriff's number, Vida sat back in her chair, wearing a smug look. "It's about time. I thought you were going to sit there all day and slurp coffee, just like Ed.''

I gave Vida a wry glance. At the other end of the line, I was put on hold. Before I could say anything more to Vida, Milo's laconic voice sounded in my ear. He was mildly interested in the information I'd gleaned from Mrs. Hoffman. One thing that I've learned from dealing with law enforcement agencies is that their representatives in general—and Milo Dodge in particular—rarely get excited over what the average lay person would consider a hot lead. They deal only in facts. Guesswork is anathema.

But Milo agreed to get on Carol Neal's trail. He'd call the King County sheriff's office in Seattle right away. My so-called tip was the only lead he had, after all.

Vida had resumed her doodling. Six circles and an evergreen silhouette later, she put the pad aside. "I'm going to do the Whistling Marmot story after all,'' she announced, just as I was heading back into my private office. "Oscar is eighty-two. He might not be around by the time we get to the Marmot's official seventy-fifth anniversary. Oh, I know, Lars lived to be ninety-three and still had all his faculties, such as they were to begin with, but I don't want to take a chance. As far as that goes, *I* might not be around.''

That didn't strike me as likely. Vida seemed about as indestructible as any human being I'd ever met. She had a point, however. "What's the hook?" I asked.

"The Capra movie," Vida answered promptly. "Oscar has shown *It's a Wonderful Life* every Christmas now for going on twenty years. I want to ask him why he thinks people keep coming back to pay for something they know by heart. He won't have any answers because he's never thought about it, but it's a feature story and I can speculate. It also gives me an excuse to be at your house when he comes over tonight."

"Crafty," I remarked. "By the way, I'm leaving early. I want to go to the mall and do some Christmas shopping."

On my way out, I met Carla and Ginny, who were each carrying a rather small paper bag. "Didn't Harvey have any decorations?" I asked.

"Sure," Carla replied, rustling about in her paper sack. "Look, isn't this adorable?" She pulled out a six-inch figure of Santa Claus, or more precisely, Father Christmas, since he was decked out in a nineteenth-century satin suit of blue trimmed with white fake fur.

"It's charming," I said in admiration, as the wind blew snowflakes before my eyes. "But I was thinking more of—"

"See this," Ginny interrupted. Her paper bag held a pair of candlesticks shaped like angel heads and two green tapers. "We can put them on the reception desk instead of those crummy Wise Men."

Somehow, I'd been thinking more in terms of evergreen garlands, tasteful plastic holly wreaths, even a small artificial tree with a few handsome ornaments. "These are very nice," I said with a weak smile, "but they don't make much of a display. Maybe we could get a couple of other items. How much did these cost?"

Ginny dug anew into her paper bag. "Here's the bill. They came to $53.73. We kept it under fifty dollars, but of course there's the sales tax."

I clenched my teeth. It was no good criticizing my staff members for their ill-chosen method of eroding my finances. I had, as Vida and other Alpiners would say, sent a boy to the mill. Or a couple of them, in this case. They'd gone, they'd seen, they'd purchased. Ginny and Carla simply weren't up to the task. A veteran Christmas decorator had been required, and neither of them qualified.

I brushed snow off my nose. These two pieces were at least a start toward improving the quality of our holiday decor. Maybe I could find some other decorations on sale after Christmas. But for now, I wasn't about to deplete my checking account any further.

At least not on behalf of *The Advocate*. I was, in fact, about to make a large dent in my current balance by filling some of the gaps on my Christmas list. The parking lot at the mall was full of slush, with big piles of plowed snow around the outer edges. I'd taken care of most of my shopping on two weekend trips to Seattle during October and November. But there were still a few presents I wanted to buy for Adam and Ben. And Vida. It wasn't so much that she was hard to please, as that she never seemed to want anything. I took a chance on bedroom slippers and headed for Barton's Bootery.

The Alpine Mall isn't very large by big city or suburban standards. There are only fifteen stores and two restaurants, though Ed has been trying to track down a rumor that Fred Meyer and Starbuck's Coffee plan to open in the coming year. We've heard other such stories, usually concerning big chains, but so far nothing has come of them. In my dreams, I see an honest-to-goodness department store, with three or four floors of merchandise. But I don't think that will happen soon in Alpine. Too many people are out of work. Even now, so close to Christmas, the large parking lot was only half-full. A couple of cars looked as if they had been sitting there for a week or more. Snow was piled high on their roofs, hoods, and trunks. If their owners had suffered from mechanical problems, I wondered why they hadn't pushed the cars across the street to Cal Vickers's Texaco station.

The merchants at the mall had done their best to make their shops look festive. The light standards in the parking lot wore gold garlands and sprigs of plastic holly. Inside, more garlands hung from the ceiling with more holly and clusters of shiny colored bells. The display windows were jammed with Santas, reindeer, angels, snowmen, trees, wreaths, fireplaces, and candles; at Tina's Toys, Snow White and the Seven Dwarfs were dressed in holiday finery.

In Barton's Bootery, I saw several people I knew, including Annie Jeanne Dupré, music teacher and the organist at St. Mildred's; Heather Bardeen, Henry's daughter; and Charlene Vickers, whose husband Cal owns the Texaco station. I had just made my purchase of turquoise blue high-top slippers with little bows when Arnie Nyquist came into the store. At his side was a plump middle-aged woman who I realized must be Mrs. Nyquist. Yes, I probably had met her, but on closer inspection, I realized that not only was Louise Nyquist mousy; she was the type of person who looks like everybody else; a bit under medium height, a bit overweight, a bit of gray in her brown hair, a bit of this and a bit of that. She was utterly average, though I suspected that in her younger years, she had probably been pretty.

Arnie was prepared to breeze by me, but I executed a quick step in my fur-lined boots and barred his way. "Hi, Arnie," I said cheerily, then beamed at Mrs. Nyquist. "Louise, right? We've met . . . uh . . . ah . . ."

"At Doc Dewey's funeral reception," Louise replied with a diffident smile. "I poured."

The senior Doc Dewey had died of cancer the previous month. His funeral had been held right after Thanksgiving. Less than two weeks had passed. I felt like a fool. I couldn't believe Louise Nyquist could be so forgettable. I must be having a memory lapse.

"Everyone was so upset about poor Doc," Louise murmured, as if excusing me for my obvious gaffe. "If it isn't one thing, it's another."

I'm never sure how to respond to that particular cliché, especially since I've never figured out exactly what it means. I gave Louise a weak smile and turned to Arnie, who was all but tapping his foot in his impatience to move on.

"Any luck with the sheriff?" I asked brightly. "We'll be running your complaint in the weekly log. You don't happen to have a description of the guy who's been lurking around Travis's house, do you?"

Arnie Nyquist bristled. "Ask Travis. I got problems of my own."

Louise was obviously embarrassed by her husband's manner, and not, I figured, for the first time. She patted his arm and gave me an apologetic smile. "Arnie is so upset by all these incidents, and who can blame him? Really, there's not much to say about this person, whoever he may be. Very ordinary: medium height, stocky, a working man, mid-thirties, perhaps."

Arnie looked fit to spit. "Mid-thirties! How the hell could Travis or Bridget figure that out? They've only seen him two or three times, and never up close. What a bunch of bunk!"

Surprisingly, Louise Nyquist held her ground. "By the way he moved. Or so Bridget told me. And he wore workmen's clothes, like a logger or a millworker. That's not much help, I know."

She was right. In Alpine, that description could fit at least two hundred men. Not wanting to further annoy Arnie, who would probably take his anger out on his wife, I wished them a pleasant shopping trip and made my exit from Barton's Bootery. Arnie didn't exactly heave a sigh of relief, but he did relax a little. Louise, however, looked as if she was sorry to see me go. As I headed for SportsWearWorld, I wondered why.

Ninety minutes and two hundred dollars later, I was loaded down with parcels and heading back to the Jag. Two sweaters for Adam, a lightweight jacket for Ben, the slippers for Vida, and, as an afterthought, a little something for Milo. If, I reasoned, he was coming for Christmas dinner, I ought to have a token gift for him under the tree. I opted for a trio of alder-smoked sockeye salmon, rainbow trout, and kippered king salmon, then added a bag of Ethiopian coffee beans. I was at the Jag when I suddenly thought about Teresa McHale. Would she be alone at the rectory for Christmas dinner? It was possible that Father Fitz would be out of the hospital by then. As the snow drifted around my inert figure, I debated the matter: Teresa had been in town for about a year and should have made some friends among the parishioners. If memory served, this would be Teresa's second Christmas at St. Mildred's. But Alpine was slow to accept newcomers. On the other hand, surely someone in the parish would remember what Christmas was really all about and take her in. I decided to bide my time. Ben would find out about Teresa's plans, if any.

I was at the arterial on Alpine Way when I realized that the one person I hadn't bought anything for was *me*. If Milo and I were going to dinner at King Olav's Saturday night, it would be nice to have a new dress. It was after four o'clock and already quite dark. I hadn't planned on going back to the office, but Francine's Fine Apparel was only two blocks away, across Front Street. I parked the car in my usual slot and cautiously walked over to Francine's. Even though the main byways had been sanded that morning and rock salt had been put down on the sidewalks, the below-freezing temperatures and the new snowfall made footing hazardous.

The apparel shop was deserted, except for the owner and one customer I recognized as Roseanna Bayard, wife of Buddy Bayard, the photographer we use for our darkroom work. Like Francine, the Bayards were fellow parishoners. Roseanna greeted me with a friendly wave.

"I *love* your brother," she declared, her wide-set blue eyes dancing. Roseanna was an enthusiast, a grown-up Carla, but intelligent and well-grounded. When she wasn't helping Buddy run the photography studio, she tutored children with reading disabilities. Roseanna was a tall woman, rather rangy, with short blonde hair and incongruous dimples. "Not that I don't think the world of Father Fitz, but let's face it: he's been gaga for years. I don't care what that old bat up in the rectory says, it's great to have a priest who's got all his marbles."

My proud smile endorsed my brother. But I had to ask Roseanna about the old bat. "You mean Mrs. McHale? What's she got against Ben?"

Roseanna sniffed. "She's a typical parish housekeeper. Remember Mrs. McPhail? She thought *she* ran the church, and Father Fitz along with it. That's why those women take those jobs. They're on a power trip."

Francine Wells's carefully plucked eyebrows arched. "That's true, Roseanna," Francine said in her amiable retail manner. "They don't have a vocation, but they want to be involved with the Church. So they become housekeepers. What do you think?" She held up two tweed skirts, one in soft tones of heather, the other in creamy browns.

Roseanna seemed caught off-guard. I'd watched Francine in action before and knew some of her tactics. This one involved forcing a customer to choose between two garments, rather than rejecting a single item out of hand. It was a trap, and both owner and customer knew it. But like most women, Roseanna would prefer to have than have not. She merely needed a little coaxing.

"The heather," she said, giving me a rueful smile. "I haven't a thing to go with it. Now Francine will sell me a new sweater, a blouse, and some damned scarf I'll never take out of the drawer."

We all laughed, but Francine was shaking her head.

"No, I won't. I'll wait for Buddy to come in here looking hopelessly baffled. Then I'll whip out the blouse and the sweater. Buddy will practically kiss my feet in gratitude, and you'll end up with something you really want for Christmas. Your kids can give you the damned scarf.''

We laughed some more. After Roseanna had gone out into the dark late afternoon, I told Francine what I was looking for. She led me not to the rack of moderately priced dresses, but back up front to the display window where three mannequins stood on a sparkling snow-covered floor and huge crystal snowflakes were suspended from almost-invisible wires.

''The dark green is you, Emma. You've got a nice figure and it will emphasize your height.''

I gazed at the green wool crepe with its surplice bodice and gently draped waistline. In my head, I also translated Francine's comments: *Your bust's okay, your hips aren't bad, you don't have much of a waist, and you're kind of short. This dress will make for good camouflage.*

''I'll try it on,'' I said, ''but I hate to have you wreck your window display.''

Francine was already heading for the back room. ''That's an eight. I've got a ten out here. I was saving it for Dr. Starr's wife, but she didn't think the color looked right on her. She got purple silk instead.''

The last words were spoken from behind a mauve velvet curtain. I looked around the shop, marveling as always that Francine could make a go of it in Alpine. Her clothes were in what retailers laughingly call the *moderately priced* designer range, which meant that anything under a hundred bucks could be found only on the clearance sale rack. Vida once told me that Francine had made out like a bandit ten years earlier when she'd divorced her alcoholic attorney husband from Seattle. Apparently, she had taken the money and run—back to her hometown of Alpine, where she'd opened Francine's Fine Apparel. It was the only store within sixty miles where a woman could buy clothes that didn't look as if they were designed primarily for spilling beer down your front at the bowling alley. Despite the dearth of customers on this dark December afternoon, Francine obviously did enough business not only to keep going, but to make a profit.

"Roseanna Bayard's off-line, of course," Francine announced as she emerged from the back room. She held the green wool crepe up for my inspection, not unlike a wine steward proffering a bottle of champagne. I wondered if I should ask to sniff the sleeve.

"About what?" I finally inquired, coming out of my shopper's daze.

"Teresa McHale. I don't think she's spent her life as a parish housekeeper. She applied for a job here first."

I'd already stepped inside one of the two small dressing rooms. They were also curtained off by velvet draperies. "She did? You mean after she moved here?"

"No, before that." Francine's voice was slightly muffled by the curtain. "She'd worked at a couple of apparel stores in Seattle. Nordstrom's, I think, and then some place in the Westlake Center. But I don't need anybody full-time. Gerry Runkel fills in whenever I have to be out of here."

Geraldine Runkel was one of Vida's numerous in-laws. She was married to Everett, Vida's husband's youngest brother. Or so I recalled from the complicated and extensive Runkel-Blatt family tree.

I stood back a few paces. More than my bangs needed a trim; I realized I was at least two weeks overdue on a haircut. Most of my makeup had worn off during the course of the day and the harshness of the elements. Still, I looked good in the dress. Or did the dress look good on me? I peered at the price tag: Francine's dollar amounts were always printed in round numbers and so smashed together that it practically took a magnifying glass to decipher them. Two hundred and fifty dollars, the tag read. I gulped, and visualized my rapidly sinking checking account balance.

"Let's see," Francine called.

Dutifully, I walked out of the dressing room. Francine beamed at me. "I was right. What a difference—Carrie Starr couldn't handle that color. It's great with your brown eyes and that almost-olive complexion. Here, Emma, let me show you something.'' Francine dashed over to the display case where the cash register was located. She whipped out a single strand of pearls set with random dark green oval beads. ''Put this on. There are earrings to match. It's going to be dynamite.''

It was. I guess. In fact, after I left Francine's Fine Apparel, I felt as if I'd been blown up by a ton of TNT. The dress, necklace, and earrings had set me back three hundred and forty-seven bucks, sales tax included. I'd had to use my bank card.

As I drove home through the swirling snow, all I could think was *Did I do this for Milo*? The answer was *No*. I'd done it for me.

And, just in case he might show up over the holidays, I'd done it for Tom Cavanaugh. It occurred to me that if Alpine had a contest for the Christmas Fool, I could win it hands-down.

Chapter Eight

VIDA ARRIVED AHEAD of Oscar Nyquist, stamping snow off her buckled boots and shaking out a long plaid muffler. Her black hat looked like the sort that Italian country priests are supposed to wear, but in this informal, global era, I suspect they lean toward Mets baseball caps.

"You didn't come back to the office," she said accusingly.

"I didn't say I would," I countered, taking her coat.

"I thought you might want to check in with Milo." She plopped down on the sofa and gazed around my living room. "Now this looks very nice," she said approvingly. "Why is there a camel on your Nativity stable's roof?"

I stared at my cherished set. Sure enough, the standing camel, as opposed to the other two which were seated, appeared to be stalking across the stable. "Ben," I muttered. "He must have come by to get the rest of his stuff. The camels don't go up until this weekend." I whisked the little figure away, putting it back in the desk drawer.

"Milo didn't call," Vida remarked, apparently willing to excuse me for my truancy.

"He probably won't know anything until tomorrow," I said, going out into the kitchen to fetch us an eggnog. "Rum or not?"

"Half milk," Vida called back, and I winced. I like my eggnog pure and simply fattening. I only put liquor in it when I figure I need to cut my cholesterol count. Happily, I rarely gain weight. I have too much nervous energy.

I told Vida about my encounter at the mall with Arnie and Louise Nyquist. Vida was mildly interested in Louise's description of the so-called lurker. She had been more intrigued by Milo's suggestion that Bridget knew the man's identity.

I was putting another slab of wood on the fire when Oscar Nyquist arrived. He looked like a snowman, having walked— uphill—the six blocks from his home on Cedar Street. Snow was caked to his overcoat, his stocking cap, his boots. I practically had to pry him loose from his outerwear. Yet at eighty-two, he seemed none the worse for his exertion.

"I been here all my life," he said, easing into the beige armchair. His voice bounced off the walls, but he wasn't operating at full bellow. "You get used to the snow. The rain, too. The weather's good for the movie business." He nodded sagely, as if he'd invented the climate.

"Good," Vida retorted. "We're going to talk about just that in a minute. Meanwhile, tell us about this pest and what's worrying you."

Oscar squinted at Vida. "You think I'm nuts?"

"Of course I do. Most people are." Vida sounded impatient. "But why are you so concerned about your granddaughter-in-law?"

Oscar didn't respond immediately, but gazed into the flickering flames and barely seemed aware that I was shoving an eggnog at him. Absently, he took the mug and sipped. I'd laced it lightly with both rum and milk. I had a feeling that Oscar Nyquist could have drunk Drāno and had neither a reaction nor a complaint.

"She's an odd girl," he finally said. "Different. Maybe that's because she comes from the city." His gaze lighted briefly on me, as if I, too, might be pretty odd. "She's up, she's down. You never know. She seemed so scared the other day, then she's happy as can be. I figure it's this fellow, hanging around and making her nervous. He can't mean any good."

It was time for me, the official interviewer, to speak up. "Has Bridget expressed a fear of this man?"

Oscar's bald head tipped to one side. It seemed that he never answered any questions impulsively. "Not outright. But she's scared. No doubt about it. When she isn't being happy, she acts like she's scared to death."

Scared to death. Vida and I exchanged swift glances. Two young women, approximately Bridget Nyquist's age, were already dead. Was there a connection? If Carol Neal was missing and Bridget knew it, she had a right to be scared. To death.

But her erratic behavior was strange. I kept thinking of Milo's explanation. "Do you think Bridget has any idea who this person is?" I asked, hoping to sound casual.

Oscar shook his head. "Why should she?"

I was sitting on the sofa next to Vida. I leaned forward, trying to gauge how far I could go without riling Oscar. "Travis said Bridget didn't want you to talk about this. Why? Is she embarrassed?"

Oscar made a stabbing movement with his right hand. "Nyaaah! She's silly! She's a kid, she still thinks everybody's decent! She's a city girl, she ought to know better." His voice dropped to a rumble.

"You should give Sheriff Dodge a description," Vida said crisply. "You and Arnie may not think much of Milo, but most people agree he's a good lawman. It seems to me you're making a mountain out of a molehill with all these petty complaints, and in the meantime, ignoring the mole. The deputies cruise around town all the time. They should know who to be on the lookout for."

Oscar all but sneered. "I did tell them, this afternoon. Tall, skinny fellow, young. Big jacket, jeans. Maybe jeans; I forget. Bridget told me."

I gave Oscar a skeptical look. "But told you not to tell?"

Oscar's chin jutted like the prow of a Viking ship. " 'Don't bother, Popsy,' " he mimicked in a girlish voice. " 'This is

such a little town. What else do people have to do but look
in other people's windows?' Pah!''

Bridget wasn't entirely wrong. Since moving to Alpine,
I'd gone on a few evening strolls with Vida. While I admired
the sunset or commented on the gardens, Vida's eyes fixated
on windows. Her usual long-legged stride always slowed
when we came upon a house where the drapes hadn't been
pulled. "Daleys—new picture above the mantel, a Maxfield
Parrish,'' she'd murmur. Or, "Eversons have company—out-
of-town plates. Seattle, I'd guess.'' She didn't consider it
snooping, merely doing her job of keeping up with the local
news. I suspected that a lot of Alpiners did the same, but
weren't in a position to give their curiosity such a noble name.

Again, I glanced at Vida. She was frowning into her eggnog. "This is all very vague. I hope Bridget uses good sense.
If you're worried about her, it's up to her to see to her own
safety.''

With a grimace, Oscar nodded. I felt it was time to make
some sort of professional commitment. He had trudged
through the snow to unburden himself and not received much
in return.

"I'll tell you what,'' I said, darting a quick glance at Vida.
"We're going to do an article on the Marmot. If we slant it
so that it's as much of a family story as it is about the theatre,
then we can work in some of the problems you and Arnie
have had with vandalism and such.''

I couldn't tell if Oscar Nyquist was alarmed or mollified.
Something sparked in his blue eyes, but his only verbal response was a grunt. Vida was regarding me with a vexed
expression. I knew she thought I was compromising myself.

"We'll need photos,'' she said, and it was my turn to feel
a sense of relief. "Old ones, as well as new ones. We have
some, but yours might be better.''

Oscar nodded again, this time with more assurance. "In
the basement. At the Marmot. Come by tomorrow around
nine. I can show you a lot of old stuff. If you're interested.''

Vida didn't respond, but I did. "That's wonderful," I enthused. "If I have time, I'll come with Vida. I like old movie mementos."

Now on his feet, Oscar gazed at me as if I were a bit lacking. "It's junk," he asserted. "We should have thrown it out a long time ago. But we didn't."

Visions of lobby cards from *Casablanca* and *Rebecca* and *Gone with the Wind* danced in my head. Publicity stills of Chaplin, Pickford, Gable. Souvenir programs from blockbusters such as *Ben-Hur*, *2001: A Space Odyssey*, *The Godfather*. I am not a movie buff in the true sense, but I definitely appreciate the art form.

"What have you got?" Vida asked dryly. "W. C. Fields's false teeth?"

Oscar Nyquist took Vida seriously, but at least his denseness averted bloodshed. It was probably a blessing that I intended to visit the Marmot the next morning. My House & Home editor's lack of respect for the movies and their local purveyor might land her—or him—into trouble.

I never thought to include myself in that equation. Foolish me.

There were compromises to be made. In the summer, a University of Washington professor had devised a plan to thin out or prune almost two million acres of ten- to thirty-year-old forests in Washington and Oregon. The process would not only increase quantity, but would also enhance quality. If the trees were not cut, their density would choke out animal life and create a sterile environment.

That was just one of the proposals I included in my editorial. Naturally, we had run the story when it first broke in *The Seattle Times*. The article had elicited enthusiasm—and criticism. While most Alpiners are pro-logging, there are quite a few people who have moved to town because they love the wilderness. They would just as soon melt every chain saw in the Pacific Northwest as prune a limb from an evergreen.

I typed away, trying to balance my editorial, while at the same time taking a stand. I noted that one of the problems was that the spotted owls were—and I phrased this more gently—screwing themselves by not screwing each other. The birds had resorted to miscegenation, mating with different owl species. While that might not be a bad method to resolve racial tensions among human beings, it wasn't good news for the owls.

"Ready?" Vida stood in my doorway, muffled to the eyebrows. It was two minutes to nine.

Out on Front Street, Oscar Nyquist was furiously shoveling the walk in front of the Marmot. The snow had finally stopped for a while, but during the night another eight inches had fallen on Alpine. Walking carefully over the frozen patches, Vida and I wished him a good morning.

"What's good about it?" demanded Oscar, a big scowl showing under his stocking cap. He waved the shovel up at the marquee. "See that? More mischief!"

It took some effort not to laugh or even smile. The letters of *It's A Wonderful Life* had been rearranged to read *Saw One IUD Triffle*. Vida, however, was up for the occasion.

"I like it," she said. "It might be a science fiction movie about birth control."

Oscar looked mystified. "What's a triffle? What's IUD? Is it like Averill Fairbanks and his goddamned UFOs?"

It was now Vida's turn to hold back a smirk. "Well—not exactly." She gave me a puckish glance. "Let's say that it certainly beats rhythm, which is the Catholic version of science-fiction birth control. Speaking of which," Vida went on as I raised my eyebrows, "was that what Arnie found at the bowling alley site? Birth-control devices?"

Oscar Nyquist looked shocked. He was of a generation and a disposition that did not discuss such matters, especially between the sexes. Vida's frankness embarrassed him.

"Nyaaah," he replied, shaking out rock salt in an almost frantic manner. "It was clothes, women's clothes. A sweater. Slacks. Shoes. Underwear." He mentioned the last item as if he shouldn't know that women wore underwear. "Come inside, see the pictures."

The exterior was not what I'd call typical Alpine architecture. While less flamboyant and much smaller than many of its urban kin, the Marmot's turrets and dome were nonetheless more evocative of the Middle East than the Central Cascades. For all the grief it was causing Oscar, the marquee was a handsome affair, running across the front of the theatre and set off with row upon row of lights. The double-deck *Whistling Marmot* sign stood above the marquee proper, with a carved stone marmot at each side, like bookends.

In the lobby, Oscar flipped some switches, flooding the area with light. The concession stand had been modernized, but the Middle Eastern/art deco interior had been left mercifully intact. A wide, green carpeted staircase swept up to the auditorium, giving an illusion of vastness, despite the fact that there were a mere six steps in the ascent. Briskly, Oscar led us into the empty auditorium, down the wide aisles, and past the comparatively modern seats that had been installed in the 1960s and reupholstered two years ago. I glanced back at the balcony and the darkened projection booth. The frieze that ringed the ceiling showed a series of whistling marmots—running, jumping, sitting. On the walls, scatterings of silver specks set off dark green, three-dimensional scallop patterns, giving an impression of trees clustered in the rain. The recessed sounding board in the high arch of ceiling above the stage was dappled with silver stars and snowflakes, buffeted by the west wind at one side, caught by a crescent moon on the other. The chandelier that depended from the ceiling held tiers of petal-shaped lamps. Metallic scallops ringed the stage with its heavy midnight blue curtains edged with silver bars. I appreciated the decor anew, realizing that if Lars Nyquist wasn't blessed with artistic taste, he'd had enough sense to hire someone who was. And Oscar Nyquist hadn't been tempted to modernize. The Whistling Marmot was a little gem of a theatre, a reminder of the days when the movies not only had faces, but places in which to show them.

We went out through the exit at the left of the stage, then down a flight of stairs. The air immediately turned damp and musty. Oscar turned on more lights, revealing an awesome hodgepodge of equipment, storage boxes, and just plain junk. The heating system was on our right; the old prop room used in the days of vaudeville lay dead ahead. Dressing rooms, or more precisely a changing area with a divider for males and females, could be entered by edging around a stack of discarded theatre seats, a life-sized pasteboard cutout of a zebra, a bear suit, half a dozen buckets of paint, and a large wooden barrel filled with film cans.

I paused by the barrel. "Are these old movies?" I asked, pointing to the big tins.

Oscar, who was clearing a path for us through the debris, looked over his shoulder. "Nyaaah. When I was a kid, my father would save any extra cans for my mother. She stored cookies in them. At Christmas, she baked so many that she gave them away, wrapped in those tins. Now, we keep little stuff in 'em." He lifted the top tin out of the barrel and pried up the lid. Nuts, bolts, screws, rubber bands, and paper clips rested inside. "It's the barrel I like best. In the old days, my father kept it outside the social hall, where he first showed the movies. It'd fill up with rain water. Sometimes the fellas would come by after they'd been fishing and throw their trout in there to keep while they went to the movies. 'Course, during the winter, the water would freeze. One year, after the thaw, we found a ten-inch rainbow in there. It was still alive, swimming like crazy."

Vida apparently had heard the story before, but I exclaimed and laughed. Oscar, however, didn't seem to find the anecdote all that remarkable. It was merely part of Alpine's lore, neither unusual nor amusing.

Inside what was the real storage room, we were confronted with stacks of boxes, trunks, and grocery bags as well as shelves piled high with notebooks, ledgers, and files. Oscar scanned the boxes, finally choosing a battered cardboard container that had once held Crisco. A smiling half-moon and stars looked vaguely familiar, a logo I had seen in my childhood or perhaps in old magazines.

"Here," he said, opening the top, which was secured with ancient tape that had lost its glue. "You'll find the pictures of the old social hall in there, then the ones while the theatre was a-building. Opening night, too, with Carl and Mrs. Clemans and a bunch of other old-timers who were the guests of honor."

Vida, who knew *The Advocate*'s morgue far better than I did, took over. The pictures were all in albums, black imitation leather with tasseled cords. But like the tape that had held the box together, the hinges had come unglued, causing many of the photos to fall out of place. Flipping through them quickly, Vida selected five.

"I've never seen these," she said, holding up an eight-by-ten sepia print documenting the early stages of the Marmot's construction. In the background, I could see the original Methodist Church, so new that its wooden spire was still surrounded by scaffolding. At the edge of the photo, another structure was just getting underway. It was the Clemans Building, I realized, which stood directly across the street from *The Advocate*.

"What was on the site of the newspaper office then?" Oddly enough, I'd never asked Vida—or anyone else—that question.

Oscar's endless forehead furrowed. "The Dawsons' house. Mr. Dawson worked in the mill. He liked to act. Sometimes the townspeople put on plays, first in the social hall, then here. Mr. Dawson especially liked to play bums. His brother-in-law, Mr. Murphy, was a wonderful singer. One of them Irish tenor fellas."

I nodded, gazing at the photo, thinking about Alpine's early residents with their propensity for hard work and their proclivity for home-grown entertainment. Except for Lars Nyquist and his movies, what else was there to do, particularly during those long winters? There were no radios, no TV, no electric lights in that first decade of Alpine's existence. If Alpiners wanted to be amused, they had to amuse themselves. Obviously, they did.

We left Oscar to fix his marquee. But Vida wasn't inclined to return to the office. Rather, she stood at the curb, her attitude alert.

"Travis," she said, nodding her padre's hat in the direction of the Venison Inn. "That's him at a window table with Rick Erlandson. You know, Rick, with the orange sideburns, at the bank? Travis and Rick went to high school together."

"So?" I replied, trying to match Vida's long strides across the sanded street. "Is Rick a lurker?"

"Of course not," huffed Vida. "He's a most respectable young man, even if he does have comical hair. Especially for a loan officer. The point is, Travis is over there, and not at home. Let's go see Bridget." She pounced on my car. "Come on, come on. What are you waiting for?"

It took less than five minutes to drive from *The Advocate* to The Pines, otherwise known as Stump Hill. The gracious homes that nestled among the evergreens were situated between the mall and the ski lodge, with Burl Creek running through the west end of the property. Colonial, Tudor, Spanish, and Cape Cod architecture, all with a Pacific Northwest twist, somehow managed to avoid aesthetic conflict. Maybe it was the half-acre on which each house stood; maybe it was the buffer of tall trees; maybe it was the hilly ground that permitted the homes to sit on different levels. Whatever it was, it worked—and Arnie Nyquist had been responsible. It occurred to me that Tinker Toy wasn't a complete dunce.

We didn't attempt to get up the steep drive, but parked behind a PUD truck across the street coyly known as Whis-

pering Pines Drive. Even with the chains, I'd had a bit of
trouble negotiating the narrow road through the development. Residents of The Pines neither sanded nor shoveled.
Maybe it meant they all had four-wheel drive. Or that they
didn't have to worry about getting to work. They were too
well-heeled to care.

Travis and Bridget's Cape Cod looked picture-perfect in
the snowy landscape. The firs that had been left standing
formed a semicircle around the house, as if cradling it in
their snow-covered branches. Off to one side of the sloping
front lawn, a single old cottonwood lifted angular limbs up
to the sky. Lower down, someone had hung out suet for the
birds. A huge silver wreath with a bright red bow clung to
the front door, while a matching garland wound its way up
the mailbox post. The two front windows, presumably in the
living room, sported smaller versions of the front door
wreath. The younger Nyquists' home could have posed for a
Christmas card.

And Bridget could have posed for *Playboy*, I thought nas-
tily, as she warily opened the front door and revealed just
about everything in a skintight plum-colored leotard.

"I'm exercising," she said, somehow managing to beat
Vida to the verbal punch. "Excuse me." She started to close
the door.

Vida was not to be bested. Sticking her galosh inside the
door, she managed to kick it open. "Now, Bridget, you don't
want us to go away mad, do you?"

Bridget pouted. "I just want you to go away. I've got a
video running."

Vida barged right in. "We'll wait."

Bridget glared at both of us. "You're trespassing. I'll call
the sheriff."

"Fine," Vida replied, taking in the handsomely appointed
living room with its French country accents. Pickled pine
finishes, woven rush chairs, delicately painted wood, and
wrought iron proved that money could buy class. I wondered

who had chosen the furnishings. Not Bridget, I fancied. Maybe she and Travis had hired a decorator.

The TV, which was encased in a beautiful armoire, did indeed show a vigorous young woman leading an equally vigorous group of enthusiasts in an exercise routine. Such displays make me queasy.

"Well?" demanded Vida, looking over the rims of her glasses at Bridget. "Are you going to call Milo or just stand there and perspire?"

Bridget shot Vida a rebellious look, but marched over to the TV and shut the set off. "What do you want? I told you, I'd rather not be written up in your paper."

"We don't intend to," Vida responded, admiring the painted faux marble walls. "We're doing a big piece on the Marmot. And we're curious how it has affected your life as a Nyquist." Vida never took notes; her memory was prodigious.

"The Marmot?" Bridget wore a baffled expression. "What do you mean, *affected* my life? I've seen some movies there. So what?"

"So it's the original family business," Vida said, tilting her head to one side. "The theatre, along with your father-in-law's construction business, has helped pay for all this." Vida waved a hand, taking in the living room, and presumably the entire house.

"No, it didn't." Bridget had turned smug. "Travis paid for all this. He made a fortune in the stock market."

I wasn't sure why Vida had been so insistent about calling on Bridget Nyquist. It was too soon to ask Bridget about Carol Neal. There was no point until the dead woman was identified—or Carol turned up missing. This particular line of inquiry on Vida's part baffled me. So did Bridget's attitude. Her initial hostility had dwindled into inertia.

"How did he do that?" Vida inquired, now moving to the mantel, where half a dozen gilded cherubs dangled from a golden holly garland.

Bridget blinked, then looked vague. "Stocks. Bonds. You know—investments." She shrugged, muscles and curves rippling under her leotard.

"My, my." Vida chucked one of the cherubs under the chin. "How clever. Did all his clients get rich, too?"

"Of course." Bridget's jaw was thrust out.

So was Vida's bust under the tweed coat. She had deftly moved across the living room's flagstone floor to stand directly in front of Bridget. "And his partners? Which brokerage house was it, Bridget? My nephew works in one of them. Piper something-or-other, I think."

I'd never heard of Vida's nephew the Stockbroker, but that didn't mean he didn't exist. Given her extended family, Merrill, Lynch, Pierce, Fenner & Smith might all be related to the Runkels or the Blatts.

Bridget fingered an arrangement of pine and cedar boughs in a terra-cotta container. "Sampson. Or Frampton. I forget. Travis had already quit when we got engaged." Bridget didn't look at either one of us.

The names meant nothing to me. But I hadn't lived in Seattle for years. And even if Bridget was referring to a national firm, I'd never been in a position to get cozy with brokers. If they didn't advertise on network TV, I probably wouldn't have heard of them.

Vida pushed her glasses back up on her nose. "Cramden's?" she offered. "Very reputable, old-line Seattle."

"That's it." Bridget nodded energetically.

"Very good." Vida started for the entry hall. I trailed along, feeling about as useless as Rudolph without his red nose. "You like movies?" She threw the question at Bridget over her shoulder.

"Sure," Bridget replied, coming along behind me. "Popsy gives us free passes."

"I should think so," murmured Vida. "By the way, have you seen that pest lurking around lately?"

Bridget almost ran into me as I stopped next to Vida on

the threshold. "The pest? You mean that guy? No. That is, not this week."

Vida's eyes were keen as she peered at Bridget. "What did he look like?"

Bridget shifted from foot to foot. "I'm . . . not sure. Ordinary, I guess. It was always dark. And snowing," she added hastily. "He was just a form."

"Of course he was." Vida started down the front steps, which had been swept clean of snow. "Thank you, Bridget. Generally speaking, you were courteous."

We had started down the walk, which had also been cleared. "You should have pulled into the driveway," Bridget called after us. "The Amundsons across the street have been having trouble getting their car out with that PUD truck parked there."

I decided it was finally time for me to stop acting as if I were Vida's mute stooge. "Did you lose power out here the other day?"

Bridget shook her head. "No. We were lucky. G'bye." She closed the door before we got to the Jag.

"Liar, liar, pants on fire," muttered Vida as I turned on the ignition.

"What?"

"Bridget." Vida was resettling her hat. "There's no such investment house as Cramden's."

I gave Vida a sly smile. "Well, well. And there's no such thing as a PUD truck parked where there isn't any problem."

Vida gave a faint nod. "It's been an interesting visit."

"So it has." I steered the Jag carefully down the little hill that led away from The Pines. "But to what purpose?"

Vida made a face. "I wish I knew."

So did I.

Chapter Nine

CAROL NEAL HAD disappeared. According to Milo, she wasn't missing; she had merely dropped out of sight.

"There was a forwarding address after she moved out of the apartment on Fifteenth Northeast in the University District," he explained over the phone. "It was for another apartment just a few blocks away, on Eleventh. But my Seattle source tells me she hasn't lived there for the past two years."

"What about a work address?" I asked, looking up at Vida and shaking my head.

But Milo hadn't dug that deep yet. His theory was that Carol had probably moved in with a roommate, male or female, which might account for the lack of more forwarding addresses. "Let's say she had another girl living with her on Eleventh, then they moved together but put the new address in the other girl's name. Maybe Carol was avoiding her creditors. Or escaping from some guy who'd made a pest of himself."

"What about parents? Relatives? Friends?" I was unwilling to let go of the possibility that the dead girl was Carol Neal.

"We're checking on it," replied Milo at his most laconic. "We need someone to ID her, after all."

I almost suggested that Milo ask Bridget. But that was a ghoulish idea. The victim might turn out to be a stranger. Why put Bridget Nyquist through such an ordeal?

576

"The thing is," Milo continued, "if this is Carol and Carol had a roommate, why hasn't said roommate reported her missing? It's probable that she's been dead for almost a week."

"Maybe she can't," I replied with another glance at Vida. "Maybe the roommate is dead, too."

Evan Singer lived in a cabin two miles out of town off the Burl Creek Road. I decided against maneuvering the Jag up his winding, snow-covered drive and parked in a small turn-out some fifty yards down the road. Although it had stopped snowing, the gray clouds hung low, almost touching the tree-tops. The temperature seemed stuck in the mid-twenties.

Cabin was probably too extravagant a term for Evan's dwelling. The one-story frame shack might have been a summer retreat at one time, or more likely a hermit's lair. Tar paper stuck out from under the uneven cedar shakes, the tin chimney was crooked despite being wired to the roof, and several panes of glass in the two front windows were pock-marked with BB pellets and bullets from a .22.

Evan Singer met me at the door, standing on the top step that also made up the entire front porch. He was wearing a loosely woven slate-gray sweater, paint-stained khaki pants, and workmen's shoes, laced halfway up his calf. A bandanna was tied around his red-gold hair. The reek of marijuana wafted from the cabin.

"This is truly remarkable," he announced, ushering me inside. "Everyone gets to be famous for ten minutes, right?"

"Something like that," I replied, taking in the single room that made up the entire cabin. Happily, the interior was an improvement over the exterior. A Franklin stove stood in one corner and a Christmas tree in the other. Several sketches and a movie poster for *Patriot Games* were held up by thumbtacks on the unfinished walls. There were candles everywhere, including on the tree. The shapes were both exotic and erotic, no doubt fashioned by Evan himself. He had clearly put his stamp on this ramshackle old place, and I marveled at his hardiness. A Murphy bed was folded into the far wall. There was an icebox and a sink but no pipes for running water. Two Coleman lanterns hung from nails, but only one of them was lit. It was extremely cold, and I wondered how Evan kept from freezing to death at night.

"Have a seat," he urged, pulling out one of the three chairs that circled a small wooden table. "This is amazing. Why me?"

For the first time, I took in Evan himself. He was probably in his late twenties, with an angular face and a few freckles. His nose was slightly hooked, his blue eyes seemed to be in constant motion, and his entire lanky body appeared to be charged with a set of powerful batteries. I couldn't tell if he was nervous, exhilarated, high or merely wound too tight.

"You're new in town," I said, getting out my notebook. Unlike Vida's, my memory is flawed. "Our subscribers like to read about newcomers. They're always particularly interested in why anyone would exchange city life for a small town. I suppose they want their own attitudes reinforced."

Evan, who had been drumming his long, thin fingers on the knotty pine tabletop, stopped. "Is this like *The Visit*? You know, the movie that Anthony Quinn and Ingrid Bergman starred in? Am I going to die?" The question seemed rhetorical, but given recent events in Alpine, I wasn't about to make false promises. Evan apparently didn't want any; he didn't wait for an answer. "You know where I'm from? How?"

"How?" I tried to gauge his expression. Alarm? Pleasure? Curiosity? I hadn't the foggiest notion. That constant motion of the eyes made it difficult to read Evan Singer. "Somebody told me, I guess. Henry Bardeen?"

"Oh, Henry." Evan rolled his blue eyes. "Henry's a case, huh? People like him can never die."

"Really." I waited for Evan to explain.

"That's right. They've never lived. So how can they die?" He gave the table a light tap with his fist and grinned at me.

I couldn't disagree completely with Evan Singer's assessment of the dour ski resort manager, but I felt a need to defend him all the same. "Henry has given you a job," I reminded Evan.

"Right! He's wonderful, he's caring-sharing-daring—and wearing. But up your nose, if you think he's got blood in his veins." Evan was still grinning and wagging a finger at me. The ill-fitting sweater slipped a notch in the sleeve, revealing a Rolex watch. I tried not to stare. "People always give me jobs," Evan went on blithely. "I can do a lot of things. I'm the stranger in their midst, like Alan Ladd in *Shane*. And if I've never done something before, I'm willing to try it. Ever skinned a snake?"

"Alas, no." It was time to gain control of the interview. "Where did you learn to drive a sleigh?"

Evan sobered and stared straight into my eyes. "Saudi Arabia." He waited for my startled reaction, got it, and burst out laughing, slapping his knee all the while. "Ha-ha! You almost believed me! Henry Bardeen did!"

I doubted it, but decided to forge ahead. "What do—"

"It's not driving a sleigh that takes any training," Evan interrupted, growing more serious. "It's the horses. I've worked at a couple of riding stables outside of Seattle. Tiger Mountain. You know it?"

I did, vaguely. In my youth, the area east of Lake Washington had been a sleepy Seattle suburb. But no more. Bellevue, Kirkland, Redmond, Issaquah, even North Bend were rapidly becoming congested, overdeveloped bedroom communities. For all I knew Tiger Mountain was laced with condominiums and shopping malls.

"You grew up on the Eastside, not Seattle?" I inquired.

Evan stomped on the floor with his workmen's shoes. "I grew up in the world. We moved a lot. Chicago. Paris. Cairo.

Philadelphia. Toronto. Rome.'' He shrugged, then grinned again and leaned across the table. ''But not . . . ?''

''Saudi Arabia?'' I tried to keep a grip on my patience.

''Right! Never been there. In this lifetime, anyway. I used to be a toad.''

And I used to be a newspaper reporter, I thought through gritted teeth. This interview was out of hand. Should I humor him? His fancies could make a sprightly feature. As long as he didn't sue me.

''When did you start to paint?'' I held my breath, dreading the answer.

But Evan had turned serious again, his jaw resting on one hand. ''I always made pictures. It runs in the family. The visual arts, that is. But it's not a career with me. You have to please too many other people, especially the ones with lots of money and absolutely no taste. I do what I do for myself.'' Jerkily, he pointed to a large sketch of a gnarled tree. An oak, maybe. Its bare branches appeared to shelter mistletoe, its twisted roots hunched into the earth. ''You see that? I call it 'Lost Love.' Stripped bare, yet still alive. Are you moved?''

''It's very forceful.'' That much was true. More to the point, I could tell what it was. I'm not a fan of abstract art. At least Evan Singer had painted a tree that looked like a tree.

''I make jewelry, candles, some sculpture. I can sing and I can dance. One summer, I was a mime at Lake Tahoe.'' He plucked at his upper lip, suddenly acquiring a brooding expression. ''It was a bad idea. Those holiday gamblers only care about this''—he made yanking motions with his right hand. ''I should have dressed up as a bowl of cherries. You know, like on the slot machines . . .''

I gave him a faint nod. I was well acquainted with cherries, as well as plums, lemons, watermelons, and Harold-in-a-barrel. There had been a gang of us at *The Oregonian* who had made an annual pilgrimage to Reno or Vegas. It wasn't any riskier than listening to advice from the paper's business editor.

I complimented Evan on being so versatile, trying to bring him around to his educational background. He was vague about high school, dismissing those years as "an abyss." College was another matter.

"I liked Reed," he remarked, referring to the somewhat unorthodox private school in Portland. "Stanford was okay, so was USC. And Pepperdine. But give me Baylor or give me death!" He rolled his eyes again.

"Is that where you got your degree?" My head was spinning from his whirlwind of higher education.

"Degree? *What* degree?" He laughed so hard that tears filled his eyes. I waited, not too patiently. Even in my heavy car coat, I felt chilly. If there was a fire going in the stove, I wasn't benefitting from it. But Evan Singer didn't seem to be suffering in the least. "A degree . . . is just a . . . waste of . . . paper," he said between gasps for breath. "What's . . . in a . . . diploma? All it says . . . is that you have completed the required courses as stated by a specific institution. Now what does that mean?" He had recovered himself and was gazing at me in an imploring fashion.

For me, it had meant a great deal, including my passport onto a daily newspaper. But it was pointless to argue with Evan Singer, who was probably a candidate for Averill Fairbanks's UFO collection.

I steeled myself for the final, and perhaps most important, question: "Why did you come to Alpine, Mr. Singer?"

His gaze traveled to the sketch of the gnarled oak. The long pause made me wonder if he'd ever considered his own actions. But of course he had. I waited some more, my eyes drifting to the Christmas tree with its eclectic ornaments. I'd noticed only the traditional glass balls and fantastic candles earlier. Now I saw some unusual objects dangling among the fir branches: an ivory skull and crossbones; a tiny, shiny pistol; a dagger with a carved hilt; a small Kewpie doll in a body cast. I had a fervent desire to get the hell out of Evan Singer's cabin.

Apparently, Evan wasn't quite as self-absorbed as he appeared. "You're admiring my ornaments?" he asked with a big smile. "You find them odd?"

"A bit." I tried to smile back.

He nodded sympathetically. "Of course. I'm not a Christian, you see. The original trees were a pagan rite. I put together the best of both worlds, though I belong to neither. Intriguing, huh?"

"Very." My voice was a little faint. "Now about your decision to . . ."

"Oh, yes." He sounded wistful. "Can't you see it?" He inclined his head toward the sketch.

"The tree?" I frowned at the picture. "There aren't any oak trees around here."

"That's not the point!" He seemed positively shattered by my response. Or perhaps he was disappointed in my lack of perception. "Consider that tree, in all its ramifications."

"I will," I promised, getting up a bit awkwardly. "I don't suppose you could give me a hint?"

Evan Singer had also stood up. He threw his hands high above his head. "A hint? It's all there! Everything! My whole life!"

"Yes," I agreed, making for the door. "Thank you so much."

It was just as well that I couldn't run through the snow. It would have been undignified. But I was ecstatic to reach my car. All but jumping inside, I locked the doors before I started the engine.

A glance in the rearview mirror showed no one in sight. Of course Evan Singer wouldn't follow me. He was nuttier than a Christmas fruitcake, but probably harmless. Then again . . .

I decided against asking him to paint my house. Photographs would be cheaper. And safer.

* * *

Milo Dodge was coming out of his office when I pulled up in front of the bakery in the block between *The Advocate* and the county sheriff's headquarters. My usual parking spot had been usurped, presumably by one of the holiday shoppers taking advantage of the lull in the weather. I paused to gaze at the display of Christmas confectionery, which, appropriately for Alpine, leaned toward Scandinavian delicacies: Berlinerkransar, fattigmand, sandbakkelse, spritskransar, yulekake, rosettes. The breads and cookies looked wonderful, but as an old family friend from Bergen, Norway, had once told my mother, "The bakery is well and good, but never like homemade." She might have been right, but The Upper Crust's offerings looked pretty tempting to me.

"Emma!" Milo called from the opposite curb. "Got a minute?"

I was debating between stuffing myself on Scandinavian goodies or going to the Burger Barn for something a shade more wholesome. It was well after one o'clock, and I was famished. Fleetingly, I wondered what Evan Singer cooked for himself. Bat wings and puppy dog tails came to mind.

"I need some grease," I said, gesturing across the street. The Burger Barn's roof exhibited a fake red brick chimney with a jolly Santa waving with the hand that didn't carry a packful of toys. "Have you eaten?"

Milo met me in the middle of the block, both of us jaywalking. A couple of cars, a flatbed truck, and a Jeep slowed to avoid running us down.

"Yeah, I had lunch with Sam and Jack," Milo replied, "but I wouldn't mind another cup of real coffee. Jack waters it down at work."

Milo also had pie—apple, with a wedge of cheddar cheese on the side. I dug into a burger, fries, and a small salad. Ben was coming to dinner again, but probably wouldn't make it until after seven. I didn't worry about spoiling my appetite.

"We got some background on Carol," Milo said after we'd been served and I'd finally wound down in my recital of the interview with Evan Singer. "Parents are divorced, mother remarried and living in the L.A. area, father somewhere in central Oregon, which is where he came from. Probably a rural type who never adjusted to the urban jungle, but I'm guessing. There was a brother, but he died when he was about ten, some kind of accident on a bicycle."

I looked up from my hamburger. "Where did you get all this? Did somebody clone Vida for the SPD?"

"Actually, it's out of the King County sheriff's office, but my contact got hold of a neighbor who still lives next door to the Neals' old house in Greenwood. That's close to Blanchet, right?"

"Sort of." Blanchet is just a few blocks from Green Lake. The neighborhood that bears its name borders on the Greenwood area in the north end of Seattle.

"Anyway," Milo went on between bites of cheese and pie, "the house was a rental. The Neals didn't have much money, but somehow they managed to send Carol to private school. By the time she was a junior, she had a nice car, expensive clothes, a fancy CD player that had a bass loud enough to cause earthquakes. Or so said the neighbor." Milo raised an eyebrow. "Interesting, huh?"

"Very. Did she have a job?"

"She did, at least for a while. In a place like this." He waved a big hand, taking in the Burger Barn with its rustic decor and paper cutout Christmas decorations.

"Hmmmm." I was gazing at a cardboard angel with blonde dreadlocks. "Minimum wage, probably. Not enough to buy nice cars and clothes and CD players."

"Not enough to *pay* for them," Milo noted. "Carol left home right after graduation. I gather that Dad left before that. Mom headed south a few months later."

"And?" I looked up expectantly.

"And nothing." But Milo was looking smug. "Except

this.'' He reached inside his heavy jacket, pulled out a piece of paper, and handed it to me.

I studied the words carefully. It was a faxed copy of a complaint, filed the previous day by Stefan Horthy, owner/manager of the Villa Apartments. The complaint stated that Carol Neal and Kathleen Francich had defaulted on their rental agreement and vacated Unit #116 without giving proper notice. Horthy wished to confiscate their belongings, which had been left behind, to cover the outstanding monthly rent payment of $1,025. The damage deposit would not be refunded.

I looked at the address, which was on Capitol Hill, south of the University District and east of downtown Seattle. ''When was the rent due, I wonder?''

Milo shrugged. ''The first, I suppose. Why?''

''Because most apartment houses in Seattle—and Portland—ask for first and last months' rent, in addition to a damage deposit. It's only December twelfth. This Horthy is covered for the last month. His tenants must have owed for November, too.'' I pushed the complaint back at Milo. ''More to the point, they left all their belongings. Doesn't that suggest they intended to come back?''

''Sure.'' Milo gave me a wry smile. ''If you want to stretch it, you might say it suggests they were murdered. First Kathleen, then Carol.'' His expression turned bleak.

''Damn all,'' I breathed, though I'd already had a whiff of this particular fear. ''Any chance to find out about Kathleen Francich?''

Milo shook his head. ''No. I'm wondering if we should get Horthy up here to ID our victim.''

It was better than my brief brainstorm to ask Bridget. I didn't know Stefan Horthy; I wouldn't feel any responsibility for him if he turned blue and passed out. ''Did you learn where Carol worked?''

Again, Milo hadn't had the opportunity to make further inquiries. ''Horthy should know. I'm afraid he's our pigeon.

We can't force him to come up to Alpine, but it would be in his best interests.''

I agreed. Milo's revelations had driven Evan Singer into the shadows. As we paid our respective bills, I realized that I still had to write a feature article about the strange young man with his baggy sweater and Rolex watch. I hadn't the vaguest idea how to approach the story.

Indeed, I was still mulling over a lead when Ben called. To my mild dismay, he informed me that on an impulsive Christian whim, he had invited Teresa McHale to join us.

''What?'' I yipped into the phone. ''Shall I ask Milo? Is this a double date?''

''Listen, Sluggly,'' my brother admonished me, ''you're the one who was thinking about having her over for Christmas dinner. This will let you off the hook. And me. Father Fitz either fasted a lot or didn't have a big appetite. Teresa's been cooking up a storm since I got here. She won't let me near the stove or the fridge or anything resembling a frying pan. You give Teresa a meal and finish up Advent with an extra star in your crown.''

''Bull,'' I replied. But Ben was right: including Teresa was an act of charity. And possibly of endurance. I told him I'd pick up a small salmon at the Grocery Basket. ''They've got some silvers in this week. Naturally, Ed Bronsky wanted to keep it a secret.''

Vida was amused by my brother's invitation. She was also vaguely alarmed. ''If I were you,'' she cautioned, ''I'd drive over to the church and pick them up, then take them home. I don't trust that woman an inch.''

''You don't know her.'' It was true: Teresa had kept herself to herself, as they say, at least as far as non-Catholics were concerned. For once, I had the upper hand with Vida.

''I've seen her around,'' Vida muttered, giving me her gimlet eye.

''So? She and Ben are all alone at the rectory. What's such a big deal about them driving back and forth to my house?''

Vida's eyes narrowed behind her big glasses. "Cars. They're always dangerous when it comes to sex. Cars liberated Americans, giving them an opportunity to become promiscuous. I'll bet you've never seen a rumble seat."

"Of course I have!" I countered. "Don't you remember the Classic Car Rally last June?"

Vida ignored the remark. She was pounding on her typewriter when my phone rang. It was Milo.

"Durwood's been found!" he announced, evincing more animation than was customary.

"Huh?" I'd forgotten that Durwood was lost. "Where was he?"

"He took Crazy Eights Neffel for a snowmobile ride up Mount Baldy. Crazy Eights hopped off halfway to the top and Durwood had to go looking for him. He found the old nut making snow angels and talking to a goat."

"Swell." I put the phone down. Durwood and the town loony weren't a news item. In Alpine, they were merely a way of life. As my father used to say, you can get used to anything, including hanging. After three years, I was obviously getting used to small-town ways.

Teresa McHale wore a gold charmeuse blouse with a black and gold wrap skirt and matching shawl. Her dyed red hair was carefully coiffed in a side part that curled just under her ears, her makeup was flawless, and at the door, she exchanged her sensible boots for a pair of sling platform pumps. She did indeed look as if she were on a date.

By contrast, Ben wore an Arizona State University sweatshirt over blue jeans and kept his boots on. I was determined to watch Teresa like a hawk. At the first coquettish glance, I fully intended to smack Teresa in the kisser with the silver salmon.

But as we chatted amiably through cocktails, Teresa McHale's demeanor was irreproachable. The hard edges I had observed earlier were now softened. Maybe it was the vodka. Or the sociability. Perhaps Teresa really did lead a lonely, isolated life as the parish housekeeper.

Still, there was a girlishness about her that struck a discordant note. Her ensemble was smart, perhaps expensive. It might have flattered a woman who was ten years younger and twenty pounds lighter. As it was, the shimmering gold and black made Teresa McHale look like a large Christmas bauble.

Up until we served dinner, Ben had dominated the conversation, not out of a desire to seek the limelight, but at Teresa's urging. He recalled his years on the Delta. His new life on the reservation. The three trips to Rome in two decades. The life and times of a priest in the home missions. Teresa never ran out of questions. I had to assume that she and Ben didn't talk much at the rectory.

"Father Fitz must know these people inside and out," Ben remarked after giving the blessing. "How long has he been at St. Mildred's?"

Teresa looked at me. I looked blank. "Years," I finally said. "Fifteen? Twenty?"

Teresa lifted one shawl-clad shoulder. "I guess so. Someone said there was no regular priest in Alpine before he came."

"Probably not," Ben said. "It would have been a mission church, served out of Monroe or even Everett."

"And will be again, I'm afraid." Teresa sighed over a forkful of salmon. "I doubt that he'll be back. At least as pastor. He can't possibly resume his duties."

Ben was slapping butter on his baked potato. "You may be right. Dr. Flake isn't too optimistic about the prognosis."

I hadn't thought beyond Ben's stay at St. Mildred's. It was so wonderful having him here in Alpine, with Adam due to join us shortly. I didn't want to look beyond the holidays to the New Year when I'd have to wave goodbye to both my brother and my son. Regrettably, Father Fitz hadn't been preying on my mind. It hadn't occurred to me that I might have seen the last of our pastor.

"He *is* up there," I commented, "and has certainly served the Church well. What will you do if he doesn't come back, Teresa?"

The housekeeper's green eyes avoided my gaze. "Oh—I don't know. I take one day at a time."

Ben had added sour cream, chives, and onion bits to the butter. His potato looked like Mount Baldy. "Have you considered going into pastoral administration?" he asked. "With the shortage of priests, parishes need more lay people to staff the rectory."

Teresa gave a sharp shake of her head, the red locks flipping this way and that. "No, that's not for me. Too much politics. It's hard enough being a housekeeper."

"There aren't a lot of jobs in Alpine just now," I noted. "The economy is bad everywhere, but especially in a logging town like this one."

Teresa's green eyes now met mine head-on. "As I said, I'm not going to worry about it. Something will come along." She gave Ben a smile that was more coy than coquettish. "We have to trust in the Lord, don't we, Father?"

Ben smiled back, albeit crookedly. "It makes more sense to trust in the Help Wanted columns."

I passed Teresa the bowl of buttered baby carrots. "I take it you want to stay in Alpine?"

Again, she avoided my eyes. "I like it here. It's a beautiful town." Then, as if she suddenly remembered railing against the rural life earlier, she continued on a more breathless note: "That is, the scenery is beautiful, even if there isn't much to do. But location can make up for a lot, isn't that so?"

Ben agreed, though he immediately launched into what evils could lurk behind the scenery in, say, Tuba City, Arizona. I'd already heard Ben talk about snakes and scorpions and small dinosaurs or whatever else crawled and slithered in the desert. My mind drifted, engaging itself in debate over whether or not to ask Teresa why she'd moved to Alpine in the first place. But I'd tried that once already that day, with Evan Singer, and received a wildly enigmatic answer. I decided to refrain from putting the same query to Teresa McHale.

My guests departed shortly after ten. It had been a pleasant enough evening, with the conversation turning again to Ben's adventures. Teresa had led him down the garden path with more questions, reserving a few for me regarding my newspaper background. But a full work day, dinner preparations, and playing hostess had drained me. I was not in top form as a *raconteuse*. It was only after Ben and Teresa had driven off in Father Fitz's Volvo that I stopped marveling over Teresa's interest in others and wondered if the truth was that she didn't want to talk about herself. Did Teresa have a dark secret in her past? It's amazing how many people do. Or *think* they do.

I was affixing an angel to the roof of my Nativity stable when I noticed that one of the shepherds was smoking a cigarette. Ben had rolled up a small piece of paper and taped it to the figure's mouth. Funny Ben. Naturally, I laughed. Not for the first time, I thought how essential a sense of humor was to Christian faith. Or to just plain getting through the days that spin out over a lifetime. While I giggled at my brother's puckish stunt, there were people suffering and dying out there in the winter landscape. There was nothing funny about that. But if I couldn't laugh, I couldn't live. It was that simple. I turned out the lights and went to bed.

Chapter Ten

"THE RENAISSANCE MAN has come to Alpine."

It was the worst kind of overstatement, but I couldn't think of any other way to write the story about Evan Singer. I spent Saturday morning working at home on my word processor, trying to fill a two-column by six-inch space about the bizarre young man with the erratic emotions and multifaceted personality. It was easy to make him sound interesting; it was damned hard to make him sound sane.

And I'd forgotten to take my camera. Ordinarily, I could send Carla to cover for me. When she remembered to use film and take off the lens cap, she was a better photographer than I was. But Carla wasn't keen on Evan Singer, so I decided to bring the camera to dinner at King Olav's. I could get a picture of Evan driving the sleigh up to the ski lodge.

The afternoon was devoted to cleaning house for Adam's arrival Monday. Not that my son would notice if I had a Dumpster parked in the living room, but it made me feel like a proper mother. I even ventured into my son's room, something I usually did only under duress or when certain odors threatened to drive me out of the house. He had left his belongings in no worse condition than I'd feared, which meant I could probably apply for Federal funds under the National Disaster Act.

At five o'clock, I emerged, feeling virtuous and weary. But the prospect of a good dinner and relaxed companionship buoyed me.

My companion, however, looked as if he'd been beset by Vandals and Huns. Or spent a week in Adam's room, precleaning. Milo Dodge was far from his laconic self when he arrived on my front porch. His long face was far longer than usual, his sandy hair was disheveled under his ski hat, and his long mouth was set in a thin, angry line.

"I'm going to kill him," he announced, stalking into my living room.

I had been prepared to twirl about to show off my new green $250 dress. "Who?" I demanded, planting my feet firmly on the floor.

"Arnie Nyquist, that son of a bitch." Milo started for the Scotch, thought better of it, and turned around to jab a finger in my face. "Arnie's going around town saying you told old Oscar you were going to investigate me! What the hell is going on, Emma?"

I was abashed. "I told . . . Oh!" Enlightenment dawned. "Hold it, Milo. I told Oscar no such thing. Sit down, relax, take a break." I all but shoved Milo onto the sofa. Giving him a moment to collect himself, I lighted a pair of big red spiral candles on the mantel, turned on the CD player, and let Bing Crosby dream of a white Christmas.

"You may have one short Scotch," I announced, heading for the liquor cabinet that was actually part of a big bookcase. "You are a law enforcement official, though off-duty. I hate it when you have to arrest yourself."

Milo was now pouting. "I wasn't drunk the other night. Neither was Ben. We were just . . . upset."

Milo and Ben may not have been drunk, but they hadn't been exactly sober, either. I refused to argue the fine point. "Here," I said, shoving a Scotch and soda at Milo. "Oscar is muddled. I stalled him with a promise of an in-depth study of the sheriff's department. You know what that means—nothing. Then I placated him further by letting Vida do a story on the Whistling Marmot—and the Nyquists. If that doesn't make Oscar forget, then you'll have to pour him full of these.'' I hoisted my glass of bourbon and water.

''The Nyquists don't forget *anything*,'' Milo lamented, but he suddenly looked a bit less miserable. ''Emma, do you realize how long memories are in this town?''

''Not as well as you do,'' I admitted. ''Take it easy. You got re-elected by an overwhelming majority last month. And I'll bet the Nyquists all voted for you.''

Milo looked askance. ''I've got a murder investigation that's going nowhere. I don't need distractions like the Nyquists.''

I had sat down in an armchair opposite Milo. I'd given up expecting him to notice my new dress. Or how nice the house looked, with all the Christmas decorations. Only the tree was missing. Briefly, I visualized it standing in the corner between the bookcase and the window next to the carport.

''Speaking of Nyquists,'' I said, hoping to steer him a bit off course, ''I'm puzzled about their peeker. Oscar and Louise gave two different descriptions. Bridget is vague.''

''Bridget is brainless. Travis didn't marry her for her mind.'' Milo tugged at his polka-dot tie. He hated getting dressed up. His concession to King Olav's dress code was a herringbone sport coat, flannel slacks, a pale blue dress shirt—and a tie. ''You ought to know that eyewitnesses never see the same event.''

''This is different,'' I persisted. ''Louise said the guy was medium height, stocky, in workman's clothes. Oscar described him as tall and skinny, wearing jeans. They were both relaying what Bridget said, and when Vida and I asked her, she insisted she only saw an outline. What's the official rundown on this bird?''

Milo sipped his drink and shrugged. ''As I said, people aren't good at giving descriptions. It can make us law enforcement types crazy, especially when they testify in court. Or at a lineup. Now there's the worst possible scenario. About four years ago last summer, Darla Puckett filed a complaint about some guy who'd broken into her house and stolen some money and a watch and a berry pie. Shaggy hair, a beard, big son of a gun. We actually threw together a lineup and . . ."

I have never considered Milo Dodge loquacious, not even after a shot of Scotch. He's a good conversationalist—direct, candid, humorous. But he never runs on. I half-listened to his elaborate account, which I'd heard a long time ago from Vida. I knew the punch line, which was that Darla Puckett had fingered a visiting state law enforcement official from Olympia, she'd given the money to the milkman, the watch had fallen into the garbage, and the berry pie had been eaten by a bear. It was amusing, it was cogent, it was very Alpine. But it wasn't like Milo to talk my ear off. I suspected him of fobbing me off.

". . . And the bear had left the empty pie plate out by the woodshed!" Milo chuckled richly.

"And you're dodging me, Dodge." I stood up, glancing at my watch. "We've got a seven-thirty reservation. Let's go. You can tell me all about it over dinner."

Milo was still protesting his innocence when we got to the turnout for the ski lodge. The Overholt family owned the property bordering the county road that took off from Front Street at the edge of town. The big old rambling farm house was ablaze with Christmas lights, and a Star of Bethlehem glowed on the barn roof. The Overholts were close to ninety, but their son-in-law, Ellsworth Griswold, still actively farmed the land and kept a few cows. The family had leased the big rolling front yard to Henry Bardeen to allow diners to park their cars before getting into the sleigh.

Milo and I weren't the only customers waiting for Evan Singer. Neither of us recognized the other two couples. From their excited talk about the snow and treacherous driving conditions, we guessed they were Seattleites. Milo regarded the quartet with bemusement. He clearly considered them effete.

The sound of sleigh bells jingled on the cold night air, signaling Evan's approach. Sure enough, the sleigh pulled off the Burl Creek Road, with Evan at the helm and two giggling young women passengers. They looked vaguely familiar, and Milo nodded to them both after they allowed Evan to assist them in alighting from the horse-drawn conveyance. Evan was dressed in a Regency coachman's costume, complete with a tall black felt hat. He looked quite imposing, especially when he flicked his long whip.

The two other couples got in first, then Milo and I squeezed in. There were lap robes to ward off the chill and a tub of popcorn to alleviate hunger pangs. Evan had greeted me politely, if indifferently, as if he'd forgotten I'd spent part of yesterday in his rude cabin. Maybe he had. It wasn't easy to figure out how Evan Singer's mind worked.

Discreetly, I clicked off a few frames of 35mm black and white film. Evan must have been used to having his picture taken. He paid no attention to the camera.

Our companions were exclaiming about the quaintness of the sleigh, the endurance of the horses, the beauty of the snow-covered wonderland. Indeed, for a man whose imagination usually seemed to be set at simmer rather than boil, Henry Bardeen had come up with an enchanting idea: the small bridge that crossed Burl Creek halfway up the hill to the ski lodge was decorated with tiny white lights and big green wreaths. Lamp posts, also of the Regency period, stood at each end. As our route wound through the trees, more fairy lights twinkled among the branches. The effect was magical, a charming mesh of Old World beauty and contemporary commercialism.

The sleigh glided ahead; our fellow passengers chattered on. Evan cracked the whip, but spared the horses. Milo and I remained silent. This was hardly the place to discuss a brutal homicide.

Evan Singer stopped for the arterial at Tonga Road, which was well traveled, since it hooked into Alpine Way over by

The Pines. A single car went by, perhaps heading for Arnie Nyquists's Ptarmigan Tract west of town. The horses plodded on across the road, their big hoofs making comfortable clip-clop noises that seemed to provide a bass note for the jingling bells.

Through the trees, we could hear the rushing sound of Burl Creek as it tumbled down the mountainside. There were more fairy lights, and somewhere a discreet speaker sere-naded us with a choir singing "It Came Upon a Midnight Clear." I couldn't resist grinning at Milo.

"This is the best thing to hit Alpine since Vida," I said in a low voice.

Milo grinned back. To my astonishment, he took my hand under the lap robe. "You're a Christmas nut, Ms. Lord. Whatever happened to your hard-bitten newspaper cyni-cism?"

I was about to reply that I put such negative emotions on hold every December, but the sleigh was suddenly zipping along at a surprisingly rapid speed. We were almost to the ski lodge; perhaps the horses sensed it and picked up the pace. They weren't exactly galloping, but my guess was that they were executing either a canter or a very fast trot. The two other couples had finally shut up. I tightened my grip on Milo's hand and gave him an inquiring look.

Before Milo could say anything, a car came down the road from the opposite direction. It moved slowly, since the ac-cess was narrow and had been cleared of snow to allow pas-sage of only one vehicle at a time. I noticed the familiar Mercedes symbol first, then recognized the occupants: Bridget Nyquist was driving; Travis was at her side.

Evan Singer let out a howl, and the horses both reared up, pawing the freezing air. The Mercedes rolled past us. Instead of getting his steeds under control, Evan turned around and stared at the car. With a shudder, the sleigh sprang forward, then sideways. The horses were making for the trees. We hit the piled-up snow along the roadside with a jolt. The sleigh tipped over, and we all fell out. The horses kept going.

I was still clinging to Milo's hand when I tumbled into the snowbank. One of the other women was screaming, while her male companion cursed a blue streak. Now hatless, Evan Singer sat wide-eyed, virtually dumbstruck. The horses had stopped a few feet away, balked by the deep snow and the heavy underbrush beneath its surface.

Milo sat up, pulling me with him. "You okay?"

I wasn't sure. I felt stunned, battered, and bruised. Otherwise, I decided I'd live. My main concern was that I hadn't ripped my new dress. "Yeah, except that black and blue aren't my favorite Christmas colors. How about you?"

Milo was shaken, but also unharmed. The couple that hadn't been screaming and swearing had descended upon Evan Singer, berating him and threatening lawsuits. The other two were also on their feet, still making nasty noises. Milo hesitated, then finally let go of me and approached the city folks.

"Excuse me, I'm the sheriff. If you have a complaint, file it with my office," he told the quartet of strangers. "However, I'll testify that there was no negligence involved. It was an accident. If you're going to go for a sleigh ride in the mountains this time of year, you'd better be prepared for just about anything."

Our fellow passengers didn't exactly look mollified, but at least they stopped yapping at Evan Singer. He had retrieved his hat and appeared indignant. He didn't bother to thank Milo for intervening, but made straight for the horses.

"You'd better walk the rest of the way," he called without turning around. "Enjoy your dinner."

The parking area for the ski lodge was just around the bend in the road. Of course Milo and I knew that, but the others didn't. They were still bitching when we turned the corner and saw the lodge in all its yuletide glory.

The slanting roof with its dormer windows was decked out

with yet more fairy lights. Garlands of evergreens hung from
the eaves, tied with huge red bows. Off to one side at the
parking lot entrance was a miniature Dickens village, complete with rosy-cheeked carolers, a gaunt lamplighter, frol-
icking children, and a terrier wearing a green scarf. The
photo that Carla had taken didn't do the decor justice. I found
myself smiling again. Indeed, even the out-of-town foursome
was beginning to pipe down and cheer up.

Inside the lobby, a huge spruce soared up into the high
beamed ceiling. There were smaller trees placed in various
spots, all touched with fake snow and trimmed with blue and
white ornaments. The restaurant continued the color theme,
but highlighted Scandinavian traditions: St. Lucy with her
crown of candles; a sheaf of grain tied with a blue and silver
ribbon; Jul Tomten, the tiny old Swedish Santa, with his
hunk of bread and bowl of milk; a Danish horn of burnished
brass; the Norse god, Baldur, holding a sprig of mistletoe; a
small evergreen hovering over silver straw to commemorate
the manger. Henry Bardeen—or his decorators—had done
their homework, casting a Christmas spell from out of Europe's northern reaches.

Milo and I were shown to a table near the massive stone
fireplace. The restaurant itself might be brand-new, but the
design had taken up where the original lodge left off. More
high ceilings with great beams, natural pine, and a Swedish
floor gave the room a spacious, open look. The Indian motif
which was featured in the other public rooms had been discarded in favor of a Viking theme. The longboats, horned
helmets, furs, and spears now took a backseat to the holiday
decorations. However, I imagined that once Christmas was
over, the old Norse decor would fit the dining room just fine.

We started with cocktails and an hors d'oeuvre of pickled
herring in sour cream. I didn't badger Milo until he was
halfway through his drink.

"You're holding out on me, Sheriff."

"No, I'm not. I won't hear from the folks at King County until Monday."

"I don't mean about the Seattle angle," I said, noting that the quartet from the sleigh now seemed to be happily draining wineglasses at a nearby table. King Olav's cellar was rumored to be an improvement over the Venison Inn's limited stock of domestic red, white, and rosé that could be purchased for a third of the price at Safeway. "I'm referring to Bridget's lurker. You know something you're not telling me."

Milo looked faintly exasperated. "And if I do? I'm the sheriff, for God's sake."

I gave him my most wide-eyed stare. "You want Vida and me to muck it up for you?"

"You two . . ." Milo speared another piece of pickled herring. "Okay, let me clarify one point. Just one." He tapped his index finger on the linen tablecloth. "There may be two men hanging around the Nyquist house. I don't know much about the tall, skinny guy in jeans. But the so-called workman is from the PUD truck."

I made a face. "The PUD? Why? Are the Nyquists wasting electricity?"

Milo slowly shook his head. "I didn't say he worked for the PUD, I said he was from the PUD *truck*." His hazel gaze fixed on my face. I had the feeling he thought I was being stupid.

"A cover? Are you talking about a stakeout?"

Milo hummed an offkey tune and looked beyond me to the sextet of high school students who were dressed à la Dickens and singing "I'll Be Home for Christmas" to a table of eight near the bay window.

I wiped my fingers on my napkin and leaned my elbows on the table. "Okay. To what purpose? Who is this man watching? Bridget? Or Travis?"

Milo kept on humming. I was getting annoyed. He was playing a game, supposedly keeping his confidences while

forcing me to guess what was going on. This was not like
Milo. Which, I realized, meant he was out of his mind or
out of his league. I opted for the latter.

"FBI," I asserted. "Or some such Federal agency. Keeping an eye on . . . Travis." I had a fifty-fifty chance. Usually,
I make the wrong choice. But this time, I could tell from
Milo's swift glance of approval that I was right. "Why?" I
demanded.

Now Milo stopped humming and ended the game. "I'm
not sure. We've been asked to cooperate, but only to give
these guys permission to maintain surveillance. If we need
to know more, they'll tell us."

"Travis," I murmured, recalling Vida's attempt to pin
Bridget down about her husband's former place of employment. "Have you checked him out?"

Milo made a dour face. "What for? As far as we're concerned, he hasn't done anything except break his leg."

I had to admit that Bridget's uncertainty was no indictment
of Travis. Still, I persisted. "Do you know where Travis
worked in Seattle?"

"Sure, Bartlett & Crocker. Jack Mullins went to high
school with Travis. They weren't best buddies, but they kept
in touch."

Bartlett & Crocker struck only the dimmest of bells. Or
half a bell, since I remembered Bartlett, but not Crocker.
"Local?" I asked.

Milo shrugged. "You mean in Seattle? I guess so. Not one
of the big international houses, but well established. What
are you driving at?"

I didn't know. Our waiter, whose name was Vincent and
who looked like a ski bum, stopped to ask if we'd had time
to consider the menu. Milo had—and ordered the Danish
roast loin of pork, which went by the name of Stegt Svine-
kam. I scanned the entrées swiftly, choosing the Norwegian
duck stuffed with apples and prunes.

The conversation turned to Evan Singer. Milo dismissed

my idea that the unexpected appearance of Bridget and Travis Nyquist had anything to do with our crash landing.

"You've got Nyquists on the brain," he chided me. "Evan Singer's a terrible driver. He's already been picked up by us three times, once for speeding, and twice for illegal turns."

"Drunk?"

"No, just out of it. He's not a world-class driving disaster like Durwood, but give the guy some time. Evan isn't thirty yet." Milo wore a pained expression. If there was one thing his deputies didn't need, it was a contender for Durwood Parker's reckless driving crown.

"He's weird," I asserted as Vincent showed up with our beet salads. "Very weird." The high school chorus was coming closer, now serenading the next table with "The Twelve Days of Christmas."

Milo made no further comment on Evan Singer. Except for exceeding the speed limit and turning out of the wrong lane onto Alpine Way, the multitalented, mega-bizarre Mr. Singer didn't seem to trouble Milo. Yet I knew the sheriff had something on his mind, and it didn't take a swami to figure out what it was.

"You've been getting calls about the bodies?"

Milo sighed and put down his fork. He had gobbled up all his pickled beets, which was more than I could manage. "You bet. Winter's a bad time to have a murderer loose. People feel trapped, especially the old folks. On the face of it, we've got two dead young women. There may or may not be any tie-in—except for their youth and gender. But try to convince an eighty-year-old arthritic woman living alone up on Icicle Creek that she's perfectly safe, and you might as well talk to a Norway spruce. Of course there are the calls from worried parents who have daughters in that age group. That makes more sense."

I thought of Carla and Ginny. My spine tingled. Between Ted Bundy and the Green River killer, we of Western Washington weren't strangers to serial murderers. "Do you really think these women were killed by the same person?"

Milo's hazel gaze was steady. "I don't know. Hell, I don't even know who these women are. We may never figure out who the first one was if we don't find more than that damned leg."

It wasn't the right moment for Vincent to bring Milo's loin of pork and my carved duck. Milo sucked in his breath; I regarded the drumstick with dismay.

But I ate it anyway.

It was delicious.

After Milo polished off his lingonberry mousse and I devoured my egg flip with a side of macaroons, we climbed back into the sleigh and headed down the mountain. Evan Singer seemed subdued, even glum. There were three other couples crammed into the conveyance, two from Alpine, though they were merely nodding acquaintances to Milo and me.

Milo walked me from his Cherokee Chief to my front door, but declined my invitation to come in. It was just as well. We had talked ourselves out over dinner, and one—or both—of us might feel compelled to do something foolish. I suspected that we didn't want to ruin a beautiful friendship. Or that we were chicken.

Virtue cannot dispel loneliness. In the cold quiet of my living room, I set a Wise Man up next to one of the camels in my Nativity set. I should be accustomed to being alone, I told myself, or at least used to not having a male companion. Oh, there had been men in my life since Tom Cavanaugh, but only a few, and never for very long. A single working mother has to give up many things. Intimacy is only one of them, but it may be the greatest sacrifice. Raising a child alone takes time and energy. As the only parent who can drive, clean, cook, cheer, chastise, teach, nurture, and listen, you discover there aren't many minutes of the day left to yourself. And even after that child has gone away, the mold in which life has been cast for almost twenty years has grown virtually unbreakable. After all, it's a safe haven, with those thick, high walls, like the womb that put you there in the first place.

But Ben was close by, and Adam was coming home in less than forty-eight hours. No doubt my son was within driving distance, somewhere in Kirkland, snug in the bosom of Erin Kowalski's family. As for Tom, he was probably in San Francisco, surrounded by his unstable wife and insecure children. I could imagine their beautiful home, their lavish decorations, their expensive presents. Graciousness and good taste would flow from their holiday festivities. Mr. and Mrs. Tom Cavanaugh's photographs would grace the pages of the Bay Area newspapers as they attended a whirlwind of parties, galas, and candlelight suppers. To the casual observer, it would look like a fairy tale—until Sandra Cavanaugh got hauled off for trying to eat the plastic grapes in an I. Magnin display window.

Poor Sandra.

Poor Tom.

Poor me.

Chapter Eleven

BEN GAVE A terrific sermon Sunday morning, transforming St. Luke's account of the barren fig tree into a clear-cut forest on Mount Baldy. *Patience*, my brother urged; it takes time to grow a stand of Douglas fir, but even longer to live a fruitful life. Logger or lawyer, don't just stand there, but reach, stretch, *grow*. Ben's words could be taken on a couple of levels, which may have been lost on some of the parishioners, but they seemed appreciative all the same. At least they weren't being called upon to drive out bad thoughts or avoid suggestive entertainment.

Ben was going to entertain himself by joining Peyton Flake on an excursion to Surprise Lake. I didn't ask if they would be armed. It was scary enough to think that it might snow before they got back.

I spent the day wrapping presents and catching up on Christmas cards. I'd had mine ready to go the previous weekend, but had held off mailing them. As usual, I'd already heard from several people who weren't on my list. I'd ship the whole batch off in the morning on my way to work.

By late afternoon, the snow began to drift down again. I baked spritz cookies, squeezing camels, dogs, trees, wreaths, flowers, and every other imaginable shape out of my copper pastry tube. Adam loved spritz. So did I. By the time I'd finished, I'd already eaten about a quarter of the dough. My original intention to take a couple of dozen cookies to the office went by the board.

I was beginning to worry about Ben when he called just before seven o'clock to say that he and Dr. Flake had returned. I asked my brother if he'd like to pick up something and eat with me. But Ben had been invited to join the ecumenical celebration of St. Lucy's Day at the Lutheran Church. I had attended the previous year, enjoying the Scandinavian custom of crowning a young girl with a wreath of candles and serving strong hot coffee and piles of pastry. Carla was covering the event which would star a thirteen-year-old Gustavson, yet another shirttail relation of Vida's. I've always secretly questioned the wisdom of allowing an awkward teenager to waltz around with burning tapers in her hair while pouring out quantities of steaming liquid, but, I must admit, I've yet to hear of a St. Lucy Wannabe incinerating herself or scalding her family to death. Still, I decided to conserve my resources and stay home.

Monday would be a busy day. We were publishing twenty-four pages, to capitalize on holiday advertising. Naturally, Ed Bronsky was in despair. He had scarcely recovered from the thirty-six pager the previous week. Gleefully, I warned him that we wouldn't get back to sixteen pages until the second week of January. Promotion had been Tom Cavanaugh's key advice when I'd consulted with him about making *The Advocate* more profitable. While he'd insisted that a special edition could be published almost every week, I'd been too timid to try. Once, maybe twice a month was the extent of my ambition—except for wonderful, lucrative, dazzling December. Of course it would have helped if my advertising manager hadn't preferred to sit around on his dead butt and drink coffee.

Twenty-four pages, however, doesn't require more work only from Ed. It also means that Vida, Carla, and I have to produce enough news copy to carry the non-advertising part of the paper. Consequently, we were all busy banging out stories first thing Monday morning. I polished the Evan Singer piece, Vida pried information about the Marmot from

Oscar Nyquist, and Carla concentrated on a Russian Christmas customs feature. Although she'd plagiarized most of it from a library book, she'd taken the trouble to interview a family who had recently moved to Alpine from Minsk via Vancouver, British Columbia, and Bellingham.

I was getting back to my editorial when Milo called. He'd heard from his contact in the King County sheriff's office. Stefan Horthy said that Kathy Francich worked as a cocktail waitress in a bar near the Kingdome. Carol Neal was a table dancer at a seedy nightclub on the Aurora Avenue strip. They'd moved into the Villa Apartments in July. He had never met Carol or Kathy, so he wouldn't be coming to Alpine to identify bodies. Horthy also managed the Riviera Apartments two blocks away, which was where he lived. He would certainly like to know if his tenants were dead or alive.

So, of course, would Milo. I was about to ask if he intended to send someone to talk to neighbors in the Villa Apartments who might know Carol and Kathy, but Ginny Burmeister rushed up to my office door, signaling that I had another call, long distance. Reluctantly, I hung up on Milo and pressed line two. Adam's voice sailed into my ear.

"Mom! I missed the bus! Can you come get me?"

"What bus?" There was no bus service from Seattle to Alpine, only to Everett, with a change for Monroe.

"Huh?" Adam sounded amazed. "Hey, I remember a bus. You know, last summer. It came right up Front Street and stopped at Old Mill Park."

I gritted my teeth. "That was a tour bus. Where are you?"

"Kirkland." Adam had regained his aplomb. I envied and despised the resiliency of youth. "You need directions?"

I did. Like the rest of Seattle's Eastside, Kirkland is a suburban maze. Indeed, my son's proposed route so confused me that we finally settled on a landmark, rather than the Kowalski residence. At one P.M., I would meet Adam at the carillon bell tower by the lake in downtown Kirkland.

My day was virtually shot. It was now after ten, and the

round trip would consume almost four hours. What had I been thinking of? That Erin or her parents would drive Adam to Alpine? That Ben would volunteer to collect his nephew? That Durwood Parker and Crazy Eights Neffel would zip down Stevens Pass on the snowmobile?

As usual, the burden fell on good ol' Mom. I abandoned the editorial, not wanting to rush through the conclusion, and instead devoted what remained of the next hour to a few local news briefs and reading proofs. As usual, Carla had made several typos, including the fact that Alpine had been blanketed with four feet of *snot* and a reference to the Episcopal *rectom*. If necessary, I could start working on the layout in the evening. Meanwhile, it occurred to me that as long as I was going to be in the Seattle area, I might do a bit of sleuthing on my own. As ever, Milo seemed set on going through channels. That could take forever. Or at least until our deadline had passed. I very much wanted to get an ID on one of the nameless victims before we went to press.

It was snowing fitfully as far as Sultan, but the trees along the highway were bare and the ground was visible. I was in a green world again, with the temperature climbing into the forties. I actually rolled the window down an inch or two. The rain pattered steadily on the windshield, but I didn't mind. As a native Seattleite, I was used to it. The snow was another matter. When I was growing up, there were winters when we never saw a snowflake or even a hard frost. The same was true in Portland. Yet after almost three years in Alpine, I thought I was growing accustomed to a seemingly endless world of white. Twenty miles down Stevens Pass told me otherwise. I definitely preferred rain to snow.

I arrived at the appointed spot almost ten minutes early. The wind was coming off Lake Washington, and its sharp damp chill cut to the bone. I didn't mind too much. Unlike a lot of people who can't wait to spend part of winter on a sun-soaked beach, I prefer clouds to sun. Gray days invigorate my mental processes; heat smothers them. I sat on a

bench, admiring the modernistic cluster of bells in the carillon and the whitecaps on the lake. A few hardy souls hovered about, sipping lattes and nibbling on muffins. As the
bells chimed one o'clock, Adam crossed the square, a pair
of skis slung over one shoulder and his hands clutching three
large vinyl bags.

We hugged—briefly, since Adam is still young enough to
be put off by excessive displays of affection. Indeed, our
latest parting had been of a remarkably short duration. Adam
had been home for Thanksgiving, just two weeks earlier.
Tom's generosity had guaranteed the airfare for frequent trips
between Fairbanks and Alpine.

After the requisite questions about Erin, her family, and
the Sunday ski trip to Crystal Mountain, I informed my son
that we were heading into Seattle. I half-expected him to be
excited at the prospect of detecting, but he was surprisingly
indifferent.

"As long as we're going up to Capitol Hill, could we stop
at REI? I need to get some new ski bindings."

"You could do that in Alpine," I replied as we headed for
the Evergreen Point Floating Bridge across Lake Washington.

But Adam shook his head. He was a confirmed believer in
REI, the sporting goods co-op that serves not only as a pro-
visioner of outdoor gear but as a fashion guru. Seattleites are
known not for their tailored three-piece suits, but for plaid
flannel shirts, all-weather pants, and Gore-Tex jackets. In
fact, most big city inhabitants would, in terms of apparel, fit
nicely into Alpine's woodsy milieu. And that goes for men
and women. REI may be the mecca of unisex clothing. Seattleites wouldn't have it any other way.

I, however, am an anomaly. I prefer fitting rooms with
classic covers of *Vogue* and sales clerks who tell monstrous
lies to bolster the customer's ego and pad their commissions.
In Alpine, Francine Wells suits me fine. And in Seattle, I
still lament the demise of Frederick & Nelson, one of the

world's great department stores until greed and mismanagement got the better of it.

Consequently, I dropped my son off to wander in the wilds of REI while I drove north on Broadway to the Villa Apartments. Located above downtown Seattle, Capitol Hill is only eighty miles from Alpine, but demographically it's a world away. The land that climbs above the city center reaches to the ship canal on the north and the fringes of the International District to the south. The neighborhood is made up of large, stately homes and bunker-like condos, legendary watering holes and trendy boutiques, old money and new drugs, college students, artists, panhandlers, lawyers, punk rockers, homosexuals, chiropractors, philanthropists, and every hue of the ethnic rainbow. It's the big city in a nutshell—crazy, colorful, vibrant, and depressing. I love it and yet fear it. But after almost three years in Alpine, my first spotting of a transvestite startled me as much as the sight of a black man and a white woman pushing a baby stroller made me smile.

The Villa Apartments, a block off Broadway, wore a tawdry air. The four-story brick facade had none of the charm of its English Tudor neighbors, and the once-sweeping view of Elliott Bay and the Olympic Mountains had been obliterated by a block of new town houses.

I pressed the buzzer for number 116, next to a strip of paper that read K. FRANCICH/C. NEAL. As I expected, there was no response. I tried R. Littleriver in 115, then D. Calhoun in 119, and finally, V. Fields/T. Booth in 117. Nothing. I got back in the Jag and drove over to the Riviera Apartments, two blocks away. The building was about the same vintage as the Villa, but larger and better maintained. I found S. HORTHY—MGR. at 101 and buzzed some more. To my relief, a woman answered, her voice heavily accented.

After identifying myself, I launched into fiction, stating that I was a friend of Carol Neal, over at the Villa Apartments. I had lent Carol some photographs of my family reunion. They were the only copies I had and they meant much to me. My tone hinted that though I knew Carol, I realized she was irresponsible. I, however, was an honest, if sentimental, fool. "I understand Mr. Horthy plans to confiscate Carol's belongings. Could I please get my pictures back?"

There was no immediate reply. I wondered if the woman had understood what I was saying. A scratchy sound emanated from the small wire speaker; then I heard muffled voices in the background. They weren't speaking in English. Hungarian, maybe, judging from the manager's name.

The woman spoke again into the intercom: "Wait," she commanded, and the speaker shut off.

A moment later, the front door with its wrought-iron grille swung open. A gaunt man of middle age and medium height eyed me warily. He introduced himself as Stefan Horthy but didn't offer his hand. He, too, had an accent, but not as pronounced.

"You know where are these pictures?"

"No." I had trouble meeting his stern gaze. I was a lousy liar. "But they shouldn't be hard to find. They were in a big manila envelope."

Stefan Horthy shifted from one foot to the other, scowling into the rain. Traffic moved cautiously up and down the hill. A trio of black teenagers in Starter jackets walked by, drinking pop out of big plastic cups and eating onion rings from a small cardboard container. Across the street, an elderly woman hunched under a drab wool coat pushed an empty grocery cart into an alley. Nervously, I waited for Stefan Horthy's response.

"Come on." Horthy stalked off in the direction of the other apartment building. I wondered if he would mention being contacted by the sheriff's office.

Stefan Horthy, in fact, didn't mention anything. I hurried to catch up, deciding not to mention my car. He unlocked the Villa's front door, led me up a short flight of stairs past an ungainly Douglas fir that was adorned with bubble lights, and down a stale-smelling hallway. Horthy opened number 116, and stepped aside.

Whoever and whatever Kathleen Francich and Carol Neal were, they would not have qualified as conscientious housekeepers. My initial reaction was that the place had been ransacked. But I'd had some experience covering crime scenes for *The Oregonian* and I could recognize the aftermath of an intruder. There is a certain method to such madness. Unit 116 was merely a slovenly dump.

Even if I'd really been looking for something specific, such as the nonexistent family reunion pictures, I wouldn't have known where to start. Dirty clothes, fast food cartons, wine bottles, magazines, pop cans, grocery sacks, and even a rotting jack-o'-lantern were strewn about the room. My eyes fastened on a bunch of unopened mail lying helter-skelter on the shabby carpet. It all seemed to be addressed to Kathleen Francich.

Stefan Horthy was watching me like a hawk. Casually, I picked up one of the empty grocery bags. "Do you mind if I take this mail? I understand they didn't leave a forwarding address. Is there any more downstairs?"

"Maybe." His ambivalent answer could have referred to either my request or my question. Horthy scowled at the litter of brochures, bills, and mail order catalogues. He might have been considering the legal implications, but I suspected he was calculating monetary value. "Go, take that much. But all else is mine."

I gave him a flinty smile. "Except my photos. Let me check the bedrooms." I was already heading for the hallway, staving off Horthy's anticipated protests. He said nothing, however, but followed me as far as the first bedroom door.

I tried to overlook the chaos, zeroing in on the dressing table with a framed picture that was almost obscured by cologne bottles, cosmetic jars, and underwear. A young, pretty face gazed out at me from under dirty glass. Curly dark brown hair, brown eyes, a disarmingly self-conscious smile. The

subject was posed in a high-backed rattan chair. A typical
Blanchet High School senior photo. Was it Carol? I didn't
know what the victim looked like. I grabbed the picture and
put it in the grocery bag.

"Hey!" Stefan Horthy growled. "You're not taking that!"

I gave him a steely look. "Yes, I am. I'm sure you know
something terrible may have happened to Carol. I'd like a
memento."

Horthy made a face, but didn't argue. I opened drawers,
perused the closet, even looked under the bed. I didn't know
what I expected to find, but if Milo Dodge could ID our
victim from the photo, he could get a search warrant for the
apartment. I brushed past Horthy and went into the other
bedroom. It was only slightly less of a shambles. There was
no graduation picture, but a dozen snapshots had been tucked
around the mirror on the dresser. They featured a fair-haired
young woman with dancing eyes and a dimpled smile. I selected three of the pictures and put them in the grocery sack,
too.

"No luck," I called to Horthy, who was standing in the
hallway, hands jammed into his pants pockets. He turned
away just as I tripped over a tennis shoe. On impulse, I
snatched it up, then followed Stefan Horthy back into the
living room. Next to the battered, tattered sofa was a small
table where the telephone stood. The table had a little drawer.
I opened it and sucked in my breath. A square, blue spiral
address book was too much to resist. My back was turned to
Horthy.

"Here are the pictures," I said in triumph, allowing him
to hear but not see the address book join my little collection.
Inspired, I picked up the phone, grateful to get a dial tone.
I'd half-expected it to be disconnected.

"Hey—what you doing now?" Stefan Horthy leaped
across the room, no mean feat, considering the obstacle
course he had to overcome.

Waving Horthy off, I hit the redial button. A female voice

answered on the second ring. "History Department. This is Rachel Rosen. How may I help you?"

"Oh!" I made flabbergasted noises. "What number is this?"

Rachel told me. I recognized the prefix as belonging to the University of Washington campus. "I'm sorry," I apologized. "I misdialed."

Stefan Horthy's patience, which I judged to be chronically on the thin side, finally snapped. "Hey, you—get out of here now. You got your pictures. You waste my day."

I smiled, this time more amiably. "You're right. I just wish I knew what happened to Carol."

Stefan Horthy obviously didn't share my concern. With another scowl, he closed and locked the apartment door. When we reached the foyer, he indicated a row of brass mailboxes. "Letters may be inside or in that pile by the stairs. People are careless pigs." He selected another key from his big silver ring and unlocked the slot for 116 with a show of grudging condescension. "Let yourself out," he said, abruptly, and then banged the door as he made his exit.

Five minutes later, I put my stash in the Jag and headed back to collect Adam. He was standing in line to pay for his purchases at the cashier's counter.

"Nick o' time," he said with that engaging grin so like his father's. "I can pay cash for the bindings, but I need some of your plastic to cover the gloves and the boots and the ski wax."

"Adam . . ." The motherly lecture died aborning. With his six-two stature and his once-boyish features sharpening into Tom's chiseled profile, I knew I was sunk. Nor was it just the resemblance that turned me to jelly. This was my baby, my son, the only man who had been a real part of my life for the past twenty-one years. I produced the plastic; Adam offered a pat on my head. It was, I suppose, a fair exchange.

* * *

I hadn't planned on serving dinner for five, but that was the way it worked out. Adam and I had stopped for a late lunch at the venerable Deluxe Tavern on Broadway, so it was going on six o'clock by the time we reached Alpine. We swung by the newspaper office, where I discovered that Vida was still working. I invited her to join us for dinner, at which point she informed me that Ben had called and said he'd be able to come, too. My brother was anxious to see his nephew.

I was anxious to show Milo the photos I'd filched from the Villa Apartments. I took a chance that he was also still on the job and asked him to eat with us. No arm-twisting was required. Adam and I rushed off to the Grocery Basket, where I tossed chicken breasts, French bread, cauliflower, two bottles of Chardonnay, and a frozen lemon meringue pie into my basket. Dinner would be late, but, along with the rice I already had at home, it would be ample.

Milo and Ben studied the framed photograph with somber expressions. At last Milo looked up, his hazel eyes showing pain. "It's her. She looks different here, but I'd swear to it in court."

Milo didn't need to explain that his memory was based on Carol Neal being at least four years older and maybe three days dead. Ben concurred with Milo's opinion.

For the first time, my son evinced interest in the case. "She was a mega-babe," he murmured, looking over Ben's shoulder. "What a waste! Who'd do something like that?"

I eyed Adam carefully. He'd turned pale, and it occurred to me that in Carol Neal, he had come face-to-face with his own mortality. Twenty-two-year-old women shouldn't die. Neither should twenty-two-year-old men.

"The worst of it," put in Vida between mouthfuls of trout pâté and crackers, "is that there are two of them. Let's see that tennis shoe again, Emma."

I handed it to Vida. It was an Adidas, but, like the Reebok Milo had found, it was a size seven and a half. Vida looked up at Milo, who was now on his feet by the fireplace, fiddling with a candle in the shape of a choirboy. "Inconclusive?"

"Of course. But suggestive, if nobody knows where Kathleen Francich is. The King County people will be on this first thing tomorrow. It's their case now, too." Milo wore a faint air of relief. The law enforcement officials in Seattle had far greater resources than he had in Alpine. Indeed, Milo was still smarting over the failure of a bond issue on the November ballot that would have allowed him to hire two more deputies and acquire more sophisticated equipment. Skykomish County voters had also turned down a proposal to expand the fire department. My editorials urging passage of both measures had gone for naught.

I went into the kitchen to turn the chicken breasts over. Vida was perusing the address book. I'd only had time to glance through it. I wasn't sure if it belonged to Carol or Kathleen, but whichever it was, she had certainly jotted down a lot of masculine names, and strange ones at that. Corny. Stitch. Porky. Big Wheel. Diver Dan. Shaft. I was curious to know what Milo would make of it.

The cauliflower was aboil, the rice was steaming nicely, and the buttered bread loaf was heating along with the chicken breasts. I returned to the living room, where Vida was tapping the open pages of the address book.

"Prostitutes," she asserted. "These names are clients. Disgusting. But part of life. What else would you expect of a table dancer and a cocktail waitress?"

"I don't know about cocktail waitresses . . ." Ben began.

"You don't know about prostitutes," interrupted Vida. "At least I hope you don't. You're a priest." She whirled around on the sofa to give Adam a sharp look. "I hope you know better than to get mixed up with that sort of woman. They'll take your hard-earned money, give you a dreadful disease, and tell you you've had a wonderful time. Men are silly enough to believe them. Oh! It's maddening!"

Milo, either out of professional duty or in an attempt to

ward off his turn on the spit of Vida's tongue, ventured that prostitution was a good guess. ''Which means we may have a typical serial killer on the loose. Most of the Green River victims were hookers, or at least runaways who turned a trick to make survival money.''

On the face of it, Milo's argument made sense. But the Green River ran its course near the Sea-Tac airport strip, a bit of real estate notorious for its vice crimes. The Skykomish River was far removed from the sins of the city. I had to disagree with Milo.

''If Carol and Kathleen are both dead, and even if they were both part-time hookers, they still had something else in common,'' I pointed out. ''They were roommates. That means they were probably also friends. They had more in common than just turning tricks.''

''An excellent point.'' Vida nodded vigorously, then carefully turned the pages of the address book to the middle. She studied the listings, gave a slight shake of her head, and then flipped back toward the front section. ''Ha!'' She waved the little blue book in triumph. ''Just as I thought! Dunne, Bridget!''

All three males looked puzzled, but I practically jumped up and down. ''Bridget Dunne Nyquist,'' I cried, for the elucidation of Milo, Ben, and Adam. ''Is there an Alpine address?''

''No.'' Vida offered the book to Milo. ''It looks like a Seattle number, no address. But one—or both—of these girls knew Bridget.''

''Of course,'' I said, squeezing in between Vida and Ben on the sofa. ''They went to high school together. I wonder if Kathleen Francich went to Blanchet, too.'' I poked my brother. ''Call Bill Crowley. He'd know.''

''Now?'' Ben regarded me with reluctance. I poked him again, harder. He got up and went to the phone, then turned back to look at me. ''I don't have his home number. He used to be in residence at Christ the King, but I'm not sure he's there anymore, with priests being moved all over the place lately. I'll call Mrs. McHale. My address book is at the rectory.''

Teresa McHale, however, did not answer. Ben remembered that she was taking Father Fitz's Volvo out for the evening, to visit an elderly shut-in. He promised to call the Blanchet chaplain first thing in the morning.

Milo was going through the little blue book page by page. I told him to check on a listing for Rachel Rosen. Ever methodical, Milo told me to hold my horses; he was only as far as the Gs.

He'd gotten to M by the time I announced that dinner was served. Speculation was rampant, but I must admit we didn't get much beyond what we already knew or guessed. There were so many *ifs* in the case. *If* the other dead body was Kathleen Francich. *If* one or both of the young women had been prostitutes. *If* Carol had maintained contact with Bridget Dunne Nyquist. *If* Kathleen had gone to Blanchet.

We ran out of conjecture about the same time I ran out of chicken. By then, everyone was full, sleepy, and content to stare into the fireplace. Milo offered to drive Ben back to the rectory. Vida wanted to help clean up, but I told her to head home. It was starting to snow quite hard. Adam could lend me a hand.

Adam, however, had dozed off on the floor by the hearth. Apparently, his exertions on the ski slopes the previous day had worn him out. After throwing an afghan over him, I went out into the kitchen. I was emptying the second load of the evening from the dishwasher when I realized that I hadn't finished my editorial, let alone even begun to lay out the newspaper.

It was after eleven. I dithered briefly, then decided it was better to get off to an early start than to make a late finish. I put the last of the silverware away, wiped off the counters, and headed for bed.

I stopped at the Nativity scene to add the second Wise

Man. The first was hiding behind a palm tree, peering out like a German spy from a bad World War II movie. Adam was still asleep in front of the dying fire. I left him there, offering up a prayer to keep him safe and happy. As I kicked off my shoes, I wondered if Carol Neal's parents had ever said the same prayers for her. If they had, their supplications had been stamped denied. Of course Ben would tell me it didn't work that way. Prayer acknowledges faith; it's like sending a thinking-of-you card to God. And sometimes even that gets returned to sender.

Chapter Twelve

We can't turn back the clock. But neither can we turn our backs on history. Washington State was built on a firm foundation—of logs. Trees are still our major crop. Scholars and scientists tell us we can have both a healthy environment and a prosperous timber industry. People must remain our top priority. We can keep the spotted owls in the trees, but let the logs keep rolling. And let the good times roll again in Alpine, and in other logging communities of the Pacific Northwest.

I hit transfer, save, and print. The editorial was finished, though my day had only begun. I turned my attention to Vida's story on Oscar Nyquist and the Whistling Marmot Movie Theatre. It was long, and, as was Vida's style when she got her teeth into a meaty feature, a bit rambling. She started with the theatre's early history in the social hall under the reign of Lars Nyquist, moved up to the new building site, mentioned that the Marmot had been designed by Isaac Lowenstein, a well-known West Coast architect specializing in movie houses, and then jumped to the postwar renovations and the most recent updating in the 1960s. The exterior had been repainted last summer, another product of the film location company, but with happier results than our garish yellow facade. The quotes from Oscar were mundane, but Vida had done a telephone sampling of local Marmot aficionados, who had waxed eloquent over such varied historic occasions as the first talking picture, a visit by Betty Grable on the vaudeville circuit, Bing Crosby passing through on a fishing trip during World War II, and the crush of females who had showed up for Elvis's movie debut in *Love Me Tender*. Amazingly enough, Vida had managed to track down Mabel Hubbert Bockdorff, who had played the piano for Lars during the silent-screen era. Mabel was ninety-seven yeas old, but still sharp and living on her own in Wenatchee.

Only in the next to the last paragraph did Vida allude to the Nyquists' recent rash of pesky problems: "Running a movie theatre isn't all roses and popcorn," wrote Vida. "Oscar Nyquist and his son, Arnold, have experienced their ups and downs, including an outbreak of vandalism on both their private and professional properties. The elder Nyquist has expressed a strong desire to see these culprits apprehended, but so far no arrests have been made." Vida summed up with a lengthy paragraph about all the excitement and romance and laughter and thrills the Marmot had brought to Alpine. She gave credit to Lars for being farsighted, to Oscar for his perseverance, and to Arnie for bringing a bowling alley to the town. I suspected that the last remark was made tongue-in-cheek, but I let it ride.

"Nice work," I told her, as Carla handed me the pictures of Evan Singer in his coachman's costume.

Vida made a harumphing noise. "I wasn't exactly interviewing Sol Hurok. If Lars Nyquist had owned an insurance agency, Oscar would have peddled policies door-to-door. If Lars had been a blacksmith, Oscar would still be pounding on the forge, and never mind that the horse and buggy has been gone for three generations. Oscar has no imagination. I doubt that he ever watches the movies he shows. At least Lars had enough emotion to get a crush on Greta Garbo."

Carla was looking at the photos Vida had selected to go with the story: the social hall, the Marmot's opening night, an amateur production of *You Can't Take It With You*, a head shot of the late Lars, and three generations of Nyquists standing under the marquee with *It's a Wonderful Life* in big block letters.

"When did you take this?" I asked Vida.

"Yesterday, while you were out gallivanting. See, Travis has thrown his crutches away, just like Tiny Tim."

I edged closer to Carla and scrutinized the photo of Oscar, Arnie, and Travis Nyquist. I noted Oscar's bald head, Arnie's receding hairline, and Travis's wavy brown locks. "I wonder how soon Travis will start losing *his* hair," I mused.

Carla gasped. "Don't say that, Emma! He's so cute!"

"Knock it off, Carla," I said, trying to keep my tone light. "It's a shame my son is too young for you." Of course it really wasn't. The role of Carla's employer was bad enough; being her mother-in-law would be worse.

Carla gave me an irked look. "You're a washout when it comes to helping me meet men. Adam's still a college kid and your brother is a priest. Don't you know any eligible guys?"

"If I did, I'd have first dibs," I replied, shoving one of the Evan Singer photos in her direction. "Here, don't you think he looks dashing in that coachman's rig?"

Carla's dark eyes grew very wide. "With a whip? Why not shackles and chains, too? I told you he was weird, Emma. You were pretty brave to go out to his cabin the other day. I would have taken Milo Dodge along."

Milo, in fact, was entering the door. He looked very purposeful this snowy December morning. "Things are beginning to hum," he announced. "The King County people are sending up one of Carol's co-workers to officially identify her. Whoever it is knows she had a tattoo on her backside."

If Milo was expecting congratulations, he got more than he'd bargained for. Carla zipped across the room, grabbed the sheriff, stood on her tiptoes, and kissed him soundly. "Mistletoe!" she chirped. "Hey, Sheriff Dodge, *you're* eligible!"

Milo reeled "For what?"

"Never mind," I sighed, shaking my head at Carla. "The sheriff's taken. Honoria Whitman, remember?"

Vida, who had removed her glasses, drank from a mug of hot water. "How is Honoria? I haven't seen much of her lately."

Milo was pouring himself a cup of coffee. "She left for Carmel Saturday. She isn't used to the snow and doesn't like to drive in it. And I've been pretty tied up. I wasn't able to get down to Startup last week."

I made sympathetic noises. The sheriff's current lady-love was hampered by more than a lifetime in California's warmer climate: Honoria's ex-husband had taken out his rage against the world by throwing his wife down a flight of stairs. Mr. Whitman had paid for his temper tantrum with a bullet fired by Honoria's brother. He'd served ten years, but had told his sister it was worth it. Honoria's sentence was longer—she would never walk again.

We were expressing our admiration for Honoria's independence and spunk when Arnie Nyquist stormed into the office. I'm used to irate readers, so I braced myself for a tirade. Arnie's target, however, was not me but Milo Dodge.

"That's it! You're a waste of the taxpayers' money, Dodge! Haven't you ever heard of patrol cars? Not only are those morons still screwing up the Marmot's marquee, but my house has been robbed!" Arnie Nyquist flailed around the office, gesturing wildly. I had a perverse wish for him to stand under the mistletoe so Carla could kiss him.

Keeping calm, Milo held his coffee mug in both hands. "Have you reported this?"

Carla jumped in between the two men. "I should take a picture! What does the marquee say this time?" She could hardly contain her glee.

Arnie glared at her exuberant form. "What the hell difference does it make? Some damned fool silly thing—'*Under A Low Stiffel.*' Jesus!"

Carla clapped her hands. "Cute! A Stiffel's a kind of lamp, get it?" She dashed to her desk to grab her camera.

"No, you don't!" yelled Arnie. "My dad and I don't want you poking fun at the Marmot!"

I shook my head at Carla. She hesitated, then docilely put the camera back on her desk. "You've got to admit it's clever," she muttered with a flash of dark eyes for Arnie.

Arnie ignored her, turning his ire back on Milo. "I reported it, all right. The robbery, I mean. That's how I knew you were here." He was still barreling around, bumping into Vida's desk. She gave him a frosty stare.

The sheriff had kept his expression bland. "The robbery happened this morning?"

Arnie finally stood still, just as Ed Bronsky came in, grumbling and brushing snow off his overcoat. "The mall! How can those merchants want all that advertising next week for end-of-year clearance sales? The paper will come out the day before Christmas Eve! Nobody'll read the damned ads!"

I would save my lecture on the importance of post holiday bargains in a depressed economy until after Arnie finished pitching his fit. And Arnie was indeed blustering away: "The robbery was last night, while Louise and I were gone. We drove down to Sultan to visit some friends. It was late when we got home, almost midnight. We went right to bed, and didn't notice we'd been robbed until this morning." He shot Milo a defensive look.

Ed was pouring coffee. "Robbed, huh?" he said over his shoulder. "You know, Arnie, if you didn't take out those two-inch ads every week for Nyquist Construction, nobody'd know who you were. Then they wouldn't realize you had anything worth stealing. You plaster your name all over the paper, and there you are—a sitting duck."

Not for the first time did I resist the urge to strangle my advertising manager. In fact, I secretly hoped Arnie Nyquist would do Ed in and save me the trouble. But Arnie chose to ignore Ed, which was probably what I should have done, had he not been on my payroll.

Milo raised his sandy eyebrows. "So? What was taken?"

A slight flush enveloped Arnie's round face. "Priceless stuff. Keepsakes, two cartons of 'em. How do you put a value on a lifetime of memories? They're irreplaceable!"

Milo's beeper went off. He gave Arnie a cool look, started to pick up the phone on Carla's desk, changed his mind, and announced he'd better go straight back to the office. He took our coffee mug with him.

Arnie was now leaning on Vida's desk. "Well? Aren't you going to put this in the story about our family? About how we're being persecuted?"

I watched Vida gaze up at Arnie. She looked a bit owlish. "I could. What's actually missing?"

Momentarily appeased, Arnie began to tick off items on his thick fingers. "A lot of family pictures, especially from when Travis was little. Maybe our wedding album—Louise isn't sure, she's been too busy crying. My discharge from the army, my diplomas from Alpine High School and the University of Washington, my yearbooks, and Travis's baby book. Letters, postcards, invitations, announcements—all the stuff people save. You know."

Vida gave a curt nod. " 'Arnold Nyquist—The Early Years.' Yes, I've got it." She put her glasses back on and blinked twice.

Now that Arnie had quieted down a bit, I posed a question of my own: "How did they get in?"

Arnie looked exasperated. "Walked. Louise forgot to lock the basement door." His voice dropped to a mumble.

Carla made a clucking noise with her tongue. "Oh, gee, that's not too smart, especially with a murderer on the loose. You know, Mr. Nyquist, you can't blame the sheriff for everything, not if you don't take precautions."

I felt like applauding Carla; Arnie Nyquist looked as if he wanted to slug her. But he refrained. Instead, he heeled around and slammed out of the office. We were not sorry to see him go.

"Neener-neener-neener," chanted Carla, putting her thumbs in her ears and waggling her fingers. "What an oaf!"

Vida snorted in apparent agreement; Ed shrugged and took a bite out of a sweet roll he'd picked up from the bakery. I retreated into my office to lay the paper out on the computer. The Pagemaker program has simplified my life, though sometimes I miss the immediacy of hot type and cold sweat. I was never very good at translating words into inches. Translating other people's incoherent words was more my line.

I had finished the front page when Milo called. The summons he had received had not only gotten his day off to a jolt, but also upset my carefully computerized Page One. Duane Gustavson, a shirttail relation of Vida's on the Runkel side, had been out fishing at first light on the Tye River at the mouth of Surprise Creek, near Scenic. He had caught an eleven-pound steelhead, a worthless white fish—and an arm. Duane had netted his dinner, but he'd lost his lunch. Or, in this case, his breakfast.

And I had another piece of the story. So to speak.

Doc Dewey and his wife had gone into Seattle to attend a conference and to visit relatives. Doc wasn't due back until Wednesday night. He had delegated Peyton Flake to take over as medical examiner, should the need arise. It had—unfortunately.

Dr. Flake cruised into his private office, sangfroid intact. Milo and I didn't share his equanimity, though, as professionals, we tried. The sheriff had studied Flake's impressive credentials; I had admired his collection of duck hunting stamps. The ducks were another matter: there were six of them, stuffed and glassy-eyed, with handsome plumage and unfamiliar pedigrees. I suppose they went well with the moose, stag, cougar, and lynx heads. I half-expected to see

a couple of his patients mounted on the wall, but I was probably letting my imagination get the best of me.

"I don't like guesswork," Peyton Flake announced flatly.
"It's going to take a while to get all the lab results back. But
if you want my *opinion*"—he stressed the word, curling his
lips over his teeth—"I'd say the arm went with the leg."

Milo nodded. "Do you think it had been in the river a
long time?"

"Definitely. Two, three months." Flake fiddled with the
rubber band that held his ponytail in place. "Unfortunately,
from your point of view, there were no rings, no watch,
nothing identifiable. You want a look?" He gazed at me, and
I could have sworn that he was trying to keep amusement at
bay.

Milo, of course, had already seen the arm. He was duty-
bound. I wasn't. I shook my head. I didn't even want to think
about where Dr. Dewey and Dr. Flake filed spare append-
ages.

Dr. Flake had leaned back in his chair, putting his hiking
boots up on the desk. "Interesting," he mused. "Amateur
at work. A saw, I'd guess."

"Gack!" I closed my eyes and shuddered. Then I berated
myself. It was all part of the job—the reporting of news, the
discovery of facts, the search for truth. "Gack," I repeated,
with less force.

Milo's suggestion of going to lunch fell on deaf ears. Not
only had I lost my appetite, but I was up against a deadline.
Milo didn't press; Carol Neal's co-worker was supposed to
arrive at the sheriff's office around one.

Carla was out, Ed was working on his advertising layout,
and Vida was munching carrot sticks between spoonfuls of
cottage cheese. Ben had called while I was gone. Vida relayed his message.

"He talked to the chaplain at Blanchet. There is no record
of a Kathleen Francich attending the school."

Somehow, I was disappointed. But the information goaded

me into calling Rachel Rosen at the University of Washington. I went into my office and closed the door, not to keep secrets from my staff, but to avoid distractions. I had the feeling I would need full command of my wits.

Luckily, Rachel had not gone out to lunch. She answered in the same manner as she had done the previous day when I called from the Villa Apartments. I wondered if she would remember my voice.

"Ms. Rosen," I began, using my most professional tone and trying not to jar Rachel too badly, "I'm the editor and publisher of *The Alpine Advocate*, on Stevens Pass. We're running a missing persons story about someone you know. Her name is Carol Neal. Could you tell me when you last saw her or talked to her?"

"Carol's missing, too?" The words were blurted out.

"You're referring to Kathleen Francich?" Milo should be doing this, I thought. Maybe he was, through the auspices of the King County Sheriff.

"Yes." Rachel Rosen paused. I could imagine her sitting at a desk, pondering the disappearances of Carol and Kathleen. When she spoke again, there was a note of caution in her voice. "I haven't seen Carol or Kathy in a long time. But I did talk to Carol a month or so ago. She was worried about Kathy."

"Worried because she'd disappeared?"

"Yes. It wasn't like Kathy to be gone so long. Excuse me, Ms. Lord, I have someone in the office here." Rachel had become brisk.

"Ms. Rosen—where did you go to high school?" The question flew out of my mouth.

"Seattle Hebrew Academy. Why do you ask?" Rachel sounded suddenly tense.

I ignored her query. I was a journalist; I could ask whatever I damned well pleased. "And Kathy?"

"Kathy? Holy Names, I think. Goodbye."

The phone clicked in my ear. Holy Names was a private

all-girls' Catholic high school at the north end of Capitol Hill. The Seattle Hebrew Academy was coed, but also private and located not far from Holy Names. What was the link between Blanchet's Carol Neal, Holy Names's Kathleen Francich, and the Academy's Rachel Rosen? Was there any link, other than all three young women had gone to private schools? And where, if anyplace, did Bridget Nyquist, also of Blanchet, fit in? I ignored my computer screen and drew strange rectangles on a piece of scratch paper. I wished I had been able to keep the little blue address book. But of course Milo had confiscated it, along with the mail I'd brought from the Villa Apartments.

A firm knock on the door jolted me out of my reverie. "Well?" Vida stood on the threshold, her green cloche hat askew, though with a cloche it's hard to tell. "Who have you been grilling?"

I told her, adding that while Rachel Rosen hadn't exactly been a font of information, she had made one telling remark. "She said Carol was worried about Kathleen because she was never gone for such a long time. That tells me Kathleen occasionally took off for a few days. I assume she went with a man."

"A fair assumption," said Vida, nodding. "It's also fair to assume that if Carol called Rachel a month or so ago, it was more likely back in October, not November. People lose track of time. And that could mean that the other body is indeed Miss Francich."

"Ugh." I put a hand to my head. "I hope somebody in Seattle is going to question Rachel. I got the impression she wasn't real eager to share what she knew."

My phone rang before Vida could comment. The call was from the sheriff's office, but it was Vida's nephew, Bill Blatt, not Milo.

"Sheriff's interrogating this Desmond woman," Bill reported in his youthful tones. "She positively IDed Carol Neal. Then she fell apart. But Sheriff Dodge said you'd want the information right away, because you've got to get the paper out, right?''

"Right." And God help Billy Blatt if he didn't deliver the goods to Aunt Vida and company first. "Does this Desmond person know the other girl, Kathleen?''

"Couldn't tell you," said Bill Blatt, then, lest his aunt and I accuse him of keeping secrets, quickly added, "That is, I don't know. I imagine Sheriff Dodge will ask her. We'll keep you posted.''

I thanked him and hung up. It was an easy matter to add Carol Neal's identity to the story about the discovery of her body. We were a week late with the news anyway, having missed last Wednesday's deadline by a matter of hours. I'd already inserted Duane Gustavson's grisly catch on the Tye River. The front page of *The Advocate* was turning into a gruesome travesty. The lead story of a double murder juxtaposed with a picture of Fuzzy Baugh in a Santa suit wasn't going to make for the jolliest of holiday reading.

Vida was lingering in my doorway. "We've got to talk to Bridget again," she announced flatly. "We can't leave it up to Milo. He's too busy following *procedures*." She made a face as she spun out the word.

"Bridget doesn't want to talk to us," I pointed out.

Vida sniffed. "Of course she doesn't. But she will."

"How?''

"I'll think of something." Vida finally started toward her desk, then turned back to face me. "Say—if you need more filler for next week, I've got some fascinating background left over from the Marmot piece. That Lowenstein fellow designed several of the old movie houses in the Pacific Northwest, most of which have been torn down. The Marmot is the only one left on this side of the state. Besides, he lived in Alpine for a time, while the theatre was being planned.''

I considered Vida's suggestion. "Sounds good to me. But it might fit better in the New Year's edition.''

"Fine," Vida agreed. "That will give me time to see if I

can track down any old coots who might have known Lowenstein. Besides Oscar Nyquist, of course.''

For the rest of the afternoon, I tried to put murder from my mind. It wasn't easy, but by five o'clock the paper was ready to roll. Milo stopped in just as Carla and Ed were leaving.

"Lila Desmond," he said, sitting on the edge of Carla's vacated desk. "I hope I never see her again."

"Carol's colleague?" I signed my initials to the note for Kip MacDuff, who would truck the paper to Monroe in the morning. "What happened?"

Milo was looking bemused. "She cried, she got hysterical, she threw up. Trying to get any genuine information out of her was like walking in a swamp. All she could say was that Carol was a sweet kid and lent her a pair of earrings. Hell!" Milo made an impatient gesture with one hand, as close to anger as I'd seen him in ages.

Vida pursed her lips. "Now, now. Surely this Lila knew when she'd last seen Carol?"

"Sort of." Milo gave Vida a disparaging look. "She was vague about that, too. But she thought it was over the Thanksgiving weekend. I gather table-dancers don't keep to strict schedules. And no, she wasn't acquainted with Kathleen Francich. She knew—vaguely—that Carol had a roommate. But that was all." The sheriff now wore a disgusted expression. Alpine is not without its depravities, but table-dancing isn't one of them. Milo could cope with drunken brawls, domestic S & M, drug addicts, and even grisly homicides. But scantily clad young women bumping and grinding for bug-eyed lechers was beyond him. His idea of an evening on the wild side was four beers and a bowl of popcorn at Mugs Ahoy.

"What about Kathleen?" I asked. "Has anybody in Seattle come up with news about her?"

Now solemn, Milo nodded. "She hasn't shown up at work since October the sixth. She had a couple of days off at the bar and never came back. Nobody got excited. It happens, I guess." His hazel eyes suddenly sparked. "But on October fifteenth, Carol Neal reported Kathleen missing."

"Ooooh!" Vida whipped off her glasses and rubbed frantically at her eyes. "Why didn't you say so? Honestly, Milo, you are as slow as mold!"

Milo resumed his stoic expression. "One thing at a time. The bottom line is that Kathleen never turned up."

Vida stopped rubbing. "So Carol went looking for her?"

"Maybe." Milo shrugged. "Carol probably hoped the police would find Kathleen. Or that she'd show up on her own. What I want to know is why did she come looking for her in Alpine? If, in fact, that's what Carol did."

"We can't know that," I murmured. "And yet . . . If that other body is Kathleen . . . The tennis shoe fits, should she wear it?"

"Carol gave a description of Kathleen as five-six, a hundred and twenty pounds, light blonde hair, deep blue eyes, a small scar above her left eyebrow. Doc Dewey and Peyton Flake can figure out height, maybe even weight. But not much else. Yet."

I grimaced at Milo's implication. Vida, however, appeared composed. "Well. If Carol was out searching for Kathleen, Alpine may not have been the first place she went. But I have a feeling it was the right place, don't you?"

Milo nodded slowly. "I'm afraid so. It was also the last place she looked."

From that point of view, it was the wrong place as well.

Milo was taking his leave when Cal Vickers came into the office. "Just the man I want to see," said Cal to Milo, after acknowledging Vida and me with a tip of his greasy duck-billed cap. "Bill Blatt said you'd be here."

"What's up?" inquired Milo of the strapping gas station proprietor.

Cal was the sort who liked to spin out a tale, a habit forged while standing next to an open hood and putting off the moment when the car owner learns that it's going to cost him dearly to have his vehicle repaired.

"I got a call yesterday from Clancy Barton at the Bootery. You know Clancy, he's a fussbudget. The mall was busy over the weekend, and at one point they ran out of parking places. Clancy and the rest of the merchants wanted the sheriff to impound those old heaps that have been sitting there for weeks and have me tow 'em away." He stopped, taking off his earmuffs. "Actually, there were only two cars. Dodge here said fine, go get 'em; he had other fish to fry. So did we, with all the jackasses sliding into each other or landing in ditches. You'd think people around here would know how to drive in snow. Anyway, we finally got down to it this afternoon. The old Malibu belongs to some kid from Gold Bar. Starter went out, near as I can tell. You know kids, they'd rather give up on something than take the trouble to fix it."

Behind me, I could hear Vida emit a low, impatient sigh. I, too, wished Cal would speed his story along. Milo, however, appeared unflappable.

"Then we checked out the Barracuda. Man, it had been there a *long* time. Everything's froze up, no antifreeze, but almost a full tank of gas." Cal shook his head.

"Stolen?" The word was Milo's mild attempt to hurry Cal along.

Cal Vickers shrugged. "Could be. I figure you ought to run it through the computer." He removed his cap again and brushed his stubby fingers through the fringe of dark hair that grew from ear to ear. "The car's from Seattle. It's registered to a Kathleen Francich."

Chapter Thirteen

THERE COULDN'T BE much doubt that if Kathleen Francich's car had arrived in Alpine, so had Kathleen. How her car had ended up at the mall while she seemed to be appearing in various other places remained a mystery. Maybe Milo could wave his forensics wand over the Barracuda and come up with some answers. Meanwhile, I was going to rely on intuition. Sometimes it actually worked.

I had been bothered by Louise Bergstrom Nyquist ever since I'd run into her and Arnie at Barton's Bootery. Maybe I'd imagined that she had wanted to talk to me; maybe I'd misread the appeal in her eyes.

Nevertheless, on this snowy Tuesday night I felt compelled to talk to Louise. The timing was good: I'd put aside the cares of *The Advocate* for another week, and the planning commission met on the third Tuesday of each month. Arnie Nyquist was on the board. Louise would be home alone.

I arrived shortly after seven, my nerves frayed by the brief but treacherous drive up First Hill. Arnold Nyquist had built himself a house on Icicle Creek. Two stories of brick and cedar, the showpiece dwelling was set among the evergreens, but commanded a ravishing view of the town and Mount Baldy. Everything seemed to fit, from the cathedral ceilings to the Aubusson carpets. Everything, that is, except Louise Nyquist, who looked as if she would have been more at home with faded mohair and braided rugs.

"This is a surprise," she said in apparent pleasure. "I

633

was just going to bake some Christmas cookies. Would you like an eggnog?''

I said I would indeed, but to skip the rum. I had to face the tricky downhill drive to get back home. ''I wanted to tell you how sorry I was about your burglary. It's one thing to have VCRs and CD players stolen, but it's terribly sad when keepsakes go. Arnie said your wedding album might have been taken, too.''

Louise beamed at me from across the kitchen island where she was pouring homemade eggnog into tall mugs. ''I found the album, thank goodness. It had fallen behind a box of Travis's high school mementos. But you're right,'' she went on, leading me back into the living room. ''Those were treasures we can't ever replace. Now why would anyone take them?''

I was sitting in a tapestry-covered armchair; Louise was perched on an amber brocade sofa. Even with its cheerful Christmas decor, the room seemed stiff and formal. But it was also very beautiful. I wondered if the same person had done both this house and the younger Nyquists' decor.

''Mischief, maybe,'' I replied, taking in a Lalique vase, a Baroque mirror, and a brilliantly colored bowl that might have been crafted by Dale Chiluly. If the thief had had a pack like Santa's, he could have thrown in those three items and made off with six figures worth of goodies.

''Drugs,'' Louise was saying. ''That's what Arnie suspects. Whoever it was thought we might have some—or cash lying around—and when they couldn't find anything, they just grabbed the first thing that came to hand. You know how those people are. They don't think rationally, like the rest of us.''

I tried not to look dubious. But I recalled that Vida had said that Louise was no dope. Perhaps I could trust to be candor. ''You know, Louise, that doesn't seem likely. If the burglar was a drug addict, he would steal something he could sell or pawn.'' I waved a hand to take in the vast living room with its many-splendored things. "You have some valuable pieces. Sterling, too, I'll bet. Who designed all this? It's lovely."

Louise's gaze wandered around the room, from the demilune-inlaid console table to the satinwood urn filled with holly. "Designed it? We did. I mean, Arnie, really. But we always discuss what we're going to buy. Once in a while he comes up with a clinker."

I gaped at Louise. I couldn't imagine that Tinker Toy could possess such elegant tastes. But of course the houses he built—at least the ones that didn't fall down—were handsome structures. I had assumed that he used an architect. I said as much to Louise.

"Sometimes he does," she said. "He did for this house. But Arnie has quite an eye. He has to, since there's no real architect in Alpine. He couldn't be running into Seattle all the time for consultations. Besides, talented architects are very expensive."

It seemed to me that if Arnie Nyquist was going to spend money, he preferred to do it on himself. However, Louise and I had strayed from the point of my visit. If there *was* a point—Louise wasn't exactly pressing confidences on me.

I steered the conversation back to the burglary, but Louise dismissed my remarks with a small smile and a shake of her head. "What's the use? Maybe it's just mischief, like stealing Christmas lights and rearranging the Marmot marquee. I have to be honest, except for Travis's baby things, I won't miss any of it. Who really looks at old birth and wedding and engagement announcements after thirty years? As for the rest—it was Arnie's, and I don't think I ever took the trouble to go through his Tyee yearbooks from the UDUB in my life. I went to Pacific Lutheran." Her smile grew quite merry.

"But your M.A. is from the UDUB?"

Pride surged through Louise's plump body. "I wanted to do that for years. Arnie couldn't see why. But nowadays you have to have a master's to teach in most districts. The truth is," she went on, lowering her eyes, "I enjoyed my time in

Seattle. Being in the city was an adventure. Of course I would never admit that to Arnie."

I could see why not. "You went to high school together, right?"

Louise abandoned her memories of independence and nodded complacently. "I was two years behind Arnie. We didn't date until he graduated from college. It was cute, really." She settled comfortably onto the brocade sofa, looking more at home with her memories than with her furniture. "It was summer break, and I came back home to work at the Marmot, taking tickets. Grandpa Lars was still alive, and on weekends he liked to get all dressed up in a suit and tie so he could greet the customers as they came in the door. We were showing a Paul Newman film that night—I forget which, I think his wife was in it, too—and I just adored Paul." She emitted a girlish sigh, and I responded with a flutter of my own. I was not immune to Mr. Newman, either. "Grandpa Lars teased me about my crush and said if I wanted to meet a handsome young man, why didn't I come to dinner at Popsy's on my night off ? Popsy—Oscar, I mean—and Mother Nyquist had huge meals—courses, really—with soup and salad and fish and meat. Everyone said they ate like kings and queens. I wasn't as anxious to meet a handsome young man as I was to see the spread they put on. And they did." Louise rolled her blue eyes. "Gravlax and sweet soup and butter dumplings and veal sausages and potatoes cooked with anchovies and onions— oh, it went on and on. I was such a skinny little thing then, but I ate until I almost passed out. Then Grandpa Lars said, 'See this wee one. She can eat like a logger, ya? Maybe she can cook, too. You better marry her quick, Arnold, before she gets away.' " Louise's laughter bubbled over.

"That fast?" I asked, eyebrows lifted.

"No, no. I'd barely noticed Arnie, poor dear. And to be frank, he wasn't exactly bowled over. But we did agree to go to a church picnic, and the next thing I knew, I was having

dinner at the Nyquist house whenever I had a free evening. I
still had to finish college, but we wrote letters. Arnie was quite
a good correspondent. We got engaged the day I graduated.
His family welcomed me as if I already was their daughter.''
She gave another little shake of her head, apparently still overcome by the memory of such familial warmth.

''That's a charming story,'' I remarked, now racking my
brain for a way to get Louise Nyquist to open up. I must have
been mistaken. The pleading look I'd seen in her eyes at the
mall had sprung from an urge no more specific than a need
for female companionship. I'd risked my neck and my Jaguar
for nothing. Except, of course, to be kind to another human
being. Sometimes I'm surprised by my own crassness.

''We've done the same with Bridget, I hope.'' Louise had
gotten up, going to the kitchen to refill our eggnog mugs. I
followed, with an eye on my watch. It was almost eight, and
planning commission meetings seldom lasted more than an
hour unless there was something controversial on the calendar.
According to Carla, who was covering the session, tonight's
agenda was pretty tame.

''Bridget could use a maternal figure,'' I noted, admiring
if not particularly liking the stark black and white modernistic
design of the kitchen. ''Her own mother and father are dead,
I hear.''

''Yes, very sad.'' Louise handed over my replenished mug.
''She never speaks of them. I must say, it hasn't been easy.
Making her feel loved, I mean. Oh, she's agreeable enough. I
was so afraid she might put up a fuss about being married in
the Lutheran church.'' Louise kept talking as we headed back
into the living room. I noted with some alarm that the snow
outside the tall windows was coming down so thick that I
couldn't see anything but a film of white. ''She was raised
Catholic, you know. That can cause problems. That is,''
Louise went on, a bit flustered, no doubt because she suddenly remembered that I was one of Them rather than one

of Us, "it *used* to be that way. Things have changed, I'm told. Bridget didn't protest at all."

Frankly, I wasn't surprised. Catholic education has become so ecumenically-minded since Vatican II that the younger generation has problems telling the difference between a Christian and a Jew, let alone understanding the finer distinctions between Catholics and Protestants.

"But you're fond of Bridget," I said, allowing only the hint of a question in my voice.

"Oh, yes," Louise replied quickly. "So is Arnie." She hesitated, caressing her eggnog mug. I had noticed that while my portions were as pristine as I'd requested, hers contained a fair dollop of rum. I wondered if the second shot would make Louise more prone to revelations. "The truth is, she's not an easy person to get close to. I suppose losing both parents while she was still young has made her a bit guarded. And I can be *too* affectionate. Or so Arnie tells me. He insists I spoiled Travis. But what could I do? Arnie was always so busy and Travis was our one and only."

"So's my son," I remarked. I didn't add that Adam wasn't spoiled, at least not as far as I was concerned. I'd had enough trouble just keeping up, financially and emotionally.

"Once the babies start coming, I'm sure we'll grow closer." Louise's expression was now sentimental. "Babies have such a way of bringing people together, don't you think? If you want to know the truth, Arnie and I never had a lot in common until after we had Travis."

I murmured something inane about babies, but my thoughts were wandering. Louise Nyquist had a lot of love to give—I didn't doubt that for a moment. But Arnie's courtship of her sounded oddly perfunctory, as if it had been orchestrated. Not once had I heard exclamations of "love at first sight" or "mad about the man" or any such indication that Arnie and Louise had been drawn together by a strong romantic attraction. The beautiful house with its handsome furnishings suddenly spoke volumes. Under that brusque, burly exterior, Arnold Nyquist aspired to champagne and caviar. Louise was satisfied with eggnog and cookies.

I hadn't worn out my welcome, but the Baccarat clock on the mantel told me that it was time to go. Louise protested, insisting that I have one more eggnog, a piece of homemade fruitcake, a taste of her Mexican wedding rings. I demurred, and after nervously negotiating the steep curves that led down First Hill, I slowly drove home through blinding snow.

Adam and Ben surprised me. They had brought my tree inside and set it up in the sturdy cast-iron stand fashioned by my father thirty years ago.

"It's been out there for a week," Ben said as Adam turned the tree to display the best side. "We thought we'd start decorating it."

I had planned on leaving work early Wednesday to put up the tree, but as long as my son and my brother were willing to help, there was no time like the present. Having decided on the fir's best angle, Adam began testing the lights, while Ben unwound the tinsel garlands and I opened the first box of ornaments. I had four cartons of them, each individual piece wrapped in tissue paper. Every year, I went through the same ritual, smiling and sighing over the ornaments' history: "This bell belonged to my parents . . . That reindeer came from Aunt Rylla in Wichita . . . The skinny Santa was a freebie at a toy store . . . Adam made this one with his picture when he was in first grade." Naturally, it took a long time to trim the tree, but every ornament was like a present, a gift from the past, a garland of memories. My son thought I was a real sap.

The topper went on first, an angel from Germany clad in blue velvet and silver tissue, with spun-glass hair and a golden halo. My grandmother had bought her over fifty-six years ago for three dollars, ignoring Adolf Hitler and his schemes to conquer the world. Hitler was gone and so was his ruthless ambition. Germany had been conquered, divided, reunited, and gone on to produce copies of this same ornament at twenty times the price. No wonder my angel looked a little smug.

The lights were next, no easy task. Adam didn't start them up high enough. Then he left gaps about a third of the way down. One of the plugs wouldn't reach the outlet to the previous string. The white electric candles tipped every which way. The last set, miniature colored bulbs, went out as soon as it was connected. Like the lights, Adam also blew up.

"Jeez, Mom, you're so picky! You've got six strings on the tree already! You want to blow a fuse?"

"I always have seven," I said doggedly. "Try plugging the little ones into the wall."

Muttering, Adam did as I suggested. Nothing happened. Ben intervened, fiddling with the plug. No luck. "I think these are shot, Sluggly," he said. "You got a spare?"

I did, but it was old, another hand-me-down from our parents. Some of the wires were frayed. I was a bit nervous about using them, but Ben assured me that there was no danger as long as we didn't keep the lights on too long at a time.

The silver tinsel was next, wound carefully around the tree by Ben and me. Adam had decided to take a break and watch TV. I would lure him back with popcorn later. We were halfway through the first box of ornaments when Vida called. She was practically chortling.

"I figured out a way to get Bridget Nyquist to talk to us," she said.

I was momentarily distracted from admiring a bright pink pine cone made of glass. "How?"

"We tell her that Evan Singer has been asking impertinent questions about her." Vida sounded as smug as my angel looked.

"Vida!" I protested. "That's unethical! You'll have to come up with something better than that. It's not worthy of you."

Vida harumphed into the phone. "It most certainly is. I

don't need anything better." She paused just long enough to speak sharply to her canary, Cupcake, who apparently had not settled down for the night under his cloth-covered cage. "It's true, Emma. Evan Singer left here not five minutes ago, on his way back from the lodge. He made some very strange remarks about Bridget. I wouldn't like to repeat them over the phone. We'll talk more in the morning." On an imperious note, Vida hung up.

Ben, who had been inserting a Jessye Norman Christmas CD into my player, stared at me. "What's up?"

Jessye's rich voice filled the room with the strains of "The Holy City." I tried to explain. "This is all very strange. What did your buddy at Blanchet have to say about Carol Neal and Bridget Nyquist?"

"Bill Crowley?" My brother turned Jessye down a notch. "Not much. He remembered them both, but they weren't very active in school. He wasn't even sure if they were friends. Or if they *had* friends."

I had resumed decorating the tree, clipping on a red and white mushroom, Santa climbing down a chimney, and a bird with a silvery tail. "If Bill Crowley was the chaplain, why didn't he help Bridget and Carol fit in?"

"Probably because they didn't ask him." Ben had joined me, hanging a yarn snowman with ebony eyes. "I got the impression they went their own way and were perfectly content. What are you getting at?"

I put up a gold glass rose, a silver pear, and a purple cluster of grapes. "I don't know, Stench. I really don't. But it can't be a coincidence that Carol Neal came to Alpine and got herself killed. I mean, why come here except to find Kathleen Francich, who probably was also murdered?"

"But Kathleen didn't go to Blanchet," my brother pointed out. "Why would she come to Alpine?"

I gave my brother a blank look. Somewhere, there was a common denominator. Was it Bridget? Was it the private school connection? Was it someone or something else we hadn't thought of?

"Let's face it," I said, opening another box of ornaments. "There are only four thousand permanent residents in this town. Oh, sure, people come here to hike and ski and fish and camp. Maybe that's what Kathleen Francich did. But Carol Neal didn't think so. Otherwise, she would have reported her missing to the Forest Service or to the sheriff up here. I figure that in the beginning, Carol didn't know where Kathleen went. But six weeks later—more or less—Carol comes to Alpine, too. Why? What did she learn in that time period that led her to believe Kathleen had come up here? And why didn't she go see Milo?"

My brother knew my questions weren't idle speculation. "If those two girls were engaged in prostitution, Carol may have been chary of contacting the police. Oh, sure, she called King County to report Kathleen as missing, but she waited quite a while, right? Maybe she was going to see the sheriff here after she saw somebody else."

"Somebody like Bridget?" I raised my eyebrows over a pair of turtle doves.

"You keep harping on Bridget," Ben remarked, getting on his knees to hang some of the heavier ornaments down low on the sturdiest branches. "Are you sure she's the only Blanchet High grad in Alpine?"

"She's the only one who went to school with Carol Neal," I replied. Seeing Ben look up at me with a mildly incredulous expression, I waved a plastic Rudolph at him. "Vida would know. She keeps track of every newcomer, every bride, everybody who arrives in town other than on a slow freight. It's not just being nosy, it's watching out for a story angle."

Ben stood up, rustling through the ornament box. In the background, Jessye Norman put her heart and soul into "I Wonder As I Wander." I wondered, too, about many things. So, apparently, did Ben. "Did Vida do a story on Teresa McHale when she took over at the rectory?"

"No." I set Rudolph on an inner branch, his red nose poking out between the thick green needles. "We ran a paragraph in our Community Briefs column about her." I paused, fingering my upper lip. "You know, that's kind of odd—as I recall, Vida wanted to do more, but Teresa said she wasn't interested."

Ben had resumed crawling around on the floor. "Not everybody is keen on publicity. Some people like to keep their private lives private." He put a plush calico cat on the lowest limb just as Adam resurfaced, seemingly refreshed by his thirty-minute break in front of the television set. My son admired the tree, hands jammed in his pockets. It was, I thought, an unconscious attempt to pretend he didn't have hands and thus avoid work. "Hey, cool! You're almost done."

"Guess again," I replied, nudging an unopened carton with my foot. "Get with it, Adam my son. The hour grows late and the old folks grow weary."

With a heavy sigh, Adam unwrapped a crystal snowflake. I wasn't kidding about being tired. It was after ten, and we were an hour away from completion. A glance out the window showed me that the snow was still coming down hard. I could barely see the outline of the Jag in the carport, a mere four feet away. Ben was going to have a difficult drive back to the rectory.

"Why don't you stay here tonight?" I suggested.

But Ben declined. "I don't want to take a chance on being marooned and missing morning mass. Besides, I walked. Teresa needed the car."

Thinking of my brother blinded by snow and lying half-frozen somewhere along Fourth Street, I started to protest. But St. Mildred's was only a half-mile away. Ben could practically slide down the hill from my house to the church. Instead of arguing, I shrugged, and ditched another one of Aunt Rylla's homemade concoctions close to the tree trunk, out of sight. Somehow, sequin-spangled furnace filters don't appeal to my Christmas spirit.

But one big bowl of popcorn and an hour later, I rallied. After a quick pass with the vacuum cleaner to pick up spare needles and spilled icicles, we switched off the living room lights and turned on the tree. Ben chuckled; Adam whistled; I gasped. As always, it was a miracle: Magic lights and glittering balls, silver garlands and shimmering rain, old memories and renewed promises. The tree was cut fresh each year, yet never changed. I glanced at Adam, at Ben. We were together. Christmas was nigh. I felt peace wash over me, and let out a weary, happy sigh. The moment was sufficient unto itself. Tomorrow and its troubles would have to wait.

I had no idea that they were only a few minutes away.

I had just put my book aside and was about to turn off the light when I heard the sirens. Shortly after midnight, by my bedside clock. My first thought was of Ben. The weird little fantasy I'd had of him struggling through a snowbank had come true. An ambulance was pushing up Fourth Street, desperately trying to rescue my brother.

But I can differentiate between the sounds of the various emergency vehicles. This was a fire truck—*both* fire trucks, in fact, and farther off, perhaps over on Alpine Way. It was hard to tell, with the wind blowing the sirens' wail in erratic directions. I settled down into bed and drifted off to sleep.

It might have been the middle of the night, it could have been early morning, but it was really only one-fourteen. Fumbling for the phone, I managed to knock my book off the nightstand and hit my elbow on the headboard. My brain was fuzzy with sleep.

"Emma?" It was Milo Dodge. His voice was tense.

"What?" I finally managed to turn the light on.

"Sorry to bother you, but I know you're sending the paper to Monroe first thing in the morning." He paused, and I heard shouts in the background along with the grinding of wheels.

"Right, right," I muttered, fighting to get my eyes open in the brightened room. "What's going on?"

"We're at Evan Singer's place. It burned to the ground. No known cause yet, no damage estimate."

I sat up, feeling a draft around my shoulders. "How sad!" In my mind's eye, I pictured the dreary exterior, the bizarre artwork, the strange Christmas tree. With candles. Maybe that's what had started the fire. The rickety old shack would go up like kindling. Even if Alpine had more than four full-time firemen and a dozen volunteers, there probably would have been no way to contain the blaze. In ten-degree weather, the water in the hoses would no doubt freeze. "How is Evan taking it?" I asked.

Milo expelled a little grunt. "I don't know. We can't find him."

My knees jackknifed as I clutched the phone. "What? You don't mean . . . Was he in the cabin?"

"We don't know yet." Milo's voice was grim. "I've got to go, Emma. If we have anything new, I'll call before you ship the paper out."

Clumsily, I set the receiver in its cradle. With a groan, I fell back onto the pillow. Surely it wouldn't take long to determine if Evan Singer had died in the fire? The cabin was small; the furnishings were sparse. The image of his Christmas tree with its dangerous candles and grotesque ornaments wavered before my eyes. Evan Singer was odd, maybe even unbalanced. But he shouldn't have been foolish enough to set his home and himself on fire.

Then, as I switched off the light, it dawned on me that maybe he hadn't. Perhaps someone else had done it for him.

Chapter Fourteen

I SLEPT FITFULLY, upset about Evan Singer, and aware that the phone could ring again at any minute. Milo, however, didn't call back until after six A.M. I was already up and dressed, having decided that as long as I wasn't going to get any more sleep, I might as well start the new day.

Milo reported that no remains had been found in the ruins. I heaved a sigh of relief, then asked if they'd figured out how the fire had started. They hadn't, but it had originated inside. His voice foggy, Milo announced that he was going to bed.

Vida was an early riser, so I had no compunction about calling her. She would want to hear the news, and for once, I had scooped her. Or so I thought.

"My nephew Ronnie called an hour ago," she said, sounding vexed at my insane notion that she should be uninformed. "He's my brother Winfield's son and a volunteer fireman, you know. It's all very peculiar. I think we should run out there. We'll need a picture, though I suppose we couldn't make the deadline for this issue."

We couldn't. But I was faced with an editorial problem. On page four I had a photo and a feature on a young man who was apparently missing. I had to pull the whole spread and move something from page one to fill up the hole. The cabin fire was late-breaking news and took precedence over everything except our female body count. *The Advocate*'s front page was getting grimmer and grimmer. As for going out to Burl Creek, a peek through the window revealed that we had at least another eight inches of snow. It wouldn't get light for two hours, and the county road probably hadn't yet been plowed. Nor would there be time to take the picture, get Buddy Bayard to develop it, and run the thing in the paper.

"Damn!" I exclaimed. "I wish we knew where Evan Singer was. We could fill up that hole with quotes from him." Only fleetingly did I chastise myself for my callous attitude. At six o'clock in the morning of press day, I tend to let a crisis make me a journalist instead of a human being.

Vida, however, understood. "We could hold off sending Kip to Monroe until eight or nine. Wouldn't you rather be late than inaccurate?"

Of course I would, but the printer would hate me for it. *The Advocate* had a specific time on the press. Missing it screwed everybody up, and cost me money. "We've got over an hour to hear anything new," I pointed out, trying to keep panic at bay. "I'm walking to the office. I'll be there in twenty minutes if I don't fall down and break my neck."

Vida said she'd come in early, too. Hurriedly, I drank a cup of coffee, ate a piece of toast, and bundled myself up for the foray out into the snow. Peeking in on Adam, I saw only a patch of dark hair etched against his old Superman sheets. It occurred to me that I should replace them. Maybe bedding could be added to his Christmas gifts.

It was still dark, still snowing, but the footing was decent. A few cars were plodding along Fir Street. I crossed it carefully, noting that several houses along my route had left their outdoor lights on overnight. They provided cheerful beacons as I made my way down Fourth, mentally waving to Ben as I passed St. Mildred's and the rectory.

Except for a couple of delivery trucks, Front Street was virtually deserted this early. By the time I got to the office, I was stiff with cold. It didn't seem much warmer inside than it did outside. I turned on the heat, made coffee, and didn't take off my coat. Vida arrived before I could switch on the computer.

"Where do you suppose Evan Singer is, if he wasn't at home last night?" Vida demanded, yanking off her heavy knitted gloves. "Ronnie told me the fire probably started around eleven-thirty. Nobody would have noticed it way out there if Sue Ann Daley Phipps at Cass Pond hadn't gone into labor. She and her husband saw the flames on their way into the hospital and called from the emergency room."

"What time was Evan at your house?" I asked, staring stupidly at the computer display of page one.

"About nine-thirty. The snow got so heavy that he couldn't get the sleigh through it. Henry Bardeen had to use a four-wheel drive to haul the diners back to the parking lot." Vida gave me a flinty look. "Don't say it. No, Evan did *not* tell me where he was going after he left my house. If he had, I would have told you already."

I fueled myself with more coffee and wrote the sketchy story about the fire. It filled up a scant five inches. I needed twenty. I could run Evan's photo with a new cutline—but only if I knew whether he was dead or alive. I scowled at the layout. It was after seven, and Kip MacDuff would be along any minute. To my astonishment, Vida was emptying a string bag on her desk. At first, I thought it was our mail, but the postman doesn't usually show up until around ten. Then I recognized the bag of letters and bills and circulars I'd brought from the Villa Apartments.

"How'd you get hold of that stuff?" I demanded.

Vida gave me a superior look. "Billy let me borrow them. He and the rest of those dimwits haven't had time to go through them yet. They only opened a couple of bills. Now that we know Kathleen Francich was in Alpine—or that her car was—we can proceed without further doubts." She waved a green-edged piece of paper at me. "See this? It's an oil-company bill with a charge for the BP station in Sultan, October seventh. I do hope Milo is going over that car with a fine-toothed comb."

I stared at the list of billings; Vida was right. The Sultan charge was also the last one made on the account. The bill itself was dated November the first. Vida held up another BP invoice.

"December. No payments, no charges. Nothing on any of her credit cards since early October, either." She was haphazardly organizing the mail into categories: catalogues, circulars, bills, and personal mail. "They both have a lot of creditors, their bank cards are up to the limit, and neither seem to make many payments. Dun, dun, dun—done." Vida pushed the bills to one side. "There are some Christmas cards, but no letters. Most of the cards are absolutely hideous, as you might expect with a person of Kathleen's low morals. Vulgar, too. I really don't care to see Santa exposing himself. There are some for Carol, too, but read this one."

Vida handed me an envelope containing a card that didn't seem to bear out her assessment. The return address, in Redmond, was for one Murray Francich. The card itself was a handsome cutout of a dove with an olive branch in its beak. Unless it produced bird droppings when I opened it, Murray Francich's greeting seemed to be the exception to Vida's rule.

Inside there was a note: "Kathy," it began, "it's Christmas, let's try to be a family for a couple of days. I'm heading for E. Wash. Dec. 21. Why don't you come with me? No matter what you may think, the folks want to see you. Call me. Love, Murray."

I hazarded a guess. "Her brother?"

"That's what it sounds like. Their parents must live on the other side of the mountains." Vida gazed down on her untidy stacks of mail. "Frankly, that's the only one of real interest I found. The rest are signed with names and at best—or worst, considering—the occasional ribald remark."

"Milo has to get hold of Murray," I said. "Maybe the

parents, too. And Carol's. It sounds to me as if those poor girls had problems with their parents.''

''No wonder.'' Vida grimaced. ''Carol's background sounds unstable, but that's no excuse to sell herself into prostitution. Imagine! Private school backgrounds, good educations, a bright future—and now this.'' She slapped at the pile of allegedly obscene Christmas cards, symbolic of depravity. ''What could have made them ruin their lives?''

I lifted an eyebrow at Vida. ''What? Or who?''

Vida regarded me with approval. ''A good point.''

The door opened, and of course I expected to see Kip MacDuff. Instead, Oscar Nyquist blundered and thundered into the office. This day was definitely not off to an auspicious start.

''Now this! What next? Who do I sue?'' Oscar was one of the few octogenarians I knew who could still jump up and down. His bulky body made the furniture shake.

Vida, however, was unmoved. ''Sue the ACLU. Claim you're a minority and then get them to represent you against themselves. It should be an interesting case.'' She gave Oscar a tight smile.

As usual, her irony was lost on Oscar Nyquist. ''I'm not kidding!'' he bellowed. ''I get down to the Marmot first thing, like I always do, never mind four or forty feet of snow. And what do I find? A trespasser, that's what! I made a citizen's arrest. It's come to that, I tell you!''

I edged a bit closer to Oscar. ''You actually took this person to the sheriff?'' Why did I doubt it? Oscar Nyquist looked as if he could have hauled off the entire loge section of the Marmot.

''You bet.'' He nodded vigorously, the tube lights lending a jaundiced cast to his bald head. ''They'd better lock him up, too. He's dangerous. He was smoking dope!''

My heart gave a lurch. ''Who? Who was this trespasser?''

Now Oscar shook his head, just as vigorously, but from

side to side. "That punk, you know, the one who drives the sleigh. Henry Bardeen must have been nuts to hire him."

I slumped against Ed's desk in relief. "Evan's alive, then?"

Oscar's bushy brows drew close together. "Evan? Is that what he's called? What kind of name is that? Only my sister could come up with such a silly moniker! She called her kid Norman!"

"It's no worse than Travis," Vida pointed out. She saw Oscar start to boil over again and shook a ballpoint pen at him. "Simmer down, Oscar. Haven't you heard about the fire last night?"

Oscar hadn't, though he recalled sirens somewhere between dusk and dawn. The burning of Evan Singer's cabin didn't faze him, however. "No wonder," he muttered. "He was probably smoking that dope and set it off himself."

It took some doing, but eventually we got a rational account out of Oscar Nyquist. He had come to the Marmot shortly before seven. Walking through the auditorium, he had noticed what he thought was a coat that someone had left on a chair in the third row. Upon closer inspection, he discovered Evan Singer, slumped down and fast asleep. Irate, Oscar had bodily hauled Singer out of the theatre and down the street to the sheriff's office. Trespassing charges had been filed with Deputy Dwight Gould, though Oscar didn't doubt for a minute that they'd be dismissed and that Evan Singer would be merrily on his way to go off and smoke more weed. Would we put the story in the paper? Oscar assured us that we needed to run this kind of publicity. Vida informed him that we didn't—at least not in this week's issue. We'd have to see the formal charges, talk to Dwight Gould, get a statement from Evan Singer, and take another picture of Oscar the Valiant Hero. Since the paper was due to leave for Monroe at any moment, our hands were tied.

Amazingly, Oscar seemed to understand. What was even more amazing was that after only another outburst or two, he left. Frenzied, I called the sheriff's office to make sure that Evan Singer really was alive and reasonably well, then redummied the front page, threw in Evan's picture, and added a semi-happy ending to the fire story. Three minutes later, Kip MacDuff was on the road to Monroe.

As for Oscar's prediction, he wasn't entirely wrong. Given the circumstances of the fire—which was news to Evan—Dwight Gould showed mercy, asked for a five-dollar fine, and tore up the charge.

"So where is he going to live?" I asked Carla, who had done the legwork on the latest developments.

"Evan doesn't know," she said, "and I didn't want to get close enough to ask. He's really upset. His artwork was destroyed, you know. I gather he figures Henry Bardeen will give him a room up at the lodge. Of course the cabin is owned by somebody else." She threw an inquiring look at Vida.

"Elmer Tuck," Vida responded promptly. "He lives out by the fish hatchery. Retired from the Forest Service. Originally owned by an offbearer in the old Clemans mill. Bachelor. Went up for auction in 'thirty-four and Elmer's dad, Kermit Tuck, bought it for two hundred dollars as a retreat from his wife, May. Awful shrew, but a fine cook. Kermit drank, but only on weekends." Vida summed up several lives without glancing away from her typewriter.

Wednesdays are usually slow days at *The Advocate*. Next week, however, we were aiming for forty-eight pages, which meant that there was a lot of copy to write. Now was the time to get a jump on it. I culled the wire service for anything that might have a local angle. Timber industry, ski resort, environment, state department of highways—often there was a tie-in. I handed several items to Carla and kept a couple for myself. By the time the AP got to business news, I gave the stocks and bonds my usual detached glance. But a dateline out of Seattle startled me:

The State Attorney General's office today announced the indictment of Seattle broker Standish Crocker on unspecified charges of gross misconduct. Crocker is the president and CEO of Bartlett & Crocker, a local investment firm. Pending further investigation, all activities of the firm have been suspended. Crocker, who lives at Hunts Point, refused comment.

I read the item to Vida who wrinkled her nose. "Hunts Point? Isn't that where all your rich city people live across the lake?"

It was. Or at least it was an enclave where many wealthy persons had palatial homes. Hunts Point spelled prestige, exclusiveness, affluence. And, in the case of Standish Crocker, gross misconduct.

"I wonder how Travis Nyquist feels about this?" I mused. "Shall we get a comment from him regarding his former employer?"

Of course, Vida agreed, and a moment later, I had Travis on the line. He was shocked; he was incredulous. Standish Crocker was the soul of integrity. There must be some mistake.

"Cutthroat," asserted Travis. "That's what the financial business is like. I'm glad I'm out of it. Poor Mr. Crocker—he's obviously got some sharks swimming after him. He'll be fine, trust me."

I didn't, of course. Not with a stakeout in a PUD truck sitting across the street from Travis Nyquist's house. I wondered how deeply Travis was involved. We were a week away from the next edition, but I felt a sense of urgency. It wasn't yet noon. Milo Dodge was probably still asleep. I called his office and left word for him to get in touch with me as soon as he checked in.

Ed Bronsky was moaning over a double-truck co-op ad from the mall. "Look at this! Every store there is wishing our readers Merry Christmas! And after gouging us for presents! That takes nerve!"

It also took money, which I was only too glad to accept. I

let Ed groan on while consulting with Carla about a feature she was planning around holiday reunions. To my pleasant surprise, she'd gone to the trouble to track down several Alpiners who were getting together with relatives they hadn't seen in years, either here in town or some place else. If she could carry through with her writing, the story should make heart-tugging, tear-jerking Christmas copy.

Ginny had just delivered the mail, which was late and not of much interest. Having skimped on breakfast, I was thinking about lunch when Vida announced that it was time for us to leave.

"For where?" I asked, startled.

She gave me a look of exasperation. "For Bridget's. I told you we were going to talk to her this morning."

"But . . ." I started to protest, watched her shrug into her tweed coat, and gave up. "I mean, I thought that after the fire, you might want to lay off Evan Singer."

Vida gave me a hard stare. "Why? He's not dead, is he? Let's go."

We did, taking her big Buick up to The Pines. The snow had let up a bit as the morning moved along. As difficult as it may be to conduct modern life in a world of perpetual winter, it is always beautiful. Each new fall obliterates the blemishes, accentuates the magic, and enhances the peace. Christmas lights, indoors and outdoors, sparkle all the brighter against a backdrop of white. No wonder the old pagans lighted bonfires for their winter festivals. Even less surprising is our modern urge to tear the rainbow apart and fill our homes and hearths with twinkling lights and dazzling baubles. We have not come so far from the barbarians; we merely have more means.

Bridget and Travis were both at home. Neither was pleased to see us. "I just talked to you," said Travis, as if once a day with Emma Lord was quite enough.

"You didn't talk to *me*," Vida asserted, breezing past our

host. ''The truth is, you might want to make yourself small, Travis. We've come to call on your wife.''

If Vida had used a lasso, she couldn't have come up with a better way of ensuring Travis Nyquist's presence. He still wore the walking cast, and though he limped, I saw no sign of a cane. Reluctantly, Travis offered us seats in the living room, where a graceful blue spruce had been added since our last visit. Its gold, silver, and red decorations harmonized with the rest of the holiday accents. I marveled anew at the Nyquist family's good taste.

Bridget perched on the arm of a chair, as if she weren't quite sure if she intended to stick around. ''I told you, Mrs. Runkel, I don't know anything about this Evan Singer. From what I hear, he's totally strange.'' Bridget's voice had grown very wispy.

Unwinding her muffler, Vida made a clucking sound. ''Strange or not, Evan says he knows you.'' Her gray eyes darted in Travis's direction. ''*Both* of you, from way back.''

Travis threw back his handsome head and laughed. ''Poor guy! He's probably in shock. My dad said Singer's cabin burned and he had to spend the night at the Marmot.''

That was a different twist to Oscar's version, and not necessarily an incredible one. But while Travis looked more amused than concerned, Bridget was wriggling nervously on her perch.

It was my turn to play interrogator. ''Bridget, where did you work before you were married?''

I caught the swift exchange of glances between Bridget and Travis. Still, the answer came promptly enough. ''I was a temp. I met Travis when I was working as a receptionist for Bartlett & Crocker.''

I noted that Bridget seemed oblivious to having contradicted herself about Travis's place of work. There was no point in chiding her; obviously she had been protecting her husband from a possible scandal.

''Could Evan have met you there, too?'' I asked.

"No." Bridget shook her head emphatically.

Travis, however, fingered his square chin and tugged at one ear. I was reminded of a third-base coach giving signals. Was Bridget on first? "You know," Travis said amiably, "Evan might have come through the office while you were there, honey. He was never a client of mine, but he could have consulted someone else. Didn't you have a nameplate on your desk?"

Bridget's eyes grew wide. "Did I? Maybe so, I don't remember." She grew more flustered. "I worked at a whole bunch of places."

I saw Vida draw herself up to imperial proportions. The moment had come. I braced myself for her next query: "Bridget—what about Carol Neal? When was the last time you saw her?"

The color drained from Bridget's face. Travis merely looked puzzled. "Who?" he asked.

Vida's lips were clamped shut. With a mighty effort, Bridget regained some of her poise but none of her color. "Carol Neal!" she echoed in wonderment. "Now there's a name from out of the past."

"Yes," agreed Vida, her fingers playing over the surface of the twining vines that adorned the armchair. She didn't speak again, allowing the sudden silence to fill the living room like the aftermath of a death toll. I was tempted to prod Bridget, but I understood Vida's tactics.

"At commencement, I suppose," Bridget finally said in a small voice. "The cruise, I mean, afterwards. It's been a while."

Vida nodded once, her buckled boots planted firmly on the tiled floor. "You didn't see her last week before she died?"

Bridget's mouth opened; Travis let out a short exclamation. Their surprise seemed genuine.

"Carol Neal *died*?" Bridget slipped off the arm of the

chair and fell onto the upholstered seat. "How? A car accident?"

"Why do you ask that?" Vida inquired, sounding bemused.

Bridget's hands fluttered. "Why—a lot of people do.
Young people. What was it?" Her voice had taken on an
edge.

Having failed to elicit more than shock, Vida grew impatient. "She was murdered. So, I fear, was Kathleen Francich. You can read all about it when *The Advocate* comes out
today." She stood up, seemingly oblivious to the horror on
Bridget's face. I couldn't see Travis's reaction; Vida was
standing in my way. "I don't suppose you've seen Kathleen
for years, either?"

"Kathy! Oh, no!" Bridget reeled. Travis rushed to her
side.

"Please leave," he said, very low, very tense. "Why did
you come?"

"We're going," Vida replied blithely.

We didn't need to be shown out, but when Vida turned the
brass doorknob, Bridget called after us: "Wait!" She was
pushing at Travis, scrambling to get out of the chair. "It must
be him! Tell the sheriff! I need protection!"

Vida and I had turned around in the foyer. Bridget stood
under the archway that led into the living room, trembling
and distraught. Travis had moved toward her, but stopped
short, favoring his bad leg. He, too, looked stunned, but
another emotion played across his handsome features. Fear?
Anger? I couldn't be sure.

"It must be who?" asked Vida, her voice more kindly.
"Protection from what?"

Bridget was making short, chopping motions with her right
hand. "From whoever killed Carol and Kathy. He must be
going to kill me, too." She was starting to cry, her pretty
face crumpled like a mangled Christmas ornament.

"Who?" repeated Vida.

Limping, Travis stepped up to Bridget, putting a firm arm around her shaking shoulders. "Calm down, honey. You don't know anything of the sort. Terrible things happen in the city. You know it. You were raised there."

Slowly, Bridget turned to look up into her husband's face. "In the . . . Oh!" She gulped and pressed her face against Travis's chest. He looked at us over her head. His curt nod indicated that we should be gone. I half expected Vida to linger, to ask more questions, to raise more cain. But she didn't.

"I'm a monster," she muttered, trooping down the walk to the drive where we'd left the car. I noticed that the PUD truck was gone. "Think of it, Emma—Bridget could be innocent!"

I stared at Vida through a fitful fall of snow. "You don't seriously believe she might have killed Carol and Kathleen?"

Vida had to jiggle the handle on the car door to open it. "No, I doubt that very much. Of course, all things are possible. Certainly we learned that Bridget and Kathleen knew each other, even if they did go to different high schools. But didn't you notice Travis's coaching? About *the city*?"

I broke my stare only long enough to get in on my side of the car. "He assumed Carol and Kathleen were killed in Seattle. He couldn't know—yet—that their bodies were found so close to home."

Vida gunned the engine, craning her neck to reverse down the drive. "No, no," she said impatiently. "Just because *The Advocate* isn't in the mailboxes doesn't mean the whole town doesn't know. You realize what gossips these people are. I mean that Travis wanted us to think he and Bridget didn't know anything about Carol and Kathleen. Now why, I ask you, is that?"

My guess came promptly. "Because Bridget knew they were in town? But even if Bridget had heard from one or both girls, that doesn't mean she did them in."

"True. But she's got something to hide, and that's what I

mean about her innocence, or lack thereof.'' Vida cornered in front of a greenery-topped mailbox on a red-and-white peppermint stick stand. ''Vice, its various forms such as prostitution and drugs. Or whatever Travis was mixed up in. Gross misconduct, in Standish Crocker's case. What does it mean?''

I didn't know. ''My guess is that it's financial misdeeds. You know, inside trading or embezzling clients' funds. Why are you suggesting something more seamy?''

Vida was keeping her eyes on the road, which was a mercy, since the chains on her car didn't seem to have too firm a grip in the snow. ''How long did Travis actually work? Four years? Five, at the most. Now how many brokers or investment advisors or what have you make enough money in that span of time to retire? And why retire at all when you're only thirty? You don't think there's something fishy about it?''

I had to admit that I hadn't thought much at all about Travis's life decisions. ''Maybe he wants to take over The Marmot when Oscar pops off,'' I suggested. ''Or go in to the construction business with his father. It's possible that he burned out early in the financial world.''

''Oh, yes, anything's possible,'' Vida conceded as she pulled onto Alpine Way. ''But I'm definitely dubious.''

Vida had a point. Certainly there was something suspicious about Bartlett & Crocker; ergo, there was something suspicious about the firm's former employee. Milo must know who had been keeping an eye on Travis Nyquist's house. But I doubted that he'd tell Vida and me who or why. Yet. I wouldn't underestimate Vida's powers of persuasion over Milo or his deputy, Billy Blatt.

Front Street was freshly plowed and sanded. ''Vida, you've never told me what Evan actually said to you about Bridget.''

Vida inclined her head. We were passing City Hall, a refurbished red brick building of two stories with swooping strands of gold Christmas lights draped across the facade. ''It didn't make a lot of sense,'' she admitted. ''He called

Bridget and Travis a pair of selfish philistines with no sense of loyalty. Bridget was a parasite, an interloper. Evan had some harsh words for Arnie Nyquist, too. He called him a despoiler of the earth. He said the Nyquists in general had betrayed their trust. The line was diluted. Or was it deluded?'' She glanced in the rearview mirror, preparatory to backing into her usual parking place. "Really, he did go on.''

I didn't doubt it. But I still couldn't see any connection between Evan Singer and the Nyquists. Why pick on them? Until Oscar had ejected Evan from the Marmot, there had been no encounters between the family and the newcomer.

Ben was waiting for us in the office. In truth, he wasn't exactly waiting, but in the process of writing a note to me.

"Aha!" he exclaimed as Vida and I trudged inside and stamped snow off our boots. "I'm taking in the homeless. Evan Singer is going to stay up at the rectory."

I shook out my car coat, which had accumulated a few snowflakes in the walk from Vida's car. "How does Mrs. McHale feel about that?"

Ben shrugged. "I didn't ask, I told her he was coming. There's plenty of room with Father Fitz gone. The place was built for at least two priests. What's the problem?"

I heard Vida sniff loudly, and knew that her thoughts were running parallel to mine. Occasionally, my brother's priestly naïveté gets the better of him. "Teresa McHale doesn't strike me as the Hospitality Queen of Alpine," I said. "I don't see her opening the rectory door to anybody, let alone a non-Catholic."

Ben tipped his head to one side and ruffled his dark hair. "Well, well. Then I guess I won't tell her that Evan was raised in the Jewish faith. Not that he follows it, being a freethinker and a world-class loony. For Teresa's sake, we'll pretend that Evan is something more ordinary." Ben glanced at Vida. "A Presbyterian, maybe."

Vida groaned. "He could never be one of my brethren. We only have *sensible* people in our congregation."

I was about to remind Vida of some of the less sensible—and more insane—members of her church when Evan Singer ambled into the office. He was unshaven and hollow-eyed, but the leather jacket he wore looked expensive, as did the calf-high snakeskin boots.

"How," Evan Singer demanded of Ed Bronsky's empty chair, "do you place a value on art? Insurance people are number-crunchers. They just don't understand."

I gathered, rightly, that Evan had been with the State Farm people in the Alpine Building. As it turned out, he had no insurance of his own, but was expecting his landlord to cover his losses. I wished him well, but had the feeling that Elmer Tuck, retired, wasn't about to reimburse him for the loss of his paintings.

Bill Blatt, however, wanted to be helpful. His eager face appeared in the doorway, greeting his Aunt Vida, nodding at Ben and me, swinging a plastic Grocery Basket sack at Evan Singer.

"We may not have saved your picture," said Bill, his cheeks pink with cold, "but we got the frame. Maybe you can clean it up. It looks like real silver."

Evan Singer, along with the rest of us, stared first at Bill, then at the charred object he was taking out of the sack. It was indeed a picture frame, eight-by-ten size, the glass blackened by fire and the silver melted around the edges.

Evan glared at Bill. "That's not the picture I meant! This is commercial trash! You savage! I was talking about my paintings! My artwork! My life! Up in smoke! Gone! Destroyed by the gods who envy mortal talent! A pox on them all! I'm going to a higher authority!" He yanked the frame out of Bill Blatt's hand, stared at it malevolently, then dashed it to the floor. The glass shattered into tiny shards. Evan Singer ran out through the open door.

"Well, there goes your houseguest," I said to Ben. "Now where did we put the office broom?"

Ben, however, was undismayed. "He'll show up." He

saw my skeptical look and gave a short nod. "He has nowhere else to go."

"The lodge? A motel?" I was at the little closet in the
corner, getting out the broom and a dustpan. Vida had come
around from behind her desk and was inspecting the charred
silver frame.

"Now where did he get that?" she murmured. Carefully,
she picked up the frame, shook off a few bits of glass, and
began to rub at it with her handkerchief. "That's a Buddy
Bayard frame," she announced. "They cost at least a hundred and fifty dollars. Two years ago I bet Buddy he wouldn't
sell more than one. Why do I think he didn't peddle this to
Evan Singer?"

"Why shouldn't he?" I asked, whisking up glass.

Vida took the dustpan from Ben, who was trying to be
helpful, but managing mostly to get in the way. "Did you
see that picture frame in Evan's cabin?"

"No," I admitted, "but I might have missed . . ."

"No, no, no," Vida interrupted, dumping the dustpan's
contents into Ed's wastebasket. "It was one room. You said
you saw all those peculiar things stuck around. You'd have
noticed something prosaic—like that frame. What would be
in it? His parents? If so, wouldn't that have struck a normal
note among the discord?"

"Vida," I inquired, a trifle annoyed, "what are you getting at?"

It was Bill Blatt, not his aunt, who answered. "Arnie
Nyquist's van! He said a framed photo was taken with all
that other stuff. It was a picture of Travis and Bridget."

Vida nodded in approval. "Very good, Billy. A photo Evan
wouldn't display, for obvious reasons. He stole it."

Bill's deep-set blue eyes widened. "Wow! You mean he
was the one who broke into Tinker Toy's van?"

"It wouldn't surprise me," his aunt replied, and then
scowled at no one in particular. "Wait—what time did Arnie
say the break-in occurred?"

Unfortunately, Bill Blatt couldn't remember the specifics. His round, freckled face grew troubled. Felons were a cinch compared to Aunt Vida. "Jack Mullins took the report. Do you want me to check the log?"

"Well, certainly," Vida said, though she softened the response with the hint of a smile. "You weren't going to rush out and arrest Evan on my say-so?"

Judging from the startled look on Bill's face, that was precisely what he'd been prepared to do. At least until he thought twice about it. Ben and I exchanged amused glances as Bill Blatt dutifully headed for the door. He almost collided with Carla. She took one look at his youthful, engaging face, glanced up at the mistletoe over his head, and planted a firm kiss on Bill's lips. The young deputy staggered, stammered, and blushed furiously. Carla released him and swished over to her desk, long black hair swinging under her red ski cap. Bill Blatt stumbled out the door.

She beamed at Vida. "He's eligible," said Carla.

"You're crazy," said Vida.

"So?" Carla was still smiling as she took off the red ski cap and shrugged out of her quilted parka. "Couldn't your family use a little loosening up? All the inbreeding that goes on around here must be producing a lot of idiots."

Vida's eyebrows lifted above the rims of her glasses. "So that's what causes it," she murmured. "Now why didn't I think of that before?"

Chapter Fifteen

WEEKLY LULL OR not, the season brought its fair share of news that Wednesday. Trinity Episcopal Church had collected two hundred pounds of clothing and four hundred pounds of food for the needy of Skykomish County. A California couple had gone off Stevens Pass four miles below the summit and were being treated for minor injuries at Alpine Community Hospital. Two Sultan residents had been arrested for cutting Christmas trees on U.S. Forest Service land near Martin Creek. The number three lift at the lodge had broken down, stranding a half-dozen skiers for almost an hour. Mayor Fuzzy Baugh's Santa Claus suit had been stolen from his office in broad daylight. The usual number of outdoor lights, none of them at properties owned by the Nyquists, were reported as broken or missing.

Returning from a late lunch with Ben and Adam at the Burger Barn, I had just waved my companions off when I saw Arnie Nyquist getting out of his van in front of the bank. I paused at the corner, and he waved me down.

"Hey—you heard the news?" he called, causing a half-dozen shoppers to turn and stare.

"What news?" It wasn't a response to add luster to my reputation as a journalist, but it just sort of tripped off my tongue.

Arnie approached, jerking his thumb in the direction of City Hall, two blocks down Front Street.

"Fuzzy's suit. What did I tell you? This town's going down

664

the drain. Now the crooks can walk into the mayor's office and steal the clothes right off his back!''

I gave Arnie my most ingenuous look. ''Fuzzy was *in* the suit? Funny he didn't notice.''

''No, no!'' Arnie waved a hand, batting at a few drifting snowflakes. ''It was hanging up. He was in a meeting with the Chamber of Commerce. But what's the difference? Milo Dodge has a crime wave on his hands. Murder, arson, robbery, vandalism—what's next, riots, like L.A.?''

Since the racial mix in Alpine is virtually nonexistent, and a Welshman is defined as a minority, I didn't bother to attempt reasoning with Arnie Nyquist. His remarks, however, had given me an idea.

''Say, speaking of clothes, what did you do with that stuff you found last week at the bowling alley site?''

Arnie looked momentarily blank. I waited, gazing at the city's Christmas decorations, the garlands and bows and bells and candy canes touched with snow. The lone traffic light blended in: red, green, amber-gold.

''Oh, yeah!'' Arnie finally responded. ''I tossed them in the Dumpster. Any floozy who uses my property to make out doesn't deserve to get her stuff back. I hope she froze her butt off.'' He stopped, suddenly embarrassed. ''Sorry, I got carried away. These kids nowadays, all they think of is sex, sex, sex. In my time, a fellow might sow some wild oats, but he didn't hop into the sack with every girl he dated. He had some respect for her. And she respected herself. Now that's the way it ought to be.''

Arnie Nyquist was only a decade or so older than I, but his romantic experiences were a world apart. The men I'd known in my younger years had used every ploy imaginable to get a female into bed. By my junior year in college, I'd heard everything from the possibility of facing certain death in Vietnam to suffering from hypothermia. A member of the Husky varsity crew had told me that sex would keep him from catching crabs. Justifiably confused, I had refrained, not realizing it was a rowing term.

I had not stopped to talk to Arnie Nyquist about sexual mores, however. At least not about the philosophy thereof. "Were you able to pin down about what time your van was broken into?" I asked.

Again, Arnie's expression was temporarily blank. "Heck, that was a week ago. I was at Travis's place for an hour or so. Eight, nine o'clock, maybe." His eyes narrowed as he looked down at me. "Say, are you deputized or something? Why do you want to know?"

I gave Arnie a big smile which seemed to thaw him a bit. "No, it's just that if we do this in-depth piece we mentioned to your father, we need to know details. Besides, I think we've got a picture frame of yours at the office."

"What?" Arnie would have jumped up and down if he hadn't been mired in six inches of slush. "How come?"

I explained that it had been recovered from the rubble at Evan Singer's cabin. Nyquist's reaction was less than I had expected. His high forehead furrowed, and he gave a little shake of his head. "Singer? That goofball who drives the sleigh for Henry Bardeen? He may be nuts, but he doesn't strike me as a thief."

My assessment of Arnold Nyquist shifted yet again. Originally, I had considered him a typical rough-and-tumble small-town builder, shrewd, but not smart; cunning, but not canny. Yet he was a UDUB graduate, which didn't stamp him as a genius, since I knew several people with college diplomas who could barely tie their own shoes and wouldn't qualify for anybody's brain trust. However, he'd gotten through the school, and that meant that he wasn't as dense as I'd figured. Then I had discovered that Arnie was blessed with inherent good taste. That had come as something of a shock. Now, it seemed, he wasn't entirely a things-oriented person as I'd suspected, but was occasionally given to accurate perceptions of people. Tinker Toy was full of surprises.

"I agree with you," I said, because it was true. "Evan Singer isn't a thief. Maybe he was looking for something." I watched Arnie carefully.

But Arnie merely shook his head. "Like what? My granddad's fountain pen? Or those photographs? How would he know what was in the van in the first place?"

"I take it you don't know Evan?"

"Heck, no," Arnie replied, looking mildly aghast at the mere idea. "In fact, when I heard he was out of work after he got canned at the video store, I was on my guard. I thought he might come around and ask to go to work for me. No thanks. I know trouble when I see it. I'd heard enough from Dutch Bamberg. If you ask me, Henry Bardeen made a big mistake hiring him. You hear how he dumped all those folks out of that sleigh the other night and they ended up in the emergency room at the hospital?"

"Not quite." I didn't want to press the issue. It's useless to try to squelch rumors in a small town, either in print or in person. Besides, Arnie Nyquist had told me what I needed to know for now. And a good thing, since I had a feeling that when Travis revealed how Vida and I had barged in this morning up at The Pines, Arnie might close up like a clam.

"Scratch Evan," I said to Vida as I entered the news office.

She glanced up from a spread of engagement photos. "I know, Billy already told me. According to the report, Evan Singer would have been driving the sleigh up at the ski lodge when Arnie's van was broken into." She looked vexed. "So how did he happen to have that picture frame? Is Arnie going to come get it?"

"I don't know—to both questions." I got out of my car coat, which had grown quite damp and even frozen in places while I had stood on the street corner jawing with Arnie.

"Unless the fire was set, and whoever did it left the photograph at the site."

Vida rolled her eyes. "Honestly, Emma, that makes no sense! I expect better of you!"

So did Ed Bronsky, who all but begged me to call the mall owners and ask them to cancel a full-page ad for a three-hundred-dollar shopping spree drawing to be held on New Year's Eve Day. "Now why would they go and do a thing like that?" Ed groaned, wringing his hands. "Are they so rich they have to *give* stuff away? Why not just donate it to the poor and keep quiet?"

His rationale sent me to the phone, not to call the mall, but Milo Dodge. The sheriff was back on the job, but sounding harassed. I hesitated briefly, but went ahead with my suggestion. Milo's reaction was predictably grudging.

"The Dumpster? What if it's been emptied since then? What do you think we'll find?"

"I told you, clothes. Carol Neal's, maybe. It's worth a try, isn't it?"

Milo started to mutter, mostly incoherently: ". . . Other agencies . . . Seattle . . . Damned computers . . . The brother, he's not so surprised . . ."

"Stop!" I ordered. "Whose brother? Speak up, you're talking into your socks, Milo."

"What?" Milo seemed to get a grip on himself. I could picture him behind his cluttered desk, his skin a sickly green under the fluorescent lights, his bony hands delving into his pockets for a roll of mints. "You mean Murray Francich? I talked to him about thirty minutes ago. He works for some software company on the Eastside."

"And?"

"He was afraid of something like this. He hadn't heard from Kathleen for six months. He figured some crazy john did her in."

"And?"

"It's possible."

"You're waffling, Dodge." I could picture him squirming in his fake leather chair. "You don't really believe that."

"We can't discount it, not with either of the girls." Milo sounded slightly affronted.

"So Murray knew his sister was hooking?"

"He guessed. They haven't been close for years." Milo paused, and I heard papers being shuffled. "Kathleen was the youngest of a family of four, sort of an afterthought. Murray is closest to her in age, some seven years her senior. The other brother and a sister live out of state, California and Illinois. The parents, who are retired, moved to the Spokane area a couple of years ago. I gather they wrote Kathleen off."

I waited for Milo to go on, but he didn't. "That's it?"

"What else? He hasn't seen Kathleen in over a year. They talked on the phone last spring. We're *presuming*, remember? We can't ask this guy Murray to identify limbs. But finding the car is pretty conclusive." Again, Milo sounded put out that I wasn't waxing enthusiastic over his disclosures. "I got some background on Evan Singer, too."

I decided it was time to give Milo a verbal pat on the back. "You've been busy. I'm surprised you've gotten so much done, after being up all night."

"Hey, Emma, this job's a backbreaker. We're understaffed, underpaid, and with jerks like Arnie Nyquist, underappreciated. Now Fuzzy Baugh is on my trail because his damned Santa suit got swiped. I told him to go ask his elves about it."

"Hmmmm. Good for you, Milo. What about Evan Singer?"

"What about a drink? I'm not officially on duty, wouldn't get paid for it if I were, so why don't I meet you at the Venison Inn? I could go for a hot toddy about now."

I started to say yes, then went into a stall. "Give me twenty minutes. Say," I added, apparently as an afterthought of my own, "what's Murray Francich's phone number?"

"Why?"

"Why not? Vida will get it if you don't give it to me."

Milo heaved a deep sigh, but capitulated, relaying both the work and home numbers. As soon as he hung up, I called the software company in Redmond where Francich was employed. It took three transfers, but I finally got him on the line.

I introduced myself, offered condolences, and explained that we were planning to do a background article on the murder victims. This was not a favorite part of my job. Murray Francich and his sister may not have been close in recent years, but he was obviously shaken.

"I was about to go home," he said a bit curtly. "I'm going to leave tonight for Spokane to see my folks. This is a hell of a thing to happen at Christmas."

"I suspect it actually happened back in October," I pointed out, wondering how families could become so estranged that one member could be missing for months and the rest wouldn't notice. Or give a damn.

"Kathy was too trusting," Murray Francich's remark came out of nowhere, except some sad corner of his soul. Was he making excuses for Kathy? Or for himself? "She was such a cute little kid, dimples, big eyes, curly blonde hair. But shy. My brother and I used to tease her about . . ." He stopped abruptly, aware that somebody was actually listening to his reminiscences. "What do you need to know, Mrs . . . ah . . . ?"

"Lord," I filled in quickly. "She went to Holy Names, I understand. How did she get off track?"

Murray let out an exclamation that was part snort, part hiss. "How do *I* know? She was the baby, and my folks spoiled her. No, that's not fair—they were older when they had her. They couldn't do what they'd done for the rest of us, like driving to music lessons and soccer practice and debate team meets. So they made up for it by sending her to private school—the rest of us went to public—even though they weren't well off. They tried to give her the right clothes and all that fad stuff, whatever was the craze that particular year. But Kathy never had many friends. She didn't date much, either. And then . . .'' His voice faltered. "Is this what you're after? I don't like it.''

Neither did I. "We're not a tabloid, Mr. Francich. We probably won't use most of what you're telling me. Does it help to talk?''

He sounded bleak. "I've tossed this around a hundred times with the rest of the family. What good can it do now?''

Of course he was right. I shifted to different ground. "Was Kathy a good student?''

"Oh, yes." His voice brightened a bit. "At least until her junior year. That's when she changed. But she did graduate.''

Ginny Burmeister appeared with a bundle of *Advocate*s, fresh off the press. I signaled my thanks, then glanced at the grim headlines:

SLAIN WOMEN FOUND
IN ALPINE AREA

ARSON DESTROYS
SECLUDED CABIN

As always, bad news looks even worse in bold, black type.

"What happened when Kathy was a junior?" I asked as Ginny discreetly made her exit.

Murray Francich sighed. "That's it—we never knew. At first, my mother thought she had a boyfriend, some creep who wouldn't make muster with my folks. Kathy started wearing a lot of makeup, flashier clothes, keeping odd hours. My folks confronted her, but she wouldn't tell them anything. There were some godawful fights. I was still living at home, and it got pretty ugly. Kathy moved out for a while— with a friend, I guess—but my mother was so frantic that she begged Kathy to come home. Then Kathy bought a car, with her own money, and more clothes, and she was gone every weekend. It was hell, I can tell you. I got an apartment that winter, and as soon as Kathy graduated, she was gone. The next day, in fact. She came home once, to pick up some tapes she forgot. My folks were heartbroken.''

My own heart went out to Mr. and Mrs. Francich. How do children go wrong? Where do parents fail? Who's to blame? I may not be my brother's keeper, but I am my child's custodian. Still, I don't like pointing the finger at parents who haven't been as lucky as I have.

''What about drugs?'' I knew I was pushing my luck with Murray Francich. He'd been far more loquacious than I'd expected. Maybe he'd underestimated talking through his sister's troubled life.

''It's possible. I wondered at the time. I know there was alcohol.'' Murray was beginning to sound weary. It was going on four o'clock, and he'd had a terrible day. The trip to Spokane still lay ahead.

''One last question.'' My tone had turned ingratiating. ''Did you know Carol Neal?''

''No. She'd been Kathy's roommate for quite a while, but I never met her. I don't know how they teamed up. A mutual friend, maybe.'' He gave a sudden, harsh laugh. ''They weren't good for each other, I guess.''

They certainly weren't. And someone had been very bad for them both.

Milo's generic hot toddy turned into his standard Scotch. I, however, kept to the season and drank what the Venison Inn called a Yule-a-Kahlua. It tasted better than it sounded.

''Who gets these girls together?'' Milo mused after he'd scanned the front page of *The Advocate* that I'd brought along for him. ''How many were there? So far, we've culled four out of that address book, which, by the way, must have been Carol's. There were no Franciches, but there's a Burt Neal in Grants Pass, Oregon. Her dad, it seems, but there's no answer.''

Burt Neal didn't interest me as much as the four culls. "What do you mean? Who are they?"

"Rachel Rosen. Bridget Dunne, now Nyquist. Tiffany Matthews. And April Johnson. Tiffany went to Bush, April to Seattle Lutheran." Milo was reading from his notebook. "Tiffany overdosed two years ago on Christmas Eve. April married a soldier and is living at Fort Hood, in Texas."

Bush was an exclusive private school near Lake Washington. I didn't know much about the Lutheran setup, except that it was over in West Seattle. "Has anyone contacted April?" I inquired.

"King County did, this afternoon. She hung up on them. They also tried to reach Rachel at the UDUB but they've gone on Christmas break. There was no answer at her home number." Milo regarded his Scotch as if he expected it to elude him, too.

I was silent for a bit. The sound system played "The Little Drummer Boy." Pah-pah-pah-pum . . . Pah-pah-pah-pum. "How about Tiffany's family?"

"Kid gloves," Milo replied, again on friendly terms with his Scotch. He signaled for the waitress to bring another round. "The Matthewses are very rich, very influential. Old money, big house on Lake Washington Boulevard. To complicate matters, they're in Europe."

"Swell." I gazed around the room, with its red and green streamers, big paper bells, and real stockings affixed to the fireplace's temporary cardboard brick mantel. Half the tables were occupied, and a handful of customers sat on stools, joshing with each other and with Oren Rhodes, the full-time owner and part-time bartender. It was too early for any of the clientele to be drunk or unruly. Serious daytime drinking in Alpine was reserved for private homes and the Elks Club.

Oren himself brought our drinks, ribbing Milo about having his hands full. His attitude toward our recent tragedies was detached. Like all good bartenders, he took death, divorce, and other debacles in professional stride.

"Why single out these girls?" I asked after Oren had re-treated to his post behind the bar. "That address book had a lot of names."

Milo nodded. "They'll all be checked out. But a red flag went up at King County on anybody with a private school background. It may mean nothing, but it's the only link we've got between Carol, Kathleen, and Bridget. And Bridget is the only Alpine link to Carol and Kathleen."

"Bridget's scared," I admitted. "Or pretending to be. But she denies seeing Carol and Kathleen recently. I have a hunch she's lying. I don't suppose you want to tell me who was doing the surveillance at the young Nyquists'?"

Milo grimaced. "I don't know why, but I could say who. It'd be off the record, though."

I hate off-the-record information. If I know something, I feel that the public ought to know it, too. But I can keep a confidence when necessary. "Who, then?"

"State police," said Milo Dodge. "They went home yes-terday."

"Having been successful?"

"I wouldn't know." Halfway into his second Scotch, Milo had visibly relaxed, although he still looked tired. "Evan Singer went to Lakeside."

I wasn't surprised. "Rich, huh? Lakeside costs a bundle. Where does the money come from?"

Milo again consulted his notes. "Father is Norman Singer, a prominent plastic surgeon. Mother, Thea, is a rabid patron of the arts. Grandfather was an architect. One sister, dab-bling in the New York theatre scene. Varied academic career, no degree. Arrested twice, once for disturbing the peace, the second time for disorderly conduct. Plea bargains, fines, but no jail time." Milo closed the notebook.

"Spoiled rich kid," I murmured. Evan's claim to have lived all over the world was probably pure hokum, invented to add exotic zest to his suburban upbringing. "Has he ever invested with Bartlett & Crocker?"

"His money's tied up in trusts. Dr. Dad apparently realized Evan wasn't stable." Milo was grinning at me. "Well? Have you and Vida solved the case yet?"

I sniffed at Milo. "All this stuff is interesting, but not very helpful. Evan's too old to have known any of these girls in high school. We need some serious leads."

"We need another drink." Milo waved his empty glass at Oren Rhodes. I, however, demurred, and urged him to do the same.

"You're still beat, Milo. Go home, eat something, watch TV until you fall asleep." I stood up, ready to head back to the office to see if the place had gone to hell in a handcart during my absence.

Milo was gazing up at me with an off-center grin. "Emma, are you mothering me? Haven't you got enough men in your life at the moment?"

With Adam and Ben around, I certainly should. But without Tom, all the men in the world weren't enough. The ridiculous thought crossed my mind in a haze of rum and Kahlua. "I'm a jackass," I announced in my best imitation of Vida. "Go home, Milo."

He was still grinning as Oren appeared with another Scotch. But before Milo could take a sip, Bill Blatt hurried into the bar. I stepped aside as the young deputy nodded at me in greeting and addressed his boss.

"We found the clothes, Sheriff. They're girl's stuff. Jeans, sweater, jacket, and . . . ah, bra and panties." Bill blushed, though not as deeply as he had when Carla had kissed him.

"Damn!" Milo drained his glass and got up. "Back to work. We need the lab to check the stuff out, match it with the victim, see if . . ."

Milo and Bill had outdistanced me. I shrugged and wandered out through the restaurant. Oscar Nyquist was sitting alone at a corner table. A napkin was tucked under his chin, and he was engrossed in the *Advocate* story about the Marmot. I hesitated, then saw the waitress approach with his order. Oscar put the paper aside and began to eat.

"How's the story?" I asked, resting a hand on the vacant chair across from Oscar.

He looked up from his meatloaf, his blue eyes wary, his bald head shining pink under a grouping of red Christmas lights. "Okay, so far. That Vida writes like she talks. A lot of words, blah, blah, blah. It sounds like that architect fella built the Marmot instead of my father."

"Lowenstein? Vida wanted to make sure he got credit because the theatre is such a structural gem. Apparently he was well known for his work all over the West Coast."

Oscar speared a chunk of over-browned potato. "Yeah, sure, he was clever. That's how he got rich. My father paid him a bundle." His wide face turned sullen, making him look like a big wrinkled baby due for a crying spell. "Better to have run him out of town."

I shifted in place, wishing Oscar would ask me to sit down. "Why is that?" I asked.

Oscar waved his fork. "Never mind. What's done is done. I'm too old for grudges. You eaten?" He pointed the fork at the spare chair.

I rested one knee on the seat cover. "No, I still have some work to do. I'll eat later at home."

Oscar nodded. "I always eat early, except on Sundays. For forty-eight years, my wife had supper on the table every night at five. Then I'd go to the Marmot to open the doors at six-fifteen. Astrid's gone, but I still eat at five. And I still go to the Marmot at six-fifteen." He spoke with pride.

"Let me know what you think of the rest of the story," I told Oscar with a smile. I almost wished I could join him. How many nights did he eat alone? I was feeling sorry for him as I walked up the street with my head down to ward off the wind and snow. The Burlington-Northern whistled as it started its climb to the summit. There was more traffic than usual on Front Street, caused by Alpine's usual exodus from work and the Christmas shoppers returning home. The amber headlights glowed in the scattered snowflakes. I glanced up, seeing the town perched on the mountainside, windows shining, trees lighted, decorations ablaze. The sight cheered me. Oscar Nyquist not only had family, he was probably the object of many Alpine widows. He was also the type who enjoyed his solitude. I realized that he hadn't exactly jumped for joy when I showed up at his table.

Everyone was gone at the office except Ginny, who was finishing the weekly mailing to out-of-town subscribers.

"I'll just make it to the post office by five-thirty," she said, dumping the last bundle of papers into a mailbag. "We had more calls than usual after *The Advocate* came out. They were mostly people upset about the murders, but some of them phoned to say they liked your owl editorial. Then there were some who didn't."

I laughed. "I expected that. If it weren't the Christmas season, I might get bomb threats."

Ginny, always serious, gazed at me from under her fringe of auburn hair. "You think people really behave better this time of year?"

"No. They're just too busy to make mischief." I glanced at the old clock above Ginny's desk, with its Roman numerals and elaborate metal hands. It was 5:24. "You'd better hurry, Ginny. But be careful."

She was putting on her blue anorak. "I'll get there. I made one trip already. I couldn't find our mailbag. This is a new one I got from the post office this afternoon." She hoisted it over her shoulder, looking from the rear like a small Father Christmas. "See you tomorrow."

"Right. Good night." I went into my office, swiftly sorting through the phone messages. Nothing urgent, nothing startling. Ginny had made notes on some: "Green River killer loose again?" "Saw stranger Monday night in Mugs Ahoy. Saw man from Mars there last week." "Owls have big hooters." "Bride wore teal going-away suit, not *veal*." "Buckers got robbed on charging foul in last twenty seconds against Sultan." "You're an idiot."

It was the usual assortment, many anonymous. The only one that held my attention read, "Ask Oscar Nyquist about Karen." The space for the caller's name was blank. I wondered if Ginny had recognized the voice. She often did.

Karen, I thought, as I started my uphill climb for home. Who was Karen? The name rang a bell, but I couldn't place it. Vida might know. I'd call her after Adam and I had dinner. Ben was dining with Jake and Betsy O'Toole. The zealous Teresa McHale couldn't coax him out of eating with the owners of the Grocery Basket.

My son, however, had spent the afternoon with my brother. To my amazement, Adam had helped Ben with some fix-up chores around the church. They'd repaired pews, shored up the confessional, replaced light bulbs, and gone through the decorations which would be put up on Christmas Eve Day.

"Tomorrow we're going to do some stuff at the rectory," Adam declared matter-of-factly as we dined on pasta, prawns, and cauliflower.

I couldn't help but stare. Here, in the home I'd created for the two of us, rafters could fall down, sinks could overflow, walls could collapse, and Adam would wander through the rubble, looking for the TV remote control. "Gosh, Adam, what happened? Did your heretical Uncle Ben introduce you to the Protestant—gasp!—work ethic?"

Adam didn't get the joke—or didn't want to. I dished up tin-roof-sundae ice cream for him and listened to his account of Ben's Tuba City chronicles.

"They've got all these great Indian ruins around there, way back to the Anasazis. There's Betatakin, with dwellings just like big apartment buildings carved into the cliffs from over eight hundred years ago. It's real green at the bottom of the canyon, not like the desert up above. Uncle Ben says there's aspen, elder, oak, and even Douglas fir. I want to go there next summer.''

I gazed fondly at Adam, who was finishing his ice cream. Over the years, he had seen Ben an average of once, maybe twice a year. They rarely wrote and never talked on the phone. Yet there was a closeness between them, born of a solitary man's need to love and a child's instinctive response. Adam had only recently met his own father. They had started to forge a bond, and I was glad. Typically, my son hadn't regaled me with details, but his attitude toward Tom seemed friendly. And now, he was seeing Ben, not just from a nephew's point of view, but man-to-man. I was pleased by that, too.

''You ought to go down there,'' I agreed. ''Maybe you could get a summer job.''

Adam nodded, a bit absently. ''That would be so cool— archaeology, I mean. Or is it the other one—anthropology? I wonder how long it takes to get a degree?''

I said I didn't know. I refrained from adding that it probably wouldn't take as long as it had for Adam to declare a major. At twenty-one, it seemed that it was time for him to decide what he wanted to be when he grew up. Or, having grown up already, he might consider his future in terms of . . . a job. I would say this later. Maybe it would be better coming from Ben. Or even Tom.

I caught myself up. For over twenty years, I'd never delegated an ounce of my parental responsibility. I wasn't about to start now. I rose from the table and went to call Vida.

She wasn't home. I'd forgotten that she was going to her daughter Amy's house for dinner. The question about *Karen* could wait. So could relaying Milo's various pieces of information. I settled down to watch a video that Adam had picked up earlier in the day. It was the remake of *Cape Fear*, and it scared me witless. How could anyone be as evil as the Robert De Niro character?

"Hey, Mom, it's only a movie," Adam said, laughing at my dismay while he rewound the tape. "Lighten up."

Adam was right. It was only a movie.

But out there in the drifting snow, among the festive lights, with the sweet strains of carols in the air, evil, real and terrifying, was on the loose. *Who was the killer?*

The only thing I knew for sure was that it wasn't Robert De Niro.

I would do Elvis. And the Wise Men. Ben had to attend the St. Mildred's Christmas Pageant, so I decided to join him on Thursday night and cover the event. Adam was noncommittal. He had met Evan Singer's replacement at Video-to-Go, and her name was Toni Andreas. I vaguely recognized her from church. She looked as if the wattage in her light bulb was pretty dim.

The day had dawned crisp and clear, with the wind blowing the snow clouds out over Puget Sound. Alpine sparkled in the early morning sun, and I could have used my sunglasses. Native Puget Sounders are like moles—for nine months of the year, they see the sun so seldom that their eyes can't take the glare.

The first thing I noticed downtown was the Marmot's marquee. It was the last day for *It's A Wonderful Life*, which was just as well, since the letters had now been rearranged to read *A Wide Full Fir Stone*. The Nyquist staring up at the scrambled title wasn't Oscar, but Louise.

"Now why do people do things like that?" she asked in exasperation after hurrying over to meet me at the corner. "Popsy will be wild."

"Where is Popsy?" I asked, as Louise fell into step beside me.

"He slept in," she replied, her brown boots mincing through the rock salt. "He needed his rest after last night." Her profile was uncustomarily grim. When I made no comment, she turned to give me a sidelong look. "You haven't heard? It's that same demented young man, Evan Singer. Two nights in a row he's caused problems for Popsy! Really, something's got to be done about him!''

"What now?" I asked. Trucks from UPS, Federal Express, and the U.S. Postal Service were already out and about, making early deliveries of Christmas presents and mail order gifts. Something about the vehicles rattled my brain, then melted away. Maybe I'd forgotten to mail a parcel. Or a greeting card. It'd come to me, hopefully before Christmas.

"It's crazy, just crazy," Louise was saying. "He came to see the movie—again—but this time, he was dressed as Santa Clause, complete with a pack over his shoulder. That was strange enough, but then he got into an argument with somebody because he insisted on sitting in their seat. The usher came, then Popsy, and finally the other person moved, just so they could start the movie. It's not as if there was a full house—the picture's been showing for over a week—but Evan Singer wouldn't back down. Popsy should have thrown him out, but he didn't want to upset the other customers."

We'd reached *The Advocate*. I invited Louise to come in, but she said she was going to the bakery. "We're having Travis and Bridget to dinner. Travis is so fond of the Upper Crust's sourdough rolls. Maybe I'll get a dessert, too." She gave me a faintly wistful smile. "I *could* make one. But the last few days have been so upsetting. Arnie thinks Evan Singer stole that Santa suit from the mayor. If he did that, then I think he was the one who robbed our house and van. But Arnie doesn't agree with me, he says just the suit. I think." Louise looked confused over her own words, and I could hardly blame her. Confusion seemed to have the upper hand in Alpine these days.

I said as much, and Louise heartily agreed. Certainly anything was possible with Evan Singer. I had to talk to Ben, to ask if Evan had showed up at the rectory. But it was eight o'clock, and my brother would be saying the morning mass.

Louise scurried off to the bakery. Inside the office, I found

Ginny and Carla, both still wearing their coats and fiddling with the thermostat.

"No heat," Ginny announced, pulling off her white earmuffs. "It's freezing in here. The pipes are okay, though."

"I can't type with my mittens on," Carla complained. "I'll make a lot of mistakes."

I suppressed the obvious rejoinder. But she and Ginny were right about the heat. The electrical unit wouldn't turn on. Otherwise, we had power.

"Call Ross Blatt over at Alpine Service and Repair," I told Ginny. Ross was, of course, a nephew of Vida's, and thus Bill Blatt's first cousin.

"How old is Ross?" asked Carla, loading her camera. "Is he married?"

"Yes," I replied. "He's got a couple of kids. He must be ten, fifteen years older than Bill. Why? Are you giving up on the local lawman?"

Carla shrugged, heading for the door. "Maybe. You did." She left.

"I never . . ." But there was no one to hear me. Ginny had gone into the front office to call Alpine Service and Repair. It was useless anyway to point out that Milo Dodge and I had never been a romantic item. Everyone assumed that because we were peers, single, and enjoyed each other's company, we ought to fall in love. Everyone, that is, except Vida, who knew better, and who was crossing the threshold carrying a Santa Claus suit.

"I found this in my front yard," she announced. "I'll bet it belongs to that old fool, Fuzzy Baugh. Why is Carla taking a picture of the Marmot's marquee? Haven't we given the Nyquists enough coverage?"

I thought so, too, but apparently Carla couldn't resist capturing for posterity one of the scrambled movie titles. It was the kind of photo we could use as a novelty: "Alpine Outtakes," or some such filler feature for a slow news week.

"Vida, what do you know about somebody connected to the Nyquists named Karen?"

Vida was taking off her coat. She cocked an eye at me from under the brim of her red veiled fedora. "Karen? She's Oscar's sister. Why?"

I told Vida about the anonymous phone call. Vida put her coat back on. "Oooooh! It's like ice in here! What happened?"

My explanation was brief. Vida gave a curt nod. "Ross knows his craft. It's too bad he's such a noodle otherwise. Now what's this about Karen Nyquist and asking Oscar? What's to ask? She moved away from Alpine when she got married back in 1938."

I sat down on Ed's desk. He'd be in late, this being the morning of the Chamber of Commerce's Christmas breakfast. "You mean she never came back?"

"Of course she came back." Vida yanked the cover off her typewriter. "She and her first husband, Trygve Hansen, and Oscar and Astrid were all close to Lars and Inga. Then the war came, and Trygve got a patriotic urge to serve. Maybe it was because Norway was occupied or some such silliness. He and Karen had no children yet, so the army took him just like that." She snapped her gloved fingers. "He was killed in North Africa. Karen went to work for Boeing, where she met her second husband, a scientist. He was a Jew. I told you that already." Vida fixed me with a reproachful look.

"I forgot." Vida was right. She'd mentioned that someone in the Nyquist family had married a Jewish man. But their genealogy, like that of so many Alpiners, was too complicated for a poor city girl to follow. "What happened then?"

"Nothing." Vida sorted through a stack of news releases, discarding most of them in the wastebasket. "Old Lars disowned Karen, more or less. He never mentioned Karen's new husband by name. Oscar went along with it like the lump of a lamb he is. Arnie was still a boy. Goodness, I was in high school at the time." She rolled her eyes at the marvel of her youth.

"So you don't know what became of Karen Nyquist Hansen after that?" I saw a note on Ed's desk from Francine Wells; she was having a pre-Christmas clearance, with twenty-five to fifty percent off on all designer dresses. I winced inwardly, trying to calculate what I would have saved if I'd waited to buy my green wool crepe. It had certainly been wasted on Milo.

"I know she and her second husband had a family. Karen hoped that the children would soften up old Lars, but of course he wouldn't give in. Finally, she stopped trying. I hate to admit it, but I lost track of her." Vida looked uncommonly rueful. "I suppose everybody else here did, too. Including the Nyquists."

I was lost in thought. Vida had begun hammering on her typewriter, having better luck with her gloves on than Carla would with her mittens. Or without. "I wonder who called," I finally said aloud. "And why."

Vida looked up but didn't stop typing. "Some busybody the Marmot story set off. You know how that goes. Shouldn't we call Milo about that Santa suit?"

Since I was still wearing my car coat and it wasn't any colder outside than in, I carted the suit down the street to the sheriff's office. Ross Blatt honked as he passed in his repair truck, presumably headed for *The Advocate*.

Milo shook his head as I handed him the suit. "Let's see if it's got a Fantasy Unlimited label. Irene Baugh remembered that much, even if Fuzzy wasn't sure which parts were red and which were white."

The suit indeed bore the proper label. Milo had heard about Evan Singer's latest escapade at the Marmot, courtesy of Sam Heppner, who had been in the audience. Deputy Sam had not wanted to interfere, since he was off-duty as well as loaded down with popcorn, soda pop, red licorice, and Milk Duds.

"The question is, did Evan Singer swipe the suit," said Milo, offering me some of his dismal coffee. "If so, why?" He bit into a glazed doughnut, which I presumed was breakfast.

"Because he's nuts?"

Milo wasn't amused. "First the Nyquists on my case, now the mayor. Who's next? The KKK and the ACLU?"

I got serious, too. "Do you think Bridget Nyquist needs protection?"

"She hasn't asked for it." Milo poured himself another mug of coffee. I realized he was using *our* mug. Maybe this wasn't the time to request its return. "Let's face it, Emma, we've got zip. Oh, those were Carol's clothes, hair and fibers match, right size, all that. But so what? The killer dumped the stuff at the construction site, and any traces have been covered by snow." He paused, rummaging through the file folders on his desk. "Here—how's your stomach? I got some details from the M.E. in Everett. Are you up to it?"

I blanched, then lied. "Sure. Go ahead."

Milo perused the typewritten form. "First victim, presumably Kathleen Francich, was dismembered with an axe. Do you want to know how?"

I told the truth. "No. I mean, I can guess. Do I need to know?"

Milo shook his head and finished his doughnut. The man had nerves of steel and a stomach to match. I had to give him that. "But consider what a mess it would make. Where does the killer do it? Outside, where the snow will eventually cover the blood? Off on some logging road? A hiking trail? How do you transport the remains to the river without staining your car or truck or whatever? In a sack? Maybe. Still, I think you're taking a big chance. There are too many people out roaming the woods, especially in early October."

"Stop saying *you*. I feel as if I'm about to be arrested."

Milo gave me a thin smile. "Okay. But what do *you* think?"

I preferred not to think about it at all, but just to sit in Milo's crowded office, feeling the warmth of his space heater and drinking his dreadful coffee. However, I was a journalist with an obligation. "If it was an inside job—literally—where? A private house? If you could be assured of privacy and then clean up like mad, maybe so. But that's risky, too."

An enigmatic expression crossed Milo's long face. "What if your place was secluded and you burned it to the ground?"

Milo's theory had some merit. It also had some flaws. "Why wait two months? Kathleen Francich was killed in October. And, if the same person killed Carol Neal, why not dispose of her in the same way?"

"No time. There was a rush on with Carol. If we knew why . . ." He let the thought float away.

"Motive," I said, looking into my coffee mug as if I were reading tea leaves. Maybe it *was* tea, not coffee. That would explain why I could see the bottom of the mug with an inch of liquid left. "If Carol and Kathleen were hookers, was Bridget, too? What about the others? It sounds as if you're envisioning a ring of private school prostitutes."

"I am." Milo didn't look as if the idea agreed with him. "Carol, Kathleen—and Bridget—all suddenly had money to burn in their junior year. Drugs or prostitution? Both, maybe, but I lean toward the sex angle. If we can nail Rachel or April, we may find out."

"Tiffany was rich already," I pointed out. "Why would she get involved? Drugs?"

"That's a decent guess," Milo replied. "Nobody's ever rich enough to afford a serious drug habit. Especially not a young woman who was probably on an allowance."

Milo made sense. "How did they get together? Carol and Bridget went to the same school, but not the others." I frowned at the mounted steelhead behind Milo's desk. He had decorated it with a strand of green tinsel. "At dances? Football games? Summer camp?"

"Hey!" Milo grinned at me. "You're sharp. We'll see if

King County can find out if they were counselors. Going into their junior year, they'd be sixteen, seventeen, too old to be regular campers." He scribbled a note to himself.

"I still think Bridget may be in danger," I said, swallowing the last of the ersatz coffee.

Milo's phone rang; he ignored it. The caller persisted, which meant that Bill Blatt wasn't intercepting in the outer office. Resignedly, Milo picked up the receiver. His indolent form snapped to attention.

"Is that right? . . . I'll be . . . Yeah, right, we figured that much. . . . Oh? . . . Well, now . . . When? . . . Sure, okay. . . . Thanks. By the way, here's something you might want to run through the . . ."

I stood up, now too warm in my car coat but unwilling to take it off when I knew I was on the verge of leaving.

Milo continued to give instructions to the person on the other end of the line. At last he hung up, and gave me a self-satisfied look. "Standish Crocker is being charged with racketeering, money laundering, and drug dealing. He used that investment firm as a front for providing cocaine and call girls to businessmen from Seattle to Singapore. What do you think of that?"

I sat down again. "Whew! That's incredible! I thought Standish Crocker was some stuffy old Brahmin. What'd he do, go into his second childhood?"

"He died. Standish Crocker II, that is, in 1989. His son, Standish Crocker III, is only thirty-four, a real swinger. But he swung too far. Maybe Travis did, too." Milo was still looking pleased. "He's being taken into Seattle for questioning today."

My first, irrelevant, thought was for Louise Nyquist and her dinner party. I didn't admit as much to Milo. "So maybe that's how Travis met Bridget? She was one of the call girls?"

"*Was*. Maybe." Milo was now frowning at his hastily scribbled notes. "Bridget Dunne, Carol Neal, Kathleen Francich, Rachel Rosen, April Johnson, and Tiffany Matthews all have arrest records for soliciting. But only Kathleen and Carol have been busted during the last year and a half. That figures—Tiffany died, April and Bridget got married. Rachel . . . maybe she reformed and went to college.''

"Let's hope. All of them had some advantages. It would be reassuring to think they didn't have to come to a tragic end.'' I suddenly felt weighed down by Milo's news. It was one thing to make suppositions; it was quite another to be confronted with the bald truth. Six girls, from decent families with good intentions, sent off to private schools to develop their intellectual and spiritual potential—and they'd ended up selling themselves to international thrill-seekers who hid behind three-piece suits. "Is Standish Crocker in jail?'' I hoped he was hanging by his thumbs.

"He was released on his own recognizance.'' Milo saw my disappointment. "No doubt he's languishing in the quiet splendor of his Hunts Point mansion.''

I stood up again. I felt a perverse need to make Milo feel as glum as I did. "You still don't know who the killer is.''

Milo's hazel eyes studied my gloomy face. "No. I don't. But we can start grilling Bridget Nyquist. With Travis gone, she'll be vulnerable.''

She would indeed. And not just to the sheriff. Bridget would also be vulnerable to the killer. I was sorry I'd taunted Milo. Most of all, I was sorry for Bridget and the other five girls from fine private schools. Three of them were already dead. Was April Johnson safe in Texas? Where was Rachel Rosen?

Bridget Nyquist was in Alpine, and everybody knew it. Including the killer.

Chapter Sixteen

THE REST OF the day was not nearly as eventful as the first hour on the job. It took Ross Blatt less than ten minutes to restore our heat. The bill came to $87.34, a cut-rate bargain, Ross asserted, due to the presence of Aunt Vida. I hated to think what it would have cost if there had not been a blood relative on hand.

There was more reaction to this week's edition of *The Advocate*, with two dozen letters to the editor arriving in the mail. Eleven upheld my stand on the spotted owl, two denounced it, four criticized the sheriff for not having arrested the murderer or anybody else, three had their own memories of the Marmot, and the rest were miscellaneous. As usual, I'd run them all.

The fire department and the insurance people still hadn't decided whether or not Evan Singer's cabin had been burned deliberately. Evan had admitted that he didn't always lock up when he left. This revelation was made to Ben after Evan arrived at the rectory around ten o'clock the previous evening. He was not wearing a Santa Claus suit.

If Milo had learned anything new about the murder case, I didn't hear it. The details of the charges filed against Standish Crocker III came over the wire, but they didn't provide further enlightenment. Bill Blatt had called around eleven to say that Travis Nyquist had been taken into Seattle. He had put a good face on it, claiming he was being summoned merely to help out with the investigation. To my relief, Bridget went with him.

The pageant was scheduled for seven P.M., but Ben suggested that I join him for dinner at the rectory. Teresa McHale was leaving for the evening, but planned to put out what she termed *a cold collage*. Adam's date with Toni Andreas was on, though he allowed that they might show up at the school hall later. Toni's brother, Todd, was playing Colonel Parker.

I left work early, arriving home in time to go through the mail and check in with Adam. He had spent the afternoon at the rectory again, but hadn't accomplished as much as expected.

"Mrs. McHale insisted we work on the front porch," Adam said, haphazardly unsorting the laundry I'd set out for him that morning. "She's really picky, and insisted the porch was rotting and somebody would fall through and sue the church. But Uncle Ben and I couldn't figure out where it had gone bad and even with the sun shining, our fingers got so stiff we had to quit. We ended up hauling a bunch of junk from the church basement."

I had been in St. Mildred's basement once, when I had volunteered to help set up for Easter. If the bowels of the Marmot contained a history of Alpine entertainment, the church vault was a religious museum: the purple draperies that once shrouded statues during Lent, a set of wooden clappers used on Good Friday in the pre–Vatican II millennium, a carton of outmoded Baltimore Catechisms, and an actual nun's habit, complete with wimple. Relics, I'd thought, not in the true theological sense, but certainly of a different era in the Church. I suspected that the first item that Ben threw out was the Baltimore Catechisms.

I left before Adam did, again walking. The sky was still clear, and the stars were out. Almost every house now had its tree—fir, spruce, pine; tall, bushy, angular; flocked, artificial, traditional. Christmas trees are as individual as the people who decorate them. Mine was as big as the room could hold; its branches were as loaded as they could bear. Was I compensating for a hole in my life? Probably. Weren't we all?

When I got to the rectory, Teresa McHale was about to leave. "There's ham, macaroni salad, bread, sweet pickles, and cheese," she told me, jiggling a set of car keys. "I may be late. I'm meeting an old friend in Edmonds."

"What about Evan Singer?" I asked. "Is he eating here, too?"

Teresa bent down to pick up a large canvas shopping bag that bore a recycling logo. It was crammed with red tissue paper. Maybe it was recyclable, too. Fleetingly, I wondered if Teresa was one of the environmentalists who disapproved of my stand on the spotted owl.

"Evan Singer!" she exclaimed. "Really, that man is deranged! I'm all for being a good Christian, but there *are* limits! Your brother is very naive about people. He's spent too much time with all those blacks and the Indians." With a nod, Teresa exited the rectory.

Ben popped his head around the corner of the pastor's study. He was grinning. "Do you think I'm naive, Sluggly?"

"Eavesdropper! Yes, in some respects. Or maybe it's just that you're not a complete cynic like most of us."

Ben led me into the parlor, which was aptly named, because it was right out of a 1930s time warp. Overstuffed mohair furniture, solid but dull end tables, a glass-fronted bookcase, and a cut-velvet side chair with curving wooden arms were crammed into the room, along with a somewhat newer TV console of bleached mahogany. The brown wall-to-wall carpeting dated from the 'Sixties, and was worn but curiously unfaded, as if the drapes were seldom opened. It was a room more suited to listening to Notre Dame football than to the tribulations of a troubled soul.

Since liturgically the Church was celebrating Advent, rather than Christmas, the only holiday concession was a velvet-covered wreath with an electric candle, which glowed in the front window. The walls were covered with religious art of the sentimental school—a proud-as-punch Virgin Mary and St. Joseph showing off the twelve-year old Christ as if He'd just won first place in a debate contest (come to think of it, He had); St. Cecilia, with plucked eyebrows and marcelled hair, being showered with roses as she played her harpsichord; the Holy Family on the flight into Egypt, a term that has always thrown me since they couldn't possibly have gone more than three miles an hour with that plodding little donkey. My favorite, however, was the one picture that attested to Father Fitz's humanity and to the fact that somewhere, at some time, the man had possessed a sense of humor: The art work dated from the turn-of-the-century and showed two red-robed altar boys hiding behind the corner of a huge stone church, about to launch snowballs at an unsuspecting young lad in civilian clothes. I loved the scene. I loved Father Fitz for displaying it.

"We can't eat in here. Mrs. McHale is afraid we'll ruin the furniture," Ben said wryly, opening the cupboard doors on the TV cabinet. He got out a bottle of Canadian whiskey, two glasses, and a bucket of ice. "Father Fitz was down to his last drop of Bushmills. No wonder he had a stroke. It's a good thing I like rye."

"Where's Evan?" I asked, accepting a glass from Ben. It was Waterford crystal, cut like diamonds, and felt good in my hand.

Ben sat down in the other overstuffed chair. "Who knows? He's been gone since noon. He didn't get up until eleven."

"Did you talk to him much?"

Ben shook his head. "Last night I got him settled down in Father Fitz's room. He acted upset, tired, so I didn't push it. Of course I didn't know about the latest incident until you told me this morning. Evan was out of here before we could have any meaningful dialogue."

"Will he be back tonight?" It was chilly in the rectory, and I eyed the empty fireplace with longing.

"Who knows?" Ben followed my gaze. "Forget it. Mrs. McHale says fireplaces are a bother. Now you know why Father Fitz wore two sweaters."

Teresa's cold collage was adequate. The pageant was endearing. Elvis learned much from the Wise Men, despite Colonel Parker's lousy advice to ignore them. But even the colonel capitulated at the end, joining the rock 'n' roll shepherds in a stirring version of "O Come All Ye Faithful." Elvis, as it turned out, was a girl.

After partaking of refreshments, Ben and I returned to the rectory. There was no sign of Teresa McHale or Evan Singer, but it wasn't yet nine o'clock. The clouds were rolling in again from the north. Ben and I had a dollop of brandy before I headed home. Adam and Toni hadn't showed up at the pageant, which didn't come as a surprise. It did, however, present a new set of worries. When Adam was away at school, I had put his love life out of my mind. But while he was under my roof, I fretted. I was visited by visions of an irate Mr. Andreas, who grew taller and broader with every passing minute, pounding on the door and demanding that my son make an honest woman out of his daughter.

But Adam was home when I got there, comfortably ensconced on the sofa, watching *Cheers*. "Toni's brain is unfurnished," he said at the commercial break. "What's with people around here? Some of them think the big city is Monroe."

I was about to explain small town mentality to my son when the phone rang. It was Ben.

"I found a mailbag under Evan Singer's bed. It's got a tag on it that says it belongs to *The Advocate*. You want it?"

I frowned into the phone. "Sure. But . . . I don't get it. Why did Evan Singer steal our mailbag?"

Ben chuckled. "He needed something to put these old film cans in. You ever heard of a movie called *Gösta Berling's Saga*?"

I had—and recently. "Listen, Stench, don't you read *The*

Advocate?'' I heard Ben squirm at the other end. He'd read *most* of the paper, at least the front page. But a pastor's life was busy, especially when you were new in town, and it was Advent . . .

I cut Ben off. "*Gösta Berling's Saga* was Greta Garbo's first big hit. It was also the film that Lars Nyquist used for the grand opening of the Marmot. Now what the hell are you talking about?''

Ten minutes later, I was back at the rectory, this time driving my car, which took five minutes to warm up. Four big round tins of film lay on the parlor floor, clearly marked in English and in Swedish. "Where," I asked in amazement, "did Evan get these? They must be worth something.''

Ben got out the brandy again. "Think about it," said my brother, his usually crackling voice slowing to a drawl that he might have picked up in Mississippi. "Evan Singer spends Tuesday night at the Marmot. How long is he there? What's he doing? We don't know, Oscar doesn't know. Oscar finds him asleep in the theatre's auditorium. Cut to Wednesday. Enter Evan dressed as Santa, suit stolen from the mayor, mailbag taken from your office. Now why does he need the sack?''

I eyed my brother in the dim amber light of a three-way lamp, conservatively set on low. "To carry something . . . And," I added, suddenly remembering Vida's barbed remark of the previous week, "because Fuzzy Baugh didn't use a pack. He has lumbago.''

We were silent, both of us staring at the film cans. "Evan found the tins Tuesday," my brother speculated. "Where?''

"The basement?" I had been down there, but Ben had not. "It's full of old stuff, but I didn't see anything like this.'' I closed my eyes, trying to picture the clutter. Oscar had shown Vida and me almost every nook and cranny. Where had the film cans been stashed? "The rain barrel! Lars saved it from the old social hall. It was probably empty, and somehow these cans were put in it after the movie ended its run.

Lars Nyquist was a great fan of Garbo's. Maybe he wanted a souvenir.''

Ben nodded. "Could be. It was illegal, unless he worked out some kind of deal. In any event, I'll bet Evan Singer found these cans and took them up to the auditorium, ditched them under the seat—and fell asleep. Oscar found him and threw him out before he could get away with the reels. So he had to come back—and sit exactly where he was the previous night. That's why there was the ruckus. Somebody else was already in that seat. During the movie, Evan slipped the cans into the mailbag. Who would stop Santa with his pack?''

I had to laugh. Evan Singer might be crazy, but he wasn't stupid. "How did you find these?" I asked.

Ben lighted a thin, black cigarette, one of his rare tobacco indulgences. He knew better than to offer me one. I would have accepted. "Teresa McHale will kill me for smoking in here, but I'll remind her I'm the pastor. How, you ask? Same reason—Teresa. She's so damned fussy, and I was afraid Evan might have trashed Father Fitz's room, so I went in to check. It was tidy enough, he hasn't got much left since the fire, but when I looked under the bed, I found this." He waved his cigarette at the mailbag and film cans. "Now what do I do? Confront him?''

I didn't like the idea of Ben confronting Evan Singer. My brother was a big boy, and reasonably fit. But he had no killer instinct. I was beginning to think that I couldn't say the same for Evan Singer. "We'd better find out if these reels came from the Marmot.''

"Where else?" asked Ben.

"Right." I watched Ben's cigarette smoke spiral up toward the ceiling, drifting into the old-fashioned light fixture of orange bulbs shaped like candle flames. "Ben—we're asking the wrong questions." My brother blew a smoke ring, forming his unspoken *oh?* I stood up and began to pace the room. "It isn't enough to know how Evan Singer stole this movie. We need to know why. We need to know how he knew it was there in the first place. Most of all, we need to know who in hell *is* Evan Singer?''

I lingered at the rectory, unwilling to leave Ben alone. At last, I openly questioned my brother's safety. He might be sleeping under the same roof as a known thief and a possible killer.

"I'll admit I can't see why Evan would kill those two girls," I said as the old marble clock on the mantel chimed eleven, "but I'm worried. Maybe you should put those film cans back under Evan's bed before he gets in."

Ben shook his head, his customary indecisiveness coming to the fore. "I can't. If Evan's got the nerve to ask for them, we'll talk it over. But I need to think this through. Now go home, you're stalling to give me protection. I don't need it. Teresa McHale is strong as an ox. She could put Evan Singer on the ropes in the first twenty seconds of round one."

"But she's not back, either," I protested. "Where are you going to put those film reels?"

Ben picked up the four cans, placed them in the mailbag, and pulled at the sleeve of my red sweater. "Come on, Sluggly, I'll show you."

The rectory was built on a simple, practical floor plan. The parlor and study were at the front; the housekeeper's room and bath were separated from the two priests' rooms by the kitchen, dining room, and another bath. The long hall gave the impression of a dormitory.

The priest's guest room was spartan, with a twin bed, a bureau, a desk and a chair. A crucifix hung above the bed, but otherwise the walls were bare. Ben opened the closet to reveal his limited travel wardrobe. He put the mailbag on the floor at the rear of the closet, then set his ski boots at such an angle that the sack was obscured.

"Okay?" He gave me a tight smile. When I didn't respond, he sighed. "All right, come here. I'll show you my life insurance policy." He went over to the bureau and pulled out the top drawer. Socks and underwear were folded neatly. Ben reached under a pile of T-shirts. I waited. Ben reached some more. I glanced out the window to see if it was snowing yet. It wasn't, but the clouds were low and seemed to press in on Alpine.

Ben swore. I jumped. Under the tan, his face had lost its natural color. "It's gone, Emma," he said hoarsely. "God help me, it's gone!"

"What?" Ben's reaction baffled me. It annoyed me, too, since he seemed to think I knew what he was talking about.

Ben slammed the drawer shut, rocking the rickety bureau. "My gun. The Browning high-power. It's gone."

I was adamant. Ben was either coming home with me or I was staying at the rectory. He refused to leave. So did I.

"You're irrational, Emma," said Ben, sounding angry.

"You're a fool," I countered, dialing my home. Adam answered, half-asleep. I wasn't sure my message sank in, but maybe he'd figure it out when he woke up in the morning and found me gone.

At last, Ben gave in, but insisted that I take his bed. He'd sleep on the davenport in the parlor. We'd just settled this minor dispute when Teresa McHale came in. Seeing her solid, no-nonsense figure made me feel a bit foolish.

Ben, however, took command. "Please sit down, Mrs. McHale," he requested, indicating one of the mohair chairs in the parlor. "I want you to tell me who has called at the rectory this past week."

Teresa was still wearing her handsome plum-colored wool coat. She set her handbag down on the floor next to the chair. "The last week? Really, Father, I don't know if I can remember everyone. The entire school faculty and staff at some point. Most of the parish council. Mary Beth McElroy, the CCD teacher. Annie Jeanne Dupré, the organist. Oh, the choir, after practice Monday night. Mrs. Nyquist from the Lutheran Church. The eucharistic ministers. The dishwasher repairman."

"Mrs. Nyquist?" I interrupted. "Which one?"

Teresa eyed me with distaste. It was one thing for a new pastor to invade her domain. It was something else for the pastor's lippy sister to butt in. "Mrs. Arnold," she replied coolly, turning to Ben. "Louise Nyquist. She came by Monday, after you attended the St. Lucy service. You forgot the Swedish Christmas chimes they presented to the clergy, Father."

"Oh. Right," said Ben. "Who else?"

Teresa continued her list of names, which made up most of Catholic Alpine and a dash of Separated Brethren thrown in for good measure. At last Ben revealed the source of his anxiety. The housekeeper was appalled.

"A gun? You carry a *gun*, Father?"

"I need it in the desert, believe me," Ben replied, a trifle testily. "I've got a permit. I brought it with me because my quarters are being renovated while I'm on vacation. The workmen had to pull the safe."

Teresa did not look appeased. "I see," she said between taut lips.

I dared to interject myself once more. "Mrs. McHale, when Louise was here Monday was she ever alone in the rectory? Waiting for you or something?" Louise Nyquist wielding a Browning high-power seemed incongruous, but so were a lot of other brutal truths.

"Certainly not," Teresa answered, taking umbrage at my suggestion that she somehow might have been derelict in her duties. "I let her in, we chatted, she said she'd never been in the rectory before. Mrs. Nyquist joked that her parents had told her horror stories about the place. You know, the usual Protestant mumbo-jumbo—orgies, Black Masses, human sacrifice, all that nonsense. She seemed interested, so I showed her around. She stayed so long that I thought she was thinking about converting." Teresa laughed softly at her own small jest.

Ben and I exchanged glances. I knew we were thinking

alike: while Louise Nyquist detained Teresa, someone else might have sneaked into the rectory. It could have been pre-arranged; it could have been by chance.

Teresa still seemed unconvinced about my reasons for spending the night. Indeed, I was beginning to change my mind. But when the housekeeper headed for bed and Evan Singer knocked at the door, my resolve was renewed.

"I've been out to the cabin," he announced, looking mournful. "It's all gone. Everything. I communed with the spirits. They told me to go to Hoquiam."

"Hoquiam?" Ben and I chorused. There's nothing wrong with Hoquiam, which is a small city in the Grays Harbor area out on the coast. Still, it struck both of us as a strange choice by the spirits.

"I leave tomorrow," Evan said, drifting down the hall-way. "My task here is finished." He went into Father Fitz's room and quietly closed the door.

I grabbed Ben's arm. "What if he sees the film reels are gone?"

Ben shrugged. "He'll ask. I'll tell him. Stop fussing, Sluggly. It's after midnight. Go to bed." He kissed my fore-head.

It was very chilly in the rectory, so I slept in my clothes. I didn't have much choice, unless I borrowed one of Ben's sweatshirts. As late as it was, I couldn't settle down. The bed was too narrow, too hard, too unfamiliar. I wondered how Ben was faring on the davenport.

I tossed and I turned. I thought I heard a wolf howl. Was Adam okay? Should Ben have reported the missing gun? Or the discovery of the film reels? Maybe I should call the sher-iff's office. Dwight Gould was on night duty this week. But I might wake Ben if I went down the hall to use the phone in the study.

A frantic knock sent me bolt upright. Evan Singer de-manded to be let in. On stockinged feet, I hurried to the door. Evan flew into the room, wearing jeans and a T-shirt.

"They're going to kill me!" he cried. "It's horrible! The rack, the boot, the Iron Maiden!" He fell on his knees, wringing his hands. "Save me, Queen Isabella! Tell Torquemada I'm innocent!"

"Oh, jeez!" I rolled my eyes, then collected myself. "Okay, I'll send Ferdinand. Get up, you're safe. Hey, Evan, come on. You've reached sanctuary."

Slowly, Evan Singer got to his feet. He gave me a pathetic, grateful smile. "You're a good person," he said, sounding almost sane. "I know the Inquisition is passé, but that room scares me. Think of it, a priest occupying it all these years! Do you think he wore a hairshirt and flogged himself?"

Evan might like to think so, but I didn't. Such extreme penitence wasn't Father Fitz's style. He'd be more inclined to give up fudge for a week. But I didn't expect Evan to believe that.

"You want to trade rooms?" I inquired.

He considered the offer carefully, then accepted. Ben was at the door, looking bleary-eyed. Teresa McHale, wearing a brilliant satin quilted robe, stood behind him. Without makeup, she more than looked her age. She also looked upset.

"Really, Father," she murmured to Ben, "didn't I warn you?"

Ben ignored the remark. He stood by while Evan and I switched sleeping quarters. Teresa padded off down the hall.

"Well?" I whispered to Ben after Evan had closed the door to the guest bedroom. "I don't think he noticed that the film was missing."

Ben gave a little smirk. "That's not all that's missing," he said, starting back toward the parlor. "And I don't mean the Browning."

"Hmmmm," I said, and yawned. Evan's outburst had broken the spell. It seemed normal for him to be crazy. I went to sleep almost immediately.

Chapter Seventeen

BEN WAS STILL hemming and hawing over telling Milo about the missing gun. As for the film cans, my brother would hide them in a safer place. Evan wasn't going anywhere. Milo had seen to that. He had arrested Evan first thing Friday morning for the theft of Fuzzy Baugh's Santa suit.

"Honestly," Vida exclaimed as Milo joined us in the news office around nine o'clock, "you can't hold him long on such a flimsy charge!"

"It's Friday," Milo replied. "We'll be able to keep him over the weekend. Besides, he's got nowhere else to go unless he wants to stay on at the rectory and get himself harassed by Torquemada and the Spanish Inquisition." Milo gave me an amused look. "By the way, Travis and Bridget are back."

I turned away from the AP wire, which was spewing out national news. "What happened?"

Milo took a maple bar from the sack of goodies Ginny Burmeister had brought for a special Friday treat. "Not much. Travis insisted he didn't know what Standish Crocker was up to. They didn't charge him, so I have to figure the surveillance team didn't turn up much." He dug inside his down jacket. "Except these."

I took the four photographs from Milo. They showed a man standing in the driveway of the younger Nyquists' residence, then on the snow-covered lawn, leaning against the gnarled cottonwood tree, and finally up against the side of

701

the house. Although the pictures were fuzzy, there was no mistaking the tall, thin figure of Evan Singer.

"The guys in the PUD truck took these shots a week ago Tuesday. I guess I was wrong about the lurker's intentions. Or was I?" Milo looked bemused.

I handed the pictures to Vida. "Bridget and Evan as lovers? Well . . . maybe."

Vida huffed as she studied the photos. "I don't call this lurking. He's bold as brass. The least he could do is hide in the shrubbery or climb up that tree."

I practically fell over Vida's wastebasket. "Let me see that again!" Puzzled, Vida handed the pictures back to me. I scrutinized all four in turn. The big tree at the edge of the front yard was prominent in each shot. "Isn't that a cottonwood?" I asked.

Vida didn't bother to look. "Certainly not. It's an oak. George Jersey, who felled the first tree when Alpine was still called Nippon, planted it back in World World I."

I felt half-silly, half-euphoric. I described the gnarled tree Evan had sketched, told how he had said his entire life was pictured there. A family tree, I realized, with its roots in Alpine. It was the same tree that grew in the front yard of Bridget and Travis Nyquist's house.

"Vida, think—is there any way Evan Singer could be related to the Nyquists?"

I heard Milo guffaw. But Vida merely adjusted her glasses. "Now that's an interesting question, Emma." She picked up a pencil and began to draw lines on a blank piece of paper. "Let's see—Arnie's sister, Thelma, had twin girls who must be in their late twenties. Thelma and her husband, Peter, live in Spokane—he works for a packing company." Vida drew another line, in reverse. "Oscar's sister, who is, of course, Arnie's Aunt Karen, had no children by her first husband, Trygve Hansen. But as I told you, she had three by the second marriage to Mr. . . . Well, if that doesn't beat all! I never knew his name! None of the Nyquists would mention it because he was Jewish.'' She looked to Milo for confirmation.

''Hey,'' said Milo, holding up a big hand, ''I was a baby when all that happened.''

I turned to Milo. ''Can you find out what Karen Nyquist's married name is?''

Vida was dredging up the Seattle White Pages. ''I can. If I'm following your thoughts.'' She dumped the book back on the floor. ''I don't want that, I want the Eastside, don't I?''

''I don't suppose,'' Milo said in his laconic voice, ''that anybody's going to tell me what's going on?''

Vida looked up from the Eastside directory. ''Oh, hush, Milo! It's obvious.'' She bent her head over the pages again. ''There are four of them in the Bellevue area . . . ah!''

''You found Karen?'' I asked eagerly.

Vida regarded me with dismay. I felt as if she were about to crown Milo and me with dunce caps. ''Don't you pay attention either, Emma? I'm not looking for Karen Nyquist, I'm looking for her son: Norman Singer.''

I had forgotten that Oscar Nyquist had told us that his sister had named her son Norman. Vida, naturally, had absorbed that piece of knowledge like a sponge. Milo and I waited quietly while she dialed the Bellevue number. We were as fascinated by the excuse she would come up with as we were by the possible confirmation of my theory.

''Mrs. Singer? Yes, this is Vida Blatt, from West Seattle. I understand your son, Evan, is an artist. . . . Oh, really? No, it doesn't matter if he's sold previously. I was thinking of a commission. A mural for my backyard fence. Your mother-in-law suggested it. Karen Singer, is it? I met her at Bel-Square a while ago. . . . Confined to a wheelchair? Since when? Goodness, maybe it's been longer than I thought. You know how time flies. . . . Oh. Oh, that's a shame. I'll have to find someone else. Thank you so much.''

Vida put the phone down and smiled in triumph. "Now you see how easy that was? The personal touch. No computers, no data whazzits, nothing but pure human communication. Thea Singer, Mrs. Norman, says her son has moved out of town. Surprise. Grandma Karen has been stuck in a wheelchair since she had a stroke a year ago. What else do you need to know?"

Milo grabbed a cinnamon twist and started for the door. "Plenty. Evan Singer's got some explaining to do. We may have cracked this case." He left.

Vida snorted. "This case isn't cracked. Milo is." She dropped the Eastside phone book back into the pile of directories.

I'd sat down at Ed's desk. He was breakfasting with the Rotarians this morning. Ed Bronsky might not enjoy selling advertising, but he certainly relished the job's fringe benefits. "Listen, Vida—Evan shows up here in early October. Kathleen Francich is murdered about that same time. Then Carol Neal. Evan is photographed hanging around Bridget's house. He said he knew her in Seattle. Now how much more . . ."

"That's not what he said," Vida broke in. "Evan was never clear on that point. It *sounded* as if he'd known Bridget and Travis for some time. And he had—not personally, but as his long-lost relatives."

"True." My hypothesis wasn't totally destroyed, but it certainly had suffered some dents. "I suppose we could ask Evan."

Vida looked as if she considered the idea worthless. But before she could put her reaction into words, Ginny Burmeister appeared with the mail. I remembered to ask her if she had recognized the person who had called with the message about Oscar and Karen.

But Ginny had no idea who it was, other than that it was an adult female. "I don't think I ever heard her voice before," said Ginny, filling Vida's in-basket with an assortment of items addressed to the House & Home editor. "She was brief. Businesslike."

I sighed. It could be anybody. But it wasn't Evan Singer. "Okay," I said to Vida after Ginny had finished her delivery chores and returned to the front office. "With or without Evan Singer, we need a motive. Why kill two out of five prostitutes—the sixth one being dead already?"

Vida looked up from the typewriter. "Blackmail. There's no other reason, except a mania. This is not a maniac, not in that sense. A true sociopath would have killed any young woman he encountered. She might be a prostitute, she might not. But Kathleen and Carol had something in common. They were chosen deliberately. And before that happened, they chose to come to Alpine. Deliberately. Carol probably came looking for Kathleen. Why did Kathleen come here? Why has nobody come forward saying they saw her?"

Vida had made some good points. I decided to tackle the last one. "As far as we know, Kathleen didn't check into either of the motels, the hotel, or the lodge. Her car ended up in the mall parking lot, but the killer might have driven it there. Where did Kathleen go after she got to Alpine? Where did Carol go? Did they call on Bridget Dunne Nyquist?"

Vida was sitting with her hands folded under her chin. She seemed to be staring at the opposite wall, where Carla had hung a cardboard cutout of a jolly gingerbread man. "Of course they did," she said in a hushed voice. "Where else would they go?"

Evan Singer had come down with a case of Constitutional rights. He demanded to call his attorney, who turned out to be a senior partner in one of Seattle's most prestigious law firms. He was also Evan's uncle, on his mother's side.

I felt my breath catch as Milo Dodge finished his recitation. Another piece of the Singer-Nyquist puzzle might be falling into place. "What's the uncle's name?" I asked, leaning on Milo's desk.

Milo looked down at his notebook. "Benjamin Stern. You know him?"

I felt deflated. "Mrs. Singer was a Stern before her marriage? Drat! I was sure it would turn out to be Lowenstein."

Slouching against his imitation leather chair, Milo frowned at me. "Lowenstein? Who's that? Composer? Third baseman? Furniture-mart mogul?"

I bit back the urge to ask if *he* ever read *The Advocate*. "I had this crazy theory—except it wasn't so crazy, since I figured out that Evan Singer was related to the Nyquists—that somehow the guy who designed the Marmot was also a relative. Evan's maternal grandfather, maybe." I saw Milo lift his bushy eyebrows. "Hey, it's not so weird—it would explain where Evan got his interest in art and how his sister ended up in the theatre back in New York."

Milo gave me a patronizing look. "His mother's a big art buff, remember?"

"Patroness of the arts. It's not the same." I turned mulish, reluctant to let go of my idea.

Milo ambled over to the hook that held his down jacket. "Let's eat," he said. "It's almost noon. I suppose Evan Singer is halfway to Monroe by now."

"Heading for Hoquiam," I said with a sigh. We started through the reception area only to be confronted by Carla, who flew in the door. She was coatless, and her long, black hair was dappled with snowflakes.

"Emma, your brother is on the phone! He needs to talk to you quick!"

Running in the newly-fallen snow was prohibitive. All the same, the three of us hurried as fast as we could, covering the block between the sheriff's office and the newspaper in less than a minute. I took Ben's call in the front office, where a startled Ginny Burmeister was waiting on a customer who wanted a classified ad.

"Emma," said Ben, his voice crackling more than usual, "those film cans are gone! Mrs. McHale thought she saw

Evan Singer rushing out of the church about ten minutes ago!''

''Out of the church?'' I stopped myself. There was a covered walkway that connected the rectory to the church. I'd momentarily forgotten. ''Evan's still in Alpine then.'' I turned to Milo, my comment as much for him as for my brother. I put my hand over the receiver so Ben wouldn't hear. ''I have a confession to make, Milo. Evan stole an old movie from the Marmot. He's got it with him.''

''An old movie?'' Milo looked unimpressed. ''The guy steals Santa suits and old movies? Whatever happened to bearer bonds and diamond rings and *money*?'' All the same, Milo was out of the office like a shot, presumably to launch a manhunt.

Ben had lost Evan Singer, and I'd lost my lunch date. I went into the news office, where Vida was munching on a carrot stick, Carla was brushing the snow out of her hair, and Ed was getting ready to go to the Kiwanis Club Christmas lunch. The bells went off on the AP wire, signalling a late-breaking bulletin. We all ignored the sound. It was hardly unusual.

''Santa Claus,'' chuckled Ed, letting his belt out to the final notch. I didn't know if he was referring to the AP bells or his ever-expanding girth. ''I'll be late getting back. If Gus calls from the Toyota dealership, tell him this isn't the right time of year to sell cars.''

I tried to coax Vida into going to the Burger Barn, but for once she was adamant about sticking to her diet. ''There are too many temptations this time of year. If I eat my carrot and celery sticks and hardboiled egg and cottage cheese, I'll be able to have two pieces of Grace Grundle's pecan pie at the John Knox Christmas Fun Fest on Sunday.''

I started to remind Vida that John Knox had been virulently opposed to the celebration of Christmas in any form, but decided against it. If we Catholics had survived Vatican

II, there was no reason the Presbyterians shouldn't have their own share of revisionism, too.

Takeout was the only answer. Carla said she'd go fetch me a hamburger, fries, and a Coke before she and Ginny went to lunch up at the lodge. "It's our pre-Christmas treat," she explained. "We might be a little late."

Absently, I nodded. It was, after all, the last Friday before Christmas. I wasn't in a position to hand out holiday bonuses, only modest presents. Why not offer the hired help a gift of time? Carla scurried off to pick up my meager repast. I dialed the rectory to check in with Ben. Teresa McHale answered.

"Father is counseling an engaged couple," she said smugly. "His afternoon is quite full. He plans to join the school faculty's Christmas party, then he meets with three sets of new parents to give Baptismal instructions, and this evening, he intends to start going over the parish books for year's end. May I give him a message?"

I was hungry, frustrated, and annoyed. "This is his sister, not somebody selling a new format for the parish bulletin." I paused, seeking a more conciliatory note. "I'm upset. Teresa, what happened with Evan Singer?"

Teresa McHale also became more human. "Evan Singer! What did I tell you? Now he robs us blind. See how much good it does to extend charity to people who don't deserve it? I can guess who stole Father's gun."

I could, too. Probably. Except that if Evan Singer had taken Ben's Browning, Milo would have found it on him. At least that was a plausible scenario.

Ed left for Kiwanis. Carla returned with my lunch. Vida snapped off more carrots and celery between bouts with the typewriter. I worked on my next editorial, which would be benign and brief. It didn't take many words to wish our readership a Merry Christmas. They could save their eyes and I could spare my brain. I polished off my hamburger and fries, then went out to check the wire. It shut off at two P.M. Carla had let about two hours worth of news pile up on the floor. That wasn't so strange. Most stories that come in after eleven are late-breaking developments from earlier pieces, sports summaries, stock market reports, and other details that don't suit a weekly's needs. Indeed, I often wonder if we could get rid of the wire and save some money. The only time we really need it is on Tuesdays, when we might otherwise miss a hot story with a local angle. The rest of the week, it's just a legacy from the Marius Vandeventer era.

Still, I always scan the long strip of paper to see if we've overlooked something. Once in a while there's a feature on Fridays that's aimed for weekend editions that we can pick off for filler on Wednesday if *The Times* and the *Post Intelligencer* don't use it first.

"Oh, my God!" My jaw dropped as I clutched the long ream of news. Vida looked up from a set of contact prints. I ripped the paper midway off the wire and brought it over to her. "Standish Crocker is dead! He died in a fire last night at his Hunts Point home! Are you thinking what I'm thinking?"

Vida took off her glasses, regarding me with unwavering gray eyes. "Of course. Shall we go see Bridget?"

"What about Milo?"

Vida was getting into her tweed coat. "Milo's out playing sheriff. Let him have his fun. Meanwhile, let's go catch a killer."

Travis Nyquist met us at the door. His handsome face looked tense. The walking cast was gone, but his limp was more pronounced. He didn't ask us in.

"Bridget's not home," he said curtly. "Excuse me."

For once, Vida's protests went for naught. We were left staring at the red and gold wreath on the front door. Vida frowned at the two-car garage. It was closed on both sides.

"No fresh tire tracks in the new snow," she noted. "Don't tell me Bridget walked. It's not her style."

We had started down the drive to the road where I'd parked the Jag. "You think she's home?"

Vida didn't answer. I glanced back over my shoulder. The big oak's branches framed the front window. Travis was looking out, watching our progress.

We got into the car. "It's just a matter of time," said Vida. "Travis is as guilty as sin."

I gave a little jump and accidentally hit the brake instead of the accelerator. The Jag stuttered, then eased down the winding road. "Of what? Murder?" I sounded incredulous.

"Maybe. Certainly of other things, à la the late Standish Crocker." Vida twisted around in the passenger seat, trying to look out through the rear window. The Nyquist house had disappeared from view. "If only we knew where Bridget is . . . I feel as if I'm swimming in cheese soup."

Vida insisted that we stop at the sheriff's office. Milo was still out, looking for Evan Singer. Bill Blatt was manning the front desk. His aunt had orders for him.

"Billy, I want you out there combing this town for any sign of Bridget Nyquist. *Any* sign. Do you understand me?"

Bill's freckled face grew distressed. "But Aunt Vida, I can't leave until Sam Heppner comes back from highway patrol!"

"Radio Sam and get him over here right now. Hurry, Billy, this is a matter of life and death. Start with Travis Nyquist's house."

Torn between his appointed duty and his aunt, Bill Blatt naturally gave in to Vida. After a few more instructions, Vida led me back outside. "That's all we can do for Bridget. Let's hope I'm wrong."

We left my car in front of the sheriff's office and walked to *The Advocate*. It was snowing harder, and the air felt raw. "Do you really think Travis killed those girls? And set fire to Evan Singer's cabin and Standish Crocker's house?"

Vida was trudging along in her flat-footed manner. "Heaven help me, I don't know. But the killer is somebody close to Bridget. I'd stake my soul on that. Who could it be but Travis? Oscar, Arnie and Louise wouldn't want it known that their daughter-in-law is a former prostitute and their son is a crook, but none of them strikes me as a killer. As for Evan Singer . . .''

Across the street, Evan Singer was coming out of the Marmot. He wasn't alone. Oscar Nyquist was at his side, an arm draped around the younger man's shoulders. My first reaction was that Evan was being forcibly ejected. Again. But as Vida and I plunged across Front Street, we saw that the pair was engaged in deep, intimate conversation.

Most people wouldn't have dreamed of intruding on Oscar and Evan in what was clearly a private moment. Vida, however, was not most people. She was Vida, and she marched straight up to confront the two men.

"Oscar," she nodded her cloche, then jabbed a finger at Evan. "Milo Dodge is scouring the town for you, young man. You stole something besides a Santa suit."

Evan, looking bewildered and very young, started to answer, but Oscar broke in: "He didn't steal anything. He borrowed it. Come here." Oscar led us back into the empty Marmot, which would be showing *Fantasia* that evening. I glanced at the lobby's sidewalls, divided by art-deco columns, and featuring individual murals of forest creatures in sylvan settings. We climbed the half-dozen stairs to the upper foyer where the auditorium was dark behind the parted velvet curtains. "In there," said Oscar, his voice unusually hushed, and his eyes never leaving the blank screen, "we watched greatness. Greta Garbo in her first important moving picture. It runs three hours. My father, Lars Nyquist, ran it every year on his birthday. He was Garbo's biggest fan. I haven't seen it since he died."

The words were spoken simply, and I felt slightly embarrassed. Oscar Nyquist was not given to emotional outbursts, except anger. Yet he could not have made more of an impression had he wept and wrung his hands.

Some of the steam had escaped from Vida. "Well, now."
She turned to Evan Singer. "You returned the reels to Oscar?"

Evan took his time replying, and when he did, his voice
was very thin: "I wanted to see it. This is the only full-length
copy of *Gösta Berling*. The director, Maurice Stiller, died in
1928, and his assistant cut the movie by half. A few years
ago, the Swedish Film Institute tried to restore it, but some
of the footage was lost. Only the Marmot has the complete
motion picture."

"It must be worth a fortune," I remarked, noting Vida's
frown. "How did you know it was here, Evan?"

"My grandmother told me." He darted a look at Oscar
Nyquist. "May I, sir? What difference does it make? It all
happened almost seventy years ago. Your father and Mr.
Lowenstein are both dead."

Oscar's barrel chest lurched as he emitted a big sigh. "My
sister talks too much. I always said so."

Evan's usual gawky animation began to return, but he
seemed oddly in control of himself. "Isaac Lowenstein came
to Alpine to design a new movie theatre. He was brilliant,
but like a lot of creative people, he short-circuited now and
then." Evan gave us a self-deprecating smile. It was obvious
that he considered himself both brilliant—and short-circuited. "Lowenstein had a passion for beauty. He also had
a yen for little girls. My grandmother was eight years old,
golden-haired and pretty." He looked at Oscar for confirmation; the older man gave a single nod, his eyes half-shut.
Evan continued in quiet lucid tones: "Lars Nyquist, my great-
grandfather, caught him in time. He told him to leave Alpine
and never come back. But Lars had already paid a portion of
the money for Lowenstein's work. He'd bragged to everyone
that Alpine would have a theatre designed by the great Isaac
Lowenstein. So he ended up paying Lowenstein off to *not*
design the Marmot. Lars Nyquist did it himself, creating one

of the first art-deco movie palaces in the world. He was very talented, don't you think?''

My eyes scanned the graceful columns, the elegant arches, the charming frescoes. Lars Nyquist was indeed a talented man; he might have been a genius. I was flabbergasted. But Evan's story explained a great deal, at least about the Nyquist family's inherent good taste. It was in their blood. Arnie, perhaps Travis, and now Evan had all come by their artistic talents naturally.

Vida wedged herself between Oscar and Evan. "Honestly, Oscar, after all these years you're going to acknowledge Karen's family as Nyquists? What's come over you?''

In the lobby's soft blue lights, Oscar's face flushed. One bearlike hand gestured at the classic flocked wreaths that adorned the walls. "It's Christmas,'' he muttered, then added under his breath, "it's about time.''

Vida spent the rest of the day fuming over Oscar's change of heart. "Why wait so long?'' she'd say at intervals. "Karen is an invalid, Norman and Thea have never known the rest of the Nyquists. What a waste!'' Or, "Stubborn Norwegian. Oscar wouldn't have caved in now if Evan hadn't played on his sympathy by showing an interest in that old movie. But Lars was such a sap about Greta Garbo—and Oscar fell for the soft soap.''

In between grousing about Oscar, Vida fussed over Bridget. By late afternoon, Milo and Bill hadn't turned up any trace of her. They had finally obtained a search warrant and showed up on Travis's doorstep. Travis told them that Bridget had left Alpine. He also told them to go to hell, but Milo wasn't listening. He and Bill went through the house, finding nothing. Some of her matched luggage was missing, as was a chunk of her wardrobe. The lawmen began to wonder if Travis wasn't telling the truth.

"I hope Bridget is far from here,'' Vida said as we prepared to close up for the weekend. "I don't like it, though.

It's easy to ditch some clothes and a couple of suitcases. Of course it's not so easy to ditch an entire person.''

I shared Vida's concern, but I had no idea what to do about it. Finding Bridget was up to Milo. Perhaps a check of the airlines, trains, and buses would turn up a lead.

''With both cars in the garage, how did she get out of Alpine?'' I mused, looking up and heading into the heavy snow.

Vida's car was parked in front of *The Advocate*; mine was still down the street, in front of the sheriff's office. Vida gazed into the flying flakes, chewing on her lower lip. ''I called Louise Nyquist. She said Bridget went to Seattle with Travis yesterday. She never came back.''

Chapter Eighteen

I CONSIDERED STOPPING in to see Milo before I got in the Jag, but Peyton Flake was coming out of the sheriff's office, carrying a sleek medical bag.

"Why don't they deputize me and get it over with?" he grumbled. "Dodge and Blatt are out, Heppner's off-duty, Gould's on the desk, and Mullins is trying to break up a fight at the Icicle Creek Tavern. Your editorial pissed off some people." Behind the wire-rimmed glasses, Flake's eyes were gleeful.

"My editorials are often controversial," I sighed, then pointed at his case. "As you off to patch up the losers?"

Flake shook his head, the ponytail swinging under an Aztec print wool cap that matched his fleece pullover. "I'm rescuing Durwood Parker. He took that freaking snowmobile up to the ranger station and ran over himself. Let's hope I can find the old fart in this weather. If not, I can cut some firewood." He pounded on the rear door of his Toyota van. I could see a gun rack, an axe, a maul, and a brown paper bag that may or may not have contained a fifth of Wild Turkey.

I wished Dr. Flake well, musing on how different he was from his predecessor, the late Cecil Dewey. Or from Gerald Dewey, who was almost as tradition-bound as his father. Maybe Peyton Flake's brand of medicine would eventually catch on in Alpine. Certainly he seemed to have the skill and the dedication. I watched the rust-colored four-wheel drive

715

pull into Front Street and wondered why the forest rangers hadn't brought Durwood back to town. Probably, it dawned on me, because Peyton Flake relished taking off into swirling, hip-deep snow with his medical case and a mission. He might not seem suited to Alpine, but Alpine was certainly suited to him.

At home, I discovered that Adam was going night-skiing with Carla and Ginny. I shuddered at the lack of visibility, but he laughed at my fears. Then I shuddered at the thought of my son in Carla's clutches. But this was a buddy event. They were a threesome. Surely Adam would be safe. Carla was two years older. Nineteen months, actually. Put like that, I shuddered some more.

The lamb steaks went back in the fridge. I wasn't in the mood to cook for myself. Maybe Ben wasn't as busy as Teresa McHale had let on. I dialed the rectory; there was no answer.

Adam came into the living room, carrying his skis. He saw my worried look. "I forgot to tell you," he said, running a finger up and down one of the skis to test the surface, "the phone's out. Or some of them are. I got disconnected from Carla, and when I called back, it rang and rang, but she didn't answer."

I sighed. First the electricity, now the phones. It was annoying, but it wasn't unusual, given Alpine's hard winters with so much snow, ice, and wind. I decided to walk down to the rectory after Adam left.

I felt restless. Anxious, too. Vida's concern for Bridget Nyquist was contagious. I wondered if Milo had made any progress. Maybe Vida was right—Bridget had never returned to Alpine. She was in Seattle, staying with friends.

But Bridget had no friends, except for the girls who had formed the ring of hookers. Three were dead, one was in Texas, and the other's whereabouts were as big a question mark as Bridget's. My anxiety mounted. Irrationally, I started to worry about Ben.

But at the rectory, all was well. Ben was in the study, poring over Father Fitz's files. He wasn't aware that the phone was out; he was merely thankful that no one had called to distract him from his duties. Teresa McHale was in her room, watching television.

"This isn't your responsibility," I told Ben as I sat down in the room's only other chair, a straight-backed oak number that probably had been part of a dining room set sixty years ago.

"I know, but somebody's got to do it. Peyton Flake told me today that Father Fitz isn't rallying. He may have to go to a nursing home."

I sighed. "I'll miss him. We all will. He's a good man." I gazed around the small study with its open bookcases, filing cabinets, and more religious artwork. Our Lady of Mount Carmel, holding Baby Jesus, stood on a slim wooden pedestal. *The Agony in the Garden* was painted in murky colors above the desk. "Can I help?" I asked.

Ben shook his head. "I'm not balancing the books or anything like that. The parish council can do it. Mainly, I want to make sure all the masses have been said by people requesting them, that any queries from potential converts or fallen-away Catholics have been answered, that I'm covered on weddings and baptisms—you know, all the usual parish stuff. Bridget Nyquist, by the way, put her father's name in for All Souls' Day masses. She was generous—fifty bucks."

"I'm surprised," I admitted. "Given what she's been through and her marriage in the Lutheran church, she might have given up on Catholic trappings."

"Old ideas die hard," Ben muttered, checking names off a list. "Bridget's been a Catholic for a lot longer than she's been a Lutheran. Or was a whore."

"Right." I sat back, watching Ben go through file folders.

"Gripes," he said, putting one aside. "Kudos," he said, setting down another. "Crackpots," he said, fielding a third.

Ben kept at it. I felt useless. After ten minutes, I saw a

well-worn book of devotions on top of the nearest filing cabinet. I got up and flipped through the pages. It was very old,
with fragile paper and heavy ink. Red rubrics and line en-
gravings decorated the beginning of each section. Prayer
cards, mostly for deceased priests, marked favorite passages.

"Father Fitz's?" I asked when Ben reached a lull.

He smiled and then, surprisingly, turned quite serious. "I
was looking at that this morning after Evan Singer vacated
Father Fitz's room. You know, I shouldn't be surprised when
I discover that every priest has suffered some pretty severe
temptations. Nobody knows it better than I do. But with an
old guy like Father Fitz, it still brings me up short."

I gave my brother a curious look. "Temptation? Like what?
Wild women?"

"Worse. Determined women. Or just one." Ben opened
the middle desk drawer. He took out a single sheet of pale
blue stationery. "This was stuck to the back of the prayer
book. Look at the date. Father Fitz must have been in his
late fifties. I guess that's not too old for midlife crisis, especially for us socially retarded priests."

I took the flimsy paper from Ben and began reading the
close-knit handwriting. It wasn't easy to decipher.

May 23, 1960

My darling:

I can't believe you don't [won't?] love me. I saw it in
your eyes. I felt it in your arms. No matter what else you
are, you're still a man! Act like one and defy old laws [?].
Why should you care about generations of cold-blooded
robots who blindly obeyed instead of following their
hearts? Why does religion have to put up barriers [farriers?
fanciers? financiers?] between people? Isn't love [?] everything? Please! I'll wait forever, if I have to!

With all my heart,
Your loving MA

"*Ma?* Isn't that carrying the Irish mother bit too far?'' I handed the letter back to Ben.

"It must be initials. I wonder what happened to her?'' My brother looked wistful as he studied the letter again. "He must have thought something of her, or he would have thrown this out.'' Ben returned to his file folders. My watch told me it was almost eight. I hadn't eaten dinner and was suddenly ravenous. I asked my brother if he might be hungry, too.

Ben shook his head. "Mrs. McHale fixed me a crab omelette and a green salad. Delicious.'' His puckish expression showed that he still delighted in taunting me.

I waited until he seemed absorbed in his work. "Any leftovers?'' I, too, could be a pain.

"What? No, I ate the whole thing.'' Ben looked very pleased with himself. "The salad, too.''

I got out of the chair. "In that case, I'll go forage for myself.'' I headed for the kitchen.

The rectory refrigerator was not only immaculate, but virtually empty except for the usual dairy products, condiments, and a crisper drawer full of vegetables. Except for a wedge of cheddar cheese, there wasn't much with which to make a meal. The freezing compartment was small and looked as if it had been recently defrosted.

"Try the big one in the basement,'' said Ben, lounging in the doorway. "But don't let Mrs. McHale find out I said it was okay. She lives in mortal fear that somebody will screw up her food-filing system.''

"She files food?'' I wrinkled my nose. "What is she, a frustrated Department of Agriculture clerk?''

Ben chuckled. "She's the most organized woman I've ever met. Peyton Flake keeps telling me how Father Fitz tries to give orders and practically gets himself worked up into another stroke. The poor old soul needn't worry—Teresa McHale will keep this place running like a Swiss watch.''

We headed out the back door. The basement stairs were at the rear of the house, off the small porch. "Father Fitz is lucky to have her," I noted, as a blast of snow and wind hit us. "He ought to stop fussing and put his energy into recovering."

"I know," Ben agreed as we carefully trod the dozen wooden stairs that led to the basement. Although the steps were covered, snow had drifted onto them, making the descent treacherous. I worried about Adam skiing. Then I worried about Adam *not* skiing. But if he was sipping mulled wine in the lodge with Carla, Ginny would be there, too. Somehow, I wasn't consoled.

Ben tried the door; it was locked.

"Damn," he muttered, unhooking a set of keys from his belt. "Which one is it? I've never been down here before. Front door, back door, church, garage, car ignition, car trunk . . . here, it's got to be this one. . . ."

It was. The hinges creaked, and we couldn't see a thing inside. Ben felt for a light switch, but couldn't find one. At last he made contact with a thick string. One pull illuminated the unfinished basement. The usable area wasn't much bigger than the parlor. Above four feet of concrete and several beams, we could see piles of dirt and some large rocks. The mountainside pushed up beneath the rectory. It was no wonder that the basement smelled damp, even rank.

"This place needs airing out," Ben remarked, grimacing. He moved toward the old freezer, which was wedged between a large fruit cupboard and a stack of cartons tied with twine. Next to me was an ancient, black steamer trunk with rusted locks. I wondered if it had made the original crossing from Ireland with Father Fitz. Like its owner, it would probably never see the Emerald Isle again.

Ben put his shoulder to the heavy freezer and lifted the lid. I was wrinkling my nose. The basement really smelled terrible, an odor I couldn't define. Ben bent over the freezer. And let out a horrible cry. I think I made an exclamation, too, of shock. Ben allowed the freezer to slam shut. He reeled, then stumbled toward me and held on for dear life.

"Ben . . ." He was clinging to me so tightly that I could scarcely speak. "What . . . ?"

Taking deep breaths, Ben kept his arms around me but steered us to the door and onto the stairs. The snow swirled around us; the wind howled in our ears. Ben's face was in shadow from the basement light, but I could see that he was pale under his tan.

"It's a body," he finally gasped, then groaned. "*Some* of a body . . . Oh, God!" He let go and crossed himself.

I fell back against the side of the house. "Ben . . ." I couldn't think clearly. Had he said it was *somebody* . . . or *some body*?

My brother put his hands over his mouth and took more deep breaths. Then he squared his shoulders. When he spoke, his voice had lost its usual crackle. Indeed, he sounded faintly giddy. "Oh, Emma—I think we found the rest of Kathleen Francich!"

Maybe I always knew we would. Or that someone would. My knees turned to water. I kept leaning against the house, oblivious to the snow that blew in under the overhang, impervious to the sharp wind that came off the mountains. In truth, I was turning numb, and that was just as well. Maybe I could go to sleep and not have to deal with what was left of poor Kathleen. . . .

But Ben rallied. "Come on, let's call Milo." He snatched at my hand, which hung limply at my side.

"Milo?" I spoke his name as if I'd never heard of him. "Oh. Milo." I felt Ben tug at my hand and I gave myself a shake. "Yes . . . Milo." We started up the stairs but I stopped behind Ben at the door. "Wait—the phones—maybe we'd better drive over and find him in person."

Ben's brown eyes darted this way and that, indicating he was considering our options. "Right. But we'd better tell Teresa. What if she happens to go down to . . .'"

He saw the awful look on my face and his jaw dropped. "Oh, Jesus . . . Emma . . . What are you thinking?"

My voice came out as a rasp. "Ben—that letter. Quick, let's take another look. Please."

Furtively, we moved through the rectory, past Teresa's room, which was now ominously silent. Ben closed the study door behind us and locked it. I grabbed the blue sheet of stationery and put it directly under the desk lamp. The cramped handwriting wasn't improved by the illumination, but my brain was illuminated instead. "Oh, Ben—this doesn't say *defy old laws*—it says *defy old Lars*."

"*Lars?*" He sprang toward me, reaching for the single sheet. "Let me see!" Scanning the page, Ben was incredulous, then puzzled. "So what does it mean?"

A kaleidoscope of seemingly unrelated bits and pieces of knowledge spun in my brain: Bridget's mother's suicide, Arnie Nyquist's former girlfriend, Teresa McHale's desire for a public swimming pool, Francine Wells's remark about Teresa seeking a job, Ben's comment about Bridget's request for masses for her father, and now, the letter signed *MA*.

"This wasn't written to Father Fitz," I said in a hushed voice. "It was sent to Arnie Nyquist, from his Catholic girlfriend. Who, I might add, was quite a swimmer." Ben's puzzlement deepened, but I rushed on; there wasn't time for detailed explanations. "This woman was begging Arnie to defy his grandfather, Lars Nyquist, and not let religion stand in their way of getting married."

"I don't get it." Ben's forehead wrinkled. "What's it doing in Father Fitz's prayer book?"

"It wasn't in the book, remember? You said it was stuck to the bottom. I'm guessing there were more letters, which have been destroyed." I swallowed hard, trying to figure out what to do next. "They were stolen from Arnie's house, along with his UDUB-yearbook and that other stuff. Ben, let's get out of here."

But my brother was still looking baffled. "Hold it, Emma. Are you saying . . . Oh, come on, Sluggly, you don't think . . . ."

A noise in the hall made both of us freeze. Ben's face turned grim as he positioned himself at one side of the door. "We've got company," he whispered. "Do I attack first and ask questions later?"

Frantically, I shook my head. "She may have your gun," I whispered back.

"Oh, God!" Ben glanced at the doorknob and recoiled. Maybe he thought that Teresa McHale was going to blast her way into the study. Maybe he was right. "The window," Ben breathed, shoving me across the room. "It opens. I smoked one of Flake's cigars in here today and had to air the place out."

It was only a two-foot drop into the snow. A last look over my shoulder caught the doorknob turning. Of course Teresa had a key. Ben and I ran as fast as the snowstorm would permit. We were on the side of the rectory directly across from the darkened church. To our left was the garage and woodshed; to our right, the street. Teresa hadn't followed us through the window. My guess was that she was going out through the front door. Ben was already heading that way.

"Wait!" My voice sounded hoarse. Ben turned, cocking his head. "Let's go the back way and around the church," I urged, shivering in my green sweater and flannel slacks. "We can get to Fourth Street. There's bound to be some traffic there."

Looking as chilled as I felt, Ben followed my lead. As I fought through the snow that had drifted up against the sanctuary, I kept looking back. To my relief, there was no sign of Teresa. Maybe she had decided to make a clean getaway. Maybe she didn't feel threatened. Maybe my hypothesis was dead wrong.

There wasn't time to open the garage and get out the old Volvo. Across the empty church parking lot, Cascade Street was obscured by the blowing snow. A dash for the nearest house might be smarter than trying to get down to the intersection. I felt Ben at my elbow as I tried to make out any nearby lights. My face stung from the cold, and my feet felt numb. We pressed forward, and I uttered a sigh of relief to find that the snow was only a few inches deep in the parking lot. Apparently some Good Samaritan was keeping it plowed.

But nobody could keep it from icing up under foot. I slipped and would have fallen had it not been for Ben. We teetered, then started forward again, moving at an agonizingly slow pace. On any given Sunday, the lot always seemed too small; tonight it was vast, windswept, like the frozen Arctic tundra.

The voice came out of a void. Or so it struck me at first. Then, when I turned, I realized it had come from the rear entrance of the church. Teresa McHale's shadowy form was barely perceptible through the flying snowflakes. She had used the covered walkway between the rectory and the church. No wonder we hadn't seen her.

"Come here," she called, her voice strong and steely.

I glanced at Ben. He gave a faint shake of his head. We plunged forward. Teresa called out again. We kept going.

The single shot ripped past us, maybe between us. It was impossible to tell. We were both jarred, and fell against one another.

"Stop." Teresa's voice now sounded very near. I looked around Ben to see her approaching, the Browning high-power clutched in both hands.

"Is that what you used on Standish Crocker before you set his house on fire?" I had no idea what prompted me to make such an inquiry under the circumstances. Begging for mercy would have been more appropriate, but a journalist's quest for truth dies hard. Right along with the journalist, it suddenly occurred to me.

Teresa was now within ten feet of us. Still, I could barely make out her heavy orange jacket and brown slacks. "You don't need to know about Crocker. Get inside the church."

Priest or not, this was one time Ben didn't seem drawn to the altar. Neither was I. Our only hope was for someone to drive by, realize something was amiss, and bring help. But Cascade Street was obliterated by the snow, and seemingly untraveled. On this stormy Friday night before Christmas, Alpine's residents must be keeping cozy at home, wrapping gifts, sipping eggnog, listening to carols. There was no reason to expect them to cruise the town in a blizzard, looking for a homicidal housekeeper and her would-be victims.

"Listen, Mrs. McHale," Ben began, the crackle back in his voice, "you're going to get caught. If you shot Standish Crocker, the police have found the bullet. The law will exact its price. But you *are* a Catholic. What about the higher law? Have you thought about your soul?"

I couldn't see her expression, but I could hear the contempt in her voice. "My soul died with my heart a long time ago. What did being a Catholic ever do for me? If I'd been something else—or nothing at all—I wouldn't have lost the only man I ever loved. I've been dead for thirty-two years. The only pleasure I've had is watching Bridget marry into that stiff-necked bunch of Lutherans. That, and making money by making fools out of men. Don't give me a homily on the state of my soul, Father. I've been in hell since I was a girl."

Despite the imminent danger of dying in the freezing snow, I was aghast. "You turned your own daughter into a whore just to avenge yourself on the Nyquists?"

Teresa gave a little snort. "On *all* men. A woman has the power to reduce any man to the status of an animal. But I did it for the money, too. My husband ran his trucking business into the ground. He'd even let his life insurance lapse. When that oaf died, I had nothing. I couldn't make ends meet as a sales clerk in a boutique." She gave a toss of her head. "So I put Bridget and the others to work. They loved it. It was party time, 'round the clock. Young ladies of the finest backgrounds, groomed to please silly businessmen. Catholic, Protestant, Jew—take your choice. I was sorry I never had a real minority. That was my goal, but the girls graduated first."

For someone who didn't want to tell us anything, Teresa McHale seemed to be revealing a lot. And why not? Where else could she brag about her brilliant call-girl scheme? Maybe she wasn't going to shoot us; we could freeze to death instead.

But I was too optimistic. Teresa gestured with the Browning. Maybe she was cold, too. "Enough. You're trying to stall. Let's get on with it."

An even stronger gust of wind blew down from Tonga Ridge. Briefly, Teresa disappeared in a flurry of snow. Siblings have their own wavelength. Ben and I ran for the street. We slipped; we slid. Teresa screamed at us to stop. The gun fired again, not quite so close, but near enough to make my heart skip. No doubt she was right behind us, more than halfway across the parking lot. Or maybe we'd reached the sidewalk. It was impossible to tell. If there was a streetlight in the vicinity, we couldn't see it. Teresa shouted another warning. The people who lived in the houses across the street didn't hear a thing. The sound of the wind muffled not only her voice but the shots from the gun.

I turned to see if she had us in range. She did. I made a misstep, and fell off the curb. Ben reached down to help me. Teresa stopped at the edge of what must have been the sidewalk.

"I'd rather not do it this way," she said grimly. "but you're giving me no choice. Maybe it's just as well. The snow will cover your bodies. I'll have left the country long before the thaw sets in." She laughed, a hideous, grating sound.

Ben got me on my feet just in time to see Teresa aim the Browning at us. I was so cold, I could barely react to the incredible notion that my brother and I were about to die. My heart was pounding, and a strange rumbling sound assaulted my ears. Teresa seemed to appear and disappear between flurries of snow. I heard a click; the safety? Ben would know. I gazed up at him—my brother, my friend, my only close family besides Adam. . . . How ironic that we should die together.

The large black form seemed to rumble out of nowhere, sailing along the sidewalk and striking Teresa with full force. The gun went off, and this time I saw its flash. I also heard a masculine voice, letting out an obscene exclamation. I gasped; Ben swore. Teresa lay on the ground, writhing in pain. A thud echoed on the wind, then more curses. Dazed, I grabbed Ben's arm and followed him to where Teresa lay. The Browning was a couple of feet away, already dusted with snow.

"My back!" Teresa groaned. "I can't move!"

Ben was kneeling at her side. "We'll get help!" He put a hand on her forehead. There was blood along her hairline and a gash in one cheek. Her left leg protruded at an unnatural angle. "Mrs. McHale, would you like me to hear your confession?"

The laugh was twisted, agonized. She stared up at Ben, her eyes glassy. "You're incredible, Father." Her face was wrenched with pain. "You really believe all this swill, don't you?"

Ben nodded, an offhand response. "So do you. The day Father Fitz had his stroke, you went to confession. Why?"

Teresa let out a series of little keening cries before she answered. "Habit, I guess. What difference does it make?" Her eyes closed and her body went limp.

Ben made the sign of the cross on her forehead. "It made a difference to Father Fitz," he muttered, sounding angry. "Her confession probably gave him the stroke."

"Is she dead?" I was shaking all over, from relief, shock, and the aftermath of terror.

"No." Ben was standing up again, peering into the snow. "Now where did . . . ah!" His shoulders slumped as he waved a hand. Peyton Flake was limping toward us, looking furious.

"What have we got here? I told that goddamned old fool

he ought to let me drive that snowmobile.'' Flake, his vocation as automatic as my brother's, bent down to examine
Teresa McHale. ''She's a mess. We'll have to get an ambulance. I feel responsible. I was supposed to be rescuing one
patient and now I've got another one. Shit.'' He turned back
in the direction he'd come. ''Hey, Durwood, let me see if I
can get a can-opener and pry you out of that freaking snowmobile.''

''Actually,'' I said, trooping along after Dr. Flake like a
pet pup, ''you saved our lives. We'll explain all this later,
but now I'll go see if the phones are working.''

Flake didn't seem to hear me. Or at least he didn't seem
to understand. He tripped over the Browning. ''Hey—is this
yours, Ben? What happened, did your housekeeper make you
a crummy casserole?''

Ben's smile was thin. He was still standing next to Teresa's
inert form. I was struck by the irony. She had tried to kill
us, had murdered at least three other people, had corrupted
six young women, including her own daughter, and yet my
brother wouldn't abandon her. Peyton Flake and Durwood
Parker might have saved our lives, but for me, Ben was the
real hero.

Chapter Nineteen

THE WHISTLING MARMOT Movie Theatre's marquee had again suffered at the hands of pranksters. Overnight, *Fantasia* had turned into *Ana is Fat*. I'd seen the rearrangement on my way to the sheriff's office Saturday morning. Milo Dodge had put off taking depositions from Ben and me due to our half-frozen, totally exhausted state.

Teresa McHale had been transferred from Alpine Community Hospital to Harborview in Seattle. She was in critical condition, but despite internal injuries, a concussion, and broken back, ribs, and leg, Peyton Flake thought she would recover to stand trial. Frankly, it was a good news/bad news prognosis.

Of course she wasn't Teresa McHale, but Mary Anne Toomey Dunne. Vida was still shaking her head over the events of Friday night when she approached the impromptu buffet supper I had prepared the following evening.

"It's bad enough that I never knew Lars Nyquist had designed the Marmot, though I still can't imagine him being so clever. He certainly hid it well. But I'm ashamed of myself that I didn't figure out Teresa McHale," she complained, spearing slices of ham and roast beef. "Of course, I'm not a Catholic." She managed to say the words with a mixture of accusation and relief, as if she was sorry that I had a venereal disease but thankful that she didn't.

"You never heard her make a fuss over Alpine's lack of a public swimming pool," I pointed out, handing Milo Dodge a paper plate etched with boughs of holly. "You never saw the letter she wrote to Arnie Nyquist. And you didn't know she'd applied for a job at Francine's Fine Apparel."

Ben looked up from his mound of potato salad. "If I'd known that about Francine, I might have wondered. I assumed she'd been sent up here by the Chancery. But of course she was already in Alpine and only needed an okay from the Chancery office. It was just a coincidence that Edna McPhail died not long after Teresa followed Bridget to town."

Milo dumped horseradish on his beef, tossed two dill pickles onto the plate, and scooped up a spoonful of black olives. "This has been the damndest case I ever saw. Jack Mullins threw up when he opened that freezer in the rectory basement."

Ed Bronsky nodded from his place in my favorite chair. The springs would have gone if he'd had any more food on his plate. "It was pretty bad, I guess. You'll have to get a new freezer, Father. Alpine Appliance is having a sale after New Year's. If they get pushy, you'll see the ad in next week's paper." He sighed with resignation.

Shirley Bronsky, who was squatting on the floor at her husband's feet and revealing a great deal of fat white thigh in the process, clasped both hands to her bulging bosom. "Honestly, what's this world coming to? A mother who turns her daughter into a prostitute? But I still don't understand why Mrs. McHale—or whatever her name is—had to kill those poor girls!"

"Simple," said Milo, sitting down next to Vida on the sofa. "Blackmail. Once Bridget got her hooks into Travis Nyquist, Teresa figured it was time to retire and gloat. She staged her own suicide with that phony cancer story, jumped off the Bainbridge Island ferry coming into Seattle, and swam over to the Smith Cove marina. It's not that far, at least not for a strong swimmer."

"Which," I noted, "Teresa was. Olympic class, in her youth. It appears that without Teresa running the show, the two girls who wanted to continue hooking didn't do so well on their own. Until Teresa comes around—or Bridget opens up—we won't know exactly what happened, but one theory is that Kathleen came to Alpine to hit Bridget up, and Bridget panicked and told Kathleen to go to the rectory. I doubt that Kathleen knew Teresa was still alive, so imagine her shock at discovering Mary Anne Dunne taking care of a small-town parish and a deaf old priest. I can imagine how Teresa met a demand for money.'' Sadly, I shook my head.

Milo made a crunching sound with one of his dill pickles. ''The body had to be disposed of. Father Fitz apparently never went in the basement because of his arthritis. There was an axe in the woodshed which has bloodstains on it.'' Milo glanced at Ben. ''Didn't you say something about how she wouldn't let you use the fireplace? She didn't want you near that woodshed, just in case there were some incriminating traces left.''

Ben ran a hand through his dark hair. ''There I was, eating omelettes and oyster stew and oven-fried chicken, and meanwhile Teresa had already confessed to my predecessor that she was a murderess.'' He pulled his hair straight up on end.

Vida wagged a finger at him. ''Now just a minute, Father Ben. I thought you priests weren't allowed to tattle about what you heard in confession. Don't tell me that old fool of a pastor *blabbed*!''

Ben gave Vida his most somber expression. ''Mrs. Runkel, how could you? An upstanding Presbyterian gossipmongering? Tut! I can only speculate on what Teresa said to Father Fitz in confession. But a few minutes later he suffered a stroke. And then Peyton Flake said Father's been acting agitated, passing on instructions. I wonder if he wasn't trying to give a warning instead. Without naming names or deeds, of course.''

''Poor old guy,'' remarked Milo. ''He was oblivious to everything that happened. Not that you could blame him,

given his age and health problems. Teresa sure took her time
to hack up. . . . ''

Shirley Bronsky let out a squeal. ''Stop! We're eating!
Please, Milo, I have a very delicate stomach.''

I tried not to lift my eyebrows. Shirley's stomach looked
about as delicate as a blast furnace. Ben came to Milo's rescue. ''Teresa had the luxury of time with Kathleen. But then
Carol Neal came along looking for her friend. We assume
she went to see Bridget, too. And got the same response:
head for the rectory.'' He shrugged. ''Same result, except
that I showed up, neither deaf nor feeble. Teresa must have
put Carol in the freezer for a couple of days and then used
the Volvo to transport the body to the river, at which point
the temperature rose—which explains why Doc Dewey noticed some signs of thawing.''

Carla flipped her long, black hair over her shoulders. ''Really, it's too dumb! Why not get another pimp or madam or
whatever? I mean, it's totally weird to expect somebody to
hand over money for nothing.''

There were days when I felt as if I were doing the same
thing with both Carla and Ed, but this was hardly the time
or place to say so. ''It wasn't that simple,'' I pointed out.
''Kathleen and Carol were over their heads in debt, and they'd
have a tough time finding anybody as efficient as Teresa.
Remember, she was a terrific organizer. She booked her stable with several different businesses at first, then got in thick
with Standish Crocker, who was also peddling cocaine. So
was Travis, which is what made him wealthy, if nervous. He
didn't get out of the investment business because he was tired
of making money. He was afraid he'd get caught. And, along
with Crocker, he did.''

Adam, flanked by Carla and Ginny, brought their plates
over to join the circle. ''So Teresa bumped off Standish
Crocker with Uncle Ben's gun and set his house on fire because she was afraid he'd squawk about the call-girl ring?''

Milo nodded. "You bet. And he would have. Travis will do it now instead."

Ginny, with her usual serious mien, fingered her small chin. "How can Travis do that when his own wife is involved? And why didn't Mrs. McHale get rid of Travis, too? Then Bridget would have been a rich widow."

Milo sipped from his tankard of ale. "Travis might have been next, but I think Teresa was hoping he'd never have to testify. As for Travis and Bridget, that marriage was doomed from the start. Bridget dazzled Travis, and of course Teresa egged her on. It was the perfect revenge, full circle on the Nyquist family. But let's face it, I wouldn't call it a love match. Bridget is better off back in Seattle with Rachel Rosen."

Vida heaved a sigh. "Thank God Rachel and Bridget are safe. Where did you say Rachel had gone for a few days? Portland?" The question was for Milo.

"Eugene. But she came back a day or so before Bridget went to Seattle with Travis," Milo explained. "At that point, Bridget suspected what was going on with her mother. I don't think she knew—or would believe—that Teresa had killed Kathleen and Carol until she couldn't duck the truth any longer. Bridget had to get away. She used the trip to Seattle with Travis as an excuse. She told him she wanted a trial separation."

My idealist's scenario called for Bridget to follow in Rachel's footsteps and go to college, to put Travis and prostitution and even her mother in the past, and to try to pick up the pieces of a life that had been broken at seventeen. It could be done, but the realist in me painted a grimmer picture.

Adam had gotten up to turn the CD player on. The Mormon Tabernacle Choir sang "Hark the Herald Angels Sing" at less than the usual ear-shattering decibels my son preferred.

"It was the masses," Ben said, seemingly apropos of nothing. We all looked at him. "For All Souls' Day. Bridget had asked Father Fitz to remember her own father among the dead. But she didn't request any remembrance for her mother. That made Sluggly here wonder why. The answer was obvious. Mrs. Dunne wasn't dead.''

''That and a lot of other things,'' I said, ''including all those trips Teresa kept making with the Volvo. She didn't appear to have any friends in town, and yet she went out quite a bit. As it turned out, she was disposing of bodies, setting fires, and shooting people.''

Carla leaned back in her folding chair, the long hair dipping toward the carpet. ''Talk about a hectic holiday season! Wow!''

Ed, however, was once again looking puzzled. ''Now wait a minute—you mean Mrs. McHale set the fire at Evan Singer's place? Why?''

Sometimes Milo's patience astounds me. Maybe it wouldn't have been so exemplary if he'd had to work with Ed on a daily basis. ''She was trying to divert suspicion. Evan was a likely target because he's a bit strange. She also needed to burn all that stuff she stole from Arnie Nyquist's house and van. The old letters he'd saved, even the college yearbook with her pictures and inscription had to be destroyed, just in case anybody ever found them and made the connection. I don't think she and Arnie ever ran into each other, but if they had, the middle-aged Teresa McHale didn't look much like the young Mary Anne Toomey. I figure she hoped Arnie's van was unlocked with the keys in the ignition. She probably wanted the one for the house. Teresa couldn't count on Louise Nyquist not locking up. The picture of Bridget and Travis was a bonus. It was the sort of thing a lovesick swain would take—and burn.''

I was gazing into the fire, listening to the Mormon rendition of ''Away In A Manger.'' ''I feel sorry for the Nyquists. Travis is a terrible blot on the family escutcheon. Poor Louise. But maybe reconciling with Evan's side of the family will help.''

"Evan will help," Ginny announced, surprising all of us. "I hear he's going to stay in Alpine and work at the Marmot. He's nuts about movies. After all, Oscar can't live forever."

"He's working on it," Vida said without enthusiasm.

I got up to get the dessert out. The Upper Crust had provided me with a *buche de Noël* that looked too good to eat. Almost. To my surprise, Adam came out to help me. To my amazement, Carla and Ginny tagged along to help Adam.

Ginny and Adam busied themselves with plates, forks, and more napkins while Carla lounged against the counter. "Now why couldn't Travis turn out to be a good guy so he could dump Bridget and become eligible?" She uttered a dramatic sigh. "He was handsome, rich, charming."

"And a crook," I noted, carrying cups and saucers back into the living room. I checked my big pot that stood on the dining room table; the coffee had finished perking. Vida would probably want tea. The phone rang on my desk across the room. Ben volunteered to answer it. There was no one at the other end, but the answering machine clicked on.

"The phones still aren't working quite right," I said. "If there's a real message, I'll get it later." It couldn't be an emergency affecting anybody I cared about, since they were all under my roof. If it was for Milo, his beeper would have gone off. I went back into the kitchen.

Adam, Carla, and Ginny were clustered together like a baseball conference on the mound. They were laughing and whispering in a conspiratorial manner.

The only words I caught were Ginny's: ". . . *Bugsy* starts next . . ."

All three jumped at my intrusion. I stared. They grew awkward. I frowned in puzzlement. And then it dawned on me. I dove for Adam, grabbing him by the front of his beige sweater.

"You! I don't believe it! How could you?"

"No, hey, really, I only . . . uh . . ." My son tried to

escape my clutches, his eyes darting back and forth between his accomplices.

Carla doubled over. "I can't help it! It's too funny!" She held her sides, giggling and jiggling away.

Ginny was the first to regain her composure. "Carla's right. It *is* funny. And what else is there to do around this town in the winter? What's the harm? It's good publicity for the Marmot. Who can resist checking out that marquee every day?"

I released my son and bit at my cheeks to keep from smiling. My gaze remained on Adam, who was adjusting his shirt collar and straightening his sweater. "When did you join this merry band, my boy?"

"Uh . . . last night. We couldn't ski. The weather was too crummy."

I gave a shake of my head. "I can't condone this."

Carla had gotten her giggles under control. "You don't have to. Would you rather we shot out Christmas lights or stole wreaths off doors?"

I sighed. I would rather they acted like responsible adults, but that was expecting too much. At least Carla and Ginny weren't selling themselves to the Alpine Kiwanis Club and Adam wasn't hustling crack to the Rotarians. Maybe I ought to count my blessings. I started back into the living room, made a quick change of direction, and went into the bathroom.

And laughed my head off. Carla could spell! Ginny had imagination! Adam wasn't rolling around with either of them in the snow!

Or maybe it was Carla's imagination and Ginny's spelling. It didn't matter. At least I might be right about Adam. Then again, we don't always get our wishes, not even at Christmas.

By eleven-thirty everyone had gone home, and Adam was in bed. I started the dishwasher and put on a German boys' choir Christmas CD. Except for the tree, the living room was dark. No, I was mistaken. The answering machine light was on. I turned the volume to low and played the tape.

"You must be out reveling," said the mellow voice of Tom Cavanaugh. "Sandra and I are leaving for London tomorrow. She's always wanted a Dickensian Christmas, so I'm going to let her shoplift Royal Doulton at the Olde Curiosity Shoppe. I'll be back in San Francisco the twenty-seventh. Sandra's going to spend a few days with her sister up at Lake Tahoe. Any chance you and Adam could fly down to welcome Baby New Year? The trip's on me. Merry Christmas." There was a pause, then Tom's voice deepened. "Every Christmas I miss you like hell. Now that I've finally met Adam, I miss him, too. Damn and double damn. Why is life such a pain in the ass? I'll call you the twenty-eighth."

I replayed the tape three times, foolishly drinking in his voice, savoring his sentiments, wishing I weren't such a sap. There would be no New Year's party for Tom, Emma, and Adam. Ben would still be in Alpine, and I couldn't run out on him. Oh, he'd try to make me go if I told him about the call. But I wouldn't. Tom had his principles, which some might call excuses; I had my own sense of honor. And I'd call it what I pleased.

I hung the last angel above the stable. All the sheep were on their backs, looking as if they'd been mowed down by an outbreak of anthrax. I righted them, then adjusted the angel who seemed intent on flying off to the port side. Through the speakers came the pure, youthful voices of the boys' choir. *Stille nacht, heilige nacht.* I stood next to the tree, the lights shimmering, the icicles dancing, the ornaments sparkling. Outside, it was still snowing, though not nearly as hard as the previous night. *Silent night, holy night.*

Christmas was five days away. There was one more Sunday to go in Advent. The last ten days had taken a terrible toll. I realized I was exhausted. But tonight I felt contentment wash over me. I unplugged the tree, but paused again by the crèche. The tiny manger was still empty. Baby Jesus wouldn't bide there until Christmas Eve. I smiled and headed for bed.

Sleep in heavenly peace.

Now that you've enjoyed the first three books
in MARY DAHEIM's thrilling Alpine Series,
don't miss the rest of the Alpine alphabet!

THE ALPINE DECOY

THE ALPINE ESCAPE

THE ALPINE FURY

THE ALPINE GAMBLE

THE ALPINE HERO

THE ALPINE ICON

THE ALPINE JOURNEY

THE ALPINE KINDRED

THE ALPINE LEGACY

THE ALPINE MENACE

THE ALPINE NEMESIS

THE ALPINE OBITUARY

THE ALPINE PURSUIT

THE ALPINE QUILT

THE ALPINE RECLUSE

"The characters are great, and the plots
always attention-getting."
—*King Features Syndicate*

"Daheim writes . . . with dry wit, a butter-smooth
style, and obvious wicked enjoyment."
—Portland *Oregonian*